GREY REDEMPTION

Scott D. Covey

iUniverse, Inc.
Bloomington

Grey Redemption

Copyright © 2011 Scott D. Covey

This is a work of fiction. All of the characters, names, incidents,
organizations, and dialogue in this novel are either the products
of the author's imagination or are used fictitiously.

iUniverse books may be ordered through booksellers or by contacting:

iUniverse
1663 Liberty Drive
Bloomington, IN 47403
www.iuniverse.com
1-800-Authors (1-800-288-4677)

Because of the dynamic nature of the Internet, any Web addresses or
links contained in this book may have changed since publication and
may no longer be valid. The views expressed in this work are solely those
of the author and do not necessarily reflect the views of the publisher,
and the publisher hereby disclaims any responsibility for them.

Any people depicted in stock imagery provided by Thinkstock are models,
and such images are being used for illustrative purposes only.

Certain stock imagery © Thinkstock.

ISBN: 978-1-4502-9637-3 (pbk)
ISBN: 978-1-4502-9638-0 (cloth)
ISBN: 978-1-4502-9639-7 (ebk)

Library of Congress Control Number: 2011902449
Printed in the United States of America

iUniverse rev. date: 2/22/2011

I want to thank Cathy and Crystal for all the hard work editing a story and making it a book. Without whom this story could never have been told. Thanks to all my test readers you know who you are. You got me through the Inky Black.

For the Ice Cube Fairy.

For my father, and other vets like him, that fought for our freedom in WW2. So writers could write whatever they like. Thanks Dad.

PROLOGUE

I AWAKE TO A HOT, humid hell. I'm lying on my side outside a small boma, one of many circular grass huts in the village. It must be a cooking boma. I can still smell the food from last night's meal. "Sunday" the black in our Grey team lies beside me. We're so drenched in blood our fatigues feel like cardboard. Stiff and unyielding, they reek of the day's contacts and will no doubt draw leopard or hyena come sundown. Not that we are likely to see that spectacle one more time. We have multiple hits past our body armour and we're exhausted. We don't need to talk, we know the situation is far past dire. Sunday props himself up and is rewarded for this heroic effort with a bullet grazing his head. It moves his black beret like an unseen hand and I hear the mad bee-like buzz as it passes over my left shoulder to end in the red earth a meter from my knees. Sunday falls into my lap as I try to see if I can spot the sniper.

Another mad insect of death buzzes past into the wet earth with a light thump. Light Russian sniper rifle, in all likelihood, but the shooter can't correct for the down angle shot he needs. I feel Sunday rummaging around and stop when he hears my pistol clear its holster. I lean my body's mass against him in an odd, erotic-looking shooter's brace, as I catch a glimpse of a scope flash. I raise my weapon, a .44 magnum. My army buddies had teased me about my Israeli arms Desert Eagle.

"Compensating!" they taunted.

But now the gun's long distance afforded me a chance, albeit small, of hitting the shooter. The shot was 100 meters up and angled, in humid conditions. I didn't have a scope on my pistol so it was going to be a best guess. I aimed carefully at the opposing scope's reflection and I raised it up to the point of aim. Sensing, far more than sighting, I started a gentle squeeze. Another round whizzed by to the right of my head. But this time I saw the shooter's muzzle flash. With a strength and steadiness that belied my condition, I continued to squeeze. The retort of the gun was deafening. It rocked backward out of my grip and hit Sunday's head on its way to the blood-soaked red earth. I never knew if my round had found its mark or if the shooter had decided to move on, but no more rounds came our way. Snipers hate to be spotted.

Sunday had dug out our last bag of "Bleed Stop," which contained a white powder-like material to help clotting and stop serious blood loss. The problem was it burned like a bitch, as if you had thrust the area of skin into a swarm of blister beetles. Those little bugs could push out a fluid that would immediately cause second degree burns on exposed flesh.

Sunday pointed to my side and pushed the bag at me. I debated using it. I was in serious shock and pretty much dead. I figured why die in more pain or of heart failure from the shock to the system. But I remembered God's words: "Thou shalt not fall." The General was not really God, but I would have angered God far more quickly than him. I ripped the bag open and jammed the open gash of the bag to the open gash on my side.

The pain was immediate and unbearable. Thankfully, I passed out. When I awoke the sky was crimson red and I wiped my eyes figuring this was from the blood in them. No change, the clouds were unreal in the way they stood out against the red sky. I was reminded of my old man saying "red sky at night, sailors delight"; too bad I wasn't in the Navy! I chuckled a little and noticed Sunday had moved us into a little better hiding position inside the cooking boma.

Sunday saw my eyes and signed in battle language, a rough slang sign language all of us knew to various degrees. "The extraction chopper was on its way."

The effort to hope was almost too much. Sunday saw it and spoke.

"That big hand cannon of yours probably saved our butts."

I nodded in agreement and for some odd reason wanted – no, needed to – know how The Greys got their name. Despite being a member for three years, it had just occurred to me: I wasn't sure of our origins, so I asked. Sunday most certainly saw this as an odd request; I could see it reflected in his eyes. He slid down close, granting a dying wish or distracting a mind to abate shock, and told me.

The Greys, he explained, probably got their name from the Grey's Scouts, a Rhodesian mounted infantry unit created in 1975 and named for George Grey, a hero of the Second Matabele War. They were based in Salisbury, then the capital of Rhodesia, now Harare, Zimbabwe. The General probably heard of them there. Or he was just being a racist bastard! With that Sunday laughed (more of a gurgle, really) and continued.

"As a Black there are places I can go where you can't. The opposite is true as well. Another rumour is that he needed to create a team that could go anywhere, kill everything and disappear into the grey mist." I passed out once again.

Before the time of Moses there was only one Commandment.

Thou Shalt Not Fall!

In the Special Operators Unit called The Greys it was the same.

Thou Shalt Not Fall!

Very few of us ever broke that edict from "God." Yet for those few, the falls were such glorious examples of death and bedlam that one could almost forgive them of their transgressions. Almost, except that if one of the Grey's fell it meant the total destruction of that Grey Team.

The "Greys" comprised one Black and one White Special Forces Operator. Their combined skills were far greater than the sum of their abilities. They were the terror battle-hardened soldiers told each other to insure they stayed alert in the inky black, on watch. In reality, alert or not, if a Grey wanted your life it was theirs for the taking, for the dark caressed them like a cloak. Allowing them to move and exist in the zero point fields of reality and between an ethereal "not there" region. That's until they chose to unveil their existence with the fury and love of death only a truly super predator understands. Then, alone and dying, coming to terms with your own frail identity, the cold creeping along your spine you would understand: they were not the Operators legends celebrated in the annals of soldiering. They were creatures of myth that hunted the hunters.

Then it stopped. Our world no longer needed us and we were banished, separated and tossed aside to live out the remainder of our days. Broken and alone, many of us chose to end this fresh hell created by this new world order. Acknowledging there was nothing in this world honourable and deserving of our blood. Refusing to die slowly, rotting like some great forest giant only to fall soundlessly out of this world. Oddly enough, when one of the separated Greys took their own life the other would come to the same conclusion. Despite being separated by the thousands of miles and cultures each still worked as a team: a harmonic and gorgeous ballet of fatality.

CHAPTER ONE

I'M SITTING IN A RUN-DOWN working-class bar, looking at the bored faces around me. Tears, unseen or unfelt, seem to fill up the glasses of booze that mark time between us. The tepid boredom grates on us all. You wear it like a robe from a fine hotel, the cloying reality warm and secure across your shoulders. To me it feels like horsehair.

We've been friends since high school; you're a successful man, father of three. I've been to your home and shared many meals with your family. Despite this I want to smash your banal face and destroy the weak, limp mirror of me, which you represent. I feel no ill will toward you, yet my mind reels at your effortless acceptance of this nauseating world: a world of the familiar, built within the shelter of humanity. I want to smash my glass into the side of your neck, and let it tear a gash across your throat and then rip through the truth in which you have wrapped yourself. I want to wake the sleeping masses huddled in this familiar bar with the spray of your blood — using you to do nothing more than to get them to change expression! I feel, at my core, that to do this would be a better use of your life than the path you have chosen.

But I hold myself in check. I'm my own oppressor and jailer of emotions that I desire to feel and roll in. Like a dog with something dead I crave to rub the stink of this safe world from my skin. I yearn for the smell of men voiding their bowels in fear! For that sickly ammonia smell that underlies, and is usually missed; the copper smell of blood. I look at you and for a second can almost smell your flesh burning, the sweet smell of frying of human fat.

My expression must have changed for you turn to look over your shoulder, saying,

"See something you like?"

I pick some young girl my brain had cataloged while I spent time within my own thoughts and reply.

"Blue dress, three from the end."

You nod in acknowledgment of her beauty and I feel my horsehair get a little more uncomfortable. The press of this sheep-like humanity has brought me to the edge of fury and I know I must leave. For a brief moment I fantasize about what it would be like if I let loose the reins of my self-induced oppression. Let the fury and hatred of this banality grip me in ecstasy and love and turn on all of you as a grand display of mortality rendering flesh and bone in a magnificent dance of death and confusion. The "machine" behind my consciousness has cataloged the humans in the bar and knows the fear of this death spectacle would grip them like the sheep they are, allowing me to kill with impunity and precision more than 85 per cent of those here.

You dig for a pill out of your little bottle. An Ativan, no doubt, to ease the anxiety you're feeling.

"What's it like," I wonder?

An anti-depressant to get out of bed to live in the depressing world you chose and created. Then an anti-anxiety one to dumb down your own truth that this is not right.

I sip the remainder of my scotch and think, "Perhaps we have something in common after all? Perhaps my choice of drug is just older and more predictable. Perhaps I should tear out your heart and spare you this slow death, out of friendship?"

"I have to work early tomorrow," is all I say in the place of what I should say and do.

"Need a lift?" I ask.

Thankfully, you decline and I get up. The pain in my back is like a knife, reminding me of the world I was made to live in. I could get it fixed, but like the tattoos on my arms they serve a purpose – a purpose I'm trying hard to hold onto.

As I leave the overheated bar, the cool rainy night air of Vancouver flexes over my skin and I wonder what Sunday is doing. As I often do, I inhale the faint salt air and for a second can almost smell the tang of a lion. I feel him. Sunday, you're thousands of miles away, yet I can feel you sleeping like a coiled spring, wrestling in the shadowy darkness with tomorrow! Will tomorrow be our day to burn brightly like a berserk Nordic death star? An ambulance flies by, lights gleaming and siren wailing, shaking my focus — no doubt to pick up another rotted tree fallen from disease!

I walk toward my car, suddenly aware of the temperature difference between my feet and head.

"Why is 'the machine' still in high gear?" I wonder.

Sensing and probing past normal awareness levels into the damp darkness, scanning, aware and crouching, I see the mouse a second before I sense the approaching alley cat. I feel as though I can hear the static charge building on its fur as it rushes its prey. Its eyes narrowed in tight focus it moves past the dumpster on its killing run, unaware of me till it's almost on the sidewalk.

I can smell its dank fur; this alley tom is obviously an old street predator. I sense a motion as the cat imperceptibly changes its gait to allow its claws to come into the fray. Tail swirling for balance it swings its right paw at the running quarry. In the same instance the tom becomes aware of me. Even though it was only about a foot away on its death trajectory, he swirls and spins, claws grating the concrete like nails on a chalkboard. The sound makes my hackles rise.

I'm certainly down in the zone now. Why?

The cat, sensing an alpha predator, hisses and spits violently as it backs away to the far dumpster. The noise and fury increase as my foot touches the pavement. The howls are of terror and fury — a mask to hide the creature's true instinctual understanding. Froth explodes from the cat's mouth and nose as it involuntarily empties the contents of its stomach. In the same breath I smell the human, no doubt hidden. That's what had "the machine" on high alert!

I spin, turning my attention above the closed dumpster, on the fire escape I see the shooter. He has a long rifle, a Remington 700 with a large tactical scope. He's dressed in semi-military looking gear. My hand drops to the small of my back. There, warm against my back is a butter-soft leather holster, custom designed and worth almost as much as the small Walther PPK pistol it holds.

My thumb touches the back of the slide and my fingers wrap around the familiar grip.

"Slow down," I tell myself, "You're home!"

I reassess my situation. The silhouette has just become aware of me, his focus a tenth of a second ago on the screaming, frothing feline.

My pupils blow wide open. Years of operating in the dark have allowed me to increase the pupil dilation ability letting in much more ambient light. Almost to see in the dark! It lets me distinguish the darker shade of black and slightly less reflective area of cloth that clearly says "Police: ERT."

I let my hand drift casually away from my back while raising my left hand in a diversionary wave. The open raised palm an instinctual and universally recognized signal of, if not friendship, then submission. The officer, slightly startled, if his pinched voice was any indication, quietly says,

"Careful, that thing looks rabid; I'd suggest crossing the street, sir. This is the perimeter of a police situation."

I dip my head in acknowledgement and jaywalk across the street.

I cross back at the next corner and make my way toward my car.

I could have parked much closer to the bar, but out of habit I park at least 200 meters from my destination. It allows me to survey my surroundings during the walk over and back. I allow "the machine" to take in the surroundings and mark the changes. As precise as an accountant, it sees everything. Assorted street debris could be a bomb, the dark hotel windows could hold a sniper, and the lady waiting for the bus could be an assassin. Subconsciously, like breathing, "the machine" takes it all in. Nothing. The area is clear of potential threats. There are low-level thugs, drug dealers, and whores, but they ignore me like elephants ignore lions during the daylight hours.

Most have done time in jail and developed that sixth sense that allows them to sense a threat. Probably too dumb to really understand this skill they just know — I'm not a cop.

I'm six-three, with a lean and muscular frame. People often find my presence as intimidating as a cop's. My size and calm demeanour in this seedy neighbourhood might project that. No, they just know I'm not a cop. But they also know I'm not approachable; not a man you would proposition for sex, not a junkie. I make eye contact with some of them as I walk past. Most instinctively break my gaze and look down and right, like mountain gorillas do to the lead silverback. Some of the women search my eyes for some sign of compassion or contact; finding none they scan the oncoming headlights. Others, so broken they use the 100-yard stare of burned-out soldiers with too many hours on point.

I reach my car - one of my few displays of luxury. It's an Aston Martin Vanquish. Black, with a V12 engine, forged black-and-silver mag rims and red calipers. Inside the leather is black and grey and as soft as a supermodel's inner thigh. I saw my first Aston Martin head on and thought it looked exactly like a sleek black panther I once noticed stalking me in a tree on the African veldt! I walked onto the dealership lot and fell in love. One of the powerful machines was being moved into the work bay as I passed.

The raw power and furious sound of the engine connected with me like no woman ever has. I immediately ordered one – in black — and was amazed to discover it would take almost four months for delivery.

When that day came I was awestruck. Inside and out this was the projection of power and strength! The paint was liquid and flawless. Inside the engine compartment, snuggled over the light and dark power plant, was a plaque stating the car had been hand built in England with a plate indicating it was engine number 556 and that Mark Buller had inspected it. The driver's seat was more like a fighter jet cockpit than a car, the white face gauges and the red start button under the clock true classics. A little gold commemorative inscription on the dash stated the car had been "Hand built for Rhys Munroe." When I acquired it I felt what proud fathers must feel seeing their newborns for the first time!

The security system chirped off from about thirty feet away, the car announcing the happy arrival of its human. The engine sprang to life with a light push of my remote, and this time, like every time, I was pleased there was no accompanying explosion!

I slid in behind the wheel, the gentle vibration only a very quiet indicator of the immense power the vehicle possessed. I immediately felt the world become a little more correct. This vehicle was dangerous and a modest amount of throttle could create an unrecoverable slide. It was not a gentle mistress, more like the sturdy women clad in black leather who punished the flesh of public school Britons in London's classroom "dungeons."

I pulled out onto the dark street and chased the lights toward my home far away in the valley. The tires protested under the extreme torque, the dark shadows that had gripped me earlier lost in the squealing smoke of the punished tires.

I spent the time locked in my thoughts as the freeway disappeared behind me. The cranes that had become the unofficial bird of pre-Olympic Vancouver stood silent, as if in harsh judgment of the unfinished structures. The lights of Vancouver polluted the night sky, erasing any hint of star shine. I hate the city. Not that Vancouver isn't a beautiful city, it is! But the unnatural light and tracks of roads contribute to an inefficient transportation system. The road was clear but at one a.m. this would be expected. However, the speed limit was still 90 kph. It was hard to keep the speed below 100, as the beast wanted much more rein. It idled and ran rough at this slow speed as if it wanted to proclaim its pedigree like some proud stallion made to give trail rides to fat tourists. I itched to give her what she wanted! Another inch into the throttle and she would be rocketing down this wide-open stretch of road. But there would be a cop between here and the Valley.

Even at this late hour the RCMP would be out filling their quota of speeding tickets! Another example of how we have to dumb down the society to the lowest common denominator. The tires under me were worth more than some of the cars I was passing now and a brake job was in the neighbourhood of what these drivers made in a year. Yet they could do the same speed as me? How much safety could be built into a car worth nine grand? Three empty lanes were calling me forward like a seductive lover. But the system included points and at 12 points they can pull your license, so once again I found myself bent double in restraint. If it were a "fine only" system this drive would take forty minutes and not an hour and a half. Even that was pushing the limits a little.

The lights of the Port Mann Bridge over the dark expanse of the majestic Fraser River signaled an increase in the speed limit, now allowing us 100kph. This had originally been a toll bridge and the speed then was 70 mph in the old scale, or 112 kph in the current metric system. As we progress, we take two steps back.

I approach a black Acura, its windows darkly tinted. Right before I overtake it the vehicle strays into my lane. It's obvious the driver is either drunk or distracted by a cell phone, as he doesn't stop.

I brake hard, hitting the horn, and to add insult to stupidity the driver panics and hits the brakes. I swerve into the lane he had just drifted out of, knowing there was no other car there behind me, and tap the accelerator. The Aston leaps forward reminiscent of the cat it reminded me of when I first saw it. I'm past the idiot in less than a second. I glance at the side window as I pass and notice a young man on a cell phone. Being the stellar and courteous driver this poster child for "why we have to do such slow speeds," decides to try and put out the fire of my growing rage with gasoline! He flips his high beams on and then pulls behind me! My fury boils to the top and flows over me like molten lead.

The scenarios run through my mind in an instant. Change lanes and hit the brakes, while lowering the passenger window, and shoot this pathetic egotard in the head? Simply roll my window down and put three rounds, warning like, across his hood? From this distance the specially designed truncated arcane rounds fired from the 10mm Glock secreted under my seat would punch through his engine like hot piss through snow. Floor it and disappear into the night like a sodomized cheetah?

All of these take less than a second and I settle on one. I straddle the two lanes and slow down to 70, and the egotard comes up to ride my ass. I drop two gears using the paddle shifter on the steering wheel and tap the brakes while pushing the throttle to the firewall. The tires take off as easily as if we were on black ice. I shift, keeping the tires going and let off the brake. The tires are tearing at the road, as billowing burnt acrid rubber smoke obscures the car and, in less than four seconds, most of the bridge. I take my foot out of the throttle, ready to be crushed into the seat's back. The tires slow down and find traction, and with that traction, slams me back and rockets down the road like a fighter jet on an aircraft carrier launch. I ease off and look behind me to see only smoke. I'm just past the Department of Highways building by the time I see the annoying Acura lights again. They are back on low beam. I wonder to myself if the egotard driving knows how close he came to oblivion?

CHAPTER TWO

I ARRIVE HOME WITHOUT FURTHER incident.

Home is a simple Cape Cod house with a gated entry programmed to the car's signal. It's fully open before I turn into the driveway. The lights are on in the basement. My student tenant is still up. I find having a tenant helps keep the place looked lived in while I'm away fulfilling contracts. Pretty good gig for my tenant, too. While I'm gone she gets a 4,000-square-foot house in which to live — as long as she feeds the love of my life, Ruben the cat.

Ruben is a spotted Savanna, weighing in at about 35 pounds, a little fatter than he would have been in the wild. I see the blinds move, indicating he's aware of my arrival. He's a big cat who likes only me, and my tenant Andrea. Everyone else is viewed as an intruder and treated as such. Several friends have suffered wounds needing stitches for forgetting his one rule: Ignore me! As long as the intruder ignores his presence they are safe. To make eye contact is at your own peril!

I pull the car into one of the four parking stalls in the garage and notice that Andrea's car is not there. Odd, as the lower lights are on sensors, turning on with motion. I switched off the engine and got out of the car.

I walked away from the crouching, silent beast and heard the chirp as the security system locked the doors. The monitor on the house security system tells me the upstairs is armed. Downstairs and two of the exits are off. I tap my key fob near the panel, turning the whole system off.

As I opened the door I was greeted by some of the trance techno music of which Andrea is so fond. I entered the vaulted foyer and dropped my keys on the side table. Stepping out of my shoes I sensed her scent, fresh with a hint of baby powder, prior to her opening the heavy door. The house is soundproof between levels yet the doors, although steel and sheathed in wood, are the weak point. There is a door to Andrea's domain and then another to this area. She must have been waiting up for me, with her door open for the sound to be noticed here in the main entrance. There is a knock at my door, that's rarely locked, and then it swings open, her scent racing ahead of her thin silhouette.

"Rhys," she says nervously, slipping quietly into the entry hall. She's dressed in a housecoat of a soft blue, satiny material that reaches to her mid-calf. Her bare feet make little noise on the ceramic tile as she crosses over to me.

"Yes, Andrea," I answer, curious as to her nervousness.

I tried to remember if it was rent time. Most of the time she just deposited it to my account, but on a few occasions if she was late she would hand it to me personally, with an apology.

"Someone stole my car!" she blurted out.

I can see the concern etched on her young face. She's in her late-twenties, finishing a degree in human behaviour at university. She has lived in the house for three years, yet I'm still stunned at her beauty every time I see her. It's made more so by the fact she has no idea how exotic a creature she is. Her long limbs frame an athletic body, her elegant, long neck supports a slightly European-looking face under long, flowing blonde hair. Her large breasts push hard against the cross of her housecoat, its tie accenting her full hips.

"Where?" I ask.

"From the campus parking lot! It has the code for the gate. I waited up to make sure you changed it."

"Thanks, Andrea. That was very thoughtful of you. I'll disable it until the car is found"

"They've found it already! Burned!"

She's close to tears and from the redness of her eyes she has obviously been crying. Her scent is also a little sharper than normal. Not in a bad or unclean way, but like the tart smell of people under stress. I move to a wall sconce and press the hidden button making it slide up and reveal the security computer. I punch in the code and make the changes required, and explain,

"Well, I guess the insurance will cover it," I try to reassure her.

"But, but … they say it was only worth two grand!" she cries.

"I can't replace it for that and I can't afford to spend any money right now on a new one, or even a decent used car."

I shake my head at the injustice, pressing the "close" button, watching the sconce slide down into position. Andrea's car was perhaps not worth much more than three or four grand, but it was certainly worth more than two!

"I'm going to be away for a while," I tell her, "and I need to get the truck and the Cutlass's oil changed. Baby will need a few baths while I'm away too, to keep the dust off her. Why don't you do the oil changes and use it for school. Drive the Cutlass until you graduate. If you can't think of a better graduation gift you can keep her."

The lines in Andrea's face shift like lines in the desert sand on a windy day. Her eyes light up and a smile creeps hesitantly across her pretty face.

"Really?" she blurts out. Then her brow furrows as a thought intrudes on her joy.

"But, you only bought the car when I first started renting three years ago, and and … and," she stammers, "You fully restored it just last year! It has to be worth a great deal more than two thousand!"

I smile to myself. Obviously she's not a car chick. The paint alone cost twice that!

"That's why you're not buying it. You're borrowing it till you graduate — and doing me some favours for the privilege. When you're done school and if you get good enough marks so that I'm comfortable letting you mess around in my head we can work out a further trade. Therapy straight across for my first car!"

As I said it I knew it was a lie. I would never let anyone know my true motivation. Therapy was for people who could not come to terms with their true nature. Furthermore, I was not that attached to the Cutlass. Not that it wasn't a perfect example of retro muscle, it was! I preferred the precision engineering and styling of the Aston.

Andrea's face opened into a full smile and without a word she ran over and hugged me hard against her body. It was very out of place and awkward. I couldn't remember so much as shaking her hand before this! Now she was crushing me with a heartfelt hug, her leg between mine, full breasts crushed flat against my chest. I could feel the warmth of her body and her scent was more than a little alluring! I felt my body start to respond and I damped the sensation down and let my arms fall somewhat awkwardly on her shoulders. I fought the urge to lower my face to her blond hair and inhale deeply. Sensing my discomfort, she stepped back, her cheeks flushed.

"Sorry Rhys. I have just been so upset by this that, that, um, well I couldn't concentrate and I … I mean this is just so great and it's not like I have anyone to help, and … and … like I never expected this! Not that you're not a great guy! I don't mean it that way! I just, well, I just never expected anything to work out so well. Nothing in my world ever does! So this is just fucking — oops, sorry — frigging awesome! That's such a cool car — and I do look good in red!"

I smile, suddenly feeling far more paternal than I would have liked. It was strange, too, as she had always seemed so self-assured, almost too distant in her approach to me. Then again, it was a landlord/tenant relationship, nothing personal.

"Great. Well enjoy it. It's a good car and you deserve a break," I said.

I would have preferred to continue the conversation upstairs in more comfortable surroundings. Would she follow me if I made a pass? Her demeanour suggested it was a good possibility. But this would complicate the real role she played here.

She stepped further back. Now both of us were feeling awkward, not knowing how to break the physical connection with grace. I smile and say with some levity,

"Hey, isn't it past your bedtime? It's a school night," again, sounding more like a father.

She smiles taking my lead and says, "You're right!"

Turning, she pulls her robe a little tighter, bouncing those gorgeous fruits and retreats back to her side of the door.

It was going to be a long night!

I wander up the dark stairs to be greeted by Ruben. He's sitting at the top of the stairs but back near the wall, as if giving the humans privacy. He looks at me with the knowing look of an animal. I can almost see a judgmental expression reflected in his yellow-green eyes.

"What?" I ask. He responds with a non-committal meow.

He gets up and greets me with a rub. Then he sniffs loudly at my pants, smelling the tom of earlier this evening.

"Yeah buddy, I'm stepping out on ya."

I get no response as he wanders over the teak floor, claws clicking and waits knowingly as I get him some dry kibbles.

Cat satisfied, I go to the built-in fridge and retrieve a bottle of Talisker 15-year-old scotch from the freezer. Setting it on the textured concrete counter, I grab a crystal tumbler and pour myself a large measure. I have never acquired the habit of drinking warm booze when I don't have to. I also like my scotch neat. This compromise seems to be a good one. As the scotch warms slowly in the tumbler it changes flavour, without the watering down effect of ice. I sit in my favorite chair; a black leather massage chair made by Human Touch, its design looks more like an executive office lounger than an easy chair so common in massage chairs. I flip on the programmed massage and revel in the realistic sensations this chair provides. I look up to the dark sky, past the heavy Damask drapes, and through the triple pane, Lexan enhanced windows. No light pollution to obscure the stars here. Although the angled Lexan that provides a threat level three bullet resistance does distort the view to a degree. I swivel in the chair and retrieve an H. Upmann mag 50 cigar from my custom made humidor. I can never open this fine piece of furniture without rubbing my hand over the rich one-inch thick Spanish mahogany, and the carving on top that mimics the Executive Outcomes tattoo on my right shoulder. Executive Outcomes — a world, no a galaxy away. A day never goes by without me thinking about someone or some contact that I lived through! The aches and scars on my body could be a texture storybook like the ones popular with preschoolers. I reach for my ST DuPont cutter and lighter blindly, they are together exactly where I set them down last time. The sharp blades of the cutter neatly snip the end of the cigar. Picking up the James Bond ST DuPont lighter I feel its heavy weight. Flipping the top open elicits that hallmark ping. I roll the bullet igniter on its side and it springs to life. Perhaps not as easy to use as a jet-style flame lighter, I prefer the elegance of the simple orange flame. The cigar slowly comes to life. A few lighting puffs and the rich, chocolate, buttery smooth smoke fills my mouth. Despite having quit smoking for 10 years, I attempt to inhale and stop myself, wondering how long it will be before I lose that typical cigarette smokers desire?

I move the computer mouse and open my mail and my browser. One screen displays my mail and the other displays my Aston Martin as Safari opens my last bookmarked page, reverting to a scantily clad red head astride a motorbike. Looking at naughty pictures so close on the heels of the downstairs incident some how makes me feel like a dirty old man so I flip over to my mail.

I scan down the unread messages and notice an invoice for something bought at the iTunes store. I didn't recall making the purchase so I check the invoice. It's for some music purchased, that I didn't buy. Hmmm?

Then I see it in the special instructions; "Hello Captain."

My heart rate increases as I check the amount — $103.56.

I flip over to my browser and point it at a secure server. I check my account, nothing. Then I check another older account, one I haven't typed in so long my computer doesn't auto fill the address!

When it asks for a password I type in "Captain."

Nothing. I type in "Executive Outcomes." Again, nothing.

I take a long pull on my cigar. It's gone out so I relight it. Two more pulls and once again the smoke curls up past the computer screen to the ceiling. A sip of scotch jogs my brain.

I type in "10356."

Success!

The browser starts to open the mail and even though my bandwidth is big, it seems to take forever. It opens on the inbox frame and I know there will be nothing there! Nothing sent over the net these days. There are too many high-end alphabet agencies with snoop programs out there to be sure of confidentially. I click on the drafts page and it opens and my heart skips a beat as I read the subject line of the saved draft.

"Re: Simon Alexander."

Simon Alexander! My mind stretches back, making the reach to the time I met the Colonel in Liberia, the light humming of the chair and the tasty cigar replaced by a remembered scent that must be like the unwashed testicles of an old goat.

He was quite a commanding figure for a rather diminutive man. Small, but with a coiled core seemingly to denounce the laws of physics. He projected a sense of self that, despite my personal dislike of Paras, touched me even then on my first meeting. He was a confident, true leader of men, one that knew the price of war and was ready to spend the lives to achieve his goals. Being from the Para Regiment he was well versed in small squad tactics, capable and not one of us thought otherwise. You could simply read it on the man like so many of the "Caution Land Mines" signs that littered the African veldt.

There was quite a bit of excitement at the meeting. He was, after all, a movie star mercenary, having starred in a film about the Irish troubles. A man schooled at Eton and forged at the Special Air Service School in Hereford, England, when the selection process for the SAS routinely killed men. I had to admit that despite my abject hatred of the British SAS, or any other Brit that served in or near Free Derry, Ireland, I was won over by him and his charm. You just had to respect the strength of the man; his focus and intelligence were diamond sharp.

I was sitting on the back of a non-tracked military truck, smoking what served for a cigar in this lousy place and having a cup of coffee. I had a little cook pot heating up a stew like concoction and was trying unsuccessfully to make dumplings out of the corn flour common in these parts. I was wearing a set of the Grey's battle fatigues, the special fabric pattern different from the others. My battle shirt was off and only a t-shirt kept the hot sun off my back.

I remember the t-shirt. The men and I had found a custom silk screening shop in the most unlikely of places just outside the shantytown of Firestone, and had a few made. This one had the EO crest on the left breast and the slogan "Fit in or Fuck Off". The fuck off part was written in Afrikaans to highlight our speech preference. A common cultural anomaly of the area is despite both speakers knowing each other's language neither speaks the others. Each speaker stubbornly speaking in his or her own tongue, despite possessing a complete understanding of the other's. On the back of the t-shirt it read, in Afrikaans, "I'm not a UN soldier, go die someplace else".

I heard Simon Alexander approach, although his practiced walk was very stealthy and the soft tropical dirt cushioned his step. I figured he was coming over to meet me, as I wasn't in the throng of people that surrounded his arrival, yet was distinct being white and uniformed. I heard the intake of air past his thin lips as he prepared to speak and announce his arrival. I spoke first.

"AithnÃonn cÃarg cÃarg eile." Translated from a Gaelic proverb it means, "One beetle recognizes another beetle." It caught the military tactician completely off guard. He stopped, and he took a long inhale through his nose before speaking.

"I'm Colonel Simon Alexander and TIA."

TIA was a phrase used to comment on many things and situations found on the Dark Continent. Like Aloha in Samoan, it could mean good things or bad things depending on the inference. Literally translated it meant: "This Is Africa."

I was impressed; he had done his homework and was getting the lay of the cultural land that was so important. He moved around to my front and took a great interest in my cooking pot. Quite suddenly he produced a spoon, curled at one end with an old well-used leather lanyard attached. This took me back. "The guy walks around with a spoon in his fatigues?" I thought.

"You trying to make dumplings with the shit the locals use as flour?" he asked.

"Yes, Sir."

"If I go get some biscuit flour will you drop the sir?"

"Yes, Sir."

With that he turned about and walked off to where his gear lay. I watched him go. He walked confidently and quietly, his eyes scanning the area and taking in as much as he needed to and yet his gaze wasn't rapid like a scared rabbit. His personal gear was squared away correctly for a combat situation reminding me this man had seen his fair share of hotspots. He returned with a bag of flour and sat down beside me. "Got another mixing bin and some fresh water?" He asked.

"Yes, Simon I do." With that and the sharing of my stew we both agreed, silently, to forget, or at least suspend, whatever shared dark history we might have. He ignored the tattoo on my wrist that said in Irish, Sniper at Work, and I ignored his cap badge, TIA.

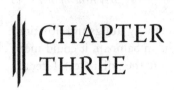

CHAPTER THREE

I'M STARTLED BACK TO THE present. Ruben decides he must see what I'm up to. He lands in my lap and extends his claws to gain stability. The slight pain is a pleasant, familiar one. He turns to face me and bumps my face with his. Smelling his kibble breath I set down my cigar and run both my hands down his soft sides. I'm rewarded with a rough tongue lick to the nose, followed by a love bite. He looks into my eyes and I return the gaze. I see an understanding. I'm sure he knows I will be leaving.

People often tease me when I comment on this. They scoff at the idea our house pets possess this level of intelligent thought. "They don't understand us" or "they can't communicate." are statements usually made to debase me of my fantasy that Ruben can and does understand.

I usually just smile and acquiesce to their position, knowing I can't very well tell them the truth. The truth being that, as a Grey, I knew what Sunday was going to do without any verbal communication. He would be on the other side of a compound incursion and I could sense him, waiting. Sunday, in better physical shape, was usually to the lying-up point, or LUP, minutes before I was at mine. When I would reach my LUP I would usually need a minute to get my breathing under control. There in the darkness, I could feel him patiently waiting for me. Then, projecting myself to him I would think, "Now!" and together we would slide very slowly toward our objective, masked by the darkness. I knew there was some form of non-verbal communication between Ruben and me, just as I knew there was between Sunday and me. Ruben was a cat so it was disjointed and the focus time was short, but it was there as surely as his hind claws were digging into my thighs.

Bored with this he climbs onto the desk and under the big screens. How many hours had I watched this exact moon trace across its predictable path in the African sky? The sky there is much more expansive and bright. The amount of stars visible to us on this side of the world are much more diminished. It was never boring listening to the eco-tourists that shared some of the same hotels with the less than eco-friendly. I loved to sit in the grand dining balconies of the hotels that surround the area of Victoria Falls, and listen to people certain they were in the deep of Africa. Look! They would exclaim at all the stars; it's like someone threw a million more lights up there. This identified them as North Americans — usually from the west coast. If they identified Orion's belt as being so much higher, then they were Europeans, and so the course would go. Their national origin would allow me to place a cultural milieu to their observations.

Listening to others talk in English helped me stop the running ticker tape in my head prior to, or post operation. It served as a generic form of re-entry therapy, something private contractors did not receive from their employers. Listening to the mostly naive observations of these people brought the machine to normal levels and was often very amusing.

Many of these tourists comment effusively on the dangerous wildlife, completely ignoring the horrific death sitting so close. So close in fact that its wings moved as they reached for their glasses filled with wine — the tiny killer's stature so much smaller than the ones found in Vancouver. Her long proboscis, bounces rhythmically with the night air, as she sniffs for the exhaled carbon dioxide that identifies her meal. Finding her prey she takes flight, her short sharp edged wings making that familiar high-pitched whine, circling upward through the moist hot air. Targeting the carbon dioxide source, as accurately as a GPS-guided drone, she lands on the nape of the tourists' neck.

The landing is softened by the lemon yellow Egyptian cotton, blouse. It's one of the worst colours to wear in the bush or on a safari. While attractive to humans, it's also attractive to insects. She sets to work, proboscis vigorously testing the temperature on the surface, like a sounder looking for oil close to the crust. Finding her mark she secretes a painkiller and anti-clotting agent down her long tube and drives it into the woman's neck. The lady doesn't sense the attack and takes another long pull of her cheap merlot. The predator's middle starts to glow crimson from the meal.

Then, as quickly as she arrived she pulls out and is gone. The tourist reaches up and feels her neck, without looking, and has no idea the danger she's in. Later, when she realizes she has been bit she will comfort herself, secure in the knowledge that she's taking an anti-malaria drug and will be fine. This error in thinking is akin to believing one can swim across a river known to have crocodiles because they can swim faster than the crocs. The deaths that result from each mistake may be different in ferociousness and suffering, but it's death just the same. Having battled and won two fights with the little predator I think that I would rather take that swim.

The mistakes made by these visiting sheep are not really their fault. Tour operators lead them to slaughter. Perhaps they don't die in the millions like the locals of the area, but die they do. Simple advice could spare them. The nets around your bed are not just for ambience. If you're not covered, be sure you're wearing lots of Deet.

I remember one such conversation like this I had in an airport lounge with a rich, granola-fed environmentalist. I say rich as we were in the first class London airport lounge in Heathrow four. She was going on about citronella and how good it was at keeping most mosquitoes away. She was much younger and naive and perhaps I was more compassionate than I am now.

I suggested using Deet. She rolled up her nose as though I had vomited on the table.

"Oh. That's a harsh chemical and not good for you. Besides, it smells like crap"

I looked at her oddly as she slapped away this sage advice. She went on,

"Anyway, very few areas in South Africa and Zimbabwe have malaria."

I continued to look at her, unbelieving. It was if she was denying the existence of air.

"Really?" is all I could bring myself to say.

Then with a sharp tongue and the insolence bred of youth and money she mimicked.

"Really?"

The disrespect in her tone was as evident and intentional, as if she were speaking to a servant. She had obviously judged me and found me beneath her in class, despite our sitting in the first class lounge. I travel in light shorts and t-shirts, so perhaps she thought I was some traveler lucky enough to enjoy a free upgrade from coach, instead of paying the full $13,000 flight.

My anger was not as venomous in those days as it is now, but I still pulled her up short.

"Well I'm sorry you feel that way dear, cause if your citronella lets even one infected mosquito bite you the smell of you sitting in your own shit and puke will be far worse. Let's hope you have personal fortitude so you can tell them to call dear old daddy to save you. God help you if they think you're just an armpit-hair braided, dope smoking, friend of Jesus. All those elocution lessons and finishing schools will be burned out of your fevered brain like carpet under a blowtorch!"

Her mouth flapped like a fish trying to draw raw non liquid air across its gills as I got up and left her to her ideals.

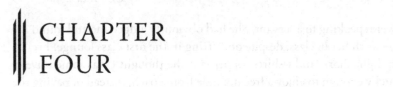

CHAPTER FOUR

THE RINGING PHONE INTERRUPTS MY thoughts. I look over at the glowing display and there it is — 053 area code in South Africa. Pomfret!

Pomfret a shantytown the South African government set up on Defense Force Land to provide a place for over 3,000 soldiers and their families. It was known in the industry of private contractors as the place to go to hire good talent. Most of the soldiers were part of the infamous "Battalion 32," known as the Buffalo Squadron ("Terrible Ones"). Most South Africans saw the predominantly black squadron as a brutal force, which did the dirty work for a repressive apartheid regime. But they were also taking on Marxist guerilla movements in Angola and Mozambique, backed by Havana and Moscow. The Squadron was led by Ben Visser the notorious Commander who had started Executive Outcomes. The town was destined for destruction because of asbestos poisoning, but in reality, involvement of the former South African soldiers in Simon Alexander's plan had infuriated President Thabo Mbeki's Government. As a result, most of the families were moved and scattered across the republic.

I looked at the phone again. The call would be coming from "Chiwa," whose name means death in Malawi. He was one of the few people I knew who had stayed in the old asbestos mining town of Pomfret.

I reached for and slipped on my headset. I expected the conversation to be a long one — and in Portuguese, the language we had usually used when we were together. Chiwa spoke several languages. Some I understood, but most I couldn't do much more than muck through. His grasp of English was decent but my understanding of Portuguese was better. The Bluetooth connected to my phone system chirped, ready to go. It was nearly 2:00 a.m. here — lunchtime in Pomfret.

"Hello my friend" I said in Portuguese, followed by the traditional "How'z it" — African slang for how are things in general?

Chiwa answered slowly, in English.

"Things are as they are. Life is hard, more so now that my family is in a new place without me. How is your pussy?"

The traditional polite structure of asking about one's family had been taken care of, spoken in the language of the listener, demonstrating respect.

"We should do this in Portuguese," I commented.

"I imagine you don't have too many people to practice English with."

"True," he responded. Then he continued in Portuguese.

"I have been contacted by some old friends to organize the removal of another old friend from a slightly poor nursing home. Have you too received this request?"

"Yes" I answered, while I checked for security, more out of habit than anything else. The current line voltage on the phone was -49.3 volts, probably secure unless the "Officials" had my phone on a list.

Chiwa asked, "Have you made your decision?"

"What choice do I have, Chiwa? He's a friend and a brother. I'm in."

I had decided that as soon as I received the request.

"What is lacking are the particulars."

"True, I meant no disrespect. Only so many have sat on their hands for so many years I thought there might be an edict not to!"

"Chiwa, I don't have a £293 million-pound three-year contract with anyone to motivate me! I'm a contractor, just like you, but wise enough not to sit in a car again with the man who messed up so dramatically in Papua New Guinea."

I was referring to the total fiasco that Simon and Tom had got into in Bougainville. It had spelled the start of the downward spiral of the industry in Africa.

"True, sir. I totally understand and agree. But this is in contrast to the money that seems to be behind this plan. My salary and advance was a most generous offer. This is the only indication I have that this is backed by some big money interests."

"Perhaps someone grabbed a sense of honour, Sergeant Chiwa," is all I can add.

"I have no other particulars regarding the grandfathers' re-location. How many people are in the game at this time from the rank side of things?" I asked.

"Seventy-five, sir. Each has received a £2000 pound advance to secure their services. We have also been promised £1000 pounds a month."

I thought that this was indeed a great deal of money for the sharp-end men to make. There had to be some very deep pockets organizing this little dance in the jungle.

"Glad to hear it, Chiwa! You guys deserve to be taken care of this time! How many of the originals?"

I was referring to the ones that had been arrested in Harare.

"Thirty-eight. They want to redeem themselves. I wish Mabeko and Seni had of lived to see this. They both would have desired to be in the fray with you again, sir!"

"Thank you, Chiwa"

It was the only response I could muster thinking about the two men who had died in the Zimbabwe prison. Good men, both of them brothers. The memory silenced me long enough for Chiwa to continue.

"Anyway Rhys, I guess we will be seeing each other soon enough. I should let you go to bed"

"Roger that, Chiwa. It's late. Take care. Your adopted parents (making reference to Chiwa's adopted citizenship in South Africa) are really not cool with these types of church services."

"True, sir! I will make sure to take all pains to hide it from them."

"Goodnight, Chiwa. Thanks for the call"

"Goodnight Sir. It will be good to see you and Sunday together again."

With that I heard the insects of the area, their sweet trill joining me on the line for a moment as the receiver was moved from Chiwa's ear and replaced in its cradle.

I checked the line voltage again as it bounced with the disconnection. I stayed on the line for a count of three, more out of habit than tactical necessity. If any agency was listening I knew there would be no indication on this fiber optic first world line. But habits, good ones, were sometimes rewarded. There was nothing and I pushed the button on the headset ending the call. I pulled up the draft message and wrote two lines:

"Roger. Retirement home relocation idea. I'm in for the move. Details of meeting time and place required at earliest possible option."

I clicked the "save" button, and then reopened the saved draft to insure my text had been added to the message. I logged off to wait for a reply later on.

CHAPTER FIVE

I RELIT MY CIGAR AND thought back to the debacle that had started us down this road so many years ago. It had started, like so many of these endeavours, with just such a phone call. I had been sitting in the dark watching my friend, the moon, walk his usual path across the night sky, his reflected light creating shadows for my mind to chase across the office.

The shadowy world I live in now started very much the same way, watching my friend's shadow trace its path. A whole world and many destroyed lives had passed since that fateful day. The choices we make at one junction of our lives forever stain the world to come. It was odd how a decision so early on, made innocently and without any real forethought could cast a shadow that forever coloured the world I was to live in.

How many lives had I taken? How many times had the reverse almost been true? Would I have made that decision so many nights ago in that dark apartment if I'd known then what I knew now? Probably! Life is spent like a gambler at the Black Jack table! The knowledge is there. The odds are against you but betting against those odds makes the chips so much more valuable.

After five years of military service I had been given a honourable discharge from the Canadian Armed Forces Special Service Force. Leaving had left a poor taste in my mouth, but I had made a decision that if I were to be re-coursed again out of sniper school I was going to quit. I had been trying to get that module from the week after I finished airborne school. I was technically not even a regular member, as I had been brought in from the reserves. I had finished basic training and trade qualifying courses one and two within the reserves. The

Royal Westminster Regiment then offered me the chance to go onto Reserve Class C status to take the program. I agreed and was sent to the airborne school, run out of Cold Lake, Alberta. It was significantly more brutal than I had expected. My sergeants and other non-commissioned officers knew I was reserve and they did everything in their power to get me to quit. What they ended up in fact doing was forging me into the perfect soldier I would have never believed I could be.

To say they disliked me would be an understatement. I was taking 'their' course and I wasn't even a sworn regular member. The other program participants were career soldiers from various elite units in the CAF, brought together to create airborne units within their own home units. I had no home unit other than the Reserves. "Weekend warrior units" they called us — only part time soldiers. It made life a little more than difficult and I was set aside and alone from my course mates. This created a sense of focus that for me was a first in my life. Instead of going on leave with the rest of my course mates I stayed and practiced my training and focused on the modules with a concentration that I had never shown before in my life.

A regimental sergeant major, RSM, either found this loner interesting, or took pity on him, and took pains to engage me when he could. He helped me find further reading material and course work to occupy my time alone. He also introduced me to my now love of cigars. One night I was doing the obstacle course, alone I thought. I had done this on many nights practicing the track with the added difficulty of darkness. The blue-black of the night sky added to the danger of the treacherous course! This was forbidden as many of the classmates had already been RTU'D, or Returned To Unit, having suffered training ending injuries running this circuit in the day! I had managed to practice and get a course passing time in this inky black. Doing it in the day was a cakewalk and I was sure my times would stand for years to come.

One night I had just finished the course and collapsed at the end, lying on the ground trying to drag enough oxygenated cold air into my tortured lungs to allow me get back on my feet. Lying there sucking air and dirt, I tasted an acrid smoke. Looking up and into the surrounding dark I saw a red ember like glow that cast its light up into a cold set of grey eyes. This apparition floated closer to me and the scent of the smoke got stronger. The eyes reappeared, now only a few feet from my face, cold and angry. The red light reflected the evil these eyes had seen. Following the exhalation of scotch tinted breath and smoke there was a voice attached to this surreal apparition.

"This area has a fence around it for a reason, Private. That locked gate is a pretty damn good indication that we don't want you here alone. Running this exercise at night is folly, my little retard!"

Now I realized this dark demon was in fact the RSM. I would have felt a little more comfortable thinking this was the demon Baal! My mind raced at the potential outcomes. RTU'D being likely; a black stroke on my record at this early point in my career would follow me for years!

"Get off your chin strap, retard and stand the fuck up when I address you," he barked at me.

I jumped to attention, brought back from my dark reverie. My legs screamed in protest and my mind was straining to remain conscious.

"Do you smoke cigars, retard?"

My mind searched for the actual question, disbelieving what it had just heard.

"Sir," I stammered stupidly. "Say again, sir."

"I asked you if you smoked cigars, you simpering retard. Easy question really. Did you have a fucking stroke while your dope- smoking hippy ass, sent to my unit by the Kremlin to fuck it up, was running MY course?"

"No sir", I stammered. I was feeling like a cornered possum.

"I don't smoke anymore. Quit years ago. Bad for your health!"

The RSMs' hands moved in the dark as he replied;

"I asked you a fucking question, not for some bullshit armchair doctor opinion."

With this I felt his hand enter the space between us and I braced, ready for what might come. A slap? A punch? My muscles were tensing, for the impact to my chest I was sure to come. When it didn't I looked down to see his hand holding a brown stick that looked like a four inch long piece of dog shit. Stunned I stared at the hand and offered dog rocket. Again my silent reverie was shattered by his voice. "Boy, I'm thinking you might not be as smart as I think you are!"

I reached out and took the offered stick. It was already clipped and ready for smoking, but at the time I had no idea that this had been done having never smoked a cigar. I placed it in my mouth and the acid taste was pungent on my dry lips. There was a flash and a flame under the cigar. I took a pull to light the cigar and immediately inhaled like a reformed smoker always keen to fall. I coughed as the thick smoke scoured my lungs as tear gas. "Don't inhale, it's bad for you, or so some retard arm chair doctor told me." It was the reward for my smoking transgression.

He sat down and pulled out a flask. I joined him on the large log and listened as he unscrewed the cap of his flask and took a long pull. He offered it to me,

"Here. This stuff is cheaper than therapy, and you won't get some simpering chick or priest raising their eyes at you when you tell them you liked killing the asshole."

I accepted the flask and took a pull of the strong liquor. The sharp taste was good and instantly made my mouth significantly less dry. I could talk and wasted no time taking advantage of this renewed ability.

"Sir, I meant no disrespect. I figure a great deal of the operations I'll be on will be at night so I figured you should train as you'll fight."

I let the statement hang like ice in the air.

He took a long pull of his cigar before responding.

"I told the lead ass brass the same thing a year ago but was overruled as they thought it was too dangerous!"

Then he added, partially to himself.

"Not like were creating people to teach fucking school — war is dangerous!"

We said nothing more for over an hour as we shared cigars and the rest of his flask. I was aware he was gone when I heard, from several yards behind me,

"Get some sleep retard. You need bunk time as much as you need time on this course."

I had not heard or sensed him move. He was there and then just not there!

I was awoken in the morning in the usual noisy manner. Today it was a trash can being insanely beaten. The noise was deafening.

"Get up, get up! Get up, you fucking maggots!" was the call.

The sound in the barracks was the music of chaos. Men were jumping to their feet or rolling to the floor, grabbing rifles before identifying the threat as a friendly one – albeit loud and obnoxious.

We all struggled in various degrees with our consciousness and set to getting our bunks squared away, ready for inspection. This was the last day of the course so everyone knew what was expected from them. The inspection that was to follow would hardly be the two-hour affair it had been at the beginning of the course. Then most of our bedding and worldly possessions, such as they were, ended up on the floor. Today would not be such a day. Today we would be spared this course-specific treatment. Specific in that it was designed to make the candidate feel hopeless and quit. Nothing was quite good enough. Out-of-order transgressions were harshly rewarded with a complete dump of all goods to the floor. No today, being the last day, we would be spared this. We assembled in front of our bunks, stiff from poor sleep on the hard mattresses — mattresses we would yearn for in the very near future.

The RSM entered the barracks. His tightly controlled pace exactly twenty-eight inches, and with a crack like a shot from his ancient side arm his leg came "up six inches and down eight."

He stood there at attention for a long time. My eyes were boring a hole in the far wall. I allowed my peripheral vision to expand, taking care to not allow my eyes to move. I could see him looking down the line at all of us. His steely grey stare accessing and appraising us as though he was an appraiser from Sotheby's looking at a fine gem. His forehead was furrowed and his shave, while razor-close, had been made several hours earlier.

It was 5:30 a.m., and I thought, "How early does this Methuselah of war rise?"

"Perhaps he doesn't sleep," I thought. "Perhaps he's just waiting like the dusty machines of war to be started in times of need." My thoughts were pulled up short by his look and sharp inhalation as he prepared to address us.

"Retards," he started, his tone crisp, precise. "Today would have been the water drop exercise and with it the completion of your training. Following that would have been the masturbatory backslapping and general jocularity following the completion of this course. A ceremony officiated by myself and whatever brass ass saw fit to drag themselves away from their secretary ogling to pin you all with your new Airborne wings and salute you — like smashing champagne on a new boat.

Today your chest should push out like the little bantam roosters you all are and you would toast each other's elite status within these ranks!

Today all this would happen and make you feel so proud. Some of you would shed invisible tears wishing your long dead parents, grey in the grave, were here to share your moment. Others here would inhale the love of your spouses lying to them as you did that your special status made you safer in the battlefield.

So close your fucking eyes! All of you!"

We shut our eyes.

"Good, now imagine all of that! All the pomp, circumstance and ritual that this standing army can provide your frail little egos!"

With that he turned left and with precise measured steps marched to the left and turned toward the end of the barracks.

"Imagine, he bellowed, "the band is struck and playing God Save the Queen."

His measured steps continued down the rank of men and I smelled his sharp scent as he passed me, pausing briefly, only to continue to the man on my left, his scent leaving my presence like the warm sun passing behind a cloud. I heard him reach the end and then crossing to the other side of the barracks he continued in the oddly directed standing visualization exercise.

"The fly-over by the big C-130 aircraft happens now, as you all stand in the hot sun. You can feel your hot little wings that have been presented to you in your chubby little hands. You can't wait to sew them on your combat shirts! You yearn to press the sharp little points through your dress uniforms, to be momentarily blinded by the short flash as they catch the sun."

He continued back up the right side again pausing briefly at each bunk and pair of soldiers. Reaching the front he again sharply turned right and marched smartly to the center. His halt again a like a shot. He turned right and once again faced the hollow square! Congratulations gentlemen, you're all Canadian Armed Forces Airborne! Take a moment to feel proud."

He paused, and continued a moment later;

"Enough! Open your goddamm eyes!"

The command shattered our personal reveries.

"That's it, and that's as good as it gets and it will never get quite that good again. A situation has occurred in the previous Soviet state of Kosovo and you're all flying out at 2130 tonight to join your home units and deal with this threat. Those of you attached to fluffy support groups will be re-assigned to a Special Service Force.

Retards, we're putting you into harm's way and it's very unlikely all of you will share turkey-fucking dinner with your families this year. I will not apologize for the abrupt nature of this graduation ceremony, nor will I coddle you like some surrogate mother or wife. This is life, reality hard-honed and sharp men. This is war!

The water drop will go ahead at 10:00 hours, and for those of you who complete it, a further terror awaits you after your flight to the Balkans.

For those of you that fail … "

He let the statement hang in the air.

"Do yourself a favour and drown in Cold Lake and save yourself the pain and suffering I will deliver unto you."

"Your orders will be given to you on the flight over. Operational security is dark on this one, no calls to loved ones or your mangy cat. The human resources department is in full swing; calling your contact numbers and telling them you're going on maneuvers in the high Arctic.

"Ladies, take an hour to get yourselves and your weapons in battle shape. Strip the oil from your rifles and the cobwebs from your head. Munroe, see me in my office directly after dismissal. Airborne Class 1984-6, Dis-missed!"

We all turned right and marched the required three steps and broke off to look at one another. I spent only a moment exchanging glances with my newly "badged" teammates. On our bunks were both the distressed combat wing patch and the black box that contained our gold dress wings. As I made my way directly to the RSM's private office I wondered how many would actually get the chance to wear them.

I arrived at the cheap wooden door, adorned with two strips of white medical tape with "RSM Exner" roughly printed in black marker. I hesitated only a moment and knocked. From behind the door a voice called out. "Enter."

I walked into the small space, closed the door, and came to attention. I stood there for about six seconds until he spoke. "Munroe, stand easy, take a chair."

I sat, very un-relaxed, in a hard wooden school chair. I could see from the folder in the RSM's hand that he had my file and was reading it with immense concentration. He opened with two questions.

"Munroe, have you ever read your file?

There is no next of kin on your file. Am I to take this to mean there is no one in your life?"

I answered. "No sir. Yes sir!"

He looked over his reading glasses and said.

"Wow, what a chick answer. Mixed in message and confusing as hell. Relax and answer the questions would you."

"Sir," I responded, "My parents died when I was six years old. And no, I have never read my file."

"Well you should. But as time is short and I have other things to do, allow me to summarize. I'm reading a direct quote here:

"Rhys Munroe seems to be an individual created by both nature and nurture. He scored a full 17 points out of 20 on the Hare's Psychopath Checklist-Revised. Losing his parents at an earlier age has severely hampered his ability to form lasting, loving, normal relationships. He presents with an extremely high IQ and seems to feel comfortable within the artificial structure of the Military. It's this psychologist's professional opinion that he will excel at and thrive within this structured environment. However, care should be taken when viewed within the command structure for promotion."

Exner allowed me only a few moments to digest this before continuing.

"During a recent training exercise Private Munroe presented to the clinic with a severe tear across the back of his left hand. The skin was avulsed and open, damage to three tendons on the metacarpals was evident and the patient had a marked reduction in mobility. Although this type of injury should be accompanied by severe pain, Private Munroe was not presenting as such. His resting blood pressure was one hundred over a systolic of sixty. Blood tests were ordered to see if there were any drug-related reason for this muted response in keeping with policy for suspected drug use. These tests were negative. Private Munroe's hand was repaired using only local anesthetic and the patient did not ask for pain medication. A script was, nonetheless, given for Tylenol 3. It was never filled."

"Do you know what this tells me, Rhys?" the RSM asked.

"No" I said, feeling a little like an outsider. I was surprised they had tested me for drugs without consent. Even more surprised that they kept such detailed records.

"It tells me you're very much like me! I could be reading my own records. You're a special kind of soldier. One who survives to get the job the done. It also means you'll never rise above my rank. The top brass don't like predators calling the shots up to those above!"

"Okay, back to the subject at hand," he continued.

"You completed the Combat Diver course at the top of your class, right?"

"Yes sir, I did." I answered proudly.

"So am I correct in the assumption that this drop into water would be a walk in the park?"

"I don't anticipate any problems, sir," I agreed.

"Great. Then I will just tick you off!

You are unfortunately currently on Reserve Class C status. Is that right?"

I nodded.

"Well that's a United Nations service designation and we need an advance group in place prior to the main force insertion. The good news is you won't be jumping into the unknown dark, like I will be, tomorrow. The bad news is you'll be on the ground calling the drop point in and holding the position with a long-range reconnaissance Special Service Force team until we get there."

I nodded once and, in doing so, acknowledged my agreement and understanding.

"Congratulations, Munroe you're now a Corporal and a member of a very elite team. It's one I trained in myself years ago. You'll get my nod and recommendation to the team leader. I don't do this lightly or because I need to. You've earned it."

With that he handed me my new rank: two chevrons. I had some sewing to do.

He didn't say anything for a while and then reached into an elaborate box and pulled out two more cigars and handed one to me.

"We will smoke these when were on the ground, in harm's way"

I took it with the hand already holding my new rank.

"Your flight leaves from the main hanger in 30 minutes, get kitted up, son, and we will see you on the ground."

I got up, taking this as an informal dismissal. His stare froze me at the halfway point between standing and sitting. Steely, dark and like a man that could see and take my soul if he so desired. A smile slipped into place and he waved me off. I left the office quietly closing the door behind me and re-entered the main barracks. I faced the quizzical stares of my teammates with silence and walked to my bunk.

I quickly made my kit bag up and headed for the main hanger without a word to anyone.

Exner and I would never smoke that cigar. Enemy fire crashed the plane without any jumpers clearing. There were no survivors! It would have been nice to save the cigar if only to smoke it later in his honour. Saving myself and completing as much of the mission that could be salvaged was the predominant concern. I had barely managed to do that!

CHAPTER SIX

I LOOKED AT THE SCREENS again, their brightness muted by long inactivity. I shook the mouse and the screens illuminated the room, but only marginally.

Ruben stirred and looked at me with one eye. Sensing my answer to his unasked question he closed it again to continue his nap. Only when I got up and made the way to my bedroom would he come up and check his crystal tumbler to ensure it was full of water. Content he had enough water and would not need to use the toilet bowl overnight, he would look at me in the darkness and jockey for position with the hand holding my scotch on my chest. Satisfied I was indeed going to sleep he would complete his house check, jumping off the bed to wander into each room of the house as if searching for unseen guests. Once certain we were alone he would return to take up position in the crook of my arm or rear of my legs, depending on what state of sleep I had fallen into.

That time was a long way off and I refreshed the secure anonymous website and logged in to see if the draft had changed. It had. During the course of my call and silent thoughts someone had logged in and made some changes. The draft now had three more lines:

"Glad to see you're still up late these days, Captain. Awesome you can help. Meeting is set for Amsterdam, Tuesday afternoon, Russian Tea Room — 1500 hours. Bring your overnight bag. You'll be carrying on from there."

There was no Russian Tea Room, of course. There was, instead, a Russian mob-run brothel and bar. It was not a place frequented by tourists. Some stumbled across it on occasion, but they were effectively dissuaded from staying for more than one drink. But only if they made it past the door. A giant man held the entrance like the fabled three-headed dog guarding the gates of hell. His real name was Koyla but everyone called him Cerberus.

He was huge — seven feet tall and probably more than 400 pounds. Looking at him it was easy to believe the Russian Military had either done genetic experiments, or placed some sort of cybernetic enhancements into his body. Perhaps most disturbing were his eyes. One was ice blue. The other was blank white with a small black dot. The dead eye's black dot pupil followed the other pupil giving the illusion it worked. No one knew the story behind this malady and few had the courage to ask. I had once asked him if it had been from birth. He had simply looked at me, fixing me hard with his stare, and answered,

"No! I looked at something too closely and now I see it forever."

The bar had ultraviolet light in the entrance as most of the operators had ultraviolet tattoos on their faces. The specialized ink was made from the carapace of the Emperor scorpion. Ground down and powdered ingredients were added to wash out the black pigment, leaving a white powder that was mixed with mineral oil and produced a consistency like yogurt, which was then stuffed under the skin to make a design.

Some had animal designs done on their cheeks, others tribal. I had the traditional dots and lines, opting for the larger design to be placed on my forearm. This ink and the scars that accompanied its placement were almost invisible in normal light. However, I had been a little concerned with having any symbols added to my olive-toned skin. My skin scarred far easier than the milk white or blue-black South African flesh did. However, the dots were clear enough, announcing my membership. It ensured I would not be challenged at the door, even if Kolya were taking a rare day off.

I moved my mouse over to the draft and opened it. I typed two words; "Roger. Wilco."

The misunderstood slang meant, "Roger. Will Comply."

I switched to the British Airways website and typed in the required password for my account. I clicked on the date for tomorrow and for the back flight picked a date a month later. I picked "first unrestricted" from the class dropdown tab. I chose Flight 84 out of Vancouver, which left at 20:35 and arrived in London at 13:40. My connecting flight left Heathrow at 14:00 and arrived in Schiphol at 1600 hours. I mused over the fact that this flight was worth about the same as the Cutlass I had given Andrea earlier. She deserved it more. I confirmed the details and hit the "purchase now," completing my transaction.

I would not print the tickets, nor would I e-mail them to myself. No, I would show up at the airport and hand the counter girl my passport, my Platinum club card and similarly designated BA credit card and listen as she tells me how I could have done this all online and just proceed to the lounge. I would smile and nod, not telling her that this was a far more secure way to travel and a good practice as my seat wasn't assigned until 40 minutes before the flight and so harder to put a plant beside me. "Paranoid" was another word for safe and alive!

I clicked the house security icon on my desktop and 42 cameras around the house jumped up on to the three large monitors. I looked at them all in quick succession. Most of them were invisible to the naked eye, only three being actually visible. Two outside front and back with pelican weatherproof enclosures and one in the main foyer. I had two in Andrea's section although out of respect they were blanked out, still recording, but could only be viewed by accessing a special section. I opened those two now and was pleased they were working well. She was still up and writing something at the kitchen table, dressed only in a blue slip. I clicked the two hidden cameras back to "record only" and switched to the main display screen. I clicked on the long-term away option and entered my private cell connection number. I changed my passwords to the offsite monitoring option and enabled it. I liked to watch Ruben when I was gone. One of the reasons I was so fond of Andrea was the long hours she played with him while I was gone. She treated him well.

I clicked the house security system and confirmed I had cancelled Andrea's car code. I then brought up the function called "Away." The system was set to randomly cycle through 12 options and when viewed outside was nearly impossible to discern a pattern. Adding Andrea to the mix made it impossible for anyone casually viewing the house to discern whether or not I was home.

I made a purr sound at Ruben. He stirred and looked at me.

"Time for bed, fuzz nuts," I grinned.

He answered with a chortled "meow."

I clicked the shutdown option and let the main server shut down. I touched my spent cigar to ensure it was cold and got out of my chair, its massage program long since completed. I picked up my glass of scotch and made my way to the master bedroom. The hallway ceiling was ten feet high, and the soaring arched bedroom ceiling shot up past where a second floor should have been. It was impressive and complete waste of building space, but I didn't care. I loved the open-air feeling and expansive feeling of the room.

The large Extreme Ultra king bed measured 12 feet in width and ten in length, yet it was dwarfed in this space. I reveled in the enormity of the bed that in a normal room would have dominated the space. The house looked to be the usual size from the street, but it was deceptively large inside. The upstairs contained 3,000 square feet, but the layout was totally different from a regular three-bedroom house.

The house had been custom designed for me and me alone. I was told numerous times that this design would severely hamper re-sale. I thought that was a stupid idea — to build a house for yourself only to make compromises for people you didn't know. The house was set down into the foundation, which allowed for the high ceilings yet still gave the appearance a normal height from the street.

The downstairs had a more traditional layout, with two normal-size bedrooms and one large bathroom. Since it was designed as a suite it had a larger living room and a small kitchen.

The upstairs was completely different. The kitchen was large and used the "Euro" design to make very effective use of the space. The living room was huge, with vaulted ceilings similar to the master bedroom. The audio and video components were built into the wall studwork to eliminate the need for cabinets and enclosures to take up floor space. The wall was overbuilt, using 2x8 studs rather than the normal 2x6 internal studwork for the rest of the house. That, itself, was two inches bigger than the industry standard. It allowed me to build in the components and hold the large 150-inch plasma TV. The feature style wall gave the illusion of looking through another set of windows set on the internal side of the house.

The massive seven-piece sectional sofa, wrapped in red soft leather easily sat nine people and dominated the far wall under the window. It continued into the corner and along the wall for another eight feet. This position allowed every seat to be far enough away from the huge screen for comfortable viewing. The middle section contained a queen sized pullout bed.

There was a large bathroom containing both a three-person shower and a separate two-person soaker Jacuzzi tub. The bathroom also had a bidet, which never failed to elicit questions and interest as they are rarely installed in North American bathrooms. However, anyone who has traveled to Africa or other regions hard on the digestive system understood immediately. Down the hall was my office and further down was the computer server room.

On the other side was workout room that also contained a hidden "Panic Room." Although I rarely showed this hidden room to anyone, it was the one I was most proud of.

The workout section contained various weight devices that looked more like torture equipment from a London dungeon. All the equipment was custom-painted red. The floor was a very hard bamboo, its pattern tight and gloss reflected in the three floor-to-ceiling mirrors that served as walls. The far right side of the room was the mat area, used for stretching or practicing hand-to-hand skills. There was a heavy bag and a wooden device that had various protruding arms that, when struck, would spin and require a block or dodge from the opposite side.

The mirrors on this side had an almost imperceptible seam down the middle — that was the entrance to the panic room. The mats had to be pulled out of the way to allow access. The room could be opened three ways, via the house security key fob or automatically if the alarm went off. Finally, depressing the light switch three times in quick succession could open it. The mirrors swung out to the sides from the middle revealing a 20-x 30- foot room.

That hidden room was hardened against fire and contained a water cooling system and external air supply that would allow the house to burn to the ground around it with the temperatures inside never getting rising 100°F. It contained enough supplies for five days and had security computer access to the rest of the house. It also contained a stash of weapons and devices more suited for the battlefield than a quiet residential neighbourhood. I had once been served with a search warrant allowing the RCMP to look for weapons, no doubt after one of my suppliers decided to toss me to the wolves after some transgression on his part. They had been in the house with their team of specialists for 14 hours and had not found this room, choosing instead to be very concerned about some pot they had discovered in Andrea's bedroom.

Tired, I walked into my bedroom; the deep pile carpet and extra deep underlay cushioning my step. The 70-inch TV on the closest wall was set to randomly show pictures of areas of the world I had been to. Random, except that the time of day was accurate. At night, it showed dark city skylines and darker African veldt scenes. The room was bare of furniture other than an enormous bed wrapped in expensive Egyptian cotton sheets, and a small Victorian wood writing desk and chair.

There was a hall that led to a large walk through closet that had at its center a round table compartmentalized for shoes and ties. Further the closet opened to a bathroom one could play baseball in. Well, perhaps not that large, but large enough to include a massive glass enclosed shower and a four-person Jacuzzi tub. The skylight above could be opened via a remote switch. The design allowed me to sit in the warm tub and still enjoy the elements, like rain or snow to fall down and into my little sanctuary.

The floors and walls were sheathed in imported Italian marble and were installed by Italian masons I had flown over to do the job. The seams and joints were indistinguishable from the tiles to either side, giving the effect that the marble was one solid piece. The colour transitioned from a deep black on the floor to dark blue flecked with gold around the fixtures and lower wall, continuing to slowly change shade till it reached the ceiling middle blue.

The cost for this indulgence was more than many of my neighbours' entire house and took a full month for the four men to install. It would easily be the centerpiece of any house showcase book. To date less than 10 people had ever seen it. I didn't see that number increasing anytime soon, as I guarded my privacy and indulgences like a Tolkien's Lord guarded his magic ring.

I stripped off my clothes and tossed them into the hamper. With Ruben running interference I walked over to my bed and climbed in under the cool sheets, the soft plush top of the mattress forming around my body. Once again I marveled at the floating sensation it provided. Ruben jumped up and checked his glass of water sitting on the built-in headboard side table. Happy it was full he wandered over and perched himself on my chest.

I retrieved the remainder of my scotch with my left hand while rubbing his head with my right. "Bed time buddy," I said into his face. Taking a sip I reached again to the side table and turned off the light master switch. The dark fell like a warm curtain and my eyes adjusted to the light, Ruben slowly coming back to my vision. I finished the last sip of my scotch, tipping the heavy tumbler and letting the last of the golden liquid flow into my mouth. Setting the glass on the side table I ran both hands down Ruben's powerful sides. I heard and felt his loud purring which helped lull me into that in-between time of asleep and awake. The pressure on my chest shifted and Ruben was gone. My last thoughts before sleep captured by me were of Ruben, unseen, completing his nightly house check.

CHAPTER SEVEN

THE EXPLOSIONS WERE LIKE ROLLING thunder; each impact highlighting just how wrong this engagement had gone. They had obviously found a few big, old Russian HM 38's — the "38" not being the caliber but the year in which it had been designed. These big, bad babies tossed a 120-millimeter sized round, weighing in at sixteen kilos of high explosives! I guess the good news in this is that they were more than three kilometers away, roughly gauged by the sound and timing. They were capable of six kilometers, and while it was doubtful they had a spotter up this close to call the firing solutions, they were getting lucky. I have always maintained that, on occasion, it's better to be lucky than talented.

The next volley of rounds landed 200 meters to the right and its impact, like Thor's hammer, picked us up off the soft red dirt and dropped us again like unwanted toys. I spotted a ditch to our right and signaled Sunday. He had seen the depression as well and we rolled like tightly wrapped carpets toward the fire and the depression. As luck would have it the depression was bigger than it appeared, and we dropped well below the angle the shrapnel needed to find purchase. Explosions blow up off the ground so even a shallow ditch past the shock wave meant safety. The next four rounds hit slightly left of the previous impact by about twenty meters! The sound of the sizzling casings shredded the foliage directly above us and covered us with a rain of leaves and dying insects.

We shook our heads. It was as though they had a spotter! Usually it's better to move toward the impact, as the next grid pattern firing solution should be several hundred meters left or right of the previous impact point — unless they knew our position. Unlikely, as we had been on the move for well over three hours following our runback, and had covered about 20 kilometers. No one could have stayed with us for that length without our knowing it.

However I reminded myself that TIA (This Is Africa). The enemy was getting lucky. A direct hit would give this ditch, (as deep as it was) a new designation — our graves! As if to highlight this thought the following volley was shorter than the previous one and only about 50 meters to the left of our new position. The torrent of water at the base slowed to the trickle as we watched, and then stopped completely. The ditch had collapsed above us!

Moving quickly, we did our best rendition of river otters slipping and sliding down the mud-slick ditch. Covering a surprising amount of terrain in a short period of time was a good thing. However, the risk of breaking a leg was the steep price for this newfound mode of escape.

I remembered when Sunday had come to Canada to relax and enjoy some time with me outside of the dark environs of Africa. It had been funny to see such a capable man removed from his comfort zone. We had indeed watched river otters on that trip, while enjoying a drink on the deck of one of the many hotels near the Vancouver airport. He had just arrived and had marveled at the ease in which he had entered the country.

"It's so beautiful, and the art in the airport was incredible. The customs officers were so polite — and me without a visa! They just asked me a few questions and issued me one for three months multiple exit. No problems and so polite and they even said they had people that could probably speak my language if I didn't understand," he had enthused.

Flying in on the British Airways afternoon flight he had seen the city of Vancouver framed with majestic mountains and the Pacific Ocean. Landing on the island on which the international airport sits had been stunning. "You can see the muddy river staining the blue sea for miles out past the airport, and those huge snow capped peaks! Incredible! Why would you ever leave such a paradise"? Sunday had marveled.

The city itself had been a treat too. I had made reservations for him to stay at the Fairmont Waterfront hotel for three days, just to show him the sights of the jewel of the Pacific. It was a comfortably luxurious hotel, located downtown near the water across from the old Vancouver

Board of Trade and Convention Center. He had been truly amazed at its opulence and had commented that lesser digs would have been fine. I explained that it was the off-season and the prices weren't that prohibitive, but this did nothing to ease his uncomfortable feeling at being surrounded by such grandeur.

Sunday was, by his own account, between 50 and 55 years old. He had grown up in northeast Zambia and had been pressed into military service when he was very young. Long before the atrocities of child soldiers captured the headlines around the world it was common practice for rebel groups to refill their ranks with the children of whatever village they were close to. Sunday had been one of these kids. He was certain he had not yet taken the rites of adolescence, as his foreskin had not been removed, as was the practice. He was less than 12 when he first was forced to pick up a rifle. But he had never been able to find his parents after his initial engagement to ask how old he was or regain his family. Being forced into service and removed from his village had been as traumatic as one might guess, but the length of his first war had been seven long years: an eternity in the small rural communities of the Zambezi area.

He tried to return to the simple farming life in a village he thought had been his after the war. This had been folly, as the headman didn't know who he was, and the obvious scars and military bearing marked him as a rebel. With sides as fluid as the sliding economy he was not accepted. He was viewed with suspicion and, despite having some wealth, he was not allowed to buy land or take a wife.

This had condemned him to continue the profession. By this same luck a war had broken out between the white Rhodesians commanded by Ian Smith and the black Rhodesians commanded by Robert Mugabe. The war of independence from British rule was a difficult one, politically and ethnically. Sunday's stature and build marked him as ethnically Shona — in direct contrast to the largely Matabele ethnic background of Mugabe's armies. Tribal identification is almost always front and center in any African conflict, politics and policy taking a back seat.

Sunday joined the British Special Air Service Squadron C in 1968, and took his initial selection training in the Matopos just outside Bulawayo. His years of combat allowed him to excel within the ranks and marked him as an outstanding asset to the regiment and he was promoted from the ranks to that of Warrant Officer. It was one of the highest ranks a black man could hold in the service at that time.

The regiment was moved to Ndola, Rhodesia in 1969, along with the Selous Scouts. It was here where Sunday found his true calling. The Scouts were a clandestine unit, practicing hit-and-run guerrilla tactics, specializing in small unit operations, unsupported and alone in the bush. Sunday's previous experience allowed him to survive easily in the dense veldt and jungle that his units found themselves in. He took on the role of teacher that culturally was very easy for him. In 1971 the units had taken such causalities that they were almost completely destroyed. The men forged in battle and left alive became the stuff of legends, and Sunday stood out among them.

The unit was moved again; this time to the Cranborne barracks in the city of Salisbury that today is named Harare and is the capital of Zimbabwe. Life in the city environment was difficult for Sunday to adjust to. The large buildings, bleak and Russian in design were cloying and made Sunday claustrophobic. He preferred being in the field training and working with his men. When orders came down that the unit was moved once again in 1979 to Kabrit. Sunday was happy and by now well respected by the two operational units he floated between. It was natural then, for him to continue with Ben Visser into the private world of soldiering.

CHAPTER EIGHT

THE CONTINUING TRAVERSE DOWN THE ditch shook me back to reality as my leg wedged into a root and spun me with significant force into the ditch wall. I felt my knee scream in pain as I torqued it harder to remain in control. The effort failed and I slipped onto my front. My weapon jammed itself, unyielding, into my chest and marked me for the effort. I felt a hand grab my boot, then a body on top of me in an effort to spin me back into control. My heel caught the side and by jamming my shoulders into the slippery side I extended my legs and my dangerous, out-of-control descent stopped. Sunday slid into me face first. His black face, covered in mud, broke in half with a chocolate-milk-stained smile. He righted himself and wiped the muddy camouflage from his face.

Kneeling at my side he used battle sign language to indicate we should pop up and take a look at where we were. I signed back I needed a second to clear and insure my weapon could be used. He nodded understanding and agreement.

I dug my Heckler and Koch suppressed MP5 out of my chest. I could feel the warm blood flowing down my chest where the rough weapon's sharp points had marked me. I tilted the barrel down and was satisfied to see a trickle of water exit the barrel. I pulled the action fully to the rear and caught the ejected round, while holding the action open. Thumbing the hold open device, or HOD, caught and held the breech open, as I rotated the weapon to look directly down the business end of the gun. The barrel was clear and I thumbed the HOD letting the return springs force the breach forward, catching and chambering a round. My thumb intuitively checked the weapon's safety insuring it was off safe and ready to go. I signaled to Sunday;

"You look and I'll cover," I signed, and we popped our heads out of the ditch and into a rogue patrol of the enemy.

If it weren't for bad luck, today I would have none!

They spotted us just as we saw them.

I opened fire and the advance rank fell making significantly more noise than my silencer-suppressed weapon, gurgling like a coffee maker announcing its finish. They were bringing weapons to bear as I saw Sunday flip a can at them. The "can" was, in fact, a white phosphorus grenade, or WP, its range and effective killing radius about 30 meters, or well inside our perimeter! I dropped below the edge and adopted the "legs tight" missile position, so popular with children on waterslides. This was no waterslide, but the fear of having a leg snapped like a twig was replaced by the greater fear of melting, fat burning, in a ditch. I stretched the frozen moments with that fear rocketing down the ditch with rocks and roots tearing viciously at the exposed areas on my underside not covered in body amour! I sensed more than felt Sunday's boots on the top of my head. A bump of hard stone tore viciously at my butt, like some deranged headmaster wielding a copy of Mein Kampf. My stomach sank as my legs found air.

The fall was only about ten meters and my ditch exodus was marked with a muted "whumph" as the WP grenade detonated. I felt the heat across my neck despite what I believed had been a safe distance. My mind raced trying to determine if the evil white material had in fact, contacted me. Were my screams soon to join those of the dying behind me? I landed hard, distracted by my fears and Sunday plowed into me forcing me down further into the mud. I rolled forward and half crawled; half swam to the edge. I gained the bank and with it solid footing and dropped to one knee, scanning the bush.

"Clear!" the machine screamed in my mind.

I checked behind me and saw Sunday clearing the rear section and high point from which we had just fallen. He signaled "clear" and I pumped my fist up and down to suggest we get the hell out of there.

We followed a game trail back into the bush and disappeared into its sweet safety, the screams from above trailing off as we moved quickly away from the point of contact and toward the LUP extraction point.

I awoke rested, the dream fragments trailing like baby spiders riding webs in the wind. The dream was remembered fondly. While it had been a very dangerous contact experience it had also been comical.

Sunday throwing the wrong grenade and then landing on my head brought a smile to my face. I was glad I was here to smile about it. I was never troubled by my dreams like some private contractors I knew were. As I stretched, I recalled a line from *Apocalypse Now*.

"When I was in the jungle all I wished for was to be back home. When I was back home I wished I was in the jungle"

"Soon", I thought. "Soon."

Soon I would be back in my element, back in my world, back in my jungle.

CHAPTER NINE

RUBEN'S ABSENCE WAS THE FIRST indication I had that something was wrong. Normally I awake slowly, and he's there to greet me. Curled on one side or the other, watching me with anticipation, knowing it would soon be wet food time. This morning he was absent. I rolled to the left and picked up the control pod. Opening it, I clicked the remote and the house cameras jumped onto the TV screen in mid-rotation. Split into six smaller screens on the TV screen I looked for Ruben, as I grabbed my bottled water and took a sip trying to eliminate the taste of morning in my mouth. Sometimes I could swear the damn cat pushed his tail down my throat when I slept. But I knew it was really only the snoring that, oddly, I didn't do in the field. The next sets of six screens displayed, and there he was in the front window watching. I gave a chortling meow sound and with a bolt he sat upright and instead of running off the frame and to me, he meowed back. Very unusual. Normally he would stop what he was doing and run full bore back to the bedroom and, with agility belying his girth, jump from the floor to the middle of the bed. Today he continued to look out the window. The next six frames were displayed and I immediately saw why.

There was an unmarked police cruiser parked just left of the gate behind the large fir tree. It was parked perfectly to be just out of view of the visible main front camera — which was why this camera had been hidden on the tree. The angle showed the two-man team providing surveillance perfectly. Yes cops, the haircuts and general dress gave them away. They were playing cards, a foldout crib board between them keeping score.

"Fuck!" I thought, "How had this unfolded?"

Did someone intercept the e-mail action? Even though the message never gets sent, there were communication packets that went between my modem and the remote mail service.

Andrea, perhaps? No, despite her living with me for three years my mind, or more accurately "the machine," forced me to look at the possibility. No, impossible!

Then what? The phone call? Did they have a warrant for an intercept on my phone? Could they have got one for a long-time after the local gunsmith had tried to toss me in front of some charges they had on him.

"Damn," I thought, my pre-coffee brain refusing to work. "When had that been?"

Almost a year since they produced a warrant and searched the house, after the gunsmith tried to deal me to avoid a tax evasion charge. He got what he wanted, I remembered with a smile. He hated paying taxes to the "corrupt" and "Illuminati run false government." Well, even they didn't collect from dead men.

"Coffee!" I thought.

I pulled on fresh clothes on the way to the bathroom. With a fast look up I checked the large skylight. Nothing. I and moved low and quietly to the fixtures. I rinsed my face and hair in the bidet and tugged a brush through my hair. Inelegant perhaps, but certainly clean and quiet, and it prevented me from casting any shadows on windows, turning on any lights, or running any water as the cistern supply was more than adequate for a quick rinse.

They might not have listening devices placed on the water and electrical meters, but I would have. Listening for the telltale click as one turns on the facilities as surely announcing my awake state as if I retrieved the morning rag in my underwear. Moving down the hall, past my office I checked, took a second to retrieve two handguns in the room, one inside my humidor secured to the lid and the other under the desktop. There were others, another in the drawer and in the safe, but I had permits for those and so I just checked the drawer gun to insure it had its trigger lock secured. It was its only use secured as such — a paperweight.

I moved into the safe room and moved the mats back and checked the blinds. Lucky, I thought as the blinds where down and turned to not allow any visual intrusion. I reached up and pushed the light switch button toward the back three times, quickly. Soundlessly the big mirrors swung on hydraulic trams into the open position. Dimly, lights set into the floor edges came on blue, similar to the ones on an airplane that are supposed to come on and lead you to an exit.

I tossed the three guns, one from my bedroom, and two from my office onto the beige couch and checked to insure the battery meters had lots of juice. They did.

Before leaving I opened a can of tuna or, to Ruben, "Kitty Crack." I passed him on the way to the living room and he gave me a knowing glance, happy to see I was switched on and dealing with the threat he had been watching for several hours.

I quickly collected the three guns from the living room and two from the kitchen and returned them to the safe room. I thought about just closing the door and pretending I wasn't home, but then I would learn nothing about why they were here and what they wanted.

I gave Ruben a head rub and he growled, letting me know how much he loved tuna and just where I stood in the hierarchy of his world. He wasn't sharing without a fight. Pushing the close button, I quickly stepped past the edges of the doors, as they swung shut.

I walked normally now, and checked to see if there was any additional activity at the unmarked car. None, the two cops were still playing cribbage.

"Wait!" screamed the machine.

"What am I missing?" I thought as I looked again.

Coffee! Two new paper coffee cups were in place of the old thermos tops that had been there a few minutes ago. Sure enough there was steam coming from both cups. The scene still pulled in tight on the amazing duo and now, looking this close, one officer even had white powder on the edge of his mouth, marking him as a doughnut addict. Someone new had entered the perimeter.

I retrieved my iPhone from beside the bed and thought about calling my lawyer, James. That staunch Catholic would be up eating eggs, against his doctor's orders, before going to morning prayers to ask forgiveness for being selfish and weak, just as he did every morning. He would hate if I interrupted his routine. Could I use the house phone? No, probably not. The same went for the cell. It took me thirty-five seconds to work out this challenge, further highlighting my need for coffee. On the way to the kitchen I grabbed the satellite phone out of my always packed "jump bag" from the office.

I put water on the stove for coffee. The blue flame licked the bottom of the kettle. The water came to a boil the same way that James's personal cell number came into my head — painfully slow. I dumped a practiced measure of coffee into the French press as the squeal of the kettle announced it had beaten me in the task of dialing James. I poured the hot liquid over the coffee and pushed the "Send" button on the phone at the same time. Three minutes 'til coffee. Hopefully James would answer an unknown number at 6:45 a.m.

He picked up on the sixth ring, with a tentative and pensive "Hello?"

"James! Rhys here. "Cops at my house. Using satellite phone."

I said this like most drunks talk, without any punctuation, all of it strung together. I listened as the echo of my voice bounced up and down, the weird distortion caused by beaming a signal 20 miles into space to bounce off a satellite and then come back to a ground-based unit to transfer to a regular phone. It sure messed with newbie users. They would hear themselves and stop and start and repeat as the echo messed with them far worse than the worst cellular connection. James did just that.

"Rhys. Oh. Ok ah ... Rhys shit can hear myself Rhys ah ... crap." I cut him off,"

"Get here A.S.A.P!"

He stammered, "Okay ... Yeah. OK. Bye. OK."

I had forgotten how confusing conversations on these things can be and laughed at my very smart and talented lawyer's problems with technology. I wondered if a call to British Air would be prudent, then thought better of it. Vancouver, Space, London, India then back would mess with the most talented user. Instead, I settled for checking the security cameras again.

I punched up just the outside cameras and saw that a few others had joined the original party. There were now two "Tac" guys, as they loved to call themselves, hiding next to my shrubbery, as well hidden as clowns in a snow bank. Two others were by the back door and two more on my front steps, backs pressed so hard against the walls on either side of the doors I could probably tell who had high blood pressure.

There was gear all over the place — lots of it. They looked like TV cops. No doubt they told themselves they were the real deal. But they were as far from the real thing today as pre-schoolers playing cops and robbers. I pressed the handle of the French press down and poured a mug of coffee. The crib-playing duo had finished their game and looking alert with shirts tucked in and all signs of donut addiction wiped from their chubby faces.

"Well, I guess the GIS (General Investigation Services) boys are here," I thought to myself as the coffee fueled brain listened to "the machine" highlight a problem.

Shit, there was a gun in the Aston Martin. Under the seat and well hidden, but the searching section was far better than a usual cop and would probably find it. I rushed down the stairs softly and with coffee cup in one hand took great pains to quietly open the garage door. I opened the door manually with the key, so not to let the security system chirp. This gun was registered to me so I simply slipped it into my waistband at the small of my back. I exited the garage into the foyer and went to go upstairs and stopped. I took a long pull off my hot coffee and thought, "Nah, fuck this."

I turned and walked to the front door and in one quick motion flipped the lock and pulled it open. I smiled as I heard both heads hit the walls of my house. Striding with a purpose I didn't really feel I walked out the door into the brisk fall morning to retrieve my paper like I never, ever did.

The shouts were immediate and loud, from directly behind me I heard "get on the ground" repeated and in stereo but like with the treble turned way up on the left one. I allowed a slight flinch to be shown in my shoulders and I turned around to face the duo.

The one with a little more bass in his voice said; "Sir, can you hear me get on the ground, do it now."

I responded, "Constable, of course I can hear you, my elderly neighbours can hear you. The ground is wet so no, I won't get on the ground and your safety is on."

To my surprise he looked at his safety taking his gun off me for a spilt second. Part of me wanted to say "Fucktard rookie says what?" just to see if he would. They would have this section on video and would be recording this in real time to play it back at their debriefing. Then gathered, like a murder of crows, they would sit, as if on a fence, and watch themselves on video, cawing comments about their exploits, bravado apparent. Still dressed in black suits they would not be viewing this feature with the same jocularity as their usual cast of characters.

"Gun!" was called out behind me and I felt the warmth of six laser points as the other crows brought their weapons to bear and went active. The two in front of me on either side of my door also squeezed additional switches and their laser aims came to life and traced nervous patterns across my chest.

I yelled out in my best drill sergeant voice.

"Yes, I'm armed this is my house and my land and I'm licensed and allowed to carry this gun. I haven't finished my first cup of fucking coffee and I'm not going to prone out in the wet. Unless you tactical Nancies are going to shoot me, on camera, with my weapon holstered, I'd suggest another plan."

A new voice, projected — not screamed, took over.

"Hands out to your sides, palms up."

I thought, "The boss," as I followed his direction, yet still holding onto my coffee cup. I felt the aim point of the laser get significantly hotter, followed by the voice.

"Don't move. I'm going to approach."

I stood where I was.

I felt a hand tug the Glock pistol from the small of my back. Then the voice said,

"Turn around slowly." I did and came face to face with the boss.

It was the same boss cop who had been here before to execute the search warrant. Why all the hardware this time?

He yelled, "Stand down everyone, situation is clear and secure."

I asked. "What is the search warrant for this time? Penguin abuse? Or did you all do that with each other before showing up?"

"Actually, Mr. Munroe I don't have a warrant yet, as the Judge hasn't issued it yet."

"Well," I paused, waiting. "Fetch my newspaper and I won't make you stand outside till it arrives."

I started to walk back to the house and door sentinels one and two moved together to block my path. I heard the footsteps behind me retreat as I looked down to see the aim points of various weapons making red dots on the ground around my feet.

"Are we going to have to stand on my front lawn all fucking day?" I asked of no one in particular.

"No," was the response from behind.

"Sorry, Mr. Munroe but everyone is a little jumpy this morning. This was supposed to be a high-profile take- down and arrest."

"Arrest?" I exclaimed. "What the hell for, bad fashion?"

The boss cop, an officer O'Neil, returned from the front gate with my paper and answered for him.

"Yes, sir!" He handed me my paper and continued.

"We recovered two prohibited weapons from a car registered to this address and with the last search warrant issued for illegal weapons it flagged. I didn't realize that it was your address until I got here."

"Well?" I exclaimed, letting a hint of displeasure enter my tone.

"Is it all right if one of the officers comes inside with us?" O'Neil asked carefully.

"Yes, that's fine," I answered as I turned to look over my shoulder as O'Neil moved up beside me.

He pressed his hand to his chest mic and ordered the situation to stand down. His left hand holding my Glock signaled he was left handed. A peripheral check confirmed his "Sam Brown" holster was tucked up under his right arm. These holsters were the ones preferred by cops and hated by gunfighters, underlining their less-than-reactive ability and public protection view. It held the weapon hard and high making a quick draw impossible, but also making the weapon invisible to the casual observer.

"This is Sunray," meaning the tactical overseer and commander.

"Situation is clear, target is in custody Delta 2. I will be entering the target house to continue investigation. Stand down all units and switch to regular radio one after clearing."

I couldn't hear the replies as everyone was wearing earpieces, but I could see O'Neil using his fingers, tightening each one in turn as each station answered his order.

Twelve responses. Wow! They had been serious on this one.

I moved slowly to the door and the doormen moved out of my way as I reentered the foyer. O'Neil and "Delta 2" did the same, the latter closing the door behind him.

"No Andrea," I thought. The sleep of the innocent!

The two officers were looking at me, waiting for me to continue upstairs.

"Shoes," I responded to their unasked question.

It was time to take control and impose my will. Time to let them

know this was my house and without a warrant they were my "guests."
O'Neil stepped on the heel of his conservative — both in price and
quality — black shoes and slipped out of each shoe in turn.

"Delta 2" leaned over and his submachine gun caught on his gear,
struggling face flushing with the effort, he stretched to reach the laces
on his combat boots. Failing, he relented and went to one knee and
pulled his bloused pants out of the top of his left boot. O'Neil stopped
him with a gesture and asked, "Ok if he just stays down here?" "Sure"
I said, and gestured to a chair and continued, "If you need anything
just wave, I'll see you," I explained, pointing to the camera.

"Sir" the booted officer offered in protest. O'Neil silenced him
with a look and I started up the stairs with the investigating officer
behind me.

O'Neil commented as we reached the upstairs landing;

"This place is bloody amazing, I forgot how big it was. It doesn't
look that big on the ... outside."

Hmm, I thought, "On the outside?" There had been a very slight
hesitation in his speech between "the" and "outside". Was the officer
going to say plans, or drawings? The correct version of speech should
have been "from the outside." Odd, perhaps they had pulled the filed
drawings of the house? That was likely the case, I thought, smiling
inwardly at the cost to have two sets made and having the safe room
design architects hired directly from New York. That room wasn't on
any filed plans or drawings. Money well spent. Being paranoid had
paid off again.

I continued into the kitchen and O'Neil followed me. I picked
up the French coffee press and refilled my cup and looked at O'Neil.
"I know you're fond of Tommy's coffee, but can I pour you a cup of
this?"

"Yes, please."

Taking down a second mug from the cupboard that minutes ago
had contained a handgun I poured him a cup and handed it to him.

"Cream is in the fridge," I offered.

"Black is fine" he responded.

I moved to the large oak table and sat down. O'Neil joined me a
second later.

"Mr. Munroe," he started, "we recovered a burnt-out vehicle
registered to this address. The registered owner was not you, but a

woman named Andrea Perch. Inside the vehicle was a laptop and — more significantly — three assault rifles. We are attempting to recover the drive on the laptop but the techs are not too confident they will be able to do that."

He stopped and looked at me, and placed my Glock on the table to our left. His eyes narrowed slightly and his pupils followed suit.

"Here it comes," I thought.

This was his move to regain the upper hand.

"That Glock feels pretty heavy, Mr. Munroe. It wouldn't have an illegal high capacity magazine would it?"

While the handgun was legal it was law that it had to come with a "stamped" or blocked magazine. That allowed the gun to carry only five rounds in the magazine instead of the 18 for which it was designed. It was legally loaded with only six rounds. However those rounds were special. They were custom-designed truncated arcane rounds. Machined from depleted uranium they were much heavier than the alloy rounds common for this pistol. While technically as illegal as amour piercing, they would punch through light amour, like a hot knife through soft butter, and heavy plate with only a slight decrease in velocity. They weren't sold as such, making them legal. They were in fact not sold at all. These were custom designed and created by a very talented gunsmith in Colorado.

"Your feel must be off, Officer. The gun only has the legal mag. I find if you need more than six rounds you're not in a police action anymore, you're in a war. Please feel free to check."

A line raced across his brow, betraying his failed trump play. He picked up the pistol and ejected the magazine. Pulling the slide slowly back he allowed the chambered round to fall noisily to the table. I thought the move looked rather amateurish for a man who always carried a pistol. He should have caught the round in is hand.

He picked up the round and looked at it.

"Wow, this is a heavy bullet".

"Yeah, it's real lead — not that alloy crap, covered with a 929 silver to keep it from fouling the barrel."

"Silver bullets, Mr. Munroe? Were you expecting werewolves to break in to your house?"

I didn't answer. Instead I put my hand out to receive the gun. He smiled and said

"I think we'll leave this over here for now. You don't mind, Mr. Munroe, do you? Just for my safety."

Taking advantage of the officer's slip I said. "Officer O'Neil, I hope you don't fear for your safety! I assure you I have nothing but the utmost respect for the law and those that enforce it. Really, O'Neil, what can I do to make you more at ease? Perhaps you'd like to cuff me to continue this Q and A?"

O'Neil was Irish in more than name. My comment stung him as I had intended it to. His nostrils flared, announcing his aggression even before he was aware of it. His pupils pinned and he squared his shoulders for his response.

"Sir, (spoken more like cur) you don't scare me in the least," his eye twitched again, betraying the lie.

"I know you're a bloody mercenary and have been involved in more bloodshed and amassed a body count probably higher than all the murderers we put away every year! That does not impress me!" (Again spat like a curse)

"Nor does your fancy mansion, or your exotic cars. You're a parasite, profiting from the misery of others and I'm going to find something to bust you on. I intend to put you away for a long time!"

He continued, his anger rising.

"Your local gunsmith gave us a lot more than was in the depositions your fucking mouthpiece subpoenaed! If I thought I could get away with, I'd put you down right here and now like the fucking rabid dog you are."

I smiled and let the smile stretch across my face. Leaning back in my chair and setting my elbows on the back I could see my relaxation brought out the opposite reaction in O'Neil. The man was really very upset — almost ready to snap. I softened my response slightly.

"Officer, the car and most likely the laptop belong to Andrea, my downstairs tenant. She told me her car had been found burned. The fact that you found assault rifles is disturbing. As an upstanding member of society I'm disheartened that we are experiencing this seemingly uncontrollable gang problem. I can only hope that no one was hurt with these illegal and previously undetected weapons. Perhaps it would be best to focus on that issue, rather than harassing and threatening tax-paying, law-abiding citizens like me."

O'Neil pushed his chair back and placed both hands on the table, his milky-white face filling with blood and going red just as that backs of his hands emptied of blood and went white.

"Look you fuck, don't tell me my job and save the con for someone else. Get your little girlfriend up here. I wanna' see if her story is the same as yours!"

I watched him closely; aware he was no longer in control of himself. He obviously did not share my observations. I was somewhat relieved when I saw on the monitor in the corner that James had pulled up in his big black Mercedes.

"Certainly, Officer O'Neil. I will call her immediately."

With that I rose and went to the side table, my body thus blocking the computer monitor. I pushed the gate button and the big solid steel fencing moved quickly to the side. I picked up the phone and hit the speed dial for Andrea. I couldn't hear the phone ring downstairs but a sleepy "hello" cut short the fourth ring.

"Morning, Andrea. Sorry to wake you but there is an officer here to discuss your car problem. Have a quick shower and toss on some clothes. The officer and I will wait upstairs with James."

I pressed the button to end the call and another for the front door so that James could let himself in.

Still furious, O'Neil blurted,

"What the hell is with the 'take a shower' routine? I got lots to do and don't need to sit up here half the day while your live-in tart gets ready!"

Scowling into his now-cold coffee he muttered something I missed. I was concentrating on picking up any sounds from the downstairs foyer. No doubt the officer there would challenge James. I heard none and once again moved back to my chair.

CHAPTER TEN

O'Neil regained some of his composure. In an effort to bring the situation back under control he tried to make small talk.

"Is James your cat? I saw the dish when we sat down."

The answer came from behind him.

"No. I'm his lawyer, James Taylor. We've met before, Sgt. O'Neil."

O'Neil was completely taken off whatever game he thought he still had. His mouth flopped open and his expression could have been a billboard for "How the Hell?"

James, still holding out his hand for the officer to shake, was quite enjoying himself. He was a tall, yet slight man with little physical muscle. His genes must have determined that someone this smart would not need any physical prowess at all. They had been correct. James was probably more feared in the courtroom than I was on a field of war. Finally, the officer took James' skinny hand and shook it.

James turned to me, raising one eyebrow in a gesture that always made me think he looked like Mr. Spock.

"Rhys," he started, "I thought I told you that talking to police without me here was a rule we were not going to break? Not that I mean to suggest in anyway that you should not co-operate completely, but just with Counsel present."

I smiled and looked at him, then at Officer O'Neil. Pulling a small hand-held recorder from my pocket I continued. The mini-sized device was one thing the cops' frisking hadn't found.

"I taped the whole thing so you could review it later! That's legal right? You told me that to tape a conversation in Canada you just needed one of the parties being recorded to consent right? James looked puzzled, but did not let it reflect in his voice when he said,

"Yes. Correct."

O'Neil looked as though he had just shit his pants.

I continued, looking directly at O'Neil, the mask of "nice" now discarded completely and said,

"Officer O'Neil is going to be very nice with Andrea and this investigation, or he's going to have to figure out how to feed his wife and litter on fucking Kraft dinner for the rest of his life. Aren't you, you illiterate, proddy fuck?"

Broken, knowing his career was gone should I wish it, he could not bring himself to speak. He just nodded. O'Neil's dreams of busting me lay at his feet like the evidence of an uncontrolled bladder. Police work was sometimes like pissing yourself in black pants. You get a warm feeling and no one notices. I caught the scent of Andrea as she entered the room. I slipped my "nice" mask on.

"Andrea, this is Sgt. Paddy O'Neil. He's a friend and will be looking after your car issue. I was just going to have bacon and eggs with James, but he can stay with you while you answer some questions."

"If you don't mind, James. That would be nice," Andrea responded politely.

"Police make me nervous."

O'Neil spoke like a man trying to catch his breath.

"No problems, Andrea," I explained. "Just some basic stuff. Would you like a coffee?"

"Yes. Please," she replied.

I poured a cup and brought it over setting it down between them and gave Paddy a friendly squeeze on the shoulder, communicating in one squeeze that I owned him as much as if he had signed a contract with me in blood.

The interview process took about 20 minutes. I never heard James interject once as I scanned the headlines in the rag that served as our local daily.

I put the paper down and pulled up my laptop to look at my stock portfolio. I was more uncomfortable with the people in my house than the freefall losses I seemed to be taking on the market. It was only money and I couldn't take it with me.

The kitchen interview ended and O'Neil walked into the living room. The TV was on showing shorelines from around the world. The 150-inch screen set in the way it was made it look like a cruise ship window. He shook his head and nodded to me and made the long walk back out to his world — a world that would forever look different to him. Andrea and James came into the living room, saying nothing. I could see James needed his breakfast fix. Tall and skinny, the man had no reserves and a noticeable shake was developing in his left hand. I really needed a shower, so I suggested,

"Why don't you guys head down to Spike's for breakfast. I'll join you shortly and pick up the tab."

"Sounds good," James said. His reply made me smile as they walked down the stairs. From the foyer I heard James offer to drive as I went over to let Ruben out of the panic room.

I pushed the light switch three times in quick succession and the big mirrors swung left and right. Ruben was sitting there looking as though he had heard me. He couldn't have, as the panels are far too thick. He sensed me, course that kind of thing didn't happen! I headed for the shower followed by tuna-breath Ruben. We were both eager to get back to our routine.

I arrived for breakfast having been quicker than I like in my morning rituals. Spike, a rake-thin classically trained chef had landed here after a failed marriage and a brief stint on a cruise line. He was a better chef than most top end Vancouver restaurants had and he knew it. He was raising two kids by himself and needed the cheap rent and freedom living in the Valley provided. Spike saw me come in and grabbed a coffee as he headed over. Despite the early hour he was dressed in chef's whites with a red scarf tucked in around his neck. I never ordered off the menu and so Spike never brought one. He said "good morning" and waited for me.

"I don't know, Spike. Something with fruit, lox and low carbs."

My weight had gone up a little, washing out the "washboard abs" and carbohydrates were making me feel bloated again.

"'K" was all he said as he turned and disappeared into his kitchen. I had been invited into the back on one occasion and I got the feeling he was interested in showing it off about as much as I liked to show off my bathroom. I smiled to myself. James commented:

"Happy with yourself today, Rhys?"

"Yes," I replied cheerily. "I'm really happy. The cops are moving along nicely on the theft of Andrea's car — and I'm going away for a while."

They stopped eating and looked, waiting for me to continue.

"Not long. Probably only a few months if I'm lucky — a few being three.

Standard stuff, really. A few people to see and a simple problem to fix."

Their grunted response signaled they didn't believe me, but weren't going to ask me to elaborate on the lie.

My breakfast arrived, a small corn fritter with some lox on the top. Melon balls, their green-and-yellow colours mixing and contrasting nicely with the yellow corn bread and red salmon, surrounded it. There was a sharp cheddar sauce lightly drizzled on the top.

"Perfection," I thought, as I caught up with my friends.

CHAPTER ELEVEN

THE CONVERSATION WAS LIGHT AND spirited, drifting from topic to topic. James, wiping his sins from his lips, explained he had to be in Court in two hours and needed to stop by the office first. It was a small lie. He rarely went into the office — he had become totally mobile a year ago. The office in this case, most likely the church. I found it interesting that this lethal attorney was such a devout Catholic. It didn't fit the mould into which I tried to push him.

Andrea had been removed during the conversation, chasing egg yolk around on her plate with a piece of sourdough bread, lost in thought. Perhaps the morning's meeting with the police had caught up with her. She looked at me and smiled as James shook my hand in departure.

"Same policy and procedures I have locked away in the safe?" He asked somewhat cryptically.

Shit I thought, "Yes. Same old, same old."

The usual procedure for me going away was for James to have power of attorney over my affairs in order to take care of the day-to-day stuff and all of my affairs should I not make it back. We hadn't really got to get into it with the morning's excitement. Thinking about the previous instructions I wanted to make a few changes. My investment strategies could have used some tweaking but perhaps I would just leave them as is and hope this global depression turned around faster than they expected, at least for Canada. He saw the conversation in my head as surely as if I had said it out loud. Again, he raised that eyebrow in his "Spock" pose.

"No really, James. It's good, some minor tweaks but I can work around them without having to meet up."

Nodding his head he said; "Ok. You're leaving tonight; I'll take care of the bills and stuff. Stay safe my friend and perhaps we can celebrate the New Year together!"

I nodded agreement and said, "You Bet" as he turned and walked out of the rustic building.

I turned to Andrea, who was still lost in thought.

"You okay?" I asked, startling her.

"Me? Yeah I'm good. Just thinking about something. Nothing important. Sorry, I tend to fade out when other people are talking about things that don't concern me."

"I didn't mean to be rude." I replied.

"Just forgot to take care of some housekeeping and you know lawyers; the devil is in the details."

"You weren't being rude, I get it. This trip is really dangerous isn't it?

Andrea had never commented on any of the "trips" I had taken before. Why now? The "machine" peered from the black of my mind, assessing the ground. Was this a trap? Was the limping gazelle really hurt or drawing me away from an easier kill? I dismissed the notion and smiling, said,

"No more than usual."

She smiled in response, but it was a smile tinged with bitterness.

"A non-answer if I ever heard one, Rhys. But that's ok, I don't mean to pry. You know you're really quite broken. I think you'll definitely get your money's worth when I get board certified. Did you drive down? I have to use the ladies room and would prefer to use the one at home. But if you walked I won't make it."

"I drove," I said, and could feel she wanted to say something more.

"Shall we?" I said, getting up tossing $50 on the table. I had no idea what the bill for breakfast was. The special, which James and Andrea had was $6.99. But Spike and I had come to an agreement years ago. Order from the menu and pay the menu prices, order off and pay what you like.

She rose and moved toward me.

"Thanks for breakfast" she said, and without warning leaned in for a kiss to the cheek. This public display of affection really took me off guard, and as she turned to walk out I found my eyes drifting down her long blond hair to her perfect apple-shaped butt. I looked around quickly, happy there was no one in the front, and followed after her.

We arrived home and I could see the gathering. The neighbours were hanging about doing menial chores. I had four and at the present time two were across the street seeming to discuss the required pruning before the potential snowfall. The other one, to my right, was watering a hanging basket near the border of our properties, its withered dried flowers unaware of the effort.

"I'll just run inside for a moment, okay?"

As she sprinted towards her door, she turned and said,

"Park her outside, Rhys. I want to get some of the dust off her while it's sunny. Besides it appears you have a little debriefing to give."

And with this she laughed. The earlier gloom she displayed seemed to have vanished.

"Great. 'No one expects the' Valley Inquisition!" I mimicked Monty Python and to my surprise she got it and laughed. I looked at her and she read my face.

"I'm not that young, Rhys. I've seen Monty Python reruns!"

Then, with a scolding look, she went inside.

I shut the Aston down and climbed out, leaving the keys in the ignition. The gathered inquisitors waved, as welcoming as cake and about as sickly sweet. I reached in and pushed the gate button, stopping the gate midway and reversing its direction. The two neighbours lost interest in the pruning and slowly took their marks at the edge of the road. I slipped on the mask and moved to take my place in this rural play of obscure title!

"Morning, Rhys."

The chorus line chimed together, almost as if on cue.

"Morning. Sorry about the excitement. I hope they didn't wake anyone!"

"What was going on? It looked like a war zone out here?"

The question came from Richard, my neighbour across the street to the left.

"Yeah" added Markus my other across-the-street neighbour. I could hear Roxy, the single lady next-door neighbour walking across the street. I turned to allow her into the circle and waited for her to arrive. Both Richard and Markus involuntarily sucked in their more-than-robust stomachs.

Roxy was the enigma on the block. She served to draw a great deal of attention away from me, and for that I liked her. I professed I was a travel writer and used that cover to explain my wealth. Rumour on the block was she ran a dungeon in her basement and was a practicing dominatrix. She was always dressed in black or grey and always with high heels.

We employed the same gardener and had chatted on numerous occasions about yard stuff. She liked her flowering plants but how she tended to them in heels was beyond me. Yet somehow she did just that. Today she was dressed in a sheer black blouse that allowed an easy view to the corset that was pushing and shaping her more than ample breasts. The skirt was to her ankles, but with a slash that opened to her hip. She walked with a confidence and grace that did little to enhance her reputation with the other wives in the area, and did a great deal for the men's libido. She was not a pretty woman in the classical sense. She was severe and powerful and commanding — sexy and erotic, for sure.

"Hi, Roxy. I was just about to explain to Richard and Markus about all the excitement."

"Yeah I noticed, guys in black playing around in my beds this morning! A few of the flowers got abused," she said with a sly grin and a double entendre.

"Sorry" I continued; "No real drama actually. Andrea's car got stolen form the university and was used in a crime," I lied.

"They found a couple of machine guns in the trunk and figured there might be a gang connection so they overreacted. The totally weird part is I know the investigating officer really well. We have worked together on some corporate security stuff and he has been to my house before," I lied again.

Their faces all projected they had bought the lie. Roxy was the first to comment.

"Typical cop reaction to stuff they suspect or don't understand"

Her cell phone started to ring and looking at it she said; "It's my Mom. I need to take this. Excuse me."

The three of us watched her walk away, her hips grinding to her own rhythm and our eyes must have made her bottom hot as she brushed some unseen element from it as she walked back to her house. Markus and Richard held the view far longer than I. Mouths slightly agape with desire and eyes lined with apprehension at the cost one would have to pay in pain to see more of her!

"So," I said pulling the two men from their leering, "Planning on doing some pruning prior to the snow flying?"

"Ah yeah well, have to plan so we can figure out how best to get at it" was Richard's response, as Markus shook his bald head in agreement.

"Well I will let you get back at it then. You don't need me distracting you anymore today." Again, like a chorus, they chimed together signaling the curtain for Act One, Scene One. I walked quickly back to my own house.

CHAPTER TWELVE

THE HOUSE WAS SET BACK on the lot, the biggest on the street on a half acre of land. Like so many others on the block it had originally been scheduled to be two houses on small lots. To create the illusion that the house was a normal size the builder had set the house back and down into the foundation so the height wasn't so apparent. The driveway was angled slightly, no parallel sides and the concrete stamping was gradually different — small to large to further enhance the effect. Three cars could be parked on the driveway, in a row end to end and yet still allow the gate to close. The fir trees lining the drive were also shaped to provide privacy and enhance the illusionary effect. It worked well.

Andrea was just coming out of the garage when I walked up the long drive. She was dressed in a white t-shirt and what could only be described as "Daisy Duke" shorts. They rode low on her waist and were cut off high on her thighs, the white pockets clearly visible. She smiled at my expression.

"They're for the Halloween party at campus. I'm going as Daisy from the Dukes of Hazards movie. I wanted to see how they fit before I wore them to the party. Well?"

She twirled around struck a pose and tossed out her hip looking over her left shoulder.

"Wow! They look really…" I hesitated. "Sexy. In a good ole boy kind of way," I added.

She laughed. "Great. That's what I was going for but I didn't think I could pull it off, I don't have a nice butt."

I got to the end of the Aston and stopped and thought about how to respond. I watched as she put the bucket down, her ample breasts strained at the cotton; nipples reacting to the pull of the soft fabric.

"You have a very nice butt, Andrea. I don't know who told you differently, but they're an idiot," I stated, more emphatically than I had intended.

She looked up, soapy soft sponge in her hand, and smiled.

"Thanks. I didn't think you noticed young blood."

Her tone was teasing, with just a hint of sarcasm.

"Well," I continued, "I may be older but I'm still a guy, and we all notice that kind of thing. The day we don't is the day they lower us into the ground in a box."

She had brought the sponge down from the top of the car and was making long strokes along the fender, still bent over double but this time in profile. My eyes locked on her as I walked up past the rear of the car toward the open garage.

As I passed her, she continued,

"Well, it's pretty hard to notice sometimes."

I could see the top of her red t-bar as it rose like a tempting snake above the waist of her shorts; on the small of her back was a tattoo, in pink, the read "Girls, Girls, Girls."

As I walked into the garage directly behind her, I allowed myself a longer look. The shorts were pulled tight, barely containing that taut little apple-shaped bottom.

"Well" I answered, "I guess I get points for being discreet."

She finished our brief volley; "Yeah? You think so, eh?"

Two thoughts rushed into my head at the same time and collided. That seemed like a pretty blatant come on. Yet the tattoo suggested she might be gay. Confused, I continued past the parked truck and let myself into the house. Young women were confusing. Unlike Roxy next door, they were hard to read and harder still to understand what the conflicting information meant. Surely a woman wouldn't get a pink "Girls Girls Girls" tattoo if she were straight?

Had the last comment suggested I had been indiscreet? Had she seen my head turn as I dragged my eyes across her gorgeous ass reflected in the ink black paint? Why now, was she so overt? Surely last night's hug hadn't been orchestrated?

The "machine" was scratching away in the background, suggesting far more sinister angles. But the "machine" was devoid of feelings past those of self-preservation! Man, I needed a drink.

I entered the office and pulled out a cigar from the humidor. A

Partagas Double Corona, its seven-inch length of chocolate brown wrapper as promising and enticing as Andrea's shorts. I sat near the window and clipped it. I tried its draw, and found it to be perfect. Aged for nine years, it should be sublime. I reached for a glass in my mini bar and poured myself a measure of Cuban rum. I reached into the small desk fridge and pulled out the ice tray, relieved that the housekeeper had refilled it. I dropped in three cubes of ice and swirled the light brown liquid in the glass.

Then I allowed myself to look out the window. There she was, directly below me, her long arms reaching and caressing the Aston. I immediately wanted to change places with the car. From this angle the cheeks of her butt were well displayed. The milky white replaced by white alabaster the higher one went. She reached and leaned to one side to dip the sponge into the bucket and countered her balance by stretching the other leg out. There was just a peek of red lace where the material of her panties met at the apex of those gorgeous legs.

"Wow," I thought and looked away. She was twenty-eight and an adult, but to me she was still just a näive kid from the Okanagan Valley. She once told me the longest trip she had ever taken was with her family to Disneyland. She did not deserve to have me complicate her life. What could I offer her past uncertainty and — most likely — loss? Then why was I building white picket fences? Perhaps a little fun and a dalliance was all she wanted? But did she want that with a man or a woman?

I stepped away from the window and caught my reflection in the mirror. I wasn't bad looking for forty-three, toned and muscled and with sandy brown hair cut in a newer style. In fact, I hardly looked my age. Most people guessed I was ten years younger. I had no wrinkles around my blue-grey eyes and when I had got surgery a few years prior to fix a gash on my forehead I had had the doctor put in a few hook sutures to tighten my brow. The doctor had explained that a scarring would be less noticeable if these were placed in my hairline to pull the skin taunt. The sutures were like small stitches that had little hooks like Velcro that went in one way and then when pulled back would catch and pull the skin tighter. They had worked very well. My 6'3" frame was well proportioned and I had been blessed with powerful legs, unlike most of my Irish ancestors. My gut still had the suggestion of abs. While not a washboard six-pack anymore it was still more defined than most kids half my age. Yeah. I had to admit I was in pretty damn good shape.

I went to the window again, stopping just before the edge of the seat. At this angle I could see down, yet someone on the ground couldn't easily see me. She was cleaning the mag wheels with a special spray designed for the Aston's alloy wheels.

Then she looked up. I moved very slowly to one side of the angle and again leaned forward till I could just see the top half of her. She was finished spraying the left wheel and was moving to the right one. Again she squatted down and began spraying the wheel, and again she glanced up. Just a brief glance, but she was definitely watching to see if I was watching her. I moved to the window and sat down, looking directly down at her and in plain view. Her head moved a little to the right and I could tell she was using her peripheral vision to check my window again.

Her left hand grabbed the tire as if to steady herself and I could see her weight shift to her heels as if she were leaning back to get a better look at a missed spot. Then she opened her legs, letting her ass rest on her ankles, the cut-off shorts providing less than an inch-and-a half of material coverage for her sex.

That brief little acrobatic move done she stood and, as casually as possible, she looked up at the window. The move was overdone and forced and I smiled in spite of myself. Seeing me she waved. I waved back and took a long pull on my cigar and then my drink. Well if those weren't signals, I wasn't much of a man. Still I thought what was with the "Girls Girls Girls" thing? I decided to go ask.

I placed my cigar in the ashtray and tossed back the rest of my rum. I was a tiny bit surprised that my heart rate increased at the thought of going back downstairs. This for me kind of sealed the deal and I walked out of the office towards the stairs and, perhaps, toward a point to no return.

I entered the garage and said loudly, "Got enough spray or should I order some?" She looked over and said,

"Well, if you're going to be gone for three months the car isn't going to move and I have more than enough for another application. She went on.

"You came down here to ask me if you needed to order more magic cleaner?"

"Ah no, I came down to ask why you had "Girls Girls Girls" tattooed on your lower back?"

"Here we go," I thought, "into the fray one more time."

She looked directly at me and her face took on a very serious expression. Shit I thought foul ball, strike one. Then she smiled.

"Hmm. Well, 'cause I like having sex with women."

My expression must have indicated utter surprise, and she burst out laughing.

"No, I'm kidding. But everyone thinks that. I was a huge Motley Crue fan when I was younger. I loved the song; "Girls Girls Girls." So I got a tattoo one night after a concert and have been dealing with the fallout ever since!"

I joined in her laughter and commented; "Yeah I have been dealing with the fall-out from my tattoos as well."

"Do people think you're gay?"

"No!"

"Then you hardly know what it's like. Grab the hose and spray this sexy beast down," she said gesturing at the Aston Martin.

I walked over and picked up the hose and started spraying the car off. The soap ran off the black surface leaving a black sky in its wake. She picked up her bucket and the rest of her supplies and walked the over into the garage and replaced them in the cupboard. Walking back she stood off to one side as I moved around the car removing any residual soap. I retraced my steps pulling the hose out from under the wheels and returned to the front of the car giving it a last once over from top to bottom. I was standing about eight feet away spraying the roof when Andrea ran in front of the stream.

The spray caught her along her neckline and she squealed like a young schoolgirl. Stopping and turning a circle in the wet spray she proclaimed; "It's cold!"

I held the hose away. In shock she had run into the spray and that the thin white top was now transparent.

I released the pressure on the spray attachment and the water stopped. She stood there, about six feet away, her gorgeous breasts as exposed as if she just stepped from a shower. She did not move to cover herself, choosing instead to run her fingers through her wet hair, pulling it back and wringing it out into a ponytail. Her heavy breasts moved up and down with her breathing and activity. Then she fixed me with a grin and walked right up to me and stopped her tits about an inch away from my chest.

"When we're young we're allowed to do things that are impulsive. I'm not trying to complicate our lives or our arrangement as landlord/ tenant. Quite the contrary, I don't have time for a boyfriend and I think you're probably too broken to start a relationship. But that doesn't mean we both don't have needs and desires. Until last night I didn't know you were into me, or women for that matter. You have never brought anyone home in three years. You're good looking, dress well, and you're in great shape. Let's just say you weren't the only one with a "homo" question!

"I'm going to go have a shower and you can decide if you want to join me or not, up to you. I know you leave tonight, so I figured I'd better make an obvious pass or forget it. No strings, Rhys, really!"

She turned and without another word disappeared into the house, leaving me holding my hose like some cheese-eating high school kid!

CHAPTER THIRTEEN

I KICKED THE HOSE INTO the garage, climbed into the Aston, parked it and hurried after her. As I reach the foyer I was held back by my thoughts for only a moment. She thought I was gay?

I guess living all alone with a pampered cat, dressed stylishly all the time and in good shape could give that illusion. I could understand the confusion.

"No strings," she had said.

"Hmmm?" I wondered at that. Rarely in life do things come without strings. But I had been through several months of self-induced celibacy, so the desire was winning over the thought process.

"Slow down, Rhys. Think with the big head!" I told myself.

My mind continued with the questions.

"What is the potential down side to this?

She could get weird and leave, and then I would need to get Ruben another cat sitter.

She could want more than this arrangement.

She could want …"

My thoughts were scattered, I was not used to thinking past all this emotion.

I walked into the cellar and selected a bottle of wine.

"A 10-year-old Merlot should add to the adventure," I mused.

She would have been 18 when this was bottled! It was a good wine. I continued out of the cellar and crossed the threshold into her apartment. I could hear the shower running as I entered her domain.

I wandered into the living room and retrieved a couple of glasses. Not finding a corkscrew in plain view I pulled out my multi-tool to open the wine, and set the bottle on the table to let it breathe.

I heard the shower stop and waited, hesitating, unsure. I moved from chair to couch and back to the chair, trying to decide on a place to sit. This was difficult! I was out of my element and I knew it. The desire to be with her was like an overpowering scent, not exactly pleasant yet not disagreeable. She came out of the bathroom and wandered up the hall, her wet footsteps making their mark. She looked into the living room and saw me.

I reached to pour some wine and looked at her. She had on a white terry towel, tightly wrapped around her creamy body. Her full, voluptuous breasts held the towel easily in position.

"Wine?" I asked, as a safe preamble.

"I thought you decided not to join me? Did I stutter when I said to join me in the shower?"

This jockeying for power took me off guard, and in doing so put me on alert.

"I thought we could start off slowly with a drink," I offered.

She shook her long flowing hair loose of her towel and I couldn't tell if there was a comment attached to the action.

"Rhys," she says calmly, and drops the towel around her hair and, without concern, pulled her wrap open and dropped it to the floor.

"This is not a date, paid or otherwise. This is desire — fueled by lust. I like you. I want to have some fun with you, plain and simple. Nothing more is on the agenda here. Do you want me?"

I gape as she takes another step towards me and awaits my answer. Her long athletic body is gorgeous. She's smooth and toned, her long limbs fading in colour as she cools from her hot shower.

"Yes," is all I can manage in a now-subdued voice.

"Good. Then stand up and get naked! After you do that you can pour us both a glass of wine."

I stand, unbuttoning my slacks, fumbling with the belt and she stifles a laugh.

"Slow down soldier, I'm not going anywhere." With that she steps up and starts unbuttoning my shirt as I step out of my shoes. The belt now loose, her comment reaches my brain.

"Soldier?"

Where had that come from? I look into her emboldened eyes, now only inches from mine.

She senses my question.

"Do you really think I don't know what you do Rhys? Do I seem that innocent and näive to you?"

I didn't answer.

"I know you're a mercenary Rhys. And I know what that entails. I understand society needs people like you to enjoy the cheap goods people like you provide for people like me. But I don't really care about that right now. Right now I care about this."

She reaches past the border of my underwear and grabs my half-erect cock. Dropping to her knees she straddles my leg and I feel her warm dampness on my foot as she takes me into her mouth. In one motion she devours me whole. My hands fall to the top of her head as she engulfs me with her mouth. The wine plan is lost in the bliss of the moment. I pull one hand from her head and, reaching back to find the table, steady myself as she continues. Her hands trace an erotic path up the back of my powerful legs and reaching my ass she cups it and lets out a long moan. She drives me deeper in her mouth and a long, low moan escapes my lips.

Her hand continues up passed my abs onto my chest. My legs shake as she pushes me back into the chair. Her warmth comes off my foot and onto my leg and she grinds herself against me, sucking with reckless abandon. She unfolds off me and her long legs easily encase mine, her beautiful tits pressed against my face. Like a baby, I reach for a nipple with my lips. They are hard and long and I find one and pull it past my lips and into my mouth, sucking hard as I cup her perfect apple-shaped bottom with my hands. She slides herself against my cock and I feel the sticky warmth of her desire. I feel her hand grab me; to direct me into her core, I think. Instead she once again rubs me, hard, through her wetness. I feel her shake with a building orgasm as she continues to rub me hard across her sex.

"Hold me," she mouths breathlessly.

I move my hands to her upper back and feel her legs tense in anticipation. She continues her manipulations and I can feel her covering my cock, now wet with her effort. Her breaths come in quick gasps as she slaps my rigid firmness against her spot and shakes in her arrival and drops her spent weight on my thighs.

She takes a breath and rolls her hips forward bringing her face to mine. She kisses me and lifts her hips a little higher and I feel the tip of my cock contact her searing sex. She brings her mouth to my ear and with a hoarse voice whispers, "God, I needed that!"

I involuntary react to her sweet passion and bounce against her opening. "Not without a condom, Rhys." Her comment pulls me up short. She rocks back and looks at me directly with eyes half closed in passion, smiles and continues.

"This is the day of AIDS, Rhys. I know most of your lovers have probably been professionals. Not trying to be rude, but the truth can sound like that, can't it?"

I nod, feeling like a parishioner making a confession. Smiling she continues, "Are you close?" I shake my head no. "Ok" She continues and slides her body forward and I slip into her unyielding wetness. Pushing she yields and slides onto my hard cock.

I can feel her heart beating rapidly and her hard clit pulsating and joining mine in her tight soft wetness. She arches away from me; tossing her head back lets out a long sigh. "God, that feels so good"

Then, just as quickly, she slides off and I feel the cold room air as it replaces her warm core. Then with a gymnast's dexterity she rotates her legs and slides back onto my leg. Coming to rest on my foot takes me once again into her mouth. Her hand grips my base and slides easily up to meet her pouty lips.

"Mmmm, I taste good," she says, partially to herself. She reaches up, with her hand, for me to partake of her wine. I lick at her fingers as she slides her mouth down my cock. She pushes against my face and I'm enveloped by her wonderful sweet scent. Pushing her fingers into my mouth I suck at her slippery wetness— the sharp and sweet tastes contrasting deliciously. Her head movements increase, as does her grip on my cock and I can feel my orgasm building!

Faster now, she pulls and drives me deeper into her mouth, tongue pushing against my underside only to wrap deliciously around the head of my straining cock before once again going down. I build much faster than usual, and have to tap her head in a bit of a panic to signal my coming release. She drops one hand to cup my balls, shrinking now with the impending release. She continues faster and I once again signal that I'm more than close and she drives her lips down hard past my base and I feel the tip of my cock slip past her throat. I explode with the fury of the many months of neglect and feel her gag point reflexively grip the head of my cock.

I make sounds, more animal than human; I lose all sense of time as the crushing wave of my orgasm takes me like the power of a Hawaiian wave! Spent, and feeling like I had just been spit out on the beach of this same Hawaiian paradise I open my eyes to see her looking up at me.

Smiling with more than just her lips, red from her effort, she says; "Not bad for a youngling, eh Rhys?"

I can't speak at the moment but I guess my face is all the answer she needs and she gets up. Her flesh is goose-bumped and covered in a slight sheen of sweat that collects on the downy hair of her lower belly like the fresh dew of an African morning! She reaches across me and lifts the wine bottle and looks at it appraisingly. Smiling she pours two glasses and sets it down. Her sweaty breasts swing deliciously in front of my face and she moves to retrieve the two glasses and handing one to me she asks.

"Did I ever tell you my family made wine in the Okanagan?"

I shake my head "no," and she sits on the couch, placing her towel down first. Casually, she sits in repose, her legs slightly apart, reclining back. She takes a sip of her wine and smiles, rubbing her tongue first across the roof of her mouth and then her lips.

"Hmmm, great year," she says, checking the label. "It was bottled when I was 18. I remember when Carl – our local vintner — and my uncle had the vintners' tasting. They let me taste it with them, it was the first time I had been allowed to drink wine. I doubt they thought it would go so well with me. It does, doesn't it?"

I was stunned by this revelation and caught midway with glass on it's way to my lips. My expression was all the comment she needed to know this was all fresh news to me. Nodding she urged me on. I took a drink and she was right! The tasty base and fresh finish was the perfect complementary arrangement. As if some sommelier that specialized in post-coital wines had selected it.

With a mischievous smile reveling in my slow realization she burst out laughing and I quickly joined her, feeling closeness for the first time in years.

She smiled and was silent for a moment or two, then brought the topic back to reality.

"Are you taking the local limo company to the airport this afternoon?"

I hadn't yet called the only company that served this area of the valley, but I didn't imagine there would be an issue midweek.

"Yes, I had intended to, but I haven't called yet. Why?"

"Well she started, "I have never done anything like this before and I thought I would end the experience with a ride in a limo, as I have never done that before either."

"Could have fooled me," I said in a teasing voice.

She responded by hopping up and tossing the towel she had been sitting on at me.

"Pig!" She mimicked in false indignation.

I watched as she walked across the room and disappeared down the hall, a wonderful spectre of beauty. I picked up the towel and inhaled her heady scent and was brought back to the reality that I was leaving and had yet to pack and still make more arrangements, although I could easily spend the day repeating this exercise.

"Well?"

She had returned wearing a long and clinging t-shirt and was eyeing me as I held her soiled towel.

"Limo?" she continued.

"Sorry. Sure. No problem."

I tried to shake the stupid out of my head. Swearing at my own gender's inability to have blood flow to the two organs at the same time.

"I should really call him and make sure he's free. I have to pack yet." I said more to myself than Andrea.

Chuckling, she responded,

"Well get going, I'm not looking to cuddle. Besides, you will have to explain your new scent to Ruben. He'll be asking for details, so you boys should do the locker room confessional while I clean up."

Dismissed, I stood and made my way to the door and she stole a kiss as I passed by, slapping my bare ass hard with her hand.

"Forgetting something?"

She laughed.

"I don't do laundry!"

Shit, I had got up literally forgetting my pants.

"Sorry, having a hard time getting everything working." I said.

"You're sure good for a girl's ego!" she responded, as she tossed me my shirt. I caught it and made my way back to my side of the house and hopefully to full conscious thought.

I carried my clothes down the hall and closed Andrea's door, then closed the second door into the foyer, consciously replacing the boundaries and trying to make myself come back online.

CHAPTER FOURTEEN

I WALKED UP THE STAIRS to be met by Ruben. He purred loudly and approvingly then chased me down the hall to the bedroom, nipping my heels. I picked my cell phone out of the jumbled wreckage of my clothing and dialed the limo driver. The ringing was cut short by a quick answer. "Yes, Mr. Munroe?"

"Hello Charlie, sorry for the last minute booking but I need a ride into the airport for a 1930 departure. I'm checking bags so need to be there for 1800 at the latest. This isn't just a drop off, one passenger will be returning home. Can you do it?"

"The 15:30 pick up is fine, Mr. Munroe," he answered. "But I have a wedding rehearsal dinner pick-up at 20:00 back in Chilliwack. Will it going to be a long good-bye at the airport?"

"No. Just long enough to pop the trunk and go," I answered, thankful I had an excuse to move into the terminal quickly. Charlie responded back over the static of his cell phone. "Great Mr. Munroe, I'll be outside at 1529."

"Thanks," I called into the cell. Charlie was a great limo driver. His car was always meticulously clean and he was never late. I checked the time on the phone before putting it away. It was now 1320 — barely enough time to get everything done on the list, that I couldn't recall. I moved into the bathroom for a much-needed shower and with it hopefully get some focus!

The hot water blasted my skin and turned to a mist that, caught like prayers to God, flowed upward to the open blue sky past the skylight. The October air cool, even now in the early afternoon, completely fogged the bathroom as it mixed with the shower's heat. My skin was red in the downpour and I watched the swirling mist circle the large glass enclosure like sharks around wounded prey. It was judging me, looking for an opening, preparing to strike and bring home its point. I heard Ruben's call like a siren's call threatening to dash me on a reef. Ruben liked Andrea. She played with him and loved him when I was away. He liked the idea of Andrea and me. The whirling demons in the mist did not.

"Never fall in love and never live with anyone you wouldn't walk away from in 30 seconds or less."

I wasn't sure where the quote or advice had come from, but it was something I had lived with forever. I had pushed what little family I did have away and my friends in this world had purposes — nothing more.

"What the hell have I done?" I thought through the swirling torture. She will be riding to the airport with you. No doubt to say goodbye, with a kiss and perhaps a tear. Waving like the Queen Mum: a false acknowledgement of recognition and a very real acknowledgement of power. Power over all her subjects' adoration.

But I wasn't powerless here. I wasn't under a spell! I raged against the misty inquisitors. They responded by clearing slightly and showing me my pants. My argument as diminished as my resolve and position returned.

The sex had been good. "Okay, really good," I allowed myself. It was only because we had lived in the same house for so long that this connection was made so quickly. The mists were not convinced, but yet were not ready to retire in judgment.

"I'm just feeling the connection because I like her as a friend, she's good to Ruben, and I trust her."

The machine rushed out of the mist, scattering it like the wake of a motorboat.

Trust? Really, that soon? One BJ and you're happily in trust mode, eh? It was sex, simple, and base — like on the educational channels. People do it all the time and because it was real for her, unlike paid partners, you trust? Reality was fighting with the returning mist, and the mist was winning the fight and rewriting reality. It had been just sex, fun and enjoyable. Just a weird and fun afternoon. Nothing more. No, it was nothing more.

I stepped out of the shower and into the convinced mist and fumbled for the wall switch to activate the fans. Finding it I turned them on and pushed the button to close the skylight. I watched it close tightly and lock into place with a click. I also watched the mist swirl up and then part, as if cut in four and like ghosts to retreat into the three foot-long metal grilles set in the walls.

I toweled off and forced the thought of dropping white towels out of my mind. I grabbed my toiletries bag and checked its contents. I shaved a second time and was rewarded for the effort with a nick to the underside of the nose. This nick gushed blood as if I had slashed a femoral artery. The steady drip of dark red blood was accompanied perfectly by the tickle-pain that threatens to make you sneeze a Jackson Pollock original onto your mirror.

I stuffed a piece of toilet paper on it and walked out of the bathroom. I got dressed in the hallway closet and instead of jeans and a t-shirt picked out a winter suit. I wanted to breeze through customs and I decided on the consultant look. I went to my watches and decided on The Breitling Emergency. It was showy enough to signal success, but it was not over the top. It also had the added benefit of having a built-in transmitter that, if engaged, could signal passing aircraft in an emergency, just like a downed plane. I slipped it on my wrist and checked to verify the storage unit had worked in preserving its time.

It was nearly 1500 and I still had to go through my jump bag to ensure everything had made its way back in, like the Satellite phone that was still on the kitchen counter. I figured I'd better tell Andrea what time we were leaving.

While I walked to the kitchen tying my tie, I made some mental notes. The excitement this morning had bought me lots of time, I concluded, as the guns were all safely hidden, or stored correctly and the safe room had been checked. I reached the kitchen and picked up the Sat phone while I dialed Andrea from my cell phone. It rang twice before she picked up.

"Hello Rhys — out front at what time?"

I replied using the civilian time, '3.30.' "

"Okay," was the distant reply, and she hung up.

I went into my office and was greeted by Ruben sitting on my jump bag. I reached for its handle and he swatted my hand.

"Ruben, I have to go."

I pleaded with the cat and was rewarded by a hiss. Yet, despite this show of aggression he jumped to the desktop and settled down to watch me. Most of this stuff would be checked and I went through it all very quickly. I replaced the sat phone inside its Pelican hard case and tossed fifteen cigars in a similar Pelican indestructible case. The only differences were the colours, red and black. Red was for the phone. Everything was there and ready to go so I placed the soft duffle bag into a hard-case Tumi roller and secured it with the FAA certified locks. They were certified as the FAA had a master key to allow inspection and would usually lock them again if the bag were chosen for hand inspection. This would keep an honest thief from making off with your stuff. I got my laptop case and wardrobe bag, again made by Tumi. It was foolish to travel with bags made by anyone else, as these were trial tested and just worked perfectly.

I turned on my Mac laptop and watched as the 17-inch screen sprung to life. I wanted to insure there was nothing that could create problems entering the United Kingdom. I deleted the history of all recent computer activities. I packed the clothes needed for the trip, added the computer and zipped up the Tumi carry-on.

I checked my watch. It was 3:25. Looking out my window I saw that Charlie was early and that she was already outside talking with him, both ready to go. I moved all my stuff to the stairs and sat it down three steps behind me and turned to pat Ruben who had appeared at the top in his designated spot.

"Bye," I said. In response he bit my nose lightly and held it softly between his incisors. He made a purr mixed with a "Meow" then turned and walked off. I thought, "Thirty seconds or less!"

I rolled my bags toward the black stretch limousine.

Charlie broke away from his conversation with Andrea and moved to intercept me.

"Thanks, sir," was all he said as he took my gear and made for the enormous maw of a trunk.

I walked over to Andrea; she was dressed now in a simple white blouse and swingy dark blue skirt. Casual but still elegant and enticing. She smiled and winked, saying,

"I brought some entertainment!"

I was wondering what she meant when Charlie came back and opened the door for us. Turning completely around, being totally discreet, as she bent and climbed into the limo. I did not share his sense of discretion, watching the tartan skirt ride high as she entered, and followed quickly behind her.

Inside, the limo was set up like a small den, with a large C-shaped grey leather couch dominating the ends and one complete side. The other long wall contained two bar sections, both with ice, and in the middle a 42-inch LCD television complete with DVD and live feed from a rooftop mounted satellite receiver.

Charlie closed the door and in the blue glow of the floor lighting I saw Andrea's socks, the blue/white glowing with an ultraviolet quality. The windows were all black and the overhead lighting was off and this made it hard to see my scotch bottle. My eyes had trouble going from very bright to very dark. A laugh signaled she could see my confusion.

"You look like Mr. Mole, blinking away over there."

"I can't go from bright sun to cave dark in seconds anymore," I laughed.

"Would you be so kind as to pour Mr. Mole a few fingers of Scotch from the bottle, if you can find it? Glasses should be on ice in the end compartments."

I was now aware we were moving, the big land shark banking left off my street. I sat back and closed my eyes, willing them to recover. I was rewarded by the sound of a high-pitched squeak as an old cork was pulled out a bottle by young hands. Then the sound was followed by another, the clink of glass on glass and finally the soft pouring of liquid amber.

I smelled the peat-smoke mix with her natural scent as she moved closer to hand me the glass. My eyes had now adjusted to the light as I took in her pretty face as it loomed and then retreated back to her place on the end of the couch. She was keeping her distance, or making me come to her? Exactly what I wasn't sure but I wasn't playing any games. I sat in the place I always sat, the middle, and stretched my feet out toward the far dark window past the flush mounted TV. Reaching up above my head I pushed a toggle that slid the long sunroof open a tad and opened the square sunroof down where we entered a bit more.

She started, "I have a video I would like you to watch and give me your opinion on. Would you mind?"

She was moving to the DVD slot just under the big TV right above the toes of my feet.

"No" I answered her "I don't mind at all. What is it?"

Cryptically she just said; "documentary," returning to her seat at the far end of the couch.

"Ok. I like real stuff," I replied. "If you're going to sit way over there do you mind if I smoke?"

"Nope, I figured you were going to when you opened the sunroof."

I lit the Bolivar Petite Corona, despite the signs admonishing me not to, and relished its sweetness. These cigars were fast becoming my favorites and I was glad I had packed a few. The closet-like dark was replaced with a blue glow as the TV sprang to life and announced it was about to play a DVD.

The logo was splashed across the screen like a big deal. Perhaps when it had been first installed it was, now my cell phone could play a movie. The title: "Shadow Warriors" sprang onto the screen in a little too dramatic a fashion. But I guess it worked for the name. I hoped this wouldn't be a long film.

The countryside got a little less sparse as we moved further toward the city and so did the film. I was pleasantly surprised that the film did not live up to its title and drama. Instead it showed a pretty well balanced view of the war in Iraq and the role private soldiers were playing in it.

There was some cowboy stuff, but then again the biggest PMC, Private Military Corporation, working in the Green Zone were cowboys and a group I wouldn't think of attaching myself to. Then there was a very unnecessary and probably very expensive animated section telling the story of some contact. The teller had so many details it was hard to believe he could have been there. But as he was on TV it must be true. I chuckled to myself.

The limo was moving fast now, entering the city of Richmond running along side the wide muddy river that separates it from Vancouver. The next section of the film came on focusing on Executive Outcomes and included two great interviews done in that country.

It was a real treat and made the watching of the boring early footage and base storyline well worth the effort. Too soon the credits ran, as the towers of the airport loomed in the distance.

Andrea was looking at me across the car,

"So? Is that about right? Would you agree with the guys on the disk?"

I couldn't tell her mood at that moment, but recognized she would make a good therapist. I was a master at discerning human emotion, having had to mimic it most of my adult life.

"Agree with it? Hell the Hind-helicopter pilot quoted me! I used to work with some of those guys and have shared a beer or six with many of them!"

She remained quiet for a few moments as if taking it all in. Then she smiled and said,

"Ok, I get it. I wanted to understand it all better. A professor of mine told me it was pretty unbiased. Simple, but not sensational. Hearing you agree puts it in perspective for me."

The bump of the limo signaled we were approaching the drop off point and going up the overpass that always made me reflexively duck my head. The big car slowed and pulled to the curb as perfectly as a space station docking. I heard Charlie's door open and close and saw his shadow move across the darkened window on the way to the trunk. Andrea wasn't moving or saying anything more so I thought I would make a remark to stir her from reflection.

"Hey, I never said what I did wasn't sensational. Sometimes it was very sensational!"

This attempt at humour appeared to go unnoticed and any further attempt was cut short as Charlie opened the back door. I moved out of the subdued light, into the glaring, harsh aperture of daylight, searching for something to say. I got to the end of the couch and bent low to exit. Andrea stopped me with my name.

"Rhys!"

I turned and looked down the long couch to where she was sitting. Spreading her legs enticingly, she continued.

"This is sensational. When you get back I would very much like you to get to know it better and the person behind it, just as I would like to know you. Still no strings. I just kind of like you more when you're off your guard. Funny thing is I think you like you better then, too. Otherwise you wouldn't be grinning like a school boy now!"

I snorted, and then laughed in response. She was right. I was grinning. Facing the bright light I exited the car thinking, "Thirty seconds or less!"

I gathered my luggage from Charlie and he gave me a knowing wink, reminiscent of high school.

"Good trip, sir." He said through a grin.

"I hope it will be, Charlie." I responded and headed into the departure terminal of Vancouver's International Airport.

CHAPTER FIFTEEN

THE DEPARTURES AREA WAS AS austere and plain as the arrival area was decorative and artistic. I always wondered, "Why such a contrast?" I understood the rationale for impressing visitors when they arrived. But, why the cafeteria-like cattle line design for departures? Surely we wanted to impress and remind visitors and locals alike when they left? Moving past the shops, selling food that would sit in your stomach and magazines that would fill your carry-on I walked toward the British Airways check in counter. I smiled; yes, the class system was alive and well in London. Instead of First and Regular lines like most airlines had, BA had Coach, Upgraded Coach, Business, and First. Four clear distinctions of service and, unlike in Vancouver where there was only one first class lounge, London Heathrow had four levels of lounges. In fact Heathrow had a private restaurant for its first class passengers that provided a truly fine dining experience.

The first class line was empty. I was a little shocked to see the other lines contained lots of people. There was only an hour and a half before departure and the recommended check in time was two hours for international flights. Most people arrived three hours early. BA only flew this one flight out of Vancouver tonight so all of these people must be for that flight. I walked down the line, aware of the stares of the people threading through the cattle maze, clearly two lines removed from the unwashed masses. Yes, the class system was alive and well. I liked it that way. Perhaps "unwashed" was harsh but with luggage carts looking like overloaded African porters and strollers containing squalling noise machines that line would be hell. Caught in that position people feel the need to socialize and "get to know" their fellow travelers. I wanted to share nothing with them. I had nothing in common with those sheep, winding their way through the abattoir-like maze. I didn't have to stop at the end of the line as the attendant at the first class desk had seen me approaching and had not waved anyone over to her desk from the other lines.

"Afternoon," I said, handing her my ticket, passport and platinum frequent flyer card. Her eyes darted to the frequent flyer card and she reacted like a woman at a reunion who had had a crush on you in school.

"Hello, Mr. Munroe, Glad to see you again. I see you haven't picked a seat yet? Did you know you could do that online? That way you can just proceed straight through security and go to the lounge."

"Yes, I know" I answered. I could see her brow furrow at the confusion at my answer. I wasn't about to tell her,

"I did it this way to make it harder for anyone to put a plant in the seat next to me."

Instead I replied,

"But then I wouldn't get to talk with you and perhaps get a seat with no one near me if the section isn't full. And I like walking past all the sheep in the other lines. Makes me feel special."

She was either very good, or as arrogant as me. There was no physical response to my statement. She continued smiling and punching buttons on her computer.

"Well, first is only about 20 percent full. Getting you a quiet spot should be easy. Unless we fill up in the next half hour and need the space you should be all alone."

She looked up and smiled. Then, taking my bags she placed them on the moving belt. She handed me my boarding pass, luggage tags and documents.

"Thanks, " I said slipping them into the outside pocket of my carry-on.

"You're welcome. Thanks for choosing British Airways. Have a great flight," she responded with a warm smile.

Walking away I scanned the line of other passengers. Most of the people who had been at the counter when I arrived were still there, fumbling with passports and papers. It wasn't just lack of money that made them sheep. They were half asleep, moving through life like grazing beasts. It should be obvious to them to have all their travel documents ready. Yet most of them didn't, choosing instead to gab to the people around them, like cows chewing cud.

I cruised quickly toward the international section, separated from the US international section that cleared you into the USA while still in Canada. I thought this odd, too, and probably costly. There must be some security reason for it. The woman at the "real" international gate checked my boarding pass and passport with tired eyes and a blank expression before waving me through. I arrived at the baggage screening area and moved to the line for First Class passengers. It was empty. I walked past a handful of people in the regular line. Again they were waiting until they actually got to the end of the line before preparing for inspection. I had already started undoing my belt, wondering if this was going to be shoes off or on month, as it seemed to vacillate between the two.

"Shoes on or off?" I asked.

He waved me forward without answering.

I didn't beep.

I collected my things on the far side of this drama and thought how stupid it all was. The cleaning closets and shops on the other side of this artificial barrier contained all the products I would need to bring down a plane. There were weapons available, if one knew what to look for in every shop. The only smart thing they did post-September 11 was to harden the cockpit door. Although this meant that no small children got to go sit up in the cockpit anymore like I had the year my parents died.

As I made my way to the first class lounge my mind drifted back along the grey fading to white halls of time to the last vacation, I open the private door and walked into the quiet surroundings handing my boarding pass to the receptionist I could almost feel my Dad's big hand on mine.

We had gone to Disneyworld in Florida the year I turned six. It had been a grand trip, and one I had anticipated for months. My parents rarely planned trips, preferring to go last minute and I would usually have to stay with my grandmother. Not this time! My grandmother had passed away that year and one day at breakfast my father announced we were going to Disney World. I couldn't finish my breakfast. My Mom had just responded with "In Florida?"

My father continued to lay out his plan. We were going for two weeks at Spring break and I would have to miss three days of school. Spring break was over two months away; it was the longest two months of my life. I was on my best behaviour, marking the days in red on the fridge calendar. When it finally came I was in heaven. I didn't sleep the night before but did fall asleep in the car on the way to the airport. We were in first class and one of the stewardesses had come over and asked if I'd like to see the cockpit and meet the pilot. I had almost jumped out of my seat at the invitation. I looked at my Dad and he nodded approval while admonishing me not to "touch a damn thing."

The cockpit had been dark. We had been flying late in the day and the sun was behind us. I remember thinking how small the windows were, and how many buttons and dials and switches there were. The two pilots talked to me and pointed out things I couldn't understand. I was a big kid for my age so grownups always thought I was much older than I was. They asked if I had any questions and I remembered I asked if they had parachutes. They had both looked at each other and then back at me and broke into a laugh! They explained that they were going far too fast and too high to even use a chute, before shooing me back to my seat.

Six months later my parents were killed in a plane crash. It had been much smaller private jet, chartered for a quick, romantic getaway. When I was told of the crash I remembered wondering if that plane had flown too high and fast for chutes, too? Not that I had that much time to worry about it. My life was now to get a great deal more complicated than any six-year old deserved.

My parents had been very well off. Not that I really knew anything about finances then. With no siblings or other family members still alive, they had left my guardianship up to my fathers' company lawyer, John, as we had no close relatives left. John was a great lawyer and kind of a hired gun to solve problems in the corporate world.

John was not a good replacement for my parents. Rarely did I have a bedtime or any other real structure imposed in my life. The fact I was very much a type A personality and hyperactive made a lack of structure detrimental to my development. Add to this John knew lots of people that "fixed" things. My transgressions as a young child were handled with the same efficiency as John handled things in his corporation — they were just made to go away. Instead of parenting John did the second best thing he could think of and enrolled me in courses. These courses provided the only real structure. I had riding lessons, swimming, fencing, karate, boating, and shooting.

Shooting was the only thing we did together. John would take me to the range every Sunday. I loved those days and recognize now that at the time I was yearning for loving contact. Instead I spent time learning how to handle and shoot many different guns. John was an avid collector and knew lots of police officers that joined us on many occasions. John would always have a gift of some sort for these officers, hockey tickets to a game no one could get tickets for and so on. I didn't know it then, I just thought John was generous like he was with me. But these gifts were for help and consideration for helping him fix things. John enrolled me in a special school when I was 12. At the time I thought it was out of discipline, as I had just been involved in some nonsense, as he framed and called my transgressions. The private school was out near the University of British Columbia. It was called St. Georges and provided a great deal of structure, far more structure than I was used to. My first year saw me in the headmaster's office more than in class! How John managed to fix my transgressions and keep me enrolled was beyond me. Our Sunday outings had turned more into mini pep rally's to keep me acting appropriately and no doubt saving John lots of favours. I settled down and started enjoying the school and opportunities that were there however I never really fit in as most of the kids that went there were from rich families and I was not from any family whatsoever. I lived with John in a very nice penthouse apartment in the west end of Vancouver but he had his space and I had mine. We were like an age separated "odd couple". I had karate and fencing to occupy my evenings, determined by my homework. John had his cases. I never once saw him go to court for these cases, as most of them were settled with a mutual understanding, as he called it. He never attended any school functions and I never thought to ask him. I withdrew from the world I never really fit into with and focused on personal achievement.

I was in my final year when I came home one day to find John sitting at the big kitchen table. A half-empty bottle of scotch was sitting in front of him. He had been crying – his eyes were red and swollen. He had beckoned me over to the table and told me to sit and poured me a small measure of scotch. This was odd behaviour to be sure, but alcohol had never been forbidden. We routinely had wine with dinner, but I could tell this was different. John fixed me with his red eyes and after a long exhale gave me the bad news.

"Rhys, this fucking sucks, but believe me it's worse for me. I have pancreatic cancer and my doctor has just given me three months to live."

I started to speak, but he waved off my comment.

"Wait till I'm done. You're going to be fine. You're graduating soon and there is lots of money in your trust account. I will be leaving you the apartment and the cars, but you need to socialize more. I worry about you. I think I kind of failed your Dad in raising his kid. You don't have any close friends, Rhys, and I think I'm to blame for that. I've been a poor influence and I should have really worked on that. It was just one of the many things I didn't get around to. I have enrolled you in a program that's going to take you to Europe this summer, after you graduate. Promise me you'll go and try to make a few friends."

Finished, he fixed me with that hard negotiator stare for which he was famous and I felt myself nodding before the answer croaked out of my throat;

"Yes, I promise."

John lived only another three weeks and was so heavily medicated during his last week I think he preferred death. I kept my promise to go traveling and really tried to make friends, but I failed. I found the effusive emotional connections people made difficult.

It was on the European trip that I realized I was different from other people. It wasn't just that I didn't fit, I simply didn't feel things to the same depths other people did. The stresses of travel and being foreign didn't affect me as much either. I realized I was lacking a basic human condition, the love and compassion most humans feel towards each other.

I had reached that conclusion after one of our traveling companions had been run over by a bus near Bern. I had worked quickly and had done everything I'd learned in the many first aid courses I'd taken. The head trauma had been massive and I was really unsure at the time of who had been hit. I was unable to discern the gender until I started CPR. Lori was her name, and she lived for three hours after the incident, thanks to the expert care of the Swiss system and, if the doctors were to be believed, my immediate actions.

After she died the hospital set up a meeting for us. It was an optional meeting but we were all encouraged to attend. I was flat about the experience; upset I had not been successful in saving her life. But the loss was not mine, I hadn't known her well. She had stepped out in front of the moving bus. I had not really intended to go but one of the other girls came to get me ten minutes before it started. Rather than explain why I wasn't going I just went along.

The man running the meeting was a whale of a man, easily 350 pounds. He looked as though he would be more at home behind a sleigh with his white hair and beard. He had an open, friendly face, further enhancing the Father Christmas effect. He began by telling us there were only three rules in the meeting. Once it begins everyone stays till the end. Only one person speaks at a time, and we are to only speak about our personal feelings and not comment on others' observations. Continuing he said.

"This meeting is a Critical Incident Debriefing. My name is Doctor Kurt Schuller. You may call me Kurt or Doc. This is based on the program started in Canada called Critical Incident Stress Management or CISM. We have adopted it nationally to help curtail the stress that's associated with these kinds of incidents. There is a basic structure we follow as we move through the process, which is why we ask that no one leave. There are cookies and juice at the rear of the room and you may get up to help yourself if you need a break or get hungry. My two associates are Gert Strand and Emma Steinbrink. They are here only as observers."

These two associates were seated outside the circle at opposite sides and I immediately got the feeling I was white, fuzzy, sporting a scaly tail. Each of them wore glasses and while they didn't have white lab coats and clipboards, their facial expressions were that of researchers. I admonished myself quietly for opening my door and attending this meeting. "Santa Kurt" continued on but I wasn't listening. Instead I was trying to figure out why I found this far more stressful than the actual critical incident! The eyes of my fellow travelers were doe-eyed open and hopeful, expectant of an experience akin to the wisdom of Buddha. That this was going to wash their souls clean, and put the experience into some form of cosmic renewal. I felt trapped like they would discover something about me, that I was a fake, an alien in their world to be exorcised and banished from society. This feeling was enhanced to near panic levels when I realized everyone was looking at me expectantly. Fuck I had missed something critical, my mind spun, rewinding the last few seconds clawing for meaning, the urge to bolt from the room swelled along my back and joined the wet panic sweat. NAMES! We were going around the circle saying our names. "Ah sorry, Rhys Munroe." The eyes remained on me, expectant as Nuns looking for an apology after farting in church. Thankfully, Santa Kurt provided some assistance, or I would have indeed bolted from the room.

"What part did you play in the incident?" he asked.

"A part? I didn't think this was a fucking play. I held her brains in, stopped the massive bleeding, and restarted her heart." I responded harshly.

Kurt answered, "Sorry Rhys. I didn't mean to suggest this was a play. So you provided aid to Lori and were able to get her stable until the ambulance came. Ok good, thanks."

The looks lingered on me for just a second, accusingly, Lori shit I should have used her name. The microscope got a little closer, magnification turned up like it just spotted something foul and cancerous. But thankfully the guy next to me burst into tears and the drama drew the attention of the two-seated watchers. I took steps to slow my breathing and regain my composure. I forced myself to pay attention and not be taken off-guard again.

The rest of the group shared what they had done at the incident for the initial few minutes. Most of what they shared did not match what I remembered. People were getting blankets, directing traffic, and helping me. My recollection was they all grouped into a huddle and started screaming. I remember having to get a lady to call an ambulance, yet three others remembered me directing them to call. One of them didn't even have a cell phone! How was this possible I thought? Seventeen other people saw the situation so differently than I did? Was it me that was all fucked up? Did they all get together to concoct a story so they didn't look negligent? Did I have it wrong? "No" was the voice inside my head. Like a frozen razor slicing along the soft tissue on my brain I heard the "machine's" voice for the first time. I was not mistaken, but I was unsure and unnerved by this new psychological addition.

The debriefing went on with people filling in what had happened and what they did but this part was voluntary. Each person was building on the others observations and filling in missing details and everyone showed me in a good light so I relaxed and thought the best way to proceed was to just remain the silent hero that the other seventeen were painting me as. I added nothing and just tried to look interested in the process. It moved to another level asking each of us what was the worst part for them. Again the round-table style filled in facts and details and added how each of these issues had made them feel. Santa Kurt's comments were always consoling and the phrase "normal reaction to an abnormal situation and was to be expected". It was like some sort of mantra that if said enough would cure all that ailed us. This part was voluntary as well but I figured better add something and so I searched for something meaningful to add. My turn in the circle came and I had been mulling over a few options and quickly settled on one.

"For me the worst part was when we got Lori to the hospital and they hooked her up to the machines. She was breathing on her own and her vitals looked really good and then she went into cardiac arrest. The machine beeping an unnatural rhythm its' trace arcing sharply in distress. They shocked her three times, each time a little more voltage and then the long beep, like the wind blowing through a small crack stealing her away from us."

I looked around when I finished recounting my experience. Several people were crying. Others were doing the involuntary gulp to stave of the onset of tears. Satisfied I had added correctly I let my eyes fall to the floor.

The debriefing ended with the mantra and Santa Kurt explaining how we all had been through a very intense situation and that many of us may need to continue some form of one on one counseling to move past it. He admonished us to avoid red meat and alcohol for a few days and to try and maintain our normal routines. He said that he and his assistants would remain behind if anyone wanted to talk privately and thanked us all for our honesty and sharing.

I made for the juice as I could feel my blood-sugar dropping as I had missed breakfast that morning. I tossed a cup of the overtly sweet juice back and swished another glass around in my mouth before swallowing. I could feel the sugar hit my system like a drug mainlined. I never ate sugar and avoided things that contained it. But in this circumstance it was necessary if I were to escape this room without fainting. My dream of flight was ended by one word, "Rhys" — spoken to my back.

I turned around and Santa Kurt was standing there, three feet back respecting the personal space we North Americans expect.

"Fucking hell," I thought, "what did this asshole want now?"

I didn't allow it to show on my face but he picked up something as he raised his hands showing his palms and said,

"I have a quick question for you."

This guy was good at reading people, so instead of adding to his suspicions I tilted my head and opened my posture. He took the lead and, stepping closer, asked me,

"Rhys, I think you need to talk with someone, one-on-one. Not so much to help you with this situation but with your situation. You really didn't feel sad when Lori passed did you? You were mad she died; angry you had failed to save her. Anger was your primary emotion, wasn't it? Please be honest. This is anonymous, no notes or follow up, unless you ask for it."

I didn't answer, I just looked at him. He continued.

"Ok. I get it, no problem. But while I have your attention let me say one thing. I have worked with many people like you. If I'm correct in my suspicion, if you ever want to live a normal life you have to learn to affix the mask of humanity a little better and mirror feelings you don't feel. You have to learn to feel the little emotions you have as greatly as we do with our emotional tides. If this makes any sense to you I suggest you check out this place."

He passed me a white card as I continued looking at him.

"It's for your own survival, son. You can learn these things you don't feel and learn to nurture the feelings you do possess, without it you will make a mistake that can't be fixed."

He turned and walked away. I could see the muscles tense in is shoulders; his body was in full on flight or fight mode as if he had just walked up to pet a growling dog.

So instead of following the group to Scandinavia I decided to check myself into the Swiss clinic of Sonnenhalde near Basel. It was a world-renowned clinic, in a gorgeous pastoral setting at the bottom of rolling hills. The buildings were modeled after a ski resort. Most had three floors, all white and very "old world." It was preferable over the Scandinavian retreat.

CHAPTER SIXTEEN

THE ANNOUNCEMENT FOR FLIGHT 055, Vancouver to London Heathrow, chimed quietly over the speakers, just barely audible over the background music. I got up and moved over to the well-stocked bar. I poured myself a nice measure of scotch and checked the gate location. My boarding gate was just around the corner. I decided to wait and grabbed a bit of sushi from the food area. There was no one else in the lounge tonight and I walked back to where I had been sitting. Passing the receptionist I caught her eye.

"Give me a ding for final boarding call, please."

She nodded. I wondered at why all this past stuff was coming up now? I hadn't thought of my parents in years, never mind John. They had left a hole in my life and exchanged it for cash. Like a rich divorcee I was set for life but knew intuitively it had damaged me emotionally. Like the noise of a broken car, I could not diagnose the problem. I had joined the military despite having well over $7,000,000 in the bank.

My much poorer team members never knew, expecting me to be the out-of-work slobs most of them were. Why would someone that well off choose the military? I was worth much more now, yet I was about to embark on a very dangerous operation that, in all likelihood, could end in death. What was I searching for? I knew the answer yet hated to admit it. Connection, family — and excitement. I needed to be part of something accepted and respected. But I also I needed the rapid intense stimulation to feel alive. I finished my scotch and looked over to the reception area. She was working at her computer but felt my eyes on her. She looked at me, looked back at her computer and then looking back at me again, nodded.

I picked up my carry-on, finished my scotch and thought,

"Once more into the breach."

Feeling my step get increasingly light, I walked toward the heavy doors. Beyond them lay my plane, like a modern Valkyrie, ready to drop me into my world once again.

I walked through the empty terminal toward the departure gate. The dark sky beyond the windows looked like the black curtains along the wings of a stage.

"How would this performance play out?" I thought as I approached the boarding gate.

The two people at the gate were looking at the paper manifest and comparing it to the computer one and looked relieved as I walked toward them.

"Mr. Munroe?" one asked as I approached, boarding pass in hand.

I nodded and they both looked satisfied they weren't going to have to track down a drunk first class passenger in one of the many airport lounges. Track him down as they prepared to find and remove his luggage from the plane. It was an FAA requirement that passengers must accompany their luggage. I handed one my boarding pass and passport and she marked me off the list.

"You're pretty much alone up there tonight, sir. Two pilots dead-heading back, and three other passengers."

"Great," I responded as I walked passed them and down the gangway.

The plane had two attendants at the door, watching the other passengers as they tried to organize themselves into their seats. I smiled as I approached and pointed toward the front of the plane. They smiled and one stepped out to allow me to pass to the far aisle. I continued to my seat.

It was a large lounge chair with high sides and lots of room—more like a suite, really. The blocked seats were swung to give me as much space as possible – equivalent to about eight square feet of quiet solitude. I set my carry-on down on the small shelf that fits perfectly halfway down the gorgeous burl-like wood divider.

The seats are the velvet ones and not the Connolly leather, this is good luck as the leather retained so much heat it made sleeping difficult. I've barely crushed the velvet before the flight attendant is beside me, seemingly to materialize out of the air. She's a smaller, British-looking girl, her uniform perfect and welcoming smile firmly affixed.

"Mr. Munroe. Can I get you anything before we're airborne?" she asked.

"Yes please — and the name is Rhys. A glass of champagne would be nice. Do you still serve Piper-Heidsieck?"

"Yes we do. I'll get it right away."

"Thanks," I smiled after her as she hurried to fetch my drink.

The perfect service made the cost of this fare so much more palatable. Head office knew this and so did anyone who worked in this cabin for more than a single flight. I took off my shoes and stored my carry-on in the work desk pocket, which made getting your bag so much easier than under the seat. I opened the custom designed amenities bag and dragged out the plush velvet slippers and just managed to get them on my feet before my attendant, Susan, returned and place the chilled champagne in front of me, then left me to my drink, glancing down to ensure my seatbelt was on.

The lights dimmed slightly as the shore power plug was pulled and we transferred to plane-generated power. The muted roar of the engine dragged the plane backwards in the cool Vancouver air. It had started to rain. The damp was streaking the small window to my right. We bounced a little down the jet way and took our position in line. I took a small sip of the rare champagne and was not disappointed. The wine available in first class rivaled many of those available in fine restaurants. BA took a great deal of pride in this and always had a well-stocked "First cellar" as they called it. The big beast rotated effortlessly 90 degrees and I could just see the lights of Vancouver through the far window. The jet engines roared up to speed and the pilot released the brake and the plane accelerated quickly down the runway belying its huge weight. Not quite the Aston's acceleration, but then the fuel onboard alone weighed more than four times the car!

I felt the fresh, damp salt air catch under the wings and in a moment we were airborne, starting our slow climb to our cruising height. I was "feet wet" as it was referred to in the industry. Being airborne and inbound was "feet wet" and when we landed I would be "feet dry." When we landed, I thought it odd that despite both my parents dying in a plane wreck, I never had even the slightest concern about flying.

"Hell, this was good champagne," I thought to myself. I never drank champagne except on BA flights and when a special occasion required it. But I could certainly get used to this stuff, although the sugar content alone would require many more hours in the gym. The seat belt sign turned off and Susan, once again, materialized like the Cheshire cat.

"How's the champagne? Can I get you another glass?"

"Thanks, but my glass is still half full.

She explained the dinner choices and I made my selection.

"Anything else, sir?" she asked.

"Nothing at the moment, Susan. I'll use the bell if I need you." I said by way of dismissal. She nodded and left.

CHAPTER SEVENTEEN

I HAD A FEW E-MAILS to write and some things to wrap up before I arrived in London. I pulled out my laptop to find a bright pink card on top of the keyboard. I certainly didn't remember receiving any cards. It had been a few months since I used this larger Tumi carry-on. Leaving the laptop closed I looked at the card.

"Rhys" was written on the front in a careful, feminine hand — writing I recognized as Andrea's.

"What the hell is this?" I thought, as I instinctively reached for my knife to open it. It was of course not in its usual place and I swore at my stupidity!

"Wow. You're slipping boy!" I thought. "If that had been a hijacker and not an envelope you would have just lost two seconds — two critical seconds."

I pulled at the envelope's opening. It had only been fastened at the tip and opened easily. Inside was a letter from Andrea.

The first page contained just one line:

"Ruben is going to die!"

I almost bolted from my chair in panic. The psycho bitch was going to hurt my Ruben. My pulse felt like a machine gun in my chest. My eyes narrowed with rage as I reached for my phone. She would take fucking hours to die, I'm going to peel the skin from her body and put her on a steady drip of cocaine to insure the nerves are fully online. The phone was in the safe airplane mode, but I needed the number of someone close, someone that could snatch and sit on this sick bitch till I got home.

I found it and grabbed the air phone in front of me. I jabbed at the number and heard a distant ring. Then it went straight to voice mail. Fuck! I raged and felt helpless for the first time in a long time!

"You know who this is. Call me at… " said, the automated voice.

"Shit," I thought. Operational security, his phone could easily be on a watch list and a phone call from an international flight would be flagged for sure. The eight hours of flight time would easily allow the local authorities to contact London. "Fuck that! Get to a fucking computer and contact my Yahoo account; same name as my e-mail but at Yahoo."

I placed the phone back in its cradle and opened my laptop. It sprung to life almost immediately, the screen casting a huge light in the darkened cabin.

Susan appeared again; "Everything ok? Can I get you another?" she asked, gesturing at my empty glass.

"Everything is fine" I said, the answer very unconvincing in my ears, so I added.

"I just realized I left the stove on and so I need to get a hold of my tenant to have her turn it off."

"Stove on?" the machine raged against the soft tissue of my brain, "Fucking stove on?!"

I looked up and smiled at Susan.

"A triple Grey Goose martini – burnt — with olives would be perfect."

She looked at me quizzically, but went to fetch my drink.

"Get it together, Rhys!" the machine hissed in the back of my mind, its cold breath turning my eyes an icy blue. The computer found the wireless network for the plane and logged me onto the Internet. Plane Internet access was a new thing pioneered by BA, but it was still slow. Painfully slow. I clicked on and waited for program to connect to the ether.

I picked up the letter and looked at the next page. It was full of her script and I forced myself to calm down and read it.

"By now you've probably hired someone to come get me. No need! Ruben is fine and will be fine when you get home. I just wanted to conduct an experiment to allow you to see how broken you really are."

My heart rate slowed considerably and sank back in its chest. Susan arrived with my drink and set it down without a sound.

The letter continued. "I really can't imagine what went through your head as to plans for me but I can predict what you were thinking, and for that I apologize." I continued to read her explanation.

"This experiment would never have passed an ethical review board but then you're not the typical man either. Rest assured, in case you have set things in motion, that I'm safe in a hotel enjoying a night out with the girls. I had the limo drop me off at the sky train, just in case there is a tracking device on the Cutlass. If I missed some clandestine trick then you can call me and tell me. Ok? Unless you believe this transgression was worth my life. I have no illusions about the kind of person I'm dealing with." I was surprised at her assessment of me. It was on the mark. I continued to read.

"The point of this experiment? You probably went into full panic mode and were prepared to take out another human being for a pet. Worse, you were prepared to set this in motion taking extreme risk. Why? Because for you, Ruben represents your family. The only one in your life who matters! He's an old cat and one day he will die and what will that do to you? Have you asked yourself these questions? Do you see my point? I like you a great deal and before I switched to my new honours major, which, by the way, is human sexuality, my focus area was psychopaths.

You're too smart to not know, Rhys, so I surmise that you think you're dealing with the illness well. You have a job in which people of that psychological affliction do very well at. The standard restraints are removed, not conditioned away. I shouldn't have to explain this to you but just in case. The army intentionally uses man shaped silhouettes on the range to get you use to shooting at humans as we have an inborn aversion to doing this. Well, most do. You do not. That makes you quicker and more accurate as you are wired differently. It's the reason you crave excitement and like all the cool adrenaline-type sports you engage in. It's why you are so good at what you do. Well, I guess you're good at it, as you certainly don't seem to be shy on the paycheck side of things. I haven't been snooping. I just happen to know that the Rolex Meteorite you so casually wear everyday are worth over $60,000!

Girls look at shoes, watches, and haircuts on our battlefields. You probably think I'm a gold digger, and you might be considering having James come evict me. Rest assured, I'm not after your money. If I wanted to debase myself like that I would have just stayed at home and made wine on my parent's farm in Peachland. I didn't and I don't. I just want to follow my studies to their end conclusion and I think human sexuality is very interesting. See I knew if I didn't go over the top with you, once I figured out you weren't gay, you wouldn't notice. You only notice stuff, which smashes out of the normal world into yours! The daisy dukes and the porn star moves? Really Rhys, is that not out of sync? Over the top? You know what else is?"

The computer beeped, halting my reading. I looked at the contact on Yahoo. Frenchkiss38 had come online with a one-word question.

"Yes?" I thought about what I had read and typed a simple response back.

"False Alarm." The contact winked out, a second later and I continued reading Andrea's bizarre 'love letter.'

"Your connection to Ruben. We all love our pets and we laugh and have fun with them daily but they are not our significant others. I cried for weeks when I lost my dog and to be honest if I think about it for too long I still cry. But that pain is different from the pain of losing my grandmother. What you need to get is the level of the emotion you feel may be different in volume to that which I feel, but it's no less valid. Your disease doesn't make you a heartless, asshole, killer, extraordinaire. It just makes it easier! The flip side is true too. You can be a compassionate, loving and kind person! Your disease just makes it so much harder.

I like you a lot, and I know what and who you are better than you do. Trust me. I spent four years of my life studying the disease. Despite this, if I'm honest with you, I feel a nurturing affection for you significant enough to risk my safety to point it out. I did not just kick a rabid dog in the balls not knowing it wasn't rabid. I did it because I wanted the dog to pay attention. Are you paying attention, Mr. Rhys?

I score high on that Psychopath test too. My number is seven, if you want to know. Yours would probably be 10 or better — and you're the only ten I ever met. I'm not a naive kid from the Valley. I'm a socially dangerous person, like you. I just grew up well and learned to deal with it better than you. As I said in the limo, that's if I had the heart to go through with it. I'm sensational and I want you to get to know me a bunch more when you make it home. If you don't, well rest assured I will still take care of Ruben.

The letter was signed with

"Be Safe — Andrea"

"Wow," I thought, "just when you think it's safe to fuck the tenant!"

CHAPTER EIGHTEEN

My mood changed from panic to curiosity.

I had to admit Andrea had some valid points. I thought back to my time at the Swiss institution. They had developed a method called Milieu Therapy. Basically it was role-playing and it did help me mimic the feelings of others and hide very effectively within society. I didn't get much more than that in the four months I was there.

Well perhaps a little more. I came to terms better with my parents' deaths and John's drinking and skirt- chasing. I learned that these were not normal, but I never learned why they weren't normal. No, the feeling part of the program never did fully take hold. Perhaps it was to do with their overtly Christian focus? I never believed in God and, as far as I could tell, he never believed in me.

Was she right? Could I really lead a normal, albeit risky, life and be satisfied? Could I find a connection with one special person? Perhaps. I had with Ruben so I guess it was still a possibility. I looked out at our old friend the moon as we moved in opposite directions. These thoughts were like that. Moving in opposite directions, right now I needed the asshole, killer, extraordinaire. I pushed back in the deep velvet seat and thought, "Yeah I'm ok with that," and smiled to myself.

I was not about to check the secure mail website over this connection but I could confirm the meeting was going ahead as planned and there had been no last minute snags. I pulled up the Craig's list for Amsterdam and typed in "Coffin" under the search function.

Up came a single ad for a coffin for sale. I reached forward and picked up the sky phone again. I slipped my credit card through the reader and dialed the number in the ad. It rang and I leaned out and checked to see if Susan was hovering anywhere close. The call was answered on the fourth ring.

"Hello, I'm calling from Vancouver. Has the coffin been sold yet?"

"No," came the answer.

"Not yet, although I have had six calls on it and the most interested is coming to look at it on Tuesday at 1930."

"Thank you" I responded and rang off.

So everything was on schedule and set for Tuesday. Excellent!

I settled back and checked my usual e-mails and a few of the news and cigar sites I read regularly. There was nothing new.

Susan had returned.

"I must make a pretty good martini, or you found someone to deal with your emergency."

"Yeah I did. Sorry if I was loud. It's a new gas stove, and wasn't really sure I had turned if off properly. I only got it yesterday!" I lied to cover the stupid response I had given earlier.

"Makes sense," she replied, indicating that she hadn't bought the "stove panic" story.

"Can I get you another martini before you order dinner? Do you know what you'd like to have?"

"Another martini would be great," and added, "I promise I will have a dinner decision when you get back."

I decided to book my accommodation. With everything that had gone on today I had completely forgotten. I usually liked to stay at Fairmont properties. I loved the 'Gold' level floors and private concierge service. I knew Amsterdam didn't have one. They did have a Marriott, my second choice, but it was a little ways out of the city center and in the very American section of the city.

The Amsterdam Grand hotel was an awesome place. However, the last time I was there — about two months earlier — they were pulling up the sidewalk and making adjustments to the canal and the hotel. I remembered painfully they had started extremely early. The front of the Grand looked like an old military garrison building, with a u-shaped courtyard that faced the street. The doormen wore heavy black tunic-like tops and were most knowledgeable. The rooms inside were exquisite with bold decorations and paintings. The last time my room had a line painting of what looked like Napoleon — easily nine feet high on one wall. I had complained about the noise last time and was moved to a lesser, but quieter room without this decor but still very smart. I mentioned this to the person who I thought was a concierge and it turned out to be the hotel manager, a Mr. Robert-Jan Woltering. He assured me that he would do anything in his capacity to ensure my pleasure the next time. I told him and I would hold him to his promise.

The location was perfect. Close to the areas I needed to go, eliminating the need to take cabs, and large enough to be discreet. I picked up the sky phone again and called the number for reservations listed on their website. The web price for a room was £368. The call was answered on the second ring, in Dutch, just as Susan returned with my drink.

I cupped the mouthpiece and said to Susan.

"Pair a great red with something and I'll be happy." She nodded and left.

I said into the mouthpiece. "Sorry, bad connection," I said in Afrikaans, which was like simple Dutch. The Dutch called it "kitchen Dutch," a polite way of saying "uneducated."

"Do you speak English?"

I knew they would, but it always sets a good tone to ask, and not assume, someone from another country can speak your language.

"Or Danish?" I continued in almost perfect Danish. It's a difficult language but I had learned it easily, perhaps because I spoke Gaelic. Both languages make your tongue do more moves than a Cirque de Soleil show!

He answered in perfectly accented Queen's English.

"How can I be of service, sir?"

"I need a suite for seven nights, arriving early on the tenth."

"I was there a few weeks ago and Mr. Woltering said he would leave on note for me on your customer data base. My name is Munroe"

"Just one moment please, sir." I could hear the mad typing of keys on the other end of the connection.

"Mr. Rhys Munroe?"

"Yes."

"Yes, sir, I have a note here. I'm to book you at our best rate and upgrade you to one of our newer suites. The only suites we have available are the Opera suites. They're 75 sq.m. — converted canal mansions, with a kitchen and separate living room. The current best rate for our regular rooms are €280. The regular rates for the Opera Suites are €800. Would this be all right, sir?"

"Perfect," I replied.

"What time will you be arriving with us on the tenth, sir?"

"My flight gets in around noon," I lied.

I didn't share this kind of information with even the most discreet of hotels.

"I should be there around one, but I won't need the room right away. I can just dump my luggage."

"Your suite will be ready for you Mr. Munroe, if I have to clean it myself. If there is anything more we can do for you? Please do not hesitate to inquire. My name is Percy and the suite concierge for the week is Amanda."

"Great," I said and thought, "Wow, I wonder what was written on that profile note?

"Your room is booked at the rate of €1,960 plus taxes for the week, beginning on the 10th of October. Your confirmation number is SPL389667. Confirmed early arrival and late departure on the eighteenth. Is there anything else I can do for you sir?"

"Yes, Percy. As a matter of fact there is. Could you book a limo for me with the Amsterdam Limousine Service for some clients of mine? They will need to be met in the arrivals area at Schiphol for 10:15. It's their first time in Amsterdam so a nice two-hour city tour would be perfect. They will only require the Mercedes S320, not the big Lincoln. The company name for the driver is Talisker Gold. If there are any problems with the short notice you can reach me on my cell. Would that be too much trouble?"

"Not at all, sir. Consider it done" Percy answered.

"Thanks, Percy," I said as I rang off.

Leaning back I ticked off things from my mental list. Room secured. Ride secured. The two-hour tour would allow me to get my bearings in the city. Amsterdam was in constant renewal. Basically, it was a horseshoe-shaped city amongst a bunch of foul smelling canals. The core things stayed the same but other areas didn't. The driver would have a great deal of good intelligence of the area and changes.

I loved limo drivers as they were some of the best and cheapest intelligence a person could purchase with total anonymity. Taxis were ok but they often sold information to other less savory sorts and were known to play both sides of the fence. Ask too many questions about a certain area and they were likely to go looking for the people that wanted to know when someone asked a lot of questions about the area. I avoided them like the plague and generally thought most of them were reprehensible trolls best left under dark bridges.

The hotel was booked under my real name. That would normally be a concern but I was only traveling with one passport and would have to use my real identity on this trip. I didn't have any other passports that were current nor did I have financial means to obtain another. The new procedures and banking requirements made obtaining false identification difficult. It was not impossible, but it was tricky and very expensive. Gone were the days when one could obtain a working passport in thirty minutes for €1,000. The world was getting to be a much smaller pond, and many of the sharks were getting caught.

Susan arrived with a large glass of red wine and a square plate presenting many odd looking pieces of sushi. This must be some of that 'fusion' sushi she was talking about. The red wine was deep and bold looking and I wondered what type of fish would pair with a red? She smiled reading my expression, and said.

"This is fusion sushi. This is rare beef served seared, with a sesame sauce and a Japanese horseradish cream base sauce."

I noticed the green and amber liquids mingled to make a perfect yin and yang frame around the tasty looking morsels.

She pointed to another item on the plate. "This is eel done in a sea urchin-based-brandy reduction – it's very robust. To the side is yellowtail done with an orange and cream reduction with crushed pistachios and leeks. "Finally," pointing to the middle, "these are handmade rice noodles in a pulled pork nest, with Mahi Mahi medallions in a ginger-cognac reduction. This is about the only time one can drink a robust Merlot with fish. It's a perfect pairing, trust me."

"Well," I said. "I'll believe you. You haven't lied to me yet."

She retreated and I picked up the porcelain chopsticks and let them hover over the meal. It was like trying to draw on an oil painting done by Vermeer with a dripping fountain pen. I chose a piece and paused. I took a sip of my wine, swirling it around my mouth and then grabbed the little piece of art and placed it in my mouth. The flavours complemented each other perfectly. I loved food and this was more than food or edible art — it was a masterpiece of service. To be high above the Arctic and enjoying food prepared as perfectly as for a king.

I finished dinner and turned on the BBC. After leaving me alone for the entire meal, Susan arrived, knowing it would be better than perfect even before she asked.

"Was I right? It went together well?"

"No," I replied, "It went together perfectly — awesome!"

"Great!" she smiled.

"Can I turn down your bed on the seat beside you? That way I can get you an after-dinner drink and not bug you while you catch up?" She continued while gesturing at the TV.

"Perfect, Susan, thanks"

"What would you like to top that off? Brandy, cognac, scotch?"

Normally I would have ordered a Scotch but tonight brandy caught my attention and palette and I said so.

"Ok great, I'll get that, do you want me to wake you after or before we land?"

"Well, since I won't have to fight for the bathroom how about after we land." I responded.

"Certainly. Anything for breakfast?"

"Coffee please, black as my soul, and a little fruit"

She nodded and went around the burl wood partition to the other seat and reaching down set it fully flat and pulled the Egyptian cotton sheets out from underneath and, without another word, made up my bed.

I listened to the news and weather and felt myself drifting with the newsperson's voice. My brandy had arrived and I took a sip. The harsh bite of the strong alcohol was replaced first with cherries and finished with plums. "Perfect," I thought. "Better enjoy it while you can."

I placed everything back in my carry on and moved to the bed, brandy in hand. I set the carry-on down at the end and placed my drink on the little nightstand-like shelf. Leaving on my underwear and custom BA slippers I crawled between the cool, soft sheets. I lowered the lights, reached for my brandy and took a long swallow. The plane's hum was ever-present, like the beating of a heart. I drifted into welcome sleep.

CHAPTER NINETEEN

I AWOKE TO A SOFT bump, my mind struggling for a second to discern why we seemed to be moving. Right! Flying to London. My mind reached its conclusion only to have it highlighted by the plane's heavy braking. I stayed in my position until I was sure we were finished our landing and were taxiing to the terminal. I sat up and swung my legs to the floor. I grabbed my pants and putting them on remembered something John had said once.

"Yes, we both put our pants on the same way in the morning. It's just that mine are worth $4,000."

I smiled at the memory of John's arrogance. I stood and collected my shirt from the desk and slipped it on. Turning, I saw Susan smile as she gave me a quick once over and turned away, pretending to adjust seat belts. I buttoned my shirt and grinned: men weren't the only dogs.

I sat down as Susan arrived with coffee and a plate of fresh fruit and cheese.

"You woke up early," she said, her makeup, hair and uniform as perfect as when I first sat down eight-and-a-half hours ago.

"Sorry I missed the view," I responded with a sly smile.

Blushing only slightly she replied "Yes, it was a gorgeous one, and not at all typical"

She set my breakfast down and walked away with perhaps a little more swing to her hips than before.

I sipped the coffee and ate a little of the fruit as I listened to the engines whine down. There was a slight bump as the jet walkway contacted the plane and the lights got a little brighter as we plugged into the main power at Heathrow. I finished breakfast and, looking around, found my shoes sitting on the writing desk. They had been polished. "Nice," I thought. I slipped them on and gathered my bag. Hearing once again the rookery noise begin in the back. I sensed movement to my right and saw Susan walking toward me with a white and blue BA cup.

"One for the lorry and ditch?" she said as he handed me the coffee to go. I took the offered cup.

"I'll take you out, Rhys." With that she strode off down the aisle allowing me a perfect view of her swing, which I was now sure was accentuated just for me. She reached the airplane door and spun like a dancer blocking the aisle to the back, fixing me with a knowing look and smile as I walked, unimpeded, toward the exit door.

"Thanks for flying with us, Rhys. Hope to see you again soon," and continued under her breath as I passed, "without your shirt on."

I smiled at her comment but didn't change my step or look back. Instead, I caught the reflection in the round safety mirror that's often installed in these jet ways. Without moving her head her eyes scanned me like a shooter, looking for a chink in the amour.

"Always good for the ego," I thought as I walked out in the din and light of Heathrow and headed for Gate 36.

My luggage was checked through to Schiphol, so I didn't need to retrieve it. First class passengers enjoyed a private escalator that had an attendant to check passes. I walked up and showed my Platinum level card instead of my boarding pass and continued out of the din, like a bird of flight, away from its land-locked cousins, to the private screening area. I still had to go through airport security, but there was a private one for first class.

I reached the officers and handed them my bag. They took it and set it in the scanner. I walked through the metal detector and to the waiting officer, who performed a light pat-down frisk search. I thought about what patting down a few hundred sweaty travelers must be like. I gathered my bag at the end of the belt and made for the Concorde lounge.

It was odd that, despite ending service on the Concorde, they had still chosen it for the name of their top lounge in H5. I walked in and checked at the reception desk ensuring my connection flight was on time, and which gate it left from. I took a sip of my coffee and the lady behind the desk smiled and looked down. The smile changed into a sly grin as she tapped the screen. She composed herself and left me thinking what the hell was she smirking at, as I checked my zipper.

"Your flight is on time, sir. But your gate has been changed, due to some technical issues. You're leaving out of gate 22 in H3, boarding in fifty five minutes."

"Hell," I thought as I took another sip of my cup and watched again as the woman's expression changed. I could feel my skin like a skim of old cream and I needed a shower. What was this stupid woman smiling at?

I said; "Well that's kind of inconvenient. It appears I'm destined to miss breakfast and a shower. How long is the trip over to H3 with the construction?"

"It's about 25 minutes, but we can't have Susan's super sexy and nice guy treated that way can we?" she said, pointing to the bottom of the cup. I lifted the cup and found;

"AA. Super nice and very sexy, treat well and tell him to call me. Susan."

Smiling I said;

"So, you're AA?"

"No, AA is short for "Attention All Attendants." She laughed.

I asked, "This kind of thing happen a lot?"

"Only to the real jerks and the real nice guys" She explained.

"Go have a nice shower and breakfast and be back here in forty minutes. I'll have a service cart run you over. You'll go the back way, past the construction and lines," she finished, smiling mischievously.

"Thanks" I said "I suppose if I had been a jerk I would be running across the terminal right now." She didn't answer except to say, "Go shower!"

I made my way to the lounge showers and locked myself away in what looked more like a spa. I guess being nice until it's necessary not to be pays off. No wonder Susan had been so attentive. I thought back to Andrea and her note.

"Unless it's over the top and smashes into your world."

Hmm, the water crashed into my skin hot and fast. Smart woman. Pretty observant and hides it well. I stepped from the shower, shaved and feeling human. She wouldn't go for the usual personal ad type material.

"Smart, sexy, graduate student psychopath seeks same to birth antichrist. Must like cats!"

Laughing to myself I finished buttoning my shirt and dressed in fresh clothes and made my way to the chow line.

The ride over to the departure terminal was fast and I took it from the deference the driver was showing, special. We arrived at the gate a full three minutes before the scheduled push back. This was only a short hop flight and there were only two classes: business and coach. I was seated in 1A. Everyone was already on board so I got the gopher, every aisle looking up to the front to see whom the guy was holding them up. Me! I thought as I sat down. You fucks can sit and wait for me!

The flight to Schiphol was a short one — barely enough time to get a drink. I declined my entree and my seatmate offered to eat it for me. I looked at the man smiling and turned to the flight attendant and said "Sure."

I watched as she passed my meal to him and, as he happily set the second tray on his upper fat roll and started eating. He wanted to engage in conversation; I didn't. Trying to avoid him I worked on the crossword in the New York Times I had picked up in the lounge. Hopefully I could drag it out an hour. My ears signaled it was time to pay attention again and I looked forward. Unfortunately, the stunt double for Dumbo saw this as his chance to engage me. I wanted to lodge a dinner roll in his throat as he rambled on, jowls bouncing, purple tongue wagging on about who he was. Finally he stopped and looked expectantly at me. I said in a thick Russian accent. "I don't speak English." He looked at the crossword and then at me, confusion creating eye palsy. I was saved by the bell, as the flight attendant made the announcement to stay seated until the plane came to a complete stop.

The din in the cabin rose as we got to the gate and the lemmings jumped to their feet, jockeying for position like bubble-gum pink penguins. They eyed the overhead areas like watching eggs. If hands moved too close, or luggage shifted and fell the colony would erupt in mass dissatisfaction. I sat and waited, as nothing was going to happen until the attendant got up and went to the door.

When the attendant got up, I stood and with a look moved the guy who was standing beside me in the aisle, just back a little. The colony quacked in protest. The overhead was already open and I grabbed my carry-on and moved to the door just as it opened. I stopped and waited for the ground crew and flight crew to exchange paperwork and lock out the door. The colony surged forward, as if on an ice flow, pushing the one penguin forward. My look must have been sufficient. He held his ground and clucked and shook his head.

With a nod I was off striding quickly up the gangway and into the terminal. Clearing customs and immigration was a breeze. I made the baggage carousels just as it started turning and without moving into the actual area looked for the chauffeur.

There he was, holding his sign. Was anyone else watching him? I strode around the area not looking at any carousel, talking in Matabele on my cell to no one, scanning the entire area for other watchers. I spotted two, but neither was interested in my driver. I saw both my bags on the carousel and I pulled out my boarding pass walking quickly to an empty spot in the throng of people around the carousel, grabbed them both and moved toward the driver.

"Hey, Talisker Gold. Just me today." I said as I came within talking distance.

He joined me, long Dutch legs easily keeping up. He said, "I was told there would be two, sir."

"Yes well, Percy at the Grand is known to exaggerate. You have me for two hours and this is not my first time in Amsterdam. I don't want to go look at skanky immigrant pussy in the Walloon," I said using the local slang of 'Walloon' for the Red Light District. The district was used by tourists in the know. I had identified myself as someone comfortable with the city. Very comfortable.

We reached the car. It was the one I had requested and it was grey. My driver's name was Darius and looked as though he'd worked a few nightclub doors as he looked like a dressed-up mixed martial arts fighter. I decided to ask, as he tossed my luggage into the trunk.

I grabbed a few Euros out of my carry-on and asked him. "How long have you been off the door and driving?"

Closing the trunk, he looked at me, his expression confirming my observation. He opened my door and said, "About seven months. How could you tell?" I slipped him £100 and slid into the big back seat. It wasn't really a limo in the real sense but it was as big as I wanted for the narrow streets we would be traveling. I figured I'd stroke Darius's ego a bit and when he got in I said; "I can tell by the way you carry yourself and you look like you hate the work and the boredom and love the pay cheque."

He snorted and laughed. "You're very observant for a mining executive, Mr.?"

"Munro. You ever get a £100 tip from a mining exec before you even turned the key?"

He started the powerful car and swung deftly out into traffic, answering,

"No, Mr. Munro. I have not."

"Well then, I guess you've answered both your questions. What I want to know is all the shit that's happening in the city. The good the bad and the ugly. All of it. What the cops know, what is getting torn up, where is there construction, what gang is running the park these days. What are the Americans up to, the Russians and I'm talking gangs and alphabet agencies here! The better you do the better you'll do at the end of this two hour tour. Goes without saying what gets said in this car stays in the car. Head to the Pipe market and start off with what a good Russian pistol is going for these days."

CHAPTER TWENTY

THE PIPE FLEA MARKET WAS a daily thing held in the old industrial area of town. It wasn't a tourist hang out. It got its name from all the smoke stacks that used to be in the area when it was still a heavy industrial area; the locals called it de Pijp, or The Pipe. You could find any manner of stuff if you looked. It wasn't like a London antique market either. It wasn't steeped in illegal stuff, yet it was there if you knew who to ask. Darius hadn't started talking yet so I figured I'd help him along.

"Darius", I said in Dutch. "Let me help you answer the 'how full of shit question' you're asking yourself. We could just swing by and see Cerberus and I can explain to him you got all Dutch schoolboy on me so now he has to tell me what's new in the zoo."

He looked into the backseat of the cab, terror traced across his face. "You know Cerberus?"

"Yeah, pretty well really. I'm the one that gave him that pretty eye." I lied. But it worked. His neck went all goose flesh and beads of sweat rose at his hairline. His voice was significantly less sure of himself as he started his debriefing.

He talked rapid fire and without a filter for the entire forty-minute drive to the edge of the Pipe market. The information was good, but nothing jumped out at me pertaining to our meeting.

The bigger sedan was not as inconspicuous as it might have been in other European cities. I actually stood out a little; drawing a bit of attention was what I wanted. I wanted to see if any of the other alphabet agencies had flagged our various communications and had sent someone in. I had had very little communication, but I bet I was the exception. I could have got everything I desired at The Russian Tea House, but it would have been the obvious pick-up point for any one sniffing around. We could see how that went tomorrow. Today it was time to do some good old-fashioned reconnaissance.

I slipped out my cellular toss-away phone and opened it to see the number. I gave it to Darius and told him to text me if he had to move the car. I also told him to reach out and see if he couldn't find out some more info. I opened the back door and stepped out and was almost run over by a bike.

The mad bell trilling off down the street, I forced myself to relax and become reacquainted with the horseshoe streets of the city. I walked slowly toward the rail that lined the dyke and inhaled dank water and dog crap; at least it was better smelling than in the summer. Men in business suits rode bikes, some roller bladed, a few walked. It was like the green movement's wet dream. Now if only these people would pick up after their dogs. I started a slow, careful walk toward the north end of the market.

I felt the machine really come online for the first time in several hours. I gave it a little more rein than required — just to shake the cobwebs out. I snap focused on people, teasing it like an owner teases a dog with a ball. Like the dog, it rose to occasion. The right chemistry now rolling through my veins, nothing like a little adrenalin to spice up life. I stopped at a booth and used its glass display to check behind me. Nothing. The man behind the counter asks if he can help me, in English. "Coffee" I say scanning his goods. "And one of those" pointing at the baked sandwich with three types of cheese.

"Cream or sugar, Canada?" he asked from the back.

"Black, please," remembering that the Dutch loved Canadians.

Taking my food I continue my stroll along the canal. The mix of languages and scents assault my senses. I take a sip of coffee — it's great. Looking back at the vendor I check behind me for tails while gesturing to the vendor, "Good." He smiles with pride. I wind my way past bikes, some ridden, some chained and all annoying. The machine starts tracking two police as they lazily wander past the shops. I see a black jogger; an odd bounce in the small of his back suggests a gun. The machine swings its attention away from the cops. Yes, it's a gun. And he, though dressed in a jogging suit, wasn't doing much of it. The shoes were court shoes, not running shoes — clean, colourful and trendy. I grab a bit of rail and watch. Anyone selling guns will be selling hard drugs too, but the reverse may not be true. He doesn't approach anybody and he's watching the area — almost like a cop.

Scanning slowly, precisely, carefully I wait. He's between two booths. One booth is selling bongs and water pipes; the other cheap knives and martial arts gear, the wall behind plastered with MMA t-shirts. Finally someone comes up to the booth and points at a shirt. The rapid point makes the black man's eye twitch and he shifts his weight reflexively. The movement is subtle but I notice it. Ok so he's with the booth on the left. I wait for the MMA fan to leave. I start my approach, looking for signs of danger. This could be a police operation but I doubt it. The other shops are paying no more attention to this shop than they are anyone else's. I feel the black man pick me up, his quick gaze lingers a fraction of a second too long. I stop like I'm going to go over the canal and take a slow look around me. Senses straining, looking for the one odd thing, the out of the usual, that would signal danger. Like animals carefully returning to a water hole I probe out with anticipation. The outer circle blurs with the intense focus on the immediate. Clear! Nothing out of place, a usual scene, sunny and warm for the time of the year.

I walk over, tossing the rest of my sandwich and empty cup in the garbage, and speaking Dutch, ask about switchblades. I sense movement to my right and use a reflective surface to watch my back. The black man is looking over his shoulder at me. A few cheap Chinese ones are presented from under the table along with a very good quality pair of leather SAP gloves. The glossy black leather looked very good and the lead powder in the back of the hand and knuckles discreet. I continue in Dutch;

"Those are shit; these gloves, however, are really good. Do you have any better quality spring knives, something in the £300 range?"

This got more of a response from the black man than it did from the vendor. The black man turned around quietly and appraised me in a way that could have got him slapped. I watched him, watch me, from three different reflected angles as the counter guy, saying nothing, brought a box with five knives in it. They were all automatic opening knives but they didn't look like they belonged in West Side Story. Well one did, but the rest were modern design. I grabbed two thin ones and tried the actions. Looking around as I did, to show the man at my back that I was capable of being discreet. I tucked the two knives into my pockets and put the SAP gloves into the small of my back, showing my watcher I was unarmed. "How much?" I asked.

"£250," he replied, his eyes darting over my shoulder.

I didn't hear the man behind me move, but I picked up his scent as he moved closer.

"Perhaps I can get a package deal from the Boss?" I said as I moved slightly left and turned. The black man and I looked directly at each for the first time. He looked Nigerian and I spoke a Bantu that was common around Windhoek in Nigerian, so I figured it was worth a try.

I said in Bantu; "How about making a deal, that makes us both happy."

The black man froze, a big smile spread across his face and he nodded. "Yes, yes very easy this kind of deal. I have a £300 special but also much better. Follow please."

He walked past the table of goods and I followed him and from the expression of the table vendors' face he didn't speak the language. Pushing aside the MMA shirts he disappears into a small door. I stick my head in, hands against my temples to ward off any blows and wait for a second for my eyes to adjust to the dim light.

The dim features pull into focus as my eyes become accustomed to the light. It's a small travel trailer devoid of the usual built-in stuff, with two large couches facing each other separated by three square yellow packing crates — the kind that have the "Property of ..." stamped onto the side to stop people from making coffee tables out of them.

"So you want to buy a gun?" he asked in Dutch.

"Yes," I answered in Dutch.

"Well, my odd friend of linguistic talent, I can help you. I have a few Markov Russian pistols for £300 - £400, but I also have a couple of pistols that are not shit too."

"Really? Like what?" I asked.

"I have two Ruger pistols and three Heckler and Koch 9mm USP as well one of them, the USP tactical, has a silencer too."

Wow. This Nigerian had some sources, or had got really lucky. Most of the black market stuff would be Balkan/Russian stuff.

"So package deal for the stuff from out front and the silenced USP tactical with another USP and 100 9mm hollow points?"

I watched his brow as he thought and added up the numbers. I had decided to take his deal if it was under £3,000, or just buy the cheap Markovs and not to barter. I let my peripheral vision take in the room. Where the hell were these guns? I wasn't getting into any car with this fellow. His answer cut off my thoughts.

"£2,700, but only have fifty rounds of hollow-point. Have belt holsters, though."

"Toss in the leather and we have a deal. Where are the guns?" I asked.

"Sure. I will toss in holsters, where is money?"

I set my back against the couch and lifted my hips as if to dig in my front pocket. In reality I was feeling how solid the wall and couch was. It was good enough for my use should it come to it. I pulled up a wad of Euros and placed my foot on the plastic container. If this were going to go south, now would be the time, and my plan was to use the container to break the black man's knee.

Mostly to himself he said; "I like serious men" and with that he sat forward and swatted my foot with his hand. I moved my foot and he picked up the yellow container. The floor came up with it! It hadn't been loose like I thought it was. He turned it around and I could see the two guns and a medium silencer resting on the two leather holsters. I set them down beside me and counted off £300 from my wad and handed him the rest.

He smiled and gestured with his hands,

"Please, check and satisfy yourself. We have both done this before, I'm sure. Rounds when you leave and no turning around, right?"

"Right" I answered, picking up the USP tactical and checking the fit of the silencer. It was perfect. I worked the actions of both guns a couple of times and slipped both the holsters inside my pants; the stainless steel clips gripped as if new. The sculpted leather held each pistol snugly and I dropped the silencer into my coat pocket. I stood up and said "Thank you."

Another wide smile crossed his chocolate black face and he responded, "My pleasure," as he gestured me out into the light of day. I walked past him and he held out a box wrapped in brown paper. I took the bag and walked back into the market.

CHAPTER TWENTY-ONE

THE COOLING DAMP AIR OF the retreating afternoon seemed to have a little more stench in it than before, the dog shit a little more pungent. I wanted a beer to take some of the cotton out of my mouth and get these things loaded. Unlike United Nations soldiers I never saw the point of walking around with unloaded weapons.

There was a nice Heineken pub just up the canal on the other side of the bridge. I started moving in that direction and began projecting that I belonged. I fought the urge to look around, setting my shoulders back and moving to the pub, dodging the dinging bells just like a local.

Slipping inside I caught the smell of yesterday's spilt beer and too many bodies. However, the place wasn't even half full. Yellow hard hats on almost every table answered my confusion as I walked up and got a beer. I took a long swig and remember why I never drank the swill at home as I made for the toilet. I grabbed an end stall and pulled the box of rounds out of my bag lunch. They were one hundred and nineteen grain-jacketed subsonic hollow points. Nice score. This deal was changing my mind about Nigerians. Without drawing the pistol I released each clip in turn, loaded it and placed it back in the pistol. I drew one pistol and carefully pulled the slide fully to the rear and engaged the hold open device. Then I did the same with the other. No one had come into that bathroom yet. I stood up holding the two pistols and turned to face the bowl and with my foot tripped the flush while at the same time releasing the slides of both pistols. The metallic "shnick" sound was effectively muted by the flush and I put the pistols back into their holsters. Grabbing my beer from the back of the toilet I walked back out into the pub, finishing it, and leaving the empty glass on the bar as I left and returned to the limo.

I once again let the machine keep watch as I enjoyed a casual stroll around the dog shit along the canal and back. I had to walk one block past the limo before I could get a bridge back over to that side. I continued across and at the corner stopped and sat down at a café table to watch Darius. I order and pay for a beer when the waitress cruises by. I sip this one a little slower while I watch the activity on the street. Nothing out of place, nothing that stands out. Time to check in. I need some quiet time. It's been a while since I have had this much humanity pushed against me. I need some cultural adaptation time. I finished my beer and made my way to the car. Darius saw me and I heard the mechanical click as the door locks opened.

"Good," I think to myself, "stay in the car."

I slid into the back and felt the bite as the holster hit the seatbelt and get pushed up into my side.

"So, Darius, what else have you got to tell me? Grand, please."

He fills me in as he drives. It's all good data but nothing really concerns me. He mentions that security at the Grand is going to be tighter than usual as a Princess from Norway or Sweden is staying there. Details were sketchy but it was a woman from Scandinavia. Great. This does concern me and I ask if he has the Opera level concierge number. He does and I call the number.

"Hello, Grand Executive concierge. How can I be of service?" A woman's pleasant voice answers.

"Yes. This is Rhys Munroe. I'm about twelve minutes away and I just wanted to check and make sure there were no surprises. Is the room ready?" I inquired, politely if somewhat cryptically.

"Everything is ready, Mr. Munroe. Are you driving in?" She asked.

"Limo, grey Mercedes Amsterdam Limo car number nine," I replied.

"Ok, Mr. Rhys. We have a special guest that has security a little higher but your arrival will be expected at the front area. Tell the driver to come in as usual but perhaps a little slower. I'm calling down right away." She said before hanging up.

She must be a little flustered as she ended the conversation with me and not the other way around, as it should be. Great, a flustered staff and pompous royalty. God knows what level of security and security products that would mean. Proximity metal detectors, high end eavesdropping gear, the sky was the limit for these types. The Grand was starting to look unlucky for me. I thought about the possibilities and tried to think of a few counter moves. I was going to hide the second weapon in the room and now I wasn't sure if one was safe! Something came to me.

"Darius, you keep a very clean car, provide great service and nice driving"

"Thank you, sir." He answered.

"Do they do that back in the yard or do you have to do it?" I asked.

"We have to do it, but we can take our cars home and do it or do it back in the yard and drive our own cars home, sir. All depends on the job we have in the morning." He answered.

"Good to know." I said, "as I will probably need to hire a car again on this trip. Do you have a card with your private number on it?"

"Yes, sir" he handed me back a card written on the back was a private cell number.

"Darius, I forgot to grab a bottle of Grey Goose Vodka. Could you stop on the way and run in for me? I have to make a phone call." I directed.

"Yes, sir" He responded. We were still within the two-hour 'tour time' but I got the impression he had some place he wanted to be.

He pulled into an alley and shut off the car. "Be right back sir." He said before walking off.

I had to work fast. I grabbed the bottom of the seat back on the passenger front leather seat and felt. Staples! Great! With a quick motion I pulled hard down and then back. The leather made a zipper-like noise as it came away from the seat and its Velcro seam. I pulled out the gun and the automatic knife. I opened the knife and slashed into the seat foam. I cut out a quick section of foam and jammed the pistol sideways into the hole. It fit and held snug. I grabbed the leather back and, pulling it tight, re-attached the Velcro seam. I looked up. Shit, he was coming back! I reached down and using the knife pushed the staples back through the leather and bent them over. Darius opened the door. The light came on and I got a first-hand look at my work. There was no bulge, thank God, and the leather looked tight.

I pulled out my cell and opened an application called Blue tooth dentist — used to hack Bluetooth devices. I told it to search for discoverable Bluetooth devices and crossed my fingers, hoping Darius had a Bluetooth phone and that it was enabled. A moment later up popped the device with the number Darius had given me earlier for his private phone. I pressed "copy" and the data started coming from his phone to mine. This was not a fast process but it was invisible. This allowed me to use the specific GPS identity of this phone to find it and consequently my gun anytime I needed to. It also allowed me to see whom Darius might have called, e-mailed, or chatted with while I was gone.

CHAPTER TWENTY-TWO

WE REACHED THE GATES OF the Grand and were waved through the police cars at the front, and proceeded slowly to the main building entrance. I looked over at the amoured limo and three Range Rovers that must be her escort cars. Two men stood silently watching the vehicles. Good security detail, I thought to myself. I reached forward and shook Darius's hand and palmed him another £100. My door was pulled open and I, and my luggage, was quickly and efficiently whisked into the hotel, past registration into an elevator and up to the fourth floor.

I got off and followed the bellboy pushing the luggage cart down the carpeted hall to the Executive floor lounge and private concierge. I handed over my passport and credit card as the bellboy continued down the hall and right with my luggage. She checked me in and handed my documents back and with a smile asked; "Have you stayed with us on the Executive level before, Mr. Munroe?"

"No I haven't, but I hear it's fit for a queen," I said with a grin.

"Here, let me show you the lounge and your suite," she answered, not even acknowledging the comment.

"Good!" I thought. Discreet is very good.

She walked me through the lounge, which was the same as any Club, Gold, or Prestige. Although the view out was onto the canal and street it was very nice. She led me down the long hallway to the end and opened the last door. The thick door opened and the room took even me back. To use words like opulent or posh would be an affront to this room. Seems I had summed it up earlier: "Fit for a Queen." The view from the windows was up and down the canal. It was from the corner and offered a truly panoramic view. I handed her a £100 and she left me alone to explore the luxuries of the room without saying a word.

The suite had two king beds and a separate sitting area with a couch and two chairs and writing desk to one side. It also came with a 30-inch LCD television. There was a fireplace at one end and a kitchenette up near the entrance to the bathroom. There was a master bath with a separate claw type bath and glassed in shower. I went back out to the main area and looked at the mini-bar. My vodka was on ice and I poured myself a few fingers and took off my clothes. "Time for a soak in the tub," I thought, and turned on the taps.

I picked up my new gun and took it apart. Its raw black machine surfaces were smooth and new and perfect. I put it back together again and thought about test firing it into the tub. The weapon to this point looked good but it was unproven. People who went into the field with unproven weapons usually wound up dead. The silencer would take care of the noise and the water would stop the round safely but what about the smell? The room was a non-smoking room, I wasn't really sure if you could get a smoking room at any hotel in Amsterdam. The charge was £300 applied to your final bill for cleaning. I really needed a cigar anyway. I lit a Monte Edmundo and screwed the silencer onto the front of the weapon. I opened one of the windows in the living room and collected my wardrobe bag. I looked at the full tub and thought that 99 times out of 100 this would be okay, but what happens to that one? I took two large bath towels and placed them in the tub and let them soak and sink to the bottom. I reached in and bunched them up in the center and holding the pistol vertical to the surface of the water fired into the bunched towels. The weapon made a little pop sound and the bullet punched into the water. I took a long drag and blew smoke into the blue gun smoke. I cleared the weapon, and reloaded the one round and put the spent casing in with my change of clothes.

In a country where guns were uncommon shell casings would stand out. I pulled the towels out of the bottom of the tub. There were no holes, but nestled like a blue-black pearl of death was the round. The hollow point had opened up and dumped all its energy when it contacted the water — just as it would do when it contacted a 70 per cent bag of ugly water or human. I tossed the towels in the shower and placed the bullet next to its casing. Grabbing my glass of vodka I hopped in the tub to finish my cigar and drink in peace.

I awoke to a semi-cold tub of water and hopped out, toweling off as I checked my watch. Only an hour had passed. I wonder how the water could have got that cold until I walk into the other room. The open window is like the open door on an industrial fridge. The semi warm day has been replaced by an arctic evening with the sun's departure. I close the window and turn on the gas fireplace and the chill retreats as quickly as the French military. I dress warmly, a black cashmere and silk mock turtle neck, black pants and short leather half jacket that was so popular with the KGB twenty years ago. This one was a reproduction made by Prada and made more functional by my seamstress. She had put ballistic panels front and rear and holsters under the left and right arms. The pistol slips in and disappears, stiff leather hiding the tell tale signs. I was ready for the evening's reconnaissance.

I decided to skip eating at the hotel in favor of grabbing a bite out. There used to be a great cafe, in the Walloon district across from the Moulin rouge sex club that provided endless people-watching entertainment. It was an East Indian place called the Vijaya, or something like that. I remembered there was a hotel attached to it. I grabbed my room key and another cigar and headed into the hall.

The night air was sweet, with the drop in temperature burning slightly on my cheeks as I exited the hotel and turned right. The throng of bicyclists replaced by people looking to party. They were bundled up against the cool night looking for the newest of the new to get lost in trance or techno, as it went along with the pot or ecstasy in their bodies. Most of the people passing, or walking with me were speaking English – the Queen's or other being the only real distinction. I continued up into the RLD as the kids called it and hoped I could find my restaurant. The machine was working and watching, so I relaxed and just took in the sights. It wasn't that late — only 8:00 p.m., but people were already hanging off their friends, pleasantly drunk and singing.

Turning at a street that looked like the right one I saw two men in a doorway pay me far too much attention. The bright red glow of the neon sign for the Moulin Rouge lit up the area two bridges down. My stomach growled with anticipation and need. I flicked the ash off my little Monte four and tracked the two men. One was against the railing for the canal and the other on the shop side. They were forcing me to pass through the middle. I stopped before I reach them and moved to the railing and reclined against it. They continued toward me like awkward dancers unsure of the song. The one on the rail moved up to my side, offering me cocaine in four different languages. The other came straight at me as I dragged on my cigar and turned to the guy on my left to answer.

My left arm trapped the guy on the rails arm with his hand in my jacket pocket as my right arm rose straight out and flicked the cherry hot cigar into the face of the attacker coming straight at me. I stepped back along the rail pulling my captured pickpocket with me as we both watched his blind friend, hands in front, continue on his path. As he passed I twisted my hips and drove my knee into the small of his back, just as he contacted the rail and his friend's extended elbow. There is a whoosh of exhaled air and a loud snap announcing the elbow's destruction. I step back sharply and watch as pickpockets' hand stays in my jacket as the elbow elongates and the cry of pain becomes an inhalation, followed by a collapse, his hand finally pulling free of my pocket, like a sick Marquee de Sade cookie jar. The straight-on attacker is still trying to get his breath. His diaphragm still in spasm, I walked over and retrieved my cigar from the cobblestones. I take a couple of quick drags and continue my walk down the street. The high-pitched screaming started about the time I reached the restaurant.

I sat down at a table that faced the canal, took off my jacket and placed it over my legs. The screaming continued and was joined by an off-key duet partner as the police arrived. Then an ambulance joined the chorus.

"Hmm," I thought, "Dinner *and* a show."

CHAPTER TWENTY-THREE

THE FOOD WAS AS GOOD as I remembered. The Jenever, or Dutch courage gin, fortified tea and spicy Rijstafel provided all the heat I needed. The police never came down after they had interviewed and, by the looks of things, arrested both. I watched the tourists come and go from the big red painted facade of Moulin Rouge, looking in the widows before returning to inspecting the cobblestones

I paid for my meal and casually strolled over to the canal to clip and light my cigar, another Monte 4. It was short and perfect for the times one couldn't commit to a large cigar. I looked around as I finished the clip and brought the bullet and spent casing in my left hand to the edge of the rail. Then I lit the cigar. Drawing the flame in to the end and blowing out caused it to torch a little. I hoped the flashes would ruin any viewer's vision. A quiet "plop" and the evidence was gone.

I pulled on the SAP gloves, more for comfort than anything else. It had gotten remarkably cold, considering the mild afternoon. I continued up to the bridge and crossed left over the bridge to the Moulin Rouge side of the canal and looked at the wares for sale. The planted smiles on the ladies more practiced than mine, but just as fake. We were both whores I thought; just my profession was probably older. I continued down the block and just took in the sights and sounds so tomorrow I would have an accurate read on the surroundings.

I wanted to walk by the Russian club tonight, but procedure and discipline made it impossible. The rendezvous was scheduled for tomorrow at a specific time. Everyone would move in no more than three minutes early or three minutes late. It was a casual six rendezvous or an rv6 as say opposed to an rv1/2, which was an extraction rendezvous with a 30-second window of opportunity. I could walk by an alternative place just to keep something in the wings. I had thought from the start that the Jordaan section of town should really be the place to have the meeting. The Russian club provided security, but the same type of security that was provided by sleeping inside four walls. You had to pay for that security; the price was mobility and being an easy target. This operation could be over before it got off the ground with one well-placed car bomb.

I walked past the old church and found myself heading in the direction of the park, when the machine suddenly pushed past the effects of the strong gin. It had sensed a target to the rear, shadowing me. I turned into a coffee shop and immediately regretted the decision. The heavy reek of skunk pot was like a wall. The place was old looking and, despite being quite full, was not the loud bar I had wanted. The atmosphere was more than a little muted. I grabbed a chair near the window and looked out at where my shadow had been. I saw nothing except the normal movements of partygoers and tourists unstable from the strong pot, loose laws, and loose cobblestones. A girl approached me and placed her hand on my shoulder and asked if I was looking for someone. I looked at her and nodded yes. She smiled and stretching up to my ear said in English.

"I have a place just around the corner, my boyfriend is home but he won't mind. €75."

Slipping my arm around her shoulders I let her lead me out of the bar. We made small talk as I searched for the shadow. The machine was not always right and I had learned to roll with its false alarms and accept them. After all, an assassin only had to be right once. She led me to a three-storey walk-up and looked at me, expectantly. I was prepared for this and I rolled a €100 note discreetly between my fingers. I bent to kiss her hard on the mouth as I rolled it into her waistband. Her hand went to the money as fast as a preacher's daughter protecting her chastity. Yet she didn't stop kissing me, or rubbing my crotch with her other hand.

There! I caught it. A flash of errant light had caught the side of a face. The angle was wrong to get much more, but that was what the machine had seen. My lover, almost forgotten, was pulling me into the hallway of her building. How she had managed to continue flailing away at me through my pants and open the door was amazing. Once inside I stopped her with a gesture and pulled out another £100 note.

"Can we get to the roof?" I asked.

"Yes we can, but it's too cold, even for £200." Her Georgian-mixed Russian accent was obvious now.

"Da, I have a jealous wife and I think we were followed. I want to go look. You wait here for me and I'll be back in ten minutes, Okay? How do I get to the roof?" I asked.

"Go up stairs, the door is locked but just push, in the cold it slips. I wait here for you," she finished, but her facial expression gave her away. She would not wait.

I moved up the stairs and waited at the top. A full minute had passed and then I heard the click of a door someplace closing. I reached up and unscrewed the bare light bulb. The top of the stairs went black and I pushed the door open. Crouching low I was aware of the wind up here. It had been less on the ground. I moved slowly to the edge of the facade and settled on a secure perch on my knees. There was no moon directly behind me, but the glow of the city was everywhere. I very slowly increased the angle to the edge of the building. Humans were designed to spot movement. This slow move into position should not be spotted. With the mock turtleneck pulled up under my eyes and the toques from my pocket pulled down only my eyes were visible. I looked to the space the shadow had been in earlier. He wasn't there. Shit, he had moved! But where to? I didn't move my head. I lay there letting only my eyes move and scan, waiting for car lights to provide an edge. Three cars went by before I spotted him again. Off the corner reflection across the street I saw him, seated directly under my position. He was looking at the door I had gone into. There was someone else with him.

I strained to hear the conversation, knowing it was stupid. I waited for another car to provide some faces. I got my wish and saw both men, now seated, bent together talking. They were most likely American from the dress. But I knew I had to get closer. It had taken me over ten minutes to get this much. I thought about sliding to the ledge and waiting for one of them to go inside to piss or check the door I had gone in. Then I could screw the can on the front of the H&K and taking careful aim shoot the one seated in the top of the head. From this angle if I hit just behind the center of the crown the round would punch neatly through the skull and split the two hemispheres of the brain on its way to the center. The round's speed would create a vacuum behind it, and that would draw the blood along with the air into the hole.

Sounding very much like an old pneumatic tube messaging system, sending a message the body would never receive. So long as the round continued out the base and down into the body cavity the pressure trauma would be dissipated into the soft organs. If the aim was off and in front of the crown, or to the left or right, the pressure might blow the eyes out like a cartoon sneeze. That would hardly be the quiet kill I wanted.

I had to get a closer look and I had to get one quickly. I moved to the back edge of the building. There was no fire escape. I went back inside, screwed the light back in and went back down two floors and went down the hall in the same direction as the men. The red glow at the end of the hall told me I was getting lucky. I entered the fire escape and followed it down to the street level. It was dark and smelled of piss. It opened toward the back of the building and I pushed it open. A single man rushed me. My instinctive response was to bring him towards me and close the door, stopping anyone else from getting in. I felt him reach for me, arms going around my back. I lashed at the inside of his knee with my heel and drove my hand toward his chin. The knee broke with a champagne cork pop. But my hand strike was low; his crushed larynx whistled like a teapot on a stove, both announcing it was done.

I stepped back and looked at the man. He wasn't one of the men I had seen, I could tell that even in the dark. I took out a small penlight and looked. The tiny LED white light was more than adequate to see this man was a junky. Thin and hollow-cheeked he was already a dead man walking before I had finished him. He did have a nice big, thick pillow-style coat that was going to help me get out of the building. I dragged it on expecting it to smell and was surprised it didn't. I pushed the door once more and walked into the cold night, unimpeded.

I walked down the street away from the men. Then crossed the street quickly, and turned to come back to the Shadow's corner but across the street. On the way back I swayed, looked for a place to fall and shuffled like a noodle house waiter. I slipped near a bike lockup and let myself slump as if exhausted. I never looked at my prey once. Like a Nile crocodile I didn't have to; I knew where they were. From reflections or peripheral vision I confirmed they were Americans and they weren't gang related. They were company something, some alphabet agency. But how? I couldn't think of the answer.

The cold from the ground seeped into my body. I moved only enough not to appear dead. The thick jacket helped, and I tensed my legs like a test pilot to pump blood out of my cold legs and into my warmer core. The two men were patient, far too patient for spooks. They watched the entrance without looking at it and chatted like friends. They had to know there were alternative exits to this building so why were they not splitting up to cover them? Did they have others watching those? I needed to get a better angle, so I had to move.

I raised myself onto all fours. In my reflected image, I could see them both looking at me. I crawled slowly, like a drunk, past the bike racks toward the building. Reaching the building I rolled and put my back to it. In the shadowed recess of the building it should be safe enough to risk a direct look. I needed to be sure I was clean. I needed to know that another shadow had not seen me leave the building.

I opened up my senses and looked at every possible angle. I identified every person and watched, logging their movements and, one by one, struck them off the list. After twenty minutes, I was sure. The only shadows were the two men. I was starting to believe they weren't even shadows as they sat and waited far too casually.

In the distance a police siren wailed. In this quiet neighbourhood it got everyone's attention on the patio. Then I saw what I needed. Hand sign! One of the shadows had just made a series of movements with their right hand signaling the other. "Move off this position and RV 'rendezvous' back here when clear, if required." These two were military!

The siren got louder and was beside me. Slowing, it turned and parked between my shadows and me. Two officers, a man and women got out and went around the back of the car and past the patio. My two shadows waited silently, watching like everyone else. The two officers walked to the door I had used half an hour ago and were met by a blonde, and disappeared inside. It was time to move. My shadows had come to the same conclusion and one moved off across the street while the other walked towards me.

I lowered my head, listening to his footsteps as he walked to the corner and stopped. I wanted to raise my head and look to see what his partner was doing, but knew if I did he would see me. I waited, slowing my breathing and straining to hear. When shadow moved his foot it sounded like he was right beside me. It wasn't and the footsteps moved to my left down the quiet road. Slowly I moved my head up — just enough to allow me to see his back disappear down the dark street. The other shadow was still across the street sitting with three others at a bus stop. I waited.

The bus came and my shadow was alone, watching the front of the building. Another bus came and I moved quickly and silently, using the bus as cover. I left the jacket crumpled against the building, hoping that to the casual glance it would look like I was still there. I sprinted fifty feet and then slowed to a walk, looking ahead, trying to find shadow one. I reached a cross street and peered to my right: no shadow. Turning I continued right as I considered my options. If I took this watcher down and questioned him, they would learn about as much as I would from the questions I asked. If I made the attack look like a mugging I might get some information but would I get more than I already knew?

Perhaps, if he was sloppy he might have paper or cell records to identify his purpose for following me. I kicked myself for not looking at Darius's cell phone dump, for falling asleep in the bath and forgetting. Fuck I was rusty! This had to change before I got myself killed! I doubted a mugging so close to missing one's tail and with a murder sprinkled on for good measure would be believed. "Fuck," I raged. I was running out of options. I could kill them both as they had signed to RV back at the cafe. But that would tip my hand to those that had sent them. If they had checked in; if they knew whom they were following. They were good at their craft, so those were big 'ifs.'

I noticed a car with a door slightly ajar and it gave me an idea. A hit-and-run by a drunk driver would be believable. Yes, that would work. I opened the door and the car light was bright enough to be painful on the dark street. Slipping inside I pushed the button on the automatic knife and stabbed it hard into the ignition, twisting and putting my foot on the clutch. The securing pin broke and the ignition turned. The car came to life and I swung out on the narrow street and drove to the corner. I turned left and cruised up the street, now hunting my hunter.

It's two blocks before I see him, halfway down the street to my right. I continued straight, accelerating slightly and turning right at the next road. The neighbourhood is quiet and the street empty. I stop and quickly jump out of the car. Moving to the front I kick out the front lights. They smash like a firecracker shot into the quiet night. I jump back in the car and now, driving dark, head to the corner. I swing right again and see my prey. He was walking on the dark side of the street, three blocks back from the main road. Close! Very close to the busy street. I cruised along, the little engine making very little noise. I picked a spot. A perfect spot; a small alley intersected the lane and it was two blocks back from the main road. There was a gated house before the alley and a brick building on the far side. Perfect. I increased my speed and gauged my timing; this had to be just right.

Shadow steps off the curb and actually moves into the small lane slightly as I swing the car into him. The left front bumper and hood catches him under the ass and catapults him up into the brick building hard. Hitting knees first and oddly almost in the sitting position before falling backwards, his head hitting the street hard. I pull the emergency brake slowly and the car slows to a stop. I jump out and move to the shadow. He's out cold; the odd angle of his leg suggesting it's broken. I search him quickly. Cell phone, gun, wallet, badge wallet. Shit, he's legit! The badge identifies him as Jeffery Allen Stone of the Department of Homeland Security. The picture is recent so it may be a cover ID. His wallet has about £400 and contains bits of ID that match his name but not the usual debris one acquires in a wallet over time. So his name was a cover. I open his shirt and see a set of dog tags. I check the name Emory Allen Harding. I checked his arms and noticed an eagle holding a trident. The guy was an ex SEAL. I moved down his legs to his ankles — nothing.

A voice behind me asks in Flemish, "Is he ok? I continued doing 'first aid' and told the guy to call an ambulance. Thinking, "Shit, running out of time here!"

I heard his footsteps retreating, Thank God, not everyone had a cell phone.

I flipped open my phone and my Blue tooth dentist. Then I opened his cell phone and, checking the number download the contents of his phone. While the phone was downloading I packed his jacket under his head. Closing the phone I put all the items back on his body, leaving the gun very visible. I return to the car and drive quickly to the main road and turn left, away from the other viewers.

I drive at a normal speed for three blocks and turn left into a side street. It's lit and I drove slowly, as if looking for an address, looking for any sign of people. Finding none, I park. I had been wearing the SAP gloves so there was no need to wipe the car. I get out and close the door pretending to lock it, and casually walk back down the block to the main street.

CHAPTER
TWENTY-FOUR

THE SHOWER'S HOT WATER COMBINED with the deep tissue massage and I felt the stress of the day roll off my body and down the drain. This location was perhaps not the most ideal of locations but it was completely untraceable. Sarah had truly believed I was just another date and had been paid well for her time and would probably go home for the rest of the evening. The place was not great but it was close to the Tearoom and would dump me off any radar for a few hours. I brought the bar soap through my hair and could smell the skunky pot that had been captured there. I liked the relaxed atmosphere of the city but I hated the smell of pot.

I got out and toweled off, went to my jacket and removed the pistol. I pulled the silencer out of the other side and screwed it onto the short threaded barrel. I placed it on the bedside table and pulled back the sheets. They were not obviously soiled to my unaided vision. I shuttered to think what they would look like if I used one of those fancy lights made popular by crime investigation dramas.

The weight of the night fell on my chest like some sort of gravity well. It felt as though I was being pushed down into the mattress. It was like the feeling one gets under heavy sedation and I let it claim me.

"Housekeeping!"

The word entered my head and my brain struggled first with the language and then the meaning. Crawling up out of the depths of sleep I roughly rubbed the sand out of my eyes with my left hand while my right grabbed the pistol and brought it under the sheets.

"Sir, Housekeeping."

I heard the lock in the door turn. Dutch, she was speaking Dutch, I realized as my brain took the briefest of seconds to translate.

"Just jumping out of the shower."

"Check out is in thirty minutes, sir."

I heard her feet retreat from the door. Thirty minutes? What the fuck? I looked at my watch, my eyes taking seconds to focus. Shit, it was ten thirty. I had slept nearly ten full hours. I never slept more than six. Wow, I was feeling my age like an unwelcome guest. I jumped out of bed and was surprised that the knot in my lower back seemed to be taking a break today as it didn't let me know how much it loved me as it did every morning with a stab of pain. I went back into the bathroom; the harsh lighting irritating the sand in my eyes like salt. I turned on the shower and went back out into the main room.

I walked to the window and could see the sun already high in the sky. In the street below everything looked normal. I turned on the TV as I pass by and flip it to the BBC World Service news. The accented English was droning on about some soccer match. I reached into my pants pockets and retrieve one of the automatic knives, and headed for the shower. I caught myself at the door and turned my attention back to the TV, not really listening as my brain formulated an entrance plan for Equatorial Guinea. Yes, that would work, it fit and it would allow me to put a few more feet on the ground. Smiling at the unlikely source of inspiration I continued into the shower.

The bar soap made a poor lather and the knife, while very sharp, was a poor substitute for a razor. The harsh blade pulled at the skin and caught but I managed to shave without too many cuts. I walk into the living room area and pull on my clothes listening to the weather and general world events. The bits of toilet paper drying the blood and hopefully staunching its flow. I briefly consider making coffee in the little room percolator and toss the idea along with the toilet paper bits soaked in blood into the garbage.

Four minutes shy of checkout found me in the lobby, heading for the door. A call from the front desk pulled me up short of the door.

"Sir."

It was the desk clerk, a smiling, silver-haired man in his sixties.

"Coffee and pastries are available in the side lobby." He gestured to a small alcove.

"Thanks," I said lightly. I had considered just continuing out the door but my stomach took that exact moment to protest my decision.

The rich coffee scent confirmed I made the right decision. There was no one else in the area and despite the late hour there were at least a dozen different pastries and muffins available. I picked up a Copenhagen and poured a large cup of dark coffee to go. The hard graham base was covered in a hazelnut spread and the light flaky pastry top was swirled with a honey-based frosting. It, like the coffee, was perfect and reminded me why I loved Europe. The innkeeper obviously took great pride in his hospitality. I decided to sit in one of the large leather chairs and finish the pastry in comfort.

I used the time to check my phone and see what Darius was up to. I punched up the GPS application and tagged Darius's phone and waited as the system searched. The GPS first showed Europe and then by degrees zoomed in on his phone. He was at the airport.

The meeting was in less than four hours and I had figured out how to get a large group of mercenaries into the country undetected and was feeling very good about myself. The "tearoom" was only about a twenty-minute walk away. I had enough time to do some research.

It took me a while to find the shop without the expert help of a driver. Amsterdam is an odd city in which to find shops as many are on both floors and the layout of the streets are like concentric horseshoes arching along the canals. The shop I was looking for was on the second floor and I walked past it looking for numbers. On my return trip down the other side of the street I spotted the sign.

The space on the second floor was deceptively large. In the front window display were the Ajax Jerseys made popular by the very successful Amsterdam soccer club. There were pictures of the club with trophies from many victories and it all looked very impressive. I knew nothing about soccer, or to be more culturally correct, football as they called it here.

"Can I help you, sir?"

The shop attendant was a slight lady with a boyish haircut and freckled face. Her Dutch was good but it wasn't her first language. She looked like she had stepped off a mid-west prairie corn ad.

"You're not Dutch"

"No I'm from London, is my accent that bad?"

"No it's really good, but I do speak English. I'm looking to outfit a charity teaching team to travel to Africa. I'll need everything from bags to socks and all of it with logos. Can you do that here?"

"Oh yes, sir, we can. How many squads are you fielding?"

"Ah? I'm just the money behind the operation, in fact I'm not too sure how many players are even on the field at the same time?"

"Ok, well there are eleven players on the field at one time, from each side of course. The net minder and ten players."

"Ok so two squads should do it and eight coaches"

"Do you have the sizing done yet? We'll definitely need those if were doing matching cleats as well"

"Cleats?"

"Boots, you know football cleats, shoes"

"Right, sorry kind have to help me along here."

"Not an issue sir, I'm here to help you get what you need. Are you going to need away jerseys too?" Seeing the confusion splashed on my face, she continued. "When you play at home you have one colour jersey and when you play away you have another."

"I think just the one will be good. Were just running some training schools and doing some exhibition games with the local team."

"Ok. What style and what is your logo?"

I had been feeling so full of my self I really hadn't forced myself to go into the details much. I guess we needed a logo and as for colours, Equatorial Guinea is always moist and hot so something light would be best. I was starting to flounder here and I knew it. My expertise in this area was starting to show in a bad way. Just play it out Rhys, pushed the machine.

"Ah, the colours are light green and white, and the logo is a Cape buffalo. You guys can pull one of those off an art site right? Just the head looking forward."

"Sure. Not a problem. What kind of fabric?"

I was starting to feel like I was doing a wedding, Fabric? What the fuck kind of options did I have? Cotton was all I knew.

"Options?"

"Well, we have moisture wicking, and light-weight poly that provides sun coverage. Then there is Nike's proprietary stuff that does both and is designed to bring more moisture away from certain areas. It's all really pretty cool stuff and the technological design is amazing."

Amazing and expensive I thought but we had to look the part and fit in well. In the end it wasn't my money.

"These guys are going to be playing in some bad heat so what is the newest and best?"

" The stuff form Nike is, really cool. They even have specially designed socks."

"I would expect they did, do I get a volume discount if I outfit thirty people with two uniforms each of the same design and cleats?"

"I'd have to ask my boss but I'm sure because it's a charity group we could do something. You'll need bags for each member with numbers, and some practice balls and ball bag. We could probably toss in some balls with our logo and the like. Shall I write this up, sir?"

There was some ball tossing going on here to be sure and they were bouncing off my forehead. But this was the way it went when you walked into a store knowing nothing about the product. She was being helpful and gave the impression she knew her stuff. The time for the meeting was quickly approaching and this wasn't my money anyway.

"Sure, lets do the numbers here and I'll get you the cleat sizing. We can just do fifty medium shirts and ten large. Perhaps another five extra large and thirty small, or kids medium, however that works. You can e-mail me the logo design for my ok. How long from me Ok'ing the order to delivery?"

Her pen flashed across the preprinted order sheet. It looked like they did team orders all the time.

"Are we going with Nike fabric and Cleats?"

"Yes"

"The per unit cost is two hundred and €20 for thirty units with cleats and the other 30."

"Just the total is fine." I said, cutting her off politely.

"€13,500. I'm certain the boss will provide twenty-two numbered bags, balls, and a ball bag. The delivery time is four weeks from the date of order. Delivery time is guaranteed."

"Ok, sounds good. I will give you my credit card and you can run it through when I ok the design and get you the cleat sizing. You can ship these to me, right?"

"Yes, sir. We can ship"

She took my card number and asked for my passport and took that number down as well. I gave her my e-mail and phone number and she added this to the top of this purchase order. I signed the bottom of the order thinking uniforms may change but the job doesn't!

CHAPTER TWENTY-THREE

THE WALK BACK ACROSS TOWN could have been more enjoyable with a nice cigar but I was out and the general lack of cigar shops was annoying. In a city full of excess one would think it would be easy to find a decent cigar shop. I turned left up into the Old Russian area of town and could see the change immediately. The place was less colourful as if to pay homage to the very industrial design so common in Russia. I walked past the shop and looked for shadows. I hadn't sensed or seen any following me but I wanted to make a pass here to see if our lunch had been compromised. I walked the full block and then pulled out a tourist map and studied it. Turning slowly I checked storefront reflections and cars. Looking lost and using my peripheral vision I saw no one. The venue looked as clean as fresh snow. But just like snow hides dirt and danger, something about this street felt wrong. I crossed the block and walked down again toward the rendezvous on the opposite side of the street. There was a man with a dog, in slippers so not a concern. A woman with a pram was crossing the street near the front of the tearoom. She was hyper aware and scanning back and forth. She eased the pram up onto the sidewalk and continued toward me. She checked out and I confirmed there was a baby inside the pram as I walked by, smiling. Perhaps it was just nerves. I reached the point directly across from the destination and stopped. Bringing my phone to my ear I dropped the map. I bent low to pick it up and scanned the underside of cars, nothing. It was just nerves, there was no urging from the machine so I strode directly across the street and entered, the large oak door swinging with protest.

I was one minute early and I stopped and allowed my eyes to adjust from the bright afternoon to the internal gloom. I heard slow breathing to my left and turned to see Cerberus sitting on a chair his blank eye following his good one as he looked at me. He smiled, recognizing me from previous times. It was the smile that cut through people; a cross between a leer and a grimace and it suggested evil about as much as the Mona Lisa suggested mystery.

"Cerberus, good to see you. Am I the first one here?"

"No Rhys, three here before you. You look good, no shooting my club, da?"

"Da my friend, I won't be shooting in your club."

"Good I think you're not going to like everyone here, so I need to say that. Killing inside would not be convenient."

"Why? Who is here?"

"Tom"

"Fuck!"

"Remember Rhys, my club my rules, da?"

"Da."

"Tom was the big money behind this, then." I thought as I walked toward the back. Fuck. I should have bought five uniforms for everyone and paid a premium. He was probably the one that fostered the idea that the British Government sanctioned the coup. So after seven years he was willing to put his balls and contract on the line to help a friend. I stopped, turned, and walked back to Cerberus. I didn't want to alarm him so I shrugged off my coat instead of reaching inside. Handing it to him I said.

"Here hold this for me, that way if the winner of the Stupid Twit of the Year award pisses me off I can keep my promise."

Saying nothing he took my jacket and hefted it appraisingly. I just caught the edge of the smile as I walked back toward the meeting. This was shaping up to be a really lively meeting. I wished Sunday was attending and then a step later figured it would be a bad idea. Sunday's sense of honour was much stronger than mine.

The table was in the back right hand side of the club. There were two girls standing on the edges with Dimetri, the real owner of the club. The girls were young; probably seventeen and they didn't look like waitresses. Tom was seated at the head of the table with a man I didn't know. The man was bald and in his early sixties, wearing cheap looking black glasses low on his beak-like nose. Riley, a great Irish poker pro was seated right of Tom.

Besides being an accomplished poker player Riley was a happy go lucky contractor having grown up in the troubles in Northern Ireland. He had run with the IRA for a time and then had become disenchanted with the group and had joined the US military to get away from it all. Lucky for him his father was a US citizen and gave him the out. Riley had rose in the ranks and performed well, leaving the service out of the Delta Special Forces to pursue more financially rewarding goals.

Dimetri stopped me as I walked up, speaking in Russian.

"Rhys, my good friend, how are you comrade?"

"I'm well my brother, healthy and content"

Then switching to English I asked, "How are you?"

"I'm very well, perhaps not content but good none the less. These girls will bring you food or drink but they only speak Russian so you may have to translate for your friends. I thought it prudent to insure nothing was overheard in your meeting"

"Great Dimetri, your KGB training is showing again."

"Rhys, I have told you one hundred times I'm not KGB. Never was! All Russians understand privacy. We learn it sharing small apartments with two families."

"Demetri, I might believe you were not KGB. I will never believe you shared an apartment. The sand of the Black Sea has stained your hands forever, my friend."

Laughing, Demetri grabs me with his bear-like hands and gives me a big hug, slapping my back hard.

"True, my friend, true. But I'm a simple host today, enjoy."

I join the table and Riley looks as uncomfortable as a teenager who just walked in on their parents having sex. He greets me in Irish Gaelic and I respond in kind. Then I look at Tom.

"Hello, Rhys. First off I don't want to hear any of your conspiracy theories or moral condemnation. I'm backing this operation one hundred per cent despite both you and the 'duchess' having enough money to have done it yourself years ago. I wasn't as flush at the time if you remember. Now I'm writing the cheque, and I'm putting the best people on it and that includes you – plus Riley, Viktor and Neil if you need air support. We can do the "should have" shuffle all bloody afternoon, but I would suggest we move forward as all our goals are the same. Right?"

I looked at Tom and then at his bald-headed companion.

"You go queer, Tom? Is this cue-ball your daddy or something?"

Tom flushes, his pale Welsh face betraying his annoyance at my cavalier response to his obviously rehearsed speech. The spectacled bald man looks at me over his glasses and moves to say something before Tom cuts him off.

"This is Edward Scarlett, he's my lawyer and counsel. I should ask you to be civil, Rhys and respectful. He's here to outline the legal issues and to add to the conversation in a positive manner. You may not know him but I assure you I can vouch for his discretion."

"Really Tom? You can vouch for him can you? In my experience Tom, lawyers think in terms of grey. Nothing is what it seems to be and everything is an arguable fact, not real until it's believed real by judge or jury. Would you say that's an accurate assessment Mr. Scarlett?"

"Well sir, I'm not about to get led into a conversation defending my profession. But I assure you anything said at this table will be held in the utmost confidence. Client confidentiality is of great importance and my discretion is above reproach I assure you."

"Really? Seems to me I was reproaching it. You'll excuse me but I don't know you, Mr. Scarlett. I know everyone else that will be joining us at this table. But you sir, are an unknown. For that matter you don't know me, past what Tom has told you. That makes two unknowns. Let me enlighten you. I'm the fucking antichrist. I wouldn't drop a half smoked cigar to save your life. You mean nothing to me and your presence here presents me with a liability. You're an unknown equation and one that will not be physically invested in this endeavour and your client here is someone other than me. Let me invest you into our scheme. I have no idea if you have family or what you're close to. But if you stay at this table and the operation goes south and I think for a minute you could be to blame I will find these things out sir. I will find everyone and everything in your world and I will come for them. I will skin your loved ones in front of your eyes and then water board you with their blood. The suffering I will bring to you would be past biblical in nature, let me assure you. I could give lessons in torture, in hell!"

I had to give the man credit he was frosty. His brief glance at Tom was the only indication I had got under his thick English veneer. His colour hadn't changed and his heavy jowls hid his no doubt quickening pulse. His only outward indicator he was terrified were his pupils.

They were as pinned as a rabbit caught under a descending shadow. He looked at Tom and then at me, while Riley examined his napkin.

"Well sir, if it makes you so uncomfortable perhaps I will retire to a different table until your discussion is finished"

"Ed you don' have to…" Tom attempted to interject.

"You do that." I said, cutting him short and ending this rambling.

Scarlett rose to his feet and was deftly directed to a quiet table away from ours by Dimitre. Tom shot me an infected look, his Welsh skin now crimson with anger.

"What the fuck, Rhys? This is not your show; this is not your fucking endeavour! You're here cause I wanted you here, and I'm beginning to think that was a fucking mistake."

"Tom, are you going to be feet wet on this or are you just going to write the cheque?"

"You know I can't be involved. This thing almost cost me my contract when it went down. That contract comes up for review in two years. You already know the answer to that! You just threatened a senior member of the British fucking Court system for fuck's sake!"

I glared at the man and responded with a snarl.

"Yeah, I did and if you put Satan in front of me I'll kick him in the balls too, just to watch him grunt! I don't know what colour the sky is in your fucking world but since when do we bring civilians into our world? What are you thinking and why do you think you'd need a lawyer? You gonna sue us for non-performance or something? Are you still one of us, Tom? In case you forgot our currency is flesh and bone!"

There was a thick silence at the table. I turned to order a drink and notice Viktor and Neil standing about ten feet away. Cerberus was standing behind them.

"Hey guys, great to see you. Grab a chair. Vodka all around. We have to drink to Tom swimming in the deep end of the pool again."

Dimetri relayed my order to the two girls who scurried off quickly to get the angry man at the table a drink. They were unsure of what he had said, but had seen enough violence in their short lives to know it was real and very dangerous.

CHAPTER
TWENTY-FOUR

I HEARD THE OTHERS MOVE toward the table as I turned my attention back to Tom. Viktor took the newly vacated seat beside Tom and Neil the seat to my left. The girls arrived with the glasses and bottles and quickly poured shots for everyone around the table. Then they positioned themselves at opposite sides still holding the bottles ready to refill the small shot glasses. Tom stared at his glass and I figured I better end this confrontation one way or another.

"Look Tom, I didn't want to take the piss out of you there. But fuck man you know the drill? I get you're a big corporate guy and wouldn't do an interview without a mouthpiece, but fuck man this is us. I ever break your balls about failing out of the SAS on selection? No! I didn't, did I? Cause it didn't matter, you're a good operator despite it. But this shit here; this shit gets us all fucked up. The US has green badgers working this right fucking now and I'm of half a mind to melt fatso's toes off figuring out if he knows anything."

The mention of the CIA contractors being here got everyone's attention. Tom started to speak on his consuls' behalf but I continued.

"Listen Tom, you say the guy is ok. Fine he sits over there at the kid's table. But Tom, you've got to come clean with the rest of us. I know, fuck we all know what you said to the media about the coup and when you knew what. Everyone at this table knows that's shit. All right Tom? I don't know much about guilt personally, but I do know people feeling guilty try to fix the shit they fucked up. That's where we are, right Tom? I ain't asking to rub it in your face. We've got serious, hard contractors. The ones they first sent into Afghanistan after HVT's (High Value Targets), right on us already and we don't have fucking plane tickets yet. We need to know the facts, all the truths and your own ideas on how it really went down. Tom if I wanted to blame you or get revenge I would have just shot you in the face and tipped the fuck out the door. Let's move forward. Drink with me Tom and let's have it"

Tom sat looking at his shot glass, and for a moment I thought he might get up and leave. He raised his head and looked at each of us. Reaching for his glass was a signal and all of us moved to catch up. He raised his glass and with a simple "cheers" we started moving forward. Tom spent the next twenty minutes outlining the failed coup from his point of reference. Some details were different than what I thought had happened but in the end it amounted to the same thing. Everyone had been in the know and one rat, paid by the American oil company, started squawking, loudly and officially and neither the US nor Britain could take the political black eye at the time so they tossed the group to the wolves. Or more correctly in this case the Scorpions. The Scorpions were a special police section that went after this type of crime. The only real crime being their name and obvious cheap rip off of one of the EO's intelligence officer's insignia, for their own.

While Tom was describing the details (probably for the first time) I could see it was guilt motivating the operation. His loose tongue had cost the men their freedom and a few of them their lives. This revelation was there for all of us to see and I wondered to myself if the others were thinking the same thing. His transgression had been stupid and ill advised but I doubted very much if I would have felt the same way. The inference from the State Department had been positive so this mistake was made under the best possible intelligence. It was important for the US and British governments to know, and be onside with, the operation as it was planned. The Internet had sped up the world of news and the old adage of "shoot all journos" was not enough to keep something of that magnitude under wraps.

I figured a few plates of vereniki (small Russian perogies) were desirable, with some of the cabbage rolls and bread. I ordered from the girls, as they stood ready to fill our glasses. They disappeared without a word and returned just in time to hear Viktor.

"Tom, first thanks. That took some parts. I wouldn't beat myself up over the whole opps factor. You got warned off the project and Simon, being the arrogant prick he can be, ignored you. Not that I'm suggesting I wouldn't have either that late in the operation. But he went ahead, either out of ego or desperation, despite good Intel that he should not. Rhys, I know you're pissed about this, but you have to admit Simon's fate is Simon's alone."

"Yeah Viktor, I get it. But this is the first I heard of the warn off. Thanks Tom."

"Right then, since we're all playing nice in the sand box, how about some chow? I'm feeling like a famine survivor over here," Riley said with a broad smile and all the bravado he could muster.

"Good idea," added Neil. "I flew my own ass over here and haven't had a break since I landed"

"It's all coming, another drink?" I reached for the bottle and poured everyone another shot.

CHAPTER
TWENTY-FIVE

VIKTOR WAS A WEAPONS PROCUREMENT specialist and could find some of the best gear your money could buy. He was of Russian decent but spoke it very poorly having been raised in Georgia. His past was as convoluted as his contacts and he shared little of either. But he was the guy those deep in the world of privately funded operations went to. He wouldn't work with everyone and because of this he was well respected. He only knowingly outfitted one side, which was an odd and rare principle in this world.

Neil was a pilot and loved flying as much as he was good at it. We hadn't really discussed anything prior to the meeting and I wasn't sure if we would need him or not. But, I liked him and it was good to see him. It was always good to see him, be it bloody and muddy, him pulling you out of some bug infected hot zone, or like now. His confidence was inspiring and well earned and respected. He was an older fellow that got his start flying for the CIA in the seventies, and had more stories of "close ones" than any person I knew. He loved to tell them too. His non-emotional chatter on the radio headsets over the years had earned him his nickname, Zombie. He was always "Zombie" or "Z1" on the radio. I remembered one of the close ones I was in with him. We were in a "borrowed" Russian M26 Hind helicopter.

The hot wet air rushed in the open doors and made my shirt stick to my skin. The resulting moisture made my precarious position worse. I was sitting on a large truck tire inner tube. But it wasn't inflated with air it was full of aviation diesel as were the four other bloated black sausages. A flying gas can and a very risky endeavour. We were flying at about one hundred and fifty miles per hour and about three thousand feet. The dense jungle canopy was to our right and the coast to our left.

We were getting the bird into theater having borrowed it that morning. Neil had said it had been a long time since he flew a chopper this big and heavy, but you wouldn't know it from the way he handled her. The interior was typically Russian. Not made for comfort was one thing but this thing had sharp angles that if you weren't careful would mark you for life. Why the focus on function and not on ergonomics was beyond me. I don't think I ever met a Hind Gunner that had spent any time in battle without head scars.

A plume of white smoke in the tree line was a bad thing. The inbound rocket must have been launched from a hilltop just below the canopy cover. Zombie's voice was as calm, as if he was asking for a beer. "SAM in-bound, dropping to avoid, hang on."

The floor fell away and I experienced almost true weightlessness as the big heavy machine fell out of the sky. I could hear the noise in the cockpit over my own scream which had somehow escaped my mouth, beeps and buzzers warning that life was not going as expected or how the Hind liked. The airframe popped and protested as it fell like a diving sub and not a helicopter. Zombie's voice again came calming over the headset.

"Away from the doors, ladies. I'm gonna' make her dance a little."

A moment later we were almost completely sideways, doing something until a second ago I didn't think a Hind could do. We jerked back the other way and rolled over onto that side before going nose first into what was incredibly the sea.

"Now!"

I heard Neil's voice and the side rockets fire down into the water, which could only have been two hundred feet away. Then my vision failed me. First it was like a red filter that folded in from the outer edges of my vision, and then it just went dark. I was only out a second and the first sense that came back was of being crushed. Then I could smell salt water and thought; "Fuck we stuffed a Hind into the sea." My vision returned and I was surprised to see us airborne and moving fast about forty feet above the rough coastline.

"That was a close one ladies, we're staying down here on the deck for a while."

Neil had brought the big bird down to the water and fired a series of rockets into the shallows. The steam and explosion had been enough to confuse the SAM and as choppers can slip left and missiles have to turn the confused guidance system didn't' have time to reacquire the Hind's overworked power plant before it hit the water. Close indeed! SAMS routinely splashed supersonic jets. This was one for the "you won't believe it, but."

CHAPTER TWENTY-SIX

THE FOOD ARRIVED, THE GIRLS placing three large plates full of small Russian perogies in the middle. There were plenty of chopped fried onions, sour cream, and sliced sausage. Then the cabbage rolls were added to the banquet and everyone at the table lost interest in the machination and set to making sense out of the wonderful smells assaulting our noses. The food was incredible, as always. The running joke was Dimetri had stolen the best cooks in Russia. Cooks and not Chefs, for this was good old fashion Russian comfort food, not some fancily presented morsel. All of us lost the plot for a few minutes, filling our plates and tasting each of the varieties of vereniki.

Dimetri, noticing our conversations, had stopped and loudly walked into our circle.

"Gentlemen, I hope you enjoy this simple meal. Is everything satisfactory? Can I get the girls to bring you coffee or perhaps tea?" He finished looking at Tom.

No one spoke. There was nodding of heads and sounds made with mouths filled with food. But the answers were what Demetri had hoped for. He knew the one thing all contractors shared was the love of food and eating communal meals. The tension of the meeting had been drastically reduced and the guests did not appear to be going to kill each other. Before leaving he picks up an unused fork and like a child reaches in quickly and spears a little dumpling. Deftly rolling it through the sour cream before making it disappear into his mouth.

"Mmmm, yummphf that's good! I shall leave you all to your vacation planning."

The pace of our plunder slowed and we washed a little more down when the fresh hot coffee arrived. Tom had chosen to have coffee and I took this as an effort to earn rapport and be like everyone else. Wise of him. He tapped a spoon to his cup before bringing the meeting back on track.

"Ok, Rhys I guess point one will be how are we going to get everyone into the country? The president is going to be more than a little cautious these days and my Intel says that airport security is more than a little tight."

"Can't fly in covertly either as they have new and very advanced radar. I was doing a little groundwork, before I flew over myself. You know, chatted up the pilots in lounges and the like. The system is really state of the art." Neil added past some sliced sausage.

"I have a sub. Old diesel, 629 Golf class. It was the one of three made with the torpedo tubes and launchers removed. I think officially she was called a series five. They were sold to North Korea in ninety-three along with ten of the original 629 class for scrap. She's old but sound and is sitting in a safe place in South Korea. I was going to convert her to do underwater tourism in Japan but that plan never panned out. It would be slow but she's one of the quietest designs made and lots of room for gear. I would sell her at a loss and of course provide her with a crew."

Viktor, aren't the 629 class the ones that had the ghost malfunction? That was the one that fell past crush depth off Hawaii right? All hands lost with four nuclear missiles? I'm not really in the mood to be testing my Irish luck, and not to mention my Irish ass in a cigar tube!"

"The design is sound. The one off Hawaii sunk after a collision with a US sub. Or at least that's what my sources in the government told me at the time. I have personally been inside and down one hundred meters in this very sub. Very sound and working perfectly."

"Viktor, when you say at a loss how much are we talking here — in Euros?"

Before Viktor could answer Tom's question I brought my spoon to my cup and held up my hand.

"Viktor, I'm sure it's a great deal, but I have a much simpler plan. Much more budget- minded too. We are going to field a football team."

CHAPTER
TWENTY-SEVEN

I PAUSED AND WATCHED THE looks travel around the table like a sequential light panel in a rave club.

"What?"

"A football match? We are the imported hooligans then, eh?"

"Football?"

"Hear me out, guys. Everyone that wants on the team to pull this off will play football to some level of skill. The only people who play football more than the Brazilians are the Africans. Christ, the last time I was in JoBerg they weren't talking at all about the Olympics, they were talking World Cup. We pick up a premiere league trainer and coach and send them to a football pitch in RSA and have them run the men through a few drills and games and pick the best twenty-two players. Then Tom uses some of his Ivy League contacts and talks up a charity training camp for the kids in EG. The hook is we need to get a league goalie and forward."

"Net minder and striker."

"Whatever, Riley. The point is we get Tom to use his influence to get us two ringer players to mesh with our players and then the president really can't say no, can he?

BBC, CNN and the works will be chatting this one up to the ceiling."

"Then what, Rhys? Do a prison break, while you're helping orphans? Fuck. Are you daft man? That would get huge media coverage and come back to hit me directly in my balloon knot! Fuck man!"

"The sub would be more discreet, Rhys"

"Look, let me finish. Viktor, discreet until we get caught chugging up the West African coast at eight knots with a diesel supply ship in

158

bloody tow. Really? Ok, we are in the country for two weeks, helping out the kids and doing the charity game. That gives us lots of time to do some runs past the jail. Have a good look around, right? No odd looks or tails while we do our planning stages. We are loud and in their face, so we couldn't be up to anything, right? I know this doesn't roll well with those wanting to pay homage to Forsyth, but doesn't this work better than me and Sunday dropping in pretending to be bird watchers?"

"Yeah."

"Ok, we plan our gig while the men stay in shape and create the distraction. The celeb players are going to only be out for the times the media is around, as I can't imagine them buying into the cause. But in any case we need them for legitimacy and for the final game. Then we play an early afternoon game against the country's national team complete with a sponsored beer garden and food tents and really put on a show. After the game the ringers and the non-essential people take off and a group of us stay and hide out. We hit the jail sometime in the following week. The big dog-and-pony show allows us to bring in tons of equipment. For example, we can wrap rubber zodiacs in the tent tarps and no one is likely to be the wiser. Get it?"

Tom was shaking his head "yes" and the rest of the members were smiling at one another. They had got it. The simplicity of the incursion was critical because EG was comprised of a wasteland on the mainland and several islands of wealth. The capital and Black Beach Prison was on the big island. It was very hard to discreetly sneak onto an island with thirty men and a ton of gear. This also eliminated the chance of Sunday and my cover being blown doing the first work up. Catching a white guy wondering around a jail containing another famous white guy would kind of be a no brainier. The team was all coming to their own conclusions.

"Brilliant. But I'm not your typical Irish kid, and I don't play football well.

"Ya. I fly, but not on a soccer pitch."

"Football."

"Whatever. Riley, you're a trainer. Neil, I'm thinking of keeping you in reserve for extraction if things go too far south to handle. Tom, do you have any sources and contacts with Premier football squads or the like?"

"Yes I do. I'm just working out the 'If this goes bad' angle."

Tom pushed back from the edge of the table, and from the look on his face he was having a difficult time figuring out all of the angles of my suggestion.

"How this could go south?" had been effectively limited by the ease of the insertion and cover. He was tagged to the project but not the aftermath of the escape plan. Satisfied he was golden he leaned back and once again joined the conversation.

"Go on."

"Not much else to tell you, Tom. We really need to work out the details in country after we have a look around. You're off the hook for the sub but on it for the rest of the supplies, private round trip plane, beer and party stuff, and selling it to the media. Getting us the two star players is job one. Without that we're pooched before we get going. How about you and Riley work on getting us some star power players, a coach, and trainer. Take the rest of the week and see if we can't get something firm for say the middle of next week. Sound good?"

"Ok, Rhys. I don't mind living in Tom's caviar world."

"Yeah, in your dreams. Takes too long to lock up the bloody silver."

"Look, you guys get it together. You at least know the game, Riley. And Tom, like fuck you eat off anything but gold!" Laughter signaled the end of their jocularity.

"Tom, I'll need an exhibitor pass for the Contractor Fair in Dallas — one from Sentinel. I need to pick up a few hi-tech toys and I don't need to field a great deal of questions. Don't worry; I won't embarrass you or your company. I will need access to some account to buy this stuff. Viktor is going to need it as well if he's going to get things moving next week. So perhaps dump a few million pounds in an account we can write some cheques on.

"A few million pounds? Really, gentlemen we do have a budget. I'm not the bloody government."

"Just put the money in there, Tom," I retorted. "I'm not going to go over the top. I just inserted 30 killers, with equipment and supplies for the cost of a plane trip and jerseys, for fuck's sake. Viktor, when this is a go we will need weapons and identifications. The ID work ups should come complete with working credit cards, just in case. The passports can come from anyplace in the lower half of the Dark Continent."

"You want yours from there too? What kind of weapons?"

"No, have mine from Belgium, please. I want to keep it as simple as possible so nine millimeter, Heckler and Koch units. I'm thinking along the lines of thirty short-barreled suppressed MP5's with full auto available and thirty suppressed pistols. Can you get interchangeable suppression cans?"

"No, the MP5 you're describing is the short close quarter unit and the silencer is integral. Why suppress the pistol, use it only for personal defense if it goes bad."

"Good point, Viktor. I just was trying to keep as many options open as I could. On that note I want Black Talon rounds, 115 grain jacketed Teflon coated hollow points. Each machine gun has five clips and each pistol three, so I'm thinking an ammo load of 500 rounds per man. We also need two sniper systems, nothing too exotic, set and dialed in for 200 yards."

"Ok, 15,000, non-Geneva convention, rounds and an Accuracy International .338 Lapula rifle with standard mil spec optics dialed in for only 200 yards. Nothing challenging here Rhys, what about explosives?"

"I'm worried about getting them into the country really. The have tightened security and are using some state of the art gear. I don't want the whole shipment seized because of some dirty Ion sniff!"

"True, yes true. How about we place some in a propane tank used for one of the barbeques? The added smell of the sulphur dioxide should make it impossible to pick up. Vent it and then cut the top off and voila, plastic explosive and grenades."

"Great idea, Viktor. Sounds like a good option, but I wonder if there isn't something we could design that would remove having to torch a tank in two? I'm not really cool with cutting a propane tank full of grenades."

"Yeah, I'm sure there is. Let me give it to my people to work on."

"Ok, so Neil you can do the groundwork to get us a plane charter in with gear and equipment. Liaise with Tom and see how much stuff will be needed for the beer garden and the like ok? Once we decide on the jet and company, get some familiar time in the chair with her or something similar in-case we need to change plans and the staff aren't accommodating."

"Done."

"I'm going to hang around here to see if I can tell which Alphabet agency is pulling the strings and how they twigged on to us. Viktor, I'll need that identification package as soon as possible."

"At any address in the city by noon or it's free! Credit card with €25,000 prepaid. Just need to get your picture." He leaned in with his cell phone and a brief flash of the camera made Cerberus take notice. Satisfied no one had been killed he went back to his book.

"Tell us about these tails, Rhys."

"Well Tom, what I know is they are good. Very bloody good. I just happened to pick the one guy up by fluke. They are a little out of their element in the city but don't think for a second they are easy to discount. The one guy I took down for a close one on one was carrying a nice piece and fake government ID. His tattoo marked him like I described earlier as a special forces SEAL and then special contractor. I smell oil money and influence considering our target and the seriousness of the mice they sent after us. If they didn't know the target, why send these types? Doesn't make any sense does it? I think they have an idea and I'm not sure where they got the info."

"The four of us are probably tagged in some computer to alert if we get within 20 miles of each other. Not like we meet in the village well for a pint every Tuesday, right?"

"I'm not sure of the why Riley, but I do know it most likely is tagged off me and when Rhys flew in and I was in town it probably did tweak some computer model someplace. Viktor, Neil, you notice anything around you?"

"No."

"Nope, clear skies all the way. Seems to me you guys are the celebrities on this one."

"Well, I do intend to run this down a bit but it will be interesting to see if the heat pulls off me when Tom leaves. I really doubt it will but anyway we got dealt these so we got to play them. Viktor you and I will talk the end of next week, after Tom and Riley pick us up some star talent and create a media circus. Once we get that going we can pull the rest of the pieces together. I will call Sunday or Chiwa and get them staying and practicing some place quiet and out of the way that has a football pitch. Tom, I will cover the team movement and housing costs for the men. Think of it as my contribution to the effort. I'll need that Exhibitor's pass for tomorrow."

"I'll need a name for the pass — and a picture."

"I'll e-mail the one I just took"

"Viktor. That would be a rookie mistake. The same picture on his passport and pass? I don't think so."

"Right, sorry."

"Smile, Rhys," Tom leans over and takes my picture without a flash. "At least black is your colour. I need a name for the pass."

"Dick Stumpy."

"Tommy Duke."

"Give it a rest! How about Reese Forsyth? Ladies, any comments?"

"I thought you were supposed to use your first pet's name and the street you lived on?"

"That's for porn stars, ya mick bastard"

"Ok we need…"

"Contessa Odessa!"

Laughter cuts short my train of thought as Viktor bursts into a deep belly laugh. The rest of the crew joins in the laughter and for a moment forgets the daunting tasks, which are before each of us. Viktor's porn star name distracts us all from the present. It has been almost three hours and far too long for us all to be in one location. I hesitate to pull the crew back on track and catch Tom's eye across the table. We share an understanding in the brief look, we know how serious this is but we know that team cohesion is equally important. He may be a pencil pushing SAS reject but he knows teamwork. Quietly I wave for another round and the girls move in to pour, breaking the laughter by degrees, and moving us toward the next step in the process.

CHAPTER
TWENTY-EIGHT

"TOM PUT THAT IN YOUR day planner and let everyone who knows where you are now in on it — that you're going to meet me at the Café Chris tomorrow. Do you know where that is?"

"No, I don't know. Besides, I can't meet you tomorrow I've got..." he started to reply.

I cut him short.

"You're not going to meet me. You're just going to let everyone currently in the know about this meeting know about that meeting. I wanna' see who shows up. I want to see how many tails we have leaving here too. We have been here far too long than is professionally responsible and we need to wrap this shit up. Tom, tomorrow at three. Café Chris is located in the Jordaan, forty-two Blomestraat. It's one of the oldest brown cafes in town, built in 1624, tiny bathrooms too. Make sure everyone believes you're showing up for that too. You can courier my pass to my hotel. I'm using my own name. Viktor, you and I will meet up afterwards. You can reach me via my secure cell here."

I passed Viktor a card and with that simple act both confirmed something with the man and showed a bit of my hand. The card was for the Grand; it had my room number handwritten on the back. He nodded and looking directly at me put the card in his inside pocket. I watched as he settled and took a sideways look at Tom.

"We all good then?"

Nods around the table confirmed everyone was on course and ready to get the ball in play. I looked at Tom, part of me hoping he would ask where I was staying. The other part of me knowing he wouldn't, the machine part. Tom had tipped his hand twice in this meeting. The second time was obvious enough and part of me wondered if Riley and Neil had seen it. I relaxed a little knowing Tom probably sent the shadows. But what still bothered me was why Tom would be trailing his own team members. Perhaps he wasn't, perhaps it was just me. Trust wasn't a huge issue; neither of us trusted the other. But was there more to it than that? Could he be setting us up for a fall? Why? He was certainly up to something, the machine knew it. I smiled across the table at him, and as he rose I matched his movement and reached to shake his hand. He gripped my hand and pumped it hard, saying something I never heard. The machine was looking out past my eyes, visualizing the face crying for its fat nanny as a cigar burned out each of its eyes in turn.

Viktor's profile brought me back from my fantasy, and I replayed in my head what I heard Tom say. Nothing but platitudes and general social bullshit. Viktor turned to me and gave me a nod.

"I think your breaking my balls over the sub was rude."

"Oh, come on Ms. Odessa, you're not that sensitive."

Laughing, we moved over to the bar and I loudly barked for some vodka and caviar. The girls appeared and placed a fresh, chilled, bottle between Viktor and me, then quickly retreated leaving us alone.

"So, I'm to guess that Tom never knew which hotel you're staying in?"

"Bingo."

"These Eton kids are playing us, Rhys? This would be an expensive joke to play on me but it would be, how do you put it? A kick to the balls. It could make it very hard for Tom to pick up a friendly supplier on this side of the world. Makes no sense, to do it for spite or to make us look like fools. Why?"

"I'm really not sure Viktor. It has to be money and face. He has to be either trying to get one or the other."

"Perhaps both."

"Yes. Perhaps. He's running his own game here. Notice how he didn't really protest too much about the money? Not like him at all. No, he has something else up his sleeve. He's running something, I'm not sure if it's alongside us or counter to us, but I'm going to find out."

CHAPTER
TWENTY-NINE

The girls returned with two small plates. One plate had milled crackers and dark bread and the other had a small pile of very tiny black eggs. This would not be lumpfish or dyed salmon eggs. This would be Sturgeon caviar, probably the best available in Europe. Viktor looked at me and then at the tasty eggs and using a small ivory spoon scooped some onto a little cracker and popped it into his mouth, following it with the ice-cold vodka.

"It's still on Tom's tab. Tell me about this sub you're so proud of."

"Well, it's in tip top shape. I imported workers from Kalingrad to work on it as a restoration project. It was in South Korea then and it was like a holiday and labour of love for these men, some of whom had worked on the originals in the big sub yards during the cold war build up. She has been upgraded too; engines and generators are different. She has a changed final drive unit — all very plush, very expensive changes. Remember, this was for the Japanese tourist market. All very first class, the parts that were finished. She will do 12 knots on the surface and 24 submerged, and can run submerged for 500 kilometers before surfacing for air and recharging batteries. I placed a great amount of Rubles into this plan before it went tits up."

"Five hundred k on the battery? That's really something. What about range?"

"We only have five berths done forward of the command center, so could very easily weld a tank up ahead of those and increase her range to 6,000 kilometers — or more. The engines are the best Mercedes diesels money can buy and very quiet — almost on par with a nuke boat. We added new types of sound isolation baffles and traps against the hull structure on the retrofit and the final drive's primary concern

166

was stealth as we wanted to move the boat to view sea-life. There are large viewing panels on the forward lounge areas so she can't submerge past 200 meters. But with her prop and special stealth paint you'd really have to be looking for her to see her."

"Stealth paint?"

"Yes. It's a thick plastic polymer that goes on in stages. Each stage has different properties that capture, disperse, and deflect sound. It also works as a great insulator so the boat doesn't have cold walls. Well, not as cold. All very high-class. Wait, I have pictures."

With the pride of a grandparent Viktor pushed his phone at me. There on the screen was a photo of the interior of a very plush lounge. I looked at him and then back to the screen.

"It's a picture from my secure website, just push your finger across the screen like turning a page."

The sweeping motion brought up a different, large exterior shot. This thing was huge, dwarfing the large trucks in the picture's foreground. The next shot showed a command bridge, but very un-Russian like. Gone was the frugal, sparse functionality of Russian war design. This bridge looked like something out of a science fiction movie. The center captain's chair was red and his cage chrome with computer displays everywhere. I turned the page and the engine room came into view, followed by the large battery banks dropped down into the lower hull area.

"Why didn't this project get off the ground Viktor? This looks like an incredible boat."

"Superstition. The Japanese are a very superstitious lot and the accident and subsequent drama that played out after the incident near Hawaii just wouldn't go away. Every media event came with at least two questions about the incident or curse and our investors pulled out. I was able to keep enough to mothball her and do routine maintenance but I'm afraid it's like indulging an addict you love. Eventually the hole that lets the water in cannot be plugged."

"Just out of curiosity how much were you going to offer it to Tom for?"

"€19,000,000. Crewed and delivered to a safe port after the hostilities. Why? You thinking about playing Captain Nemo off your home coast?"

"Perhaps,Viktor. It would be in a salesman's best interest not to

mock the dreams of others if one wants to sell a cigar tube for anything
other than scrap."

I said it lightly with the hint of a grin, while scooping some fish
eggs into my mouth.

"Well in that case my friend-price would be $17 million colourful
Canadian dollars. Delivered and crewed. Believe me with the current
economy in the Balkans the crew would pay you to stay."

"I shall keep that in mind my friend."

CHAPTER THIRTY

The others had left as Viktor and I talked and laughed. Most left with a quiet wave or a slap on the back. Tom, however, had moved to his lawyer's table and had the mouthpiece feverishly scribbling notes. Then he got up and went to pay the bill and shot Viktor and I a look that communicated both his common ancestry and his inability to adapt. Tom was worth millions now yet he still held on to that working class frugality. Despite wishing to be part of the finer circles of the British system he had failed to adapt his behaviour to fit in.

He left, his lawyer in tow, giving me a polite wave, his lawyer never so much as glancing in our direction. A few clients had come in and taken up positions in the corners of the room. Like people entering an elevator moving to take up a position and secure their small area of privacy.

"Viktor, it has been great to see you again my friend. Just out of curiosity how long would it take you to, in a panic, to get your sub feet wet?"

"Hmm? To sea? Five days. To build a tank upfront, test, and fill. Ten. You're thinking Rhys. It's been my experience you do this contingency thinking when you feel cornered. Do you feel cornered my friend?"

"Yeah. I guess I do Viktor. I'm starting to feel like the flashy bit of bait one uses to catch old fish like this." Gesturing to the depleted caviar.

"Tom is a 'maskarova' or you would say 'smoke and mirrors' specialist. But I don't think he's going to be purposely malicious. I do not think you have children but it's like them when they tell you everything but in truth tell you nothing. Do you have anyone in your life my friend? War is such an unsatisfying mistress and hardly makes for a long-term relationship."

"I don't know if I share your assessment of Tom. I think he's a little more cagey than people give him credit for. He's not stupid. He lacks creativity and adaptability, but I think he hires others that posses these qualities. My life? No, Viktor — no one in my life I wouldn't walk away from in thirty seconds or less."

"You should take steps to change that my friend. The eve of our lives is not someplace to be alone. But enough of me playing grandfather. You have shadows to hunt I think."

"Yes I do. Have a good night and a safe journey home. We'll talk soon."

Viktor smiled and tapped my shoulder as he stood. He turned and walked past the length of bar and skirting Cerberus walked to the door. Cerberus looked up from his book at the sound of the door closing and then over to me as I approached him.

"Thank you for being appropriate in my bar, it looked at times like that was a difficult thing and I thank you for your discretion."

"I thought it was a cordial meeting, Cerberus," I replied.

"Sure, it appeared that way Rhys. But when you look at the world through this," he explained as he pointed to his dead eye, "you see things many others don't see. He's a snake and a coward. But you already know this."

"Sure do, Cerberus, but thanks for the confirmation."

I called the last bit over my shoulder as I walked over and pulled open the heavy door. I turned right onto the street and started walking and scanning pulling out the shadow I knew with the certainty one has looking in a mirror was out there. It took me only ten paces to find the first one. There should be more. At the corner I picked up the second one. He made the mistake of looking directly at me and then up to the sky as if some celestial body had just caught his attention. This one was a rookie and, like a leopard separating a weak calf from the herd, I set my plan of attack into motion.

I walked in the direction of the train station. Even at this hour the area would be packed with arriving and departing tourists and backpackers waiting for friends. The machine watched, tracked, and never lost sight of the easy kill for a moment. The other shadow was a great deal better and it wasn't till we had walked a mile or better that I got a good look at his face. It was the same shadow from last night. I guessed his regular partner was either laid up in the hospital or still explaining the gun. So was this rookie his replacement or from another team entirely?

I had to get back to my hotel room to make the call I needed to make in comfort and privacy. But I also needed more information. Now that I had a baseline of intelligence and could be certain I would get more information than my target. I was almost certain they were working for Tom or at the very least with Tom.

The party atmosphere got more pronounced the closer I got to the train station. This made if more and more difficult for my tails to remain at a discrete distance yet be reasonably certain they wouldn't loose me in the crowd. The shadow from last night was staying to my left and had made the unfortunate mistake of wearing a distinctive lime green ball cap. I reached a set of lights and saw the familiar yellow-clad police walking squad. I edged closer to one of the female officers and said, in perfect Flemish,

"I'm a police officer from Belgium and that man over to my left in the grey jacket and bright green hat looked to me to be on our terrorist "watch for" list. When I got close to him by the entrance to the park I noticed a gun under his arm. Now I think he's following me. I'm going to the train station."

The light changed and I stepped off in the direction of the train station and watched the well-oiled machine of the Amsterdam police move in. The shadow was forced to watch me far too closely in the partying crowd and missed the increased police presence until it was much too late.

I watched from a bench as four officers moved in from behind in a perfect right and left flank maneuver they cornered him, weapons drawn and on target. He shot a look my way that screamed revenge and then defeated sank to his knees, hands on top of his head. Now it was time to isolate my prey and take him down.

I had to run a bit of a buttonhook to avoid the police who wanted to follow up. In the crowd it was as simple as turning back into the group and cutting across the park. The night was still early but each bench had an occupant in some form of intoxication, from mild to dead or at least as close as you can get and still come back. How did the Jim Carroll line go?

"It ain't cool to sink that low unless your gonna' make a resurrection."

CHAPTER
THIRTY-ONE

My mind was caught in the free associative routine it did after a structured meeting or situation requiring strict form and attention. Now, caught like in a drug of its own creation, it chased thoughts and ideas across the landscape as I avoided the police and carefully kept my prey on the hook.

I crossed the road again and saw a cigar store. The tip of my tongue curled as if I was going to whistle at a pretty girl. But my desire right now was for tobacco. The reek of the pot had been strong in the park and a brief stop and costume change would give me a little more police invisibility. The female police officer had got a good look at me, yet that would be hard to convey to the rest of the foot patrols, but a hat would make it so much more difficult.

I pulled the old door open and was greeted by a bell, not some electronic beep. This was promising. An elderly man, smoking a pipe, greeted me.

"Can I help you, sir?"

"Yes, you can, my good sir," I replied in my best baroque English. It seemed appropriate to the setting and his attire.

"Cuban, short Churchill, or larger Robusto. With all the pot my nose is feeling perfectly set upon."

"I totally understand, sir. I have just what you need. I have some 2006 Partagas No. 2s. Not quite as thick as you'd like, but are smoking great right now." He went to the small humidor and pulled out a box and offered it. I checked the box code, opened it and inhaled deeply. They smelled perfect and I felt the addiction side of my hobby wrap a cold hand around my lower spine.

"Perfect. I'll take four and that black ball cap there that says Habanos Brothers."

I clipped the one cigar and looked out the storefront, as the older man rang up my purchases. My shadow was across the street was trying very hard not to get caught up in some dancing that had spontaneously broken out around him. His efforts were not meeting with the approval of the crowd. By the look on his face I saw he was used to having people fear him. The situation frustrated him.

"May I?" I asked as I started to light my purchase.

"Officially, no sir, but I only have to tell you that. You don't have to listen."

He slid an antique lighter toward me and I lit the cigar.

"€34.40, sir."

I put €40 into his old hand and watched as he deftly made the money disappear and make change. The cigar was rich and creamy and the taste of it mixed with the scent of the old man's floral pipe smell. The outcome and mingling aroma were perfect.

"Enjoy sir, that hat looks good," he said to my back as the little bell announced my departure.

At the sound of the bell, Shadow looked directly at me. This boy was really poor at this. I walked directly for the train station now, taking care to not lose him. This was actually proving more difficult than I expected, as there were more people in the streets now than just minutes ago. I walked and enjoyed the scent of the cigar and its ability to mask the unpleasant skunk pot, mixed with crushed dog shit scent.

The train station is an ancient squat building and fills more function than it does form, in the buildings it shares the block with. I walked up the stairs to the front entrance and saw shadow literally run to close the distance. This man was following me like a waiter trying to chase down a patron that has dropped his wallet. Amazing.

I entered the building and wandered over to the washroom. I took care to catch a reflection of shadow and insure he saw me. I went in, washed my hands and entered a stall. The washroom was very busy. Without removing anything I slipped my hands inside my jacket and checked my pistol was still off safe, and the knifes were as I left them. Satisfied, I slipped on my black sap gloves and left the stall. I walked past the line of people at the urinal and out the door. Shadow was sitting on a bench using a day-old Dutch paper for cover. I thought this was getting comical.

I walked directly at him and then veered off quickly, increasing my pace in both speed and distance. I looked up in the many reflecting surfaces and was surprised to see him rise to the bait. This guy was past green. I moved quickly through the train station and out the back, to the automated boats. These boats run back and forth across the canal, ferrying lots of guests and locals alike. The whole organized chaos is controlled by a single command, as the boats are captain less crafts. There is always a crowd as new users interact with seasoned riders and not in a good way. I vault the directing railing and dash into a departing boat. Shadow does the same thing and surprisingly ends up on the same vessel.

What the man lacked in experience he made up for in ability. I chastised myself for making the assumption he would be easy because of his ineptness. He lacked skill, that was all. I moved to the doors and waited for them to open. The boat bobbed and rocked its way across the canal, the city lights and stars mixing on the waters surface as though dabbed there by an artist's brush.

The bump of the dock on the far shore signaled part two of the chase, and endgame for Mr. Shadow. Or so I hoped. The doors opened and I was off ahead of the crowd, moving like I was twenty minutes late for a 10th anniversary dinner. Shadow moved quickly behind me. I exited up onto the street and made for the darker side. We were in an area rarely frequented by most travelers and even more so at night. It was an area that catered to the darker souls desires, and in a city such as this, dark was probably the wrong word. I saw the narrow alley and widened my pace a little more and then dove head long down the alley. In a full sprint I allowed the machine to spread out, looking for a tactical advantage. I found it. Two large garbage bins with bags left in front. The next corner was only thirty feet away. Perfect. I poured on the speed and grabbed a bag and heaved it, overhand, toward the corner, the toss going high and buying me time as I ducked between the two garbage bins and behind the bags.

I heard the smash of the bag as it hit the ground in a muffled crash. The footsteps increased to my left, and I heard the muffled curse uttered under his breath. The footsteps raced toward the corner in an all-out sprint. My leg swung in a vicious arc and the impact sound and shadow's breath raced each other to the corner without their master.

Shadow's knees and elbows touched and he executed a good shoulder roll in a failing attempt to regain his footing. I closed on him quickly and stomped the back of his neck into the unyielding pavement. The click of teeth chased the previous racers and Shadow was unconscious and, unfortunately, pissing his pants.

I looked at the buildings and tried to pick something that would not likely be alarmed. Finding nothing, I swore as I dragged Shadow into the darkness and cover provided by the bins against the building wall. Fuck, I couldn't very well torture the man here! I couldn't even be sure I could ask him a question. I checked Shadow's level of consciousness and, certain it would be a while, ran to the corner. There was a residential street and nothing close by but quiet houses. Running back to Shadow I was once again impressed by his resilience. He was clutching his side aware that his ribs were broken. He was regaining consciousness far quicker than I would have liked. Damn, there wasn't time to play this out.

I scooped out his pockets and placed the contents into an empty pocket in my jacket. I patted him down and located a razor and knife. His I.D. showed him to be Derek Olsen. Nothing official, and various cards that seemed to be legitimate. Credit cards needed scratches and wear to make them appear real and these ones had just that. There was even an old picture of a little girl holding a puppy in some Rockwell-like dust town in the American Midwest. A trident tattoo on his inner right forearm suggested SEAL, and from his physical attributes his retirement had not been that long ago.

I screwed the silencer onto the end of the gun and placed the barrel to the back of the guy's head. Pull the trigger and I get nothing. Perhaps it was worth the risk. Worse case scenario, I would have to kill a few cops and make the whole thing looked like a botched robbery. It was worth the risk. I turned the barrel to the lock bolt and pulled the trigger. The lock bolt fired in, leaving a hole in the old wood. I slipped my gloved finger into the hole and physically pulled the throw out of the catch on the doorjamb. The door swung inward and there was no alarm.

I grabbed Shadow and drug him inside the ruined door. I closed it and then looked for a light switch. The pale light didn't really reach to the corners of the room but it was enough to reveal a storage room holding nothing much more than the dust of a few years. There were no windows back into the alley and only another door at the end of the room. I turned my attention to Shadow Derek Olsen.

Reaching down I took the pinkie finger on his right hand and snapped it backward at the first knuckle. His eyes shot open the pain cutting through the fog his mind was wrapped in.

"Morning, Mr. Olsen. Glad you could join the party. We're going to have a little Q and A session. I have to be honest here: the chances of you seeing Kansas, the dog, and the chick aren't very good. But, what you really need to focus on here is your cooperation determines whether I go see them!"

"Fuck you!"

"Circumcised, Mr. Olsen?" The weapon bounces in my hand as the round rips the seam of Shadows jeans. The round finds flesh and Olsen's screaming increases past his bravado grin. The pain searing him before the question has a chance for his brain to answer.

"What the fuck! You can't torture me, I'm a US citizen, you stupid fucking..."

The two rounds shatter his knees in rapid succession. His hand reaches to provide the ruined joints some comfort. Eyes blinking at the mush that once supported him, fingers crudely mocking him as he reflexively clutches the oozing pulp of blood and bone. A moaning drone escapes his lips as he begins to rock like an autistic child, senses shutting down in a vain attempt to escape the pain.

"Hey! Olsen! Stay with me. It's really important to the little lady in the picture you stay with me. Now you know I can torture you, and you know I don't like being called stupid. In fact Olsen you're the stupid fuck that brought a retard to a prizefight. I got all night to bring you new places in pain. But I would really rather go for a drink, so why don't you tell me the details so I can put a bullet in your head and end this."

"Please don't kill me! They know I was following you. They'll know you killed me! They'll come after you." The round-fired from directly above Derek's shoulder forces apart the joint, breaking the clavicle and the humourous at the same time. It continues down the bone, rolling the muscle in front of it, before tearing open the skin just before the elbow. The muscle, no longer attached, causes the bicep to contract, bringing the hand up and rubbing the broken ends of the clavicle together. Derek screams and rolls over onto his right side and into the fetal position. Sucking air past his emptying stomach he tries to catch his breath.

"Derek, you're dead! I don't care if your *they* come after me. What you need to be aware of is this: if I don't get the answers I want I'm going to do this to your little girl, and her little fucking dog too."

"Erin!" his eyes widened in horror.

"That her name? Erin?"

"Yeah. Erin. Please leave her alone, leave me alone."

"Sure, Derek. I can leave you all alone, you just need to tell me all about who hired you and why, and what your plan was."

"Gonna kill me anyway."

"Yes, yes I am Derek, because you're sloppy and took on a job you shouldn't have. But your kid lives. I have to ask you again. No answer now, she dies quickly, anything past that she takes days. You getting me, Derek? This is all about her future, not yours. I don't believe in God, I just arrange appointments for him."

"Okay, okay. Enterprise Oil hired me; they're on the side with Sentinel working on some project. I don't know what project. I just know they wanted you followed and reported on. It was a last minute thing, I was going home, home to my kid…" His sobbing stops the forward progression of the monologue. I prod his shoulder lightly.

"Go on Derek, names, places, times"

"I don't know the other guy's names. There are SEALs, too but they work for the CIA. Well, most times, but this time Enterprise has command and control and when one of them got run over they asked me to divert here from a rig security gig to baby-sit you. The other guy was supposed to be on you tonight too. We were supposed to pick you up at the Russian place and see who you met and where you went and with whom. I asked why but they just told me to follow you and I heard the Sentinel name but other than that I don't know anything"

Derek was lying on his side, talking into his chest between sobs. I believed him. He was telling the truth. He knew nothing past what he told me. The round punched a dark hole directly behind the shiny little diamond stud earring that proclaimed him alternative. There was nothing alternative about his death. The hollow point never exited his head, remaining in the skull, bouncing away his life.

I carefully checked the area for anything I might have dropped. I found nothing out of place. I flipped off the light and stood in the dark, alone with the wasted body of Derek Olsen. There were no cold spots and no phantom touches. There was only the copper smell of blood and the faint stink of shit. This time it wasn't from the leashed crap machines outside.

I emerged back into the alley and walked back the way I had come. I looked for video cameras and let the machine scan for danger. Finding neither I exited the alley and turned left on the street. Pulling out another cigar I lit it to mask the stink of Derek's passing.

CHAPTER THIRTY-TWO

I HAD TO KILL DEREK. He would have been able to confirm it had been me asking him questions. He could have died by many other hands. The area of the city was a rough one and he could have been a victim of one of the many predators in the area. He really did sign up for a game he was ill equipped to engage in. It was a waste of life; a waste of a bullet. He reminded me of so many of the contractors who thought they could operate in the African bush or jungle. The Australian operators were more suited than some of the British and American players. At least in Australia the bush was as dangerous as the African one. The bush was, most of the time, more dangerous than the bullets. Spiders, snakes and larger predators watched you all the time looking for prey or trying to scare you away from their prey or home. It was just the way things were, nothing personal you're just food.

I crossed the Walloon district and headed for my hotel. I needed a bath and some down time. I could feel my nerves, raw and alive, like a cut thrust into salt water. The sting was more all over but sharp nonetheless. Yes, a bath and a large cool drink and another cigar would be just the thing before making the calls. Calls to two very different women, calls that would illuminate two very different issues.

The lights of the Grand reached out and up into the night. Reflections danced along the canal and I could see the security types were still in the main parking area of the bastion-like hotel. I walked onto the lot and made directly for the door. I could feel the eyes of the security men pick me up as palpably as rain. They reached for radios and transferred their thoughts and ideas to the others. I was carrying myself like a professional and realized it too late. The detail had picked up on it right away and relayed it to those inside. I caught my look in the reflection in the large glass doors and the day's activity had not been kind to me. I looked hard and the challenges of the day had stained my appearance. While there was no physical blood on my face, a professional knew it had seen and spilt blood that day. The scent of the spent round would be on my hands and clothes and I doubted the cigar would have covered it completely. No I really didn't want to bump into this security detail, and yet in all likelihood I would.

The doorman opened the door for me and I watched three sentinels detach from the wall and move. They came toward me and I saw the gold level concierge walking through the lobby with a large manila envelope. I knew in a service industry, especially one of this level, I need not raise my voice too high.

"Good evening." She turned her head slightly and seeing me stopped. The sentinels were still moving in.

"Mr. Munroe, I was just coming up to see you. You received an urgent package and I was just going to deliver it."

I joined her in the lobby, standing far too close, and asked her if she'd mind talking while we walked, walking toward the elevators before she could answer. I saw the hem of her skirt dig tightly into her thighs as she stretched the fabric to catch up with me.

"Sure Mr. Munroe, I hope everything is ok."

"Well, the added security types are a bit of a pain as they seem to target anyone not in a wheelchair."

"Sorry sir. Yes. There have been complaints from other guests as well." The two sentinels either had heard this or were reading lips as they stopped and moved back to their perches.

We reached the elevator. I gestured for her to enter first and, despite the mirrors, let my eyes drop to her well-proportioned bottom. I knew she would see me but I wanted her to remember something other than my scent. The day's activities coupled with the lack of deodorant this morning had surely conspired to make my body odor go a little over the top. I entered and pretended to reach for the button I knew she would have already pressed on her side. I took the liberty to check the mirror lined walls with my peripheral vision and was surprised to see her checking me out.

We rode up in silence and to my surprise; saw more security on this floor. I let her walk in front of me and noted a significant increase in the sway of her hips. There must be some truth to that pheromone thing.

I followed her out like the cover she was and while security picked me up they didn't move to intercede. I had a hotel escort now.

She walked the entire way to my hotel room in silence and without a word swiped her card to open my door and to my surprise walked in and held it open for me. I walked in and she let the door close. Now it was her turn to stand too close to me. She held the package that she had been carrying to me and stepped in.

"Mr. Munroe, I take excellent care of all my clients on the Club floor. I'm concerned you aren't enjoying the hotel because of our Royal guest. You didn't sleep here last night and I certainly hope it was because you found something fun, and not because you felt your privacy had been impinged upon."

"Well, I didn't find anything that much fun but I did have a little too much fun and stayed with friends in the Jordaan. The security thing is not that much of a bother."

"Well," She leaned in closer and I could feel the weight of her breasts touch my chest. "If you need anything at all, I'm at your disposal and all you need to do is pick up the phone."

"I'll remember that." I placed the package on the desk and slung my jacket on the back of the chair.

"Excellent. May I turn down your bed?"

"Actually, I'm going to have a bath first, and a cigar. I need to relax and get cleaned up. I've been in thee clothes all day."

She moved toward the bathroom and the tub. "There is no smoking in these suites Mr. Munroe, but I'm sure I can persuade the chamber ladies to overlook your vice."

I followed behind her and watched as she bent at the waist and turned on the taps, testing the water on her wrist like a mother tests a bottle of milk. Her thigh length skirt rose deliciously up her strong thighs. Satisfied the water was the correct temperature she reached low into the tub and set the drain to hold the water. In doing so she exposed the tops of her stockings, the darker fabric holding the light material firm to her tanned thighs. She finished with the tub and walked over and opened the high window I had opened on my first night and went across the room and cracked the other window.

"There, that should create a nice cross-breeze and suck the smoke out." She walked back to me and stopped about a foot away. "Do you want me to get these clothes laundered?"

I was enjoying this little flirt session. I wondered what she would do if I said yes. Would it be awkward? Would it be more so if I said no? I decided on fun, she was being very subservient and seemed to like it. I felt I could play along.

"Yes, and please call me, Rhys. Should I put them in the laundry bag and hang them outside on the door?"

She reached for my chest. "No need to do that, Rhys." She started deftly unbuttoning my shirt. Her hands were steady, but her pupils were wide and her neck was flushing.

"Did you know, the reason men's buttons are backwards to ladies is so it's easier for us to remove them? When a page would tend to his master the backward placement made it simple and easier for the page. The practice is lost now except among nobility. You're not a noble are you, Sir Rhys?"

"Not the last time I checked."

"No, not with a hard body like this."

She had undone my shirt and had pulled it free from my waistband and was now running a warm hand down my chest and stomach.

"No, you're more like a gladiator aren't you, Sir Rhys?"

"Well I…" She stopped me by pressing the finger of her other hand to my lips.

"Empty your pockets on the dresser. You won't want me to wash your wallet."

I took out my wallet and placed it on the black walnut dresser. Taking great pains to try and keep the knife behind the wad of Euros in my front pocket, I set it down on the top of the dark wood.

"Shoes."

I slipped out of my shoes and she bent to pick them up and took them to the door. With the diversion I pulled the other knife out of my pocket and slid it into my jacket pocket.

She returned and reached around me from behind. Her breasts pushed into my back as her hands undid my belt and then the top button of my pants. They fell to the floor around my ankles, removing the modesty they had provided just seconds before. Her hands slipped into the waistband of my boxers at my hips. Strong hands sliding over my hips onto the tops of my thighs.

"Don't want to be indelicate here, sir. Shall I?"

"Yes."

With her thumbs bringing the waist band forward she slid the boxers down my legs. As I stepped out of them her hand came to rest on my butt.

"Left"

I raised my left foot and she took off my sock.

"Right"

I repeated the motion and she did the same.

She walked across the room leaving me standing there and went into the bathroom to check the tub.

"Sir Rhys, your bath is ready."

Walking a little nervously I adjusted my slightly hardening cock and walked into the bath. She was standing at the head of the bath looking at me unashamed and appraisingly.

"Get in while it's hot. That draft is cooler than I thought it would be."

I slipped into the warm bath and felt a little more comfortable with the modest amount of coverage the water provided.

"Are your cigars in the case I saw on the bed stand?"

"Yes."

She left the room and the warm water soaked deliciously into my skin and washed away the smells of the day. I put my head back and thought how was this going to play out? I heard the door open and close and was a little surprised at my reaction. She was done? Our little flirt, master and page scenario was done? Damn.

The door opened once again and I once again thought about what was coming.

She re-entered the bath and held in one hand a glass full of ice and liquid and in the other a Monte petite Edmundo, another from my special traveling humidor.

"Vodka on ice?"

"Please."

She handed me the drink and then with practiced hands felt the cigar for plugs, deftly squeezing and rolling it between her long fingers. Satisfied, she took out the cutter from her pocket and clipped the tip perfectly, as practiced as a Jewish surgeon.

"Do you mind my mouth on your cigar, Sir Rhys?" She asked, while looking directly at my submerged cock.

"Not at all, be my guest."

She placed the cigar in her mouth and brought the flame to the tip. She sucked at the stick, exaggerating each pull until the tip was glowing red and a nice cloud of sweet smoke filled the bathroom.

"Nice." She handed me the lit cigar and went over to the sink. Picking up my shampoo she returned to my side.

"May I?"

"Certainly."

"I have to take my top and skirt off as I don't want to splash any water on them as they are silk. Is that ok, Sir Rhys?"

"I would be delighted"

She walked to the end of the tub and turned her back to me. Reaching behind her she slid the zipper of her skirt down and holding it bent to take it off. Her gorgeous ass was framed at the top by black lace and a thin string split the cheeks. She stepped to the wall and hung it up on the hook beside one of the bathrobes. She turned and started unbuttoning her blouse. The small panty barely covered her and accented her form in the most exquisite fashion. She was obviously European, preferring a natural trimmed look and her pouty sex was clearly visible. I felt myself reacting to the show. She finished with her blouse and slipped it off. She wasn't wearing a bra. Her perfect breasts hung down and forward in a surprisingly natural swoop. The large areola, and nipples puckered hard. I couldn't take my eyes off the display.

"I see Sir Rhys finds me pleasing." Her hand dragged a line across the water as she returned to my head.

She pushed my head under the water with a gentle pressure and then added some shampoo to her hand and began rubbing it into my head. The feeling was total bliss and I relaxed and drank and smoked my cigar. She continued rubbing and cleaning my body moving down my neck and to each arm in turn. She stood over me and let her beautiful tits swing inches from my face and she scrubbed my chest and stomach, her fingers stopping right at my hips. My cock was fully erect and I longed to have her touch me. I tried unsuccessfully to capture a nipple in my mouth and she giggled with the failed attempt. She moved to the end of the tub and sat at the end with her legs spread along the edges the cheeks of her ass balanced on the end.

"Leg."

I raised my right leg and she caught my foot and placed it on her thigh and began rubbing my feet. I thought I had been relaxed but this new treat made the knots in my lower back and buttocks unwind as if a boy scout had untied them. I stared into the lovely light material that was stretched tight against her and longed to push the material to the side with my tongue. The ice had melted in my vodka and the cigar was smoking perfectly. My reverie was broken sweetly.

"Other leg."

I raised my other leg and was once again treated to an amazing foot and calf massage with my rough foot resting on her soft warm thigh.

"Sir Rhys," She called pulling me from an almost dream-like state. "Is there a Mrs. or Ms. in your life?"

"Ah well yes, but I don't know if it's serious."

"Well then, my own personal rule is it has to stop here."

I was crestfallen. I wanted this woman badly and was aroused past the point of turning back. But part of me thought of Andrea and I really didn't want any secrets between us. I lived with far too many of them and if there were a chance she and I would continue with a relationship part of me agreed. I hated that part!

She got off the edge of the tub and calmly and wordlessly toweled herself off as I watched. She slipped back into her blouse and did each button up as I watched, wishing she would stop and hoping she didn't. She slipped back into her skirt and zipped it shut right before my eyes. Then she reached up underneath and slipped her panties off. Fixing me with a wanting look she walked back to the head of the tub and placed them over the side. She bent and kissed me full on the lips.

"I'm sure those will help, you seem to have well enough in hand." With a sly grin she walked out of the bathroom and I heard the door close as she let herself out.

CHAPTER THIRTY-THREE

THE TUB RELAXATION WAS GOOD but I sit knowing I have two calls to make. The kind of calls I never make. But this has been a week of changes. I look at the phone as I towel off. Who to call first? I guess I should be prudent and call South Africa first before it gets too late. The no calls after ten rule firmly driven home. I picked up the phone and scrolled through the address book to find the number. I pushed the number and heard the call ring through.

It was picked up on the second ring.

"Hello?"

"Hello Countess. If you recognize the voice please don't say my name."

"Uh yes, yes of course I know who this is. I don't give my private cell to too many men. How are you?"

"I'm good, really good actually. Just thought I would call and see how life is and say I might be in the area in a day or two."

"Really? You're coming to the Cape, excellent! I have good news, ah um ok my husband's ex racing partner is working with, ah some lubricant types to get him out of his contract."

"U.S. types?"

"Yes. It looks really promising He's in good spirits and we're hoping for between two weeks to a month."

"That fast. That's really good news Countess. Well, I won't keep you, but I will be sure to give you a call when I'm in town. Probably Thursday, ok?"

"That's great. I'll wait for your call."

"Good sleep."

"You too, my gentleman caller."

I heard her laugh to herself as she hung up the phone. I waited. No click. Not that it meant anything; another click would have meant something. It had been a risk to call her, to tell her I was coming into town. But I had to know. Now I was glad I had. That fucking snake Tom was playing both ends toward the middle. Hedging his bets like he hedged his investments. To Tom they were one and the same.

So, he was working with the US agency. They probably had tagged me all the way from Vancouver. Obviously oil, and with deep connections into the spook store. It had to be Enterprise Oil. They were brokering a deal to get at the clean, rich crude. Probably getting a great concession and Tom was going to get Simon out via that route or our route. The problem was he had compromised us from the starting gate. If this deal got brokered while we were in country then it could go very bad for us. He would have to tip the apple cart to insure he stayed spotless on the deal. What a fucking snake!

Before I made the next call I had to call Viktor. I looked at the manila envelope and picked it up. I ripped it open and found in the middle: two complete identities, credit cards, and a note.

"Here is one Belgium and one Russian identity. I figured you might need a second one. The credit limits are fifty thousand each and are clear cards. I would take it as a great favor if you didn't burn these identities, as I would like to use the Russian one again. Please pay the credit cards off if you can so I can keep the passports active and not flagged for fraud. I figured two would be good considering what Tom is doing.

Your Friend, Viktor"

I picked up my phone and called Viktor's cell.

"Hey, you know who this is, right?"

"Da."

"Ok. Look, I have the goods on what our little snake is doing and I have a play to run of our own. Think you can stand the heat?"

"Da."

"Ok, you know that pleasure craft you were talking about? What would you say if I could get exclusive offshore rights for whomever you gave the nod to?"

"I'd say you're cooking with more than Sterno. What's my exposure? Ah, how would you say, commitment?"

"You'd need to crew it and get it up to say the place we had dinner and the waiter dropped your drink. I'll personally cover $200,000 Cdn. either way it goes."

"$200,000 Cdn. for both ways if it goes bad?"

"Done."

"I hope you know what you're doing?"

"I do, but I want an option if egotard pulls a fast one. Night."

"Goodnight comrade."

I doubted we would need the boat, but I doubted Tom more. I was certain he was going to hang us out to dry and in one perfect swoop, play us off for his reputation and make himself look like the good guy. Not in my world, and this most certainly was my world!

The next call waited, the cell phone looking at me like an evil box not to be played with. I had never called 'home'. I had never had anyone at home to call. The idea of just leaving and not talking to Andrea was unsettling. More over it was wrong. Nothing about our relationship, shit I was thinking of it, as a relationship now, was normal. But I liked very much what we had started. I looked at the phone. If I invited her to come stay a few days in Amsterdam she might come. It would be safe as I was pretty sure I had enough pull to get her another room under my new assumed Russian identity and card. She would enjoy the city and since I was paying for this suite anyway it seemed better than a bunch of flowers. The phone and I debated in silent deliberation. I picked it up.

"Hello?"

"Hey Andrea, how is it going?"

"Ah well, ok. Is everything alright?"

Fuck, that hadn't started well!

"Yeah, everything is fine, but I'm running off and I can't get a refund on the room so I was wondering if you'd like to have fun in Amsterdam for the week."

Great now I sounded like a cheap fuck!

"I have classes, Rhys."

Sorry that didn't come out right. What I'm saying is I have to jet out tomorrow. If you hop a plane tonight at 7 you'll be here tomorrow and if I remember correctly you don't have classes on Thursday. All you'll skip is Friday. I'll fly you first class so you can sleep both ways and be ready for class Monday morning. Think of all the research you can do. You can eat all your meals at the hotel so it won't cost you anything."

"Well, I don't have any tests or anything. You don't have to do this Rhys. I'm ok waiting for you and what about Ruben?"

"I know I don't, but I want to. Ruben will be good till Linda comes to clean the house on Friday. Come. You'd have a good time."

"Ok. Twist my rubber arm. I have never even been on an overseas flight. How do I get the ticket?"

"You call the limo and tell him to add it to my tab and I'll have the ticket waiting for you to pick up at the British Airways counter. Just go to the first class section and ask. They'll take care of you."

"Ok, I'll 'jet' to Europe on your dime and have fun, but I wish it was with you."

"Next time. How is your name spelled on your passport?"

I collected the details and wrote them down on the stationery pad near the phone, and rang off. She sounded so excited. It made me feel … Yeah it made me feel good. I caught a reflection of myself as I dialed British Air and waited to make the arrangements.

"This doesn't feel like thirty seconds or less," I scolded myself.

The arrangements were made and paid for on my company Visa card. The "travel writer account" I kept for such purposes should provide enough security. I took the pad I had written on and tore off another four sheets and took them into the bathroom. Lighting my second cigar of the evening I touched the flame to the papers and tossed them into the toilet. I dialed Andrea again.

"Hello?"

"You're set. I will have a limo at the airport to pick you up and bring you to the hotel. The reservation will be under your name and I'll leave a message for you with things you must see and places to avoid."

"Cool Rhys, I'm so excited. The limo's going to be here in an hour, I want to be early so I can pick up a couple of things I'll need at the airport."

Her enthusiasm was infectious and I managed a laugh.

"Take advantage of the lounges and let them know this is your first time so they take care of you. In London you may have to transfer to another terminal. That shit can get confusing so ask the flight attendant for help."

"Ok, I will," she replied, sounding slightly out of breath.

"Have fun and sweet dreams at 50,000 feet."

"Oh my God, I'll need to get one of those mask things to sleep on the plane."

"No, you don't. Everything will be provided. Wear comfortable clothes and pack light, you're allowed two carry-ons and I would suggest using only that. I have two spares in my office closet. Just make sure they are completely empty, check all the pockets, ok?"

"Ok Rhys. Thanks, this is so fucking cool. Oops, sorry."

"Fucking rights it is. Enjoy it. 'Night."

"Bye" she returned brightly and hung up.

CHAPTER THIRTY-FIVE

I NEEDED A DIRECT FLIGHT to South Africa. British Air would take me through London. I flipped open the laptop and looked for a direct flight. I was pretty sure KLM had a direct flight from Amsterdam and I was right, flight 0591 left at 10:30 in the morning. It went straight to Jo Berg or Temba as it was now called. I called KLM direct to see if there was space available on that flight in first class. There was. Then I called Darius.

"Darius, I need you at the Grand at 8:30 tomorrow morning until about noon. Can you do it?"

"Not a problem. I'll be there."

"See you tomorrow."

"Right."

The house phone rang. I pushed "end" on the cell and looked at the phone again. It rang once more. Perhaps my concierge had lost her morals on the trip down in the elevator.

"Hello, Mr. Munroe. Sorry, I know it's late, but I have a David Archer who wishes to speak with you."

"Is he alone?"

"Yes, sir"

"Does he look American?"

"Yes he does."

"Send him up."

"And sir, there was a package delivered just now. Shall I send it up with the porter?"

"Yes, please have the porter escort Mr. Archer up, and bring the package."

Who the hell was David Archer and how had he traced me back to the hotel? He wasn't police or at least it wasn't an official visit as there would have been no advance warning. I tugged on a fresh shirt and pair of pants and put the pistol under the pillow on the bed. I looked around the room and finding nothing that would tip my hand got set to receive Mr. David Archer.

There was a knock on the door. I opened it to find a short porter holding an envelope and a tall, thin man carrying a briefcase. The porter handed me the envelope and stepped aside.

"Mr. Archer, good to see you again. Come in."

"Thank you, Mr. Munroe. Please call me David."

Archer entered the room and looked around, obviously impressed with its size. I watched the porter disappear down the hall while tracking Archer.

"Have a seat. You don't mind if I smoke do you?" He didn't wait for a reply.

"Can I get you a drink? I offered. Vodka, or something from the mini bar."

"Vodka is fine."

His voice was curt but polite. He obviously wasn't armed, as he opened his jacket when he sat down. He placed the briefcase to the left of his chair as I poured two drinks from the open bottle of vodka.

"To what do I owe the pleasure of your visit, David?"

"Well, I wish to avoid anymore staffing issues. Human Resources get pissed when I have to make the kind of calls I've had to make tonight. But you would have no knowledge of this, would you Rhys?"

"Nope. Not at all, someone call in sick?"

"Yes. One sick. Really sick. The other is resting with a fractured hip and skull. My substitute is in police custody answering questions. Embarrassing questions. You could say it has been one hell of a week."

"Sorry to hear that. I had a nice lunch and stroll today."

"Cut the crap, Munroe. I got a shit storm going on and part of me, a large part, wants to toss some of it your way."

"Ok, perhaps you start off with telling me who you are and what your interest is with me, and I'll quit playing the duck."

"I'm David Archer and I'm a representative for Enterprise oil. We have similar interests in Equatorial Guinea — we're on the same fucking side. We both want the same thing. Except you had to fuck that up, didn't you? You had to drive over one of my team and get the other arrested. Not to mention torture and kill a third. For Christ's sake man, the guy has a wife and kid, what the hell are you doing?"

"Open your briefcase. Take off your jacket and toss it on the bed, along with your shirt and pants."

"What?" his eyes showed his disbelief, and a slight hint of fear. He had every right to be afraid.

"Only a fucking retard would continue talking to someone who very likely could be wearing a wire and trying to implicate a simple tourist in a crime. Clothes."

"Hell, you're paranoid — but fine," he snarled as he reached for his briefcase.

He opened it and put it on the bed. There were pictures of me, and some files, but nothing electronic other than a cell phone charger and adaptors for foreign plugs. The clothes landed on the bed. They were clean as well.

"Ok, get dressed."

"You CIA then?"

"No, I work for the State department as special liaison to Enterprise Oil. But believe me I can make a call and get a CIA team in place in a heartbeat."

The last bit was said with as much bravado as an aging out-of-shape man can muster while hopping around naked on one leg with the other leg stuck in his trousers.

"Really? Like the last retard that had no business being in the same bar with me?"

"He was a security officer. He'd worked for us for six years."

"He was an idiot, probably learned all his shadowing skills from Tom Clancy novels and Soldier of Fortune magazine. Really David, you've done your research haven't you? If you're that much in the know, you have to know whom you're operating with. That is if we are on the same side."

"I have your full brief from Tom. Yes, I know who you are and all about the others on the fallback plan."

"Briefing from Tom? Fallback plan? Your gonna have to be a little more specific. Tom doesn't know shit about me other than stories he's heard. The last time that fuck saw blood on soil was when his upper class mates in high school fucked him in the ass and called him bitch.

He's a desk jockey, and judging your lack of conditioning so are you. David, I'm sure you're feeling pretty safe coming up here with all the security and the Sentinel guy waiting in the car. Let me divest you of that misconception immediately. You're far from safe, as far as you've ever been. I'm Charlie Manson, Ted Bundy and the Zodiac killer all wrapped up neat as a present on Christmas. Tom, if he sent you, has tossed you into a rabid fucking dog's lair and I'm getting more pissed by the second."

The deskman's demeanour changed, as though I'd flicked a switch. His face registered anger and fear. He looked around the room like he was looking for either an exit, or support.

"Look, I'm here to try and fix this shit and try to keep anyone else from getting killed or this operation gets blown before it begins. That's all. I'm not trying to have a swinging dick contest."

"Okay, then bring me up to speed."

"There are some things I can't tell you out of operational security but…"

I cut him off. "Like the fact you representing Enterprise oil put two SEAL green badge operators on me while the lot of you negotiate Simon out of prison? How am I doing so far?

"Then after you get him out you're gonna leave my team looking like fucking assholes holding the bag. Sound about right to you?"

"How did you know we were in negotiations? The contractors have…"

"You better start telling me something useful, David. You're about as helpful to this operation, as you call it, as great tits on a nun."

"Ok, ok, I don't know how you came to be privy to all that but yeah, you're right. Except, we weren't going to leave you hanging. Everyone is getting paid. No one is going to be left holding the bag. We are negotiating with a barbarian here! We needed a failsafe backup plan. Tom suggested the prison break idea and the team to do it. This way if our diplomacy fails we have a hammer in the wings. Tom just suggested we keep an eye on you, as he doesn't trust you. Frankly with your actions here I tend to agree with him. But everyone had strict orders not to interfere."

"Why the interest?" Now I was curious.

Archer continued, gaining a bit more composure as he did so.

"Enterprise Oil has proprietary technology for drilling shallow, horizontal wells and the area and type of crude is really set up to exploit this. We want in and we want the royalties to remain in the margin of profit. Shallow horizontal drilling isn't cheap. It's far cheaper to drill regular wells with traditional methods, but this area was made for it. He lets Simon go, and Simon apologizes for the attempted coup and the President looks like a humanitarian. He signs off on our project and we agree to the rights and the State Department views him as a friend to the USA and relaxes its scrutiny of the President's and others' banking practices"

"Okay. Makes sense, you're starting to earn your keep here, David. What do you want from me?"

"Don't kill anyone else on the team!" he exclaimed.

"Sure, but keep them the fuck out of my way."

"Tom isn't going to like that."

"Fuck Tom. He isn't running this operation, I am, and in my jungle Tom is just another fucking blue- balled monkey. You want this to go smoothly and do I. You want Simon out and do I. We on game now? Playing nice no one gets hurt, sound good to you?"

"Yeah, I guess it does."

"I think it best we keep this little talk between us. No reason for Tom to know I'm this far into the loop, is there?"

"Yeah. You're right, no need, really." Archer breathed a sigh of relief. He realized he was going to get out of the room alive, after all.

"Great then, finish your drink and get the fuck out."

David looked at me oddly, no doubt wondering if I was kidding. These indigent corporate types are all the same. "Negotiation Predators" they call themselves. Like worms they mull over a dead horse until it finally breaks down and the one with the most goo on it wins! Not my idea of negotiation. Capitulation is the masturbation of cowards. Where had I heard that before? The type of negotiation David was a master at was more like a group jerk.

I continued to look into his pasty face. My eyes were burning with anger. This was supposed to be a quiet relaxing evening and had been frustrating in more ways that one. My truth about Andrea had shocked me as much as it had dissuaded the entertainment. Why had I been forthcoming? Had Andrea got under my skin that much? I guess I had already answered that question, hadn't I?

"David, the successful end to this negotiation doesn't mean I like you. You're a corporate parasite feeding on the remains of deeds done by men like me. If you knew the cost of those remains you'd puke every time you started your Mercedes. People call me a dirty word. The say "Mercenary" like others say "Judas."

The difference is I'm there, in the field, earning every bloody dime. Stepping on the backs of my brothers, some of them dying but not dead to achieve the goal. The "operations", as you call them, forever held fresh in my mind waiting for an external cue to bring them back. The smell of a barbeque or the waft of a baby's diaper. I see every moment, and every dime I killed for. You cash the cheques and make the calls miles away from the stench and above the screaming and the deals with God. You don't get your hands dirty. You're not used to getting your hands dirty, which is why you showed up on my doorstep all shaken and upset at your first dead contractor that you had to see. I'm glad I wrapped it up nice and clean for you. Ease you into the world, so to speak. But we're not friends or co-workers by any stretch and this is not a team fucking effort. I will do what needs to be done to secure Simon's release and you will pick the marrow from the carnage. That's all."

David opened his mouth to speak and then, thinking better of it, picked up his briefcase and made his way to the door. I stand where I am and he walks around me like a man encountering a Puff Adder. The door clicking closed added to my growing frustration and I poured another stiff drink and flip on the TV. Fucking suits.

CHAPTER THIRTY-SIX

IT HAD BEEN SUITS THAT had made this whole deal go south in the first place, the reliance on the corporate machine interfacing with government. How could that not go wrong? How could Simon and the others believe it to be secure? These ass wipes would sell their own grandmother into sexual slavery to simply dodge an embarrassing situation. I'd be willing trade my life for any member of the team. The difference was not only lost on these people, it wasn't even considered. We were subhuman tools used to force economic change, usually through regime change and always for the profit of the corporate elite.

While I struggled with the right and wrong of what I did they struggled with the profit margin. I have long maintained the true antichrist will have started out an accountant. The dim blue light of the TV flashed images from around the world as the soft bed and cloud like sheets, combined with the vodka helped to ease the tension from me. The dark curtain fell, stealing away the rest of the day and, despite having had a wonderful bath, I felt dirty. The stench of David and what he represented tainted my room.

The cell phone woke me and, as always, I looked around in an attempt to orient myself to my surroundings. It buzzed again and then began to ring.

"Yeah."

"Hey, sorry comrade for the early call but I have good news"

"A welcome change, Viktor, What is it?"

"The company I know was more than a little interested and you're off the hook for the return trip. They are willing to front me the entire sum and a rather generous kick back, that I will of course share."

"Good to know, you're playing this close to the chest, right?"

"Yes, yes, no concerns at all. He's a brother-in-law and happily married to my nice sister. I only had to say shallow well and he was on me like a dog. How do you say, 'humping my leg?'"

"Great news, but they know this is a long shot right?"

"I told them and he said drilling off the coast of Odessa was a long shot this was as sure a thing as they get."

"Ok, well their dime I guess. What time is it?"

"Eight your time."

"Shit, Viktor. I have a plane to catch and gotta' run."

"Bon Voyage, Comrade."

I ended the call and marveled at the vodka glass sitting half full on the mattress beside me. How I managed not to spill it was beyond me, but there staring me in the face was the enigma. I grabbed the glass and swung out of bed. I had thirty minutes to shit, shower, and shave and be gone. The room was cool and the shower made steam and obscured my vision, but not the plan. I let the machine roll and it came back with a few options and ideas. All of them worked out with the shit landing on all the right players. I liked it. I liked it a lot.

I met Darius in the front of the hotel. Switching the reservations to Andrea's name had been very easy, the barriers dealt with by my bathing partner. I had left Andrea €2000 Euros and told her in a message to have fun and buy something nice. The luxurious interior of the car was clean as pristine as ever. The ride was quite and uneventful, Darius made small talk until it was obvious I wanted to be left alone and he was quiet for the rest of the drive to Schiphol.

We arrived with lots of time to spare. The big car pulled up in front of the arrivals area. When Darius got out to open my door I took the opportunity to kick the seat back where I had hidden the pistol. It was still there. I handed Darius another E200 and told him when Andrea's flight was arriving, its number, and explained she'd never been here before.

"She'll be staying at the Grand and no one other than you, I, and the Grand know she's coming into town. There is no connection at the Grand with me. The only thing connecting me to her is you. I don't need to be concerned about that, do I?"

"Our secret, Mr. Munroe. Not a word to anyone I can assure you."

"Great. Give her the full-meal-deal tour around the city and let her know about the different areas. Areas to avoid, at any time, and especially the ones to avoid at night. You know the drill. She may not know what to tip either, but I think I've taken good care of you."

"No worries, sir, her money won't be any good, even if she tries. Sounds like she's pretty special to you."

I caught his eye and fixed his look, letting the machine come closer to the surface.

"No more special than cute little blond, Natasha, you're seeing in the south end of the Jordaan."

He blinked twice and I could almost see the process as he went from question to understanding. His brain asking how I knew about his girlfriend, and then sliding down to cold fear at the implied threat.

"I understand sir, no problem. I'll leave her my personal card in case she needs anything, anything at all."

"I would be most appreciative, if you did. Thanks, Darius."

I left him still holding the door; mouth slightly agape, no doubt wondering what I would do to him and his girlfriend. That image flitting through his brain no doubt included Cerberus's dead, white eye.

I was still carrying serious hardware on me and I had to figure out if I was going to toss the stuff or stash it. I had that morning, cleaned it of all fingerprints and fibers and placed all of it in two zip-locked bags. Both of the bags had contained weed and hopefully finger prints from some dumb littering tourist. I still had the gloves, as I knew I would need to handle the bags either by tossing or stashing them.

I walked into the large departures area and checked my departure and Andrea's arrival. Seeing both were on time, I felt a brief bit of disappointment knowing I wouldn't see her. But I knew my flight didn't get into Jo berg till 2300 and it was going to be a long day. I was going to spend over twelve hours on the plane and most of it would be on the phone. I approached the KLM check in and baggage drop and was greeted by a smiling Amazon. Easily six foot seven this was one of the tallest women I'd ever seen.

"Good morning, sir. How can I help you?"

I went to answer and found that I'd forgot the damn name on the Belgium passport. I replied good morning in perfectly accented Flemish, dug out my passport and handed it to her. Then I made a show of digging out my wallet and retrieving my credit card, even though I had just pulled it out from behind the passport.

"Sorry, Mr. Finnes I don't speak Flemish very well. I never got the chance to learn it in school," she replied in Dutch.

"Sorry, I replied with a grin. "It's early. I should be speaking in Dutch too, forgive me."

"Not at all, I wish I spoke Flemish better. I have you confirmed as a one-way trip, in first class to Tembo. Ah sorry, that's the same thing as Johannesburg. Leaving at 10:00 from gate A36. Do you prefer an aisle or window, Mr. Finnes?"

"Actually, I will be on the phone for most of the flight, friend's wedding, perhaps as far away from others so I'm not a bother would be best. Aisle or window — doesn't matter."

"Ok, let me see what I can do here. We're only about 30 percent full in first, and almost everyone has checked in already. Ok, I have you in a window with no one behind or beside you. The seats in front of you are bulkhead seats. They should remain empty as there aren't any tiny travelers with their parents in first today."

"Good to know," I acknowledged.

"Any checked bags today?"

"Not sure. Are these legal for carry on in first?"

She looked over my shoulder and I couldn't help but think of a giraffe, helped along by the fact she pursed her lips as she decided.

"Put that one on the scale, please."

I slid the Tumi onto the scale. Its weight came up as 12 kilos, about 26.5 pounds.

"Yes, you're fine, Mr. Finnes." She said, handing back my boarding pass and passport.

It took me a few steps before I wondered if she was making a funny.

"You're fine, Finnes"? Guess the joke was on her.

Before I got to the security checkpoint, I needed to get rid of my hardware. I really didn't have a great deal of time. I checked the first washroom I found. I looked in all the stalls that were free for some type of access panel. There was none, so I left. I walked toward the food court area for this hub of the large airport and spotted another bathroom. This one was busier than the last one but in the last stall I spotted an access plate behind and to the right of the toilet. The plate had security screws securing it but like most they were loose enough to turn with the tip of a switchblade. Security professionals design and build safe airports. But plumbers fix toilets. Plumbers just see these fancy screws as annoying; after all why secure a toilet? I placed my one carry-on in front of the door and my other to the side, hopefully blocking the view. The screws turned out quickly and I had the panel open.

There was a ton of space inside and I took my time to feel above the open panel. I found the shelf I was looking for. Not even a regular inspection would turn up these weapons. I placed the plastic bag on top of this shelf, closed the access door and fastened the screws in tighter than they had been. I flushed the toilet, removed my gloves, and went out to wash my hands. I watched to see if I got any odd looks as I made my way through the white sterile washroom. No one paid any attention to my following proper male bathroom protocol known the world over.

I left the washroom and made my way to the lost and found department. On the way I grabbed a coffee and a bagel from a busy little kiosk serving many people in uniform. I took a couple of more napkins and, using these, picked up the knife in my jacket pocket and wrapped it, before tossing it in a trash can. I stopped and took a few moments to enjoy the bagel and coffee. It would be a while before I enjoyed good coffee again. Despite being surrounded by the best coffee growing areas in the world, South Africa had shit coffee, the majority preferring that red tea that was supposed to cure all that ailed you. Fucking crap! The soft honey cooked bagel soon to be replaced with rusks, basically stale dried flavourless bread that tore at your gums like an insane dental assistant. I finish my bagel while writing "AA" in each of the gloves to match the Andre Arloski of my Russian passport.

I walked up to the lost and found and dropped off the gloves, telling the lady I had found them on the bathroom floor in the toilet by the food court near the hub of this area. I figured she wouldn't handle them too much if they came off the bathroom floor of a men's room. Walking away I could tell I had been right. She lifted the first glove and noticed the weight and her face went from puzzled to disgust as she dropped it into a bag and reached for the next one.

I made my way to and then through security feeling quite pleased with myself. Saving gear for later use could be very rewarding; as enemies know these days you're landing pretty much naked. The next time I came through here there was a good chance I would have a pistol when I walked out the front door.

The plane was boarding by the time I made the gate. I joined the line and got out my passport and boarding pass and tucked one inside the other while I took another quick look at my name. I hate rushed mornings, but I knew I had better get used to them. Otherwise, the next time I forgot my name could get me in a jackpot. The lady scanned my boarding pass and gave my luggage the once over. Most of the people in line had only one carry-on while I had two and a large laptop bag. I continued down the jet way and handed the flight attendant my boarding pass.

"Welcome aboard, Mr. Finnes, let me show you to your seat."

I followed her toward the front of the airplane past two sets of curtains into first class. It was an older decor and design than BA, but actually appeared larger and more spacious. Perhaps it was the colour scheme, it was much brighter, or maybe there was more space. In either case it was more than comfortable, made more so by the empty area around me. I placed my two bags in the overhead area and set my laptop under the shelf to my right. I took out my phone and flipped it onto airplane mode, then put it to one side, my mind drifting over the mental list of calls I had to make, like Santa with Alzheimer's. I pulled out a pen and picked up a scrap of paper and started to do some planning.

"Good morning Mr. Finnes, hot towel?"

"Yes, and it's Rick, please."

"Here you are, Rick. Careful it's still quite hot. Can I get you a coffee, or a drink?"

"A coffee would be great — even better with a couple of shots of Grand Mariner."

"I'll be right back."

She left and, while the plane was pushing back to the taxiway, returned with a large mug of coffee. The sweet smell of orange mixed with the strong coffee. I set the mug down on the armrest and tried to remember what it reminded me of. Something was scratching at my memory. It came back in a rush of imagery and remembered scents.

The whir of insects, and the rush of the river beside the veranda on which I was sitting replaced the plane's noise. Then, like a bad movie edit, the aircraft intruded on the thought and the cabin, became real again.

I recalled that day. Sunday and I had been sitting on this grand sweeping deck beside the river, which was protesting loudly at being forced to go through such a tight area, and over rocks, churning and crashing like an angry mob. I had asked our host for the same drink: coffee and Grand Marnier, half in jest. To my surprise he nodded and disappeared into the house. When he returned the coffee and orange scent mixed with the hot humid jungle like an exotic model crashing a frat party.

I asked our host how he made it. He described how he bought the over-proof moonshine from one of his neighbours, and filled an old large pickle jar to the halfway point. Using a white nylon stocking he had obtained from a British nurse in the 70s, he dropped an orange into the stocking and suspended it inside the pickle jar about an inch above the surface of the moonshine. Then he screwed the lid back on and put it under the sink until the next year.

After a year had passed he would pull it out from under the sink and the liquid would be almost up to the bottom of the stocking, dark amber in colour. The stocking was then removed and he would fill up the rest of the pickle jar with bottled water until the liquid was light amber. The result was a less sweet and perfect liquor.

Now I took a sip from my cup and realized the homemade stuff was better. Perhaps it was the stocking.

CHAPTER THIRTY-SEVEN

THE PLANE BOUNCED INTO THE air and started its long climb. As the seatbelt sign went off I reached for my phone and list, trying to determine how best to make all these calls. Most of South Africa was an hour ahead of London and the flight time was 11 hours and 45 minutes long. Might as well start off with Sunday.

"Hello," came the familiar voice over the miles.

"Hello, Sunday how are the wives and children?"

"Rhys? Thanks. They are good, healthy, growing too fast or I am. How are you and that demon you call a cat?"

"Good, everyone is good. I land tonight in Jo Berg ya. Pick me up?"

"Ya, can do. What time?"

"2300 hours."

"Shall I pack then? Is this thing a go? Where are we staying?"

"Easy, my friend. You don't have any clue what is up then, ya?"

"Nothing Rhys. Two calls from Chiwa and one from London for account info, then nothing."

"Well my friend, it's safari time. Going to go out to Hazy View, relax and play some football. Sound good?"

"Safari? Can I have a white driver and tracker?"

"You can have anything you want my friend, as long as it's not me. But seriously, we're going have some fun, ya? The camp to the south a bit that has the big thatched common room. That had a soccer field if I remember right. Do you recall?"

"I recall it having a field filled with red and golden orb spiders. Along the river, on the south of the main house. No hippos or many crocks. I guess I can put up with the spiders."

204

"Ok, then can you phone and get a hold of everyone you know. Tell them to make their way to Hazy View. Designate it Camp "Sunny Ball.""

"They know we're coming?"

"They will as soon as I get off the phone with you. Tell the men to bring shorts and receipts for travel and I will reimburse them with cash. They won't need any money while at the camp, or until we go or they are let go."

"They're gonna' like that, my friend. Going to like it a lot. See you at 23:30 at the arrivals level. Are we driving straight there?"

"Yeah, we are going to rent something nice for the drive."

I hung up the phone and as soon as I had done the flight attendant walked over quickly and asked what I would like for lunch. I hadn't looked at the menu and did so quickly as she hovered. The bill of fare wasn't quite as fancy as BA but there was a good selection and it all sounded tasty. I ordered a butternut squash and Gorgonzola cheese soup and ham and Swiss combo on rye. She disappeared. I called Dave Allen, the manager and part owner of the safari camp near Hazy View, which I had now designated as "Sunny Ball. "

"Hello?" Allen's tone was business-like.

"Dave! Rhys here. How's it going man?"

"It's going well, ya. And you?"

"Better, now that I have my vacation planned."

"Where ya going?"

"Your place. Are you full?"

"Full? Shit, I wish man. We're empty. You'd think we got hit with Lassa fever or something. Had to even cut the staff back by half. Right now I have four guests, then nothing till the big school break."

"Is that still around the third week in December?"

"Yabo."

"You're gonna love me. Call your staff back and stock up on booze and good food. I'm coming with about 55 other people, all on my dime. I don't want you shaving Rands here, ya?"

"Really? Full board and the works?" He sounded dumbfounded.

"Well, they're Bat 22 boys. I think we can skip the game drives and the like, but I do need the soccer pitch in top shape."

"Soccer?"

"Football, whatever the fuck you want to call it, Dave. I need the pitch totally set up, cut, patched and sprayed. Goals and nets on order, along with balls."

"You're hosting 55 of the 'Terrible Ones' to play football for a month or so?"

"Yup."

"Three meals a day, and booze on your account?"

"Yup. Three meals and snacks."

"Any guns on my property?"

"Probably. Only me and Sunday will be armed."

"Promise?"

"Yeah, it's all good."

"Something else is up, Rhys."

"Yes it is, but you won't know anything about it till you read it in the Standard two weeks after its happened, and many flying hours away from you. For now it's a football training squad on training. Cool?"

"Very cool my friend, very cool."

"Sunday and I will be getting in there tonight around 0300 or so, depending how fast we drive and what he gets for a vehicle. Have your staff looking for us. I'm gonna need a big night cap and a little something before bed!"

"Staff? You insulting fuck. I will be waiting with a drink in my hand and you ain't going to bed till you catch me up on the shit and we toast a few. Crew flying into Hazy View airport?"

"Some will. Others will be driving in. I wanted a vehicle around, just in case. Sunday is renting something and picking me up at 2330, after I clear customs."

"Why don't you fly into Hazy?"

"Can't fly commercial, armed, my friend."

"So don't fly commercial. Hazy has a budding rental biz right now. We got some 206 Helios and a few private planes, even a Lear. I'm friendly with all of them. Why don't I call them and see if they can pick you up and save you the tickets. The enforcement is pretty heavy, as general revenues are down. That way I don't have to stay up so late and Sunday is already making a huge drive. You're in the air for 12 hours or so. Makes better sense, my friend."

I liked his idea and responded.

"Book me a 206 if you can. He can drop us off right at the ranch, right?"

"Yabo, he's an old pro. We can circle a few cars in the south field and turn the lights on and let him put it down there."

"Ok. Lets do that. I'll call Sunday and tell him just to fly into Jo'berg; I forgot to ask where he was. I assumed he was in Rosebank. Do you know something?"

"Nope, just know it's a hell driving these days so I figured I would offer the option."

"Ok my friend, let me know if there is a problem. If not, should I just be looking for a pilot in the arrivals area or is there a heliport?

"He's used to meeting guests at the airport; what do you want on the sign?"

"Sunny Ball."

"Sunny Ball? Ok, now I know something is up." He laughed again and hung up.

Staring down as we flew over the continent made me think how it was gong to be a long week of flying.

I punched in Sunday's number. The phone only rang twice before it was answered.

"I don't hear from you for close to a year and then twice in the same day."

"Sorry buddy, but I wanted to catch you before you did anything. Whereabouts are you?"

"Well Boss, I was being a good floppy and staying close to home, ya."

"Seriously?"

"Well, I have been going back and forth to the Cape but now I'm home."

"Why to the Cape all the time?"

"That's stuff we can talk about later. What's up?"

"Ok, we're flying into the Sunny Ball, not driving. Apparently it's a great deal easier now to fly to Hazy View than it was. We can meet at the airport. You won't need a car. If we find we need one in Hazy View we'll just rent one then."

"Okay. So. Same time, no car. See you there."

Something was up with Sunday. I could hear it in his voice and I could feel it too. Like the phantom pains some amputees report, I could feel something was not right. He was distracted and too anxious. A few days alone would sort it out, or so I hoped.

The food was good and the bright sun improved my mood. I put my head back and tried to relax as I sipped my drink. Several calls still needed to be made. I marked them off as I completed them. Focusing at the task at hand made the Sunday issue diminish. I called the football outfitters and gave them the shipping address in Hazy View. That finished, I called the Marriott hotel in Dallas, and booked a view suite without asking about the convention rate. The Contractors' Convention was a week away. I had, until now, assumed that was what had been in the envelope delivered with last night's guest. Remembering, I dug it out of my carry-on and tore the envelope open.

It was indeed an exhibitor's pass in my real name with my picture that Tom had taken in the Tea Room.

"Great," I thought, "Now the alphabet agency wouldn't have to work hard to keep tabs on me."

There was no note, only a brief itinerary of topics and dinners. We, being Sentinel, even had a hospitality suite. There was also a list of suppliers and exhibitors. I looked on the Sentinel blurb and was happy to not see my name under exhibitors. Thank fucking Christ for some discretion.

I picked up the phone and looked up a number in Canada. It had been a while since I had called this number. In fact, since I did the man the favour I had never called this number and he hadn't ever called me. But the debt this number owed me was a huge one.

CHAPTER THIRTY-EIGHT

IT HAD STARTED WITH THE usual father-and-daughter struggle. Moral conflict was the theme. Add to the mix that daddy was a rich industrialist and it gets interesting. Move it all to Africa and it just gets deadly. Stephanie was a very typical twenty year old and had done enough reading to know oil was money and money made Africa tick along nicely for the very few. She had orchestrated the conflict and created the drama before daddy had known he was in the play. Before he had a chance to get this situation under control his daughter was on the other side of the world being little Miss "save the children."

This man, who led companies to greatness, and savoured a hostile take over bid like others did carrot cake, was out of the game before he knew what the rules were. I've seen it played out time and time again. The men with white collars that looked down their noses past the judgmental expression. The hapless tourist that falls in love and just needs to stay and build a home in the quaint, simple, countryside. The rich industrialist's kid that gets tied up in one scene or another. Then they come looking to you. The dirty word. The man who loves only money and is capable of doing more than just appearing busy. An art the African cops have perfected the country over. These people show up like an apparition next to you in the bar. Tear stained faces below hollow eyes straining to see hope appear, they touch your arm or shoulder to insure you're real and their desperation is too at this point. They understand what Shakespeare meant, when he wrote "cry havoc, and let slip the dogs of war."

I never charged any of them; some I never helped. Some of them I didn't listen to past the first sentence, I didn't need to. I proclaimed their loved one dead as simply as Caesar. The Priests and Clergy I made beg. Good old fashioned, on your knees, before me pleading. I could save their child or free their nuns, but why doesn't your God do this? You come to me, in your darkest hour, and then beg like the hypocritical myth selling worms you are. Some didn't and I respected them for it, others had less faith. The rich industrialists I just made swear a boon, a favour, a little call in the middle of the night you didn't say no to. They all promised and they all paid, as powerful men have too much to lose to be suddenly overcome with moral virtue.

This had started off the same way. I'd been sitting in a quiet bar, enjoying a quiet drink when suddenly a man appeared in the seat next to me. Most people in these kinds of bars knew not to sit next to a white man carrying more than one gun. Like dogs and the English in the hot sun he was beside me. I looked at him. He had been a strong man at one time. That had changed to fat a few years ago but the large frame still hung it well. He was dressed very well and had the sense or luck to make his personal security team wait by the door.

"I was told I could find you here, I need your help and I will pay you a grand US just to listen."

Turning to face him, I wipe my mouth with my sleeve; "Not too many fucking details then mate as I'm a little sloshed. Get to the point, I get you're serious."

"The rebels in the east have taken my daughter and are trying to use her for leverage on a mine we have in the area. They say unless we leave they will kill her. Even if we pulled out another company would step in so no one knows what to do. My kidnap and rescue insurance doesn't cover her and the corporation is basically stalling me. Please, sir, she's all I have and I love her. You understand that, right?"

"Nope, no I don't. What I do understand is you got a major problem with no easy solution. To end this kind of situation takes serious action."

"I have money."

"It isn't about the money. It takes the kind of action that wakes men like me up in the middle of the night screaming. Are you ready to live with that?"

"Yes."

"Not so fast, I'm giving you a chance Faust never had. You really need to think this one through. Lots of people will die so that your daughter can live. That, and one day, I will tap on your shoulder and ask for something. Something you will not refuse me."

"Well, I imagine you won't ask for my grandson or something like that!"

"No. But I may ask for your liver. I may ask you create an industrial accident that kills people you had Christmas dinner with last year. I may ask you for all the money you have. Are you ready for that?"

"Yes."

"Ok, I already know about your daughter's kidnapping. Your last name is Goetz, correct? Good. Ok, so they want you out of the region because you're hiring workers from the village by the river and not theirs. I know to you it's one big village, but it's not. It's quite separate. Anyway, this isn't an anthropology lesson. When they call you next you be hard and tell them to let your daughter go or life will be very bad for them and hang up. Do nothing more and be prepared, she's going to get bloody on this, no way around it. The strength needs to come from you, fuck that up and they will rape her dead. We clear?"

"Crystal clear, sir. What is the plan?"

"The plan is for you to do what I've told you, and when you need to know more, I'll tell you."

It had taken me two days to line up the big Hind and get it diverted over and loaded with the correct gear. Two very long days for Mr. Goetz, who had received a baby finger and nipple by special courier. He had been in anguish the night I had called him. That had been many years ago. I had saved his daughter at the cost of many innocent African lives. Nothing personal really, they're just food.

CHAPTER THIRTY-NINE

FINDING THE NUMBER I CHECKED the time difference — almost one in the morning. The phone rang three times and was answered in a very hushed tone.

"Hello, do you know what fucking time it is?"

Yes, not that I care Goetz, do you know who this is?"

No, but rest assured when I do you won't be fucking pleased with the outcome."

Goetz I'm the guy that knows why your daughter doesn't go to topless beaches. I told you I would call one day. I believe I said it would be in the middle of the night, too."

Ah — ok sorry, I thought it was…never mind, what can I do for you Mr."

Names aren't really needed between friends. I'm flying right now and have a shipping issue you can take care of for me. Is your firm still doing work in EG?"

Yes."

Offices in Amsterdam still?"

Yes, but only a satellite, no one there I trust."

Then I guess you'll have to go there yourself. I need a bunch of machine parts shipped or flown into EG. They are very sensitive and will need to be there in 3 weeks. They can go in pieces or however best suits you. I'm sure you have people in place with customs that can just give it the nod, you've been doing business there for enough years."

How big are the machine parts?"

One box will be 500 pounds and the other is 230 pounds. Each one, about 42x42 inches. They can't be opened. The other box will be computer, GPS, and radio stuff and while it will pass visual inspection as sensing equipment you don't want it gone over too closely either. The big stuff has to be picked up in Amsterdam and the computer stuff I will give to you in Canada."

I will be at an annual stock holders meeting in two weeks and we are shipping, via air, a ton of new computerized heating and ventilation equipment. It will be in country in nineteen days. We are deciding between a European company and an American one. Guess Europe wins. We can piggyback it on that shipment. I guess you're not telling me what I'm on the hook for, but am I to assume it will be very bad if these crates are opened."

The worst kind of bad."

Ok, well I will do everything in my power to make sure that doesn't happen. My man in the field down there is Manfred. He's totally trustworthy and I will put him personally in charge of the storage issues. Can you meet me in Lake Louise, at the Fairmont, in two weeks with the computer stuff?"

"Yes, that works for me."

Ok, well I guess I will see you then."

See you then, Bye."

It was time to call Viktor back; I flipped my phone and read off the number he had called me from this morning. It only rang once.

"Da"

Vik, got some good news for you. The two crates of auto parts only have to get to Amsterdam. A gentleman by the name of Goetz will take possession and load it with some HVAC equipment for delivery into the country."

"You know this Goetz well comrade?"

Well enough, he needed my help a few years ago and so will play ball completely. Is that boat moving yet? I was doing the math and figured it would take 29 days to reach its destination. That's kind of pushing it."

I called and they had already decided to put the tank in upfront so it was being fueled this morning when I called you. The crew is on route and will be there tonight and so she will leave tonight. I also added three care packages I had rusting in a warehouse there. That package will double your field supplies and eliminates the need to make fancy BBQ cylinders. I figured a back up on someone else's dime would be a good thing."

I love you, Vic."

Da, Da, Just let's not break anything on this."

No worries there. Thanks!"

Bye comrade."

Next I dug out the card for the football store and dialed the number.

"Hello Strikers Sports, how can I help you?"

"Hello, this is Rhys. I was in the other day and ordered a team full of stuff."

" I remember you, sir! The owner is giving you a 20 percent discount on your order and is tossing in twenty logo game balls as well."

"That's great news. Cleats are going to be an issue, How about you send me fifty pairs of shoes, most of them in the 8 to 10 range with a few above and below that as well. I have the shipping address for you too. They're going to Africa so you'll probably need to write some delivery directions. The address is 2548 Ibex road, Hazy View South Africa. The directions are: Take R40 south to the junction of R40 and R538 and continue south on 538 till you see Ibex road. That will be the first available right off R538. Follow that road west and it will turn south again. Follow it south to the end and the farmhouse will be at the end right where the road turns west again. Got all that?"

"Got it. Sir, you didn't seem too set on your colour choice. I only ask as when I called the company they mentioned they had a cancelled order already done with the colours blue, gold, and white. Same fabric, but the order is done. We could ship that one by the end of the week; we have everything else in stock. This order included jackets too and they would throw those in if you were interested."

"Sounds good to me. Are these colours part of any national team or anything that might get us unwanted attention?"

"No they were supposed to be away jerseys."

"Ok. Well then let's do that. Who are you using as the courier?"

"We like using DHL but you can choose anyone you like."

"DHL is fine. I will look for them next week then."

"I will complete this order today, sir, and try to get everything off by Friday."

"Great. Thanks."

"You're welcome. Bye."

I leaned my head back and took another sip from my drink. I liked it when plans came together and these were coming together seamlessly. I got nervous when it was too easy. I figured it was time to give Allen and Riley a ring and see how things were going. My phone charges were going to be as much as the damn flight.

"Top of the afternoon."

"Hey Riley, so can you talk?"

"Just a second, Sir."

"Ok shoot, what's the view like?"

"50,000 feet and all white. I'm headed to Hazy View. Got a pen?"

"Go"

"The camp is Sunny Ball, it's about two clicks south of Hazy View and a click west. The address is 2548 Ibex road. It's an old lodge with a main building and pool and then it has several rooms built up into the trees along the river. Nice and out of the way with lots of room and is set up to hold sixty. There is a new private field so easy to get in and out of by plane. I'm meeting Sunday tonight at 2330 and we're flying there. What's up on your end?"

"Well Tom, has been on the phone constantly and we have some really good prospects. Even people you might have heard of. He's doing a big media campaign and has tied up Heineken to do all the bevies and food. Lots of tents and out buildings for beer gardens and the like and a fucking ton of beer. Have we got a start date for this yet? He has to have dates to see if he can free up the players and the like."

"Lets call it forty days from today."

"Ok, you think that's enough time? I'll let him know. He has already talked to the President and he jumped at the idea and even put a hundred grand wager on it with Tom. Seems like he's playing this one straight, Sir. Treating me real well and keeping me in the loop for most everything going on. Course there is the day to day stuff he has to do in-between you know but all in all been green and shiny."

"Ok good to know. Watch him close Riley, I don't trust him."

"Will do sir. Slan."

"Bye, Riley."

I had to hang up the phone as I noticed the braided hat African dictator was standing at a discrete distance waiting for me to be finished. I looked at him and he approached my seat and sat down beside me, doing up his seatbelt.

"Going to get bumpy?"

"Huh? Oh sorry habit, you sit down you click in. Just routine. I wanted to talk to you about the incident. The Captain would have come back himself but it actually might get a little bumpy as there is bad weather ahead. He's trying to go above it now. Listen, from the amount of traffic we have been getting from the tower and corporate I'm gathering you're someone who really likes to avoid drama."

"I'm just a very well connected businessman that has a chopper waiting when we arrive in Joberg and I don't need to spend three hours talking with the South African cops about something that didn't happen in their jurisdiction. If they need to ask me questions they can phone me or arrange an interview via my lawyer. I know if I say that to them when we land. I will be waiting in lockup till morning with a 206 and pilot standing by. A costly issue, you'd have to agree."

"True, very true. Ok well they have talked with our corporate types, including lawyers and have agreed that a written statement witnessed by me and signed by both is good enough. Corporate also asked me to ask you nicely if you'd reconsider your lawsuit."

"Did they?"

"Well actually they said I should come back and offer myself to you in anyway to get you to drop the lawsuit if I wanted to be flying home in the front of the plane instead of a passenger in coach. I think they were kidding."

"I doubt it. My lawyer has the reputation of a prick amongst prick lawyers. But if you can guarantee no drama, or hold up at the airport I'm fine with the arrangement. So long as you talk to the flight attendant, I was a little harsh with her and I don't want her to spit in my food."

"She would never sir, but I will let her know everything is resolved, and I'll get her to bring you a pad for the statement along with another drink."

"Thanks."

I picked up the phone as he left and kicked myself for not asking for my airtime to be free. The attendant brought the writing pad and a fresh drink and left with my old one.

"Neil."

"Yes, Sir, sounds like you're on a plane."

"I am. I was wondering what you worked up flight wise?"

"Tom has a Gulfstream G650."

"Sounds nasty, does it hurt when he pee's?"

"Sorry Sir, it's a twelve passenger fast jet almost 13000 K flying at .85 of mach. In fact it can almost break the sound barrier with a top speed of .925. She's a pretty little ace and maneuvers like a fighter jet. She will carry 12 passengers with lots of space and cargo. He figures he'll have me fly it down to you a week before and then use it to fly the VIP's into EG and out and the rest of the boys fly charter."

"What do you think Z?"

"I think it's a pretty sweet ride and it's fast enough to get the hell gone if things go south. It's an expensive taxi but we ain't paying the bills here. I say go."

"Ok, Z, you've got lots of time. We're jumping off in 40 days from now."

"Great that will give me a bunch of time to gets some hours in the seat as Tom's going to hire me and get me carded and certified as a pilot on this one."

"Have fun Z. Bye."

"Bye, Captain."

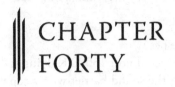

CHAPTER FORTY

I HUNG UP THE PHONE. Z was certainly in his element. I did a quick search on the plane, determining it had just rolled out. It looked pretty nice and if Z said it was an ace it couldn't come with a better endorsement in my book. Used ones of similar size were going for twenty million and they were from 1999! God knows what the brat paid for this one. Hmm that jealousy, Rhys?

The flight had been completely eventful and while I had got a ton done I really needed some down time. I flipped on the in-flight entertainment and chose a movie. It would be good to take my brain out for a couple of hours and relax. The sub was moving, or soon would be. Tom was playing nice; we had a plane, weapons. Yeah, I could afford the time. I missed Ruben and if I was honest with myself, Andrea.

Semila, my flight attendant hovered around, but as I was only sipping my drink she didn't interrupt till dinner time.

"Hey, can I get you another? Perhaps dinner?"

"Sure. How about the grilled sea bass and a nice glass of chardonnay."

She left without a word and I thought I would like to call Andrea. I wanted to give her time to get settled; see if she could handle the trials of traveling alone. I guess it was a test after all: a test to see if she was high maintenance or highly functional. Lots of people could function well within their manufactured world, but they often did poorly outside. I wanted to call her, so I did the next best thing. I called Darius.

"Hello?"

"Darius, my man in Amsterdam, how's it going?"

"Good. I got Andrea to the hotel. She was late, her Heathrow to Ship hop was delayed, but no concerns. She looked a little tired but

I tipped her to the spa at the hotel and she said she was going to look into it."

"Great. Anything else?"

"She asked about a few clubs and the RLD. I made a few suggestions and told her to call me if she was thinking about going anyplace and I would give her the 411. Told her I was at her beck and call. She tried to tip me E20. I told her everything was already taken care of and if she needed a lift, directions, or anything just to call me."

"Thanks Darius."

"Not a problem sir. Bye."

I dialed Andrea's cell and it went straight to voice mail. Shit she didn't take her phone with her? Fucking hell. It annoyed me to no end when people took their phone and turned it off to avoid charges from mistake calls from home or worse, left it at home all together.

I checked my call log on my phone and found the direct number for the gold level concierge. I dialed the number and a very familiar voice answered the phone.

"Hello, Grand gold level concierge this is…"

"Hello, beautiful, wanna' take a bath?" She didn't respond, but laughed.

"I should have left more than my underwear in your room, this afternoon when I dropped off your dry-cleaned clothes. So that's your girlfriend is it? No wonder it's easy being good. I think I may offer her a bath!"

"How is she settling in?"

"Well, I think she said 'oh my God' more than a Catholic on Easter. She got your note and care package and wandered about the room and then asked me about a spa appointment. She seemed a little overwhelmed and very tired. It was kind of refreshing really."

"Good to know. Take care of her for me, it's her first time out of Kansas and I will be back with you in no time, and would see it as a very personal favour."

"Not an issue Rhys. She's a guest — and a gold level one at that. My job is to take the very best care of her. She's in the spa right now. Do you want me to transfer you there?"

"No, I need to get some sleep. It's going to be a long night for me. But thanks, perhaps a bottle of wine, a Shiraz, with a note saying 'glad you got in safe have fun and count on you and Darius for anything you need'."

"Will do, Rhys. See you when I see you."

"Look forward to it."

My food arrived and I turned to BBC World news as background while I ate. The food was spectacular and the wine perfect with nice hints of butter. My head drifted into the pillow and I was aware my hand was looking for Ruben as sleep finally took me.

CHAPTER FORTY-ONE

I AWOKE, THE PANIC LASTING only a moment as I remembered where I was and what was going on. I changed the channel from the news to the flight progress screen. I looked at our updated status. Only about an hour out of Jo'berg. I had slept for three hours. I got up and stretched, did a few isometric exercises and, when Semila saw me, I gestured and mouthed the word "Coffee." She nodded and went to the galley. Most of the passengers were sleeping. I went to the washroom, washed my face and had a brief sponge wash then, only slightly refreshed, returned to my seat. My coffee was already there, steaming hot. I reached into my carry-on and pulled out a fresh shirt. The no-wrinkle material was trying its best and failing. I put my worn shirt into the side compartment and put the fresh, slightly wrinkled shirt on and sat down to enjoy my coffee. I found I really wanted to talk to Andrea. She should be back at the hotel, probably a little weary from the day's adventure. It was almost 9:30 in the evening in Amsterdam. I dialed the hotel and asked for her room. She was there.

"Hello?"

"How is the trip going?"

" Rhys. Its just great, I had a gorgeous time on the flight over, Holy Mother it was posh! They did everything but rub my feet the whole way over. London was a bit of a pain. I got lost and had to ask for directions. Then there was construction everywhere and it took a bit to get to the right gate. I didn't know where the lounges were so I just boarded early. They actually walked me to my seat. It was a smaller plane. Not as posh, but they brought me magazines and coffee. I needed the coffee as I had a little too much to drink on the flight to London.

Then the flight was delayed because the construction had slowed a bunch of people connecting from another flight. But it was fine. I gather there are several airports around London," she said. "Do I go back to Heathrow on my return flight?"

"Yes," I replied. "Heathrow is a suburb near London but there are two other London airports besides. Just remember to ask for directions to Heathrow. There are local trains to take you out there, as well as the Underground."

"Ok. Well then I was a little concerned about, like, getting my ride but I didn't have a number. I left my cell at home cause I thought it might not work. Bloody dumb — I won't do that again. Anyway the guy was there with a sign and he was super nice. I thought he was actually hitting on me. He offered to do anything I wanted and gave me a great tour of the city and told me the in places to go and the places I shouldn't and he wouldn't even take a tip from me. He said you had taken care of it already and gave me his card and told me to call him for anything. You took care of that too, did you?"

"Yup."

"Well thanks, and thanks for the money in the envelope. I went to the spa and the prices were out of this world. The hotel is incredible. This suite is bigger than my whole apartment. I stayed in and explored the hotel. The concierge that works this floor gave me a tour and told me all about the history of the hotel. Did you know a Princess is staying down the hall and that this suite has a better view! By the way, I didn't know you were sending me here to pick up your laundry!" she giggled.

"Yeah. I remembered I had forgot it on the way to the airport. I noticed all the body guards in the halls so I figured something was up."

"I went for dinner at the hotel and charged it to the room like you said. The prices are horrible; it was more than I spend in a week on food at home. Afterwards I went for a short walk and almost got run over by a bike. I'm pretty tired so I came back early and figured I'd take a bath and wait for your call. Where are you now?"

"I'm about an hour out from Johannesburg in South Africa."

"So I'm not going to see you?" She sounded very excited and obviously waiting for a "yes" from me.

"Not in Amsterdam. But I will be back in Vancouver for a night in a couple of weeks. If you want to drive into the city we can grab dinner and you can tell me all about your trip."

"I'd like that."

"Ok, it's a date. I'll call you on your cell when I know the actual date. Have a great bath and a better sleep."

"Oh I will, I'm going to do a ton of shopping tomorrow — with your money. I may have to buy another piece of luggage to check with all the clothes!"

"Sounds good. That's why I left you some mad money. Europe is extremely expensive."

"I wish you were here with me. The tub here is huge. We could have a ton of fun."

I was suddenly having a hard time not imaging her gorgeous body soaking in a tub overflowing with bubble bath. I managed to utter,

"Me too, but it will have to wait."

"Night, Rhys. Be safe ok? I really miss you. Sorry you couldn't join me here."

"Night, and I will be safe. Miss you, too."

I rang off and immediately felt homesick. I never felt homesick on working trips. I missed Ruben and the comfort of the house and I especially missed Andrea. Thirty seconds or less was looking more and more inane.

I pulled out my laptop and decided to do a little more research. I looked up the sub that Viktor had redirected. It was a bit of a piss off for the UN. There had been an arms embargo against North Korea at the time of the sale and while there were no real weapons on the subs when they sold them the missile targeting systems and launch controls were still onboard. Yes, the Ruskies had pulled a fast one selling them for scrap. The interesting thing was the history of the boats. One had gone down off the coast of Hawaii with nuclear missiles and torpedoes. The US government had spent a ton of money getting them up.

The project had been called "Operation Jennifer" – a joint CIA and Naval intelligence undertaking. They had built a boat to pull them up and it wasn't declassified for years. It was one of the first 'Bent Spear' and potential 'Broken Arrow' threats to the US.

A 'Bent Spear' was when an unfriendly organization had a nuke or one was lost where it could be found and used by said organizations. A

'Broken Arrow' was when one was actually in the possession of a hostile organization and launch was imminent or had occurred.

There had been far more of these accidents over the years than I knew and I was very surprised to read this. One of the first had happened near home with the plane crashing in a northern remote area of British Columbia. It was kind of scary reading. They had gotten better at it but governments were still losing their nukes. One of the latest had been the Russian sub the Kursk. Theories held that it had had a nuke torpedo blow and destroy the whole front of the boat.

The seatbelt light came on and I looked out the window at what must be Pretoria. It had been a separate city in South Africa but now the lights of humanity continued right up to the big city of Jo'berg. The big plane shook slightly as we descended into thicker air. The landing gear came down and I hoped the police interest would be as promised.

The plane taxied to the jet-way and I gathered my stuff before the seat belt sign went off. Semila arrived and offered to escort me off the plane. I nodded and we walked like a couple out of first class and only had to wait a moment for the door to be opened. I exited the gate and walked down the institutional style hallway into the terminal. I had to clear immigration and tried to pick the best line. Looking ahead at the officers I picked a line with an older officer in the booth.

"Welcome to Tenbow airport, Sir. Nature and duration of your visit?"

"Thanks," I responded as genially as I could. "Pleasure and two weeks." I handed him my passport containing my boarding pass.

"Been on any farms, or carrying any agricultural products with you tonight, Sir?"

"No."

"Ok. Welcome to South Africa; your visa is good for thirty days. If you need to extend it you'll have to see an immigration agent at any government office. Have a great trip."

He handed me back my passport and I walked past his booth expecting at any moment to hear a call for me to stop. I walked out around the edge of the building and then back into a much larger hall where checked baggage carousels lay grey and quiet. I continued out into the main arrivals area and sensed Sunday before I saw him. He was standing at the back and to the left of the terminal.

He looked older and perhaps a little slimmer than I remembered.

His eyes lit up and a broad smile crossed his face. He greeted me with the typical "Howzit' and took my hand in a two handed shake.

"It's good my friend and better now."

"Yes, yes it is my friend. The chopper is waiting and is cleared for departure, shall we?"

He turned and I followed across the terminal. I could see him scanning the area as we walked and was made aware I was doing the same thing. Like mirrors we walked across the terminal and into the warm night air.

The insect trilling was the first thing I noticed as we cleared the terminal. I had forgotten how the noise was a constant reminder I was someplace foreign. It was a good sound and one that made me remember why I loved Africa.

We walked along the building and past the car rental lots and taxi stands and made our way to a walkway that went up over a roadway into an area just south of the main terminal. There was a golf cart waiting with a driver and I hopped in the back with Sunday. We spent the trip in silence each using the time to get back in sync with each other. A security officer stopped the cart and we were held up only a moment as our driver spoke to the officer in Afrikaans. The officer picked up his mic and spoke into it and we were on our way to the waiting bird.

The Bell 206 jet ranger was a clean looking bird configured for four passengers. The pilot was in the chair with the rotors spinning when we arrived. A younger man, a kid really, welcomed us and offered to put my luggage in the storage area. I gave him my Tumi and kept the laptop case with me. He nodded and put the luggage in the hold and opened the rear door for Sunday and me.

"Headphones are on the hooks there. You'll need them to talk to each other. Water and beer are in the compartment there. Help yourselves." I climbed in after Sunday and put the headphones on and buckled up. The young kid got in the front.

"Welcome to my little airline." Came a voice with a Rhodie accent.

"Sit back and enjoy the ride. It will take just over an hour till we get to Hazy View. The weather's fine and we should be on time."

CHAPTER
FORTY-TWO

"IF YOU GUYS WANT TO chat please use channel 2. If you need to talk to the front use channel one. Don't worry about your conversation on 2, as I don't monitor it. But I can break in anytime time if I need to. If you want to listen to the flight traffic and the like you can use three but that channel kills your mic. Can't have the passengers talking to the tower now, can we?"

I flipped over to channel three and listened to the preflight chatter.

"Tenbow tower this is flight 25 requesting permission to take off from helicopter pad Alpha 3"

"Roger that flight 25 the pattern is clear to 12 thousand feet you are cleared for take off"

"Roger Tenbow tower, clear to 12 thousand, taking off."

The helicopter's blade sound increased and for a moment it felt like we were being suspended as if on a magnet. The machine rose only a few feet and then with a surge of noise we were in motion. It rose quickly through the night air and the lights of the suburbs of Johannesburg stretched out below. Sandton and Rosebank were the first to come into view and I could see there had been many changes to the area in the previous few years. I could still pick out the large man-made lake near the Rosebank mall. We climbed and the darker area of Soweto came into view and I noticed the area was much brighter than before and closer to the other communities than it had been. The urban sprawl of homes encroaching on a once "no-go" area. To the south I could pick out the city center and the tall towers that marked it. To the west were the large reactors that were a favorite target during the apartheid era. The reactors always made me feel uncomfortable. I was familiar with clean power from hydroelectric dams. I was not comfortable with having these controlled nuclear reactors so close to homes.

We banked and started heading east and got clearance for 5,000 feet from the control tower.

The noise inside was muted compared to military birds. The plush seating and comfortable surroundings were a stark contrast to the amoured floors Sunday and I had lain on in the past. I flipped to channel 2 and reached into the recessed fridge for a beer. They had stocked it with Castle and I loved Castle beer.

"Beer, Sunday?" I tried on this channel.

"Thanks Rhys."

"So, once more into the fire, eh?"

"Yeah, once more. What is the whole scoop on this one, my friend?"

I handed him his beer before answering.

"Well it's a little convoluted to be sure."

"It always is, no plan survives first contact, does it? I hope not too convoluted. We're not landing in Zim to fuel up or anything right?"

"No, nothing stupid. Just the usual cloak and dagger stuff one has to be concerned with when dealing with Tom. He had me followed in Amsterdam. I got to meet the slimy government contact he's working with after I dumped one of his less than talented operators."

"Killed him?"

"Yeah the operative, not the slimy one."

"Dangerous thing to do in that city."

"Sure. But it got us really good intelligence. Seems Tom is hedging his bets and is in diplomatic negotiations to get Simon released. Backed by the British and US governments.

"Really, I heard rumours there were some talks going on as Nick and Simon aren't too healthy. The Duchess is making noise in the upper tea-drinking circles and becoming more and more insistent. Making noise about releasing some of the e-mails that cast long shadows. Long enough to reach Government house and a few highly placed families."

"That doesn't surprise me in the least. What I have planned is a runback that puts us in the driver's seat and not playing catch up. If they release Simon early, which I think is Tom's plan, we have the option of taking the country by force."

"Really? Why would Tom put up all this cash for no payday? It doesn't make sense, Rhys. I think you're just being paranoid."

"He puts it up to look good. We're gonna be good to go and boom he's released and so Simon looks good in 'our' eyes and looks like a man of action for his employees and shuts up the duchess in the process."

"Ok. I see your point, but is he really that vain?"

"Not vanity; image. In his world image is everything. He presents an image of power and influence."

"Ok, I'm on board that sounds like him. What is your plan?"

"Well I got thirty suppressed MP5's, thirty thousand rounds of ammo, and pistols into the country. Viktor is bringing another bunch of guns and rounds into the habour on an old Russian diesel Boomer sub."

"Holy shit, Rhys an old Russian intercontinental ballistic missile sub? How in Christ's name did you pull that off."

"Well I haven't yet. She's on route from South Korea and should be there in thirty days. If she doesn't get caught and boarded by someone looking for subs."

"That's a big "if," my friend"

"Yeah I know it, but Viktor is supplying the crew and says she's a lot quieter than she used to be. Nowadays they are looking for nuclear boats so… I think he figures it has a good chance either way. Besides we don't have to go ahead with the plan unless everything is in place. The weapons will ship in two weeks and are coming in with several tons of A/C gear."

"Yes, but what about the men? Are we all going bird watching?"

"No, playing football."

"Ya, explain that."

"We're gonna fly thirteen of us in on a Gulfstream and the rest are flying commercial. To set up and run football camps for the kids. We do the recon then and if everything is in place we decide on go or no go. If everything is in country then we stick with plan A and bust out Simon and get the fuck out of Dodge either on the plane or the Sub. If things go south we determine if a coup is possible and take it down."

"You expect the US just to sit back and do sweet shit all during this."

"I doubt they will have time to react. We're going to kill the

President at the final match against the national team. He has already made a hundred grand wager with Tom so he'll be there."

"We're going to play the national team? With what solders?"

"Yeah with soldiers, and two ringers a striker and goalie from the pro's. Plus we're going to have three weeks to practice in Hazy View with pro coaches too."

"Wow! Pretty slim, Rhys."

"Yeah but we have done less than slim before."

"Yeah but what if we get a US Navy or Coast guard boat? Their interests there are huge; they aren't going to sit idly by. They can't really bring big major weapons into the fray but choppers, communications, and a few SEAL teams. That would make our job a little more difficult than slim."

"I have an option if they do. I play poker."

"Poker?"

"Yup. What has got you flying back and forth to Cape Town?"

"Hey, don't change the topic. Explain poker."

"No, I want you to be able to deny you knew anything about it if it goes south."

"I can always lie."

"Yeah well consider it an early Christmas gift."

"I'm black ass wipe, I celebrate Kwanza."

The laughter in the back was loud enough to get both pilot and co-pilot to turn around. Sunday didn't want to leave it alone but he knew he had to. This was something I was keeping him from. It meant we weren't going to be a team on that part of the operation. For me to do that meant I had a good reason for not asking him to stand with me. He hated it but accepted it and settled back into his seat after retrieving another beer. I said nothing, leaving my previous question hanging there.

"I'm not really sure how to say this. I haven't told anyone else and I haven't really had time to practice. I have been flying a bunch from Livingston to Cape Town for tests, as I had a few headaches. By the time I actually got in for tests they found a mass at the top of my brain stem. The good news is it won't hurt much. The bad news is it's inoperable. So the bullet has been fired, it's just a matter of time till it hits."

"How much time?"

"Hard for the docs to say. A year on the outside; probably four months till I start seeing symptoms, although it could be as early as two. Either way I'm good for this job."

"You sure?"

"I'm not sure about a lot of things right now. But I'm sure I will be fine for this hop. I have to be. I have to leave the kids with something other than stories about how tough their Dad was. I could have tried Chemo and radiation but that would have taken me out of this operation and there is only a twenty five percent chance it would work. I figure this op has a twenty eight percent chance so I'm going with the higher odds."

"That supposed to be funny?"

"Wasn't supposed to be but I think it is. Look I'd rather die doing what we do well than a skinny grey husk of what I used to be. This hop is supposed to be pretty profitable, right? Either way it goes. So I figure one more time, for the big dollars or a chance that leaves me broke either way it plays."

"Sunday, I would always take care of your family, you know that right?"

"That isn't your job Rhys. It's my job and besides you got to take care of yourself."

"I'm fine Sunday, money isn't ever going to be an issue."

"I'm not talking about money here. I'm talking about family and responsibility. You have neither and you're 43 years old. You have a cat. You don't know the joy of watching your own children grow. You can't know the anguish of leaving them. Sure it's functional for what you do, what we do. But what happens when you're my age? You think Ruben is going to hold your hand? Fuck, if you die in the house he will eat you Rhys'. He's at his core a predator like us. He's supposed to be, it's his nature. It's not in our nature to be. We lied to ourselves, saying commitments are dangerous, they're built in holes in the amour. But what they remove from the amour they add to the sprit. They prop us up at times like this. You know what I thought when I got the diagnosis? I thought I'm being killed by a bunch of replicating cells at the base of my brain. I'll show them, and before I knew it I had a gun pointed up through my throat at the little fuckers. I was going to kill them before they killed me! That's really fucked up thinking Rhys. But tell me you wouldn't have thought the same way. Lie to me my friend, tell me you would have gone ahead with the procedure."

"No I'm not going to do that, I've never lied to you and I'm not about to start."

"Yeah, I figured as much. Why is it ok to lie to yourself then? Saying that connection is the same as collusion? Ignoring your feelings and creating legends and stories no one will care about fifty years from now."

"I've never really had feelings that strong, Sunday."

"Yeah and if you did you killed them, rather than nurture them as you felt, fuck I felt, they made us weak. Perhaps they made us stronger, perhaps not. Fuck I don't know. I know I have someone there for me. That makes me stronger now. I have a responsibility to the people I love and that gives me the strength to do what I'm doing now. Otherwise I think I would have killed that fucking mass. If anger is all we know then that's our only tool to deal with adversity. If in doubt, take 'em out. Right?"

I sat, Sunday looking at me for an answer. I really didn't have a clue how to answer. I had never missed the quiet life as I called it. I, in fact, hated the simple day-to-day worlds I saw my regular friends enjoying. Wondered what they saw in Christmas dinners with family and friends. Sunday's words bypassed the usual filters I had for everyone. He was trusted and respected and his words had always been a source of wisdom and understanding. Now they pierced raw into my mind and created confusion.

"What, exactly, are you saying?"

"God, my friend you're broken. You're like a river that doesn't know its course to the ocean is blocked. You're supposed to adapt and grow, Rhys. Not just get better at what you do but become better than what you are. I don't mean better at the things you know how to do but better at the things you don't, the things that scare you. The things you don't do well, that's the circle of life. Grow, adapt, learn, change, and overcome. You are stuck, at the point of excellence and superiority, but you're like a croc perfect in its environment, and totally fucked outside it. The river has to dry up to force the croc to this realization. How about you?"

"I don't have an answer for you. I don't know. But I will think about what you're saying. I do have a girlfriend."

"If you had an answer, it would be a lie. A girlfriend is a nice baby step Rhys. You need to take more of them. Figure out what you want the rock to say above your head. Sorry for kind of dumping this on you but when your time is short you tend to speak a little more directly and I know if anyone else had said this to you they'd be feeding the bugs."

Sunday was wrong. Someone had said this to me, someone much younger than him. Someone who, I found to my surprise, I really wanted to see again, and soon.

We spent the rest of the flight quietly looking out the window and denting the beer reserves. Sunday usually didn't drink that much but I guessed it made not talking easier. He was right and I knew it a core level. The problem was I didn't feel it. Like an injury numbed by painkillers made worse with the activity the narcotics allowed. I was my own narcotic and I was slowly starting to accept it.

I saw the circle of lights in a small field by a river. The countryside was dark for about a mile in every direction. Hazy View was bright and I could even make out the well-lit golf course to the north of the town. The little field grew in size and slowly we descended into Sunny Ball.

CHAPTER
FORTY-THREE

THE PILOT PUT US DOWN in the center of the circle of vehicles as softly as if we were landing in a minefield. Sunday looked at me; with the headset off he had to sign "Later we talk more." I turned and as I was getting ready to exit I felt a hand pull my jacket up and at the same time a pistol was tucked into the small of my back. I signed thanks behind my back and a slap on the back was my answer. The door opened and I grabbed my laptop bag and stepped out and walked erect across the level field and toward the man holding a flashlight.

The lights from the vehicles were bright and made it impossible to see past them. The only vision cues were the flashlight held by a silhouette and the pick up truck parked with its headlights and four way flashers on. The chopper landed facing that way. Guess its better that we were blinded than him. But walking blind into the dark was making me uneasy and instinctively my hand went to the small of my back.

"Rhys, good to see you." It was Dave's voice, and I relaxed a little.

"Wish I could say the same. Can we move out of the targeting zone, I feel like a lamp-lit Panther."

"Most our guests love the light. Guys — kill the lights, kill the lights!"

He yelled above the rotors' wash. Several headlights went off and I moved to shake Dave's outstretched hand. He thoughtfully kept the flashlight pointed at the ground.

"That's better now I can see you. You remember Sunday, right?"

"Yes of course I do, great to see ya man."

"Let's move this reunion back to the house. Malaria isn't rampant here but the grass is full of mozzies and it only takes one."

He turned and walked out in front of the truck issuing directions in the local dialect as he walked. I was glad to hear him say to get our bags and take them to the Captain's house.

The property was quite large but, more importantly, very secluded. It was designed to take full advantage of the river with two large structures built into the trees to the north east of the two large houses — originally the only structures on the property. The old houses had been converted, with smaller suites on the second floors and large kitchens and dining rooms on the main floors. The kitchens, which could seat 60 guests, were connected by a breezeway.

The 'tree houses' were all one-bedroom suites with indoor and outdoor showers and king sized, or two queen-size, canopied beds in the expansive bedrooms. The main room had its own bathroom and a big queen sofa bed right in front of the generous balcony. The Captain's house was again set up in the trees along the river, to the south of the central houses. There were only three suites in the Captain's House: each a two-bedroom two-level arrangement. They were spaced to be private and apart from the regular guests.

The main floor was a large open room with soft couches around the outside walls. There was a full downstairs bathroom that had a 'Loo with a view'. It was called this as the entire outside wall in this room was glass from waist height to the ceiling. There was a privacy screen if you wanted it but I doubt anyone used it. There was a wet bar set into the area under the stairs and a small kitchenette that formed a shape like the letter D. Upstairs were the two bedrooms, one slightly larger than the other and each had king sized beds. The bed in the smaller bedroom could be pulled apart to make two twins. They each had a full bath but the bathroom in the larger or master bedroom had a larger bathroom that sported a balcony with a claw foot tub open to the world safely enclosed in only a mesh screen. It was a decadent way to take a bath, while enjoying a drink and a cigar.

We made our way up to the front of the main house and I spotted a pale green eye looking at me from under the stairs. A yellow one soon joined it and I thought for a moment it was the same creature until they both emerged from under the stairs to great the new 'marks'. They knew that with some gentle noise and rubs they could entice these new people to do something their owners wouldn't do. Drop scraps. The two cats meowed loudly and tried to enter the door at the same time. They were now dependent on the humans for food. As each had only one eye it meant their days of effective hunting were gone.

I remember asking why there seemed to be so many cats missing an eye. I had got a one-word answer, curiosity. My puzzled expression dragged the story out of my early African guide, who probably thought me quite ignorant.

"They are curious beasts, and fast. They trade on that one too many times, as it's their nature to poke and look in holes. One day the cat meets the cobra and the cat prepares to run and the cobra spits. Sometimes he missed the cat, but that's ok because the cat always comes back. Sometimes the cat loses one eye and survives the poison. Sometimes it doesn't survive. But it's true about the old saying: 'A one-eyed cat never watches a snake.'"

We made our way across the empty dining room out to the back. There was a sign on the mudroom door before we got to the screened in porch room. NO CATS! So each of us had to hold off the twin marauders with our feet as we entered the mudroom. Dave, by way of explanation, said;

"They want to follow us into the screened porch but then they play in the netting and make holes. Before we made that rule we were repairing the screen everyday. You guys remember the airlock procedures right? Turn, check your buddy for stowaways."

We entered past the first set of nets, and waited in the second netted area, checking each other, bathed in ultra violet light. It apparently wreaked havoc on the female mosquitoes. What it certainly did was show Sunday's and my ultra violet tattooing. As we checked each other for errant mosquitoes hitching a ride into the sanctuary Dave looked at the odd glowing markings.

"That shit always messes me up. It's like radioactive ink you stuff into your skin isn't it. Tells the locals you're a real bad ass, right?"

"If I told ya boss, I'd have to kill ya."

"If we were such real bad asses there wouldn't be any Kaffir locals to be telling anything to. They'd be stacked like damn black sandbags near the river feeding crocodiles."

"Jesus, Rhys. Quiet. I got lots of locals working here, ya. They won't know you're joking, man"

"Is he?" Sunday asked with a malicious grin.

Sunday pushed through the second net and into the main screen room. It was 30x50 and twelve feet high and used a double thick net for a roof to support the few monkeys stupid enough to cross it. The tight mesh would sag and pinch their feet and toes causing significant distress. The floor was angled so when the rains came it would allow the deluge to flow off the deck easily. I followed and so did Dave, looking a little shaken from Sunday and I taking the piss out of him. We walked over the center and sat below burning torches in big chairs that had large coolers beside them suggesting cold beer. The suggestion was not a tease. I cracked open a beer and decided to break the little tension the teasing had created.

"Dave, tell you what. If you can provide a simple cigar, I will break the oath and tell you the secret of the glowing tattoos."

"Right in Sunday's cooler, I thought you'd wanna face the door so I put them in there." Sunday opened the lid and pulled a beer and a box and tossed them to me.

I carefully opened the box, and picked out a nice looking stick. The climate here was hell on cigars. I rolled it between my fingers and pulled my chair closer to the middle and nodded each should follow suit. They pulled their chairs in while I lit the cigar. It's harsh taste biting my tongue and I stiffed a cough. The cigar lit and with each leaning in, I started.

"The men that carry the mark have been touched by Samelli or the white death corpse."

Sunday started laughing and Dave tried not to, but quickly followed suit. The story was true in so far as that was how many of the Liberian rebels kept their troops awake at night. For many decades the story of Sameal or Samelli, and the many other names he went by would walk the jungle at night and steal babies and children from their parents. Even before they had seen a white person, this demon or angry spirit plagued them. One only has to extrapolate then what happened when the first natives saw a boatload of these things. Now, he was said to glow with an unnatural light just like our tattooed faces so the jump for this superstitious lot was an easy one to make.

"Honestly Dave, it isn't really a huge secret. The Emperor Scorpion shell is black but under black light it glows brilliant white. What they do, after they get one, as I don't think they are indigenous, is crush it up. They drain the nasty bits and wash it out with water and they let it dry in the sun. Then they mix in some diesel, and God knows what other thinners, and grind it into a soupy mess. Next they strain it through cheesecloth a few times until the material is grey in colour and the consistency of yogurt. Then they use an old resharpened IV needle and scoop the shit up and jam it under your skin in a design. For a while it looks grey but then your body absorbs the impurities and it disappears unless you're under black light or you've 'charged' it up with a bright light first. We use it as a way to identify friend or foe quickly in covert night drops. The guy in the door of the chopper has a mounted 50 machine gun and a big black light. No glow, no go. Really that's it, no nasty witch doctor ju ju."

"Sounds like it would be painful."

"Ya, but less than getting hit with a fifty."

"So guys, how much of what is going on can you tell me?"

"Not a great deal. For no other reason, than your own safety. I picked this place because it's out of the way. I didn't fly in on my own passport and soon enough everyone will have their own I.D. No one will be going to town and no visitors. We are going to be playing football. There will be some pro coaches and trainers coming and perhaps even some celebrity players. You're going to be billing Tom from an account I will give you with my personal credit card held in reserve if Tom tries anything stupid. You just put my card through and I'll deal with Tom. No locals, no press, and you swear your staff to silence. We're going to be here for three weeks, training and testing and getting healthy, then we're gone and there is no connection to you or this place or that you knew anything."

"Ok sounds good, can I ask the football stars for their mark, you know autographs?"

"Sure, I don't see why not. We should even get a team picture."

"We should do a team clinic, within the first couple of days too, Rhys. Some of these guys may still be suffering with crap they picked up in Zimbabwe."

" I have a really good doctor. British chap, very old school type. He's kind of a novelty for the guests at times, but he knows his stuff and is very trustworthy. Besides, he wouldn't know a mercenary from a missionary."

"What's the difference? They both lead people to God."

"Sunday, the difference is easy. My conversion rate is much higher!"

The laughter brings out a couple of staff that quietly peer at us through the windows, no doubt wondering what Dave and his friends were laughing at. Knowing this visit was not just the obligatory ones that a headman has to do. No, the boss wanted to be there tonight despite him being uneasy about his guests. They were odd men to be sure. The white and black were far more comfortable than these men had seen before; they walked like brothers. Brothers that had known each other a long time.

The evening wore on and we shared news and gossip as if it were the same thing and relaxed into the night. I could see Sunday was tired and even though I had napped on the plane, the trilling insects were putting me to sleep. I tossed the cigar into the ashtray and put an end to our little reunion.

"It's been a long day and it's gonna be a longer week. That's all the time I will have here so need to get some rest and go over some ground rules. Dave, can you make arrangements to get the doc out here for Monday and again on Thursday? We should be able to get everyone looked at and blood work done by then. Ready to crash, Sunday?"

"I was ready an hour ago. You young ones have no idea how age works. How draining it really is, listening to fishwives gossip."

The laughter once again made the night security team stir. Dave had given the security men strict instructions not to shadow or escort these guests anywhere. Usually guests were to be shadowed discreetly all the time and at night escorted everywhere. The directions now were to stay away entirely, or be highly visible if you go close. Concentrate on our perimeter and not any of our new guests, especially the black and white that act as one. When some of the ex military men asked "why" with some bravado Dave had figured he needed to make this crystal clear. They are Greys, the ones that hunt the hunters, and shadows that terrify panthers. Dave didn't really have an understanding about what he was saying he had just heard the lines before. He knew Rhys and Sunday were dangerous but he wasn't prepared for the terror he saw expressed in his men's eyes.

CHAPTER
FORTY-FOUR

WE WALKED BACK INTO THE open night air, humid a floral scent as a top layer, decay and sweetness on the bottom. The sweetness was from bugs as they almost always secreted a sweet smelling scent. Africa was covered in bugs. I remembered listening to an entomologist in the field tell his class that, without bugs, Africa would be knee high deep in shit in one year. I wondered if it was an exaggeration or not. From the sound around us I wouldn't bet on it. Another scent caught my nose, a human and he was afraid. I caught his movement and when I looked at him fully he waved timidly while looking at his shoes. Odd behaviours. Dave must have given them the talk. We didn't have an escort and there were leopards, lions, and the occasional hippo in the area. I followed Sunday's lead as his eyesight would be better than mine as we made our way to the Captain's house.

"We sharing a room?"

"Well we're gonna need the space when the paid football talent shows up so I guess we should."

"Which room they put us in do you think."

"Dave knows I like the tub and the south west one lets me watch the sun rise from the tub."

The door was open and our cases were sitting in the middle of the floor. There was a basket of fresh fruit and the bar had a bottle of vodka and scotch with a full ice bucket with a card. I held the card up and had to bring it a little ways out for my eyes to focus in the low light. 'Made with bottled water.'

"First sign my friend."

"What? It's dark in here, real dark. I live with electric lights in the entire house."

"Fuck you" Sunday chuckled past the curse. His house in Rosebank was worth more than mine, as it was so large, and he had three other houses as well.

"Old my ass you dark bastard. You're looking as wrinkled as the lone toad in a dry river bed."

"Seriously, Rhys, when is the last time you did any low light shooting?"

"Yeah, ok. It's been a year or better, for low light stuff. Otherwise, I still shoot twice a week."

"Well, we should practice just in case you have to shoot someone not standing on a green sunlit field."

"Somebody needs his sleep."

"Just saying better tested in training. By the way, that was a nice thing you did getting the doctor out for everyone. It will go a long way to improve morale."

"Why should I need to do anything to improve morale? They're getting paid 1000 pounds a week to play football in a four-star safari resort and drink booze. I did it because it was the right thing to do. What? You didn't think I was listening on the ride? Shotgun the tub room, ya skinny black bastard."

"Yeah, you need to get a little more pink. You don't quite look like bubble gum, ya short-pricked dog."

The insult was called at my back, as I ran up the stairs, gear in hand. I had intended to come back down to the living room to retrieve my vodka but noticed when I came in I didn't need to. There on the large ebony dresser was another ice bucket and little card, alongside a bottle of vodka. I took a few minutes unpacking and putting things into the right places. I found my cell phone and turned it back on admonishing myself for the oversight. Fuck! I thought to myself, I needed to get my shit wired a whole lot tighter that it was. That was a good plan. I needed to create an itinerary and I could use the applications on the Ipad to do it. Having brought it along for music I had forgotten it had all of the applications the phone had without the phone. Perfect thing to do at night, in a tub suspended forty feet in a tree.

I walked out and turned on the water. It was hot right away and remembered this place when it had an old donkey boiler. A donkey boiler was a 45-gallon oil drum set on its side and suspended above a fire. The fire boiled the water and the steam pressurized the lines and turned back to a liquid as it traveled down the lines. You just added cool water to regulate the shower. A dodgy set up, but a shower in the bush after a long day was a huge luxury and the man that knew how to make a good donkey was a prize. Now Dave probably had an instant heating propane boiler someplace to service all the buildings. Yeah he had done pretty well here in Hazy View, a long way from his beginnings as an arms dealer. A long ways from the troubles of his past, troubles I had got him out of but not before it had cost him a child. I fight the images away and shake my head to clear it, those painful memories skating on the thin ice of recollection and reflection.

I pour myself vodka over five ice cubes that hiss like a snake at the contact with the liquid. I swirl them around and they crack and pop like some child's breakfast cereal. A knock at the door chases the still threatening images away.

"Ya."

The door swings open and Sunday looks tiredly into the room. He moves to the dresser and pours himself a glass.

"Sorry to interrupt the master's bath, but I humbly suggest we have a quick O group, sir."

An O group meeting was an Officer's meeting to go over the daily orders and movements and anything that needed to be done. It was basic housekeeping stuff and I should not have to be reminded. Sunday was using levity to take the sting out of it "Ya shit sorry, I was going to come back down but I found this and got distracted by it and the past."

"Well, watching the past is good unless you want to repeat it. Until you run into the present doing so and miss the future. Something other than the past that created this place is bugging you. You're not missing the cat this fucking much, so who is it?"

It was uncanny how he could sense the issues, just as I could sense his uncertainty. I had thought he was unsure about himself and the future. He wasn't, he was uncertain about me.

"Look Sunday, today has been long and one gut spilling is enough for one day. You're right, you're right, I get it. Tomorrow is a travel day for most. We'll meet with the Doctor and address health and vaccination issues. Yellow fever is an issue, I believe. Breakfast downstairs at 8am sharp and I will expect you to have some ideas about keeping the men's hands from being idle. Your turn to order breakfast too, with black coffee, none of that red tea crap. Questions in twenty seconds."

I counted to twenty in my head, and then added a few to be on the safe side. Sunday stood by quietly, looking at me.

"Dismissed Captain, have a good night."

"You too Captain. Thank you."

The ritual complete, Sunday turns right and quietly walks out of the room, closing the door as he does. There is a faint scent of iodine in the room when he leaves, and as I run to turn off my overflowing tub, I make a mental note to make sure the doctor checks him too.

I dig out my cigar case and check the time, 0230 — four hours 'til sunrise and five and a half till breakfast. Perfect time for a short Churchill cigar and I pulled one from the bottom of the case. I closed the case quickly and put it in the bottom of the wardrobe, as I didn't want to set the air conditioning to 70 degrees. The wardrobe would probably be close to that with the room at 76. I lit the cigar, got undressed, tossed my clothes in a pile and opened the sliding glass doors. The insect trill was loud and perfect. I flipped off the room light and dropped a big towel on the bench. The water was scalding hot and it took me several long seconds to finally submerge, the displaced water splashing to the deck and continuing loudly to the jungle floor. I could totally stretch out in the big tub and I felt my spine relax for the first time today. Hours of sitting on planes were not good for me at all. I took a long pull on my cigar and exhaled the smoke straight up towards the brilliant stars shining like a huge bag of spilled cut bloodstones. Another pull followed by a drink and the cool liquid tore at my overheated throat and core. Painful perfection and thoughts of scheduling all my travel and calls fell away following my bathwater to the jungle floor.

The bright morning sun pierced my dream and finding it as insubstantial as the dissipating morning mists took a poke at my brain. I shielded my eyes and in doing so noticed the prune like hand and fingers. The water had cooled completely but as it was still summer it had not got cold. My body had shriveled in the valiant attempt at absorption. I looked east at the rising sun and marveled at the green. Inuit, they say, had over a hundred words to describe snow; there could easily be that many to describe the shades of green.

I looked around and below saw two cats playing and a security officer slumped by a tree near the river, his shoulders rising and falling with rhythmic breaths. My half smoked cigar was sitting on top of my half drank vodka. I didn't remember putting them there but I must have as no one else could have. My head was clear and I checked my watch. It was 712 and I had forty-five minutes to get ready, and I had already bathed.

I lit my cigar and puffed the initial relight harshness away. I climbed out of the tub and with a little pain stood on my wrinkled feet. While smoking was forbidden inside any building I ignored the rule admonishing myself to be careful. The fire threat was high in November, the start of the summer. I took myself through the morning ritual, my skin slowly returning from wrinkle dog to normal.

I sat down with my laptop to do some flight planning. I had to leave for Dallas on Friday and needed to see what I could find for a direct flight into the US. Delta Airlines had flown direct from Cape Town to Dallas but I wasn't sure anymore. I needed to then fly to Seattle and rent a car to drive into Canada. Hopefully, anything I bought at the convention would raise little concern at the border.

From there I would drive into Vancouver and meet Andrea. In the morning, well not to early. I would fly to Calgary and take a limo truck through the snow to Lake Louise for the meeting and transfer of the high tech goods. London would be next and then back down to Hazy for final preparation. Then on into EG via commercial air for the men and private jet for the officers, ringers, and coaches. Next on the call agenda was to the exiled president in Spain. But he could wait till after breakfast. I looked at my watch, 0758.

"Good morning, Captain Sunday. I hope you slept well?"

"I did Captain Rhys, and yourself?"

"Like an Otter."

He stopped mid-dip, his rusk hovering about the red liquid. "An otter, Sir?"

"I feel asleep in the tub and woke to a gorgeous sunrise."

"One could drown that way Sir?" There was a little cheek in the way he pronounced 'Sir'.

"One from perhaps your short bus loins, Captain."

"Oh feel the love this morning."

"I'll show you love, pass me my black coffee and slowly back away."

"Glad to see your morning demeanour hasn't changed much."

"Eat your desiccated plain biscotti"

We sat in silence and enjoyed the meal and the banter. It was a long-standing ritual to eat breakfast together and apart from the men. We could plan the day, the ideas, and runbacks. I was always surly even if like today I didn't feel it and he was always jovial. I picked up some sausages and toast and thought about how many would show up today. I should probably hit the bank today as I wanted to be able to pay everyone's travel expenses in cash and I only had a few thousand euros.

"Going to be a wait-around day today don't ya think?"

"Are you going into town?"

"Yes. I have to get some money. I said I would pay travel in cash and I have a phone call to make that's best done on a pay phone. Why? Did you need me for anything?"

"Well, the men are going to want to see you. It has been a long while and we need to set down some ground rules and the like."

"Yeah I agree. Sergeant Chiwa will be here by nine, if he isn't here now, and I think the two of you can make work out of idle hands. I think it best I give one speech rather than six. I will address everyone after dinner tonight. Set a relaxed tone today I think is best Captain."

"Good, Sir. Chiwa and I will work on the bunking arrangements. I was thinking about keeping a few of the suites available for those players that excel, you know like rewards."

"Good idea, Captain."

We finished eating in silence and I watched as Sunday did some quick notes in his field notebook. I lit my cigar for the third time and poured more coffee for myself.

"Want some coffee?"

"No."

"It will put Velcro, ah sorry, hair on your chest."

"Bite me."

"Pretty weak comeback, my friend. Her name is Andrea and she's finishing her graduate degree in human behaviour. I think we're heading toward serious. She got under my skin in a way I don't understand. She's very beautiful and intelligent and Ruben likes her."

"The cat probably has better skills around this than you. Can you put her out of your mind till we finish this job?"

"I don't know, we have a date when I head back through Canada in two weeks."

"Well, I have three wives, and I like two of them. You know how I make sure I come back to see them? By not thinking about them. You need your focus my friend you really do."

"Thanks buddy, I know and I'm working on it."

"So speaking about working on it, where ya going to meet the exiled president? You go anyplace close to him in Cape Town or Joberg and the Scorpions (Special police force for mercenaries) will be all over you. Arrested you do us no good, ya?"

"I thought about that. He's going to be waiting in the first class lounge either in Cape Town or Joburg airports in transit to someplace else. I'll meet with him and the lawyer and come up with an understanding in principle just like the one he had with Alexander just in-case we go with plan B. He's past security and not entering South Africa proper so I doubt he will flag any interest. Even if he does the Immigration and Special branches never play nice, so it will be easy to spot the threat and do a work-around."

"Good plan.

"I've got to figure out the trip from this end, so I think I will have a leisurely breakfast and another cigar before I fly off. I need to really spend some time at this Contractors show. Here is some of the gear I want to make time to see. Any additions or suggestions?"

"Have you arranged for body armour?"

"Yes and no. Yes for the panels but no for the carriers. The panels are going to be used as spacers in the air conditioning parts shipment right out in plain sight. It's some really good stuff, threat level 3, resistant and feather light. One hundred panel sets are going along with that shipment. The carriers I think we will have to make in country. We are also going to have to come up with webbing kits. What I think would be the easiest is if everyone picked up two sets of under armour gear at the Rosebank mall on the way out, with a pair of black sneakers and a white walker fanny pack. You know the ones that have the concealment area for a gun."

"Sounds good. They're basically going to make their own gear in country. Turn around and fight in it. Ya, I guess it beats walking off the plane in tracksuits and combat boots. This high tech gear is great but let's use stuff that's tested, ya? I like these body mic's. They look a lot better than the old stuff, but check about radio jamming too. There is a lot of cool shit here. Kinda wish I was going."

"That would be fun. Anyway, along with getting everyone settled, I want a passport shot of everyone on my camera by the time I get back. That way I can send them to Viktor and get the passport issue taken care of."

"Done, Sir."

"Thanks Sunday.

I left Sunday shaking his head and went upstairs to retrieve my computer and cigars. Each was in its own protective case and neither more important than the other. I walked back downstairs and found Sunday gone and I continued outside. The brilliant sun was hot and my pale skin protested slightly. I knew I had to get a bit of a tan and so I went down to where I had noted the sleeping guard. I found what I was looking for, a nice depression and perfect lounging angle. I sat down, lit my cigar and opened my computer. While it was booting up I watched the people arriving. It was a mad house. Some were walking in, others on bikes, and the ever popular squashed in minivan. They were all used to significantly less and were hesitant to take the cold soft drinks offered by Dave. The bazaar like atmosphere was reminiscent of a farmers market. Inside the organized chaos I saw Chiwa and Sunday, talking with a couple of other men I knew whose names I couldn't remember.

The computer came to life and I angled my knees to prop it up out of the sun. It took me a while to navigate unfamiliar websites. It was a long flight too; 19 full hours to Dulles Airport in Washington DC and then a short three hour hop to Dallas. I could take the direct option but that gave me a six-hour layover in Dulles and made no sense at all. When I tried to back the selection up the site froze. It took me about six minutes on the phone to make the flight arrangements. I was now flying out Thursday night at 18 10 from Joburg and that put me into Dulles at six am on Friday. Actually pretty good timing if I started getting up at six tomorrow, no jet lag spin around. I called Delta and booked a first class seat for a flight leaving at eight. Two hours should be enough. Dulles was big but I would be traveling light.

I closed the computer and looked at the growing mass of people. Everyone had broken off into little huddles catching up, shaking hands, and enjoying seeing each other. I saw camera flashes. Sunday had delegated the picture taking duties to Chiwa. I moved back to my suite and dropped off the computer.

I went back downstairs and walked south along the river and cut west behind all the buildings and through the field that was receiving final preparations making it a football pitch. I carried on past the large group of workers and reached the edge of the property and then headed north. I walked along the edge of the property and by three of the perimeter guards; each was carrying an Old Russian assault rifle so I damped down the desire to scare them. When I appeared in front of the main gate the three-man team were startled. and the obvious radio banter said they were chastising their friends for missing me. I waited for a returning cab and flagged it down.

"Is there an N.E.D bank in town?"

"Yes sir, there is."

"That will be a good start then." I jumped in the back and shut the door. The cab sped off down the dusty road. We passed three more cabs on the way to the main highway.

"Busy day, ya?" I asked.

He looked at me through the rear-view mirror and responded.

"No more than usual when someone is getting married and having a bachelor party. I've seen more, but not lately, downturn in the economy is having an impact on the tourists or they're saving their money for the World Cup."

"Or the Olympics."

"Olympics? Yeah right this is the year for those. Where are they being held?"

"Canada, a place called Whistler"

"Right, I've seen an ad. Greenest Olympics ever or something. Pretty easy to be green when it rains and is cold all the time. You going, Sir?"

"To Whistler? Na too far. I got box seats for the World Cup."

"Nice. The bank is up here on the right. Should be open now, you want me to wait?"

"Definitely. You're my tour guide for the morning. Next stop is the best place for Cuban cigars."

Right Sir, good thing you're at the bank first then."

I walked into the bank and caught the guard a little off his game. I guess I was moving a little too quickly for first thing in the morning.

I smiled and waved and remembered I had a gun tucked in the small of my back. Ah well, TIA. Everything is negotiable. The good-looking woman teller had bright eyes and was ready to help.

"Hi. I need to change this to Rand," I said as I handed her 5000 euros. "Take out 70,000 Rand from my account. Here's my passport."

She punched a few buttons, trying to let the shock drain from her face. It wasn't working but I could see she was relieved she found an account with my name and that the ID matched. She wasn't being robbed, she had concluded but the lines on her forehead still indicated she was troubled.

"What's the matter, love? A little early for a big withdrawal?"

"No it's not that Sir, we can handle the amount. I'm just wondering what your taking it out in?"

"No extra canvas bags floating about?"

"Yes but that isn't very discreet Sir."

"Crooks are never up this early. The canvas is fine."

"Ok."

I waited for about ten minutes before the woman returned. She slid me the withdrawal slip for my signature and then handed me a large canvas coin bag.

"Anything else Mr. Munroe?"

"Yeah wave at Rusty over there so he doesn't try and shoot me and spill his coffee."

"Sure, have a great day."

I walked out to the cab and told him to pop the trunk. He was looking back at the bank doors and waiting.

"I didn't fucking rob the place, man. Open the trunk so the same holds true for me ya."

He popped it open and I tossed the bag in like it was dirty laundry. I got back into the cab and he was looking back at me, waiting.

"C I G A R S" I spelled out for him, slowly.

"Right. Sorry, you just kind of freaked me out leaving the bank with a huge sack of money, in a bank bag, first thing in the morning. Cigars. Right. Golf course here we come."

"It's just small Rand notes for fun games, prizes, and the like."

"Makes sense."

The golf course road was paved, a stark contrast to every other side road in the area. He pulled up to the drop off area and called back.

"I have to park back in the lot. They will report me if I sit here and wait for you."

"Ok. Not a problem. Guard my ten thousand with your life."

"I will."

CHAPTER
FORTY-FIVE

I JUMPED OUT OF THE car and made my way inside, watching the cab retreat to the rear of the lot. He parked, thankfully, with his front watching the entrance of the shop. It was packed with a huge assortment of oddly patterned knee length shorts and shirts of stranger colours. There didn't seem to be anyone around so I made my way to one end of the store past clubs and bags.

"Can I help you sir?" The voice was coming from the far end near a large window.

"Yes, keep talking so I can find you."

"Over here near the club entrance sir"

I walked along the long counter and saw a small black girl unloading a huge box of pink shirts, although their new owners would call them salmon. I approached the counter and saw her reach down into the box and pull out some green checked pants and when she held them out to fold them I noticed she had two stainless steel hooks.

The sun was directly overhead and the situation was dire. My weapons were discretely slung around behind me but the obvious gore on my shirt marked me as clearly as three sixes would have. Before me was an old Catholic Priest. The Priest we had been sent to retrieve. He was smiling and without judgment took both my blood stained hands in his. He turned the palms up and placed them together in his one hand and with the other touched my forehead and quietly uttered a blessing. The orphanage was in chaos with people running everywhere gathering children like small goats and herding them toward the three helicopters waiting in the field.

Yelling above the din. "Father, we're not here for the children, we're here for you and your contract staff. We have to go quickly. The rebels are on both sides of the river and moving fast towards this location."

"Why would you take old men over children? This makes no sense. Load as many as you can and I will wait quietly to meet God if that is his plan. I won't go, son."

"The agency that sent us, a Catholic outreach, told me I had to get you specifically. They will be more than a little pissed if I don't bring you home."

"Soldier, Sir. I doubt a small group of brothers that are short sighted will provide the likes of you any difficulties. The children are what we are here for and they are the ones in danger. Take as many of the girls as you can and then the older boys if possible."

He turned from me and ducked back into a smaller room. I pushed my talk button and spoke into the headset.

"Right listen up change of plan load the girls and older boys, as many as we can take on the birds and wait. I have a reluctant passenger."

"Father I have to insist you get on the chopper."

Two heads with white faces attached turned to me at my order. Followed by a little round black face. The little girl was 6 or 7 and was asking the younger priest a question. The look on his face showed he had no idea what she was asking. I turned my attention to the older man and saw tears in his eyes. He understood the question.

"Father, really the rebels are less than an hour away, you need to put foot and come with ya?"

"Sir, can you tell Father Michael what the little girl just asked him?"

Frustrated I turned to the younger priest.

"She said she was happy that her teeth have almost all grown in and wants to know how long it will take for her arms to grow back."

Then I addressed the older man.

"Look she's as good as dead, as heartless as that sounds. In this society what is she going to do? Who will marry her? She's weight, dead weight, but if you get on my chopper I will toss out bullets to get as many on board as I can."

The sobs of the younger priest behind me reached my ears as did the comments from the choppers. Everyone was getting anxious to get off the ground. We were all now heavy and would be sitting ducks if the time to contact was wrong.

"Son, you have lost the worst thing a man can lose…hope. I pray someday you will find it again. In fact, I will prey everyday, as I think the answer will be 'no' for a long while. I feel I'm going to be fine and so will those left behind. Take father Michael and the girl and get going please."

We had lifted off heavy and made the short flight back to Freetown and that was the last time I saw father Michael or the girl.

"Sir, you're making me uncomfortable. Is there something I can help you find?"

I realized I was staring at the girl and she was a little closer than I remembered.

"Ah sorry; bit of a flashback. Look I'm sorry I didn't mean to stare or make you feel uncomfortable. I was just remembering a lifetime ago. I'm looking for Cuban cigars and I was told you had the best selection in town."

"We do, they're right back here in the walk in."

She led me around the end of the counter and into the large and very well stocked walk-in humidor. I looked at the temperature and humidity settings; perfect. I set to looking at sticks. I was going to the US where good sticks would be harder to find.

"Sir, I don't mean to intrude but when you said 'flashing back a lifetime ago', how long did you mean?"

"About twelve years, you reminded me of a little girl I helped evacuate from an orphanage in the Kona district."

"Father Michael's orphanage?"

I turned and looked at her, the machine flared to high alert. It didn't believe in synchronicity, coincidence, or karma. The girl threw her arms up in front of her face as if I had kicked her in the stomach. Then she dropped to her knees, head bent in fear.

"Don't hurt me."

I recoiled, forcing the machine down. It was like a physical presence and I fought with it, fought to maintain control of it and not the other way around. My back reached the far wall and I slid down to a seated position.

"I'm not going to hurt you. I won't hurt you; you surprised me is all. You're from that orphanage?"

"Yes I am, and your eyes were angry, not surprised. I know anger and I remember you."

"Please, you just startled me. You're right I was angry, but I'm not now, everything is fine. Please stand up. How did you get all the way to South Africa?"

She stood up and looked at me like a scared rabbit. She looked around and smoothed her dress and carefully pushed her hair back.

"I helped run the Mission and worked at the refugee camps with Father Michael, and Father Donetilli. He was the older man that had stayed behind. I grew used to using my new arms but it was hard. I helped other kids that were amputees too and worked for a long time with others so it wasn't as hard for them. A friend of Father Donetilli's came to visit and he liked me despite my arms and we were married."

"So you learned English and…"

"English was easy, try tying your shoes."

"So you're her? The little girl with a question."

"And you're the Mercenary Father Donetilli prays for every night."

She moved toward me then and threw her arms around my waist, her metal limbs making an odd clicking as they crossed. She put her head to my chest and pulled tight. A quiet sob escaped her lips and she shook ever so slightly. She looked up; tears making her eyes look even larger.

"Thank you for saving me. I hoped and prayed I'd get a chance to say that."

I was uncomfortable and she sensed this and stepped away. I debated what to say. I'd just been doing my job. I wasn't going to save her. She had been a chip played to get the priest on board. That at the time I thought the best thing I could have done for her was to shoot her in the head and spare her the misery of growing up handicapped? Spare her the anguish of hope? Then I remembered what the priest had said he would pray for.

I stepped forward and put my arms around her and simply said;

"You're welcome. Is the priest still alive?"

"Father Michael, God rest his soul died of malaria a few years ago but Father Donetilli is still up in the Kona district. He has the Internet now too. I can write and tell him I saw you. He will be amazed."

"I doubt it; I think he has an inside track."

She laughed and I made point to get back to choosing cigars. I selected twelve nice sticks to reload my pelican case humidor and three others to enjoy today. I had a funny feeling I needed some time to myself.

"I'm sorry, I wish I could stay and catch up a little more but I'm really pressed for time."

"No, you're not. But you're uncomfortable with this type of thing and I understand. It's ok. But I would really like to know the name of the man that ended my torture and saved my life." She never looked up from ringing in my cigars and placing them in a large humidity controlled bag.

She handed me the bag and I passed her my real credit card.

"My name is Rhys Munroe, just like it says on the card. Can I ask you to keep it to yourself, other than the e-mail? I'm in the area for a while and would rather people not know what I do."

"Sure Rhys, just between you and me."

"And who exactly is me?"

"I'm Hope Visser."

CHAPTER FORTY-SIX

THE SUN IS HARD AND harsh as I walk back into it. The vehicle pulls round and parks to my left. I get in, and if the driver had changed into a monkey I couldn't be more surprised. The seat soaked me in and I reflected on Hope Visser and the prayers of an old man.

"Where to, sir?"

"Can you drive in the park?"

"Ya, I'm allowed to, but an open air jeep would be less money and give you a better view of the wildlife."

"Can I smoke in your cab?"

"Yeah."

"Head to the gate and take me for a bit of a tour. I've been to Kruger before, I need a little down time to think."

"Ok."

The big car rolls through the lot and I use the time to clip a San Luis Rey double corona. I roll the window down and the hot air drifts in to steal my exhaled smoke. The driver moves speedily through the traffic, but my thoughts race ahead faster than the car, down in time while holding on to the present. So my inadvertent actions years ago saved a child and that child helped others survive. Does that erase the sins of that time? Perhaps not, but it does put a different face on it. What was it about hope that scared me? I had realized years ago that the priest was right that I had lost hope. Hope in mankind and in the basic humanity that's supposed to guide us in our daily lives. Just because it was what I saw and experienced did it make it so? The girl was a brutal example in direct conflict to this. Perhaps I saw the things that made me comfortable with my vision of the world. The gate that marked the park was ahead and I toss a few hundred Rand into the front seat.

"Take care of it for me will you? A few beers would be good too."

"I'm on it sir."

The car gets hotter sitting and I feel my shirt stick to me like the cloying past. This is my last kick at the can. Win or loose my name will be too known to really be employable. In our world Discovery is still to be disowned. This old dog of war was howling his exit song. I knew this but until right now had not let the complete thought enter my conscious side. I was going to break Alexander out and what would this accomplish? Not a lot. The driver got back in and passed me an open beer and entered the park. We drove southeast down the paved section and he checked his speed down to the park limit. There was a grouping of cars ahead that signaled some wildlife and he angled along side a tour bus and stopped to let me watch an old lion service a female he had in a thicket. He was a mangy old boy, kind of like the old dog in the back seat of this cab. I could smell the urine he was spraying in a vain attempt to keep the cars away. He reenters the thicket and there is some growls and noise till he finishes and once again walks out and around the thicket roaring his displeasure at the gathered audience. I felt like an intruder.

"Head south to the 'Jock of the Bushveldt' site."

"Ok sir."

Going to the plague commemorating a deaf bull terrier must have seemed like an odd request but I felt I might have something in common with this deaf, loyal, and brave animal. It had protected Percy Fitzpatrick from many dangerous encounters without any real thought. It was what it did, its nature or perhaps calling. Echoing the same excuses I had used over the years. We drove by giraffes and two protesting hippos. My cigar burned away and I thought further about this little operation. Getting Alexander out wasn't really going to be that difficult so why had Tom been so agreeable to the large-scale operation? It would have been cheaper to do it more clandestinely. No he had another angle, he had to. We skirted alongside a black BMW with South African plates that had stopped to watch a family of baboons move their young. There was probably a cat around for them to move them at this time with so much traffic. I sniffed the air and caught the musky scent of leopard. Cars were safer than cats in the baboon's mind. Baboons hate cats.

We finally reached the point of interest. I got out of the car and walked over to the statue of the dog. I was alone and the statue was warm with the afternoon sun. What was the point of being just a dog? At best I would be remembered as a killer, brave perhaps. Committed, and brutal, but by whom? No statue or memorials for us. Sunday was dying and I was without hope and dead by many human measurements. I had affected the course of many countries and wars but there would be no retelling of my story in children's books, or history books for that matter. If there were would I want my parents to read them? My friends? No, probably not.

Then it came like a bullet, this was my chance to regain hope to make it right. To make it all, all right. I was going to make EG an example of what a rich African nation should be. It was a stretch, but one that had been scratching at the inside of my brain for a few days now. Why not? It was a long shot and part of me, the machine part, thought I was a fool to hope for it. But it was possible. I felt if I didn't say it out loud it would drift away half baked and unrealized like the social changes the hippies had dreamed of before getting caught up in the race.

Looking into the dog's blind eyes I said it out loud; "Jock, I'm going to take over EG and make it one of the best places in Africa. Its going to be an example of what motivated and good men can do if they replace greed with duty and honour. Or I'm going to die trying."

The dog didn't answer me, but I imagined his tail wagged at the challenge. I had a call to make. Other visitors were walking over and I was miles away from a pay phone so throwing caution to the wind and trying out this thing called hope I pulled out my disposable cell and called the exiled president of EG.

It took me ten minutes and three aides before I had him on the phone.

"Hello sir, my name is Rhys Munroe, and I'm a Grey."

"Yes?"

"Are you familiar with the Greys Sir?"

"Yes."

"Same deal you had with Simon. I'm appointed to the head of National Security and given a diplomatic passport. I intend to stay and work in that capacity with the military services under my complete command. The men that survive get citizenship and a small pension. You take over as prime minister and I can assure you no interference from the previous figureheads or regime. I get the same monetary remuneration that you promised Simon and we make more money by kicking out Uncle Sam and bringing in the Russians."

"Ok, but you will have to excuse my hesitation and skepticism. The Yanks are not just going to roll over on that."

"I will worry about the Yanks. Do we have a deal sir?"

"Yes."

"Ok, I will be in the first class lounge at Tambo on this Thursday, at 1400 hours. Book something that brings you through Joburg at that time and bring your lawyer. Have your flight continuing on someplace as it affords us a little more breathing room, if you get my drift."

"I'll be there Mr. Munroe. How will I know you?"

"I'll know you."

"Goodbye."

"See you Thursday."

I ended the call and looked out into the bush. This felt right and if I threw caution completely out the window, hopeful!

CHAPTER FORTY-SEVEN

THE DRIVE BACK WAS IN silence. I watched as a herd of antelope ran by and shadowed the car's path briefly before turning back into the bush. We reached the corner with the old lion. The cars had changed but the poor old lion was still at his task. I felt a little sorry for the old boy. Male lions could expire from the effort to pass on one's genes and this guy looked close. We turned left and headed west out of the park and back towards Hazy View.

"Anything else you need in town, sir?"

"Nope. Back to the bachelor party is fine, thanks."

The sun was starting its descent and I wanted to be back before Sunday and Chiwa and the others ran out of things to have the men do. It would be an odd operation for these men. Very different than the ones they had gone on before. But with Pomfret finished and their families scattered I thought they would jump at the chance to have a place to call home. Or at least I hoped they would.

We turned south and the driver increased his speed, probably wanting to get the quiet, "odd request" man out of his cab. First a bank then a strange ride to a forgotten memorial. It certainly qualified as an odd fare.

We reached the gate and the security men looked into the back seat and waved us through. We slowed only slightly as we made our way to the front of the main buildings. There was no meter for the cab and so I asked the driver what I owed him, added twenty per cent, and tossed it up front.

"Pop the trunk and thanks for the ride."

"My pleasure, sir."

I walked around and grabbed the bag and made my way into the main hall. Chiwa was at the front desk taking names and assigning rooms. He saw me and stood up and saluted. I returned the salute and we embraced like old friends comfortable with each other.

"What is the count Sergeant?"

"Fifty two, Sir. Three stragglers at the airport will be here within the hour. I figured the helicopter was warranted, Sir."

"Good call Chiwa. Where is Sunday?"

"I think he's still doing pictures as he got tired of doing bed assignments and left them to me."

"Good. I want all the men assembled in the main house here for a briefing at 1530 hours. That should give our stragglers enough time; correct?"

"Yes Sir."

"Then 1530 it is. Carry on Sergeant."

"Yes Sir."

I walked across the large room's floor and surveyed the men as I did. A few were in a condition other than normal. Malaria, perhaps, or just poor nutrition. But from what I saw on the whole they were mostly in good shape.

I exited the main hall and saw Sunday taking headshots near the banks of the river. The men outside were visiting and catching up. On seeing me they came to attention and one from the group, the senior man, saluted as the others came to attention. I returned their salutes respectively and thought to myself we would have to put an end to that quickly. This would have to be run like an SAS training camp where officers were not saluted in the training area. The men would be aware officers were never to be saluted in the field and that seemed the way to go with this one. Saluting Officers in the field was called "Sniper Check" and was only done to officers you did not like. I knew this wasn't the case here but the practice needed to stop before the football people showed up.

"Sunday, howzit coming, Sergeant?"

"Good sir, only two more to go and then the ones caught at the airport in Johannesburg."

"Perfect, Sergeant. Do we have the correct sizing for the South African passport?"

"Yes sir we checked them against an original."

"Thank you, Sergeant. Briefing in the main dining hall at 1530 hours, I want everyone there."

"Yes sir"

"Carry on then."

I turned and made my way along the river to the 'Captain House' and went up the stairs. Once inside, away from the din of the men, I fought the urge to call Andrea. I had to focus on the task at hand and could not afford the distraction. The old Sergeant Major's words and style floated back from the years and I sat down to prepare my briefing.

Several scraps of paper and two scotches later I looked at the time. It was 1520 and the men would be assembled in the main dining room. I checked my notes one last time and placed them into my shirt pocket. I doubted I would need them but proper planning prevented poor performance. The now-ancient words of the dead RSM drifted back to me on the hot afternoon breeze, as though it had been carried from his mouth to my ears. "Right, sir. I got the game plan laid out and this has to be a performance. I was only going to be here for one more day and I had to make an impression. These men would easily kill for me but I had to give them a reason to die for me too."

I made my way outside and the empty compound reinforced the idea of what I had to do. Dave wandered out to greet me and I stopped.

"Everyone employed by me is on the perimeter only, with the exception of the kitchen staff, but they won't hear a thing in the kitchen and I have given strict orders they are not to come into the dining rooms until someone comes and tells them it's alright to do so."

"Thanks Dave, I appreciate it."

"No worries, Rhys, you seem prepared to address the senate."

"In a way I am."

He nodded and I carried on towards the big house. I entered the back door and let it bang shut behind me. The noise of the men gathered had reached me outside, before I had reached the rear porch.

"ROOM!"

Sunday's voice yelled loudly over the men, all of who became silent. If they had been seated they stood and came to attention. I paused only a second before continuing into the room.

"Captain Sunday, is everyone accounted for?"

"Yes sir Captain."

"Thank you Captain, I'll take command."

"Yes Sir."

"Gentlemen. Stand at ease!"

There was a shuffled bang as men went to the called position, legs apart and hands behind their backs. This was not the precise movement one expected from Marines or drill candidates. Rather it was the movement of men that understood drill was to teach the unconscious movement to a verbal command.

"Stand easy! Take your seats and move till you can see me."

The movement was brief and quick and people sat and moved their chairs so they had a direct line of sight to me. I saluted all of them.

"Gentlemen, and I use the term lightly, that's the last salute I want to see on the property or in the field. We will be having civilian instructors and we have a game to play. A game requiring you to be something that you're not until I need you to be the soldiers that you are. That time will be obvious to each and every one of you. But it will not be for several weeks. Until that time you are all football stars."

I paused and let the murmurs go around the room.

"Close your eyes! Imagine you have been selected to play in an elite football league. You have been selected by some of the best trainers in the world and brought to one of the nicest training areas in Africa. The food you will be served will be top shelf all the way. You will be seen by a doctor and, if required, will get any attention you need. You will be paid to practice, train, and get in shape. Open your eyes. Then when you're done you will go kick ass and take names in one of the most risky and rewarding coups Africa has yet to see.

Sunday looked directly at me and raised his eyebrows. The men cheered and turned to one another in acknowledgement. Sunday brought the room back under control with a bark.

"Ladies."

The room fell silent and I gave a brief pause before resuming.

"As it sits right now, this is a rescue mission to free Simon Alexander. But I think it can be much more than that. But before I continue I have to ask if anyone wants out, the time to do so is now. Sunday will meet you outside and pay you 5000 Rand and your travel expenses home. Once we move past this point no one leaves the compound and all cell phones and computers will be removed from you until the end of the operation. You have 30 seconds to make your decision."

I counted 34 seconds out in my head and then proceeded.

"Good. I'm glad you all decided to stay. I'm honoured you decided to stay. You are my brothers and I will not command from any position but the front as I am now. You will not be asked to do anything I will not do. That being said this is a dangerous operation, even by our standards. The fallen, the Terrible Ones, The Grey. But I will not be like the country so many of our brothers died to create and leave you in the cold. I will not place you into harms way, only to move you and your families to a toxic new home. I will not resettle you like dogs when it becomes convenient to do so. I will stand with you and if need be die along side of you. "

The shouts from the floor in affirmation were loud and sang to my core. The machine growled that I was selling them a bill of goods I could never hope to deliver on.

"Many might say we don't have a hope or a prayer. I say; fuck them, I have both. I have hope that we will create something unseen in the African world. A new world. Following traditional ways. If a brother is more successful he takes care of his other siblings. If parents become infirm the children take care of them by any means. That's our tradition, which is our way. I'm not another white telling you your heritage. I'm a white who has had the honour of learning and adopting it. Because it's a better way, better than the greed-driven white way. If we expect this from our brothers and we expect it from ourselves why do we not expect it from our governments? Why do these rich fat brothers forget their obligations to the family that made them who they are? Because they get infected, by the lice they share a bed with. They lay down with the rich and uncaring machine of industrial America and forget their place. They rape the land without concern for their brothers. They destroy the bonds that our culture is based on. The traditional way of life that allowed us to thrive and populate the world. They pit brother against brother and say we cannot live together. That we are stupid and tribal and set in our ways of destruction and they spread these lies to whoever will listen. When we starve and watch our children die and take up arms to save those we love they point and use our suffering as an example. They create the misery or the uneven field and then use this to substantiate their lies. I'm a white, a Canadian white and few in this room have been to my land or seen my village but is there a single man here that would not call me his brother?"

The room erupted in shouts of anger and cries of no and it took several minutes for me to get the room under control.

"So we are mercenaries, we are the dirty words of society. You were used to fight for a white agenda and then tossed aside and hated by black and white alike. You only kill for money, you have no soul, no hope, and you're animals to be pulled out and set free on enemies. 'Cry Havoc and unleash the dogs of war'. For centuries this has been true. Not just here but in all countries; in all the places men like us have bled into the earth, mercenaries have been there. Then we get paid and told to move along, like dogs. I'm nobody's dog. You are not those dogs either and I will prove it, just as I will prove we are brothers."

"Sunday, Chiwa."

"Sir," the responded in unison.

"My orders are to be followed to the letter is that understood?"

"Sir." Again the cry came in unison.

I pulled out the pistol from my back, which Sunday had given me earlier. I held it up and pushed the slide part of the way back.

"It's loaded, and I'm not wearing a vest."

I walked over to the man on the extreme left of the group and handed him the gun.

"I'm going to continue to bore you with my speech. While I do this I have an order for you all to follow, everyone in this room. If you think I'm not your brother you're to shoot me dead. If you're just a Mercenary in this for the money and you believe me to be then you're not my brother and you should carry out that order. If anyone does shoot me I've made a terrible tactical assessment of the men I call my brothers and I don't deserve to live or to lead men to their deaths. Here is 100,000 Rand. The person that shoots me is free to take it and leave the compound and go unmolested.

Sunday, Chiwa — do you understand my orders?"

"Yes sir"

"Good! Then I will continue. We are going to learn the game of football. We will have trainers and coaches from England come and help you learn those skills. Then we will get football uniforms and two ringers, specialist players, from the premier English leagues that will come with us to EG. There we will set up camps for kids and teach them, while others scout out the country for the coup. We are going to play the country's national team. If things look right we will take EG for our own. Everyone will receive citizenship status for you and your families and a pension. For those that don't make it, your families will still receive citizenship and a pension. Your children will have access to doctors and schools free of charge. Your new country will take care of you like a father should."

The shouts broke out and someone banged a chair and for a second I thought I'd been shot.

"This is how I want it to go. It may not be how it goes exactly, but this is my plan. Only 25 of you will make the team the others will be moved to a distant location and will board a ship to make the final journey to EG. To wait till the plan is either go or no go. Standard payment will be made in either go or no go. We will create a better tomorrow for everyone. Are you up for it? DO YOU WANT IT?"

The room erupted again and I was happy to see Sunday was holding the gun. It had moved through the men quickly. Men, hardly wanting to touch it, as if it were tainted with disease.

"Great, I want it too. Let me reiterate. No saluting. No one leaves. No one calls out, or in anyway communicates with the outside world. We all know what happens when this occurs. You can trust me to insure your families are safely brought to EG before any harm comes to them; to you all I swear this on my life. The beer is on me, you wretched dogs of war. Dismissed!"

The group milled amongst themselves, the banter now excited and animated. I saw Chiwa disappear into the kitchen area as Sunday approached the front of the dining hall, weapon held at his side.

"That was kind of ballsy," he stated, handing the pistol back.

"Really? Do you really think so?"

"There is a lot of animosity towards authority. People are going hungry too. You hit the nail on the head though, good speech."

"Thanks. I saw Chiwa head for the kitchen. Is he getting dinner on?"

"Yeah dinner and bar service. They should be walking around with trays of beers instead of martinis any minute now."

"The men are going to think they died and went to heaven."

"Until I get them out of bed tomorrow. Then they'll be sure they woke up in hell."

"What are your plans for tomorrow? Oh by the way, I pull out Thursday for points west and have a meeting with the new president."

"Chiwa and I are going to lead them on a twenty click run and see who's been keeping up with their cardio and then let them break for the medi parade we have set up with the doctor. Why Thursday?"

"Well I have to get to Dallas for Friday afternoon and while I gain eight hours time wise it's a long flight."

"Roger that, and the bit about the boat picking up the guys that don't fly in? You're talking the sub, right?"

"Sub's a boat."

"Jesus, Rhys, that's going to raise some concerns."

"No it's not cause we ain't going to tell them till they're on the conning tower going in. By then they'll be so pumped to fight a short hop in a sub will be nothing."

"True. Well I guess I should leave you so you can hold court of sorts. All the men were asking about you so no doubt they will want to chat. Dinner is at 1830 hours and there is no seating chart. Menu is steak tonight with a creamy something pasta side or baked potato."

"Sounds good."

He turned and left me at the front alone for only a second before the throng of soldiers came to say hello. The greetings and questions varied only slightly. They always started in English and finished in Bantu dialects of one form or another. Polite questions about me, and my family. Never any questions, about the operation. They each knew those details would come on a need-to-know basis. They had the overview and they would wait.

The time flew by and in very short order Sergeant Chiwa's loud voice called the room to attention.

"Room! Listen up, there is no seating chart and the food is going to be served cafeteria style up here. But once you sit down that will be your team group. From where you are now you can only take three steps to reach a seat. No switching groups as tomorrow the group that does the best at the day's tasks will eat dinner first. The chow rules for breakfast and lunch are different; I'll go over them in a second. Right now men, take your seats."

There was some jockeying for position and some good-natured pushing and catcalls, as everyone grabbed a chair at one of the tables close to them. The food was brought in behind Chiwa as he waited for everyone to be seated.

"Alright quiet. Who cheated and took more than three steps? Good, that table of non-lying cheats can go up first, and we'll go from that table back and to the right. Quietly you cheating bastards I'm still talking. Lunch will be two hours and it's an ordered off the menu affair. The expectation is you can eat and get ready for the afternoon training session in that generous Football Star time frame. Breakfast is the same deal and is served from 0530 till 0700. The expectation is you're ready to play football at 0730 daily on the pitch. Tonight the beer limit's ten, but there is a 20 click run tomorrow morning so eat drink and be merry and god help you if you bitch tomorrow. The usual daily drink limit is six gentlemen; it's free but let's not make pigs of ourselves. There is no smoking inside any buildings and the usual security people are only on the perimeter now so watch for cat and the like inside the compound and when the football big wigs get here it will be your jobs to insure they get safely around the compound. There will be long guns by the entrances to every building tomorrow. While I'm on the topic of guns, the Grey are the only ones personally armed everyone else, no personal firearms. If you brought something please turn it in after dinner with your cell phone and computers in the other house's dining room. I'll charge you with caution not to make any calls or e-mails prior to turning them in. I know it sounds like basic again, but operational security is paramount here. One leak kills everyone, gentlemen. I found out about the Grey's plan at the same time you did. Enjoy the evening and once the last table is served you may come up for seconds."

The line moved quickly and as Chiwa spoke the tables got up, got their food and ordered drinks from the wait staff attending the tables. I could see on their faces they were not used to this level of service or cooking. Meat was the staple South African diet and they ate a great deal of it at every meal. But these men had been on lean times as of late and it showed on their happily being stuffed mouths and their too thin ribs. The three weeks would change that. They would all pack on a little weight and regain their combat ready physiques.

The last table got up and I hand signed Sunday to get into line ahead of me. It was a long-standing joke between us. He pretended to miss my gesture and wandered in behind me. In the old days the whites would eat before the blacks. To some that tradition had continued just because it was the way it had always been, not because of any ideology. Others used it to show respect kind of like the guest is always served first. This was the case that brought us this long-standing joke.

We had been in a small village and at the dinner in our honour we were to go first. I, being overtly polite, had gestured the 'headman' to go ahead of me. In doing so I created quite the social faux pas. He was upset and everyone was alarmed at my disrespectful gesture. Sunday had been quick on his feet and had told them that I did this as I liked to eat last. "He's a fat pink and he likes to go last so he can take as much as he wants knowing everyone has eaten. If he's forced to go first he can't take as much for fear of looking greedy." The villagers had laughed and one by one had cut in front of me. It was at a time I didn't speak the language and had no idea why everyone was cutting in line and some rubbing my belly.

We went through the line and I was happy to find a rare steak available and Sunday, Chiwa, and I went outside to the netted patio. We had just sat down when a server appeared with the condiments for the baked potato and cutlery. She also took our drink order and disappeared.

"I figured an impromptu O group meeting would be a good idea. Nice way to start the dinner Chiwa, thanks for going over the rules. I told Sunday already but I'm leaving Thursday."

"No problem Captain, the men will behave. My only concerns are with my football skills. I never played the game."

"Did you think I did Chiwa? The Captain has probably played more ball than me. But we're going as trainers and coaches, so we just have to run the men through the paces. But Rhys' how are we gonna pull that off as we know nothing about the game?"

"Somebody has to speak the language. No one speaks the English well, ya? You're needed to interpret, see where I'm going?"

"Yeah that will work."

"Till someone stubs a toe and starts swearing in English."

"Everyone curses in English as we have the best swear words."

"Look I'll be back in a week to ten days and we will see how the training is coming then ya. I bet the men are having a blast and picking up the game real well and having a lekker time. The uniforms should be here spot quick and the passports and working visa cards will be here before I get back. Issue them to the men as they will have to do some shopping before they fly into the country. I'm going to try to get a charter from Tambo to EG, but we shall see how it works out."

"All the pictures are on the digital camera, each shot is good as I already edited them.

"Great, and good thinking as you all look alike to a Russian."

"Russians all look alike to an American."

"Holy fuck, stereo racism."

"Ok, I will get those off tonight and leave you guys to the toy collecting ya? Cells, guns, and computers."

"Right, sir."

"Sure Captain, are we going to see you bright and early for our run tomorrow?"

"Captain, 0730 is not bright and early, and yes you will."

We finished our meal with small talk, the baiting and banter done and the week's plans basically laid out in advance. I would be leaving them in charge and they would get everyone up to speed or wash them out. I didn't anticipate any washouts in this group. But injuries did happen.

Returning to my tree house again gave me time to cut and have a nice after dinner cigar. I swung down to the river and out of habit closed my eyes and shielded the tip of the cigar when I took a drag. This basic skill made the sniper's job a little harder. Preserving my night vision was important so close to water. While gorgeous, a satin river of silver, reflecting the moon's influence it was also the most dangerous area. Like the gorgeous orchid seasoned men knew not to go near. The orchid's scent brings insects and then come the creatures that feed on insects and so on. Any one of those creatures from the insects to the cats feed on us. Hence the rule; never pick an orchid.

The machine stirred and brought me back on line. Something shifted, down closer to the water. Quietly it had moved, the sound like a fish breaking the surface tension of a lake with its fin. Someone else was out here too. I sensed him and I let my senses expand and I felt him. Sunday was only a few feet on the other side of the tree my back was against. The beer he had drank sharp in the air. As unnatural as a boy wearing pink, it stood out about as brightly too. I looked above my head, checking for branches but also for snakes. It was night, but it was summer too and it didn't get that cool at night. A Green Tree snake might be slow right now. But if I mistook him for a vine and pulled it down on me, he didn't need to be quick. The Two Step Green Tree snake, got its name not for his love of country music. But tonight the limbs were clear and I silently levered my body up and into the tree.

Quietly, Sunday walked around to the front of the tree and picked up the cigar I'd left on the ground. Then he looked up and into my glowing white face.

"Careful you don't want to surprise me, not to mention there is something down by the water."

"It was a Dossi; I saw it run past me. Probably going for a drink."

I thought about the small rodent, "Hyrax" to the world but people here called them Dossi, and how its closest relative was the elephant. A stranger contrast, than Sunday and I to be sure. I searched my brain for the rationale of this and then remembered. Both the Dossi and the Elephant had all its reproductive junk inside its body, nothing swinging in the wind.

"So did I pass your test my friend?"

"Yes you did Rhys. Goodnight and we will see you in the morning."

I swung down and dropped without a noise, my legs taking the shock and slowly dissipating it. I recovered my Cigar and followed Sunday's back up away from the river. He veered off towards the lights of the party and I continued back to our room. I had to e-mail Viktor and check messages from the group.

CHAPTER
FORTY-EIGHT

I POURED MYSELF A DRINK in the main living area and went upstairs to get my computer. I had vodka in my room but Sunday didn't really drink hard stuff and I felt like tonight could be one of those nights. I opened all the windows and the double porch doors and pulled the twin nets down like sheer drapes. Only then did I flip on the lights and find the can of Deet spray. I sprayed the floor and walls where the drape edges touched like some sort of arcane protection circle out a lost book of dark arts. I guess in a way I was.

The cool breeze blew away the smells of the spray and replaced it with the musky damp jungle scent. I loved the smell and it reminded me of the first time I came to Africa. That had been years ago with John. He had wanted to spend more time with me and was working on a banking project between a Vancouver company and a Cape Town one. We had stayed in a place like this, south east of the Cape and it had been my first real holiday with John, all three days of it. But while it had not been long, it was very enjoyable and John and I had really connected.

During the 'work time' in Cape Town I had been left to my own devices and had done the typical tourist things. Robben Island, the place Mandela was incarcerated. The beach to watch penguins and of course a hike up Table Mountain. John had got off early because of a controversy with the negotiations and had decided to join me on that hike. It had been then that John and I had bonded. He was telling me about the conflict that had him off early. Saying how the South African company had bugged the break rooms and the hotel rooms of all the Vancouver employees working on this deal. The sweat bathing our shirts and the heat rising from the rock and beating down from above had both of us wishing we had taken the tram.

"They bugged us and the bastards didn't even blink when we happened to find the little fucking thing. We called them on it and they just shrugged."

"Sounds like a reasonable plan. Are you mad you didn't do it first or that you relied on someone else to book your rooms?"

"Rhys, it's wrong, don't you see? A person has a reasonable right to privacy and when you're negotiating a deal…well, you just don't do it. I'm not the shining example of right and wrong, God knows, but you have to KNOW the difference when you're breaking the rules. Know which ones to break and which ones to bend. Hang on a second, I'm going to fucking crash, hand me the water."

He had stopped and drank some water and put his hands on his knees. Panting heavily he had looked into my eyes. Tired and with stress hormones coursing through his blood he really looked for the first time.

"You don't get it do you Rhys? Not really. You don't really feel it's wrong, just like if I asked you to feel a colour. You can't feel orange and you only know it's orange because I told you it's orange. Right?"

"Never ask a question to which you don't already know the answer, Councilor. You taught me that. You're right, but you knew that."

"Perhaps I did, and perhaps I hoped it wasn't true."

"Why?"

"Because without our wiring to be civilized, it's far too easy for us to be animals. You have to work harder than regular kids. Harder at being nice, and doing the right thing. Even when it's the hardest thing to do. I really hope you understand that. That you take it to heart and do it."

"Why?"

"For the sake of your family."

"They're dead."

"Then do it for their memory. Your old man was a rogue, yet he still tried to do the right thing. I hope you choose to do the same."

That had been many years ago and for a long time I had tried to live up to John's hope for me. Till someplace between then, and profit, I'd lost the plot and did things the easy way. But we had no doubt connected, briefly on the sweat covered rock and I think the larger picture was seeping to the surface. The machine didn't think so and it was boiling my mind with options and pit falls, not letting my mind become quiet and relaxed. I was edgy, too much so for here and I knew the perfect cure.

I set to e-mailing Viktor the photos of our football stars and drained another glass of vodka. I checked my draft box and got some updates from Riley. Tom was still playing nice and had done two interviews about the upcoming match and was working himself into the swing of things. Riley was convinced Tom was on board yet I was not. Therefore I would leave Riley out of the hopeful loop. While I might finally allow hope to enter my lexicon, there was still no place for stupidity.

The computer beeped while I drained a four-ounce glass of vodka and I opened the message. Viktor had responded that papers would be on their way in a week. Lots of time. By then the players and the second string would be decided.

My mind was addled swimming in vodka and the machine finally gave up trying to convince me there was a problem afoot. I was nicely drunk and picked up my unfinished cigar and relit it as I closed the windows and doors and went out onto the netted balcony. Sliding past the tub I perched myself on the edge and looked out over the compound at night. There was still a great deal of noise from the men and I could see the lights of the perimeter guards strolling in patterns they didn't know their minds had created. Patrols would do that if you didn't switch it up. To a hunter it signaled boredom and complacency. To a Grey it signaled death.

I heard the door to the suite shut quietly and I felt Sunday move around downstairs for a bit. I moved quietly to bed and tossed the nub of the cigar in the toilet as I passed. I flopped into bed and looked at the ceiling. I was tired and today had been a day of revelations and admissions. I wondered if I'd remember them tomorrow. Sleep slithered slowly along my spine, under the sheets and my eyes closed to chase it away, and lost.

I awoke with a start. Shit! What was the fucking time? My mind recalled the run and I dragged myself into the shower. I did the newbie rush for the shit, shower, shave routine and rolled out to find my running shoes and shorts. I checked my watch knowing without looking it was going to be close. It was. I had a full twelve minutes before the run, loads of time I chastised myself. Fuck old man set an alarm. I rushed down the stairs and saw the coffee pot and the note.

"I wasn't going to wake you but if you make it down with time figured you might need this. Twenty clicks is a long run, eat some fruit."

Fruit and coffee and a long run didn't sound like a very safe option. There was however a croissant and some real butter, peanut butter, and jam. I tore the flakey roll open and stuffed it like a taco with the condiments. I poured myself a large cup of coffee and made for the window to eat the thing. The jam was sweet, good, and completely unknown. I struggled to identify the fruit and failed. The peanuts were from a local source and the croissant perfect. The coffee on the other hand was strong and harsh and bit at my tongue like some kind of poisonous fish venom. The only things it had going for it were the caffeine and heat. One woke me up and the other tore the congealed peanut butter off the roof of my mouth. I finished eating and checked my watch; four minutes to the run. Fucking luxury, my brain screamed in an attempt to get the rest of the organs online with today's fitness activities.

I looked at my face quickly in the mirror. I looked ok, no nicks, no missed bits, and no jam. All we were missing was a stogie, a sweet punishing mistress. I clipped an RYJ Edmundo and stuck it in my cakehole and gave it a bite. That completed the look. I wasn't usually one for image but the men had to see me in a particular light. For that matter, so did Sunday.

I rounded the corner of the house and made for the field. I could hear Sunday shouting out news, and other items of concern that had come up from the previous evenings. I lit the cigar and my lungs protested as I pulled the smoke far too deeply in. I stopped my forward motion and the pending coughing jag that would have surely made me puke. Filling my lungs with fresh air I continued and carefully puffed the cigar to life.

The field was perfectly laid out and considering the condition I had seen yesterday I was impressed. The lodge must have worked overnight to get it ready. It looked great and I looked at the men and wished I could say the same. They were gathered as if at a funeral for the brain cells they had destroyed the night before. They looked like I felt and I liked that. Sunday was discussing the beer tab and moderation when he became aware of me. I saw his back flex to bark out the call for attention and then he stopped himself. Opting for a cheery; "Morning Sir."

"Good morning Captain Sunday, can you tell me what nomadic camel fisting tribe dropped these sorry excuses on my fucking beautiful football pitch?"

"No sir."

"Really, you have no fucking idea how this pile of disorganized human refuse landed here? Wow Captain you must be off your game too. How much, exactly, was the beer tab for last night?"

"Five thousand Rand sir."

"Five thousand Rand. Ladies that works out to about ten beers a piece, hardly the stuff of epics. Sunday would you mind if I led this run?"

"No Sir."

"You hang back and take the names of anyone that pukes. You may bleed into this red soil ladies, but you will not puke on it. Anyone that does is off booze for a week."

"Right, in a heap three deep and facing north, move. As much as it pains me to run you people out of step and rank let's keep it looking civilian and follow me."

I ran ahead and into the middle and took three large pulls on my cigar. The smoke hit the first group of men and had they not been black they would have been green. They had been out of operations for a good long time and many of them had let the easy creep of decay start. The first ten clicks rolled by and while there had been some retching no one had puked and thankfully my cigar had gone out two clicks back. We reached the clearing and I ran them up the north end and turned south and home. I pulled to one side and let them run past. Sunday pulled up along side and I asked for his gun.

"You left yours back at the farm?"

"Tired and I was running shirtless, so figured one was good."

"Well you're burnt, without at hat, and unarmed in the hot sun." He quoted while handing me his gun.

"I sprinted back to the men and watched how they fell into step and then thought better and fell out of step. They were in a column of sorts but were attempting to look civilian and not military. It was just working. I raised the gun and picked a tree ahead of the general group. I fired three rounds a few inches above their heads and was more than a little surprised to see everyone on the ground before the second round went off and rolling for cover. I headed down the center of the group passing the gun back to Sunday like a relay run, ran in reverse.

"It looks as though a little action makes you ladies look a great deal more impressive. But enough resting on your cocks, let's go. I'm getting a fucking sunburn with this slow ass pace you're running at." I stepped out my stride a little more and Sunday followed.

The return run was done with a little more retching and perhaps a puke or two but Sunday and I stayed out front and stepped it up a little more each click until the last click was done at a full sprint. My legs ached and screamed for fluid and my hamstrings threatened to shred up my leg. My lungs pulled air hard past the cigar and my feet protested with every step. We reached the football field and broke into a jog, followed by a walk, and then a backwards walk as we looked at each and every man running in. Most of them were doing ok. A few were limping from old wounds and doing their best to hide it and still others were walking back in but no one was farther than a hundred yards from the first group. I sparked up my cigar and waited for the rest to come in.

"I'm not disappointed, men. You all seem to be in pretty good shape and your endurance isn't bad. That said we only have three weeks to turn you into football stars so, eat and watch the booze consumption. I will have to leave you, as much as I don't want to, since I know all of you are really going to start to shine. I want to watch all that happen and I would like to but I'm going to have to meet and get our agreement signed and pick up some high tech war gear. I want you all to know I'm getting the best, better than you've seen and everything you deserve. This operation is going to be very dicey and I want you to have the tools. How many field medics do we have by a show of hands?"

Chiwa and seven others put up their hands.

"Chiwa, could you sit down with the medics and come up with a list of supplies? Remember we can't show up with a bunch of bags of 'bleed stop'. But I'm sure with some ingenuity you can repack ice packs or something. But we will need to be able to set up a mobile field unit for triage and the basics."

"Yes sir."

"I don't know how much Rand is left over after paying these football rock star's travel claims but use that and stop by and pick up my bank card from Sunday if you need more. Oh men I forgot to tell you, we will be using suppressed NEW Mp5's for this one and each of you has a set of Dragon Scale body armour. This stuff is new, tested, and is expensive. But it will bounce full size rifle rounds, and leave you standing. It also has awesome multiple hit characteristics. Truly top of the line stuff, so much so the US can't afford to buy it for their guys in the field. There is also a list as long as Santa's for other stuff I'm going to get and hopefully send here. Stuff that can be explained away as usual and regular things."

"Questions and Suggestions in thirty seconds."

"Sir?"

"Yes."

"Whatever you're looking at for tech gear can you make sure it's battle tested? We worked on a movie set last year and the radios were integrated phone/com units and they were buggered out of the box."

"Thanks, yes everything will be tested or come with test results prior to it going into our kit. Anybody else?"

"Sunday, thank you for the wonderful little run, I think I better take a dip to cool this burn. You have the men for the little bit before lunch, perhaps a little passing practice?"

"Yes sir. You all heard the man. Grab some balls and not your own or sweethearts, and let's see who has got some raw talent!"

Walking back to the compound I remembered to go talk with Dave about getting the chopper back for my afternoon departure. I found him in the back going over the lunch and dinner menus for this evening.

"Dave, you got the number for the chopper handy?"

"Yeah, in my mobile. You going someplace?"

"Yeah I have to leave your wonderful little hideaway and take car of some housekeeping stuff."

"Everything's good?"

"Everything's great."

"What time do you need the bird?"

"Around noon in the field"

"Done, I'll let you know if there are any issues."

"Thanks."

CHAPTER FORTY-NINE

THE WAY BACK TO THE room is overshadowed by a growing tightness in my calves and the walk upstairs outlines the story perfectly. Each step is more painful than the last. I should have warmed up better, and now I was going to pay for it. I find some aspirin and take two in an effort to speed the lactic acid out of my system. I climb back in the shower and rinse away the dirt and sweat. I pull out a nice suit from my travel bags and dress without putting on my pants.

On my way past the fridge I pull out the ice trays and unload each into zip lock bags and seal them. I move to the couch and place the bags down and set my calves on them. I set my watch for 20 minutes.

Sitting there looking like an odd pant less ruler I go over the operational plans for the coup. EG had a poorly trained, and badly-outfitted army. The President had handpicked all his Generals: all but two were from his family. From a tactical point this was a good thing as they would all likely be at the big game. He didn't trust his own military to provide close protection coverage and farmed that out to the Morocco specialists. This was not a good thing, as it meant foreign nationals would be killed in the assault.

The air coverage was good. They had a few jets that were slower than our brand new Gulfstream but had air-to-air missiles and we had no counter measures and while faster than the jet not faster than the missile. Basically we had no air support and this was a bad thing. Worse there was no way to get an aircraft into the country with its new radar system. The military ran its operations out of the main airport in Malabo. There was another airport on the small island capitol but by all accounts it was a mess. They also had Russian Hind M24 attack choppers and those 'Gators', as some pilots called them, were deadly.

Intelligence said there were five and it was up for debate how many would be in flying condition.

The country stole 15 Belgium Pandur amoured personal carriers in 2006. They were destined for the United Nations Mission in the Congo or MONUC. Those would be in fighting shape and the thirteen-ton vehicle was not something to be played with. It was amoured to the front and able to withstand 30mm explosive projectiles and was impervious to standard military long arms fire. It sported a 12.7mm machine gun up top or a 20mm auto cannon. Designed to carry 8 and you could stuff it with 13 for a short hop it was another problem I had to work out. It had a top speed of 100kph and was a six wheeled and very capable hunter killer platform. The Austrians built good gear and the six-cylinder Steyr turbo diesel sipped fuel and gave it a good range. Seven hundred clicks, if my memory was correct.

The actual military was estimated to be around 2500 men, but I was only really concerned about the 100-man air wing and their Rapid Intervention Force. The RIF were specially picked, trained, and equipped men and the force number was around a hundred. They would be the ones we would be exchanging bullets with. They would be using Russian made AK47's that were very capable military long arm machine guns. I knew the Dragon Scale vests would stop the 7.62 short round but multiple hits would be deadly.

The beeping of my watch pulled me from my depressing planning and I got up and put two-soaked towel into the microwave for three minutes. I packed the rest of my gear for the trip and removed all the bands from my cigars. It would be good to get picked up for importing Cuban cigars into the USA. Another beep signaled my hot packs were ready and I once again returned to my pant-less position on the couch.

There was a product that I really wanted to get. It was called Titanium Rain, made in Australia. I knew a few people involved in the company and had a hook into one of them. Getting the gear could be done. Getting the gear into the country was the issue.

The system used multiple barrels or tubes. The tubes were loaded with projectiles in stacks. So instead of the standard machine gun motion it fired these stacked rounds electronically in series. The result was devastating. The sky would turn dark, reminiscent of the Roman archer attacks of history. But instead of arrows these would be 20mm explosive rounds numbering in the thousands. All fired by remote control. Because they had a propellant and an explosive charge they would certainly set off any bomb detection devices at the air cargo center. I hadn't called to confirm my source could misship two or three of these devices, as I had no way to deliver them to the battlefield.

Slowly a plan started to form from the depths of my brain. Painfully it rolled back and forth and then I had an idea. It was possible. It wasn't a certainty but it was possible. I could piggyback this onto another plan, and that made me excited. I needed a big demonstration for the yanks and I just figured out how to do both.

I picked up the phone and called the number associated with a Dutch shipping giant.

"Hello?"

"Hey Jan, how's your wife and my kids?"

"What? Rhys, you slippery bastard, you in town? I see you're calling from a 881 8 sat phone number."

"Nope, sitting in the heat in my usual haunt."

"Too bad. I wanted to go for lunch and thought we might be able to get together."

"No this is more of an official call."

"What do you need?"

"You still hauling ammonium nitrate off the west coast of Africa?"

"Yes?"

"Big sealed container ships?"

"Yes, some of the biggest haulers in the world. Had to go big or stay home as the price point was making it not profitable with the fuel surge."

"What are you using for security these days?"

"Ah – we're using an LRAD — a long range acoustical device and some small arms. Why?"

"I want you to buy three Titanium Rain units from Australia and put them on your ship. You don't need to install or set them up or anything."

"How the hell am I going to get end use permission for that?"

"You don't. You have a secure pre-customs holding area in the places you ship from right? For sending gear, repair parts and the like?"

"Ya, but I have to declare it when it arrives in port at its destination."

"You won't have to worry about that."

"Why?"

"Because it won't be yours anymore. I'm going to steal it."

"What? I'm more than a little confused. Look. I owe you and I want to help but I really don't know how you're going to steal a 245-meter long ship loaded with 60,000 tones of fertilizer and hide it. I mean it has happened before but we have real time tracking and shit now."

"You don't have to know the 'how' of it. You just have to order the gear and get it on board a boat that's going to be in the area in the next three weeks. It would be good if you knew the Captain so he was on board with the plan. Just him, none of the crew."

"We have a boat there now. I can have her wait in dock if she finishes loading prior to the gear getting there. Engine issues, parts coming, that kind of thing. I know the skipper. He'll play ball but I don't want anyone hurt."

"No problem. Captain locks up the light arms and plays along; no issues at all."

"What about the boat. Do I get her back?"

"How is your insurance carrier to deal with?"

"Ah fuck, Rhys."

"Will you do it?"

"Do you really need to ask?"

"I'm trying to be polite."

"Don't. It doesn't suit you."

"The Hamburg Pearl will dock in four days. She's going to take on fuel — that will take two days. Loading will take another five She's set to sail Wednesday morning."

"When will she be in the sea of Biafra near E.G.?"

"On schedule. She'll be there in 15 days."

"Make it 25."

"Ok, how do I order this machine part?"

"I will have one of our happy customer service people call you in the next twenty four hours."

"Fuck you, Rhys."

"Sorry Buddy, but you just solved all my problems."

"Do you have any idea how much this is going to cost?"

"Not a clue, but if that had been the price six years ago would you have paid it?"

"Yes, of course I would have. I didn't mean to sound…"

"Then just say "Bye" and contact me only if there are any problems. Tell the Captain that a small craft will approach his ship off the coast of EG flashing a green laser. He's to stop and let us board."

"Ok. Bye."

The sound of chopper blades signaled the call was over and I got up and put on my pants. I called the Australian number as I walked down the stairs.

"G'day you've reached my mobile and know the drill."

"Clive, it's Rhys, I need you to call Jan in Holland and arrange for three 8867533Alphas to be shipped. Loaded and ready to roll. I will be on my cell at this number for five more hours if there are any problems with that. He will be buying them direct from you to be shipped to a pre-customs secure port in Africa. Thanks Buddy." The call was done before I rounded the corner of the first house. The recognition that I had just secured an LRAD device and three TR units making the pain in my calves almost disappear.

CHAPTER FIFTY

THE BRIGHT RED BELL 407 was sitting in the middle of the football pitch. I waved and waited for the pilot to signal me in. He saw me and nodded his head. I looked at my watch, it was fifteen past twelve, the 407 was a faster bird than the one we had come in on so the two hundred mile flight should only take an hour and fifteen or so. Just enough time to get into terminal four and meet the President. I tossed my bags into the back and slipped on the headset before belting myself in.

"Would you mind belting your gear into the other seat, sir? I don't like loose gear in the cabin."

"Not a problem."

The bird wound up and we were once again 'feet wet' in Africa. The compound shrank below us and I could see the men going over some passing drills and working out with the balls. The doctor would take up the afternoon and the men would have some fun things planned for the evening. I missed being on the ground with the men; I missed the camaraderie and friendship. But I had Officer stuff to do and they had ground skills to perfect. I would be back soon enough.

We banked west and I heard the engine spool up to its cruising speed. The engine was loud and cruising at a speed just ten miles per hour shy of its top speed of 162. I checked the beverage storage and found water and beer. I wanted a beer but I chose the water, TIA, I needed to stay hydrated.

"Fast bird, you like flying these?"

"I prefer Russian machines, but this is small, fast, and economical."

"Haven't seen too many Russian machines." I lied.

"Yeah not too many around. The big Hinds are fun and built like tanks. I have a ton of hours in those, although I rarely fly them anymore."

"Don't think I know what a Hind looks like."

"Oh really? I kinda thought you would have had some time in them. Pro's use them all the time."

"Really? We normally fly to games in big Bells like the 429."

"Games?"

"Yeah, we're a football club, so the players fly commercial or contract jets and owners and coaches fly in choppers on the event day"

" Sorry I had you guys pegged as something else."

"Really? What?"

"Not really important sir, just the discussions around the airfield, rumours really. Small town mentality, even if we're growing too large for our own good. Makes sense though, a black and white flying expensive trips to and from Hazy, off the beaten track training. Football makes sense. Anyone I would know practicing down there?"

"Yeah, probably."

We spent the rest of the time in silence. It was funny how in the rest of the world the assumptions would be that we were drug dealers, rock stars, or perhaps sports people. In Africa the quick assumption would be that we're mercenaries, it was only natural. Hopefully my playing the duck had worked to quell the rumours. It wouldn't be good to have the local police coming by. Mercenary activity was illegal in South Africa. I remembered I had made plans to see the Duchess and those plans would have to be changed.

"Ok to use a Satellite phone in here?"

"Federal law says no but the avionics in this bird has never been bothered by it sir, so feel free. There is a jack on the headset and if it fits your phone feel free to use it."

"Hello?"

"Hey Duchess, flying in a chopper. If it's loud sorry, now's the only time I could call."

"That's ok Rhys, I can hear you fine over the noise. Any news?"

"Not from me, other than I have an emergency at home I have to go deal with."

"Ah is that going to bugger our tea?"

"Afraid so mom, can't be helped."

"Ok, well I wish I could have got to see you, but I have news. We may ALL be having Christmas together, real soon."

"Really? That's great news."

"Ya, got a call from Tom this morning telling me things are moving ahead fine."

"Good to hear it, I will certainly make time for that party."

"Well you most certainly better. I will send you an invite."

"Looking forward to it mom. Bye for now."

"Bye Rhys. And thanks for never losing hope."

"That's me "Captain Hopeful.""

She laughed. "Hardly Rhys, but people change as they get older. Or well, ah, the smart ones do. Have a good trip home."

"Thanks, I will."

The line went dead and I wondered why Tom was keeping me out of the loop. The machine warned of a potential double cross but the rational part of my brain rejected the idea. Tom was far too involved to pull too much of a switch. He couldn't be sure I hadn't recorded our teahouse meeting. No, Tom was just hedging his bets. This time playing the margin would bite him on the ass.

The countryside flew by. It was amazing scenery and even though I had seen the area many times before I found myself watching it scroll by. The suburbs of Johannesburg started much earlier than I remembered. Flying in the daylight allowed a much better view. The view was not pretty. Sprawl had really set in. The poor were quickly eroding the nice areas. The picture of the class shift was as clear as day from 8000 feet. The middle class was being squeezed out by the rich and getting richer and the poor and getting poorer. Apartheid was alive and well and this time it was based on money, not colour.

The airport came into view quickly and the pilot deftly maneuvered the machine to the private landing area. I was not allowed to listen in this time and I focused instead on getting ready to depart. The landing was more of a cessation of movement than a bump. This pilot was very good.

"Thanks sir, enjoy your trip and I guess we will see you when we see you."

"Right. Should be about a week."

"Watch your step getting out."

I walked away from the machine and toward the terminal. I still had to clear customs but first I needed a boarding pass. The airport was busy and crowded and it took me several minutes to locate the South Africa Airlines counter. There were only two lines and both had people in them. I wasn't in a hurry as I had several hours before my trip but I wanted to get into the lounge and have a look around before the President arrived.

"Passport please."

I handed the woman my passport and she clicked away on the keyboard.

"Thank you sir, your boarding pass is here. Are you checking luggage?"

"I'd rather not if I don't have to. Are these ok?"

"Put them on the scale here, ya. Close enough to be legal sir, you can take them onboard."

"Thanks."

"Have a good flight."

I found the security lines and they were full of safari vacationers, tall wooden giraffes and various craft items in tow. It was moving about as fast as a dung beetle pushing a water buffalo's shit. I spotted the first class line and made for it. This line was nearly empty and had none of the Eco tourist ilk. Prior to the line a man was checking boarding passes. I handed him mine along with my passport.

"Sorry sir, this line is for first class passengers only."

"Ah I always fly in first, but this flight only had the two classes."

"Yabo, sir, I understand the direct flights to the USA have only two classes – no first class. You'll have to use the other line."

There was a couple approaching from the rear and so I needed to act fast.

"Yes, my good man I understand but I'm also a SAA Lifetime Platinum member as well here is my card, ya." I slipped him my card along with a 200-euro note tucked behind it.

He took the card and felt the paper and discreetly dropped the latter into his lap as he carefully scrutinized my card. It was a risk as it was not the same name as my passport. But the hour-long security wait would put me at a severe disadvantage with the President.

"Yabo, sir. Carry on."

I put my card back into my wallet as the couple arrived behind me.

Moving past the checkpoint I thought; thank god TIA. Everything is negotiable.

I cleared security easily and continued toward the escalators that would take me up to the mezzanine level and the first class lounges. I was worried that I would have to use the Baobab lounge and not the Cycad first class lounge. It sounded preposterous, as this was the highest class available for this flight. I rode the escalator with one half of my brain on this problem and the other was watching for things out of the ordinary.

Modern communications had made it more difficult to spot cops, as everyone seemed to be touching their ears to take calls on Bluetooth devices. But no one was reading a paper watching the escalators and the uniformed officers nodded politely; their eyes blank of recognition.

I arrived at the Baobab lounge to find it under construction. It had been under construction the last time I came past here almost a year ago. TIA and things were always fluid. There was a sign directing me to the interim lounge two floors up. The anger boiled in my gut and my lack of substantial food made this all the more painful. I spotted a SAA Employee and got their attention.

"Hi, I'm lost, well not lost, perhaps at a loss."

"How can I help sir?"

"I'm flying direct to Washington and they don't offer first class on the flight. I bought a full fare business class seat. Can I use the Cycad lounge or do I have to use the Baobab?"

"You can only use the Baobab lounge, sir. Unless you have a Platinum club card."

"Thanks."

She walked away and I could have committed wholesale murder. The meeting was in twenty minutes and I was stuck outside the velvet ropes. I could use my Platinum card but the name was different than the name on the ticket. Even if she didn't ask for my boarding pass the computers wouldn't show me on any flight leaving that day. I wandered slowly toward the lounge trying to come up with a plan. I passed a few restaurants and mulled over this stupid new challenge.

One of the airport stores selling gum and magazines gave me an idea. I entered and looked for a North America power adaptor. South Africa was a two prong 220 power and many devices wouldn't fit the smaller 120 power of America. I found one and picked it up along with some gum and inflatable rubber neck pillow. I paid for the purchases and left the store hoping this plan would work. I found the lounge and looked for the closest bathroom. There was one right next door and I hoped silently to myself they shared the same power grid.

I went into the washroom and checked the stalls. No power plugs were in any of them. I checked the whole bathroom and came up empty. There were some at the sinks but these would be on a separate isolated ground as they were beside water. I left, my fury growing with each step.

Beside the lounge entrance was an alcove and I slipped in there, hopeful. There was a plug to the right of the alcove on the same wall as the lounge. I pulled out the rubber pillow and pushed the prongs of the adaptor through the rubber. I left enough of the pillow out so I could wrap the device. Then I unwrapped seven pieces of gum and rolled the tinfoil into a roll and bent it to form a C. I dropped the C shaped tube over the two prongs and using my body and luggage to shield casual observation jammed the device into the wall socket. There was a bright flash and a noticeable pop as the circuit tripped and the C tube melted. The lights went out.

The system switched to a backup one and the lights came back on. I dropped the device, still hot, into the plastic bag and stood up and looked around. No one was looking at me. I grabbed my luggage and made for the Cycad departures lounge in a hurry, dropping the device in the first garbage can I passed.

I approached the lounge and tussled my hair and did my best to look harried. I entered and took on a general look of relief when the two ladies behind the counter looked up at me. I pulled out my Platinum card and flashed it at the counter. My voice high with stress I asked,

"Is everything Ok? The lights in the whole terminal just went out?"

"Everything's fine sir. Our computers are coming back online. What flight are you on?"

"Late flight to Heathrow, I'm really early. Got carjacked to start the day. I need to use the washroom and relax before I have a nervous breakdown. I've been here lots of times; don't need the tour."

"Go ahead sir. Have a nice trip."

I kept my harried look as I walked past the counter and made my way to the bathroom. The rubber pillow had kept me from any damage or shock, but the melting gum wrappers had made some black marks on my white shirt and hands. I moved through the lounge, happy the President had not yet arrived.

The soft carpet and soundproofing masked any sound from the outside. So I wasn't sure if they were looking for the source of the disruption or not. The creams and tans of the room were the same as I remembered and the African decorating was the same too. I wondered if the special smoking room was still operating. Pot lights that circled the coffered egg-shaped ceiling lighted the room. There were five people in the lounge. None of them paid me any attention as I made my way to the restroom.

I washed and changed my shirt. For the first time ever I also took advantage of the offered bottles of cologne. I never really wore cologne but in this case it was better than the lingering stench of burnt plastic. I remained in the washroom for an additional ten minutes hoping the counter ladies wouldn't get the computers up and come looking for me. Bribing my way into the lounge probably would not be effective. The back up plan was to buy another first class one way ticket to Cape Town from right here in the lounge but I preferred not to have to do this as I was most certainly on a list or two with the authorities whom would be watching the President's flight and the two together would spell an intervention as quickly as a Hilton girl in a strip club.

CHAPTER FIFTY-ONE

I LEFT THE WASHROOM AND found a remote area in the back. This position afforded me a good view of the lounge yet took me out of the direct line of sight from the entrance. I put my bags beside the two facing chairs and tossed my jacket on a third. The standing stainless steel lights had dimmers and I brought those all to low and pulled out my two hastily written contracts. Each was the same and written in Spanish. My spoken Spanish was excellent but my writing ability not as good. I hoped they were simple and easy enough to understand. They would never see the light of day in a courtroom but formed an understanding between two men: one of who would soon be in control of a country and the other its military. Any arguments presented from these contracts would be argued with guns and death.

As I had yet to get a drink, a tall round black girl approached and asked what I would like. She looked as if she came from the Xhosa speaking Thembu tribe. It was rare to see Thembu women so far from the eastern cape. I took a chance and answered her in her language. She looked at me as if I had just stood up naked. I continued in Xhosa.

"You must have mistaken me for a white American."

"Yes sir, you speak very well. You sound as if you learned the language from the Port Elizabeth area. You still have the musical rhythm and not the curt style of the mines."

"No mine work for me, child. Could I get a sandwich as well? Anything is fine. What kind of soup do you have today?"

"Lentil and seafood chowder."

Our tone and rhythm were falling into proper cadence and correct age deference.

"Seafood please, a small serving."

"Yes sir. Right away.

She had indeed meant "right away", as she brought my drink while another man brought my soup and sandwich. The services one can receive when one has taken the effort to connect far outweigh money. I heard it in my head as clearly as if John was sitting beside me.

The lunch settled my boiling stomach and I relaxed in the chair and waited. This President could be trusted; he had proved that in the trial with Simon. He had remained silent under extreme pressure from the world press. I didn't really trust him to run a country. He would quickly fall into the easy post-colonial practices of many African leaders. But this time I would be there to pull strings behind the scenes. He who controlled the military controlled the country. The figureheads were just the puppets that danced to the tune played by the commanders. I tallied up the costs so far in my head. We were easily at over eight million US dollars. More than double the yearly budget of EG's military. When the fireworks went off and we were feet dry in the thick of combat it would be ten times that. I smiled, tankers were expensive props.

The exiled President entered the lounge. Our number had grown by perhaps double and he looked around like a computer geek on a blind Internet date. I waved to him and he nodded and approached. I stood up to shake his hand, while he greeted me in accented English.

"Hello Mr. Munroe, it's good to finally make the acquaintance of such a man as yourself."

"Hello Mr. President, I could say the very same thing."

"Your Spanish is perfect Mr. Munroe. Would you mind continuing in Spanish as my English is not too good?"

"Not at all your Excellence, and please call me Rhys."

"Rhys it is, as long as you agree to call me Mbando."

"I see an easy agreement there Mbando. I hope the rest of our agreements will be as easy."

"I anticipate they will be, Rhys. You come highly recommended. I have done some research and while it was hard, I discovered you're highly effective."

"Thank you, Mbando. I do what I say I will do. It's really that simple. Won't you join me for a drink?"

"I would be honoured." He responded, while motioning to the man two steps behind him. This is my lawyer Michael Fernando, he's just here to help with language issues. But I see he won't really be needed. I can dismiss him if you want?"

"No, I think it's best he stay as my written Spanish is not as good as my spoken."

The formalities over the two men sat down. Drinks were provided and polite conversation followed about flights and connections and the like. The two men ordered food and I joined them by ordering another sandwich as my first had been incredible and I needed to be sensitive to the cultural issues of the Spanish.

The meals were finished and the lawyer picked up a copy of the contract he had been eyeing all lunch. He read it over cover-to-cover and then did so again. I thought to myself this man was very precise. While he read, Mbando talked about the country and his plans for change. It appeared as though he was genuine is his desire for change and improvement. I found myself liking the man despite my preconceived notions. Not that it mattered I would be in charge of the military and public safety and so he knew he had to play along. But as he knew nothing of my plans I was encouraged that he felt a break from US involvement was a good thing. Michael then picked up the other contract and read it over twice as well. He placed it down and patiently waited for us to finish talking.

"I see a few errors which I'm certain stem from your limited knowledge of the written language. If permitted I will make the changes and you can look them up if you like as I brought along a legal translation dictionary. Other than that these appear to be exactly the same contract Simon and you signed, your Excellence, with one exception. This exception is that the families of the men are afforded citizenship even if their spouses are killed in the coup."

"I don't see that as a problem. The men will be heroes and so their families should be taken care of, Michael. To do anything but, would be in a word, offensive."

"I understand sir, and on an aside, I agree. I only point it out, as it's the only difference. I will make the changes to correct the grammar if that's ok with both of you?"

Each of us nodded agreement and the conversation drifted toward the actual coup.

"So when is this going to take place Rhys?"

"Well to be perfectly honest, I don't wish to tell anyone other than those on the ground. The last issue was with too many people in the know and while I'm certain you're not a source for leaks, I have demanded total isolation for the men and figure that's for the best."

"I understand. I only mention it as I have some people in country that are loyal to me and could perhaps help out."

"I don't want to appear ungrateful but I would like to play this opera out with only my men. If you like I can forward you a safe place for your men to go when the shooting starts. This will not be a subtle affair and the start time will be obvious to anyone in the country."

"Yes perhaps that's best. I understand your desire completely. One of my cousins is a Hind pilot is all and I know he can stay out of harms way, but it also denies you a powerful asset."

"Well perhaps we have a work around them. He knows you well?"

"Yes, of course. Before my exile he was one of my best pilots."

"Well then perhaps a picture of you and I together with a sign written in your native tongue saying trust this man would be enough to persuade him to help me."

"Yes, that would work."

I handed my phone to the lawyer, who was finished his corrections and pulled out a fresh piece of paper and pen. I handed these to Mbando who wrote the note. Together we posed and held the note up for the camera. The lawyer took the picture and I checked to see it was useable. It was.

"I have made several corrections but nothing changes the substantive nature of your agreement Mr. Munroe. Would you please read them?"

I read both contracts side by side and then signed both copies and initialed the corrections. I then handed them to Mbando who did the same before handing them to the lawyer, who in turn initialed and witnessed them. He then put one copy in his bag and handed me the other copy. I did the same.

The formal part of our agreement now over, I looked at Mbando.

"Do you have time for a cigar and brandy?"

"I do but I didn't think we could smoke in here so I didn't bring anything with me."

"We can my friend and I have just the sticks to celebrate a new beginning. I hope you like good Cubans?"

"Very good! I love a good cigar," and I knew from his reaction that more than a good pact had been agreed upon.

We left the lawyer to watch our bags and made our way to the enclosed smoking lounge, pausing at the bar to pick up some good brandy. The women at the front desk took note of me, and then seeing I was with a man dressed like a traditional king went back to their duties. The brandy was pulled from a shelf under the bar and two large measures were poured. We entered a truly rare thing, an enclosed private smoking lounge in an airport and started toward a rarer thing. A cooperative power sharing agreement between a white and a black. Nothing new for a Grey.

We finished our cigars and only twice got the sideways glance from our fellow smokers. No one said anything; the glance was all the indignation they could muster. I had always found this odd and I talked to Mbando about it.

"We're getting the 'those stink' look, from our fellow smokers. I wonder if they know that they are the ones that smell? I don't know about you but I can pick up a cigarette smoker 20 feet indoors and 200 feet in the bush"

"Yes, I agree. When I was a boy and we were still growing yams at home I had to work in the fields. It was before we found oil, and our country was very poor. When some of the buyers arrived you could always find them by the smell. I didn't know what that smell was until I saw them light up their clean white cigarettes. People smoked but it was fresh tobacco from the field and once dried we used old newsprint as the wrapper or perhaps a larger tobacco leaf. Those didn't smell near as bad. Must be the chemicals."

"Perhaps we have another agreement?"

"What would that be?"

"We import some plants from Cuba and start growing tobacco for cigars, teach some rollers and we have a new export market."

"I think I'm really going to like working with you Munroe. You see possibilities and take steps to make them realities. That's a rare thing for a white. Normally it's more profitable to just take the resources and sell them."

"Well I intend to live part of the time in EG and there is going to be a lot of jobs to create to get people doing something. Cigars are very labour intensive. The worst thing to have after a coup is idle hands."

"Yeah you're right; idle hands may join with those of Samelli."

"You have that legend in your culture, too?"

"Not a legend Rhys, I have seen those touched by him. They are tainted and glow with his evil mark and desire for destruction of all life."

"Really?"

He didn't continue and I was once again reminded of culture. No matter how educated someone was the early teachings formed a base layer. These superstitions no matter how odd coloured the world they lived in. I bet Mbando had little carved animals on a string around his neck. These were called fetishes; perhaps the Christians would call them idols. It didn't matter and thinking about it I guessed my culture had the same silly beliefs. Turning the other cheek, I had found was the best way to end up with matching bruises.

Our cigars finished, we again moved into the relaxing lounge. My flight was in forty minutes and at a gate down the terminal. I wanted to keep my luggage close to me and so wanted to board early, as I was still unsure of this two-class system. We reached our table and to the obviously bored lawyer. I checked that my copy of the contract was still safely in my bag and standing bid them both, good bye.

CHAPTER FIFTY-TWO

THE COUNTER LADIES HAD CHANGED and I was glad they had as it made it easy for me to slip out of the lounge four hours early for my 'Heathrow' flight. I caught the reflection of both, in the glass of the big doors, as they looked up from the desk. I walked back out into the main terminal and turned left to my gate. I noticed the alcove area was taped off with workman's yellow tape. Two men were bent working on the wall plug. 220 packs quite the punch and I must have melted the plug. Five gum wrappers would be sufficient next time.

I walked along the terminal scanning for and marking potential threats. There were only a few. I passed them unnoticed. Outside was the plane that would deliver me back to North America. It was an odd looking plane as the middle section was stretched out of proportion to the rest of the plane like a Hummer made into a limo. I reached the gate and noticed that it was already boarding and joined the long line of passengers.

The line was fast and efficient, as they were not checking passports against boarding passes. The attendant, a tall Zulu women, looked at my carry on and was about to comment till she saw my ticket. Nodding she sent me down the jet way tunnel with the standard welcome aboard.

I looked at my seat designation as I approached the aircraft and turned left towards the front of the plane. The stretch was more surreal inside and I couldn't help but think this is what it must look like in a plane crash nightmare. The cabin went on far too long for anyone used to flying. I walked up, pushing my Tumi in front of me with the laptop case angled to the front. It was a long walk.

The standard curtains separated the two classes and walking into the front section was like walking into a late seventies sci-fi movie. Not that the seats and area were old or with non-modern design. It was, on the contrary, very new and up to date. But it was as if someone who had watched far too many Jetsons cartoons had been in-charge of design. The seats were white egg shaped affairs complete with a dome above like the egg chairs of the 70's era, when we were sure we would be flying in space cars in ten years. There was a great deal of separation between the capsules and the gleaming white and blue accents were kind of cool. I was pleasantly surprised that while called business class it was actually the same as first for they're in country flights.

I found my pod and sat down. It was not the country club design of British Air but it was still very comfortable and the egg design did provide a ton of privacy. A tall Dutch looking blond came by and took my drink order and I set up my workstation and was just about to turn off my cell when I realized I had missed a call. It must have come in while I was in the meeting with Mbando. Being on silent I missed the vibrating thing in my bag. I checked the number. It was an Australian exchange.

As we were still on the ground I punched the call back number and listened to it ring.

"Rhys?"

"Ya, how's life on the island of oddities?"

"Gimme a sec mate."

The line was quiet for a while and the seatbelt sign was on but we weren't moving yet and I looked up and around while I waited like a kid standing point for his smoking friends in the high school bathroom.

"Sorry, Rhys, I can talk now. Getting the products you asked for in country and on time isn't a real issue. But, what I'm worried about is exposure. I have to sign off I received proper documentation from end use country's authorization. If these things get found then the company and myself could take a real hit. With the economy and our clientele that could be a real nail in the coffin. The other thing I need is what you want the launchers loaded with and what type of software you need. So like smooth my concerns here mate as I feel like I'm about to climb into a sleeping bag with a Koala."

"Clive, I'd never put you in a position like that. The units will not be found in one piece. I'm sure you can program it to bypass the firing sequence and set off the bottom three rounds in each tube at the same time and take the units out. Or I can just rig it with some plastic. They are going to a pre-customs holding area; they don't look like weapons, to be loaded onto a ship that will never see another port again. The load should be fifty calibre amour piercing rounds with ten percent of the tubes loaded with high explosive same calibre. The other, all high explosive with the third a 50/50 mix. Software should be local area network connections and a stand alone laptop for each unit."

"Right Ok, Jan never gave me any details, just the blank purchase order. I can fudge and lose the documents I never got. Not an issue mate. But don't hang me on this one. We're in negotiations for these to be used in some really profitable venues and any word of this would trash me and the company."

"If this plan goes like it should you can look forward to a really big deal on the horizon, my friend."

"Really? That would be awesome. What are we talking about here?"

"I can't tell you Clive, operational security and all that. But, suffice to say you're going to be the primary product provider to a very rich principality. Say a thousand units and some of the mounted gun units as well."

"Ok, I understand the idea of risk and reward. I'll ship them out today configured with a failsafe fire programmed into the units. We have a new system that uses a ring coded with an algorithm that unless the person in charge is with the unit it's a box. I'll add to the code that if she gets messed with she blows the bottom half of all tubes. I'll send you nine rings, each programmed for any of the units. They were developed for our handguns but are really slick."

"Thanks Clive, I have to run; this plane is moving and they will be doing a seatbelt walk through any second now."

"Bye."

I ended the call and pushed the power button just as the attendant entered my aisle. I dropped the phone into my bag and took off my shoes.

"Another drink, sir?"

"Yes please."

She smiled and nodded and moved to the next pod. I thought about how the Titanium Rain product came to be. It had been about seven years and Clive and Owen, both avid shooters had tried the new electronic guns that were gaining popularity. These new guns used a non-moving firing pin to fire the round. Instead of a regular bolt, with springs. levers and shear points it had a glow plug device. This glow plug would receive a signal from the trigger, which was only a switch now, and heat up instantly. This heat would cause the special rounds primer to explode and ignite the powder in the round, which in turn would burn and the expanding gas would send the bullet on its way. As the story went Owen had gone home and found one of his kids trying to make the inkjet printer work. Owen, an engineer, had taken the print head apart trying to help his child print their homework. While working on the print head, Owen had come up with the idea of Platinum Rain.

The inkjet print head boils a very small amount of ink causing it to expand and 'fire' from the nozzle tube onto the paper in a rather precise manner. He wondered if this same principle could be adapted to an electric gun. It could, he believed, but the difficulty identified was the gun's traditional action of fire, eject, and reload was far too slow. Further the single barrel design was similar to the single print head of earlier printers. So he designed a multi head device like the multiple inkjet heads on today's modern printers. They added a propellant to the actual base of the projectile and Platinum Rain was born.

There was no doubt in my mind that this 'version' was oversimplified and dressed up for the public, but it was an eloquent version of the truth. Owen had then approached Clive and together, with Clive's money had started the research and development stage of the company. Five years later they had working products, which were everything they wanted it to be. Each barrel able to fire one round or up to over one million rounds per minute and just like the accuracy of an inkjet printer making a picture; this weapon could paint a picture of destruction like no other. Further making it effective for the battlefield, being solid state meant that no spent casings needed to be ejected, so the traditional power requirements do not come into play. The unit could be fired using flashlight batteries.

At issue for me was going to be getting the heavy units off the container ship and into the theater of operation. Each unit weighs in at about 300 kilograms loaded and I hoped unloaded the weight could be distributed enough to get them into play. The ship would have a gantry crane to load them onto a boat. Getting them off a boat secretly and placed into the theater without discovery would be the problem.

The flat top of the boomer sub would make this easier, I thought as a solution swam up from the recesses of my brain. If she made it there, on time. The port habour was deep enough, I knew after talking with Jan. The ability to lower the sub and roll the weapons into waiting trucks was a perfect alternative. Timing was going to be the bitch of the bunch and sitting on the runway waiting to take off wasn't lending to my optimism.

The long plane finally clear rolled into the sky and I was again 'feet wet' for the third time in two days. I needed to sleep and the calves were complaining about the run more than I hoped. My sunburn was letting me know it was there and I wished for a Viagra or two to keep my pants off my thighs.

The attendant came back with my drink and I asked for a couple of ice packs. She disappeared and returned with the ice and I propped them under my calves and tried to relax. The big issues were under control as much as I could affect them and the rest would just have to wait till we were all feet dry in EG.

Dinner was served. There had been three choices and I went for the lamb shank in a reduction that was sweet and spicy at the same time. Three glasses of wine with dinner combined to put me into a nice deep sleep as half way around the world the logistics of getting beer, tents and equipment to EG was being worked out.

CHAPTER FIFTY-THREE

THE PLANE TOUCHED DOWN WITH a jolt and I bolted awake. The pod design was a different enough to let the machine come online briefly, scanning and getting situationally aware. I was feet dry in the USA. The wet sheets of rain streaking the far windows were making it hard to see the grey skies of Washington. I checked the time. We were eight minutes late and that would likely stretch to ten. This gave me an hour and fifty minutes to catch my 8:00 am Delta flight.

"Coffee sir?"

The voice had come from behind my pod's left side. I craned to see the flight attendant as she stayed back, giving me privacy. My pant legs were damp from the ice, now water, and my feet were cold.

"Yes please, black and in a take away cup please."

"Of course sir."

I arranged my gear and wished I'd had time to change my pants, socks, and underwear. I had been to Dulles airport before but for the life of me couldn't remember where the Delta terminal was located. I wished for one of those portable printers. They seemed silly to carry most of the time but at times like this I could have checked in online and printed my boarding pass, saving precious minutes.

My coffee arrived and I took a long sip. It was good and dark, surprising for an SAA plane. They must be used to serving Americans. It wasn't the usual 'sex in a boat' coffee, fucking near water, preferred by South Africans. I acknowledged my surly morning mood with a chuckle and picked up my gear.

The seat belt sign blinked off and I moved quickly towards the exit. There was a small line of people forming as each tried to remove their bags. I politely moved past people stating I had a quick connection.

While balancing my laptop case on my carry on and holding my coffee. I was mostly successful and only decorated a few of my fellow travelers before reaching the door.

I entered what is called a moving lounge; my attempt to circumnavigate the throng of people thwarted. These were like busses that were raised up to the jet door and provided transportation to the arrivals area. They waited to be filled and I looked through the dirty looks of my previously passed passengers. I took a moment to switch passports and pulled out my real Canadian one before arriving at the building. I moved along with the group, scanning for customs, and found it just before the access doors.

The man was older. He took my passport and slipped it through the scanner before looking at me.

"Welcome to the United States. Purpose of your visit sir?"

"Just coming home via the US."

"Anything, not on your customs card, to declare?"

"Nope. I don't get into African art."

"Have a nice visit, sir."

He stamped my passport and I was glad he hadn't checked the multitude of stamps inside my passport. I didn't have an exit stamp or an entrance stamp that was current. The move to looking for terrorists by the US Custom Service had been a good one for the professionals in the world. While officially they didn't profile, they did. I fit the model of a professional consultant to a tee and therefore posed no threat to security.

Now cleared, I entered the building proper. Not having to retrieve my luggage was a boon afforded by the increased ticket price and once again I was glad about my choice. There was a United Nations list of people circling the several luggage carousels and I thought to myself there would be no way to make a two-hour connection with this crowd. It was only 6:25 and the place was packed and looked like some sort of Chaos theory experiment.

I walked past baggage carousel 15 and picked up an airport guide. This was a big airport and while I knew the Delta Airlines ticket counter would be in the main terminal I figured wandering about without a plan was stupid. So I spent the precious minutes getting one.

They had implemented a new D2 Security System for screening passengers. If I made my way to the terminal I would be stuck in the lines screening all passengers leaving. But there was a way around this. If I had a preprinted boarding pass for my Delta flight I could simply go through this system here in the arrivals building near baggage carousal four. But I needed a printed boarding pass.

There were no lounges in the area but there was a USO lounge. I had been a contractor with the US military the year previously so I figured it was worth a chance. I looked at the map and located the lounge and made my way towards it.

The lounge was empty except for volunteer desk staff. I walked up and presented my passport.

"Hi I'm a contractor and I need to print a boarding pass for my connecting flight to Dallas. It leaves in an hour and a half."

"Thank-you Mr. Rhys we don't see too many Canadian civilian contractors. Let me check your ID. Ok I have you in the system. What is your flight?"

I read him out the flight information and he tapped away quickly on the system. The printer, somewhere below him, came to life and started printing.

"There you go Mr. Rhys. Anything else I can help you with?"

"No, Thank you."

I took my newly printed boarding pass and headed for the Arrivals security checkpoint. I admonished myself I was going to get one of those silly portable printers.

I entered the empty Security Screening area, the bold black and deep red walls surrounding glass doors taking on an Orwellian motif and I wondered if anyone else made this bleak connection. The bags and I were scanned and shown to be of proper and safe configuration for travel and I made my way to the shuttle for terminal B. The shuttle was quick, not waiting till it had a full load like the moving lounges had done and we took off.

My gate was B79. I still had about forty minutes before my flight to Dallas boarded. There were several lounges located in concourse B but I figured I'd use the Delta one about gate 15. I could have used the BA or one of the others that served only to remind me I flew way too much.

I walked into the lounge and the attendants looked up and greeted me with the false smiles of overburdened sales clerks. I presented my boarding pass and passport and they confirmed my flight was leaving later than expected, but only by half an hour. So much for the rush, I thought.

"Would you like us to page you when your flight is leaving, sir?"

"That would be great, if it gets pushed back further could you let me know too."

"Certainly sir, but it shouldn't happen. It's just a luggage delivery issue with the construction of the new aero train"

"Aero train?"

"They're set to replace the Plane Mates next year?"

"Plane Mates?"

"The lounge you were loaded into when you got off your flight sir."

"Ah. I understand."

I walked to the shower area reminding myself to never again fly through Dulles if I didn't have to.

The shower is hot and the bathroom clean, North American clean, which is like Africa sterile. I feel the hot slowly start to get my body going. I hated waking up and having to move fast. In the field it was expected and fine but surrounded by the creature comforts of the civilized world it was just wrong.

I changed my clothes and realized I'd made a mistake in packing. While Dallas was usually mild in November it was still far colder than the African summer. However, as my luck would have it, Dallas was being hit with near record low temperatures. I didn't have anything warm enough. But the fresh clothes were enough for the flight and I performed the usual morning ritual wishing I were back in Hazy View.

Finished, I marked the room to be cleaned and returned to the lounge. It wasn't a great lounge but it was far better than the terminal. The high terminal ceilings made the place seem colder than it was. I ate an unremarkable breakfast, but with good coffee. Watching people slowly come in like weary travelers entering a roadhouse of old.

I flipped on my SAT phone and checked the charge. It was below halfway and I took the opportunity to plug it in. I had no messages. I plugged my laptop in too and checked to see if I had any messages there.

There were two from Viktor and one from Z. I opened Z's first and it took a while to download the large picture file of him and the new plane. It was an awesome looking jet. The belly kind of bulged slightly like an in shape woman in her late forties. The rest of the lines were sleek and toned. I had to admit it was a gorgeous plane.

Viktor's two emails were about the passports and the sub. It had made it out of the dangerous area around Korea and was heading quickly for the Philippines. It was apparently performing better than expected with the light load and quieter than the plans had proposed. Apparently the new engines and sound deadening were a marvel and fish were making more noise in the water than her. Viktor had named her Andrea's Shadow. That was almost cute, and I stopped myself from responding, as I didn't want to embarrass him. Instead I typed a brief note acknowledging I received the info.

The announcement was made the short hop to Dallas was preparing to board and I finished my breakfast and signed off. The two and a half hour flight would be quick and would get me on the ground with enough time to do a quick walk around the Convention. I had never been to Dallas although I had been through the airport numerous times. I quickly dialed the Fairmont's President club line.

"Good Morning, Fairmont President's club. How can I help you today?"

"Hi. This is Rhys Munroe. My Club number is 3477893."

"Yes, Mr. Munroe I have you staying with us tonight and this weekend in a gold level one bedroom suite at the Dallas property. Do you need to change that reservation, sir?"

"No, the reservation is fine, however I'm coming in late at eleven this morning and I was wondering if I could get an early check-in and have the hotel send a limo to meet me at the Dallas airport domestic arrivals?"

"I will put a note on your file here and send it ahead to the gold level concierge. I can't confirm availability for early check in, but it shouldn't be an issue Mr. Munroe. The concierge will take care of the limo for you and bill it directly to your room. Is there anything else I can assist you with today, sir?"

"No, that's great, Thanks."

"Thank you for calling Fairmont Presidents… " I didn't let him finish.

I ended the call and unplugged my electronics before storing them for the short walk. The lounge was getting a little livelier as friends met and hugged and I realized it was getting very close to the holiday season. While Christmas was more than a month away people were still seeing friends for the last time before the start of the rush. When I was home Ruben and I would spend the holidays together with him getting tuna and me eating a turkey dinner take out from the local White Spot restaurant. It sounded bleak but it was how we did the holidays. Perhaps that would change this year.

I re-entered the cavernous terminal and turned left toward my gate. There were the usual travelers looking shell shocked and weary, constraining children and watching luggage. I moved along with the mass as if I belonged among them. I didn't, but sheep may graze peacefully where wolves were well fed.

The machine kicked up and told me I had attracted the attention of someone. I casually turned into a magazine store and looked at the shelves allowing my perception to expand. I noticed a man in a dark suit and expensive shoes eyeing me from a coffee shop. He wasn't a cop; the shoes were worth more than a cop earned in a week. The suit was a good cut and obviously tailored for him. No weapon was immediately discernable.

I picked up a copy of the Christmas Robb Report plus some gum and breath mints and made my way to the counter. Realizing I had no US money I used my card, and the clerk shot me a funny look. For a moment I thought that perhaps I had used the wrong VISA card. I hadn't and I guessed that the small purchase, one being a magazine that catered to the stupidly wealthy fit a funny profile for him.

I walked out of the shop and continued toward my gate. Tracking the man who had once again continued in the same direction I was going. His gait was short and not obviously agile. He was about six feet tall and while not muscular was stronger than average. He moved as if he had an injury to his hip and the machine took note of this like a poker pro playing above the rail.

The gate had a plane at it but no passengers. The Machine was wondering if the delay had more to do with the shadow than the construction and carefully took in the lone gate attendant. The fact that we had just started boarding and there were no passengers waiting coiled the tension along my spine.

The gate attendant was a tall woman. Her uniform fit well if a little tight in the hips. She was wearing comfortable looking flat shoes and had the bored look seen all over the world by attendants and people who made a living waiting on people. She looked usual, not a spook.

"Welcome aboard sir, sorry for the delay. You're in one C today."

"Thanks."

I walked down the jet way toward the waiting plane and the machine made out that the shadow had just approached the attendant too. I slowed my pace and strained to hear the tone of the conversation. The other part of my brain was wondering why it was necessary to read the ticket and inform passengers where they were seated? The shadow entered the jet way.

I was met at the door of the smaller regional jet and smiled as I walked past the attendants to the first aisle seat on the right. I tossed my carry on into the open overhead compartment while I checked the other first class passengers. There were only two, a man and a woman and while they were seated together they were not a couple. The rest of the plane looked to be about half full. I put my laptop bag beside my carry on as I was seated in a bulkhead seat and had no space under my seat.

I pulled a pen from my shirt pocket and exposed the sharp end as the shadow entered the plane. He moved into the first class cabin and didn't look at me as he moved past and took a seat behind me. I watched him as he passed, the pen cupped in my hand.

The fact he had not looked at me was odd. Everyone looked at the passengers in first class on these smaller jets. They would look, trying to discern why you were seated in the special section. Appraisingly gauging why you decided to sit in the expensive seats and wondering if you were famous. The fact he had not looked had tipped his hand, that he was watching me and that he was less than a pro.

"Can I get you a cocktail, Mr. Munroe?"

Fuck. Well there was no hiding who I was now. I thought Delta would be a little more tactful. While I knew their passenger manifest had my name, larger carriers had given attendants specific instructions not to use passenger's names. While at first glance it made it appear attentive and friendly too many famous people had complained at this breach of privacy.

"Coffee, please. Black."

She arrived just as the doors were closing. No other passengers had got on and I sensed a movement behind me. The lady had got up and moved to a window seat in the second row. She remarked that she wanted to see the city to the man seated next to her. A lie confirmed by our exchanged smiles. I let the pen slip again back up my sleeve.

It was a short taxi and in minutes we were in the air. Only 20 minutes later than scheduled. I waited for the seatbelt sign to go off and when it did, got up and pulled down my carry on and belted it in the seat beside me. Getting killed in a plane crash sucked but getting killed by your laptop and underwear was pathetic.

I pulled out my iPhone and plugged in the headphones. Setting the phone to plane mode I switched to my music and turned it up loud. I placed the phone on my armrest and tucked the ear buds under my shirt collar. I then placed my noise canceling headphones on, but didn't turn them on. The picture was of someone listening to very loud music. The reality was I could hear everything in the immediate area.

The attendant made her rounds and I rudely left the headphones on appearing to read my Rob Report Christmas gadget list and tapped the top of my coffee cup. She poured more coffee and continued to help the other passengers. The shadow never moved.

The rear attendant came up and talked briefly with the first class one and she nodded and I read her lips as she said as soon as I give this group one more go around I will be back to help. The larger attendant returned to the back and ours did come round to see if we needed anything.

She left the cabin, a big no no since the September 11th attacks. The shadow picked this opportunity to make his move. The machine wondered briefly if he was coming for us or actually going to try and get into the cockpit. The result was going to be the same in either case.

The shadow moved up the four rows toward me. The machine strained. My peripheral vision tracked the shadow and saw his empty hand coming towards my neck. The pen slid into my cupped right hand again. His hand took my shoulder. My left hand shot across my body and slammed on top of his hand hurting my shoulder and trapping his hand. My right elbow shot into the man's hip hard and he yelped and fell toward my lap. My left hand transitioned to the back of his head as I brought the cupped pen into the erect position facing up. The man landed hard on his knees, the pen an inch from his eye.

"Rhys! Rhys Munroe, I'm a friend. A friend of Tom's."

I let the pen drop and taking the man's hair roughly guided him into the space between the seat and the bulkhead wall. Sitting on the floor and looking at me, at the machine yearning to drive the pen into his brain, it was obvious the man was terrified. I heard the flight attendant moving quickly towards our seat. I pulled off my headset.

"Are you all right, sir?" I asked the shadow loudly as the attendant's footfalls reached our row.

"Ah, yeah. Sorry. Damn hip gave out."

"Here, let me move my computer bag. Take a seat till you're sure you can put pressure on it. You went down pretty hard."

I got up and moved my carry on into the overhead compartment, pretending to be aware of the attendant for the first time.

"Its ok, he just kind of fell on me. I'm ok and he looks ok, but I figured it's best he sits for a minute or two before continuing to the toilet. Could have been an unsafe vascular dilation; blood pressure drop. It happens to hip replacement patients from time to time, and flying makes it worse."

"You're a Doctor, Mr. Munroe?"

"Yes."

"Ah, sorry then our manifest just says Mr. No Dr."

"Gynecology. Not much use in an emergency, I'm afraid. I changed my profile as a nurse or first aid attendant is more qualified for handling things that happen on a plane."

The shadow had painfully moved into the window seat beside me and was rubbing his hand and hip. The attendant gave me a nod and went back to the front galley cabin. I sat down and looked at the man beside me, now quivering like a mouse unfortunate enough to crawl into a puff adder hole.

"Start talking, fancy shoes, you're not out of the woods yet."

"I'm a friend of Tom's. I work for Sentinel as a lobbyist and contact person in Washington. He sent me your picture as you're working with us on a special project. I saw you when I was getting coffee and just thought I would come and introduce myself. I didn't mean to startle you. I just thought we might like to compare notes."

"I saw you in the airport. What special project?"

"Tom never said. He just said you were coming with an exhibitor pass and that I should provide you any assistance you need. He told me you were a bit of a wild card and that if there were any problems I should call him directly."

"Call him."

"But it's Saturday. He won't be in the office."

"I'll give you his cell, like you don't already have it."

"He'll be with his girls."

"Even better. Call him."

Shadow picks up the phone and makes the arrangements to place the overseas call. That done he looks at me expectantly, like Faust looking for a loophole.

"Report what has gone on, rat."

The call is connected to Tom and I can tell immediately this man is a lower functionary and Tom is not happy taking his call. The deference and fear is obvious in the man's voice as he outlined the previous events. Nodding his head but forgetting to speak he squeaks out "yes" and hands me the phone.

"Afternoon Tommy."

"Rhys, you know I hate that, you're not my grandmother. Although, you do seem to be getting long in the tooth. Look, sorry, I didn't put anyone on you or anything. You got circulated in a memo and this guy wanted to meet a 'real life mercenary'. Nothing more, and I know you can tell he isn't a pro. I'm not that stupid."

"Perhaps you should circulate another memo, before your HR department has to start paying death benefits."

"Jesus, relax man. The world isn't out to get you. You getting paranoid in your old age?"

"Only when I'm forced to play with amateurs."

"Look I'm with my daughters, what do you want me to say in the memo?"

"How about children shouldn't play with dead things."

"Really Rhys. I'll make it a little more subtle and politically correct and send it out today."

"Do what you do best Tom."

I pressed the disconnect button and looked at my corporate liaison.

"So what do I call you fancy shoes?"

"Aleister, my name is Aleister."

"So Aleister you're supposed to keep an eye on me?"

"No sir! I'm just to report if anything gets really stupid and be of any help you might need."

"Well I think we can safely say things have gotten stupid. You just about fell head first on my pen. You'd have to admit Aleister that has got to be one of the stupidest ways to die."

"Yeah."

"Ok so we are past point one. Point two is I don't need some fancy shoed fuck trying to get me laid. Do I look like I need help in that area?"

"No."

"Great! I see were looking at the monkey's balls from the same perspective. If I need your help, I'll kick those balls. Now, fuck off to the washroom and clean yourself up and get back to your seat. I don't know you and you're not my friend. Anyone asks about me what do you tell them?"

"Um, er, Children shouldn't play with…"

"Right! Now fuck off."

Aleister made his way to the can and was in there for a long time before returning to his seat. I heard the attendant ask him if he was feeling better and I heard him answer. Tom was starting to piss me off more than usual. I had blood on my hands from stupid shit and almost had more.

CHAPTER FIFTY-FOUR

DALLAS CAME INTO VIEW, a cold wasteland of nothing. I had seen advertisements for vacation plans in Texas. I wondered how many people actually followed them? In the winter it was like taking a trip to a place people wore cowboy boots in the snow and drove pick up trucks with less tread. There was a reason this was a hub and not a destination.

The airport was in keeping with the state's history. It took on the shape of a covered wagon that a smart and merciful god had stepped upon. The terminals were like wheels off a central platform. It had all the aesthetic trappings of a cactus in winter and I was certain yogurt had a more active culture.

But the state did have beautiful people. Proud, strong, and very attractive. I guess it did have some redeeming qualities, and Tom and fancy shoes probably overtly influenced my observations.

The plane touched down and I looked forward to getting settled and spending Tom's money. A gust of wind shook the plane and a few less than patient passengers took spill into the isle or the seats they had recently vacated, prompting the attendant to make another remain in your seats speech. I laughed inwardly. On big planes seat belts were an option on taxi. On these smaller regional jets it wasn't.

The sign winked off and I got up to get my gear.

"Hi, You really a gynecologist?"

I turned around to face the voice behind me. The lone female passenger in first was standing as in a ballet pose; one practiced foot pointing forward and the other behind making a T-junction, forcing out a hip. Her blouse was unbuttoned further than it had been when she changed seats and her make-up freshly retouched.

There was a bump as the jet way was rolled up to the plane.

"Why do you ask? Is your pussy broken?"

Her mouth dropped open and the expression on her face was that of a woman not used to be being rebuked. I left her standing there and walked out of the plane towards terminal E.

I walked toward the domestic luggage area and let the machine scan the area. It had been far too many hours since I had enjoyed a drink or a cigar and my nerves were ensuring I knew this. I was also distinctly aware I was not dressed for this time of year as most of the people I passed were wearing or carrying large jackets.

I spotted a Brooks Brothers sign just up ahead and figured I'd fix the issue. I went in and looked around for the jacket section. I spotted it and walked over.

"Can I help you sir?"

"Yeah, I forgot my coat at home and really need something before I walk outside into the deep freeze."

"Actually, sir, it's 37 out there today, not too bad at all, for an ex-south Dakota boy like me. I daresay it's a shock for Dallas. It is usually not this cold here. We do have some great leather jackets over here and they have zip in melton wool liners in case it does get cold."

"Well then perhaps, just in case. A 48 tall will do."

The man handed me a heavy lined leather coat. I put it on and marveled at the butter smooth leather. Black in colour it fell to my mid thigh. The sleeves were perhaps a half-inch too long but it would do.

"Great, I'll wear it out."

I reached the luggage area and spotted the driver holding a sign that simply said Fairmont.

"You here for Rhys Munroe?"

"Yes sir."

He bent and took my carry on and led the way out toward the bright snow. The air was like a surgeon's blade on unfrozen flesh and it stung my sunburned flesh. The door was opened and I blundered into the darkness of the limo's interior.

The car was more about moving people and less about opulence. It had seating for 12 and a very small bar. There was, however, ice and little bottles of booze in a miniature display. I thought this being the Lone Star state it would be go big or go home, but at this juncture anything would do. The two flights in such a short time had my nerves on edge, vodka should do wonders.

It did. The familiar bite and warmth took the edge off the after-effects of the flights and I allowed myself to relax into the deep, grey, leather seats. I heard the driver get in and the car cut melted into the flow of traffic and took off much faster than normal. I actually had to brace my foot to keep from sliding down the leather bench. Small bottles, but big motor. It was Texas after all.

The city came up fast and the traffic was light. It was certainly winter and the general lack of pedestrians proved that the locals didn't think 37F was as balmy as the coat salesman had.

The hotel came up on my right hand side. It was a twin tower building, designed with a large base. Its brown and tan colour was rendered duller, with the spackle of snow. It had three large dome windows at the front driveway and the limo pulled up the main drive to the lobby doors.

I gulped back the rest of my drink and grabbed my laptop bag as the door swung open and was greeted by the bellhop staff. The large glass doors lead the way into an expansive white marble foyer. The blinding white of it created an illusion for just a moment that the snow was inside as well. I called over my shoulder to the driver to add twenty percent to the bill for a tip and almost ran inside.

Walking into the lobby was certainly impressive. The marble work was incredible and the large pillars could have been stolen from Greece. There were two check-in areas, a large public one and a smaller one for members of the President's Club. They were all framed in rich coloured wood and had counters of black marble. I walked across the lobby and heard the bellboy coming up behind me with my bag.

"Mr. Munroe? Welcome to the Fairmont Gold, sir."

"Thanks."

"I can take you directly to the 18th floor, sir."

"Right."

I had forgot that staying at a Fairmont was comfortable but the Gold level was done like a hotel within a hotel. It usually had separate guest check in on the Gold level floor. The bell staff, vigilant in spotting license plates or any other cue this guest was a Gold level client. In my dash from the cold I had forgot.

We arrived on the 18th floor and a very pleasant women, greeted me by name. The bellboy had said eight into his mike earlier and I knew now I was guest designated eight. She expertly checked me in, confirming my rate of 375 per night, an absolute steal coming on the heels of Europe, and asked about my ride in. Before taking me to my room she gave me a tour of the gold kitchen and dining area as well as the living room. The views would be awesome in the spring but now were examples of minimalist white. The rooms themselves were impressive with a northeastern African theme making my transition seem less dramatic.

"Breakfast is served from five till nine, and evening hors d'ouvres from four till six. Is there anything else you need before I take you to your room?"

"Nope."

"Then follow me, please. We have you in a one-bedroom suite here in the north tower in 1805. I have two keys for you. Will that be enough?"

"Yes, thanks."

She took me to my room where a sand filled bag held the thick door open. My bag sat pushed to the side. The room was large and had more of an Italian theme to it than the lounges but the pillows and décor still had an eastern theme. I thought it an odd combination.

"Is everything to your liking sir?"

"Perfect. How far is the Convention Center?"

"About a mile and a half south sir, a nice walk but not in this weather."

"Thanks."

I went to the window and moved the heavy drapes and then the sheers. I was on the southwest corner of the building. I could see past the huge black monolith directly behind the Fairmont and spotted a silver dome south about a mile and a half away. I figured that must be the place. What this misplaced black building was remained a mystery. There was no advertising and it was certainly out of place in the artsy historic district; probably government.

I unpacked and put on my only remaining clean suit and shirt. I set the rest aside for in-house dry cleaning. I found my exhibitors pass and figured I'd go grab lunch at the show. I emptied my laptop case of its computer and travel things and turned on the TV as an extra measure of good security.

The receptionist was at her desk as I walked by. I stopped and dropped off my dry cleaning.

"What is the ugly black building behind us?"

"The Environmental Protection Agency."

"Figures."

"Yes. Shall I have a cab waiting for you, sir?"

"Please."

CHAPTER FIFTY-FIVE

THE ELEVATOR TOOK ME TO the ground floor and the impressive lobby. I exited and pulled my coat tight as I walked through the thick carpet and down the stairs to the marble foyer. The cab was waiting, with its door held open by the doorman. The temperature seemed to have dropped a few degrees since my arrival and I reveled in the fact that I work and live in warm climates. The cab looked like an old cop car, complete with white sides and a black top.

"Afternoon, sir."

"Afternoon. A drive-through bank is the first requirement. Then on to the Convention Center please."

"Sure thing."

The cab turned right onto the road and took another at the first corner.

"Any particular bank?"

"Nope closest one with a drive through."

"Ok."

He continued for two blocks and then pulled an illegal turn and rolled into a parking lot. He brought the car around a square building and into a drive-through lane. There were two other lanes and we don't have to wait to pull up.

"Wow three lanes, no waiting."

"Yeah 'tis the season. Or, well, I guess the start of the season. Where are you from?"

"Canada, Vancouver area."

"Ah, well I guess this is t-shirt weather then."

"Actually no, this is cold. It rarely snows in Vancouver and for most of the winter it's around 10 degrees warmer than this."

"Really?"

"Yup. I've had Christmas day at 55 degrees."

"Wow, I just thought as you were so far north it would be much colder. Vancouver a nice city?"

"Very and a safe one too. There aren't any "no go" areas in daylight, and very few at night. That's if you're a woman alone. For us any place is safe."

"Really? Can't say that for Dallas. We have our "no go" areas day and night. Deep Ellum is bad as is much of south Dallas. Actually we just got the distinction of being the third most dangerous city in the country."

"Not good. That can't be good for your tourist trade."

"Ya, tell me about it."

We moved forward to the bank machine and he rolled down my window before I moved across the seat. I used my own bankcard and pulled out two thousand dollars. The machine whirred and clanked for quite some time.

"Everything ok, do you need to go in?"

"Nope it's just taking a while to count."

The machine spit out my card, followed by the cash. I had to pull quite hard to get the big wad of bills out of the machine. Most accounts were limited to $500 or a thousand dollars. Mine wasn't. It had taken some convincing for the bank, but I was limited to $5,000 a day.

I split the wad into three parts and put one inside my wallet, one in my billfold, and the third went in my front pocket.

"All done, thanks."

The car moved on and turned left onto the street and continued to a large intersection.

"Civilians can still get permits to carry guns concealed in Dallas can't they?"

"Yes, with a course."

"You'd think that would impact the crime rate."

" It does for rapes, but violent gun crime is the issue. Most bad guys assume you have a gun so they stick theirs in your face first. The Convention Center is pretty safe but don't go under through the tunnel at night. Hookers and johns go there to park. Although with the big mercenary show I guess it won't be as big a deal."

"Mercenary show? I thought this was the American Society for Industrial Security convention."

"Yeah it is. But wait till you get down there. Tons of tough looking, dangerous men. Why are you going? You work in the industry?"

"Yes asset recovery and crime prevention through environmental design."

"Ok that makes sense; you're a tech guy."

"Yeah a tech." I didn't say Death tech as I thought back to my old days in the Canadian Armed Forces. Military Occupation Code or MOC 031. Infantry soldier or Death Tec.

The huge building loomed ahead. Simple in design it had an underpass going beneath it, just as the driver had said. We drove by the huge parking lot on the right. The sign announcing the venue was simple; a single pillar with the words "Convention Center" on it. The building was equally simple with a star I took as representative of the lone star state, cut out of the stone letting the sunshine through. There were drop off areas to the right and a long horseshoe style drive to the left. The cab swung left, and while it could be me being in three airports in one day the place looked very much like an airport. I jumped out and tossed the driver a fifty-dollar bill, the smallest I had, for the thirteen dollar fare and told him to keep the change.

The front entrance area was a zoo of golf shirts stretched by overweight men. I looked around and found the exhibitors check in line. I presented my credentials and was amazed when the mouse of a woman asked for my passport or other photo id. I handed her my passport and was given a black ASIS logo strap and a white card with my name on it.

"The black lanyard and black edged ID identifies you as an exhibitor, Mr. Rhys. Please have it displayed at all times you're inside the convention. It also allows you special access to areas where regular attendees can't go. This is also your ticket for the luncheons and dinner banquets. Do you have any questions?"

"Yes, is there a lunch scheduled now?"

"The schedule is in your folder, sir?"

"If I'd looked at the schedule, I wouldn't be asking you the question. Would I?"

"There is a meet and greet luncheon over in the A6 area, sir."

The last 'sir' was spat out like I'd heard so many times in the past. By soldiers that didn't understand the chain of command.

"Thanks Peach."

I walked away from the table and intentionally put my badge on backwards. The black strap would probably be enough for the bored security officers providing security for the event.

I checked my map and headed toward the meet and greet. I cleared the main area and moved between people brokering deals or planning various meeting plans for after. The place was huge and the crowd was filling it to capacity. I was scanned by four different security checkpoints and three times as many vendor salesmen.

The exhibition room was off to my right and it was packed with men in their forties stuffing brochures into satchels and bags as fast as they could pick them up. I found area A and moved toward a security officer and asked him where the meet and greet was he pointed and I walked in that direction.

I hated buffets but my angry stomach would not be denied. I picked up some fruit and several small wrap sandwiches before moving toward the bar. I scouted a seat and moved toward it catching the cocktail waitresses' attention. She was very busy but either she saw the need in my eye as clearly as a dealer or the cut of the suit prompted her to make a detour to my table.

"I know you're busy, love, but I could really use a triple vodka martini, burnt and dirty." I passed her a fifty-dollar bill. "I see your hands are full so don't concern yourself with the change."

"Right away."

She moved off quickly through the crowd, her tray balanced perfectly and full of empties. You had to love professionalism wherever you encountered it. Especially professionalism with an ass, like that.

She and I were about the only professionals in the place. It was packed with every type of person one could imagine. There were the fat Izod stretching salesmen and the muscle bound meat stretching Underamour and Blackwater tees. These latter had their backs to whatever wall they could find and they made a big deal of scanning the crowd. Overt and obvious, like a man standing on your nuts.

"Your name tag is backwards."

I looked left to discover a computer geek of a man. His name tag read Myron P. Eugene, Tangent Software Solutions. He was all of five feet tall and weighed less than some guns I'd carried in the field.

"Thanks Tips, what do you do for an encore?"

He locked eyes with me and in a very confident manner responded.

"Keep you alive, with situational awareness and enhanced reality. Figured you were the only non-poser here, so thought it was worth a shot. I'm at booth 45, Rhys Munroe, or should I just call you Captain Grey."

He left me standing with my mouth agape. The little shit had managed to throw me a curve and take control of the area and leave. How did he know my name? How had he known I was a Captain and a Grey was left on the floor between us.

"Your drink, sir?"

The waitress was standing there waiting for me to acknowledge her.

"Ah thanks."

"Just wave when you need another. I'll see you."

"Good."

The mass of people pressed in on me and I started feeling more than a little surrounded. No one had struck up a conversation and no one had pointed out my nametag was backwards. They preferred instead to stand about and loudly tell stories about this or that Green Zone exploit or on the way from the airport stories.

I can't help myself. I'm drawn into the circle of conversation as this group of Triple Canopy and Blackwater boys' try to out do one another in the bravado game. They are all wearing black cords so they must be exhibitors as well. They chat about roadside improvised explosive devices, or IEDS, and the children that throw rocks on the notorious road to and from the airport and the green zone in Iraq.

One of the men, from the Steele foundation, pulled me into the conversation. My famine had been satisfied and the food was now competing for space in my bloodstream with the second martini. The man asked:

"What do you think? You're standing here listening. What do you think would make operational security on the trip from the airport safer?"

The group went silent and looked at me expectantly. I wanted to turn around and leave these corporate warriors to their stupid dilemma. I knew I should leave and pretend to be an alarm installer with ADT. But the vodka won out.

"Hmm, lets see. The roadside IED's are easy. You round up all the people that had any connection with making the bomb. From the guys that provided, found, or recovered the explosives, to the man who placed it. Then you round up his family from his grandmother to the fucking goat that provided the milk for the morning breakfast, his children and the children his children played with and you chain them to the bomb and blow it up. For the little ones that toss rocks, easy you tie them to your Sarcan or carrier or what ever else you're fucking driving and you spray them with fuel and let them melt on the side of the carrier, as you drive by."

The looks were of horror. These hardened men shocked by the suggestion of the quiet man. I thought to myself, "way to be a low-profile, Rhys." But instead I just said:

"You asked me."

"What about the outcry when the journalists get wind of that?"

A tall man had asked the question. A man I knew from the many books he wrote on places in the world in conflict, a fellow Canadian.

"What journos? They all got killed on day two of the operation. Rule one kids, if it ain't profitable don't be there. Rule two, kill all journos. Rule three, if in doubt take them out. Rule four, you're not going to win the Nobel Peace prize so don't fucking try."

The Canadian spoke first, breaking the eerie silence.

"Who are you with?"

I flipped my name tag over and said:

"Pleased to meet you. Hope you guessed my name."

My food and booze requirements met, I figured a hasty advance to the rear while claiming victory was in order. The song reference was lost on many of the kids present who had no idea who the Rolling Stones were singing about years before their birth.

I left the circle and went towards the main exhibitor area in search of booth 45. The stories continued at my back and so did a few comments on how that would never work in Iraq or Afghanistan. I laughed inwardly at these naïve silly men. Thinking about how the Russians had dropped toys for the children of Afghanistan. At least they looked like toys. They were in fact mines made to look like fire trucks and cars. The children would pick them up and run to show their friends or parents. The toys would detonate killing all those within a fifty-foot radius. The Russians knew a thing or two about breaking an army's will to fight.

CHAPTER FIFTY-SIX

THE MAIN CONVENTION AREA WAS packed and movement was slow and it was hard not to be impolite to people that stopped to have conversations in the middle of the floor. I found booth 45 and looked for my computer geek.

I saw him sitting, as one would expect, in front of a large computer screen. He was typing away while watching what looked like Lego men perform various actions on the screen. The machine kicked me. The Lego men looked to be in the exact configuration as the people surrounding the booth. One of them was grey with a glowing red star above his head. He looked up from his screen directly at me.

"Myron, it worked. You got me here and you have me for the next two minutes. What have you got?"

"Please, come grab a seat for a second"

He patted the chair beside him and I moved around the booth perimeter to join him.

"Sorry about earlier, I wanted to set a hook and I figured if I just told you what Tangent Tech did you wouldn't really get it. Do you know what Enhanced Reality is?"

"No."

"Well I could tell you but it might be better if I just show you."

"Ok?"

"Put these on and go for a walk and come back in an hour or so. I'll be here waiting."

He handed me a pair of glasses. They were kind of large like the older styles of the 80's and had ear buds built in on both sides. They were black and the sides thick and wide. He then handed me a black box about the size of a cigarette pouch.

"Put the computer in your pocket and the glasses on you head. There will be a short adaptation program that will lead you through a series of tests to measure your pupil response and the level of information overlay you're comfortable with. This here is a camera and that's a microphone. I will be able to see and hear everything you do and say so please be cognizant of that while you use them. Please be careful with these as they are a prototype design and one of only three in the world."

"Ok, how do I start them?"

"Put them on and push the big button on the side."

I placed the glasses on my head and tossed the 'computer' into my inside jacket. I felt around for the button on the side. It felt like the older Ipod's scroll wheel; I pushed the center.

There was a flash across the lenses and they went dark. An image was projected on the grey-black glasses. It was hard to see exactly what it was and I fought the urge to take them off. A female computer generated voice came over the ear buds.

"New user startup, user ID six. You can skip this section if you have already set up a user ID. If you have a user ID say yes if not say continue."

"Continue."

"Setting up visual and audio for user six. Please watch the images presented and when they are clear say "yes."

I watched as a series of images were projected on the matt glass. They slowly changed till they were clear and sharp and when they were I said yes.

"Now follow the green dot with your eyes as it moves around the screen."

I followed the green dot with my eyes for about forty-five seconds.

"Good. Now, user six, I'm going to project a series of images, some near some far. These images will get progressively smaller. While I project these images I will tell you which image to look at. Please remain looking at that image until I tell you to look someplace else. Please look at the cat."

A dog and a cat came into razor sharp view floating in space and I looked at the cat. Then the images changed and got smaller and I followed the directions spoken into my headset. This went on for about four minutes with the images changing and the direction given to look at several images in sequence.

"Pupil tracking complete. Now user six please configure the tinting of the lenses to your preference by saying less or more. More is for more tint and less for less."

Then lenses went clear and the harsh lighting made me close my eyes for a second. I opened them and said more and the lenses darkened instantly. I said more a few more times till the light level was perfect. After five seconds of silence the woman spoke again.

"Light level set. The unit will try to maintain this level of light transmission as you move through your real environment. Now setting up enhanced reality overlay. Again as information is overlaid use less or more to control the amount of information displayed."

I was looking past Myron and suddenly images and names were projected onto the people and things within my vision. Myron's name was on his chest as were his company's logo. A man standing at the counter had the same information projected onto him. The gadgets on the booth table got overlaid with data as I looked at each one. It was a little overwhelming and I said less. The data overlays became less graphic and cluttered and I sat for a while to try and get comfortable with this level of enhanced reality. I looked at a man and the word searching came up and it took about twenty seconds until his name came up projected on his chest like the others.

"Thank you user six, current levels saved. You can adjust these levels by pressing the forward or back controls on the control wheel. Set up saved."

I looked at Myron. He must have been able to tell from my face that I thought this was pretty cool. I had a hard time with names and this alone would save me the issue of trying to remember people's names.

"I see you're comfortable with level five. That's really good for a first time user considering the small area the glasses allow. The combat version uses a ski mask style screen so we can project much more data with less confusion. Those versions also have other abilities, like low light and complete "see in the dark" modes. Walk around with these and I'll see you in a while."

"Yeah ok, I will. See you in a bit."

I walked out of the booth and as I walked along the aisle the computer tried to identify each person whose face I looked at. Some it got right away, others took a few seconds while the rest just didn't display. I stopped at a booth selling first aid supplies and as I looked at each product the overlay told me details like price and product code even when they weren't displayed at the booth. I was getting a bit of a headache with all the data my mind was trying to process so I made my way to the main entrance.

A women walking toward me was suddenly flagged red. I was startled and instinctively moved to flank her, the machine and the glasses conflicting on the reason for the red highlight. Then the overlay displayed 102.6, potential fever. Cool. The woman had a fever and the overlay was telling me to avoid contact with her. I continued out front and noticed that when I stared hard at a point far away a series of numbers would come up. It took a second to realize it was ranging the distance for me.

"Getting a headache yet?"

"A little bit. Just went out front to cut down on the info."

"The system will only work in the enhanced mode within the conference as it has to talk with the main server here at the booth. But if you go outside you'll get a demo of the normal mode. Give it a try."

I walked outside and was amazed when the glasses instantly darkened in response to the reflected sunshine. I looked at the skyline and as I did the glasses slowly overlaid landmarks and distances. My position was shown as a GPS coordinate on the bottom left side. My vision passed over a cab and the name and fare information was displayed.

I turned to go back inside and a larger than life Lego man walked up the street carrying a Lego gun. The machine kicked up and I moved toward cover. The laughing in my ears joined the dissolving Lego man.

"Sorry Rhys, I couldn't help myself. You see reality can be what is projected to the individual and as you get more and more accustomed to the unit it's real, and the brain treats it as such. Come on back to the booth."

I made my way back inside. As I did the image changed to a green overlay. Like night shooting mode on video cameras. With this change people were marked with red, blue, and yellow dots.

"This is for target identification. Important people are red and next blue and so on down to yellow. If you wanted to you could I.D. hostiles, friends, and civilians in this manner. Check out the girl on your left wearing the dress."

I looked left and saw an attractive woman who appeared, initially, to be naked from the waist down, her t-bar underwear clearly displayed. Then I saw the sheer dress material that clung tightly to her calves. The image went back to normal and the pink dress was clearly displayed.

"Some material goes sheer when ultraviolet light is projected on it so you get the proverbial X-ray specs sold on the backs of comic books. While it wasn't designed that way it's a cool added benefit."

I reached the booth and Myron was positively glowing with information. I took off the glasses and remembered the 'computer' and handed them back to him.

"What do you think?"

"I think it's pretty high tech stuff. Has it ever been tested in the field?"

"Not yet."

"But I'm hoping that will change soon. You've never been to one of these in all the years you've been in operation. You don't work for Sentinel so, I figure you got something in the works."

"A little less figuring and a little more selling would be significantly safer and profitable."

"Sorry, I didn't mean to pry. There are no restrictions on my product so you tell me you're outfitting your Airsoft team and we're good to go. I have a lab set up in a private room. If you want to see the whole system in action I can show you privately."

"Sounds good."

"Follow me."

I followed Myron out of the conference area and toward an area that had hospitality suites. We passed the big boys and could hear more loud stories being told by louder men. I liked it better when discovery was to be disowned. This acceptable private contractor shit was wearing very thin.

We reached a room and Myron let me in. There was a contract security guard sitting in a chair and Myron gestured for him to leave. The room was only twenty feet square and there were three manikins dressed as soldiers and a large computer table. The table had a large Apple computer and three large PowerBooks like mine.

"You use Apple?" I asked.

"Yeah I like the platform. It's more stable, but we are porting the program to the Microsoft platform as the US government won't look at it until we do."

"Good, so you could be up and running tomorrow. How familiar are you with computers and data systems?

"Working knowledge, I guess," I replied, trying to sound vague.

Myron continued, "I will lay the system out and if, at any time, you get lost stop me and I will explain."

"Ok." I was eager to hear what he had to tell me.

"The system is called "Tangent Storm." It's an individual unit-based command and control system that enhances situational awareness and asset protection. I will start at the head. The goggle system is similar to the glasses you were wearing and it overlays data to the individual on a need to know basis. The data stream is controlled by the central command and shared via any type of hierarchy structure you choose. The goggles can use enhanced reality like the glasses and receive text messages or in theater briefings just like the killer Lego man. At night they can switch to active night vision as the camera is a ten megapixal charged coupled device and sees projected ultraviolet like a camera.

The level of ultraviolet illumination is target specific. So if you're reading a map just a little. If you're shooting out to a hundred meters, max output. They will also sense and go opaque if someone sets off a flash-bang grenade, limiting the effect to the asset. The headphones in the military version are embedded into the ears and also have a sound dampening effect of 20 decibels. Normal hearing is processed and washed of combat sounds so it in fact enhances normal hearing and can amplify hearing if required.

The modules are stand-alone units and use Bluetooth, secured of course, to communicate with the other modules. Each has two "push to talk", or ptt, modules and can be placed on an individual weapon as well as the person. The brain is redundant computer each working on its own and capable of adopting the other computer's functions if one goes down, with only a thirty per cent speed reduction. They use GPS positioning and can use a large wireless triangulation as well to offset the military built in error corruption. This way you really know where everyone is both area and altitude wise.

As far as communication goes it can use regular radio, VOIP, regular cellular, and satellite cellular all two way encrypted and is able to switch to any of the available communications options present in the system currently being used in the theater. You with me so far Rhys?

"For sure. Sounds like an awesome system. Why has no one picked it up yet?"

"It's expensive and it's on a Apple platform. It also doesn't interface with the Command and Control systems the large force is currently using."

"How much?"

"Depends on the configuration. But let's say $5,000 to $12,000 a man, plus the Command center, which is $17,000 with a site license for the software. That way if you want to add a couple of backup laptops you just buy them from Apple."

"Whew. Pricey!"

"It's the best system available and is so user intuitive it takes very little training time."

"It also has a module that identifies snipers and distance to target."

"How?"

There are four microphones, one for each shoulder and one for each the front and back. When a bullet is fired the system 'hears' the shot and using Doppler time shift identifies the shooter and distance to target and transmits it to all units in the area even if the original target is hit. Further, if that target is hit the heart rate monitor sends a signal for the medics or search and rescue along the command lines you identified prior to the battle, and its smart adaptable in that if a medic is taken out it will automatically move to the closest unit with a medic.

"Sounds incredible really, like a stand-alone Command and Control system. How secure is it from hacking? If the enemy penetrated your system then they'd have all the access too."

"The unit uses a 256-bit two-way encryption system. Moreover, if you're using wireless or VOIP it uses a proprietary network encryption. It will interface seamlessly with most of the Mobile phone and Sat phone technologies as well. So you could have a layered system using all four-communication systems. If one goes down, or gets cracked then the system auto switches to the next best available system."

"What would that mean to the guys in the field?"

"The only way they would be aware is by sound quality and time delay if it went to satellite. There is nothing for them to push or do. It just works in the background letting you do what you need to do."

"What's with the Lego men?"

"I regret making that decision. We are a small firm and many of our programmers wanted to work from home. It was cheaper for development. So in order to avoid interest and detection we made the guys Lego men so if anyone got cracked or lost a computer it would look like a Lego animated war game. We're changing that as we speak and the new system should be available in about a week's time."

"Does the Lego system work?"

"Of course. It has had the utmost bug testing as it was the primary system graphics. But generals don't want to look at squads of attacking Lego men and flying Lego planes."

"I notice the modules are bright orange. Why?"

"Just for trade show visuals. The actual units can be delivered any colour from black to digital camo pattern."

"How many orange units can you get by Monday afternoon?"

"I have twenty full systems here at this trade show and could get double that by Monday if I called today."

"So, forty complete units?"

"Forty for sure, perhaps fifty or fifty-five."

"Ok, I'll take 55 units, as many orange as you can get, and a stand-alone Lego graphic server for $560,000 US."

"That price is about a $100,000 short."

"You want this system tested in battle? I'll take the risk and test it for you and let you use the info from the test in your sales literature. You want to hold onto the list price come see me when the bugs are proven to be out. Bugs in my theater equal blood."

"I knew you were up to something big. Superior force numbers, entrenched enemy? Small mobile force with superior skill, and technology, taking on Goliath? That kind of thing?"

"Yeah, that kind of thing."

Myron smiled.

"Ok, you have a deal! I'll make the calls while you set up the wire transfer. Here is my account number."

"The money is coming out of a London Bank. It's almost midnight in London, so I will call later tonight. You'll have your money first thing Monday morning."

I had one more question for Myron.

"How much space is this going to take up? You travel to trade shows all the time?"

"I use one 1730 Pelican case so you're going to need two. They have a booth here and may have deals on. You're also going to need a wireless network system and I can point you in the right direction there too. There is a company here that makes a big area unit and then smaller stand alone units that function on solar power."

"Ok well I will leave you to ordering the gear and getting it here for Monday and I'll go pick up two Pelican cases and the wireless units."

"Sounds good. There's a bit of a system for loading the cases. I have it down pat with all these conventions. Drop them off and I will load them for you. That way when you unload it you get the system."

"Right, see you in a bit."

The system purchase had been an expensive affair, but it was Tom's money and not mine. Although even if it had been my money I would have purchased it. The redundant, intuitive, and layered system made sense. We were likely to have our radios jammed and to what level was as yet unknown. I knew a plan rarely survived first contact with the enemy and while the men were good at improvising on the fly control was good too.

I went searching for the wireless network units and found them exactly where Myron said I would. The booth had several men working at it. Myron had not told me who to talk to and I wished I had the glasses on.

"Looking for anything in particular?"

"Myron from Tangent sent me over. I need a wide coverage dual channel, dual frequency wireless network and several solar powered repeaters thingies."

"You using his Command and Communications system?"

"Taking it for a test drive, real world field test."

"Ok, well you need a unit with some punch so I would use the LL 5750 base station. It has a huge bubble and great bandwidth and allows dual connections without a speed slow down. Nice unit and we have a show special price. The other units depend on a few variables, like type of use and amount of sunlight. Where are you testing it?"

"Mexico, below the Cancun region."

"Great. Lots of sun and being close to the equator gives you lots of charge time. So you could get away with these units. They will handle VOIP bandwidths and last about seven hours on a full charge, running constantly in the daytime. At night you'll get about two and a half hours before the unit goes into standby to protect its settings."

He handed me what looked like an old-fashioned wooden matchbox. When pushed open two antennas popped out the top and some additional solar cells were exposed. You simply set and forget. The unit would acquire the base unit or another of its type that was online with the base unit. Placed high it had a coverage area of 150 to 200 meters.

"How much coverage does the big unit get?"

"Line of sight about a click. But buildings, trees, and metal will affect that."

"How much are the little units?"

"One hundred and thirty."

"Volume discount?"

"What kind of volume are we talking about?"

"Two hundred."

"Wow! Yeah we can do a volume for that amount. You're going to be blanketing a huge area. Let me see what I can do."

He wandered off to a computer and I had the distinct feeling I was being watched. I let my peripheral vision check my surroundings and saw nothing. I followed the course of a pretty girl and scanned the area to my left. There were fancy shoes, watching me from afar.

He stayed only a moment before moving off with a group that had stopped to look at the Glock gun display. A chance encounter I argued with the machine. This time I won.

"Okay. We can do one hundred a unit for that kind of volume."

"Delivery?"

"Tomorrow. We're local. Were you paying with a purchase order?"

"You set up for Visa?"

"Yes."

"Here ya go."

I handed him my personal Visa card. He looked at me oddly and walked over to his point of sale machine. I signed his copy and he provided me with a receipt and copy of the transaction.

"Nice doing business with you, sir. They'll be here tomorrow, before noon."

"Thanks."

I stopped by the Apple and Pelican booths on my way back to Myron. I thought it odd that Apple would be here and was surprised to see the booth. Young girls and boys dressed trendy casual, like their computer spokesman, selling music devices and laptops to killers. The song "Mad World" came to mind and remained during my walk back to meet Myron.

Myron was waiting for me, looking satisfied with his results.

"We're all set. I got fifty-one orange units and four black ones, all tested and certified. They'll be here Monday morning before 10 am."

"Thanks Myron, here are the two Pelican cases and I picked up two additional seventeen inch PowerBooks as well. They're in that Pelican case. Can you load up the software and get them going for me?"

"For my best customer? Sure. You want the Lego version right?"

"Yes. See you Monday morning."

"Sounds good but where? The show will be over Sunday night and there will be a ton of trucks and crap here cleaning up. I'm staying at the Fairmont downtown so the stuff is being shipped there. Do you want to meet there?"

"Good idea."

"It's on…" Myron started.

"I'm sure the cabbie can find it."

"True enough. See you at the Fairmont on Monday."

CHAPTER FIFTY-SEVEN

THE DAY'S PURCHASES DONE AND everything a go for Monday left me feeling well ahead of schedule. It was a good feeling, to be sure. I once again hit the lounge area, a bit quieter now that the hog line was removed and people needed to pay for their food. I picked a booth and settled into the corner. My waitress remembered me and mouthed the words "same." I nodded my head,

The room was still full of characters and I could see the Canadian journalist waiting. The look on his face showed he had already anticipated a kill, and his prey was me. We were playing "Lion and Hyena." Observations and perceptions were like that. The lion and the hyena were a great example. Scientific observation used to be done exclusively in the daytime. After the sun came up the scientists saw the hyena trying to steal the lion's kill. But only a few short hours earlier it was the hyena that took down the prey and the lions that stole it. Perspective and timely observations are rarely made by the people that should. I had seen this lion spectacle while hunting my own prey, only to have the professionals tell me how wrong I was. I wondered what new perspective our friend the Journalist would walk away with today. From the muscle bound, tribal tattooed, pinks it would be so far from the truth it might actually be interesting.

My second martini was dropped off along with the menu. Either out of compassion or guilt she was suggesting I eat something. It was almost six and the show would be winding down soon for the evening and the extra curricular events that follow these types of things like tsetse flies follow buffalo. Even as I looked around I could see a few well-dressed ladies without lanyards appearing on the arms of the over stuffed Izod types. I left another fifty on the table and left for the main entrance.

The cabs were like crocs lying in wait, mouths open to catch the easy prey that came down the river. But the cab's eyes shone blue-white instead of the demon-red crocs' eyes reflected. I dove into a waiting cab and asked the driver to take me to the Fairmont, by way of a liquor store.

The hotel lobby was full and it looked as though a wedding procession was going through. I made for the bank of elevators with my package and hit the 18th floor. The doors closed and the din faded away like a bad dream. Weddings made me feel more than a little homicidal. Promises of tomorrow, while the stench and stains of the stag yesterday added to the lie and lies you could get used to telling and hearing.

The doors slid open and I was greeted by name by the concierge. I walked to my room, dropped off my bottles and was happy to find room in the larger-than-usual mini bar fridge. I snapped up the ice bucket and checked the map on the back of the door for the ice machine location.

Mission complete, I set off to the Gold dining area. I hated to eat alone and eating while others were around made it more palatable, even if they weren't with me.

The view was really quite impressive, lights of the city disappearing off into the black curtain of night. The kitchen would provide dinner to this special retreat and I took a few minutes to look at the evening snacks before deciding what to order.

I waited for dinner and tried a few of the evening hors d'ourves. They were fresh and tasty. I pulled up the computer and checked for mail, surprised by the amount I had. There were nine saved messages in my draft folder for the account we shared. I read them, struggling with the times. Being operational on three fronts and in so many times zones made for confusing reading.

The doctor had visited the men and everyone had received their shots: a vitamin B and one against yellow fever. A couple of the men had injuries requiring more than simple fixes. They would get them and be good to go in less than a week. Most were put on a course of antibiotics, so drinking had been banned for the next ten days and that had gone over poorly. Chiwa and Sunday were working well to get everyone in tiptop shape. A case of Guinea worm was found to be a simple cyst on one of the man's heel and nine of the men were put on intravenous antibiotics and fluid replacement. TIA; people were always carrying a host of parasites.

The preparations for the football clinics were going very well and a large shipment of tents and gear was already en route. The president had given us an area near the airfield that had access to water and power to set up our festival camp. There were no further details and I wanted to check the location on a map for tactical reasons but that would have to wait.

The Ringers had been selected and apparently Tom was much happier about his wager with the EG president. The two names meant nothing to me but from the excited level of the email I guessed they were special. We also had a good coach and two trainers that would be going to Camp Sunny Ball in Hazy View on Tuesday.

The weapons had been loaded onto the plane for delivery alongside the air-conditioning systems and it took me a few minutes to understand they were en route as I read this email. So if they were discovered we would be clear of the issue, a good safety measure.

The sub was making great time and had checked in via its satellite Internet connection with Viktor four hours ago. Apparently they had had to drop to 1300 feet and wait as a US Navy boat went over them with a towed array deployed. The array like a big powerful microphone had created quite a stir to the ex Russian submariners. The boat had passed its scary test with flying colours even managing to continue moving at a reduced speed. Looking like a hole in the water. Andrea's shadow, indeed.

Zombie had posted that he was completing certification on the Gulfstream and would likely be flying the ringers and coaches down and letting the ringers meet the men. The coaches and trainers were going to stay and set the men through some drills. The ringers had to return for some big game in Madrid. The charter flight was being arranged from Hazy View for the initial insertion in two weeks from Monday.

The plan was going ahead well. I had a sense of foreboding that was a palatable as a heart attack. Things were going smoothly and in my experience that could never be maintained. While almost everything would be in theatre prior to our arrival allowing us the ability to back out without much risk, I was overtly anxious.

I tried to uncover the reason for this. I sat back and went over each piece on the board as I slowly moved them into place. I thought of the counter moves and the most likely issues that could arise. The plan was sound. Both the machine, and brain, were at harmony for the first time in days. So why the anxiety? Why the sense of dread and doubt, had I missed something? I found the culprit. Hope. I hoped everything would go as planned. I was invested into the idea and hoped it would work and hope required faith and trust to be strong. Emotions that were sadly lacking in my repertoire.

Dinner arrived and I pushed aside my negative feelings and adopted the thinking of a man committed. I was riding this all the way into the ground, win, loose, or draw. I could adopt no other point of view. It had to work, and it would simply work because it had to. The logic of this was about as firm as the mash potatoes on my plate.

I closed off my account after adding 'read' to the strings of communications and set to work enjoying my food. Hoping the mash potatoes on my plate went down as tastily as my logic.

The following morning announced itself with brutal sunlight. I had forgot to close the drapes and the light was harsh and unflattering on the bed's strewn landscape. From the looks of things my sleep had been fitful. I felt well rested and there was only a small dent in the vodka bottle. A good sign as I needed to slowly wean myself down to a couple of drinks a day.

It was already 10 am, and while housekeeping hadn't woken me up it only would be a matter of time before they did and I set the "do not disturb sign" on the other side of the door before heading to the shower.

My freshly dry-cleaned clothes had been hung in the closet. I dressed quickly and went looking for something to quiet my protesting guts.

"Good Morning, Mr. Munroe. We missed you for breakfast."

"Yeah. I overslept."

"You probably needed your rest. Are you late for anything? Can I phone ahead and update your status?"

"No the day is mine, figured I would take in some tourist stuff after I grabbed breakfast."

"Oh good, here is a pass for brunch if you want to take advantage of the hotel dining room before you leave."

"Thanks."

I rode the elevator down and decided I really liked this hotel within a hotel concept. It was so much more civilized. It was an African concept that it was rude to ask someone to reach into his or her pockets before he was fed. A concept every hotel in the world should adopt.

The doors opened and I made my way to the dining room to start the day.

CHAPTER
FIFTY-EIGHT

The hotel was quiet. Yesterday's wedding celebrations had been vacuumed cleanly off the carpets. I wandered into the dining room and was seated by a pleasant hostess who asked about my day. She brought me the local paper and coffee along with the menu.

I read the paper, scanning the local events and happenings in the world. The convention got a three-page spread starting on page five. It was what I expected, glorifying the contractor side of things with the renewed patriotic fervor of a nation at war.

I ordered breakfast and tried to understand the article. The average American solider with six years in makes about $2,200 a month. Hazard and danger pay only adds about $325 per month. Housing and food pay if the person is married adds another $1800. So the total pay would be about $4,500 per month or $55,000 a year, tax-free.

The average contractor working for a good company makes about $350 to $500 per day. At the lower rate that's $10,500 per month – more than double the enlisted man's salary. No wonder so many men were jumping into the private side of the war. Hiring contractors decreased the costs to the State Department; assets made more money doing the work and the companies made a killing. It amounted to a good deal, corporately, all the way around.

The badly paid troops got the glory and respect by serving their country and the contractors or 'mercenaries' got rich. Not much had changed with the historical perspective of war and privateers.

Many of these corporations had ties to or were wholly owned by natural resource companies. The circle and collusion was lost on much of the public. Reading the article I picked up three of the listed companies that fit this mold. It was easy for the educated and protesting masses to draw the connection. The rank and file readers just accepted the party line. Changing lives for the better, and creating a stable government. If the food hadn't been so good I might have gagged.

Breakfast done, I decided to go for a walk around this area of the city. The bracing cold of the late morning conspired to get under my coat, making the walk brisk and quick.

My cell made me jump as it buzzed, prior to ringing. It came up as a blocked number.

"How is your day going?" It was Andrea.

"Good."

Despite myself I felt my step get a little lighter and the cool air became a distant memory. She had never called when I was away before and I hoped nothing was wrong.

"Is everything okay?"

"Everything is fine. Ruben missed you and so do I. You said something about a date so I wanted to touch base with you. I wasn't going to call as I didn't want to intrude, but I did. Do you mind the intrusion?"

"No not at all and you're not intruding. I'm just out for a walk. Does Tuesday work?"

"Yes, Tuesday works. I don't have classes till Thursday."

"Ok. I will try to get out of here Monday, early afternoon if I can and will make reservations at the Vancouver Fairmont, downtown, for Monday but I don't expect I will arrive till after midnight. Going to be a long day of flying."

"I won't ask you where you are, but that works. I have an afternoon lab on Monday. I'll see you Tuesday morning."

"Sounds good. Tuesday morning. Can you make reservations someplace nice for Tuesday evening?"

"Sure, it will be a great excuse to show off the little black dress you bought me in Amsterdam. Did I forget to tell you that you bought me a dress in Amsterdam?"

I laughed, "Yes, you did, but that sounds great. Go ahead and make a reservation. I have to fly out of Vancouver on Wednesday and I don't know what time I'm going yet so perhaps we can stay at the Airport Fairmont on Tuesday night."

"That will make it easier for me getting to class in Abby on Thursday. I don't have to fight the downtown traffic if we're out in Richmond."

"Call Charlie, and get him to drive."

"A limo out to see you, then another to pick me up and take me home? I don't know Rhys sounds like a bit of an expense. I can drive and we'll need a car to get around town."

"I'm driving up so I'll have a car at the hotel. I intend to keep you up late so letting someone else do the driving on Wednesday morning would be prudent."

"Up late? Doing what? I have to be in bed by ten. House rules."

"You will be."

"Mmmm, sounds good," she responded in a huskier tone.

"Ok, I'll call Charlie and get him to pick me up and arrange for Wednesday."

"That's good. See you Tuesday."

"Tuesday morning. Bye."

I put the phone back in my pocket, feeling much better now. I looked around and found myself close to the convention center. I hadn't really had a chance to look around and suddenly felt like doing the casual shopper thing. I also remembered I hadn't picked up a green laser to signal the ship. The devil was in the details.

I found my pass and hung it around my neck. The convention was in full swing, the announcement board had several changes and additions listed. The course material wasn't anything I was interested in. I walked past the registrar's desk and into the trade show floor.

My ID was facing the right way today and my status with Sentinel ensured that when I stopped to look at gear a salesman was right there to help. Knowing the real players in the previous secret world made me nostalgic for times when secret and private meant something. The effort to legitimize the industry had removed the protection of anonymity.

I found a company selling green laser gun sight systems. I could add one of these into the rest of the gear being shipped but it was more than obvious what it was. Anyone would know it as a weapon site. I listened as the salesman explained the various advantages to this system over others. I had never really seen the point of sticking a laser on a personal weapon other than to perform ranging for snipers. Weapons already had sights, if you needed to use them. Most of the battles I had been in had taken place at seven meters or less. The gizmo did little more than make your weapon look cool. I preferred my targets cool.

I was about to give up when I saw a lighter on the end of the table.

I picked it up and turned it around in my hand. It had the company logo and below that a button. I pressed the button and instead of the top opening producing a flame a very bright green laser made a mark on the high ceiling about a foot around.

"Pretty powerful, huh? They made a few for demos. It has to run on a camera battery. The lighter button is on the side."

I pressed the side button and a dual flame torch sprung to life. The flame was green as well. A pretty slick little unit, and one that wouldn't draw suspicion either.

"A little overkill for lighting cigarettes."

"I smoke cigars and I'll take two."

"Well they're not for sale. I used that one to light the smoke I just snuck out for."

"Well can I take this one then, it's much better advertising than a card that might just get washed with my suit when I get back to London."

"You're with Sentinel?"

"Yes."

"You a contractor?"

"No, in charge of procurement and supply."

"Oh! Ok here let me see if we have any new ones."

He went over to a large Pelican case and started rummaging through it. Since I bought my Pelican I was experiencing the same thing you do when you buy a car. You start to see them all over the place and you didn't think they were that common before. He turned around with two lighters.

"Here ya go, a new one and this one has my name on it. You can contact me directly anytime you need to order, sir."

"Thanks, I will."

I walked around for a couple of more hours and stopped by the booth to pick up my little network devices. They were ready, my order in two boxes resembling old matchbook packaging. The day's chores finished, I went out to catch a cab back. I had spotted three CIA types and figured the risk of exposure was a little too great. It was hard to be certain as many in the place looked like they could belong to some alphabet agency. But the ones I spotted were for real. Their angled glances and projected persona a little too close to the training manual.

The cab ride was quick and friendly and the hotel lobby empty. I got to my room and decided a nice soak in the tub would take the chill out of my legs. The convention center was not as warm as it had seemed. Warmer than the outside but the warmth of the suite had made me aware of how cold I really was. The quick hop from Africa no doubt.

The tub full, I lit a nice cigar, made myself a martini and climbed in. My thoughts drifted and then settled like a lost fishing lure on the coming trip home. It would be a distraction to be sure. What of the operation was I going to tell Andrea about? What should I tell her? What would she ask and what would she want to know? I didn't find any answers.

I started the computer and checked flights out of Dallas heading to SeaTac – Seattle's international airport. There was a flight at 12:37 with a one-hour layover in Salt Lake City. I was flying west and gaining time. The six-hour flight got me into SeaTac a little after 4:00 pm. I didn't mind the layover but the Salt Lake area could get snow. I was also changing planes and that meant the potential for losing luggage. I was flying with a great deal of money in gear. I decided to keep looking.

I checked with one of the many cheap seat search engines and found two direct flights. I chose Alaska Air. The flight left Dallas at 2:20 and arrived at SeaTac just in time for a rush-hour drive through downtown Seattle.

Then again I could always take advantage of the lounge and relax a little. I called the toll-free number and booked the one-way flight and inquired about overweight luggage. The fee for each Pelican case was going to be $100, a gouge on the $500 flight.

It was a direct flight and thus eliminated my concern for snow and lost luggage. I got dressed and headed for the Gold dining room. The concierge greeted me again.

"Mr. Munroe, I hope your day went well and you got a chance to enjoy our city?"

"It was cold but yes, I did."

"Good. Will you be joining us for dinner this evening?"

"Yes, and I was wondering could you check to see if Myron P. Eugene is checked into the hotel? I know it's a confidentiality issue but I was sure I saw him in the lobby."

"We're not supposed to Mr. Munroe but he was here this morning and moved up to this level. I think he's in the lounge now."

"Thanks. I won't tell anyone."

I continued into the Gold lounge area and looked around. I saw Myron sitting by himself near the jet-black window, working on a laptop.

"Excuse me Mr. Eugene but the hotel doesn't allow guest to surf porn in the living room."

"Er, I wasn't surfing… Mr. Munroe what are you doing…?"

The look on his face was priceless. He was completely taken off guard.

"May I join you?"

"Sure. I'm just setting up your last computer. I should have figured you'd be staying at this hotel. Nice up here, isn't it?"

"Only way to stay. They treat us pretty nicely up here, don't they?"

"So far so good. I was staying on a lower floor earlier, but upgraded this afternoon."

Humility, I liked that. He could have pretended to be up here all along in the "fake it till you make it" mode. But he hadn't.

"So you decided to splurge after the big sale?"

"Yes I did. It's nice to be able to work in comfortable surroundings. I usually can't justify the expense. Did you pick up the remote LAN devices?"

"Yup. Got a volume discount too. I'm getting myself a drink. Can I bring you something?"

"Sure, another beer would be great."

We spent the evening going over the operation of the software and I enjoyed the company of Mr. Myron P Eugene. He was a confident man that belied his physical stature. We told jokes and relaxed and I learned more about how to configure and operate the software.

"I would sure like to be on the ground when this went operational."

He looked at me, his eyes pleading.

"Really, what about the risk?"

"What risk?"

"Well let's imagine there was a risk of being imprisoned for life? Perhaps worse, shot on site maybe?"

"This has been my life. I figured this out from video games and created it on a shoestring. My life is totally in hock, I own nothing. This purchase, your purchase, keeps my head above water for another year at best. I'm not married; I don't have a girlfriend even. I think I would take that risk, Mr. Munroe. I would love to see my baby in action."

"Really? Could you be prepared to move with an hour's notice?"

"Yes!"

"Give me your number and I'll think about it."

"Really? You'd actually put me in the field?"

"Perhaps. Depends on how things go."

He wrote down three numbers and passed them to me.

"I can always be reached at one of those."

I studied the numbers he had given me and replied as non-committally as I could. "We shall see how things pan out."

"Your gear should be here before ten Monday," he explained. "I will let the concierge know when it arrives. You want to meet me here?"

"Sounds good, Myron."

With that I bid him goodnight and returned to my room.

CHAPTER FIFTY-NINE

THE RINGING OF THE PHONE jarred me awake. I struggled with the sheets and answered on the third ring.

"Good Morning Mr. Munroe. Tabitha here with your 5 am wake up call."

"Thanks."

It was nice to hear a real voice in the morning. So many of the new hotels had adopted the computer version. Listening to a female Stephen Hawking wake you up was not a good thing. I rolled over and brought the laptop into bed and called the bank handling the account for the operation. I had wanted to wait till Monday so Tom wouldn't have time to blink. $560,000 was a great deal of money for what Tom would only understand was communications gear.

It was 1300 London time. I dialed the bank's number as the computer opened the secure site's page. I was surprised to see £1,000,000 in the account. Tom had done as he was told.

"Accor Trust, Allen speaking. How may I help you?"

"Hello Allen. Munroe here. My account number is 7483759."

"Yes, let me bring up your account. I have it. Can you give me your verbal password?"

"Alpha delta one four green."

"Thank you sir, can you please log in via your computer using your secure password?"

I typed another password into the computer and watched as I was logged in.

"Okay, I'm logged in."

"Yes. I see you on my system here, sir. Can you confirm your location for me?"

"Dallas Texas, United States, Fairmont Hotel."

"Your IP address confirms that sir and your machine is registered to use this account. What can I do for you?"

"I need you to convert and wire $560,000 to account number 127-569044 at the Chase bank and e-mail me a confirmation letter outlining the conversion rate and the confirmation from Chase."

"Yes sir, one moment please. Fine. Your account has been debited £34,9573.96 and the transfer has been completed. I will get confirmation from the bank when it opens and will forward that to you today. I can forward the sent transaction receipt now if you like."

"That would be great. How are you going to send me the receipt transaction today as you'll be closed by the time the bank over here opens?"

"We only close Christmas and New Years, sir. Someone is here to help you 24/7."

"Wow, I didn't know a bank like that existed."

"Trying to be competitive in the global market, sir. Is there anything else I can do for you today?"

"No thanks."

Tom really had taken steps to make this as easy as possible. I wondered if perhaps my suspicions were wrong about him. To date he had done everything he said he would do.

I decided to order in breakfast and spend the day getting used to using the Lego Command and Control system, or "LCC" as we were calling it. I wasn't sure I wanted Myron along on the trip. His expertise could come in handy and he did seem like a man with nothing to lose, but I still had some doubts nagging at the back of the machine.

The morning quickly passed, as I got more and more proficient with the LCC. I ordered a light lunch and checked my e-mails while I ate.

There was one from Viktor confirming the 'machine parts' had been loaded on the airplane taking the air conditioning parts to EG. He mentioned that Goetz had been very nervous and tired looking. Ball one was now in the game and it would only be a few hours before we knew if we were alive or dead in the gate.

I made hotel reservations for Monday and Tuesday and realized I need to make flight reservations for my trip to Calgary and order a limo to take to Lake Louise. I called the Fairmont and made reservations for the Chateau at Lake Louise and confirmed arrival time and method. The drive from Calgary airport was only about an hour-and-a-half, but there would be snow and I hated driving in snow.

Flight arrangements were easy as there were at least a dozen flights from Vancouver to Calgary, leaving like a bus every hour. I picked a larger jet rather than one of the smaller E90 regional ones and made a reservation in first class for 2 pm on Wednesday. Flying in first allowed me three checked bags up to 70 pounds each. This was significantly less restrictive than Alaska. I hoped the loaded Pelicans would come in at under 70 pounds.

I called the limousine company and made arrangements for the GL550 Mercedes SUV. I didn't need the space and could have perhaps ridden in a car but I was unsure if the cases would fit in the back of the smaller sedans. I also needed to rent a car in Seattle so that call was placed next.

Hertz was the only rental car agency that allowed you to pick up at SeaTac and drop off at Vancouver airport. I booked a Chevrolet Impala. How Chevy got the look of that car and an Impala in the same continent was beyond me. But it was a big car and would fit the cases and hopefully wouldn't draw too much attention at the border.

The day's administration duties were almost complete. I knew why generals spent hours in offices and I didn't like it one bit. The tedium of dealing and making calls was more than a little annoying. I still had to book my flight back to Africa. Perhaps for the last time.

There were no BA flights out of Calgary that had first class. They were flying the bigger 767 but it only had Club World class seating. It was still a full fold down bed so I booked the flight rather than fly back to Vancouver. I left Calgary Friday at 7 o'clock at night got into London terminal five at around noon on Saturday and had five hours before my flight continued. That flight left at 8 pm and arrived in Tambo terminal A at 7, on Sunday morning. God this was getting more than a little daunting.

I opened up my e-mail and left messages for Riley and Sunday. I told Riley to meet me at Paddington station at 1 pm Saturday and Sunday to have a shuttle chopper ready for my Sunday morning arrival.

I was tired, more from a lack of activity than anything else. I was looking forward to the end of the month. To the culmination of all this stupid flying, planning, and organization. I was also looking forward to spending time with Andrea. I decided a nice run would burn off some of the sitting on one's ass all day chemicals and refresh my head.

The run had done exactly what I hoped it would and I returned to the hotel well after dark. One mile had stretched into three and then ten. I had broke into a good sweat despite the cold and parts of my shirt were actually freezing solid. The cool air abandoned, the warmth of the hotel was like stepping off a plane in a hot resort.

I rushed upstairs and jumped into the shower with everything on but my shoes. The warm water stung my skin but in a few moments revived my spirits. I undressed in the shower and wrung out my clothes. I lingered for another 10 minutes, letting the heat infuse my body.

I turned on the BBC World News and ate the salad I had ordered earlier. Then it was time for a nap.

I awoke eight hours later, stiff from falling asleep in the chair. You know you're getting old when you fall asleep in the chair. With no one around to change the channel, and wake me up. No doubt blustering, like John did, that "he was watching that!" I smiled at the memory. Yup , you're getting to be your old man, or in my case, John.

It was 9:00 am. I showered and checked the clothes I had washed in the shower. They were dry already. The dry Dallas air removes the moisture as perfectly as if in a heavy-duty dryer. I packed up and was ready at 10:10.

I checked my e-mails. There were confirmations of "read" added to my e-mails to Riley and Sunday. I checked my own e-mail and saw a message from Goetz. Panicked, I hoped he hadn't written anything telling or given away our plan. I opened the e-mail.

"Christmas care package sent and received and being held by you favorite elf at his house. Hope to see you Thursday for a Christmas drink."

The e-mail was fine and I was very happy the shipment had been diverted to the engineer's house. My brain searched for his name. Manfred. So Manfred was willing to take a nice big risk to impress. Ball two was in play and we weren't dead yet. Encouraging.

The invoice for the wire transfer and receipt were also in my inbox as was my flight information link. I clicked the link and checked in for my flight and received a boarding pass and I sent them both over the local network to print at the concierge's desk.

I left my room and headed toward the Gold dining room. I could hear the concierge's laser printer operating and I stopped to wait for it to finish. She looked at them both quickly and handed them to me with a warm good morning.

Myron was in the middle of the living room area with two brown boxes and two open Pelican cases. He was stripping off plastic and checking each unit as if it would explode. He was so intent of his job he completely missed me entering the area. He was also missing the unkind looks from the others in the lounge.

"Myron, good morning. What's up?"

"Ah, nothing really, I just wanted to be sure that the guy in the lab charged each of the units up completely before shipping them."

"And?"

"So far so good."

"Here is the receipt for the money transfer," I said and handed him the slip of paper.

"Ok, never seen one of these before."

"Just confirms I sent a valid money wire transfer and the funds are in your account and confirmed by your bank. Good thing to get before you let someone walk off with this amount of product. Transfers are easy ways to commit fraud."

"Good to know. All the units are good and charged like they should be for the first time. You should get twenty-six hours out of a unit unless you're doing super heavy overlays and the like. Less if the unit has to switch to satellite; then it's like eight hours. But LAN, VoIP, radio and cellular should be pretty close to twenty-four or so. I registered all your devices so you just have to pick a plan and dump in a credit card and all the devices will be on one account. I left you notes on this thumb drive here."

"Okay, thanks."

"No worries; customer service and all that. Anyway this stuff goes in like this and this way it's all protected and organized so you don't have to identify which part goes with what. My Mom sews the bags for me. This case weighs 64 pounds and is just slightly oversized."

"Perfect, Myron. Thanks. Tell your Mom she does a nice job."

"I will. Thanks for thinking about me coming along."

"No promises, Myron. It's a long shot."

"I know. I just appreciate the thought. Oh shit, I almost forgot. I didn't know where you were using these. The guy that sold you the

LAN repeaters said Cancun but I doubted that. So I couldn't select a satellite company to use so I just registered them with all the big players still left in the market. If you can, use a low earth angle one as the data and transfer speeds are better."

"Great, thanks again." I was impressed with his thorough work, but didn't feel the need to be any more precise about our eventual location.

I closed the two large cases and put FAA approved locks on each. I was now one of those guys. The ones that couldn't pack, and needed to take the whole farm with them. The large cases rolled easily and I put my two carry on bags on top. I found it easier to push one and pull the other.

I walked past the concierge toward the elevators .

"Checking out Mr. Munroe?"

"Just going to have breakfast and a few cups of coffee. Then, yes, I'll be heading for warmer climes north"

"Warmer? North?"

"Vancouver."

"It's warmer in Vancouver right now?"

"Sure is. We rarely go below 32F in the winter."

"I didn't know that. I'll call the restaurant and tell them you're coming. Breakfast is on us."

Breakfast done, I pushed and pulled my rolling caravan to the curb and watched as the driver and the doorman wedged my two big cases into the compact car's trunk. The cases picked up the first of their scars like young lions do when they vie for the attention of the alpha cat.

The cab pulled away from the hotel and made its way through the light noon traffic.

"Which airline, sir?"

"Alaska, domestic flight."

"Thanks."

I suddenly remembered I hadn't got Andrea a gift. When I was a child my mother and father used to bring me gifts from their trips. It was a tradition that ended with the trip from which they never returned. I could get her something in Vancouver before she arrived, but that was hardly the point.

"Any decent jewelry stores between here and the airport? Real ones, not the chain or department store crap." I asked the driver.

"Not right here along but there is a place about four miles north that does nice work. I bought my partner's ring there."

He looked into the rear view mirror to gauge my reaction to the 'partner' comment. Gay or straight meant about as much to me as blue eyes or brown eyes. What other people did with their parts was not my concern. Why one would want to play with something they already have was a mystery but to each their own.

"Sounds good. Can you swing by and wait?"

"Sure can, picking up something for the missus?"

"No, the cat."

He looked at me again in the rearview and saw my smirk. His smile changed to a laugh and I followed suit.

The store had a great deal of security, more than the structure was actually worth. Metal detectors were at the door, which was secured, and allowed entrance only by buzzer. The door buzzed and I pulled it open.

"Good afternoon sir, how can I help you?"

"My cab driver says you guys are the best in the area and I need a gift for…"

While I struggled with how to identify Andrea the man behind the counter assumed it was for another type of 'partner.'

"Ring, chain? What were you thinking about for him?"

"Actually it's a her but I'm not sure of the status right now."

"OK? How about a nice necklace? That's safe."

"True it is. Anything made local or kind of regional? This is Texas."

"Yes, we do. I don't know how much you want to spend but I made this a while back. It's a box-link chain. Each of the links is shaped like the state. See, the design repeats and it's subtle and very fine work. This is platinum, very strong and allowed me to do things that wouldn't be possible with gold."

He handed me the chain. Each link was fashioned to look like the state and turned in on itself to form the box chain style. The chain was short and delicate yet incredibly heavy, far heavier than I imagined.

"This is beautiful work. Incredibly heavy too."

"Pure platinum. Very hard to work with as it doesn't conduct heat very well."

He took the chain back and looped it around a large glass vase and did up the clasp. Slipping his hand into the loop he lifted the vase off the counter by the chain alone. Then he handed me the vase. It was heavy leaded glass with an amazing tensile strength.

"If she's a bit of a wild one you don't have to worry about her breaking it. The clasp is the weakest link. Otherwise I was afraid someone could be choked by it. It's designed to break before the others. It took a great deal of work to make. It's an expensive piece, but truly one of a kind."

"How much?"

"Six thousand."

"Will you write me a receipt for six hundred?"

"I'll write you a receipt for six dollars so long as the one you sign for me reads six thousand."

"Wrap it up."

I left the store and jumped back into the warm cab. It quickly pulled away and continued to the airport. The driver looked at me expectantly in the mirror.

"Find something nice?"

"I did. The next time you go in tell him you're the cab driver that brought the guy who bought the Texas box chain and I'm sure he'll give you a discount."

"You bought the platinum chain?"

"You saw it?"

"Did I? Hello? That was the nicest piece in the place!"

"Yes, and its going on the nicest girl in Canada."

"Someone's in love."

That kind of took me aback and I settled in for the ride as the driver concentrated on negotiating the freeway. Was I in love? What exactly is love? I thought about her daily but unlike songs to the contrary my heart didn't ache when she was gone. Would I walk away form her in thirty seconds or less? I didn't know.

The machine surged up along my spine. She makes you vulnerable. She makes me human I countered. She gets inside, she could hurt us, betray us. She could have already done that if she wanted. The argument continued and I realized the rational me was not going to win this fight with the machine. Love wasn't rational and the machine didn't understand hope. There was no word in its language for what I was feeling.

The Alaska lounge, or "Board Room" as they called it, was not in the same league as the bigger airlines. But it was quiet and the food was good and I waited for them to announce my plane was boarding. It was listed as on time which was a good thing as many of the airports north east of here were having issues with the weather. The cascade effect had yet to hit Dallas and I was glad I had booked a direct flight.

The flight was called and I waited, finishing my martini. On smaller jets I like to board last. It avoided the staring parade as everyone filed past to the back to take his or her seats. The primary boarding call was made and I got up and casually strolled toward the gate.

When I arrived the line was just disappearing into the plane. I handed the attendant my boarding pass, she scanned it and wished me a good trip.

The flight to SeaTac was uneventful. The lunch inedible and the drinks came slowly. In this case the slow drink delivery was a good thing as I had a bit of a drive after we landed.

The rainy coast appeared on the left side of the plane as we turned north to make our final approach. The rain streaking the windows created a collage effect as surreal as an Andre Breton painting, the water distorting some areas of the scene, yet leaving others untouched.

We bumped to the gate and I collected my bags and waited for the door to be opened. When it was the damp coastal air surged into the plane like a wave. I could feel the humidity climb like the anticipation of a car race. My skin, dry from Africa and Dallas, drank it up. I was a coastal person and the damp air served to drive that message home.

SeaTac airport has all the trappings of a Bolshevik office, its stark and grey concrete as appealing as Moscow tenement housing. The layout was poor and the Alaska lounge was as I remembered it. A downstairs reception area, and the upstairs lounge area sparse. I decided to just grab my bags and get driving. In this way I would be coming into Canada with all the cross border shoppers and not be the sole car at night.

My checked bags had been marked with first class stickers and I was glad to see them rotating around the carousel when I arrived in the baggage claim area. I grabbed a cart and was happy to see the cases had been designed to stack and interlock. I pushed my dolly, feeling somewhat like a vagrant pushing a shopping cart, towards the car rental area.

"Hi. Munroe. I have a one-way reserved."

"Certainly sir, let me check."

"Regrettably, we don't have an Impala for you, sir. But we do have a Mercedes. It's a luxury rental from Vancouver that you can have at the same price you were quoted for the Impala."

"Any other options?"

The counter guy was a little taken back. Naturally assuming I would want to drive up in a luxury car for the same price. I didn't. I wanted to use my Belgium passport to enter Canada as a visitor and driving a US tagged car made this much easier. Further, driving a fancy rental car screamed "search me" to the border agents. I knew the company wanted to get me to drive the car back to the Vancouver lot and save the costs of having an employee do it.

"I'm afraid not sir, this is all we have."

I could easily see he was lying, but there was no use fighting with the guy. A little power was all he would ever attain and he loved to wield it. Bribing him was out as well as that didn't work like it did in other parts of the world.

"Great. Where do I sign?"

I signed off on all the documents and he game me the keys. I looked at the pathetic little fuck and thought you just cost me twenty grand. He blanched white at my stare and unconsciously took a step back.

"Sorry sir."

I walked away without comment not wanting to be memorable to this kid. My thoughts had him swinging by his balls face down in a puff adder colony. His balls black from the constriction and face bloated with bites.

CHAPTER
SIXTY

I FOUND THE CAR — a silver SL55. Nice, but not worth the $20,000 it was going to cost to drive it. Not only was I going to be on the hook for taxes but also I had to explain what the units were and why I was bringing half a million dollars worth of military looking gear in to play paintball. It was not a likely reason, yet I was stifled to figure out another one.

I placed the two big cases in first and insured the one on top contained only orange units. Then I placed my two carry on pieces behind the cases. I was surprised at the trunk space this little roadster had. I got behind the wheel and started it. It had a GPS navigation unit and I took the time to punch in Vancouver airport. It acquired the satellites and had me pull left out of the spot.

The drive through Seattle was less painful than I had anticipated. I considered taking the 405 instead of the I5 but traffic alerts said the expressway was open and clear so I stayed on five. The computer had me going through the Peace Arch border but I thought the Pacific truck crossing was a better option for avoiding detection.

The officers at the those two borders were switched around to avoid patterns so the level of professionalism would be the same but more shoppers took the Peace Arch back. 2:32 PM. The flashy car had changed my original plan. I was now entering the country with my own passport so it made more sense to pick a crossing I lived close to. I didn't want to take the Aldergrove or Sumas crossings, as the officers there were stale and stayed a long time. I still hadn't decided what to do with my declaration. An outright lie was dangerous because if they did search I would have no run back-story. Yet if I said I was brining in half a million in computer gear that would red flag all the way to Africa.

I took the off ramp that lead to the border and slowed my breathing and heart rate. The looming border came into view as I crested the hill and drove by the duty free liquor stores. My heart rate slowed and I went over the question and answer sequence in my head. Rehearsing my responses to the proposed questions. While detection here wouldn't scrap the operation it would give it a huge dent. I took my place in line, not being able to see the officer but hoping he was bored.

The car cleared the booth and I rolled down my window and grabbed my passport, checking to make sure it was the right one.

"Where do you live?"

"Harrison Hot Springs."

"How long have you been away?"

"Two weeks."

"Total value of goods you're bringing back?"

"Five thousand."

"Any alcohol or tobacco products?"

"No."

"Goat head."

He handed back my passport and I paused only briefly, I having clearly heard him say "Goat head," not "go ahead." I slipped the roadster into gear and rolled on down the road.

I had heard that the Canadian Border Services had moved from collecting taxes to border enforcement, focusing on drugs and other more dangerous goods than charging people extra for tax reasons. What I missed was how were they supposed to find it? It wasn't like I was going to declare an Uzi machine gun?

My mood was light and I fought the urge to put my foot into this little roadster. It wouldn't do to get pulled over by an over-zealous cop while I was driving a rented sports car. I turned left on Eighth Avenue and headed for the freeway.

I was hungry but not in the least bit tired, despite it being close to midnight by my watch. It was 9:00 pm local time, and the traffic was very light as I rolled over the Alex Fraser Bridge. The large cables suspending the six lanes surface were new and clean in direct contrast to the Golden Gate's rusting façade. I wished now that I had booked both nights at the Airport Fairmont, as it was a much shorter drive. The Fairmont downtown did have one of the best chefs of the chain and I was certainly looking forward to dinner.

The sky had cleared, as it so often does in Vancouver and the beautiful city came into view. The black mountains as a backdrop, their white peaks reflecting the city lights skyward. It felt good to be home, and I thought about briefly swinging by my penthouse and replacing my dwindling cigar count. The growl of my belly won the argument and I rolled up Oak Street till I had to turn left onto East Broadway. Hanging a left on Granville I drove over the nightlife and theater area of Granville Island and into the downtown core.

The Vancouver Fairmont was like a castle in the center of the city. Found right next to the art gallery and its urban park and fountain, the hotel was in a perfect location. I pulled into the valet parking, stopped, and popped the trunk. I handed the valet $20US and took the claim card.

"Guest at the hotel, sir?"

"Yes, Munroe. I won't need her till tomorrow afternoon."

"Welcome back Mr. Munroe." He gestured to the door way and a bell hop moving quickly to the back of the car as I retrieved my two light bags.

"Can I take those for you sir?"

"No. I think those two will need all your attention."

"Wow. This thing has a big trunk."

"That's what I thought," I replied.

There was a gesture from the valet to the bellhop that I caught out of the corner of my eye. I walked a few paces away and just caught the valet whisper my name over the din of the covered entrance area.

The bellhop caught up with me. He was doing the push-pull system with the oversized bags.

"Welcome to Fairmont Gold, Mr. Munroe. I can take you directly to your suite."

"Great, I'm starving. How long does the restaurant remain open?"

"Until 10:00 p.m. sir. You have lots of time."

"Not according to my tummy."

We walked down the entrance hallway and into the main lobby area. The marble and brass was as perfect as the day it was made. The main check in was to the right across form the main lobby, bar and restaurant. We turned left instead of going into the lobby proper and walked past the President's Club check-in area and up to the elevators.

He pushed the call button and I marveled at the gleaming, old wooden doors and how they had so expertly hid modern technology behind the historic wood and brass.

The elevator arrived and he let me go in first. He followed with the bags and effectively blocked the door, annoying the other waiting guests. He pushed the ninth floor button.

"Long trip, Mr. Munroe?"

"Long enough."

The doors opened and he pushed my luggage out to the little foyer. There was a concierge at a small, but elegant welcome desk to my right. The lounge was to her left and behind and the scents wafting out made my stomach protest more.

"Good evening Mr. Munroe, welcome back to the Fairmont Vancouver. My name is Danielle. 905 Tony; just leave the bags outside, I'll take Mr. Munroe to his room.

She waited for the bellhop to leave.

"Mr. Munroe I have a delicate matter to discuss. A young lady arrived about an hour ago. She said she was your girlfriend and wanted to surprise you. She asked if we would let her into your room. We tried to contact you via phone but I guess you were in transit. We let her in but if she isn't your girlfriend we can have her removed while you grab a snack."

"Blonde? About five foot nine. Thin. Built like an athlete?"

"Yes that's her. She said her name was Andrea. She knew your home address and the Visa number on the account so we figured it was legitimate."

"It's legit."

Tony the bellhop came back around the corner and then Danielle started talking about the evening snacks. Torturing me as she did. I handed Tony a $20 US as well.

"Thank you, Mr. Munroe."

Danielle continued talking about the Gold level benefits until the elevator arrived to take Tony back to the lobby.

"Sorry Mr. Munroe, but we understand discretion. I didn't want to spoil your surprise but I also didn't want to complicate your stay in any way. Here are some toiletries and you can use the bathroom over there if you want to freshen up first. I'm supposed to call Andrea when you arrive." She handed me an elegant wicker basket, filled to the brim with Christian Dior toiletries for men.

I took the basket, grateful for her forethought, and went to the washroom to freshen up.

I came out and Danielle gave me a conspirator's wink.

"Thanks for your help, Danielle. Much appreciated."

"Please act surprised Mr. Munroe. She's as excited as a schoolgirl. It must have been a long trip."

I handed her $50US.

"Long enough, Danielle."

"Thank you, Mr. Munroe. Shall we get into our roles?"

"Lead on, Macduff."

"Your room is right down at the end of the hall here Mr. Munroe. Please go ahead sir; light switch is on the right. I'll be right behind you, with your bags."

I opened the door, flipped on the light, and Danielle held the door open as I continued in. I walked past the bathroom on the right and into the main room as it opened expansively on my left.

"Hey Mister, want some candy?" a cheerful voice greeted me.

I jumped in mock surprise and saw Andrea. She was across the room. An intelligent decision if you're going to surprise a mercenary. She was wearing a Fairmont robe that was open deliciously at her thigh.

"Hey, Wow! I thought you were going to be here in the morning?"

"Well you said you weren't expecting to be here until after midnight. That's the morning."

I walked across the room and she met me half way. We came together and kissed for a good minute. My body relaxing in her arms and my hunger, for food, forgotten.

My right hand slid inside her robe and inched down until it cupped her perfect ass. She pushed her hips against mine as I devoured her kisses. Andrea had one hand on the back of my neck and her other was against my taut belly working her way between the buttons.

She tasted like peaches and I pushed my tongue against hers as a low animal moan escaped her lips. My left hand reached for her shoulder as her robe fell open. She was naked to the waist, a slash of turquoise splayed over her hip.

She was moaning wildly as her left leg stepped past mine. I felt her wet excitement sear my thigh as she rode my leg, pushing me backwards with the exertion.

"Fuck, Rhys! I missed you. I missed you so bad. Fucking kiss me, touch me. Oh God, I want you."

Her hand was inside my shirt and pulling it free of my pants, her mouth now licking my neck and shoulder as she ground her crotch into my thigh. She tore at my shirt, forgetting the buttons and letting them bounce where they wanted. Both hands moved to my belt and she gripped the front of my belt like a scared teenager on an amusement ride.

I had to adjust my weight as she rode my thigh, while gripping my belt, her legs on either side of my leg, riding my thigh as though it was a rodeo bull. Her robe had fallen off her shoulders and her wonderful tits undulated with each of her thrusts. Her head was tossed back and her blonde hair was teasing her ass.

"Oh fuck, ah yeyes, yes, fuck yes. Rhys yes you fuck, I'm going to cum, fuck ah ah yes."

She was glowing, light moisture appearing on her toned, tanned skin. Her eyes were closed tight and she was making sounds more animal than human.

I was hard, rock hard and uncomfortable bent down to the right, the pressure on belt and pants securing my cock as completely as a chastity device. I grabbed both breasts and squeezed hard, my thumb and forefinger searching for her nipples. I found them and pressed them hard, pinching them red.

"Yes, yes you fucking fuck squeeze those, harder, yes harder."

Her direction came as short orders as her thrusts became less controlled and shorter. My leg was slick and wet with her passion and she moaned, her orgasm taking her in waves of pleasure.

I caught a movement in the window. Danielle was there, reflected against the dark pane, watching, her face a mixture of desire and disbelief. She was still in the hallway standing beside a chair and writing desk, the Pelican cases beside her, blocking her exit.

Andrea slid to her knees and tore at my belt and pants button. They came free and so did my cock. She devoured me whole. As though she was starving she sucked me deep into her mouth and soon my balls were slick with her saliva. She continued to suck on me, her hands pushing my pants and underwear to the ground before cupping my ass and pulling me deep into her throat.

I was dizzy from the action and felt very weak in the knees. My mind was swimming with desire and slight embarrassment with Danielle watching from the dark recess of the hall. My orgasm was building and as if sensing it, Andrea slowed down and pushed me backwards with her forehead.

My shirt fell to the floor as she moved me the short distance to the bed. She was still deep on my cock, allowing her throat to constrict on the tip while she tugged roughly at my balls.

I felt the back of my legs touch the bed and Andrea gave me a push. I fell backwards onto the bed and my feet came free of my pants.

Andrea stood up, as I moved up the king-size bed. Her body was positively glowing with excitement. Her inner thighs were red with the abuse they had taken riding my leg. Her panties were now deep blue at the crotch from her wetness.

"Like what you see? You were gone too long, Rhys. After two weeks, finger banging myself to your old shirts doesn't cut it. You like teasing me like that? Do you? You like making me wait to ride your fucking cock? Well you can just fucking watch, do you like watching? Hmm wanna watch me do what I have to do when you're not around?"

I wasn't sure if she was talking to Danielle or me. I didn't dare look over to see if she was still hiding in the shadows or not. Didn't dare and couldn't take my eyes off the stunning creature in front of me.

The turquoise panties came off and hit the floor as Andrea crawled onto me and up my chest. Her legs were first behind her, before moving up so that they were on either side of my head.

"Look how fucking wet you make me."

She ran the back of her hand across her soaked pussy and slowly spread herself open with her thumb.

"Does that look like a satisfied cunt to you Rhys? Does it? Well it's not and it won't be until you fuck the hell out of it."

She put one finger behind her index finger and slipped it low into herself, letting out a long moan. Then she brought it up and circled her very swollen clit. Rubbing in a circular motion she closed her eyes and I felt her ass cheeks convulse like they were grabbing my chest.

I risked a look at the hallway. Danielle was now seated in the chair.

Her legs were spread as wide as the arms would allow and her skirt was high on her legs. She too, seemed to be taking care of an urge.

Andrea leaned back further and I raised my legs, placing my feet on the bed. Her back touched my thighs and she relaxed against them while I felt her ass go rock hard.

"Watch me, watch me, oh fuck I'm getting close, fuck fuck oh yeah oh oh oh fuuuuccckkk."

Her legs shook and I watched as she first shuddered and then, rubbing herself with the flat of her hand like a spasmodic banjo player; she came. Her hips arched and bounced on my chest as she gripped her right breast so hard it was turning purple at the nipple. Her grunts of pleasure raised several octaves and she came squirting all over my chest and face.

She recovered quickly and slipped round till she was lying on top of me. Legs closed and the tip of my cock was pinched between her delectable ass. She was still breathing heavily, but I could also hear someone else, breathing nearly as loudly. Before I could follow that thought Andrea licked herself off my neck and face.

"Mmmm, that's what happens when you do it right. I fucking taste good, don't I Rhys?"

"God, you taste incredible. I want you, now!"

"Really you want this tight little pussy? You want to make it squirt again? You gonna make me fucking soak the bed with that big cock of yours?"

"Yes!'

"Well you better do a good job, you're putting on a performance. Make me cum hard Rhys and put on a good show for our voyeur."

So, she knew Danielle was in the room. She knew and was getting off on being watched.

She opened her legs and slid down the length of my cock letting out a low moan. She leaned way back and grabbed my knees and brought herself up a couple of inches before impaling herself again.

"God Rhys, I think you like being watched. Your cock feels thicker. Do you like watching Danielle? Wishing it was your pussy riding this fucking cock?"

She was watching Danielle so I figured it was safe to look. Danielle had one leg over the arm of the chair, all modesty gone, with three fingers deep within herself, masturbating like crazy.

Andrea continued to bounce on my hips and, with another shudder, came. I felt her pool out and onto my flat belly. She was more than a little sweaty and I could tell she was getting more than tired. I took the opportunity to take control and tired to spin her onto her back lengthways on the bed.

"Go across the bed, baby, give the lady a good show."

I followed her direction and slid her crossways on the bed. Slipping into her hot core was heaven. I could feel her pulse against the head of my cock. I slowly started moving back and forth lowering my head to her tits. I licked the salty sweat from each nipple as I listened to her sigh.

"Faster baby, I want to be fucked. Save the love making till we're alone, I want Danielle to watch you fuck the shit out of me. I want to watch her get off watching us get off.'

I increased my pace and instantly felt Andrea grip me hard. I felt her hand move between us as she rubbed her clit with her right and gripped her tit again with her left. The fingerprints from before became overlaid by new ones. She slid across the sheets as I slammed my pelvis into her and her moans had changed to animal grunts keeping time with my thrusts.

Her head slipped off the bed and I could see she was looking directly at Danielle. I looked and saw our voyeur roughly rubbing herself and pinching her nipple, head tossed back, eyes locked on us.

I was getting close and was trying my best to continue the pace. Andrea was tensing her legs, ass lifting into me as I felt the first wave grip her. She let out a high-pitched moan as her convulsing pussy gripped and released me like I had never felt before. Then a warm gush of fluid hit my balls, bringing me over the edge. One gigantic last thrust and I exploded inside her, my overload of cum expanding her even more.

Collapsing in ecstasy I tried to keep my weight off her, resting on my elbows. I heard grunts and gasps from the hall but was far to spent to watch.

Andrea pushed my elbow out from under me.

"You're really not that heavy, you know. I like the weight of you. You feel good."

We lay together for several minutes, arms wrapped around each other, enjoying the sensation of flesh on flesh in quiet. I was remotely aware of movement in the hall. I heard the door open and close. I could still pick out the Danielle's scent but I knew Andrea and I were now alone.

My stomach decided to protest. The carnal pleasures sated the other systems were coming online.

"Mmmm, someone sounds hungry." Andrea, giggled softly.

"Yeah. I ate at 10:30 a.m. Dallas time."

"Well, for a starving man you sure fuck well. That was cool with Danielle watching eh?"

"Did you put her up to it?"

"Nope, but I did tell her I was going to rape you as soon as you walked in the door. After that I guess she made her own decision."

"Did it bother you?"

"No, not at all. It was kind of hot."

"Kind of hot? That woman was nearly fisting herself. I bet there is a puddle on the floor as big as the one I'm lying in."

"Okay, Ok, I liked it. It was very hot."

"Cool, so did I. But let's get up and get you fed, this time with food. What time does the restaurant close?"

"Ten, I think. But we should just order in room service. I'm just too tired to get dressed again."

"You're just hoping Danielle will deliver."

"Hmmm?"

She slapped me in mock condemnation and headed for the bathroom. A moment later I heard the shower start. I looked at the room service menu. I wasn't sure if Andrea had eaten so I ordered for her as well. I was so hungry I was sure the food would not go to waste.

CHAPTER SIXTY-ONE

THE FOOD WAS ON ITS way and I could hear the shower was still running. I walked into the large bathroom.

"May I join you in the shower?"

"What? Sure but I was just about to hop out."

"That might be safer."

"Yeah, don't want you to expire from lack of nutrition."

She stepped out of the shower as I slipped in. Her hands dragged a line across my low back and ass. She slapped my butt as she left."

"I hope there are two robes."

"There should be."

"Not if I hide yours," she giggled.

"Did you decide what you wanted?" She asked.

"Huh?"

"Food. Did you decide what you were in the mood for?" She continued.

"Ah yeah, I already ordered it should be here in a bit," I explained.

"What about me?"

"I ordered prime rib and chicken parmiagano. Appetizers are wings and scallops wrapped in bacon. Brie cheese salad and a gorgonzola and pear soup to begin."

"Wow, you are hungry!"

"Figured there would be enough choices for the two of us."

"What wine did you pair that with?" she looked at me quizzically.

"You."

She laughed and left the room.

The shower washed away the evidence of our fun. I watched as the soap took the day's travels and evening's adventure down the drain. It certainly had been an adventuresome homecoming . She was a real wild one and I hoped silently to myself I was enough for her.

The food arrived before I had finished my shower. I could pick up the scents as it mingled with the after-sex scents of the two women. I found my robe and returned to the main part of the suite.

Andrea was sitting on the freshly made bed. The TV was turned on to the all-news channel. She had waited for me but was hungrily eyeing the soup, glancing sideways to see if I had noticed.

"Mmm, this soup smells awesome."

"The chef here is one of the best in the chain. They always win awards."

"Good enough for me," she laughed. "Let's eat."

We sat on the bed and attacked the food with abandon.

Comfortable with each other, the news provided the distraction until we were well into our main part of the meal. We shared and tasted things from each other's plate with an ease that comes usually only with years of cohabitation.

"Am I going to watch one day and see you on there, Rhys?" she asked, looking at the television screen.

"What do you mean?"

"The news, I don't want to hear you're not coming home over the news channel."

"It's a possibility. I don't expose myself to too much risk. You can't account for everything but you can significantly limit the risk."

"I suppose," she replied, hesitation in her warm voice. "I have to admit I do worry. I have never fallen so hard for anyone in my life." Her voice became quiet, and with a slight intake of breath she continued, "It would be more than a cruel joke to hear you've been killed while I'm eating dinner with your cat."

"Hasn't happened yet." I tried to make the response lighthearted, but felt anything but because she was right.

"Don't be cavalier Rhys. I know it's your character but it makes it seem like you're not taking my fears to heart. I think you are but I feel like your not when you talk like that."

"I'm taking your fears to heart baby, and I'd be a liar if I said this current operation isn't risky. It's risky as hell. But for the first time I'm focusing on a larger outcome than just profit for me. But I can't allow fear to cloud my judgment. Fear kills the mind and makes us react like animals. If you're just reacting you need to be lucky or you don't survive. The mind is what separates us from the jungle animals. Nature gave them claws, speed, and teeth so they are much better adapted to reactionary responses. We have the big brains, but if we let the brain get looped in fear…well we've got nothing. Do you understand me?"

"I'm the one getting the degree in psychology. Yeah I get preconditioning. I just don't know the risks so I have nothing to ease my fears. I'm not asking you what you're doing. I want to know but I don't know if I will be able to understand what you tell me. I figure it might make it worse. I also don't know the rules yet. I don't know if you're allowed to tell me. I imagine telling me would risk other people's lives. It would, right?"

"Anyone I'm involved with would trust my judgment without question. So I can tell you. You're a bright women so I know I can make you understand and grasp the concepts. But not tonight. Tonight I want to talk about your trip to Amsterdam and listen to you as you sleep."

"God, you're a secret romantic aren't you? I like it."

Dinner was done and I remembered the chain hidden in my jacket pocket.

" I got you something from Dallas."

"You did? You didn't need to do that Rhys. Having you for two days is better than any gift."

"Well you might want to hold off on that statement until you've seen it."

"Ok, what is it?"

I pulled out the box and tossed my jacket back at a chair. Her eyes were open with wonder and when she saw the jewelry, box fear replaced anticipation for just a moment. I handed it to her and was surprised to see her young hand shaking.

"Well you're not on your knee so I guess I can stop panicking. Oh God it's heavy as hell. What did you get me, a rock from the Alamo?"

"Open it."

She pulled off the top and looked inside. Confusion crisscrossed her face as she attempted to reconcile what she was seeing with the weight she was holding. She reached in and took out the chain.

"Wow! It's gorgeous and so heavy. You wouldn't expect a fine chain to have this kind of weight. The links are shaped like Texas. Is this platinum?"

"Yes, pure platinum. A man in Dallas made it to see if he could design the links like that. Gold was too soft and silver not worth the effort."

"It's absolutely beautiful!"

Then she started to cry. The sound confused me and I knew right away it was a sound I didn't want to hear now or ever again.

"What's the matter Andrea?"

"Nothing's the matter. You're just so good to me. Even before we got together you were good to me. For no reason. You're a good person; I hope you see it in yourself one day. I hope you see yourself through someone else's eyes, past those filters and blinders."

I held her against my chest, cradling her head, and running my fingers through her beautiful hair.

"I hope so too."

Together we leaned against the cushions on the bed and comforted each other, swaying together in an age-old rhythm that every child understands.

I wasn't sure which one of us fell asleep first, but I awoke with the dawn feeling very rested. Andrea was still cradled against me, her robe open, the chain still grasped in her right hand.

I slipped away and she stirred only for a second before I went to the washroom to shower. The events of the evening were running through my head as clearly as the water running down my back. We were moving fast, perhaps out of her fear that I would be killed. If I allowed my mind to go to that place, the place of fear, of shadowy "not there's", I might see things the same way.

It was easy to remember that place, ingrown in all of us, like a wayward hair circling itself instead of growing up and out of the skin. I remembered just as clearly the day I forbade my mind from going there.

I was thirty feet up a zebra wood tree, lying in a y-junction and invisible. Covered from head to toe in a camouflage sheet. I hadn't really needed the cam. It was the rainy season and the tree was in full foliage. I was the spotter for a mortar team 600 yards away. We had been waiting for three days for the suspected target to drive by. Waiting patiently for our kill.

The country's forces regularly patrolled the area. None of which had seen me. They actually hadn't come too close to this tree. It was an old one, majestically breaking into the clearing from the north end.

I had run out of food on day one and had been surviving on the water I carried. For that reason I hadn't needed to get down from the tree. Liquid waste could be easily dumped below. Day two had been long. The cam sheet was keeping most of the bugs off my skin, as I waited.

The leopard had come from the west, silently. He knew something was wrong in his world. Not being able to spot his rival made it even more wrong. Like a search and rescue team he moved in ever-expanding circles, looking, sniffing and sensing.

He had come to the bottom of the tree and picked up the trace of my urine. It was like he saw some invisible string in how he followed it up into the tree. We locked eyes. He sprayed and walked in a circle spraying the tree four more times. We had an argument he and I and from the look of him it was being settled tonight.

Then as if he heard something I didn't he bolted and leapt into the jungle. I felt my heart rate slow as I scanned for what had spooked him. Reaching slowly I turned on my radio to call in the attack.

Nothing. Nothing came into view and while I didn't have any other imaging equipment it should have been obvious.

The hairs on my neck reacted first. It should have been obvious to the cat what I was doing. It's the same action birds enact to predators, faking a broken wing. Shit, I could sense him as much as if I had his weight on my back.

I reached slowly, very, very slowly, like molasses in snow, toward my sidearm. I gripped it and cleared the holster. The weapon was almost useless against a big cat. The sound provided its best use. Scare it away. But in this case it also would bring the local troops straight to me.

I bent double and levered myself so I was looking into the trunk of the tree. The soot black shadows moved but reflected none of the moonlight. My eyes accustomed to the star shine struggled to identify the movement as real or just an illusion created by the blood flowing back into my head.

The illusion's black froze and a pair of green eyes appeared less than a foot from my face. Green eyes that had seen a thousand kills. Eyes so green they glowed like the embers of a fire. Terror replaced fear and something made me stop. For what seemed like a minute, but in reality was less than a second, my body shut down. I knew if I reacted in any way usually available to me I was dead.

I didn't react. I refused to let fear grip my mind. I simply looked at the big cat and thought this isn't going to be as easy as you think it is, fucker.

I could see my face reflected in the huge cat's pupils, could hear its heart, and I could almost taste the half rotten kill on his breath. I crouched up onto all fours. The cat drew back its lips in a snarl.

We stayed like that. Me waiting for him to attack and he waiting for me to act like humans usually acted. I was having none of it. My plan was to bite his big fucking pink tongue clean off. A folly I knew, in fact part of me wondered if I would feel myself hit the ground. But not in fear, like a child observes a falling ball.

Without warning he sniffed the air, sprayed the tree, and jumped to the ground. I was only hit with a bit of the urine but it reeked.

Movement caught my eye and I saw a small team lead by Sunday move quietly into the clearing. He motioned to me to come down. I moved quickly and silently to the squad.

"So now you can stare down leopards?"

CHAPTER SIXTY-ONE

THE SOUND OF MOVEMENT IN the other room brought me back to the moment and to my shower.

"Rhys, you in the shower?"

"Yeah, just getting out.'

"I'm going to run over to the lounge and grab us some coffee."

"Great idea," I called out as I wrapped the towel around me, suddenly grateful that I was safe and sound in a luxury hotel at home and staring down leopards was not going to be on the agenda for the day.

I got dressed and thought about how much I should tell her. Operationally she wasn't in. Therefore she shouldn't be in the loop. It was following proper operational security to keep her out of the loop. But if I never came back who would tell her the story after the fact? Most likely anyone in the failed coup would be dead and the only people I've told about her were Viktor and Sunday. How would this go? I leave and never come back. Lawyer does right by her as she takes care of Ruben and has no details. Like smoke, I'm just not there.

I made the decision. If I laid out some ground rules I was certain it would be all right to let her in on the plan, or enough of the plan so that she could at least understand the "why" part of it. Right now it might appear I was doing it out of greed.

"Hey, you got dressed. No fair I wanted to watch. They didn't have any healthy looking pastries, so I got you a bran muffin and a coffee."

"Thanks, a muffin is fine. It's gorgeous out I thought we could go for a walk on the Seawall and have a late lunch at Carderos. Sound like a plan?"

"Yeah, good one too."

"Gimme a minute to jump in the shower and tug some clothes on. What kind of place is Carderos?"

"Business casual. I'm back on the west coast so I'm wearing jeans and a nice shirt."

"Ok I'll be right out."

The shower started and I went to open one of the Pelican cases. I found the five black units and took them out. I opened the other case and took out three units and put them into the first case. The load was still stable. I pulled out the remote local area network devices and placed fifty in each case. Nice fit and weighed nothing. I relocked the cases.

I put the black five units in my checkable carry-on bag and was good to go. I had no idea what plans Andrea had in store for us tonight but I didn't want to have to remember to swap out a few so I could get the men trained up on it.

Andrea walked into the room, tugging her low-rise jeans up onto her hips, silk blouse unbuttoned. The Danish was stuffed into her mouth. She was fast; it had been less than 10 minutes.

"If we can get another coffee to go from the lounge, I'm good to go."

The morning flew by, like the perfect moments in life that can never linger. Having first walked south and then west we had walked to English Bay for the start of the seawall walk. We walked in silence, trading sides as the wind changed, watching nothing in particular and glad to be sharing it with each other. The winter air was crisp and my new jacket more than enough. Andrea's wasn't as comfortable. The wind had picked up and I wrapped mine around her shoulders.

"Thanks, but Christ, this is heavy. You're going to get cold now."

"Not if we cut through Lost Lagoon and avoid going around the Brockton Point."

"I'm okay with that. I'm actually getting rather hungry."

We turned and walked up to the tennis courts and I remembered a particularly fun lunch I had once shared up here. That time was warmer than now and as if to agree Andrea stepped a little closer to me.

The short cut was a real time saver, but we still found ourselves at the wharf restaurant of Carderos right at noon.

The waiter was used to the preppy crowd of this trendy place and expertly ran a trained eye over our attire. It wasn't necessary. I slipped $50 US into his hand and asked for something private.

He walked us down the side that faces the Bayshore Hotel explaining the popular section was the other side and we would be extremely private on this side for quite some time. Andrea had surmised my intention and her young face was marred with worry.

We were seated and our drink order was taken and filled before I brought up the topic.

"Look Andrea, all the rules of safety say I shouldn't tell you a thing."

"Then don't. I really … "

"Let me finish, please. Those rules say "no" but the right thing to do is to tell you. It's only fair. You need to be in the loop, just in case. I don't want to sound dramatic but shit does happen. What I tell you has to stay in the strictest confidence. Don't even tell Ruben out loud. Get my drift?"

Over the next twenty minutes I outlined the overall plan, explaining things she didn't understand. I described everything in detail, as best I could but in the end I could see she was taking a great deal of stuff on faith.

"You know if I didn't know you as well as I do I would say you're delusional — one of those nebbish guys who shop at the James Bond store and pretend. So excuse me but I'm caught between reality and a Springer episode."

"Well it's real; I mean you know that it's real, so I'm confused."

"Sorry Rhys, I know it's for real. It just doesn't feel that way is all. I don't expect to understand how fifty guys are going to take over a whole country. But I get it's real. I really don't get the "why" of it. I understand going after your friend but changing the government? For what purpose?"

"To improve the people's lives. They have lots of money now but no better health care or education than they did years ago. I want to change that. I want to make the place a shiny example of a successful benevolent dictatorship."

"Benevolent dictatorships are not really in fashion these days," she replied.

"Perhaps not the benevolent part. Petroleum dictators are a growing breed. The EG President's kid spent over $300,000 US for clothes on a shopping trip a few months ago. That's more than the entire country spent on education last year. It's wrong and I'm going to stop it." I heard the urgency in my voice and hoped I wasn't going over the top with this.

"What about when you leave?" Andrea asked. "What happens then?"

"Well I would like to stay. Once everything's stable and moving along towards a democratic system, it should be a very nice place."

"Democratic? What happened to dictatorship? Now I'm getting confused." Andrea's face showed the confusion, her eyebrows coming together in a quizzical motion.

I tried to explain in more detail.

"They are coming out of the dark ages really. So the first government needs to be two terms or eight years. After that it should be by the electoral process, a simple majority."

"I see," she responded slowly, but I could tell she wasn't entirely convinced.

She continued, "It sounds good. But really, what are your chances?"

"Well, I have met and talked with the president to be and he seems a bit different. He wants me to be in control of public safety and security. Therefore my influence will be vast. He remains in power only for as long as I leave him in power. I will also control the military. He should play ball very nicely."

"So you'll be the real influence behind the throne." For the first time in our discussion Andrea sounded impressed.

"Only if I need to be. I would prefer to sit on the veranda, smoking a cigar and thinking about how I fucked over the US oil interests."

The restaurant had filled up quickly and our little bastion of privacy soon evaporated, replaced by hungry, well-dressed office workers. The conversation shifted to her Amsterdam trip.

She had been impressed with the Grand, the city sights and the shopping. I was very interested in her perspective of the city. She had been apprehensive at first, but seemed to travel well.

Lunch finished, we continued our walk south and stopped in a couple of designer shops where I picked up a couple of new suits. I would be in Alberta tomorrow and it was brutally cold. I had packed for a much warmer climate.

I picked up two new winter fashion suits and one summer linen suit in a straw colour that I thought might mimic a slim Hemingway look for that "Just after I took over your country press conference."

"Where are we going for dinner?"

"I thought about the Casino but figured it might be a little too loud so I just made reservations at the hotel. We could go to the Casino for some fun before dinner."

"I thought we'd go to the hotel for some fun before dinner."

"We could do that too, but I don't want to wear you out."

We walked in the front lobby of the Hotel and past the check in area, to the elevators. We got off on the ninth floor and we both looked hopefully at the Concierge desk. It was empty. We looked at one another, and started laughing.

"You looked first."

"You had the expression of someone awaiting an impending rectal exam."

"I did not!"

"Did so."

Movement behind us in the hall made us both turn around. There was a small Asian man dressed in the hotel colours.

"You checking out now, Mr. Munroe?"

"Yes, have them bring my car around."

"Yes, sir."

We retrieved our luggage quickly and returned to the ninth floor lobby area. It was empty. We made our way to elevators but saw no one.

"Careful Inspector, Kato is around here someplace," Andrea said in a stage whisper.

I burst out laughing and she followed suit. The elevator doors opened to a rather startled and overtly stuffy couple. They looked as though they would rather stay in the elevator than come into the lobby.

We regained our composure on the trip down and hung two quick rights to the valet station. The car was waiting, trunk and doors open. I handed the valet a $20.

"Sir, I notice this is a rental. Did you know the valet service at Vancouver international can return it for you?"

"Really? No I didn't know that."

"Yeah, they're a private company that just sub contracts to the hotel there. They're not Fairmont valets. But they can return rental cars, fill them up too. Worth the hassle if you have big cases like you have here. Just thought you'd like to know."

"Thanks."

The traffic was light and we made quick time up Granville and in an easy two- bridge hop we were pulling into the hotel's porte cochere at the airport.

The Fairmont doorman was talking sports with the valet. The valet was not in the white and gold uniform of the Fairmont staff.

"Guests of the hotel, sir?"

"Yes, three cases in the trunk."

The doorman looked over his shoulder first, I guessed to see if there was a bellboy available. He then spoke into his radio.

"Name on the reservation Mr...?"

"Munroe."

The valet helped extract the luggage and moved it to the entrance with the doorman. I grabbed my laptop bag and walked over to stand with Andrea.

"Fill it, and return it for me, okay?"

The valet nodded at my shouted instructions but didn't look happy. He got behind the wheel and ran it down the departures road moving to the far outside lane.

"They're still doing that, right?"

"Sir?"

"Returning rentals and filling them up."

" Yes, sir. But it used to be a nice tip for them as they used to pocket the $30 directly. However, the company they work for got wind of it and now they offer the service, and the valet gets nothing. They all want the Fairmont to pick up the contract but the airport authority won't let it happen."

"I see. Well, pass this to him, will you?"

The doorman took the $50 and shook his head in agreement. The bellboy arrived with a trolley and started stacking the luggage on to it.

"Mr. Munroe and his guest are on the 14th floor."

The bellboy nodded and manouvered the heavy load through the doors and into the terminal. He turned left and made for the small elevator. We rode up one floor.

The hotel was over a small span that bisected the terminal below. The highlight of this bridge was a wave like chandelier that ran almost the entire length of the hotel. It was stunning and the movement suggested entrance into a calm and relaxing space. It was art that worked to set more than theme. I like atmosphere that was more than wall paint.

We traversed the span and entered the lobby on the far side. Bypassing the main desk, which sat in the center of the open room, we continued to the elevator banks. The ride to the 14th floor was quick and the bellboy exited first out of necessity. The concierge, a petite black woman, greeted us by name.

"Welcome back to the Fairmont Gold, Mr. Munroe. I have you with us for one night staying in a suite. Is that correct?"

"Yes."

"Great. I see you have reservations at the Globe tonight for 8 o'clock. Is that time still good?"

"Yes it is."

"Excellent. I have you in room 1422. It has an awesome view of the North Shore Mountains and the runways. The Lounge is open now and evening hors d'oeuvres will be served at 5:00 p.m. are two keys sufficient?"

"Yes, thank you."

"Please allow me to show you to your suite," she continued in a polite yet efficient manner.

She rounded the desk area and walked past us toward the room. From my position I saw Andrea check out her small bubble butt as she moved past. We followed behind and I marveled at the ultra thick carpet and quiet. There were planes landing and taking off every four minutes and we could have been in a monastery. This serene setting amidst that chaos made me feel like I was within the silent eye of a hurricane.

We arrived at the end of the hall and the door was opened allowing us to enter. The suite was large and the windows were floor to ceiling. The bathroom was on the left as we entered and it was separated from the bedroom by a set of sliding doors. There was another smaller room off to the right that contained a couch and a writing desk. The cream and maroon colour scheme accented perfectly with the dark wood. Andrea moved to the sheer drapes and pulled them aside to watch the planes, shaking her head.

"Is everything to your liking, sir?"

"Perfect, thanks."

I handed her a hundred dollar bill and gestured toward the bellboy. She nodded and managed to remain far more demure than the bellboy whose eyes bounced on seeing the size of the tip.

"Enjoy your stay with us. If there is anything you need, I'm right down the hall."

The door clicked shut and I moved the cases out of the way and pulled out my new suits and hung them in the bathroom.

"It's incredible, you can't hear the planes at all."

"Marvels of modern glass, eh?"

"Do you always travel like this, Rhys? Top shelf the whole way or are you trying to impress me?"

"Is it working? I'm running low on my milk money."

"I'm being serious here. The Grand in Amsterdam, last night, tonight. Do you travel like this all the time?"

"No. When I'm in modern cities I do. The old spy movie cliché that you have to stay in a dump to go unnoticed is bullshit. More to the truth if a cop or government type is shadowing you and you roll into a place that costs as much a night as his mortgage he will out himself. It's harder than you think to fit into digs like this comfortably. I mean, it's easy to feel comfortable here but to be so comfortable that you fit in is the trick. To be relaxed around money and splendour is the bitch of the bunch. When I can't stay in nice places I stay in dives just like everyone else."

"Ya, Ok I get it. Where do I fit in?"

"Wherever you want to. You're my girlfriend."

"I am, am I? You haven't asked me to go steady or anything?"

"Well...Er, do people still do that?"

"Fuck, Rhys! You're funny. I was teasing you. You should have seen your face. You really don't get this dating stuff, do you?"

"No, I don't. I never really dated. I just kind of thought, I liked you a whole lot and I hoped you liked me back. When it was obvious you did, well I...ah just wanted to spend time with you. Lots of time. As much as I could, to get to know you, to learn to trust you. Hey! Don't laugh. This is really hard for me."

She moved away from the window, the Mona Lisa-like smile still on her face. She pressed into me, and kissed me gently on the mouth. The scent of peaches again overwhelmed me. Her hands slid down to the small of my back.

"Shhh, it's ok my big, dangerous mercenary. I like you a lot, Rhys. I want to spend lots of time with you too. You can trust me, I'm not going anywhere. You're too cute when you're vulnerable."

She broke away from her warm hug."

"I smell like I have been picking grapes all day. Let me freshen up."

"But I like your scent."

"Then here, live like I have for the past two weeks."

She stepped back and pulled her t-shirt over her head and tossed it to me as she walked to the bathroom. I caught it and brought it to my face, inhaling deeply. She glanced past her shoulder as she entered the bath and smiled.

I did a brief check of the suite, more out of habit than requirement. There was nothing obvious and nothing out of the ordinary. From the bathroom I heard the noises as the toilet flushed and water started to run. They were louder than what could be heard of the landing and taxiing aircraft. I turned on the television and flipped to an all-music channel, and found something that overlapped our ages and sat down in the chair by the window.

One of the sliding doors that separated the bedroom from the bathroom opened and I watched as her shadow reflected off the white wall. She was running the tub.

She was quietly singing along with the tune and pouring bath salts into the water as I watched. All of this projected on the wall like an old movie. I heard her slide into the tub and caught just a glimpse of her side as she dipped below my view.

"Wanna take a bath?"

"Yes," I responded enthusiastically, heading for the steamy atmosphere.

CHAPTER SIXTY-TWO

WE DRESSED FOR DINNER. I wore one of the suits I had picked up earlier. It was the one Andrea liked the most. Tighter than what I usually wore, there was no way I would be able to hide a gun in it.

Andrea had kicked me out of the bathroom and closed the sliding doors. She was getting dressed with all the secrecy of an impending Academy Awards ceremony. She wanted to impress me she had explained, while slapping my ass out of the room.

I had time to check on things I had neglected for almost twenty-four hours. Everything had been going smoothly but I was waiting for that to change. I didn't want to spoil our dinner with bad news but I also knew I had to look. Twenty-four hours was a lifetime.

The drafts folder had four new e-mails. I opened them in the order they were received using that as my time reference as it was getting harder to keep track. Sunday's was first and it basically gave me a run down of the training. The pro-trainers had arrived and were working with the men. Other than a couple of slips that the pros had missed (which Sunday had severely dealt with) all was good. They were starting to look like a team. The uniforms had helped and remarkably everyone had found shoes that fit.

Riley's draft laid out all the equipment that was en route. Tom had even hired an event planner to escort them and set up all the gear. We were two weeks from being in country and we already had men in play, men who knew nothing more than this was a football event. That would take any suspicions down a few notches before we arrived. The remaining team entourage, including cooks, bartenders, and support staff, would arrive in nine days to set up tents, shelter, and training fields.

Zombie's draft read like a pilots log. It was short and in point form. He had transferred the coaches to Sunny Ball and he liked the airport as it could accommodate a mid sized jet if the pilot could fly. Therefore, flying the squad directly into EG would be an easy trip. He had also copiloted the equipment run Tom had made into EG. The airport was new and the runways good. The military shared a side of the same airport and only one Hind was visible. Security was tight and it had taken five hours and a few bribes to get the gear unloaded and onto trucks.

It was Viktor's draft that got me really excited. The sub had contacted him and was three days ahead of schedule and running better than expected. Fuel usage was twenty percent below projected and they weren't pushing her. He had also managed to secure a safe habour in Gabon for refueling and re-supply. Libreville had a huge port and the tourist sub was more than welcome to dock. The busy timber shipping industry that's run from the port had been less than busy and the extra dollars secured filling a big sub was welcome. It was a very short swim from Gabon to EG.

I heard the door open and Andrea stepped out. She was nervous, her hand was shaking as she struck a pose like a model.

"Well?"

She was wearing a short black dress that ended mid-thigh. Her legs were sheathed in black nylons with a delicate line up the back, an illusion, creating even more length. The dress hugged her form and fit perfectly. The scooped neckline framed her elegant cleavage and the platinum necklace created a border to her long neck. She was wearing makeup, this time noticeably so. It accented her perfect beauty and brought it to stunning. She truly was one of the most beautiful women he'd ever seen.

"Wow!"

"I clean up pretty good don't I."

"Clean up? You're easily the most stunning woman I have ever seen."

Her cheeks increased their colour. She reached down to her hemline.

"Nice, and naughty."

She pulled up her hem a few inches and reveled her stocking tops complete with garters, the belts disappearing under the folds of her hiked up dress.

"How naughty?"

She pulled her skirt a little higher and then in a flurry smoothed it back down.

"You'll just have to wait and see."

"Tease."

"I see little Rhys isn't complaining."

It was my turn to blush. These tight dress slacks failed to hide anything. I got up and shifted myself comfortable and took her offered arm.

The Globe restaurant was just behind the circular check-in area, separated from the lounge by a huge fireplace. The fireplace would have worked better in a chalet atmosphere and looked slightly out of place in this modern design.

The lounge was full and many looked our way as we waited to be seated. Men and women both took long looks at Andrea and I felt a pang of pride mixed with jealousy. She noticed the looks that were fast becoming stares and pulled her shoulders back just a little. Then leaned into my ear.

"We make a pretty hot couple."

"It's all you, my dear."

"Hardly, my dear."

She let her hand slip to my butt and she gave it a squeeze. I could see the looks follow her hand.

We were seated by the windows, our drinks brought in short order. They were perfectly prepared. I found myself just gazing at Andrea as if she were made of fog and would dissipate the moment I took my eyes off her. Dinner was ordered and came as we engaged in light conversation around her master's thesis and her trip. I found it harder and harder to follow even this level of banter.

"Rhys, you're making me feel...well, not uncomfortable, but overtly coveted."

"Sorry, you're just so incredibly gorgeous I keep thinking you're going to disappear."

"That's the way it's been in your life isn't it? The ones you love go away."

She had said the L word. She was right but hearing it out loud made me panic. She was also right everything I loved did go away. I fought the urge to say something like "Is this couch time?" to try to regain a little control in the conversation. She had me unstable and wanted to see if I could be relaxed enough to allow it.

"They always do."

"Well I love you, and I'm not going anywhere. I really wasn't going to say that till I was done my PhD and you were back from this operation but forgive me. I do love you and I want you to know it."

"I love you too."

"I know you do. I could see it in your eyes when you walked into the hotel room and saw me there. You hide the emotions you know very well. The ones you're not to sure of…well it's like playing Texas Hold em with a child."

"A child, you say?"

"Well, I'm a professional."

The waiter interrupted our laughter and asked if we would like coffee while we looked at the dessert menu. We both nodded and leaving the menus he went off to get coffee. Neither of us really ate dessert, but we didn't want this evening to end.

The planes landed and took off in the rain, like dragonflies skimming a dark lake. The outside world seemed cold and distant, made more so by the warmth of the room, hinting at my tomorrow. Andrea took my hand and offered me a piece of her dessert. A caramel, macadamia nut crusted apple slice. It tasted as good as her tempting eyes looked. An apple, a temptation, a promise of knowledge. I hoped this wouldn't go as poorly as it did the first time. But like the first, I'd trade Eden in a heartbeat.

We kissed in the elevator as it took us up to our floor. She tasted of apples and her natural scent had mingled with her perfume. It was a heady mix. The doors opened and we raced to our suite like teenagers.

The room was dark except for the lights of the runway and terminal shining into the room through the wide-open windows. The moon's pale glow created an almost black light effect on the white linen sheets. Andrea stepped away from me and made for the bed, hiking up her dress as she did. The garters ran up her perfect bottom and were alone there. Her dress gathered at her waist as she crouched on the bed, stretched out like a big black cat with her butt in the air, a carnal invitation if ever there was one.

I knelt at the altar she provided and pushed my face into her damp sex. She tasted incredible. I lapped at my second dessert, encouraged by her moans. She moved one hand back and rubbed her clit before sliding two fingers deep inside. Withdrawing them she pushed them into my mouth and I licked the slippery wetness, sucking her fingers hard. She went back to her clit and rubbed while I licked the length of her and shuddering, she came.

She rolled over onto her back and turned to look at me.

"God I needed that. I was so fucking horny I almost starting playing with myself at the table."

"Mmmm, you tasted like you did."

"I wanted to get that out of the way, 'cause now I want to go really slowly. I want you to make love to me Rhys. Show me how much you love me. Take me slowly and devour me. Every inch of me."

I wasn't about to disobey those orders. I stood up and took off my clothes, slowly, letting her watch each item drop to the floor. That done, I reached over her prone body and undid each garter and slid each stocking off her long, strong legs. I put my hand behind her shoulder and easily flipped her onto her tummy. I took the zipper on her dress and dragged it down her delicious spine; she arched her back as I pulled it over her tight ass. She moaned. The garter belt opened up, slipped to her side and her bra unsnapped and fell open.

I slid one leg between hers and kissed the back of her neck. My hard cock pushed at the soft flesh of her ass cheek. She shivered and tried to roll over but I kept her flat with my chest. Biting her shoulder and squeezing her ass she pushed herself back at me, the air escaping her mouth in a long moan.

I let her roll over and she swung her hips to line up with mine. We kissed deeply and I entered her slowly as our tongues jousted for position. She arched back, her tits brushing up my chest, jutting out toward me.

"Yes, just like that, Rhys."

I moved my head and caught a nipple between my teeth and softly licked underneath. Her hips thrust into mine and I continued the slow thrusts and I could feel her clench me, her orgasm building again. She shuddered, quietly this time, and urged me on. I continued.

Our passions mingled and the slow movements fell into a comfortable rhythm. In sync, and slow. Kissing with the easy motion both of us feel each other building. Non-rushed and slowly we crest the wave together,

"That's it, come with me baby, oh yeyes just like that. Ah yes now baby I'm gonna cum."

A wash of electric ecstasy ran up my legs and exploded deliciously in my loins and I came. The moment was shared as Andrea convulsed around me and under me. We collapsed together and reveled in the aftermath of our lovemaking. We were sweaty, sticky and completely relaxed.

Andrea broke the silence.

"Mmmm, that was nice. I'm going to go wash up for bed. You want me to bring you a warm cloth?"

"Sure."

"Ok, you get the bed ready, for sleeping."

Within moments we were wrapped around each other and I was feeling a comfort and security I hadn't felt in decades. And then I slept.

CHAPTER SIXTY-THREE

THE CURTAINS BLOCKED THE MORNING light and I panicked briefly as I couldn't see the clock and didn't dare move my arm, as I would wake Andrea. She was backed in against me, still sleeping soundly. The light at the bottom of the drapes was bright and I wondered, in a moment of panic what the time was. I had a 2 p.m. flight. It didn't feel that late, but my senses were raw and not to be trusted.

I slowly rise till I can see the clock. Its green numbers show me it's ten. Andrea stirs against me and rolls over. Dreamy, sleep filled eyes gaze back at me. They are barely seeing, like a baby cats; half open to the world.

"Mmmm, morning babe. What time is it?"

"Just after ten.'

"Really? Shit! I told Charlie to have the limo here at noon."

"Why so early? You don't have class till tomorrow."

"Well, I figured check out is noon so…"

"Check out time is whenever we want."

"Well I want breakfast. Dinner was great but fancy places never give you enough food. When you woke me up snoring I was going to order room service."

"I was snoring?"

"Just for a second. I told you to shut up and you did. I'm going to jump in the shower. Could you order me waffles for breakfast."

"Just waffles?"

"If they have strawberries and cream that would work too."

"Ok.

She climbed out of bed and made her way to the bathroom. A perfect a creature as I could imagine. Yeah I was in love and wasn't

388

going to be able to walk away from this in thirty seconds or less. She was under my skin and part of me was filled with dread at the possibility of losing her. Hope was such a sketchy mistress.

Charlie pulled up to the front doors right on time and I gave Andrea a goodbye kiss that could have easily heated up the surrounding ten feet.

"Hey Rhys, just in for a day?"

"Yeah, Charlie. A quick turn around. How was the drive in?"

"The usual. Good afternoon Ms. Andrea."

"Hello, Charlie. Thanks for coming."

Charlie opened the big back door and Andrea slid into the car and waved back at me.

"Be safe."

"You too. Have a good flight."

I watched the car roll away, past the departures area, until it turned the corner and was gone. I noticed the doorman doing the same thing.

I went back up to the room and packed for Calgary. Sipping the left over coffee I fought the urge to climb back into the sheets we had shared and wrap myself in her scent. I already missed her. The phone rang and I looked hopefully at it. It wasn't Andrea's number.

"Rhys."

"Morning mate."

"Clive, please tell me you have good news."

"The best! The products left this morning. Cleared customs without a hitch and are en route to your secure pre-customs destination. Jan has someone meeting the plane and will walk the thing through and onto the boat."

"Great Clive, and thanks."

"Thank me by not getting my babies splashed all over the world press, kay?"

"Done."

I hung up and felt the day get a little brighter. Packed and ready for the Alberta cold I headed out of the room and towards the departures area.

There was only a short line at the Air Canada check-in area. I walked past it up to the counter and handed the clerk my passport.

"Good Morning sir, I see you're flying out at two. Checking any bags today?"

I fought the urge to say no, I'm just dragging these crates around for exercise.

"Yes, two please."

I moved one of the cases onto the scale and she looked at the weight.

"Well they come under our weight restriction but look to be oversized by a bit."

"Really? The salesman said they were just under. Who can you trust these days?"

"You're flying in first, so I'm sure they will be fine, sir."

"Thanks."

I collected my boarding pass and headed for security screening. The five units in my carry-on might raise some eyebrows but shouldn't get flagged.

I cleared the security area and wandered down the long concourse to the Maple Leaf lounge. Two Air Canada attendants guarded the entrance. Why they put the checkpoint to the lounge on the outside was beyond me. I showed them my ticket and pushed the large frosted glass doors open and went in to wait for my flight.

The lounge has sand dark wood, burnished so brightly it hurts my eyes. I briefly think about putting on sunglasses. While the outside access is staffed by two, the inside only has one attendant. I check my flight gate and time. The attendant tells me it's gate c35 and it's on time for departure. Relaxed and thinking more about Andrea than the task at hand I swing by the self-serve buffet.

Buffet is hardly the term one would use. The spread, so to speak, is stingy and the salad looks like it's from last night. There is only one hot item; soup. There is the usual cheese plate and buns.

I pour a cup of coffee and place it on the tray with a bowl of soup and a bun. Sparse would be a compliment. The liquor, however, is free and I pour myself a nice double scotch and head for a seat overlooking the tarmac.

The view of the tarmac is exceptional and surprisingly, so is the soup. I find myself thinking about Andrea in between bites and wondering what the future held for dear Ruben and me. I had used the L word and so had she.

The boarding call of my flight ended this folly and I chastised myself to get back in the game. I had a country to steal and many people's lives depended on me being the best at the game, and the game was certainly afoot.

The plane had filled quickly and it seemed we were flying at only thirty percent capacity. The line was gone and I quickly found my seat. Thankfully they hadn't packed first class with free 'gate' upgrades. So the front of the plane was as empty as the back.

I placed my carry-on in the overhead bin and took my aisle seat. The window seat was still empty and I looked out to orientate myself. Thankfully I was not looking at the hotel. I was aware that my internal condemnation had pulled me out of my comfortable cushy warm world of Andrea and put me back in the world and role I needed to play.

The flight was uneventful and the lunch was significantly better than the lounge fare. The Costal Mountains made way for the Rockies and the cool blue white snow sparkled like a wedding cake. Calgary came into view far earlier than I remembered and I looked at what must be the truest definition of urban sprawl. Calgary had grown but not in a good way. It had spread like the asses of the sitting, chair parked, oil executives. In a very short time these same executives would see their demand increase. This reminded me to invest in the sole Canadian resource company that would be doing work in EG.

The plane touched down without a bump. A perfect landing and I was starting to consider myself an expert. We taxied quickly to the gate and the seat belt sign was turned off. I looked at my watch and found we were ten minutes early. I was immediately aware of the door being opened. The scything gusts of wind cut for purchase at the edges of the jet way. The temperature plummeted and for a moment it looked as though smoking was once again allowed on planes. Our breath hung in the air, evidence of the cold outside.

The chauffeur was waiting by the baggage carousel with a sign. I greeted him and left my two carry-on bags with him. The big machine started turning and luggage started spilling out into the chute. My two pieces were the third bags to come off, the weight of them evident as they crashed into the carousel.

I dragged both of them off and using the tried, and perfected model of push/pull headed for the chauffer. He looked a little confused as though he should offer to trade the smaller bags for the cases but I waved him off and gestured he lead on.

We arrived at the Mercedes SUV and he surprisingly lifted the cases and placed them on top of each other in the back as if they weighed very little. I climbed into the backseat and tossed my bags on the vacant seat.

"How are the weather and roads?"

"Actually they are pretty good. Is this your first time in Calgary?"

"Nope"

"Great. Would you mind if we skirted the city?"

The airport was north of the city center. It used to be out of the city completely, but the development had surrounded and surpassed it.

"Sure, doesn't look as easy to do as it used to."

"Ya, little old cow town Calgary has grown up."

"More like out."

"Ya, true sir, very true. Crazy development, although things have slowed down a bunch right now."

"Makes it hard, I imagine, to keep on top of roads and the like."

"You're not kidding. There are places some city cabs won't go."

"Really?"

"Yeah, some of the subdivisions are laid out really weird and they get lost looking for the address and then people complain because they think they are being taken advantage of."

"Sounds like a mess," I offered in response.

"It is. Traffic gets to be a mess too, with everyone heading out to the suburbs right around this time. You can't make up any lost time by speeding as I think the average age of a cop right now is twenty-four. No discretion, no warnings, you just get the ticket."

"Don't get me started. I'm from Vancouver and I drive a Vanquish."

"Wow! Nice ride. No wonder you flew from Vancouver, probably cheaper than driving. What's an oil change and service run you?"

"Well, it varies a little but around $1400 a shot as an average."

"Wow, nice ride but wow. What do you do for a living? If you don't mind me asking."

"Oil."

He grinned at me and said, "That's funny."

"How so?"

"I was going to ask about fuel economy."

We shared the laugh and then settled into our respective jobs. Him driving, and me thinking.

Things had been going far too smoothly since Amsterdam. I understood that proper planning prevented poor performance, but I couldn't shake the sneaking swirls of doubt that collected at the edges of my mind. It reminded me of a dry pile of leaves gathered by the wind and deposited at the base of a tree. One small spark and the whole thing could go for shit.

The back road finally hooked up to a main highway running north south and we turned left. The driver was making good time and I checked my messages on my iPhone. Nothing. I could check the secure e-mail site but decided against it. Typing responses in a moving car on a little keyboard was more than I wanted to tackle.

The road rolled by and I was surprised to see the animal overpasses clear of game and other than a single deer we passed the turn off to Banff without seeing anything.

"Not a lot of wildlife around."

"No. It's been kind of quiet. Good thing for us who make a living driving. Deer strikes are a real dangerous event."

"Happen a lot?"

"I've hit two while driving guests out this way. One was a bad one."

"Were you hurt?"

"No, I was fine. It was just east of Canmore and this stupid buck came running out on to the road. I was driving a 12-passenger limo and as you can imagine those things don't stop quick or swerve well. Anyway I hit this guy and he flies up the hood takes a bounce on the window and goes airborne and lands on the rear sunroof. The sunroof explodes and Mr. Dumb Deer ends up bleeding out on this bride. My window is smashed white and I hear all this screaming in the back so I'm thinking the worst, right? I stick my head out the window and get her pulled over and jump out. I open the rear door and out rushes this bride in a white dress that looks like she stepped off the set of the movie Carrie. "

"Wow. I can imagine. Would have been worse if they were vegetarians."

394   *Scott D. Covey*

"You ain't kidding."

We made a left turn off the highway and drove past a visitor center, into parking lot full of RV's and cars.

"You been here before sir?"

"Nope."

"Just to reassure you, I'm not taking the scenic route. I know where I'm going. I say that because most people think the Fairmont is in town, it's right on the shores of Lake Louise, a grand old Canadian Pacific hotel. It was famous in Europe for the mountaineering. It's a little ways up a road you'd think nothing would be on."

"Ok. You're the professional and the last time I checked this was a per trip fare."

"You'd be surprised at the people that get confused and start asking questions."

He was right. We by-passed the town completely and drove up what looked like a residential road. It was narrow and gained in elevation and seemed to get narrower the higher we went. We crested the top and I started to see signs for smaller lodges.

The Fairmont came into view and was, in a word, majestic. The horseshoe drive took us past a building on the right that looked like residences. A bus parking area had three full sized busses parked followed. The next building looked like the hotel proper as it had flags from every province flying proudly.

We passed that and entered the actual turn of the horseshoe. There were several Valets, bellhops, and doormen helping people with luggage and skies. We drove to the curb and stopped. The driver jumped out and was met immediately by a Valet. They exchanged words as I let myself out. The cold was more than I had expected. I almost retreated back into the warm Mercedes.

"Mr. Munroe, welcome to the Chateau Lake Louise Fairmont. My name is Frank. May I escort you to the seventh floor, sir?"

"Just a second, please."

I could see the driver and a bellhop removing the cases and so I went to the back of the car. I handed the driver a fifty and confirmed his return pick up time before following the Valet.

We went up to the separate Gold check on the seventh floor. This was beginning to feel a little stale and I wondered how people lived on the road for weeks at a time. The trappings were gorgeous and opulent but familiar now in the way fine dining done daily gets to be.

I was escorted to my room and after tipping the staff was finally alone. The room was a one-bedroom suite with a lake view. The curtains were closed so I went to take a look at this famous lake. I wasn't disappointed.

The lake today was white covered in snow. But the picture on the wall, taken at a warmer time, was blue. But a blue like no other glacier fed lake I had ever seen. Far more turquoise than the lake at Whistler and more like a chunk of sky pillowed by snow. I allowed myself several long minutes to take it in. The lake wasn't large and I could easily see the end and the large white glacier that fed it.

I showered, got dressed and went out to the concierge.

"Any messages for me?"

"No, Mr. Munroe. We are still serving evening snacks in the lounge if you'd like."

"Actually I'm meeting a friend. Can you check to see if Mr. Goetz has checked in yet?"

"Certainly. One moment sir. Yes, he has checked in. Would you like me to call him and let him know you're in the Gold Lounge?"

"That would be fine, thank you."

I waited briefly to she if she would dial while I was there and when she didn't I made my way to the lounge. Good privacy protocol, I thought to myself.

CHAPTER
SIXTY-FOUR

THE LOUNGE IS NEARLY EMPTY. A young couple is sitting in the corner with too many sweet things on their plates to be anything but newlyweds. They are also not used to a lot of creature comforts and check everyone who comes and goes. I sit quietly and people watch, fighting the urge to check my mail.

The hostess came in and asked me if I'm comfortable and when I answer, "Yes," informs me Mr. Goetz got my message and will be right up. I thank her and she wanders over to the newlyweds and after a brief inquiry takes away the remainder of their dessert.

Goetz walked in and I wished I had a set of Myron's glasses as his first name completely escapes me. I notice he's pale, tired and seems to be in pain. He walks in and sees me. As he approaches I see the start of a smile and I notice his pupils are pinned. Painkillers, perhaps?

"Rhys, good to see you! How is my favorite go-to guy?"

"I'm good, my friend, but you look really tired and like you have a headache. We can pick another time if you like?"

"I'm as good as I get these days. I'll be fine, really. Just can't join you for a drink, pain killers."

"Serious?"

"Depends on your point of view I guess. If I had tickets to the Men's Gold medal hockey match I would be pissed. But I don't so... Nothing to worry about."

"That's kind of cryptic."

"Sorry. I don't mean to be. I have inoperable stomach cancer. Doc has given me two months. No, it's ok. I will be fine to run this little errand for you and I like that you and I can square up."

"Wow, sorry to hear it. If you would rather spend time with your family and…"

"I would be there. Your influence is far reaching but not that far my friend. No I want to go with a clean slate. Besides, my family wants me to fight it and do the treatments and the like. I would rather go leaving a clean slate and prepare things so they are well taken care of. Dying I can accept, going into a deal I can't win isn't my style. I do have some questions for you and I really hope you'll be honest and sincere."

"Ok, if I can."

"The main question is: knowing what you do about the world and the events that will unfold would you invest in my oil company? I don't have any illusions about your goals. I saw the crates in Amsterdam and the packing material and my man, Manfred, has told me what was in them. Not that I needed to know as I had already guessed from the movie like scenario I went through in Europe."

"Manfred shouldn't have opened them. That wasn't our deal,"

"He opened them, as he's loyal to me and my company. Don't worry, he grew up in Holland during the occupation. He can keep a secret and tell a lie to cover it. Your operation is not in any jeopardy."

"Well, I'm not any good at predicting the future but I intend to invest 300 large into your company. I figure you'll get along well with the Russians and without US influence."

"That's good enough for me. I don't see how but then I didn't see how you would get my daughter home safe. She's married, now and with a son on the way. The best predictions say I will meet him. But if I don't, I want them to be taken care of."

"I understand."

"I hate to disagree with you but I doubt you do. Coming to terms with one's death lends a very different perspective to one's vision."

"I have a good friend going through the same thing."

"Well then, perhaps you have an understanding of my position as it relates to time. You don't strike me as the type of man to have family so I'm making an educated guess you miss the second part."

"True."

"Funny thing, truth. When you get close to the end you don't have time to create the lies that yesterday seemed so easy. So, back to the task at hand, what am I taking on several plane trips?"

"Fifty of these, and three computers."

I pulled out one of the orange units I had placed in my laptop bag. Goetz pulled out the visor, computer, and the rest of the pieces and laid them on the table before us. The newlyweds didn't look over. He handled them with a puzzled look."

"Ok, I'll bite. What are these?"

"Communications gear and scanning safety gear."

"They look harmless enough. But, what are they really?"

"Communications device and safety gear. That's why they are orange. That's the brain and those are sensors. Earplugs and goggles to protect the eyes and hearing. These are the push to talk modules, that go on the uniform and these are sensors that tell if a man is down. In reality they are very sophisticated command and control units, but no one will be able to tell. The computers are clean. Just the usual programs like email, word, and a computer game featuring Lego men. It can all be checked and gone over completely without worry."

"Why get me to bring them in? Why not just add it to your luggage?"

"Because it's half a million dollars worth of the finest command and control gear on the planet. Because it has to be there when we arrive. Because I'm asking you to."

"Ok, no problem. I wasn't trying to get out of it. I was just getting my head around the issue. How many?"

"Fifty and some network gear that's solar powered and so green that it looks like it's part of your company's commitment to the planet and environmental awareness. You know, the green push. They come packed in two hard case suitcases. The suitcases are ok for domestic flights but may be oversized for international flights."

"I'm chartering a jet for this run. Time is…well, time."

"Yeah I understand."

"I leave here Sunday and go directly there from Calgary. Perks of the position. I will give them to Manfred to store with the rest of your toys."

"Great."

"Ok, so if you don't mind I have a share holders meeting to prepare for. Oh, and if I were you, I would make that stock purchase before Friday. Let's get the units into my room, shall we?"

We get up, he far slower than I and head back to my room. I grab the gear and we move two doors down the hall and put them in his room. I give him the keys for the locks.

"Thanks for doing this."

"Thanks for letting me get even."

The space between us was awkward. I wasn't dying and, in fact, for the first time in years had hope for the future. My race was still in progress and his was ending. We had very different perspectives on the world. I offered my hand and he shook it. It seemed like the only way to get past the silence, which grew more awkward by the second.

I went back to my room and spent several hours looking out at the lake and thinking about the future. The four smoked cigars ensured I would be paying extra for room sanitizing.

Saturday arrived and I was happy to have spent the three days just relaxing. I had gone over emails and other basic housekeeping chores but the immediate needs had been taken care of. I had walked around the lake and taken advantage of a few free massages that my membership in the Presidents Club entitled me to. The time had allowed me to focus and engage in a few high altitude hikes and runs. The goal was in sight and I was itching to get out of the gate.

The SUV arrived and I was glad to see it was my usual chauffer. Today would be a long one. The flight to London was a little longer than it would have been from Vancouver, as the plane could not go north as it did from there. Then there was a four-hour layover in London and I had to see Riley before continuing the 14 hours to Johannesburg and Hazy View. The realization made me want to stay in bed.

"You forgetting your big bags, sir?"

"No, I sent them ahead with relatives."

The SUV pulled away and fought for traction on the circular drive. I felt the machine come online a little further as we moved toward the inevitable. The equipment was in place for the most part and soon we would be too.

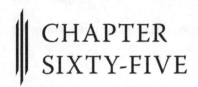

CHAPTER SIXTY-FIVE

THE DRIVE TO THE AIRPORT was completed in silence and the growing traffic was mirrored in my growing apprehension. The long flights ahead would signal the point of no return. We were committed. The small job of getting Simon out was overshadowed by the bigger concern, the Americans. This was about as much a war against them as it would be against the current government of EG. I knew I could handle the EG contingent; the American one was very much an unknown.

How much of our plot had leaked to the intelligence sources of the US? I was not naïve enough to believe they would be in the dark. But how much out of the dark were they and what were they prepared to do about it? The large question shared the back seat with me and I felt very claustrophobic.

We rolled up to the departures area drop off and I was glad to have only my two usual bags. The vehicle stopped and I opened my own door and got out and palmed 50 dollars into the chauffeur's hand.

"Thanks, Mr. Munroe. Have a good trip."

The airport was warm and there were very few travelers. I approached the BA desk and handed in my passport and got my boarding pass. I looked at the times and saw that the flight was shorter than Vancouver.

"Excuse me, are these times correct?"

"Yes, Sir."

"I thought that despite Calgary being east of Vancouver the flight time was, in fact, longer?"

"We're using different planes now. It's a half hour shorter. The website is probably still behind."

"Thanks."

"My pleasure, sir. Enjoy your flight."

I headed through security and into the large concourse used for international flights. This concourse serviced many regional and international airlines and all of them shared the Chinook lounge. It got its name from the warm wind that occurs in the winter months in the area. Some say it's from some Indian language meaning snow eater but this was just lore. The name was actually derived from the name of the race of people that lived in the area when it was first documented. It was also the standard excuse given by Calgarians when they were asked how they could live in such an inhospitable area.

The lounge was large and despite the lack of people in the terminal and concourse areas, it was full. I grabbed a seat and set down my bags. There was a warm wood-burning fireplace that added to the rustic homestead motif. The food was equally rustic and homestead sparse. It would do for the hour I had to spare.

The flight boarded and the city fell away like a business card tossed to the trash. The urban center gave way to the farms that surrounded it and the mountains that framed it. A very pretty place to be leaving.

I had to get myself shifted back to an African sleep cycle and good vodka seemed like just the medicine to do the trick. I had a meeting with Riley and then another ten hours to fly and nurse a hangover. The decision made, I ordered a large martini. This would perhaps be the last time I could drink to excess for a long while.

A soft touch on my shoulder, like a lover not willing to wake her partner, brought me back from sleep. The light streamed in the window, reflected off the very fine dusting of snow. The snow was making the old city look fresh and clean.

"We're in London, sir. You can deplane anytime you like." It was the flight attendant waking me.

I damped down my panic and took a few deep breaths. The drinks must have been strong, as I didn't remember anything past dinner. It was a few minutes after 12 and I had somehow got undressed. Completely undressed, I silently hoped I hadn't walked to the can. I slipped into my clothes and peering around the cabin saw I was alone. I headed for the washroom and passed a flight attendant picking up items left behind.

"Excuse me, how long have we been down?" I asked, sleepily.

"We have been at the gate for ten minutes, Sir. Did you have a good sleep?"

"Very. Ah, I didn't do this before, did I?"

"Sir?"

"Go to the washroom. "

"No Sir. We tucked you in and you slept like a child," she smiled knowingly.

"Thanks."

"Our pleasure," she said genially.

Her smile did little to reassure me and the smallish bathroom did little to ease my comfort level. I reminded myself I had to eat more if I was going to be indulging. I managed to scrape a razor across my face without drawing blood and had to admit that the eight hours of rest had been needed.

I left the plane and entered the lowest section of terminal five. This level was for passengers traveling further. While this was the case I had to meet Riley at Paddington station. I cleared security and realized that I was going to have to travel with both pieces of luggage. I doubted there was luggage storage anymore; the world had changed so incontinently. I figured it was worth a shot.

"Excuse me is there still luggage storage at the airport?"

"No lockers anymore, but BA still has a luggage storage in terminal four for passengers traveling on."

"All the way across to four?"

"Yes. Sorry, and with the construction it will be a pain. You going into London?"

"Yeah."

"It's not really Cricket to expect you to go all the way to four. Take the Express into Paddington. It has lockers."

"Thanks."

My nose picked up the scent of something that made my stomach rumble. It was first thing in the morning and I had yet to have coffee. But the scent was not that of coffee. There was a Krispy Kreeme donut outlet to my right hand side and I knew a Starbucks was at the top of the escalator just up one level. This was London and getting good coffee would be difficult in the city. The indulgence was worth the detour.

A few minutes later, with a doughnut balanced on my paper coffee cup I made for the Heathrow Express. The train/subway ran directly into Paddington station, ran every 15 minutes and would take only 15 minutes. The line to purchase tickets, however, looked as though it was going to take an hour.

The guy in front of me turned to his friend and asked if he had his Iphone. The conversation continued and I had nothing to do but listen. It became obvious that it was possible to buy your ticket on the Iphone and avoid the line.

The line wasn't moving at all and the next train would be in the station in short order so I took a stab at doing this.

I went to the site and after a few minutes had purchased a £39 first class ticket and now had an account so the return would be much faster. The company sent me an email with a bizarre looking 'barcode' that 'would be scanned at the gate'.

I made my way to the train platform and showed my phone to the attendant who scanned the image on my phone with what looked like a grocery scanner. It beeped.

"Have a nice trip, Sir."

I made my way onto the train and found a forward facing seat in the near empty car. Technology was sure making leaps and bounds. But I wondered why there had been no signs at the kiosk selling tickets to inform people they could do this? The age of information may be here but we weren't sharing it very well.

The train pulled away and headed toward Paddington. I looked at my watch. I would be right on time for the meeting with Riley.

In a short time Paddington station loomed in the distance. Avery big rail-yard in the middle of the city. It had been host to millions over the years. It had seen men leave for wars on foreign shores and been host to kings and queens. I wasn't a monarchist or anything but the ambience and feel of the city was hard to ignore. It was an inspiring city and huge station one, rumoured to have inspired a serviceman to write about a lost teddy bear.

The train stopped and I walked onto the platform and made directly for the excess baggage storage place. The machine took up duty scanning the area and picked Riley out of the crowd on the far end of the platform. He hadn't seen me yet.

I reached the counter and the attendant took my passport and credit card and placed my bags on a scanner similar to the ones in the airport.

"I'm only going to be a couple of hours,"

"Right Sir, we'll keep them safe for ya."

"Thanks."

I took my claim ticket and walked along the wall of the building. I watched as Riley casually looked at the arriving passengers. He looked like many other people waiting for friends and wasn't drawing too much attention to himself. I still wanted to see if Tom or anyone else had a watch posted.

The machine picked up a man wearing jeans and a blue shirt that seemed to be paying Riley a little more attention than was usual. I angled my approach and came up behind the man. He wasn't carrying anything overt, his jeans to tight to hide much and his blue shirt was tucked in. I waited at a safe distance and continued to watch him watch Riley.

Another man approached this one dressed in a business suit.

"Quit staring, people are going to think you're a wee bit daft."

"But he's cute."

"Not as cute as you, come on lover. Enough of the sights, let's get on the train."

The two men walked away from me, never knowing I was there.

Riley, drawn to the movement, spotted me standing there and without any sign of recognition headed out toward the main entrance. I followed.

"I think I'm clean, Rhys."

"You are. I just noticed a guy checking you out."

"I saw him too. But he arrived with this older guy that seemed a bit light in the loafers."

"They both thought you were cute."

"I didn't need to know that. You hungry?" He wanted to change the subject.

"Yeah I am. Lolita take away?"

"Sounds right chipper, guv."

We exited the station and facing the Hilton hotel across the street, turned left. I had thought about meeting at the Hilton; it was nice and anonymous but, I remembered Lolita where they had the best take-out fish and chips and the desire to eat there was about as consuming as the namesake book. We walked to the corner and turned left.

"Grab me a three pieces and a coffee. I've got to get some cash."

"Ok"

I went into the Bureau du Change and exchanged some US money for paper of the realm. The transaction was far faster and much better rate wise than anything at the airport.

I walked past two shops on Spring Street and into Lolita take away. Riley was still in the line and I joined him.

"I got this."

"Thanks Rhys. I've been living high off the hog pretty big these days. Tom has put me up in one of his discretionary flats down here. Nice digs and comes with a maid and the full monty."

"Yeah he seems to be playing ball real nice. Makes me uneasy. I don't trust him but I can't figure out all his angles either."

"Perhaps it's legit."

"Well then I guess I will feel a little more sorry when I fuck him over then."

"You're still ok with that part of the plan, right?"

"You should know better than to ask." Riley sounded slightly put out.

I paid for the food and we went outside to a small, cheap, chrome patio table. The street was busy but nothing out of the ordinary caught my eye. There were cameras everywhere in London and any one of them could be watching us but it was unlikely Tom would get anyone involved officially.

The chips were hand cut and the fish perfectly done. We both allowed ourselves time to enjoy it before continuing.

"Bloody hell! I should have had tea," I blurted as I took a sip from my coffee.

"Coffee no good?" Riley asked with a laugh.

"Like sex in a boat, fucking near water."

"Old joke, Rhys."

"You're not paying for it."

"Good thing, too."

"So what's the situation report?" I wanted to get down to business.

"The sit rep is good. He has lined up three players, two snipers and a goalie. Paid big money too. I was there, twenty grand. The coaches didn't come cheap either, about the same but they have to stay at Sunny Ball for a month. The players were there to meet the men and workout for two days and then are back for some huge match. They fly in three days before our match to do some press conferences, practice, and generally do the dog and pony show. He ain't holding the purse stings shut when it comes to the party either. The food and beverage budget is like two hundred large, and we're talking Brit bucks. Two lunches for 500 plus, for the two days leading up, and a month's worth of beer. In an Irish gig!"

"Good to know. He hampering much of your access to stuff?

"Nope. Anything I want to see, and I haven't had to ask yet. He's just including me in emails and the like. Zombie ran a bunch of stuff down and checked out the ground. Says everything is typical Africa, but we are getting a bit of the hands off treatment now. Some of the stuff went missing."

"Missing?"

"Yeah, like some freezer or fridge. Anyway, on the last trip the fridge was back but the customs assholes were all different. They did little more than help unload everything. No checks, no interference. What's going on in Sunny Ball?"

"The men looked good, most are healthy and with a few weeks of regular food all will be. Sunday and Chiwa have the reins and are running a tight ship."

"You sound like you ain't been there much?" Riley was curious.

"Haven't been, I went on a shopping trip in the US," I explained.

"Shopping?" he queried, one eyebrow raised as he chewed on a chip.

"Yup. Picked up this very sweet command and control software and been working on getting all our stuff into country."

"I thought you were going to get the stuff in with all the shipments Zombie's been flying in."

"Tom thinks that too?" I asked.

"I guess. He was a little concerned that no gear from you was in any of the shipments."

"Good."

"What? Am I out of the loop too?"

"No. Not at all. Things just were a bit fluid and I didn't want to email anything is all. We have sixty sets of Dragon scale ballistic vests, a complete command and control system with layered secure comms.

A crate of Mp5's and rounds already sitting in the country gathering dust."

"Really? All in and no hitch?"

"Nothing."

"That's awesome. Tom was freaking he was going to have to fly stuff in and get caught with his pants down. He's going to be happy. That is if I'm allowed to let him know."

"You can let him know we are arranging for the hardware to be delivered. Nothing more, and not that it's already in country."

"Roger that."

"We also have three Platinum Rain units, two LRAD, and a Submarine."

"What? We got a bloody sub? I thought we laughed that idea away?"

"We had and then I thought better of it."

"Three Platinum Rain units are a bit overkill, aren't they?

"No such thing as overkill in this game," I said with a laugh.

"Ok, I guess. The big issue in my mind is the Yanks. They aren't going to sit idle while we sodomize their golden goose."

"You're right. They won't. But I got that covered." I hoped Riley wouldn't ask for details, but I was wrong.

"How?" He asked, doubt and surprise creeping into his voice.

"I'm keeping that surprise to myself Riley."

"Ok, Captain."

The rest of the lunch was spent just catching up and enjoying the street scene and company. I lit a cigar and offered one to Riley. He took it and carefully took a few tentative puffs. The afternoon drifted by as each of us spent time together, yet alone with our thoughts.

The time came for me to head back to Heathrow. I took my leave, biding farewell to a slightly green Riley, who nevertheless professed to enjoy his cigar. I turned the corner and while I walked I used the cell phone and bought a return ticket on the Heathrow Express.

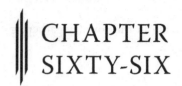

CHAPTER SIXTY-SIX

SUNDAY AND I WATCHED FROM the sidelines for another thirty minutes. I noticed the men had an intuitive sense of being a team. While they obviously weren't as talented as some of the premier players I had managed to watch on the TV they also weren't an individual playing with a group. They were teammates and their previous work as a squad was showing.

"They really play well together as a team, almost sensing the play."

"Like we do?" Sunday catches my eyes with a wistful stare.

"Like we used to, anyway."

"Don't bury me yet, ya pink fuck."

"I'm not. In fact I was going to say you look a whole lot better."

"Ya, well so did Chita Rivera when she was on stage. It's the pain afterward that gets ya."

"Well, after this perhaps we get a second opinion."

"I appreciate what you're saying, I really do. But the fact is I'm dead. I've had the best look. I've suffered through the bullshit theories and pink witch doctor crap. The bullet has been fired and this sniper don't miss, buddy. My only worry is for you."

"For me?" I turn to look directly at Sunday, slightly astonished as his concern for me.

"Yeah you. Who's gonna' tie your shoes when I'm gone? Your cat?"

"I'm serious, Sunday."

"Yeah, I know. Sorry we both do cavalier so well EH, Canada? I know ya care and I know this scares you too. We tend to go as a team."

"It's not just that…" I stumble to explain before being cut off.

"Sure it is buddy. This next hop is a bitch. I don't know what you have planned, and it doesn't matter. It's still a bitch. Fifty-something to what, 2000? Those kinds of odds are hard to even up with technology. Then there is the whole American side of things. They're going to land a SEAL team or an airborne unit and fuck us up."

"No they're not." A mischievous "I have a secret" smile crossed my face.

"You sound convinced," Sunday replied, sounding only slightly surprised.

"I have to be. It's hopeless any other way."

"So, Rhys Munroe has a sale on hope?"

"Yeah, "hope," Sunday. Without hope it ain't worth the effort and the potential loss."

"Well you sound too convinced. Personally I hope lunch is as good as usual."

"What is that supposed to mean?" I queried him and poked his arm in a gesture of camaraderie.

"It means I'm out of the loop and going into a coup on hope, with one of us being suicidal and the other one being stupid. I'll let you figure out which is which."

"I will get you up to speed later today. Bring Chiwa. It isn't suicide."

"Good, I was hoping it was just me. You got a bunch of good men out there. They deserve better. A lot better than what they got dealt. They believe you. They know you're right. They don't hope for shit. They know you're their ticket to tomorrow, and if you're selling a bill of goods I'll haunt your pink ass."

"I thought you didn't believe in that "after" stuff."

"Ya, impending death has a way of changing one's perspective," he said somberly, turning back to the field.

The game ended with a whistle blast and the men all lined up and thanked each other with rather western-looking knuckle bumps. The man with the whistle came running over and approached me.

"You must be the owner. My name is Fredrick. I'm the trainer. Got to say you have one hell of a squad here, sir. Never seen any teams come together like this one has."

"Thanks. Sunday and I were just discussing that."

Sunday cut in. "Yes, Rhys does indeed own the team. Do you think it has a chance against the National team?"

Fredrick looked thoughtful and paused a moment before responding.

"Not really, but the goal is to unite the country a bit and teach some kids the skills and show football in a national light. Right?"

"I couldn't have said it better myself, Fredrick. That said, are we going to make it interesting to watch?"

"I think so," he responded with a certainty Rhys found reassuring.

"Great. I thought we'd have to bring in something sordid for halftime," Sunday commented, jamming his hands into his pockets.

"Sunday, don't be so crass. Thanks Fredrick. Shall we grab lunch?"

Lunch was spent going over the team's strengths and weaknesses. I sat and listened, feeling like an intruder as most of the conversation was going completely over my head.

"Fredrick, I'm going to pull four men aside, in groups, to run them through some alternative testing. To see who makes the squad. But I would like you and the other trainers to come up with a list of twenty-five as well. Independent of my list. I think our teamwork is our true skill so that should be the focus."

"I totally agree, Rhys. Did you want me to break off the groups of four?"

"Yeah, that would be good. I need them for about six hours each."

"Ok, I will have a roster set and posted in the morning," the trainer said picking up the reins of responsibility.

"Thanks." I liked this football trainer, and wanted him to know it.

Lunch was winding down. I saw beer had been reintroduced and while most were taking advantage of it, no one was abusing it. It was a good sign that the men had taken this operation to heart and were ready to go. They were in for the fight of their lives, and the weight of their lives suddenly seemed heavy on me.

The trainers and players went for a post-game debriefing. I went back to my room and poured a Castle beer into a frosted glass and pulled out my computer. I pulled out one of the Command and Control units. I started the setup mode. For this training session I decided to just use radio communications.

The computer booted up and step-by-step the system took me through the set-up routine. I laid out the scenario and objectives. Then I tossed in a few known variables. The machine prompted me to make an enhanced reality overlay. I put on the goggles and went outside to design the test.

I wandered around the compound identifying landmarks and providing as much information as I could. I walked past the guards and identified weapons and movements. I tried to be as thorough as I could. The system drank up the data like a sponge. It took me the remainder of the afternoon and past dinner to complete the task. The setup system was very intuitive and worked exactly as Myron had promised. The battery low light was flashing in my heads up display (HUD), by the time I got back to the tree house.

Sunday and Chiwa were sharing drinks waiting for me. When I returned they tried their best not to appear to be anxious about my absence. I plugged the unit into the wall and let it communicate with the main computer. The laptop buzzed away and correlated its data with data gathered off the Internet. Using signal triangulation, built in maps, and Google maps it laid out the theater for the testing and familiarization exercise.

I poured myself a drink and sat down with them. The look on their faces was one of puzzlement. I knew I had a new technology to sell and it wouldn't be easy.

Two hours of conversation brought the two up to speed as to where the plan was at this stage. I ordered dinner to be brought up while they came up with questions. I attempted to answer their questions the best I could while I ate. The predominant risks were still the sub and off-loading the Platinum Rain units plus the level of defence we could expect from the President. The new CC devices were greeted with as much skepticism as I had anticipated. It was not battle proven and to this I could not argue.

I had laid out the familiarization program and so I thought the best explanation would be a demonstration.

"Look, I know it isn't tested or proven. But that's to our advantage. The US has no idea how it all works so it will be that much harder to compromise."

"They will just blanket pulse the frequency we're using Rhys and that will be the end of our 'star wars' toy."

"They won't be checking all the communication avenues we have open to us.'

"Like what?" Sunday questioned, perhaps more harshly than intended.

"We have radio, cellular, satellite, and VOIP."

"What the hell is VOIP?" Sunday asked.

"VOIP is Voice Over Internet Protocol, basically our own network with two-way communication."

"Enhanced reality and VOIP? I don't know, Rhys. It all seems a little complicated and vulnerable." Sunday was really not convinced and Chiwa, I could see, was feeling uncomfortable with this "speaking freely" type of conversation.

"The system is made to be user friendly and the signals are all encrypted. Two-way encrypted. You don't have to know how it works to use it. Enhanced reality is basically what pilots use today to fly planes," I explained, looking first at Sunday and then Chiwa.

"I don't know, Rhys," Sunday replied, sounding very skeptical.

"Right. You don't know let's test it, shall we?" I finally said in a clipped tone that Sunday finally understood.

"Now?" Chiwa asked, no doubt wanting to end the session and let the officers talk alone.

"Yeah, let's run a test. I set the scenario up for four men. I have five units but I wanted to keep one back in case one failed. So it's set for four but I will kill two of your guys right away. You're both far more than enlisted men, so you should be able to do the course without the other two."

"What about weapons?" The two asked in unison.

"The scenario doesn't call for that. Simple in and out intelligence gathering session. No weapons required."

"Okay. I'm game." Chiwa said, hoping to move this along into a comfortable setting.

"Me too."

"All right. Get suited up and be back here in five."

I called the security command post while they were gone and confirmed I had two people out on a patrolling test and that I would be firing one shot from the tree house in about an hour's time. The security command protested that no weapons were supposed to be inside the compound. I identified myself and told them to clear it with their boss.

The two men came back dressed in bush fatigues and face cam. I showed each one of them the gear and got them to put it on. They did so and each checked one another for problems. Finding none they turned back to me.

"What's the objective, Sir?"

"To go to the security post and count the men. If anything changes it will come over your devices. Questions in thirty seconds."

I waited for thirty seconds and then continued.

"There is a brief setup routine. It's simple to follow and I would like you to do that on your own, downstairs."

"Roger, sir." Chiwa was happy now this was past, his superiors arguing in front of him.

"Yes, Captain."

The two men left and I flipped on the computer. The program started up, showing me two Lego men heading out of the tree house. I took off my clothes, retrieved my gun, cigar, drink, and went to the outdoor tub with the laptop.

As the water filled the tub I watched as each man went through the same setup routine I had gone through at the convention center. I noticed Chiwa set his vision darkness enhancement a little stronger than Sunday. They had set the enhanced reality to almost full and were now looking at each other and the stuff around them getting used to the added information. I pushed my PTT button.

"Quit fucking about and get on with it. I don't want to be up all night."

"Roger, Sir, heading to objective." Sunday replied.

Sunday was the officer in charge, so his was the only response that came to my ears. Chiwa, however had answered as well. His response came up on the screen as a text. They moved off and I pushed the "start scenario" key.

The scenario let the men travel up almost to the guard shack. Then a brilliant flash and explosion would be entered into their units. The new instructions would detail that the guard post had been destroyed by an air to ground missile and the helicopter responsible had crashed near the river past the tree house. They were to infiltrate the area and check for intelligence and hostiles.

I smoked my cigar and waited.

The program ran and I heard Sunday's startled response, followed by commands.

"Shit, contact, contact, contact. Explosion front, take cover and wait for further."

I imagined the large Lego man providing the new orders and laughed, almost dropping my cigar into the tub. Once again I saw and heard the confirmation as the new orders were relayed.

I followed the slow movement of the two men on the screen as they entered the area of engagement. Hostiles could be present and they were unarmed, so they were taking great pains to be stealthy. I noticed how Sunday led the team toward the crash site, crossing his trail and doubling back before continuing. He was as sharp as ever.

They reached the area 50 meters to my left and I took out my pistol. Taking care to insure it was through the mesh before I fired I aimed at a tree near the two men and squeezed the trigger. Immediately an alarm both visual and auditory came over the system and my location was pinpointed exactly and relayed to the men. They both moved into a defensive position eliminating my shot window and went to ground.

I pressed the PTT button.

"Test run is over. Come on back up."

I jumped out of the bath and tossed a robe on before heading downstairs. Chiwa and Sunday arrived a few minutes later.

"Well, what do you think?"

"Holy crap is that ever good! The overlay is perfect and the light enhancement great. I could keep up with Sunday like it was daylight."

"Sorry Rhys, you picked a winner with this one. But what's with the Lego man?"

"Long story about the design. I take it you're both sold?"

"The shot identification software alone is worth the weight!" Sunday said convinced — his mood much improved.

"I like it, sir."

"Great. Well both of you are going to have to spend some time learning the back end command part of the program but other than that I think the men will take to it well."

"Considering this is new ground, I agree. However how hard is this program to learn?" Sunday's trepidation at new technology as obvious as if his fly was undone.

"About as hard as the setup you had to do on the system."

The two men looked tired and, while excited about the CC system, the morning would come soon for them.

"Well I'm not finished my cigar or bath so how about we call it a night?"

"Morning run at six, Sir."

"Six? I don't think so, Sergeant. It's going to take me a few days to get my legs under me that early. Sunday, I need you to join me at 0800 for computer training."

"Yes Sir, I'll be here right after the run, then."

"You can't guilt me into anything. Two hour run? Kinda long."

"Only an hour-and-a-half, sir. Breakfast is from 7:30 until 8:30."

"Well, we can order in something. Once you have the hang of it you can teach Chiwa. Then the two of you can pick two men with aptitude to each train. Questions? Or you waiting for a bedtime story?"

Laughing, they left the room, Sunday to his room, and Chiwa out the front door. I returned to my perched tub and nice cigar. The water was cooling and I topped it up looking for the small hole in the mesh I had folded over. Despite my best effort the shot had torn the net. Fixing it gave me something more to do than just smoking.

The cigar was finished and the tub was draining. I hadn't felt tired out on the deck, looking up at the stars, but once inside I felt as though I had been drugged. My shoulders felt weary and I made for bed. It was turned down, reminding me prying eyes were around and that I should clean up. The CC system was still out. I drifted to sleep, seeing conspiracies where none existed.

I woke to the bang of a door and looked at the clock, 0545. I felt rested despite the early hour and could have gone for the run. But I wasn't going to let the guilt trip win. I wondered what time it had been when I went to bed. In any case I felt refreshed and went downstairs to make coffee. It was already made.

I went back upstairs, performed the morning rituals and got dressed. Then I went back downstairs and poured myself a strong cup of coffee before opening my laptop.

The secure mail site had two unread drafts. The first was from

Viktor and provided a positioning update that was only four hours old. It wasn't so much a position but "Andrea can see her shadow on the table." As cryptic as a spy novel, and yet very definitive if you knew that Table Mountain was in Cape Town.

The second was from Z. It said he was coming to town on Friday with the hired help and would like to have lunch. I answered by adding a simple yes to the end of the message draft.

The door once again banged open and I looked up from the screen.

"Nice run, Captain?"

"Very much so, Captain. Missed you out there."

"The house bitch made me coffee so I figured I'd skip it."

"If you had said house BOY I would be stabbing you right about now, Captain."

"You might have tried to, Captain. What do you want to eat?"

"Already stopped by and ordered."

"Ordered for you, too. Does the REAL house bitch need her shoes tied as well?"

The knock on the door stayed my tongue. A tall woman brought in two trays, one carried like a traditional waiter while the other was balanced on her head. She set the trays down on the table and without a word was gone, the timing for my insult gone with her.

"Hungry? What you get for me?"

"Steak and eggs, toast and grilled tomato"

The banter done, we sat and talked more about the operation. Loading the two units on the island would be easy enough at night under a dark moon. Getting the other one off the deck, to the road above the airport was the tricky one. The area was right before the refinery and by the airport — it would be crawling with cops and security.

I agreed with him and ran out a few other options but none were as good, which wasn't saying much. So I offered a cliché.

"Hey they wouldn't pay us so much and call us professionals if it were easy."

"Humph. here is your schedule for today. It starts at nine."

"Thanks, here is your tutorial lesson."

I spent the next 30 minutes giving Sunday the basic uses of the program, then dismissed him to work with it.

I realized that the men had probably been told to meet next to the field or in the dining room. I looked out the window toward the dining hall but saw no one. They must be at the field so I went to get them. They were there, milling about in a live example for why we needed this system.

"Follow me," I called over the noise.

I went back to the tree house and paused only for a second to look back and see four people walking my way. I carried on up to the top of the house and started making some preparations, while leaving the door open.

The four men came in. Looked around and stood in front of the sofa. I told them to sit down and went through the preamble talk like I had done last night. It got about the same response, judging from their expressions, although these men were too polite to tell me. Or perhaps, too scared.

Just like last night they agreed to run the simple exercise. Just like last night I knew they would be impressed.

The four went downstairs and I monitored them running the setup windows. They all got the rigs set up but not as quickly as Sunday and Chiwa had. I gave them more time to play with and get used to the enhanced reality before bringing them back in focus and directing them toward the objectives.

The scenario played out and I watched as the four men completed the course. This time I used a starter pistol in order to save the net.

Their reactions were as positive as Chiwa's and Sunday's. Perhaps more so, as I had provided ample time for them just to look at things and get used to the gear.

CHAPTER SIXTY-SEVEN

THE REST OF THE DAY went the same way. Four skeptics in and four converts out. There were a few of the men that had problems with the level of enhanced reality they could work with. Some needed to damp it down to below level three. I took note of those and for the rest of the week the pattern was the same.

The only change in the routine was that I added the morning runs with the men. I could tell it was important to both Sunday and Chiwa for me to participate and take some of the command load off their shoulders. Things were ramping up well and the men needed to see me as a participating member. The evening "O Group" meetings now included Chiwa. He would be taking on a larger role in the coup basically being in charge of the Island station. So it seemed a good idea to get him involved and providing input.

The meeting with Zombie had been a quick one on Saturday and we got our ringers, and pro coaches back. There had been some quick handshakes and chat plane side and I had begged off the trip back saying I wanted a tour of the plane. They shook their heads in acknowledgement and understanding.

Inside I was a little overwhelmed at the level of luxury. The whole inside was like one of the finest limos I had ever rode in. Rich and very functional. Zombie invited me up front as the co pilot had gone into the small terminal for a snack.. The cockpit resembled a fantasy spacecraft more than it did any of the executive jets I had been in. There were no less than six computer screens and a very military heads up display.

"Wow Z this thing looks pretty sweet. Any bugs or quirks, being brand new?"

"Not a hitch Rhys, it even reports back to the manufacturer usage and issues for repair all on it's own. This is by far the nicest jet I've ever piloted! It handles like a military jet and looks like a Rolls Royce inside."

"So you want to keep her?" I gave Z a hard stare.

"I would love to, but even at over sixty million they have a two-year waiting list. This thing gets more attention than Shaquille O'Neal playing basketball in the nude."

"Looks a lot better, too. But seriously, could you see yourself being the Presidential Pilot? Living in country and being in charge of this and the other fleet of government airplanes?"

"Yeah, I think you could twist my arm." He said looking at me, his focus on my sanity.

"What is the plan for the craft while the escape goes off?"

"Tom is leaving that up to me to arrange. Which is why I wanted to talk to you. Do you want it on the ground for extraction or in the air?"

"Well that kind of depends. There is a road that parallels the landing strip. Have you seen it on your trips there?"

"Yeah."

"Could you land on it?"

"I can land on anything. But will she be in good enough shape to take off again is the question. I don't have any countermeasures and this pretty little cloud model won't take small arms fire, never mind big stuff. What you have in mind?"

"I want you to deliver a new president."

"What? Rhys, this ain't a wild west "lets take the bloody country" Mad Mike Hoare operation. This is a simple jailbreak. What the fuck is wrong with you? Tom is playing nice and above board on this one and you're talking crazy fucking shit here man."

My mind raced ahead, thinking of my options. Z looked to be totally outside on this one. Perhaps he had fallen in love with the new plane, or with the job, which Tom had let him in on. I liked Z, liked him a great deal. Even owed him my life. But right now he was in conflict with the coup. In conflict with the lives of those in the coup. Z had become a liability. With a wry smile I thought, "Nothing personal, old friend, but you're just food."

My mind was searching for the "how" while I continued talking. Perhaps because of the debt of honour I owed him or perhaps because my choice of weapon and method was escaping me for the moment, I continued.

"Z, you're out of the loop, flying donkey poop for Tom. Let's not forget who this guy is. He rolled Simon into this place in the first part and then let him rot. I really need to know your loyalties here, buddy. The plan is sound. I say the plan is sound and in place. Weapons and other assets on the ground, or otherwise in play."

"You're not serious? Incredulity coloured his response.

"Twenty-five guys and two talented Greys aren't taking down an entrenched and US backed military. I don't care what kind of shape they're in or what kind of toys you have. The US will be landing men in the sand and targeting my ass as soon as the first shots are fired. If you're going to do this I want to be feet wet before the first round is fired. If you're successful I will do what you need me to do, but right now, ol' buddy, you sound as crazy as a blood hound with a treed coon."

Letting the pen slide into my hand I looked at him closely. I needed to judge his conviction. He wasn't saying he was out, just that he wanted to play it safe. Would he keep our secret? The machine whispered in my ear, "A secret is only a secret if three people know about it and two of them are dead."

"So Z, can I get you to drop us off to do the four day party and tournament? I'll send you off with the ringers and coaches at halftime, so I can commit my grand suicide. You going to be ok with that?" I queried.

His response was almost staccato-like.

"No, I'm not okay with that! Simon's still in jail and two good friends are dead. How could you ask me if I was okay with that? Why would you push a simple operation into an impossible one?"

The look on his face was genuine concern. I detected no hint of deception, only fear with a hint of anger. I twisted till I was facing him, the pen in my left hand, cupped to avoid detection. I searched the area outside the windows. It was clear.

"Hope, Z — hope. Hope that I can make a place the men feel safe and comfortable. Hope for a better tomorrow for everyone in EG including Simon. Hope you'll make the correct choice to follow my lead and be onside with the coup." I shifted the pen till the end was in the middle of my palm and tensed my core muscles to deliver the blow.

"Captain, I'm with you. I'll deliver you to your deaths and I'll keep my trap shut. But you gotta know you got about as much 'hope' as a black waiter in a KKK convention. You say you can do it, and I think you know Sunday is dying and wants a last kick at the can. But you can't ask me to throw it all away with you. Like I said, I'll drop you and if you want me to make a milk run mid game, I'll do that too. Hell, I'll even make a low pass over your alternative landing strip the next time I run something into the country to give you an informed opinion about using it. But you can't ask me to die with you, sitting in a plane on a runway or road."

"I'm not. I'm asking you to drop off the pros someplace safe and then take a run into Spain and pick up the exiled president and get him coming back to EG. If it's safe we will radio you in. No radio, no land. That simple. Can I trust you to keep your trap shut and do that for me?"

"Yes, you can. But I won't land if there is any shooting. It's been good knowing you," he finished. He knew it would be his last trip for me.

"Good enough." I let my body relax and dropped the pen back into my pocket.

I could see the copilot walking back toward the plane. "What about encumbrances like him?"

"I don't need two people to fly this bird. I've got music to keep me awake. But on the big day I don't want any passengers."

"Is that easy to do?"

Turning halfway round in the pilot's seat Z fixed me with a glare. "I've been killing people longer than you. If he gets in the way he's baggage, lost baggage."

"Ok Z, I don't need convincing. On the day of, either red smoke or a fire line down the road or airport will signal we are in control, just in case we're jammed."

"You will be. Here is the flight itinerary to EG for the Officers and enlisted men. The big Russian bird is the President's and he insisted it come get you."

"Yeah, but when we're done ousting him, you come get us. Shit almost forgot, don't fly west of the island on that day, for any reason."

"Yeah I'll come get you. Why can't I fly west?"

"Just don't"

A shadow was in the door, and the co-pilot came into the plane.

He looked at me and looked decidedly unimpressed. Either that or he came from the same neighbourhood Maggie T did. They always held their heads like they had a little piece of shit under their noses. Either way he passed me on the way to the cockpit without a sound, and I left the plane glad I hadn't needed to kill Z.

I took a cab back to the golf course and was moderately disappointed the girl wasn't there. I had come of the pretext of buying cigars, that I really did need, but I wanted to talk with her a little more as well. I was in a mindset that would have given me a fresh perspective. Instead I walked out with two boxes of my favourite cigars. Partagas SD#4's and Punch Double Corona's.

I took the cab back to Sunny Ball and silently shared the afternoon on the drive back. We were stopped at the gate and I got out and paid the fare, deciding to walk back. The yells and whistle blows came from the field and I angled that way cigar boxes in hand.

The men were broken into squads and were doing running and passing drills with the ringers moving through the middle ranks picking up balls and firing them forward, before the whole column turned around and did it again. They were getting a workout and the trainers were too. It sounded like opening day at boot camp.

The ringers and the pro coaches were going to stay the entire time now till we left for EG. So basically ten days of training prior to the flight. It would be enough. The men were happy and with almost a full month of five star cuisine and varied meals they were healthier than they had been in long while.

Sunday saw me and ran over. "They're looking pretty damn good now. Even the pros are commenting."

"I can see it. Even the pros seem to be adapting into our team."

"Too bad we're not going to finish the game," he said, his voice full of melancholy.

"We are going to finish the game; the rematch two weeks later should be awesome. Have you identified who your squad leaders are?"

"Not really. We have ten days before we move. I was going to leave it till next Friday. Gives us three days to get them up to speed on things. You were thinking something else?"

"Yeah, I am, but let's talk about at the O group tonight in our flat."

"Right. You are joining us for dinner tonight?"

"Yeah. I guess I have been sticking to my room as of late. Sure."

"Then we can meet after dinner if that's good for you?"

"Good idea. Do I need to be more social?"

"Don't you always? Man, who stares down leopard?" Laughing he moved back on to the field and promptly kicked the ass of a lad whom looked at him. "Watch the ball", replacing the usual "eyes front" that would have been shouted had we not been surrounded by civilians.

I made my way to the tree house room and stashed my cigars and poured myself a drink. I hated social situations and while normally I loved the form and function of squad training the civilians had taken out the form. It felt more like a summer camp for posttraumatic stress disorder vets.

I showered off the sweat and grit of the day and took out the linen suit. A little over the top but it worked. I looked like the typical English or American Hemmingway wannabe. The men would love it. I even found a red and gold silk hankie that could easily double as an ascot. The image looking back at me was hilarious and just the kind of jocularity officers were supposed to engage in at times.

I walked in to the dining hall and let the door slam behind me. The room went silent as I walked slowly through the crowd to the front head table. I stopped briefly, engaging some of the men as I made my way. Small talk that contained landmines. Each question phrased in such a way to make the man break and start laughing. I was almost to the front, feeling I had lost my touch, when the question; "Have you seen my dead parrot, Pickles?" sparked the room as if I'd lit a match in a tub of fuel. The laughter spread in the same fashion, across the room, hot and uncontained.

I spun around, a look of mock dismay on my face. I watched as several nasal passages refused to be used as breathing apparatus, choosing instead to channel a super soaker beer cannon. The laughter went on for a good two minutes although I was hardly the cause now. The infectious and circus-like after shows had done the trick.

I tapped my knuckles to the top of the table and listened, eyes shut, till then din died down. When it did I opened my eyes and took in the room. The eyes of the men were clearer and they looked like fellows of a golf club and not the rabble of dangerous Pomfret that they were. I addressed the group.

"Right now, Ernest Hemingway is trying to figure out a way to come back from the dead and drop an airplane on your damn black villages. I'm so glad I could provide you all with such a laugh, at my expense, I might add. But on to the task at hand. In ten days we will be in EG teaching kids how to play football and why sports are important to growing boys and growing countries. Make no mistake gentleman, this is going to be a bloody war. The President will not be a happy man. The city, nay the course of that whole country, aptly named the armpit of Africa, will be changed forever. Because of your FOOTS and their BALLS. Are we gonna bring them a fight?"

The room erupted in a cheer and many pounded their tables so hard I thought they might break. The pro players and trainers looked at each other then back at me.

"Good then I'm most pleased with the money I bet the president. He gave me odds and I put up quite a sum, telling him when I was done I would own the damn country. He didn't believe me. I know you believe. But just in case I intend to import Tanya Harding as their halftime masseuse."

More laughter, and this time the pro's joined in. I waited for it to subside.

"What is not a laughing matter is this serious issue that has come to my attention. It had to come to my attention as I have been absent for much of your training. The improvements from each and every one of you have been nothing short of incredible and each of you has my adoration and respect. Thank you men. I'm proud of all of you and I look forward to the game to end all games. Cause I'll be more than broke if you lose!"

There was more than a little pounding on the tables with each man able to read between the lines of my little speech. I signed Sunday asking what was for dinner. He signed back deep cooked turkey. I figured it meant deep fried turkey.

"Men, men, men. Quiet down. We have English people among us and they get nervous when the natives get all excited. Speaking of native the dish today is native to the other side of the globe. Deep fried turkey. Enjoy!"

I went over and sat down with the pros. Introductions were made all the way around and I tried to pay attention to the conversation. It wasn't as far fetched as it seemed to actually put on a good game. They were confident it wouldn't be a blow out. I was glad to hear it and some intelligence that a few key EG players were injured, it would make the game tighter. The dinner went on and I answered questions about "my" team and tried to be an engaging host.

Dinner done, I went to the edge of the bar and held court. This entailed standing with a scotch in my hand and talking briefly with every man in the room. Each would come up in turn and chat about anything that was on his mind. Most of them were thankful for the previous few weeks of training and looked forward to showing me how appreciative they were. Others brought up their families and my promise. I cajoled some and reassured others and it was close to ten by the time each had taken their turn.

I walked toward the door signing "O group, usual place now," to no one in particular, knowing that Sunday and Chiwa would see it and follow.

I had just enough time to clip one of my Partagas SD4's and get it going before Sunday came in. The short robusto cigar was strong, it was young and the flavour had not had time to mellow.

"Jesus, Rhys. I live here too and I don't smoke."

"RHIP, Sunday. Rank Has It's Privileges."

"We're the same rank." It was spat with a mock growl.

"Yeah but I'm white. God loves me more."

"I doubt that. You're not white. You're Sameal and you learned to speak."

Sunday came over and swatted me on the shoulder. He sat down across from me and poured himself a measure from my bottle.

"When did you start drinking?"

"I'm picking up your bad habits. Actually I find it helps the medication break down or something. Pain goes away faster."

"You in a lot of pain?"

Chiwa walked in the door. He had stopped knocking two days ago. I was glad he was feeling comfortable in God land. I looked back at Sunday, waiting for an answer.

"Only when I'm alone." He remarked shuffling sideways to get comfortable.

Chiwa pulled up another chair and I held my finger up signaling silence. I went and turned on the stereo. The speakers were placed outside our circle. It wouldn't stop high tech monitoring but it would stop the ears to the walls.

"Ok guys, here is what I need, team wise. I need four men good enough with computers to work the Platinum rain units and I need those guys to go on the sub. The sub is going to have to put in at the dock here," I pointed to the satellite image, west of the airport. "Those two team leaders will go with four men to the road up here. They cover the airport, our back door, and can threaten the refinery. They also are the non high tech communication with Zombie. I would like him to be able to land on this road here. The other two-team leaders get dropped here, on this island, just off the coast. I'm staying here, less than 1000 meters away, in the Presidential suite, which will be called Dysons Folly. It's our back up command center and main communications post. The island, called Spinner, will be our primary command center. The two-squad leaders and 12 men will deploy there at night, set up and hide the Platinum rain units and dig in for a long wait. All of these guys have to be ready to leave here on Monday for travel to Gabon in order to hook up with the sub in Libreville. I need them for six hours prior to then for some training on the computer software the units will come with. Questions in thirty seconds."

Sunday was the first to speak, not waiting the 30 seconds. "These are my choices." He scribbled down four names and handed them to me.

Chiwa reached for the list.

"May I see the list, please? Yeah, I would agree with Sunday here, Rhys. Although I would love to keep him, he's good on the field."

"So, these are our squad leaders for the sub. Good. We also need squad leaders for the team in play. Chiwa, you will be the lieutenant on that crew and that branch is called "Sideline". You'll need to pick three squad leaders you can work with. Including you there are twenty-seven men so that makes two teams of twelve for the initial hot period each with their own squad leader and you in control. The stadium is going to be the bitch of the bunch. The confusion and stampede should work to your advantage but you have to stay fluid and frosty on that one. You can break your teams down later to secure hard assets like the bank and the main radio and TV broadcast station. You also have the distinction of calling in the first volley, which should eliminate the country's movers and shakers. Questions in thirty seconds."

"How did we manage to get our hands on the PR units?" Sunday shifted uncomfortably as he posed the question.

"I had them purchased and shipped to a pre-customs port and loaded onto a boat."

Chiwa looked confused. "What's a PR unit?" he asked.

"It's Platinum Rain, a multi-barreled multi projectile launcher. It can tear apart a tank column like paper maché."

"Are we getting these off a boat and onto a submarine?"

"Yup."

"Glad I'm flying in. I'm still flying in, right?" he continued, obviously wanting all the information I could provide.

"Yes," I responded.

Sunday continued, "I'm still concerned about the U.N. Technically speaking EG is a UN member and so we can expect a major response from them."

"I've got that sorted out, Sunday, and we can discuss it in a moment but I want to be clear on this part first. Any other concerns about part one?"

Both men shook their heads. I poured myself a drink and took a long swallow before continuing.

"The big Russian sub used to be a diesel nuke boat. The missiles are gone and the top welded shut. But she still has two torpedo hatches she can open. One has a real high tech camera inside and the other has an LRAD, long-range acoustical device. They put it in to call whales and talk with other animals under the water."

"So how does that hold off a US warship?" Sunday queried.

"I'm getting to it. We have a sixty thousand ton fertilizer tanker en route as we speak. We are going to rendezvous with the tanker and get two LRAD units for ourselves. We also pull the three PR units and the crew off the boat and into the sub. Then we backfill the cargo hold with diesel from the main tank, using the onboard pumps."

"Holy fuck, Rhys! That's a 60,000-ton ANFO bomb."

Sunday's eyes were alight as if they were already reflecting the explosive flash.

"Does she carry enough fuel oil to do it?"

"Yes she does, and with the seas' gentle rocking to mix it the process should only take 27 hours."

"How we going to detonate it?" Chiwa asked, picking up on the excitement.

"Remote or timer; I haven't decided," I responded, musing about it in my head.

"How far offshore?" Chiwa asked.

"I figured a kilometer would be safe and would also avoid any major wave action from hitting the mainland."

"That means two round trips to the tanker? Kind of exposes our assets doing that."

"No choice. The backfilling process can't be rushed; it has to mix slowly if it's going to mix completely."

"What about someone just staying on board? That would eliminate the dual runs and ensure the thing went off when it was supposed to. Wouldn't play out well if our trump card just fizzled because of a fifty cent detonator, and there wouldn't be time to get back out there."

"Sunday, we're talking about a 60-megaton bomb. It's going to be the largest non-nuclear explosion this world has ever seen. Probably close to the largest explosion in either chemistry!"

As soon as I said it, I could see his plan. The look in his eyes was disturbing and despite knowing the answer I tried to talk him out of it.

"No way, Sunday. I think if we use a redundant detonator we will be fine."

Sunday pondered this for a moment and then said,

"You know, it makes sense. If we're jammed, and we're likely to be right away, you lose your trump card. This way is the smartest and most tactically correct plan. Besides, what an incredible end to a wonderful life. That thing will blow parts of me into the very stuff of space! My mind's made up."

"But, but Sunday, we don't need you to die." Chiwa's voice was almost breaking and he had the look of horror on his face.

"Chiwa, what Rhys knows and you don't is I have cancer. That bullet is already coming and there is nothing I can do to avoid it. This just make the inevitable have meaning."

The room went silent as both Chiwa and I came to terms with what Sunday was saying. It made tactical sense and Sunday did seem to be in more pain and the process on the ship would be a timely one but not difficult to complete. I looked at Chiwa and could see him shaking his head but knew he was coming to the same conclusions. At issue was whether he could allow a team member to die in order to achieve the objective; an ability any good commander needed to muster.

"No need to think about this too much boys. This is how it's going to happen. Drink with me."

Sunday reached out and poured three vodkas and waited. He had used the term boys, which meant he was pulling the age card. Chiwa had to respect an elders' decision. It was cultural and as ingrained is his being as breathing.

We took the glasses and saluted our friend's sacrifice.

"Give me one of those cigars, Rhys."

"Me too." Chiwa finally acquiesced and chimed in.

I pulled out my stash and wished I had something a little more fitting for this type of occasion. The Partagas Psd4's were my favorite "go to" smoke and somehow seemed fitting for the moment. I clipped three and lit mine, passing the lighter around to everyone else.

"While we're gassing the place I want to continue. Chiwa, you're going to call in the first strike that will put everything into motion. Prior to that I have to do the overlays of the area on the CC software and this is where I have a question. Walking around with combat goggles is going to draw suspicion. But the guy that sold me the system would like to be on the ground when it all goes bang. He's a computer geek kind of guy but isn't a push over and has a set of glasses that are a little less distinctive. His name is Myron P. Eugene. Hold your thoughts for a second. He's broke desperate and will work for free. I'm thinking of bringing him in blind to Gabon and having the men pick him up from the hotel and put him on the sub. When we offload the gear on the island I'll pick him up and let him spend the next two days being a sports journalist. He can do our overlays. Questions in thirty seconds."

"What does he know about the operation?" Sunday asked, shifting uncomfortably in his seat and pouring another drink.

"Squat, and I intend to keep it that way."

"What happens when the shooting starts?" Chiwa looked at both Sunday and I.

"Holes up in my hotel room. Running the communications or at least taking care of problems. He's a capable guy, just not our kind of capable. But we are looking at a three hour window for combat so he won't have time to do anything if he loses his nerve."

"What if he fucks with the CC unit's operation?" Sunday asked, shifting his position again to get comfortable.

"Good point, Sunday. That's a risk. Let me continue with the rest of the plan and we will decide if we're bringing in Myron later."

"Here is how I see it going, but as we all know, no plan usually survives first contact with the enemy. Chiwa, you'll call in the first strike. You'll have to make sure the brass are in the stands and get a location dialed in. You can do that with the goggles. It can paint a target via the GPS and triangulation systems. The men on the island fire the PR units and you call in the strike effectiveness. By this time I should be in the stadium as well. So if you're taken out I can back the plan up. The game is scheduled to start at 1400 hours so I'm thinking around halftime, say 1500 hours. The men above the airport will see if we get a response from there and hit anything we don't own."

"What would we own, Sir?"

"There is a possibility we might have a friend that drives one of the Hinds."

"The men on the island would then hit the Presidential quarters and the military barracks with the rest of their munitions. We won't be able to call in accurate enough fire for them to do much else. The men at the airport will take out the tower and watch the road for military convoys and just hunt and kill as they see fit. Perhaps hit the refinery as a diversion if we start getting a big build up of troops in the capitol. The men on the island will then start the LRAD units broadcasting and make their way into shore and work toward the national bank and the media outlets. "

"Broadcasting?"

"Yeah, I want to get the people off the streets and out of harms way. So they will broadcast a message telling everyone to stay indoors, and that the new President is the former one in exile. The main dog and pony show for food and booze will be at the city hall area and I will work my way back there. Chiwa, if you could spare one of your units I might need the help."

"Roger that, Sir."

"That should bring us to around 1600 hours or so. That's when I have to convince the USA to not crash our party. But Sunday, either way if you haven't heard from me use the CC system's timer and blow the ship at exactly 1800 hours. That should be right around sunset, and gives us the most bang for our buck. Questions again in 30 seconds."

The two men sat and took long pulls on their cigars. Sunday poured yet another drink and slid back in his chair, while Chiwa scooted forward.

"What about the ringers and coaches?" Sunday said through a puff of smoke.

"Collateral damage. Tell them to head back to the hotel, but we can't afford to provide an escort."

"We could hide them in the stadium at halftime if we can find a place."

"Yeah, good idea, Sunday." I looked at him and smiled at the thought. It was a good plan.

Before I could say anything else, Sunday continued,

"I think this Myron fellow could be a real asset if you're going to be running all over the place, Rhys. He can stay and guarantee the thing keeps working as the US is going to jam the shit out of the standard frequencies and we're going to be lost without situational awareness. You've met him, right?"

"I have met him. He has everything riding on this baby and really can't afford it to fail. He's going to know that the world won't be pleased with who he sold his gear to, so it has to work and our success will be his."

"True Rhys, you're kind of fucking the guy over."

"He knew it was for a coup and he didn't blink. I don't think I'm fucking him over. I think he wants to poke a stick in the eye of the US and do an I told you so."

Both men shook their heads in agreement.

"So, in or out?" I looked at Chiwa first.

"In." Chiwa answered shaking his head.

"Yeah I think it will work." Sunday answered, draining his glass.

"Ok, I will get him in motion today. Any glaring fuckups with the plan?"

"Lots of 'got to happen as planned' that I don't like, but what can you do?" Sunday tossed the final third of his cigar away.

"That's it in a nutshell. We are poised to change lives and create destiny and I'm really bloody tired."

"Me too, but I doubt I will sleep at all tonight." Chiwa added, tossing his cigar into the cup.

"Welcome to the world of brass, Chiwa. Hope you didn't think it was all martinis and late mornings."

Chiwa got up and after pouring himself another large measure of vodka, headed out the door. Sunday pulled himself slowly, unsteadily out of his chair.

"You okay?" I asked. I was beginning to wonder if he would make it for the big finish.

"Just a little pissed. How do you do it? You're not even feeling it, are you?"

"The booze? Nah, good Irish genes."

"Rotten Mick," he replied with a slurred laugh. "Go! Get some sleep."

"You too my friend. Ya need a hand?" I stood and offered him my arm.

"Bugger off. In my state you might try and get all multicultural on my pretty ass."

I watched Sunday make for his bedroom. The medication had to be adding to his unstable gait. He never drank much in the past so perhaps it was just the vodka. Once alone I took a long pull of my cigar. Indeed, there was a great deal of things that had to go right in this operation and any detection prior to the game would make the situation very difficult. I guess I just had to hope everything went as smoothly as it had already gone. I tried to get comfortable with that idea and failed.

I picked up the cell phone and dialed Myron. It would be in the afternoon across the water and depending where Myron was, late or early afternoon. The phone buzzed in my ear six times.

"Yes, hello. Myron here?"

"I catch you in the shower?"

"Actually you…who is this?"

"Rhys, Myron, how's life?"

There was another moment's hesitation before Myron recognized the name and the voice.

"Rhys? Oh Rhys! It's good. Everything is good. How is the gear working out for you?"

"Good, Myron. Not too many details here, okay?"

"Sure thing." He was a fast study, I had to admit.

"Still interested in ringside seats for the big show?" I asked, already knowing what the answer would be.

"Very much so!" he said emphatically.

"You'll have to earn your keep by doing the overlays. You cool with that?" I continued.

"Hell ya," he responded enthusiastically.

"Ok. Bring your fancy sunglasses and fly to Libreville. That's in Gabon. Check into the Le Meridien Re Ndama. It's expensive but it's safe and one of the men will come pick you up Tuesday night or Wednesday. Check in under your real name and give the desk clerk $20US. Tell him you're expecting some friends to pick you up for a wedding. By the way, do you know anything about football?"

"Football, like USC Trojans?" Myron sounded puzzled.

"No, football like Manchester United."

"A little," Myron said hesitantly. I could almost hear the gears in his brain working across the line.

"Well brush up on it," I ordered, "I want you to be able to tell me players and stats."

"Ok," he said, but he didn't sound that convinced.

"Fly in first class Myron, as travel will be pretty economy class after you arrive. Besides, I think you will be more than able to afford it in the very near future."

"Not a problem. Thanks Rhys!" he said.

"Thank me after the fight, Myron. I wasn't kidding about the odds on this one."

"I understand. I'm still totally cool with this."

A couple of goodbyes and we rang off. I wondered if I had been too open with him, and then realized I hadn't had a choice. Information relayed was still pretty vague, or at least I hoped it had been.

We were in play, and as of Monday I would have men in the breech. I was not the least bit apprehensive. That worried me, so I took the time to run through the operation in my head for the hundredth time, hoping to pick out a problem. I couldn't find one.

The meeting set for Sunday night was supposed to be a quick one, but it was shaping up to be anything but. I really couldn't give any speeches with the civilians around, and the men couldn't help but feel hurt as they were cut from the team.

The roster was made and our spares identified. Those that had been cut were milling around outside licking their wounds. I knew I had to do something about it. I excused myself from the main meeting and went outside. The faces were long and using only hand signals. I told the group to follow me to the field.

I called for a tight circle and felt as each man came close and went to one knee. The mood had not improved.

"Listen up. You are not cut, you're chosen. You are going to be the advance force on this operation and believe me when I tell you the viability of this coup rests solely in your hands. Each and every one of you needs to give me all you can if this is to go ahead without us getting slaughtered. I know many of you wanted to play in the game. But we have identified your strengths and picked you for this team and this game. The football match is nothing. This is the true game and the one I need you to win if we are to be successful. Each of you has a passport and a credit card and I will provide walking around money.

You all have to make your way to Libreville in Gabon and await transport on our secret weapon. The weapon that will make this operation a success. I need you to check into the Le Meridien Re Ndama and wait further instructions. The code word for this part of the op is 'The Wedding'. From there your identified squad leaders will tell you the rest of your orders. These orders are more important than anything else we have done to date. So quit your fucking moping around and switch on. This is what we are here to do. Not play some stupid ball game. Are you football players or the takers of lives?"

The answer was a sharp exhalation of breath that reminded me of the Masi lion ritual.

"Good. I knew I could count on you. Your orders will come to you through your new Squad leaders; Hamsa and Zuberi. Questions in thirty seconds."

"Who do we report to, Sir?" Zuberi asked taking his new job to heart.

"You report to Lieutenant Chiwa."

There were looks cast around in the dark and I waited. There were no further questions.

"You'll be leaving in the morning. Keep up the masquerade for our civilian friends and have a drink on me tonight. Oh and before I forget there are lots of dollars on the cards so fly first and get your rest and relaxation as it will be a while before you're comfortable again. Remember gentlemen, no calls to loved ones."

The sharp exhalation of air confirmed they had understood.

"Dismissed."

CHAPTER SIXTY-SEVEN

THE MEN WENT BACK TO the dining hall one by one and I was left alone with the trill of insects and the wonderful night sky. A quote from my past vies for attention with the musical bugs, something about "vision." Vision is not the ability to see what is there but rather seeing what could be there. In the very same way I was seeing and focused on what could be in EG. I sat for a long time envisioning what a country like EG would look like when we were done. To make the sacrifice worth it, things would have to be better in the country. It couldn't be like all the other wars I had fought through. No, it had to be better if I was going to redeem myself.

Redeem myself? Where had that come from? There was another voice like the machine's, deep and quiet but there. Civilians would die in this coup. I was sure of that. What would they die for? Another corrupt dictatorship? Perhaps slightly more benevolent than the one before it? No, that wasn't enough to pay for their sacrifices. That would not redeem me.

"What would?" Asked that tiny voice that made me think. When you spent your adult life fighting monsters you ran the risk of becoming what you were at war with. Was that to be my fate? Did the three sisters have a web spun for me that made me into the monster that had originally started me down this road of death? Why was it I could watch a hundred staving kids on late night television barely batting an eye, yet one abused animal charity made me change the channel? The sight of an abused kitten tearing at my mind while the fly-covered bloated child was simply wallpaper?

No answer came. The little voice provided no answers. I was prepared to be the power behind the throne, the real, albeit benevolent dictator with a fancy patsy to take the fall. Would this be my fate? Were hundreds on the verge of death because I had become the thing I hated? Was the jaded response a signal of things to come?

No, it couldn't be. Andrea would not be able to love a man like that. Sunday would not call me his friend if this were true. Fifty men would not be prepared to die in brutal conflict to curry favour with such a monster. They had seen that type so many times before they were sure to see it in me if that were the case. What was my redemption?

To take a country through as bloodless a civil war as was possible and create a society and country that was an example, not only to the African continent, to the world!

The machine slid along my senses. "You're thinking like a megalomaniac from a James Bond film, Rhys. Get a grip."

The little voice, so far away it was hoarse with the effort, countered. "To hope for change and the vision to see the possibilities is not insane. Being able to do so and choosing to ignore it is. If you need to see them as kittens caught in a well to find the compassion, then do so."

I looked skyward into Orion's belt and followed it along and out toward the Dog Star, dull against the curtain of black. The Pygmy people believed we all came from there. I had heard the stories told around the fire. I didn't believe them. But I didn't believe my own culture's stories about creation either. I did believe there was a purpose for each of us in this life and until now I believed my purpose was the same as the four horsemen that were tattooed on my left shoulder. Death and hatred toward mankind. The pygmy witch doctor had even proclaimed me to be a death sorcerer. The difference between a sorcerer and witch doctor was not lost on me. I lived with them for months and I knew the difference. A witch doctor helped his tribe and others. A sorcerer used his powers to help himself. Back then I had worn his label as a badge of honour. Had I changed? I certainly hoped I had. The coming conflict had the chance of unleashing death the likes of which had never been seen on this continent. There was no telling if the American warship would be carrying nuclear munitions. They could see my ANFO attack as initiating a nuclear strike. I remembered a book by Robert Anton Wilson that had described just such a scenario that happened on Fernando Po, which oddly was the same island. I hoped fiction would not imitate life.

I walked back to my suite in the tree house, alone with my thoughts.

They were not sitting comfortably on my mind. I reached the door and knew immediately Sunday was up and in the main room. I wasn't surprised to see him sitting there looking at me.

"You look like you've been soul searching," Sunday said, putting down the computer.

"Really?" I closed the door quietly.

"Yeah. I saw you standing in the field staring off into space, you ok?"

"Just thinking." I poured myself a drink and offered Sunday another, as his glass was almost empty. He nodded.

"What are you concerned about?" he asked me.

"The op," I responded as casually as I could.

A thoughtful expression came over Sunday's face, and he paused for a few seconds before replying.

"It's easier to execute a plan than it is to plan the execution. Always been that way my friend. The water in the river just knows to keep going," Sunday offered, accepting his glass from my hand.

"What the hell does that mean?" It had come out a little more harshly than I expected and I immediately regretted it, but Sunday swatted it away like it was nothing.

"It means…" He searched for an example to help me understand. "To use an analogy you're used to, let's say Texas hold em. It's easier to go "all in" than it is to call "an all in." Right?" He crossed his legs and fixed me with a stare.

"Unless you have the nuts and were trapping." I added.

"What's the salient difference? Don't answer, it was rhetorical. The difference is knowing the outcome. If you have the nuts and were trapping you know you can't lose. If you don't, all the outs have to be calculated and weighed against the risk. That gives you the odds, correct?"

"Yeah."

"The issue for you is we already had all that calculated for us prior to going into an operation. We had to play the hand out. This time you're calling the "all in" raise and you don't know how to calculate all the outs, or if you like risks." Sunday said, taking a drink from his glass.

"It's more than that, Sunday. I'm going to be the power behind the office. I don't want to become like the people we had as targets. I worry about what happens after we do this." I slumped into the sofa.

"Purification of motives, and luck will follow. It doesn't sound as good in English but the meaning is the same. Your motivation defines your actions. So what is your motivation, Rhys?"

"Redemption." I looked up, afraid he would laugh, but he smiled knowingly instead.

"Perhaps our death has brought you as much insight as it has brought me. If that's your motivation then you'll do fine and the op will go as planned." He uncrossed his legs and picked up the laptop again.

"Sunday, I wish life were that simple."

"Life is that simple; we just think too much and make it complicated." He went back to his tasks leaving me to ponder his logic alone.

"To change the topic, oh wise one, from the mud flats of the Zambezi, I'm going to send Chiwa with the group on Monday. He can fly back when they are all loaded on the sub and underway but I want him in Gabon in case anything goes south. I figured I'd fly him out on the fast chopper in the morning with Zuberi. I want to give him the CC units to avoid any chance of issues with the EG customs."

"Mock me if you like, he who stares down leopards, but the logic is as sound as when it was told to me. As to Chiwa and Zuberi, I think it's a good idea and a sound plan. Gives Chiwa a chance to get comfortable with command before the shooting starts." He drained his glass and offered it to me for a refill.

"That's what I was thinking. You running the group in the morning?"

"Yes."

"Good. As an added incentive for the run the top five fly private to JoBerg, the next five fly commercial out of Hazy, and the rest take the bus. That way we will stagger the men getting on the planes."

"Sound planning, again. But I really need to get a handle on this fueling operation," and with that he turned his attention back to the computer.

"You really want to be standing on the deck when that thing goes off, eh?" I said in mock surprise.

"Yes I do. That ok EH, Canada?"

"Fuck you, skinny. I'm going to bed."

"Sleep well Pinky, and remember what I said."

I went upstairs, leaving Sunday with his boat schematics. If life is that easy then why the fuck didn't it feel like it?

CHAPTER
SIXTY-EIGHT

"THINGS ARE LOOKING GOOD. EVERYTHING is set for our arrival on Monday. The sub should be in place on Tuesday night. That gives me all day Monday to meet and greet officials and put any fears at ease. There is a big meeting scheduled for Tuesday with their security people."

"A meeting? That can't be good. Sounds like they know we're coming." Sunday dipped his rusk into the red tea.

"I figured they might get word of something. But to be honest I don't think they are associating it with our game. Far too much equipment already in play and if they were suspicious, they'd be going through the shipments with a fine toothcomb. They aren't, so I figure we're golden. We meet the sub on Tuesday night and the tanker is about twenty clicks out. We will start that process on Tuesday night so you'll be ready Thursday night or Friday morning at the latest. Zombie says he…" Sunday stopped me in mid-sentence.

"Operational Security says I don't need to know the rest of it. I don't intend on getting on board, but shit could happen. I intend to set trip lines to detonate if I'm taken but you don't need a loose end."

"True." I nodded in agreement with his logic.

"You all right with this plan?" His eyes scanned me.

"Yabo, I wish it didn't have to be this way. All the way around this sucks. But you're right — it's the best option," I replied with more fervor than I realized.

"Good. Make this place the way you see it in your mind and bring my girls to that place. Make sure they are safe. You could name a street after me," he said quietly.

"A street?" I locked my eyes with his, he was serious.

"Yeah I kind of always thought that would be cool. A nice street full of nice homes and happy children." He said looking away, a tear caught in the corner of his eye.

"Sure Sunday, I think that would be a good thing," I replied, trying to keep the emotion out of my voice.

"Thanks, Rhys."

Our morning was complete, with a change in the routine that made the day seem a little less comfortable than yesterday. I had missed our usual rhetoric and banter more than I thought. I also didn't have the option of bouncing my plans off him to see if he saw any problems. I guess Chiwa would have to fill that role now. The fact he was in a sub miles away didn't help much.

I could hear whistles in the distance and, in my mind, I could see the men practicing. The flight arrangements were still a mystery and I needed something to occupy my time. I could feel the electric like current that was bouncing along my nerves and I needed a place for that energy to go. I decided to call Tom. To be polite I called his regular company line. The line was answered on the second ring.

"Sentinel, How may I direct your call?"

"Morning. Rhys here. Tom, please."

"Just one moment, Sir. He may be in a meeting."

The line went dead for a moment. She hadn't recognized my name, made evident by her built-in "meeting." It was a receptionist's job, after all, to protect access to the big boss.

"Good morning, Rhys. Why the call on the company line?"

"It wasn't an urgent call Tom. So I figured I'd go through channels."

"Thanks I appreciate it. So what's up?" he asked, sounding friendly but businesslike.

"I'm just looking for a sitrep and flight arrangements." I explained.

"Oh shit, Rhys. Sorry I just kind of figured Z would have kept you in the loop."

"Z?" I asked.

There was a chuckle on the other end before he continued.

"True, true. Ok, sorry. I should know better than to make assumptions. Z is coming on Monday morning, and so is a larger transport. I'm not sure what we're going to use right now. I'm waiting for the charter company to get back to me. Not too many companies want their machines going into unstable areas these days. The security deposit's about the same as the bloody price of the machine. Right now the price of an old 737 set up for 100 passengers is about the same as a smaller, newer unit. But it does give the men lots of space to relax before they get there. How are they looking, by the way?" Tom sounded genuinely excited as he continued his explanation.

"Really good," I replied and asked, "Did the big president take your double-up bet?"

"Yeah he did. Was happy too, actually. He thinks we're throwing away our money," Tom chortled.

"Since when is betting on me throwing away money?" I laughed in response.

"Since you became a football team owner. This just became a game only play. Simon has been released and is sitting on a plane as we speak. I was going to cancel the operation but it would have looked odd. So everyone gets paid and gets to have a good time at my expense."

There was more laughter over the line.

"Anyway, everything is set up. The area around city hall is done and we have been doing pancake breakfasts and playing music every morning. The stadium is ready and the field is being touched up as we speak. The President assures me everything will be smooth for your arrival. He sends his regrets that he won't be able to meet you personally but he has engagements on Tuesday and needs to prepare for them on Monday. He's sending one of his representatives to meet you. His name is Ferdinand and he will arrange for your transport from the airport. Cars are a bit scarce, big safe ones anyway, so they gave you one of the big Dodge trucks from the refinery to use while you're there. I hope that's ok?"

"Doesn't matter to me, Tom," I replied smiling. "I'm not paying for the gas."

"Great. anything else?' he asked.

"Yeah, what is the name of your party planner you've got running things right now?"

"Bobby Anderson. Queer as a fashion designer, and very good at his job. One of the best really; he does all my engagements," Tom explained.

"Ok. Thanks Tom. Have a good day," I responded.

"You too."

The line went dead. My mood improved and Sunday must have seen my smile.

"What's so funny?" He asked as he descended the stairs from his room.

"We just got a big black refinery pickup truck to deliver the PR units. Since we're offloading one down near the refinery east of the airport it should make the process a great deal easier. Easier still is I don't have to go find Simon. Seems he is on a plane home as we speak."

"Luck follows, eh Boss?"

"Yes it does."

Monday morning came quickly and the men were as anxious to get rolling as I was. They had been away from their families for a long time and wanted to contact them. They wanted this project in motion and the tension was palatable enough for the trainers to notice.

Dave had arranged a large yellow school bus to deliver everyone to the little airport in Hazy View. Riding like a chaperon upfront made me feel odd. I turned and looked towards the back as we bounced up the road towards the town. The radio was playing some mixed tape and the song "Who Let the Dogs Out" came on. Looks were exchanged and then the bus erupted with laughter, much to the surprise of the coaches and trainers who missed the joke completely.

The little airport was a buzz with activity. The Gulfstream was parked to the side and surrounded by curious aviation types. To the right was an old 737 with a fresh black-and -red paint-job. The men would see the name "Victory" on the side as a good omen.

The bus pulled onto the tarmac and stopped. The men got eagerly to their feet and grabbed their individual gear. I headed out the door with my carry-on and shoulder bag.

There was a cart for luggage destined for the hold of the large plane and the men piled gear on it. Zombie walked out the back door and down to the tarmac. I watched the men walk up the stairs and was surprised to see the pro players following them. I had told the coaches and trainers that we would be flying in the Gulfstream along with the pros. But it seemed they took the team concept to mean they flew together. To a man they all got on the big jet. Sunday, Z, and I were alone on the tarmac.

"Should we save Tom some money and just go with the men?" Sunday asked as he shifted his shoulder bag.

"No that flight is non-smoking." I said, digging a Punch double corona out of my pocket and clipping it, while Sunday and Zombie laughed.

The big plane pulled back and taxied toward the runway as we walked over to the much smaller plane. It sat like a Ferrari ready to prove itself to all that came. The two-crew members looked disapprovingly at me as we approached. Z went past them telling them to get her ready for takeoff. Sunday followed him and so did I.

"Non-smoking flight is next Thursday, if you want to wait," I quipped to the crew as I climbed into the world's fastest private jet.

CHAPTER
SIXTY-NINE

THE PLANE ROLLED DOWN THE runway and I could feel the power coursing through the airframe. It needed very little of the actual runway to put it into the air and then went almost vertical as it climbed to it cruising altitude. The sensation was not so much like a rocket launch but that of a sports car accelerating effortlessly into traffic. It reminded me of the Aston Martin,

We leveled off into a clear and clean blue sky, so calm that it was hard to believe we were actually flying.

The time passed quickly and soon I was aware we were descending as my ears started to pop. The clouds parted and below us was the Atlantic Ocean. The coastline of E.G. was prominent and jagged. Our destination was a small island off the coast it lorded over like a czar. The capitol and the base of power were separated from the mainland by several miles. The plane banked and we shed both speed and altitude as we descended into the breach one more time.

The landing strip loomed out of the clouds and moisture streaked the window as we made our final approach. Two main roads and some small houses, just like I had seen on the multitude of aerial photos I had pored over in the previous months dissected the mass of the city. The touchdown was light and quick and the engines reversed to stop our suicidal roll down the runway.

The airport was modern and new. The angled front of the main building looked like it would be better situated in a European city. The facility was clean and busy. Vehicles were unloading gear from larger planes but the attention was focused on us as we taxied up to the gate. Like a gorgeous blonde with a wardrobe malfunction we were the belle of the ball.

We bumped to a stop and the ground crew ran to be of any assistance that would justify them being so close to such a beautiful plane. We waited in our seats like spoiled children. The flight attendants unbelted and made preparations to open the door.

The hatch swung out into the humid country of EG. The wet heat invaded the plane like a bad smell. Nothing was spared as shirt collars went limp, and we blinked to get used to the moisture. The dry air-conditioning was forgotten in the onslaught.

Sunday and I undid our seatbelts and moved to the door. The machine was in full gear and I could feel Sunday tensing up as tight as a piano string beside me. We walked into the sunlight and were greeted by a short, fat well-dressed man sporting designer sunglasses.

"Welcome to Equatorial Guinea. I hope your flight was a pleasant one." He said buttoning, his sport coat, which looked all too hot in this environment.

"Hello. Yes it was a nice flight. I'm Andre Aroloski, the team owner and this is my assistant, Mr. Urasiss." I moved into the shade of the plane as the afternoon sun threatened to set me alight.

"Good to meet you both. On behalf of the President I would like to extend to you the key to the capitol. His Eminence would have loved to meet you personally but he's detained in meetings. If I can do anything for you, please don't hesitate to ask."

"Thank you, I won't."

"Please follow me to immigration. A small formality that even I can't by-pass." He turned on his heel and walked toward the terminal, beckoning us to follow him.

We reached the immigration area and even the President's representative had to give the official looking man his passport. The man gave it a brief glance and handed it back to him with a nod. I handed him my Russian passport and the man looked at it closely before scanning it. Satisfied, he stamped it and handed it back to me with a smile. I watched as Sunday went through the same procedure.

"I have a car for you right over there. Your players and staff are about an hour out and we will have a bus ready for them when they arrive. I will see to it myself. The President would like to extend an invitation for dinner after the game on Saturday. He's unfortunately unavailable until then."

"We would be honoured." Sunday spoke up, taking his role as assistant to heart, while I nodded.

"Great. I shall pass along your desires to the President personally. The driver knows what hotel you're staying in. Enjoy our beautiful city."

The city was anything but beautiful. It started with a few shanty style shacks and moved progressively into sprawling structures that looked as though they might collapse at any moment. There was a ton of vehicles on the road as well, most in disrepair and belching smoke. The only ones that looked as though they were running well were the ones with the oil company's logo on the side.

The vehicles parted as we drove up, but the process of getting into town was a long one. It was similar to any African city; a mix of poor and poorer all trying to move in different directions at the same time. Women carried parcels on their heads and men shuffle walked as if there were no cars threatening to run them over. All of this was made worse by the non-existent sidewalks.

The road that was called the Airport Highway turned into Independence Road and there was quite a bit of recent building on either side. Even the road itself had seen recent upgrades. It was as if the country was trying to pull itself into the modern world despite the money wasted by its dictators.

We turned left through a very busy intersection and continued on 'Calle deNigeria'or "Street of Nigeria', which was confusing as my hotel, the Bahia, was on Nigeria Street two blocks north. This was a common issue with navigation in Africa. It wasn't enough to know the translation but the emphasis placed on words that proceed and ones that followed. A tourist was basically lost.

We pulled up to the Residenica Ana Jose. It looked clean and modern and I wondered how the men would do with the change from Sunny Ball.

The driver was quick to retrieve our bags from the car and wouldn't accept a tip. Shaking his head profusely and looking around as if we were on video. I allowed my peripheral vision to expand and search and was rewarded for the effort. There was a minivan parked on the edge of the lot that was riding low in the rear, a stream of exhaust coming from the pipe and no driver. No one would leave their vehicle running unattended. Yes, we were under watch.

I picked up my bag and signed; sniper left thirty meters, low. Sunday signed back he had already seen it as he shouldered his bag. We turned and walked into the hotel to check in.

The male desk clerk was dressed very well for his position.

"Welcome, gentlemen, to the Ana Jose. Do you have reservations?"

It was an incredibly stupid question. No one would travel into such a third world country without one. In fact, reservations were required for immigration. So was this another watcher? The machine looked at the thin clerk. No bulge of a weapon was visible and so I doubted it but the machine kept looking.

"Yes." Sunday said taking the lead and using his Spanish. "I'm Mr. Aroloski's personal assistant. We are with the visiting football team that is playing your national team on Saturday. He's the owner. I'm not certain what name they are under."

"Oh! Yes Sir. Welcome and good luck on Saturday. I have tickets for the game. They are very hard to come by; sold out in two days! I have a two-bedroom suite on the top floor. The rest of the team is on the same floor, most in individual rooms as per the request. Can I get someone to help you with your bags?"

"Yes, of course."

"Right away, sir. Here are your keys."

"Thank you, Madrid." Sunday said reading the man's name tag.

A short man and an even shorter woman converged on our luggage from opposite ends of the lobby. The desk clerk told the two we are in room 321 and they nod. While the luggage is heavy neither one struggles with it. Both prefer to carry it by the handles instead of rolling it. I find it odd there are no luggage trolleys and then catch myself. Labour is cheap so it doesn't matter if they use two to do the job one could do with a trolley. The lady smiles at Sunday and I and motions us to follow her to the elevator as she follows the man to the single, old lift.

Once inside she started speaking in Fang-Ntumu, a language spoken in the north and the man answers in Fang-Okah a language from the south and Cameroon.

"These men are part of the Football team I think." She says shifting the heavy bag from one hand to the other.

"Yes, I heard Madrid say so. Perhaps they will give us tickets to the match as a gratuity." He pushed the button to the third floor.

"I have no time for games of sport. I would sell mine to provide more to my family." She spoke under her breath as the doors slid closed.

"So your lazy husband could drink more? I would pay you forty francs." He responded in a nature that indicated they had worked a long time together.

"Done." A hiss of a word that mimicked the sliding doors opening.

This exchange was so typical of Africa. While each understood the others language perfectly, neither would speak the others. What would seem so rude to a foreigner was, in fact, a hold out to cultural identity. Many of the 'liberating' countries that settled Africa made it a crime to speak the native tongue; a way of homogenizing the culture to its new colonial rulers. The English had done the same to the Irish, going further, in truth, to make even native dance a crime. I smiled at my own statement; Irish native dance.

We arrived at the room and Sunday unlocked the door and went in. It was sparse but did have its own air conditioner, a phone, and small tube style TV. I turned to the two employees and switching between both languages addressed them.

"So, you would like two tickets to the game, and you would like forty Francs?"

Their eyes shot wide and they looked at each other in disbelief, then back at me. Each head was nodding yes and neither would catch my eye. They were embarrassed by their spoken confessions.

"It's alright." I continued in Spanish. "There is no need to be embarrassed asking for what you would like. I will get you two tickets for the game, and here is forty Francs. But, you must not let anyone else know I understand Fang-Bantu, ok?"

They were nodding and would not look at me. The woman took the forty Francs. "You don't have name tags, what are your names?"

"I'm Cathy BouDjou." She replied while tucking the money into her pants pocket.

"My name is Juan Mbela."

"Ok, Cathy and Juan. Pleasure to meet you. My name is Andre

and I hope I can count on you to keep our secret and perhaps provide me some information to avoid the tourist traps?"

They both nodded and each in turn launched into a long monologue about the dangerous areas and the scams that were present in the City of Malabo. Each confirmed or built on the other's recommendations. Most of it I was already aware of but there was apparently a good restaurant that overlooked the main port that I had to try. Neither spoke about the van, other watchers, or local residents using the rooms before us. The information was well worth the money spent.

"Thank you so much. I really appreciate your kindness and help. Juan, I will have a set of tickets, left in an envelope, for you at the front desk and they will be great seats."

"Andre, sir, could you just give them directly to me? I don't want to have to share with Madrid. He is, well, opportunistic."

"As you wish, Juan. But I will be out scouting and trying to get an inside line on some of the players. I don't want you to miss me."

"I will be cleaning your room Mr. Andre, so you could leave the envelope in here and I could give it to Juan. If that's convenient?" She looked at Juan, who was nodding.

"That works fine, Cathy." I replied, taking my bag and setting it on the bed.

They left and I turned to Sunday and signed to talk about the game. He followed my lead as we split the room and started searching. While no one had officially been in the room I wasn't certain the room was clean of listening devices.

Thankfully the sparse furnishings made the job much easier than it would have been in a Fairmont room. It took us twenty minutes to discover nothing. I looked at the curtains and got Sunday to turn out the room light.

There it was, a little red dot on the white curtain backing. I opened the drapes and could see the van parked just slightly off angle to our room. They were using an old school laser mike set up. The projected laser would pick up the vibrations on the glass and relay them back to the receiver that could decipher the vibrations as sound and spoken words.

I took out my iPhone and set it on the sill with the speaker pointing at the glass and pressed the button to start the music. There was over 200 hours of songs. The little device was not designed as an electronic counter measure device but it would work perfectly in the application. I laughed and pointed at the window.

"There's an App for that?" Sunday looked at me blankly.

"You know the Apple commercials...Ah forget it, you black techno heathen, that's some funny shit." I walked to the far chair and sat down.

"I have to get out of here and check in the Bahia hotel and get that place up and running. I'll be on my other cell phone should you need to reach me but I would assume they scan and listen to most calls. I didn't have this one on so it's unlikely they will know the number but it will come up as a non country phone on their system so we should be very careful. We also need a boat, something small to do some fishing with oars and a motor. An electric motor would be the shit, quiet and easy but I doubt that's possible. Wait for the men to arrive and let them know about the audience and then head down to the docks." I started changing into clothes more suited to my purpose.

"Yeah ok, I'll get the men squared away and then go to the docks and see if I can rent or buy a skiff." Sunday said, looking back out the window.

"Why don't we meet at the restaurant they were going on about?" I suggested.

"Do you always think of eating Rhys?"

"Yabo."

Laughing, he walked back to the bed and picked up his suitcase and went into the other room.

I dressed and checked the map on the back of the door for the exits and layout. There were two exists at this end of the hotel that led to the ground floor. There were two other ones at the other end of the hotel past the lobby. I chose those.

I heard the shower running in the other room as I closed the door behind me. I went to the end of the hallway and followed the staircase to the second floor. I paused briefly at door 221 and listened. Nothing. I pulled my wallet and took out a slim stainless steel card the exact size of a credit card and slipped it into the door jam and brought it down hard on the bolt while pressing inward on the door. It opened and I quickly walked inside. The room was empty. It seemed we only had one set of watchers.

Continuing down the hall I reached the end fire escape and made my way down to the ground floor. This was the end closest to the road and I walked out the south side door into the wet heat.

I continued as if I had a purpose and let the machine survey the surroundings. The diesel exhaust was almost a palatable taste. I walked to the corner and crossed. The shear volume of traffic, both vehicle and foot, made it difficult to identify any tails and I continued east two more blocks. Stopping at a shop I searched the glass for tails and found none.

I doubled back to the other Nigeria road and turned north toward the Bahia Hotel. The walk was uphill as it progressively gained elevation the nearer I got to my end point.

The white and red coloured building came into sight and I walked toward the main building, or what I guessed was the main building as it had a series of flags on top. The big red letters, Hotel Bahia, looked out of place and cheap on the top of the structure.

The door staff were absent as I entered the hotel lobby. It had African air-conditioning, otherwise known as two doors open at opposite ends. The warm salt saturated wind moved the air, stale with cigarette and diesel. There was a desk clerk reading a local paper totally unaware of my arrival.

"Hello." I said in Spanish.

"Afternoon sir. Sorry I didn't hear you come in." He set the paper down.

"Not a problem. Reservation is under Munroe."

"Senor Munroe! I was the one that took your reservation, thank you so much for the generous tip. I thought at the time you were kidding." He pulled a card and asked me to sign it.

"The room you requested is ready and there is bottled water and some fruit. The fruit's clean I washed it with bottled water myself. If there is anything I can do for you just ask Sir." He handed me a key.

"Well there is. I need to cases of bottled water, plastic bottles only and do you have two keys?"

"Two keys, yes Sir. That was two cases of bottled water?" He asked obvious he thought he had missed the number.

"Yes 48 one or two liter, plastic only, bottles of water."

"Yes sir I will get someone on that right away. Your room is on the top floor all the way down to the end. There is no extra charge for additional guests, but are expecting more than one more as I have additional keys."

"Nope, two is just fine."

I walked across the lobby to the elevators. These were new and I relaxed a little, the hotel was nothing to look at but the computer behind the desk was new and most of the furniture looked to be too. The lift doors opened to a polished wood floor.

The elevator to the executive floor was quick and silent; absent was the bouncing clicking noises of the other hotel. The doors opened to a rich red pile carpet that looked as though it had been raked. I walked down the hall to the double doors of my presidential suite not knowing what to expect.

I slipped the key in the high end Corbin lock. The hardware was serious and not common in any hotel. I pushed the heavy door in; it was almost three inches think of solid wood. Great if we had to hold up in the room exchanging rounds with the military. I doubted Russian short rounds would penetrate this thick African hardwood. The suite was out of this world. The hotel sure didn't look like much from the outside but book jackets lied.

There was a foyer with a closet and a wall sconce with a lion's head pouring water out of its mouth. The floor was polished marble and ended in rich Parduk wood paneling. I went in and the temperature and humidity was immediately significantly more bearable. I walked past the lion into what must be the great room. There was a thermostat on the wall, which read 74 degrees and 55 percent humidity, a full twenty degrees cooler than outside. The air-handling units for this room alone must be huge. The north wall was all window, the expansive Atlantic Ocean stretched forever across the room. The island we were going to use was easily visible and I was glad to see no fishing boats around it.

The great room had three large couches along the interior walls and amazingly a fifty inch plasma screen and DVD player with a small collections of movies. There was an expansive hand carved wood coffee table and a full wet bar in the corner that was delightfully stocked with Spirits and Spanish wine. I walked to my left completely in awe as a huge kitchen again tiled in marble was hidden in the corner. A doorway led to a big bedroom with its own full en suite.

I walked back into the living room and toward another doorway on the far side. This was the master bedroom and had a full view of the port and the island. There was a large desk the overlooked the water and full office style chairs around it. The bed was a canopy affair with a net for mosquitoes. This room also had a big screen TV with a selection of drama and porn. The bathroom was larger than the other and had a Jacuzzi tub. I noticed that there were several ashtrays in the suite and smiled. This was a true president's retreat. I could get used to this.

It took me two full hours to search the place for hidden mikes and I was happy I found none. I opened the bottled water, it was in a glass bottle, and poured myself a drink. There was a loud knocking at the door and I went and opened it.

It was another staff member with my water.

"Would you like this in the kitchen, sir?"

"Yes please." I watched her walk past me into the kitchen carrying 48 one-liter bottles as easy as a Canadian maid carried a tray of appetizers.

"Thanks." I handed her twenty Francs.

I would have loved to take advantage of the Jacuzzi tub, but Sunday would more than likely be finishing up soon and I needed to get the lay of the hotel. I spent another forty minutes exploring the fire escapes and hallways of the facility.

I left out the back and headed down a well-used path that took me towards the habour. I was glad not to meet anyone on this route as it was quite deserted and while I wasn't concerned for my safety I didn't need any complications. Dead bodies were very complicating.

I found the road and made my way to the restaurant that the other staff had described to Sunday and I. I walked in and was surprised to see quite a few people in for lunch.

Sunday wasn't there so I got a booth for two and a vodka martini. I only had to wait ten minutes before I saw him enter the door.

"Been waiting long?" He said as he slid into the booth.

"Nope, ten minutes. The menu is in Spanish and Portuguese. Need help?"

"I'm sure I can figure it out," he said, slipping on a pair of cheap reading glasses.

The waiter came and I ordered a white fish encrusted with local nuts and spices with a local fruit reduction and Sunday ordered a burger.

"A burger?"

"Fuck off. It's what I felt like. I managed to get us a good size skiff, and it has an electric trolling motor as well as a ten horse gas motor."

"Good. Did you have to buy it?" I took a sip of my drink.

"No I'm the same colour as the owner so he rented it to me for the week. 500 Francs.

"Good, but he saw you coming." Sunday only smirked at my statement indicating he'd paid too much, before continuing.

"The men are squared away and briefed, although I hardly had to. All they were talking about was the game. The hotel ok?"

"Yeah, you could say that. It's a fucking palace." I moved my glass to make room for my meal as the waiter arrived.

"Really? I could see it from the dock and it looks like a dump."

"Yeah well, people say you look dangerous too." I said smiling.

"The truck arrived, it was delivered by a worker. He parked right beside our tail and spooked them. They left and parked across the street. The truck is a full one ton with a quad cab, full of fuel too."

"Colour?"

"White."

"Great, well I guess it can't be all roses.

The food was as good as promised and we made short work of our meals and paid the check. The whole thing coming to twenty-five Francs with the tip.

We walked out of the hotel and back to the Presidential suite along the same back path. I ran down the plan for meeting the sub tomorrow night and Sunday listened in silence.

"What about the small arms?" He said, almost slipping on the steep slope. "I'm going to talk to this Manfred guy and see if he wants to deliver or have us come over in the truck. Don't need them right now. I want this to go as clean as possible until Saturday."

"Yeah, but if we run into problems having a few guns might be a good idea." Sunday reached the top of the bank and stopped waiting for me.

"True, but I want them used only in dire fucking circumstances. People start going missing and we're going to draw attention."

He nodded agreement and went toward the hotel, not looking very impressed. We entered the lower fire access door and made our way to the top floor. My room was only a few feet from the top doorway.

I handed him a key and he let himself in appraising the lock and door like I had done. We entered the suite.

"Holy over the top! What the hell is this place, a fucking palace?" He walked around for a full ten minutes taking it all in.

"Nice digs Rhys, I'm jealous."

"Cool. I live to make you feel like that. Come give me a hand with this bottled water."

I grabbed a case and made for the main suite bathroom off the main bedroom. Sunday followed suit and followed me.

"What the hell? You're going to take a bath with bottled water?" He said putting his case down.

"Yeah, living like a president."

He looked at me as though I had lost my mind. I started pouring the water into the plugged tub. He continued looking at me.

"You gonna help?"

"Seriously?"

"Yeah, just pour out two thirds of the water and then screw the cap back on tight and toss it in the garbage."

"Why, Rhys?"

"We're making network floats."

"Network what?"

"Floats. We're going to tie some line around the cap and attach a weight and glue the little solar powered networking devices to the top. That way our network will extend all the way to the big island out there. Probably have to use a few as they are likely to float around a bit but if we use long enough lines a few will snag on something. There didn't seem to be that much traffic between the island and the mainland. People leave other people's floats alone so we shouldn't lose too many."

"Bloody hell. For a second I thought you had been in the sun too long." He went to work filling my bath.

I found a black plastic garbage bag and replaced that as our trash can now that my little prank was played out. Sunday's sense of humour had really taken a hit with his cancer, or perhaps it was the idea of blowing himself to pieces.

That done, Sunday took his leave to go back to the men. I decided to call Manfred. I used the room phone and dialed the local number. The line noise was better than at home and I remembered that many

African countries had better fiber optics than many first world nations. The benefit of putting it in later.

"Manfred speaking."

"Manfred, Rhys here. A mutual friend said I should look you up when I got to town."

"Yes, of course. He told me when he was here last week you were coming and I should show you the sights. Where are you staying? I'll come for a drink if that is convenient?"

"Sure, the Bahai. Presidential suite."

"I'll be there in thirty minutes. I just have to finish playing with my grandchild."

"Sounds fine Manfred."

I took advantage of the time and the thirty liters of water in my Jacuzzi tub and lit a Partagas SD4 to relax; it went well with the imported Russian vodka.

I dried off and had just pulled my old clothes back on when there was a knock at the door. I opened it to find a thin, grey haired man pulling a Pelican case. Three staff members were in tow with other boxes.

"Manfred, my friend. Good to see you."

"Better to see you, my friend. I hope you have the room but I brought your surveying equipment with me."

"All of it?" I asked as they passed me to enter the room.

"I didn't know what you needed here and what you were going to transfer to the mine. So I just brought it all over". He set the Pelican case against the coffee table.

"That's good thinking. Now I know why G put you in charge."

"The rest of the stuff is in the truck, broken down into man moveable boxes. Hope you don't mind." He said, going back out the door."

"No, not at all, let me get my shoes on and I will give you a hand."

We made three more trips from his truck to the suite and all the gear was sitting in the middle of the living room. If we got pinched now the game was up and I worried about the cleaning staff. Someone would have to stay in the room 24/7 now.

"So, how about that drink?" He said collapsing into the big couch between 'machine' parts and communication gear.

"Sure, sorry what can I get you? The bar is pretty well stocked."

"Got Russian vodka?"

"Yes. Already open, a man after my own heart." I poured him a stiff drink.

"Look, sorry about exposing you and your grandkids to this. I didn't know.

"Grandkid's are two Belgium shepherd's. Sorry about opening your gear up but I had to break it down for storage and easy moving. I wasn't trying to snoop but the three crates were just too big to move to a safe location and I didn't feel good about leaving them in the warehouse." He took his drink.

"No problem. I understand. I was a little pissed at first but it makes sense." I sat across from him.

"Goetz said you were a little pissed. Said you're not the kind of man to piss off, either. I won't ask, I can kind of connect the dots anyway. But I do have two questions."

"Shoot." He looked around at the boxes and smiled before responding.

"Where should I not be?"

"On Saturday you should play with your dogs, all day long, and stay at home." I took a drink and watched his face. It didn't really change.

"Can you really do what I'm thinking you're going to do?" he shifted his legs and leaned forward.

"Yes." I caught his eye and let the machine look directly at him. He sat back subconsciously and took a long pull on his drink.

"Ok, good enough for me. I was going to get the hell out of Dodge but you seem as serious and capable as Goetz says you are."

"Thanks for your help, Manfred. I won't forget the part you played in this. The risks you took and placed on your family." I finished my drink.

Manfred finished his without comment and stood. We shook hands and without another word he left. Telling him the date had been a risk but it was no risk considering the risk he had taken for me. I watched him walk down the hall; he never looked back.

The evening's entertainment had been delivered. I had fifty submachine guns and fifty pistols to strip and get ready for combat. When that was done I had another two hundred and fifty magazines to load with Black Talon rounds. The Teflon coated amour piercing hollow points were most certainly not Geneva Convention approved killing hardware.

By the time I was done it was very late. Both thumbs were raw despite having calluses from loading many magazines over the years. The new mags were tight and I only loaded twenty-nine rounds into each. I hoped this would eliminate hard jams and limit the soft ones. Sipping vodka I wondered if this coup would go as simply as it had so far. I doubted it.

I placed a "do not disturb" sign on the door and placed a chair under the doorknobs of the big doors and headed for the couch to get some shuteye, surrounded by the instruments of war and hopefully my grand masterpiece.

The house phone woke me up. I rolled over and saw it was noon. Shit! I had slept in and was feeling the short flight jet lag.

"Hello?"

"Front desk. I have a Mr. Urassis to see you, sir."

For a moment I was confused. I thought I had left the key with Sunday on the previous day.

"What does he look like?"

"Sir?" There was hesitation in the voice and my hand unconsciously moved to the loaded MP5

"His looks. Simple question. What does he look like?"

"Black and about...Rhys it's me! Unblock the door you paranoid pinky.

"Ok, sorry." I got up and felt like I had slept in my clothes all night. Which I had. I unblocked the door and waited. Positioning myself left of the door, surprised to see the gun still in my hand.

Sunday let himself in and I relaxed.

"Working bankers hours? Here's a coffee."

"I was up half the night loading this stuff up." I hefted the small machine gun and took the offered coffee.

Sunday closed and locked the doors.

"Holy crap, everything is here?"

"Yeah." I said sitting back down, tossing the gun on the table.

"Oh here I brought you a fresh shirt, underwear and socks." He surveyed the room.

"Great, I'm going to shower. Order some food, would you?"

I got up and headed for the bathroom.

The shower finished, I walked back into the great room, which now smelled of food. We ate and spent the rest of the morning gluing network devices to the top of water bottles.

CHAPTER SEVENTY

THE FLOATING UNITS DONE, WE placed them back into the black garbage bag. We needed someone to be in the room at all times and Sunday offered to go get one of the men.

It was three and the sun was a low ball painting the water with colour. I looked and tried to pick the spot the sub would arrive. I could almost see the water shimmer, a tell tale sign of the vessel's weight and size. But it must be an illusion, or was it? I watched the surface of the ocean and wondered if they might be early. These subs were designed for just this type of task. To infiltrate and lay in wait to deliver its apocalyptic payload. A first strike weapon and one that represented the end of days. Today Andrea's Shadow represented change, a change for the better. The irony was not lost.

Sunday returned with Landry Mpondo and after the initial shock, Landry settled into the big chair near the entrance to the great room.

"Landry, it's imperative no one comes in that door. I don't want any shooting but as a last ditch scenario your weapons free. Understand?"

"Yes, Sir." He stood to address me properly.

"Good I don't imagine anyone will attempt to come in. I have left instructions with the desk that I won't need any housekeeping. But, TIA."

"I understand, Sir. If I have to I will only use the silenced weapon in a dire emergency." He looked at Sunday and I in turn.

"Great. Watch some movies, order room service, and watch the farm. There is a few hundred Francs on the coffee table if you need to tip or bribe someone."

He nodded his understanding and placed one of the MP5's out of sight of the door, yet where it could be collected quickly. I was glad to see he checked to insure it was loaded and that the safety was on.

Sunday and I left for the docks.

The skiff was older but it was wide and built out of aluminum. The engine came to life quickly with a single push of the button. Sunday checked the fuel supply as I tossed our fishing lines and bag into the front.

"Grab the lines, I want to get this over with, fisherman talk as much as their wives." Sunday settled into the rear seat to control the motor.

I undid the rear line and then the one at the front. Hopping into the boat I noticed there were no life jackets.

"Hey, no life vests. Isn't that a little dangerous?" I took my seat and looked at a smiling Sunday.

"Yeah and I'm sitting next to a fuel can with a car battery beside it. Don't fall out and I won't kick this over. Sunday gunned the motor and then put it into gear and we slipped away from the dock.

We paralleled the beach for a bit and I dug the first of the wireless repeaters out of the bag and attached a measure of fishing line to the neck, wishing I had a depth gauge. Sunday had brought my iPhone back and as it had a GPS locator built in I used it as a rough gauge for distance. The units were good for about 300 meters or nine hundred feet. The area between the hotel lands end and the island was a critical communication bridge and so I doubled up the coverage and halved the distance to be sure.

I took more care with three units. Risking them riding low in the water I added more weight so only a couple of inches of water bottle remained afloat, the wireless repeater very close to the water. They were element resistant but salt water was horrible on electronics.

"We have about an hour before sunset. Lets head up the coastline and take a look at the dock near the refinery." I shouted over the motor.

Nodding, Sunday turned the boat and increased the power and we were propelled remarkably quickly west. Must be a hull speed thing. I thought back to my Father. He had once tried to explain hull speed and how a proper amount of power was better than lots of power as a hull could only move through water at a certain speed. I had been far too young to really understand.

The shoreline was steep and jagged and I hoped that was the case underwater as well. A grounded sub would not be the best use of our secret weapon.

The trees cleared and a long concrete dock came into view. There were no boats on it and no people either. Sunday eased off on the engine and the sound returned too less annoying levels.

I dropped a few more bottles as we approached the dock. The little boat could almost go under it in places and we were very close to shore by the time I could see bottom.

"Pretty remote and quiet. The trees and angle provide pretty good cover." I swiveled around to look at Sunday.

"Yeah, not bad but this is a big bloody dock; been used recently too. Did you see the crushed mussels on the side?"

"I saw them." I lied.

"Let's hope it stays empty for a few more hours." Sunday had to shout as he had again increased speed turning back to the island.

It would be dark soon and we didn't have any lights. The port was a busy one and while quieter at night, a large ship would submerge us without knowing it. I chastised myself for not bringing a flashlight or a few radios on this trip. Some handheld portables would have really come in handy. Mistakes; well at least it wasn't too perfect anymore.

We arrived at the island with about an hour of light left. The shoreline was densely covered with plants and fell off quickly into the depths. We circled the island looking for bottom and signs of any human inhabitants. We never saw either.

Sunday picked a spot and nosed the boat onto the shore and I jumped out with the line and directly into a bunch of Red Orb spiders. I felt the stings as they let me know how welcome I was. I hated spiders, but Orb spiders especially, as they looked so alien. Their black bodies almost looked metallic, glossy and, depending on the type, had a red or golden orb on the abdomen. This colour was repeated at each of the joints on the legs. Thankfully, their bites were about as poisonous as a hornet's sting. But where there were Orbs there were others. I stepped lightly securing the boat and only received five bites for my efforts.

"Orb spiders. Be careful getting out." I yelled securing the line.

Sunday took a fishing rod and cleared the path of the offensive things. "Pretty dense in here. I don't think too many people land here."

"Probably not, hard enough to tie up a skiff." I joined him on the shore to wait.

I pulled out a little Monte 4 to smoke and keep the bugs away. The green laser lighter sprang to life and got the cigar going.

"New lighter?" Sunday looked at it.

"Boat signaling tool." I pressed the other button and a green beam cut the smoke and reflected off the slate black surface of the water.

CHAPTER SEVENTY-ONE

THE DARKNESS DESCENDED LIKE THE heavy curtain at the end of a play. Then one by one the stars arrived as if the curtain was their red carpet. We quietly watched the spectacle unfold and nearly jumped into the ocean when my phone rang. Its loud bass, line seemingly amplified in the jungle, caused Sunday to curse.

"Fuck, Rhys!"

"Sorry! Shit, I turned it on to use the GPS and thought it best to leave it on in case the babysitter called." Spoken in code out of habit, rather than necessity.

It rang a second time as I pulled it from my pocket and Sunday shot me a murderous glance. I looked at the display, which read Myron.

Myron? Where could he be calling from? Had they been picked up? A million questions launched through my brain at once and I felt the surge of adrenalin as if I had pierced the vein myself. I answered the phone before it rang a third time.

"Myron, where the hell are you?"

"Hi, ah what happened to no names? Never mind. I'm about twenty feet in-front of you. If that was your green light."

"What, you mean you're here?" Scanning the water I saw nothing.

"Yeah, been sitting here waiting for you for almost a day. Anyway enough electronic noise. Come on in the water is fine." The line went dead.

"You see anything?" I turned and asked Sunday who was now crouched down low looking out across the still surface.

"There, just left three feet high and growing slowly taller about 35 yards out." Sunday pointed.

"I still can't spot it." I said as I crouched down beside him.

"Can I see your phone?" He held out his hand.

"Sure." I carefully passed him the phone.

"You can't see shit because you ruined your night vision with this bright screen." He tossed the phone into the Ocean and I watched as it skipped twice off the surface, caught an end and was gone.

"What the hell, Sunday!"

"Isn't there an App for that?" He dove into the water and started swimming.

I dove in behind and swam after him. I had to admit he was right. Two rookie moves and a piss poor excuse. He had a right to be pissed. I should have turned the phone off as the authorities could triangulate on any cell signal and routinely would do so in a paranoid country like this, tagging all internationally identified cells. I should have turned it on every twenty minutes or so just to see if there were any messages and then turned it off again. I should have had it on vibrate even for those short checks. I shouldn't have used a bullshit excuse for my stupidity.

I felt my knee contact something and I stopped my stroke and put my hands out defensively. I felt what at first seemed to be rocks but it was far too smooth. It was the sub. I had swum a little left of Sunday's line and had contacted the side. I floated over more to my left and brought my feet down onto the submerged deck of the boat. I could see where the conning tower blocked the stars and I walked toward it.

I reached it before Sunday, who was very surprised to see me there ahead of him. I reached down to give him a hand out.

"Sorry bud, bad move and bad response." I said as he climbed onto the deck. The boat was a little higher out of the water now.

"Ok. Basics, not Bond." He said quietly into my ear as he got close.

"Captains, over here, please and quickly. We are submerging as I speak to you."

The accent was thick and Russian.

We turned toward the voice and moved, hands out in front like blind-men. I could feel the water getting deeper and it gave me the impression I was walking into a swimming pool. By the time I felt the tower it was almost to my knees. My hands gripped the rungs that led to the top and I pulled myself up and out of the rising sea.

I climbed for a good three meters before my head crested the top and I could see a red glow. A man was standing next to the rail and offered his hand. I took it and slid down to the deck. He gestured and I continue down into the boat.

Standing at the bottom of the ladder in the red light, I saw Sunday peer down from above before he climbed down the ladder. The Russian, who stopped to secure the hatch, quickly followed him. He reached the bottom of the stairs and pressed an intercom.

"Passengers on board, hatch is closed and secure, Sir."

"Roger that. Closed and secure," the intercom squawked back.

"Welcome aboard Andrea's Shadow. We are currently making our depth two hundred feet and heading for the prescribed rendezvous point. My name is Boris and I'm what you would call, in American, Chief of the boat. Let's get you out of those wet clothes, Da?"

"Thanks." Each of us chimed in unison.

The first thing I noticed about the sub was that it was not typically Russian. The corners and sharp parts were covered with soft cushion or rounded off. The second thing came as we cleared the wet room. There were red carpets and while all weather they were very luxurious looking. The lighting looked like antique gaslights and the doors we passed seemed to be made of ebony or black walnut. Even the watertight bulkhead doors between sections had gold accents and patterns etched on them. The whole thing reminded me of Vern's forty thousand leagues.

We entered a stateroom that had been converted to a storage area and Boris pointed at some footlockers.

"Surplus Russian Spetnaz fatigues are in the lockers. Find your size and leave your clothing on benches to dry."

While we found our sizes and changed, Boris continued.

"I take it you two have never been on a submarine before. Well this doesn't really qualify as a real submarine. It can go underwater but not too deep. It's well appointed and comfortable. Each man has his own bunk. These are not things found on real submarine. This is a fancy man's toy. But truth be said she's quiet, more so than any of us imagined possible. Easy to pilot, too, as it even has a front window. Come I show you, we have time."

Boris backed out of the room and waited for us in the hallway. We came after him and followed down the hall. We passed more doors and a set of stairs down and continued to the front. There was a large

468 Scott D. Covey

watertight bulkhead door, again with a gold plated handle and wheel. There was also a light on the side that had not been at any of the other doors. The light was showing green; the other colour, red, was dark.

"Listen, important thing here is colour of light. If it's green it's ok to open door. If it's red, opening the door makes you dead. If neither light is lit you're in doubt. Could be light burnt out, could be compartment flooded. Da? Little rhyme so you remember:

If it's green, don't be mean, let them free.

If it's red then you're dead.

If it's out you're in doubt, never never let them out."

He opened the door and swung it to the side and gestured for us to go in first. The room was large by any standard and had large leather viewing couches in a semi circle facing a glass wall into the ocean. There was a lounge affair on the far side with some small work stations and there, sitting behind his computer, was Myron P. Eugene, or "Minske pants" as he was known on board.

"Holy James Bond, eh? This thing is decorated like this all over the boat. It doesn't roll or pitch, even in bad seas. Nothing but that purr you hear. They let me add a cellular connection and another LAN, that's local area network, to the main mast array so that is how I called you. It will also work with the CC gear. But wait till you see this." Myron got up from his chair and moved to the glass window's center.

He flipped on some switches and then pointed above the window. It took a few seconds to come on but above the windows were two large screens that displayed what the camera could see using active infrared.

Schools of fish swam by on the screens but we saw nothing through the glass wall.

"I bet this is a blast during the day." I said marveling at the spectacle.

"It's better at night with the white lights on. Everything comes to see what's going on."

Myron flipped off the lights and screens.

"We can't do that, apparently. It could hinder the operation." Myron looked dejected.

"Captains, please follow me. We need to meet the boat Captain and your lieutenant," the big Russian interrupted.

We went back down the hall, after the Russian had secured the big, watertight door.

We reached the staircase we had walked past earlier and the big Russian went down and continued forward. On the left and right were open areas that better resembled a Russian Bordello than boat. The men were lounging with beers and seemed not to be aware we were on board. This made me a little uneasy and I decided to test that theory and turned left into one of the large lounges sporting a pool table. I entered and stopped. One of the men looked at me and then snapped his head up again to confirm what his eyes had just told him. His yell was probably heard in the engine room.

"Room!"

The activity stopped, and so now did the Russian and Sunday. I walked silent through the lounge into the middle of the room and stopped. No one looked at me; they all had picked points on a wall and were motionless. I knew if I left them in this position they would all fall into the same breathing pattern. A moment ago it had been loud and now I didn't have to raise my voice.

"I'm glad you're having such a good time. It looks as though we have good hosts. I'm going to meet those hosts now, so I thought it prudent to check to see how my Dirty Words were doing on a Russian run boat. Any complaints?"

I waited for thirty seconds, walking the isle from front to back and looking across at the men in the other areas that I could see.

"Good, I shall compliment them on your behalf. Drink your final drinks and be up in the observation lounge in twenty minutes. Bring 28 glasses and the best bottle of Russian vodka this tub has; arrange that between yourselves gentlemen. Twenty minutes from now and as a general order the Skinny White's nickname stops. Mr. Eugene will be making your life a little less hazardous, or not if he finds out you've been calling him piss pants. As you were." I walked back to Sunday and the slightly impatient Russian. He turned and led us farther forward. Ahead I could see another spill of red light.

We entered the bridge and were announced by our Russian guide. "Guests on the bridge."

I looked over at Chiwa, who was standing next to two Russians, and watched as he rolled his eyes. The Captain was sitting in his chair watching us, an unreadable expression on his face. I took a slow spin and looked at each man. They were all about the same age, except for Boris. They all showed scars on their foreheads and the look of people who served together. Boris's head had no scars, very unlikely for someone who had spent time inside Russian made machines. They were all silently watching me be embarrassed.

Sunday had his back to me. So I had to be verbal. I whistled like a zebra and let out a low grunt like a silverback gorilla. The reaction was immediate, and startled, I had to move quickly to catch up.

Chiwa grabbed the only sidearm on the bridge from the man to his right, delivering a vicious elbow to the man's neck. Then, extending the gun and his left foot simultaneously, he kicked the man on his left behind his knee and clipped the side of his forehead with the barrel of the gun and left it trained on him. The man winced in pain and joined his fallen comrade on the deck.

I stepped between the two men manning the controls and grabbed each of their throats tightly, pushing them snug to the chairs. "Nice and smooth." I said in Russian.

Sunday moved up and Boris, hearing the commotion, spun. A big paw tossed out in defence. Sunday ducked the swinging arm and chest bumped the larger Russian, who circled Sunday's small frame with his other arm. Sunday drove both his hands up, the seven-inch, slim; push dagger pierced Boris's neck and continued at that angle thru the center of his brain. Boris's eyes crossed as if he was watching the blade tip's progression, until they snapped up in his head like a dolls. Sunday let him crash to the floor like yesterdays toy, only a small trickle of blood evident on the man's jowls.

I addressed the crew in Russian.

"Skipper, I'm not a guest on your boat. I'm the Captain of this operation. I share that rank with the man who just killed your Spetsnaz muscle bound meat puppet. You are under our command and the next vodka drinking Bolshevik that fails to afford me the respect my position holds will not die as easily as your friend. I will not tolerate insubordination or any other form of cowardice. Skipper, is my Russian clear enough?"

The man sat up a little straighter in his chair. "Yes, your Russian is clear and so is your message. But I'm the Captain of this vessel and will not allow my crew to be threatened. We will perform our duties as agreed by our contract. But this is not a military engagement; it's purely a monetary one. Mercenaries are not soldiers.

I let go of the throats of the two men as Sunday walked toward me to watch them. I pulled out another Monte four and bit the cap off, spitting it to the floor before I lit the cigar.

"Your Viktor's brother-in-law's friend. Right?"

"Yes."

"Would you agree Viktor is a powerful and dangerous man?"

"Yes." The confidence swelling his chest as he concluded I knew his powerful protector.

"Well, skipper I don't negotiate very well and I really wished we saw eye to eye on this one."

I sprang, landing facing him, on his lap, his arms under the quads of my legs, ankles locked, behind his chair. The impact took his breath away and I grabbed his Odessa whore ponytail and pulled his head back, bringing the lighter to his left eye. I let him catch his breath. I flicked on the lighter, the flame tip touched the surface of his eye and he closed it and tried to move his head. I wrapped the ponytail tight and using my stomach muscles crunched myself up and held the flame to the smoldering lid. The man started screaming, the sound like a locomotive's brakes locked before collision. The lid started to turn black and then the eye below it's thin membrane burst and ran down the man's check and into his mouth joining his ending scream.

I got off the man and addressed Sunday and Chiwa in English.

"Kill the crew. We have to find replacements with less attitude. Radio Viktor to kill their families too, his sister's husband included."

Sunday and Chiwa knew I was playing a game; if I wanted them dead I would have used sign language.

"No! Wait! Please!"

The language was English and in pain. The others didn't seem to speak English as they hadn't moved when I gave the orders and they certainly had to believe my orders would be carried out.

"Hey Skipper, you're a tough mother fucker. Only went out for a second or two. You got a new fresh perspective? Seeing clearly, perhaps? Now that your offending eye has been plucked out? Well ok, that is a little overtly dramatic. Mmm, how about, 'melted out of your fucking skull?' You know what's worse? Nah, you probably don't sorry rhetorically speaking here. If you were to tell Viktor I did this to you he'd burn out the other one to make sure I knew he was in agreement with me."

"The crew can't speak English. They don't need me to do what you have to do. I will give them directions to follow your orders. Spare their lives and take mine. I beg this of you." His hand moved to touch his ruined eye.

"Make it good, skipper." I moved away to better watch the expressions on the men's faces.

"Comrades, it was my arrogance and disrespect that cost me an eye and it need not cost you anything. I apologize for Boris, he was a bad choice and I should have spoke English to the group instead of maintaining this nostalgic façade. We are not in Mother Russia's Navy any longer but we are here to do a job. A job I know you can do without me as I'm removed from command to the infirmary for recovery. Please treat your new Captain with as much respect as you have shown me over the years. He's not a sub driver so you will have to bear with his commands and follow the intent rather than what might be spoken. I'm truly sorry to have placed you needlessly into danger." He turned and looked at me.

I continued in Russian. "Thank you Captain, my actions were harsh but we are at war here and I'm glad you understood that in the end. I accept command. Helmsmen, continue on current course, speed, and depth till you are 500 meters from the target and then make our depth 30 meters."

"Yes, Sir." They both looked at each other as they answered. Then the one on the right spoke. "That will put our tower out of the water a few feet, Sir."

"I think what the new Captain wants is periscope depth at 500 meters, point of contact." The man lying at Chiwa's feet barked, rubbing his sore neck.

"Yes Sir, periscope depth 500 meters, point of contact." Said the two men in unison.

I signaled Sunday and Chiwa to watch the bridge crew. I grabbed the Captain and led him off the bridge and down the hall.

"Where is the infirmary?" I asked him as we made our way past the now empty lounges.

"We both know you're not taking me to the infirmary. The back of the ship near the engine room would be the best and I would really appreciate if you let me do it."

"Actually, I'm going to let you live. That was a brave move back there." I saw the infirmary door ahead.

"Not really, I'm blind in the right eye." He stumbled again against the wall, both eyes shut not out of pain but because it didn't matter.

I guided him into the small hospital and secured him to one of the tables. Looking around I found a medicine cabinet shaped like a mechanic's tool chest but painted white. It was locked so I jammed my knife into the lock and forced it. It gave with a dull pop. Inside I looked at the vials of medicine, which were marked in Russian and recent. I found some morphine and a syringe. I pulled 3cc's of the clear fluid and went back to the Captain.

"I'm going to give you a shot to take the pain away." I pushed the needle into his upper arm and depressed the plunger slowly. The drug would gradually go into his system as it was released from his muscle.

I tossed the used syringe into the sharps container and got another one from the drawer. I filled this one with 20cc of the drug and put the cap back on the needle and secured the drug cabinet.

"Pain any less?" I asked.

"Getting better." He said, turning his face toward my voice.

"Here is another one, it's full. More than enough to do the job. Use it all or a little, its up to you"

I left him to his decision and headed back to the bridge.

I checked the time. I had about seven minutes before I was expected upstairs. The bridge was quiet. The two men that Chiwa had dealt with were up and while favouring their knee and neck were working at stations taking care of whatever was needed.

"Sunday, you got this?" I asked, reaching the center of the room.

"Yeah, I got it. I speak enough Russian to get my point across. Perhaps give me the pistol, just in case." I handed him the pistol and went to the Captain's seat showing him the main intercom switch and how to use it. Understanding Russian was one thing, reading Cyrillic was different.

"Chiwa, will you come with me to the forward observation lounge." I started out of the room, not waiting for an answer.

"Sir." Chiwa barked and followed after me using his long legs to catch up.

"Chiwa, Am I to understand that Myron was sequestered away in the observation lounge and away from the crew?" I fought the urge to go check on the sub captain and headed for the stairs.

"Yes Sir, the Russians really didn't trust him and I wasn't sure I should make a big deal of it. He wasn't mistreated and seemed to like the solitude. I did manage to get them to let him work on his communication gear on the tower but..." His voice trailed off.

I stopped halfway on the stairs and turned around. "But what Chiwa?"

"Well, I think the decision was sound despite the reasons the Russians had used to arrive at it. We didn't know this guy and he was American and..." He looked into my eyes for the first time.

"Good decision soundly arrived at. It was my call to bring him in. Good thinking for yourself. You need to do that if you're going to work under my command. Now we need everyone to play nice and get team focused, you ready for this?" I turned and continued up the stairs.

"I hope I am sir, and thank you." He continued up the stairs.

"Thank me when it's over."

The large bulkhead door was closed and I looked at the light. It was green. I spun the big wheel and pushed the heavy door away from me. Chiwa rushed in past me.

"Room! Captain on deck."

The men were now standing at attention and even Myron had got to his feet and was slowly looking around to see how to fit in. Looking like a dance partner two-steps behind, yet eager to learn.

"As you were, Gentlemen. Boris is dead and the previous Captain of this vessel may have joined him. I didn't wish to keep you waiting to see if he had succumbed to his injuries. This was necessary as it was obvious to me these men were basic privateers and had no sense of respect or discipline. The part this vessel plays is a pivotal one and I needed people on board it that would not blink when the time came. You have been left out of the loop about a few of our end game plans. I know you understood why but I think it's only proper I include you at this time. But before I do I think Lieutenant Chiwa has a few words. I stepped left and sat down in one of the office chairs from the workstations.

"Thank you, Sir. We have a civilian contractor onboard and he has been locked away in here working at making your jobs safer and more productive. All of you have had a chance to get some time on the Command and Control units and I would like you all to meet the man that made them. Mr. Eugene. He's part of this team and is so confident in his product he's here personally to help us out. He may have some questions for you so please be as honest and forthcoming as you would with the Captain or me. Now, let me give you back to Captain Munroe."

I stood up and Chiwa took my place in the chair.

"Thanks Chiwa and thank you Mr. Eugene. Right men, this is the start of something beautiful and the end of a wonderful friend and commander. Quiet please let, me explain. No matter how much planning commanders do, things get fucked up. You've all been around long enough to know this. Part of our plan had to include something to keep the American Military at bay. EG is a UN country and as such other UN nations are required to protect her in times of trouble. Currently we have one US warship and one Coast Guard vessel within the area that can and would respond. We need to deal with that issue in a swift and deadly fashion as they could have teams on the ground within twenty minutes of deploying them. How do we do that? How do we hold the world's largest military at bay? Nuclear weapons."

The room erupted in questions and praise and emotion. Chiwa jumped to his feet. I signaled for silence and the room returned to normal. Chiwa glared at the men before sitting down.

"Please men, we're on a clock here. The problem with getting those kinds of weapons is that once you use them the big kids in the sandbox aren't going to let you get away with it. So, we have a two-edged sword. I have to make the US think I have the nukes, and will use them. But at the end of the day I can't really have them, so when we appoint the new President they will just roll over. If we had nukes they could use the age-old 'weapons of mass destruction' argument to steal the oil here too. This is where we ran into the hitch in the plan. This is where one of your brave commanders stepped up. Stepped up for you. We are on the way to meet a container tanker. This tanker is hauling sixty thousand tons of Ammonium Nitrate fertilizer. We are going to backfill the container section with diesel fuel oil at a ratio of four to one by weight. This will take a couple of days, with the ocean slowly rocking our baby to the correct mix. But here lies our problem. We couldn't get a secure method of remotely detonating our baby. Without the detonation the US comes in and saves the day and we're all dead, or in jail. A simple timer isn't good enough. Remote radio could be jammed. So, Captain Sunday will detonate the bomb. His life will end in a six-megaton explosion in order to buy us all time to finish our ground attack and get the new president into office. It's fitting he should trade his life for ours as he's like a father to all of us. A father to our freedom and the development of a truly free and prosperous African Nation. It's the duty of sons to bury their fathers and he has spared us even that. The explosion will reach space and put his atoms and particles there so that when we look at the stars we will look at him. Chiwa, pour that Vodka around. Men, tonight and tomorrow, as you prepare for this engagement and wait for it to start I want you to remember the sacrifice of not only Sunday but all the other brothers that have died to get us here. To this one moment in time. Let's drink to death as it's the only real currency, on par throughout the world. We are promised nothing more at birth, having to earn all that we are. Today we stand as we are, poised to take tomorrow. Shall we, men? TO DEATH!

The room had grown silent with the information. Sunday was going to have to set off the bomb. The men had very little time to accept and understand it so I had provided the problem, like sugar, to help it go down. It was also a good motivator. As their commander I would have been remiss to ignore it. The room erupted in a salute to death and with that salute came the promise of it. Despite setting the stage I couldn't help but get caught up in the enthusiasm.

When I finally made my way through the throng of men to Myron he was still pale, but had not pissed his pants. He looked up at me when I stopped at his chair.

"Still wanting to play with the big boys?" I asked, clinking his half drunk glass.

"To Death? We couldn't find another toast? Shit, Rhys. I'm scared. I know I signed up for this, but holy crap. I'm sitting in a James Bond plot, on a captain Nemo sub, with the fucking antichrist mixing Carl Sagan with Greek fatalism. This is beyond surreal."

"Antichrist? That's a bit harsh, don't you think? Don't leave me hanging."

I tapped his glass a second time.

"Someone said you burned out the sub Captain's eye." He lifted his glass as if to wash out the taste the words had left.

"It was required. Distasteful and barbaric perhaps, but it sent the message words could not. The scent on that bridge will be there a long while as will the echo of his scream. It will, in truth, follow those men to every bridge they walk into. But most importantly it will keep them on that bridge when required. They will put duty before self-preservation, because they know the smell of cowardice. I pulled up a chair and joined him at equal levels knowing the men would not miss this.

"I get it, Rhys. I just never anticipated I would be in this boat. I don't know what I'm doing. I've never carried a gun. I..."

He finished his vodka.

"Myron, you're going to come with me tonight to a very nice room and tomorrow you're going to walk around town listening to your iPod, doing your overlays with two of the best security people I have. Then you're going to come back to my room, finish all the overlays and get the CC program going. You won't leave the room until all the shooting is done and you get a visual Lego Creature ringside seat for the whole affair. How you view next week is beyond me. Look at the here and now."

"Yeah, yeah, yeah. I know. Eat, drink and be merry." He raised an empty glass to his mouth.

"Now, you're getting it." I tapped him on the shoulder and left to find Chiwa.

He was standing near the glass wall watching bubbles form or the refection behind him. I signed 'on me' and got my answer. He turned and moved to where I stood waiting.

"Sir?" He came to a loose attention.

"Get the booze squared away and secure. I need a boarding party for this boat; men experienced with boats or lines. It should be a simple procedure as they have orders to not give us any problems. But grab a few guns."

"The Captain had all the weapons locked up while we were in transit," Chiwa explained.

"I kept one, of course, but the long arms that Viktor had loaded are in the amouries and the key is around the Captain's neck."

He signaled to the two men as he talked.

"The Captain is in the infirmary and the key should be there. Take it and control it, and let me know immediately if the key is already gone. I will be on the bridge."

I turned and made my way to the door. Myron caught up with me and asked if he could go to the radio room and test his CC system against the three units he had brought on board. I let him follow me for a while as I thought about it. Advising him not to make any outside calls I nodded and he went into the radio room.

The bridge tension had diminished significantly since I had left. Sunday had taken the Captain's chair. I fought the urge to tease or toss a jab and simply asked how much farther. He shrugged.

"They're being well-behaved but I guess there is some sub protocol or something regarding frequent updates. The two there have been helpful and the two pilots, or whatever they're called, are scared. I think when we get back to port or rather when you get back, it would be wise to lock them up." He turned to the buzzing to his left.

I read the label. Armoires. "That will be Chiwa getting some long guns from the amoury."

Sunday nodded his answer.

"Stay here and take care of our friends while we lash the goods to the deck. Then I will relieve you, Captain." I gave him a salute.

"Aye aye, Captain." He returned the salute.

"Contact Sir, 526 meters, stationary, sounds of power generation only, screws are not turning."

"Roger that, is it our tanker?" I replied in Russian.

"Climbing to periscope depth, Sir. Shall I raise the scope?" He said, looking from me to his controls.

"Raise the scope." I walked to the cage that contained the periscope-viewing device, as the man repeated my order to raise the scope.

I scanned the horizon and saw the large ship. We were running directly to her and it occurred to me that I didn't know how to pilot this thing from above. I had seen the controls when I pulled myself over the side but I had no idea on how to use them and I doubted it would be easy to learn with the ship looming in the near distance.

"Who is the best here for piloting from above? We need to tie up to a tanker, offload gear, and secure it to the deck. Quickly now." The man that Chiwa had hit on the neck held up his hand.

"Great, follow me topside. We have meeting to make." I left the bridge the man in tow.

We all waited as the light on the upper door's light went from red to green. I watched as the Russian climbed the ladder and spun the hatch wheel and then signaled we should move. He opened the door and a few liters of seawater came in to splash on the floor. He pushed that hatch all the way up and went up in to the darkness. I followed him and was very quick out of the hatch hole. He was standing by the controls, the light beside them red.

The rest of the men came up on the deck and I instructed them to keeps the guns out of sight but at the ready, in condition one. This meant the rifles would have one in the pipe, ready to fire. They pushed them against the structure and under the lip.

I pulled out my lighter and started flashing the green laser at the bridge of the boat. Almost immediately the pilot house lights flared bright, then went off again. Then the port lights came on.

The top control's light went green and the Russian took control of the boat and deftly brought it in on the portside. There were no shots from above and the sub was easily tied up to the mountain of a boat.

"Is Captain Munroe available? I'd like to discuss the terms of our capture," came a dismembered voice form above.

"I'm here."

"Captain, will you take the lift line up?"

I walked over to the side of the boat, stepped on the sling of the lift line and was quickly whisked to the top deck.

The surrender and loading of the sub was handled well by the all-Swedish crew. While they were a little taken back at having to remain our guests for a week, there were no heroics. The LRAD units were removed and stored within the sub. The three Platinum Rain units were far too large and were lashed to the deck.

Sunday and the head engineer set to the task of backfilling the hold and running the pumps. I had wished I would have had some quiet time to say my thanks and heart felt goodbyes, but it was not to be. The last image I had was of Sunday waving to the sub as we backed away for the long trip back. The ships crew our guests for the duration. We had to remain on the surface, as the Platinum Rain units weren't salt-water immersion proof.

CHAPTER
SEVENTY-TWO

I FELL ASLEEP WATCHING MYRON doing overlays and running out "What-If" scenarios. I continued to run them out in my head as I slept, and when I woke I did not feel rested. I looked around the room in the pre-morning false dawn. Myron was asleep in his chair. a comforter pulled up around his neck. I was covered, but the salt from my late-night dip had crusted and was irritating my skin. I closed the door to the great room and went to shower. I took a long one, wondering if the mists of steam would have any insight. I was spared any Macbeth-like revelations. I knew we would probably be successful on the ground offensive, but I worried about the Yanks. I worried about the cost to the locals for this freedom. The stadium was going to be in panic, but I saw no way of mitigating the numbers. I wasn't that good of an accountant. I didn't know if that was a good or bad thing.

Myron was still sleeping when I returned. His snoring was like the mewling of a cat and reminded me of Ruben. I missed him as much as I missed Andrea. Once again I fought the urge to call her. I turned on CNN and was surprised at the signal quality, high definition, so it must have been from a satellite. Myron stirred but didn't wake up.

The door slid open and Chiwa looked in. Seeing I was awake he walked over with a cup of coffee.

"I don't usually make coffee. I hope it's ok. Most of the men are still sleeping. I know you'd want them to continue. I heard you in the shower so I figured I'd give it a try."

"It's good, Chiwa. Thanks. I want to let the men out to blow off steam. They don't have passport stamps and the op is fucked if they get picked up and checked against any database. The President will get spooked and just watch the match from his house." I took a sip of the offered cup. The coffee was as strong as any field coffee I'd had.

"I know, sir. Chiwa explained. "And so do they. I'm going to run them through a course of stripping and reassembly of the MP5 and pistol today and then I thought I would start a poker game in the afternoon. Winner gets to order room service. Just to keep them busy." He looked at the sleeping Myron.

"Yeah," I grinned. "I know he, purrs. Good ideas re: the busy work. There's a bunch of loose cash in my bag. Feel free to use it for chips."

I patted his shoulder and he left me alone with the CNN talking heads and a purring computer programmer.

The noise in the next room increased and I knew the men were waking up. The noise even woke Myron. He looked around, stunned — as though he'd woken up in a dream that was tipping toward a nightmare.

"Morning, Myron. What's on the agenda today?" I asked.

"Er, ah," he mumbled, coming awake.

"Morning. Fucking chairs. Not sure. Going to go over the units and see how they work at full power. Run a few more scenarios, I guess."

He stood up and stretched.

"Sounds good," I responded.

"I hear there's going to be a poker tournament this afternoon. You can always sit in on the morning training session. It's going to be stripping the MP5."

"Sounds like fun," he said with more enthusiasm than I thought he would have mustered. He walked past me into the bathroom.

I needed to get on my way so I dressed quickly and headed to the lobby. The smell of bacon and eggs made my stomach ache and I figured the diversion was worth it and stopped for breakfast.

I left the hotel and walked out to the truck, surveying the lot for tails. There were none. I started the loud diesel rattling and drove out to the stadium to check on the progress.

Everything was going smoothly. The coaches complained two of the men had food poisoning and had to remain at the hotel.

"TIA," I explained.

"What is TIA?" two of them asked in stereo..

"This Is Africa. Shit happens. It's to be expected. Don't let it bother you. If I know my men, they will be good to go at game time."

"I hope so. We got a real shot at winning this thing." The head coach tapped his clipboard.

"That is what I want to hear," I said, excusing myself with a wink to some of the men watching.

The next stop on the agenda today was the airfield again. I wanted to connect with the Hind pilot who was related to the president in exile. The road had a few more cars on it than yesterday and it slowed my trip considerably.

The official stop and start of the airport and military section was pretty ambiguous and I hoped to use that to my advantage. I wandered close to the fence and was immediately approached by military personnel. They were very serious types who definitely lacked a sense of humour. I was stopped, identified, and patted down. I explained that I was a guest of the President and was looking to rent some time on a helicopter. There were some calls made and I was escorted into an office to wait for an official.

About twenty minutes later a stuffed shirt came in and I could see he was well aware of my status.

"Sorry for the harsh treatment Mr..." He walked over to shake my hand.

"Please, it's André. I should have been more respectful of your sensitive areas. I jut thought it was attached the airport. I meant no harm." I shook his hand firmly.

"The officers said something about renting a helicopter?"

He sat and gestured that I do the same.

"My team is playing in the game on Saturday and I wanted to get some video from the air. I was looking to see if there was any choppers available." I looked at him as he opened a briefcase.

"Unfortunately, the only choppers would be military ones. They used to have one at the refinery for trips to boats and the mainland but it has been taken out of service. Besides, it would not be allowed to fly over the stadium. The city's airspace is restricted to military or government flights."

He shuffled some papers and looked at me.

"Is it possible to rent time on one of the President's helicopters? It would be a great angle and I would be willing to share the footage with the international reporters. I think it would show the size and freedom of the President's sponsored event. I would be most grateful."

I added the last as delicately as possible.

"It may be possible. I would have to check to see if we have a machine free. I would have to clear it with the President, of course." He placed a piece of paper between us; it had a number written down. $10,000 US.

"Certainly. I understand things are difficult to arrange. If we could look at the machine to ensure it would work, I would certainly cover your time."

I pushed the paper back to add weight to my statement.

"We could do that," he said. "I will try to arrange this for you. I don't know what the rental rates will be but I know the machines are expensive to maintain."

He gathered his papers and closed his case.

"Great. Shall we." I said standing up and reaching into my carry on for the envelope that contained the money.

"Yes," he said, standing up, eyeing my hand greedily.

"Here, please, for your time." I handed him an envelope. It contained $10,000 in hundred dollar bills.

He took the envelope and tucked it into his breast pocket as he made his way to the door.

We made our way into the military area of the airport and were checked no less than three times. The equipment looked to be in good repair but the truth was far from the appearance. There were three Hinds and two of them hadn't moved in many months. The dust on the cowling provided all the evidence I needed. One, however, was in good repair and had been at least moved in the week. The other planes were covered and I imagined they were just as flightless as the two Hinds. I recognized the man in the green flight suit before he came out of the office.

"Hey, we don't do tours, Minister," he said as he approached.

"This is André. His team is playing on Saturday and he was inquiring if one of the Hinds could provide air coverage for some of the game so he can shoot video."

"That would have to be cleared from the highest channels," the green suit responded with a sneer. He looked at me suspiciously.

"We were just checking, no harm in that. Sorry to be a bother," I explained.

The stuffed shirt went on.

"I know it has to be cleared, I told André that, thank you." The official tried to regain the air of an official.

We walked back outside and toward the main terminal. The official was aching to count his cash and had touched his pocket no less then seven times since its receipt.

"Ok. So you will check and get back to me?" I asked as I stopped outside the truck.

"Yes, I will send word to the hotel."

He took my hand and shook it, happy with his transaction.

"Great." I echoed his handshake and feeling. Ten grand was well worth the intelligence I had just bought even if the chopper was not possible.

The rest of the day was spent playing with the kids and running football camps. The men generally had a good time and enjoyed playing with the Malobo children. I managed to dodge all but two of the interview requests.

I returned to the Bahia after doing a shopping run for the men. I placed three full bags at the back door and carried one up to the suite, and made another trip to retrieve the rest. Upstairs, the poker game was in full swing and Myron seemed to be doing very well for himself.

"Any problems?" I asked, leaning towards Myron's ear.

"Nope, we're all good," he said, as he figured his outs on the hand.

I went in and ran a hot bath and lit a small cigar to enjoy with my vodka while I soaked. We were getting close to the start of this thing and I could almost feel the changes in my body as it shut down for the event. I went to bed, leaving the poker party in full swing.

CHAPTER
SEVENTY-THREE

ANOTHER MORNING, ANOTHER DAY OF waiting. Myron had made himself a bed in the corner and was mewling away. I dressed quickly and went out to the living room. The men were strewn around the room as though a transport truck had flipped over. I made my way quietly to the door, only to find one of the men propped up in front of it, sleeping in a chair. I woke him quietly and went downstairs. I ate breakfast quickly on the rear veranda and drank coffee to get me going. I looked northeast and wondered how Sunday was progressing. I decided a call was worth the risk.

"Good morning, ya old pink bastard." I made out past the static.

"Morning. How are things?" I was waiting for his explanation.

"Good, tank is full and I'm sure you will see me tonight. Car is sitting a little funny with the load. The road got a little rough last night right after I topped off the tank, but that just made it easier for me."

"It's only Friday. I was expecting to see you tomorrow night," I said.

I wanted to make sure he hadn't missed a day.

"Yes, I know. I 'm going to take my time but if you needed me 'hurry up quick' I'm all set to push this thing along time wise, is all I meant."

"Roger that. The in-laws are all safe and taking up too much room. Chiwa has really risen to the task of keeping the kids busy so no fights break out. Everything else is five by five."

The static was getting worse.

"All right my friend. Look for me tomorrow night." His voice miles away and fading.

"Yeah and every night thereafter. Goodbye."

"..bye." The line was really bad and I missed what was said before, if anything was.

I hung up the phone and felt the immense weight of this coup. Operationally it was as sound as they get, perhaps better. The cost was still more that I wanted to pay from a personnel position. I consoled myself by looking at the long view, the bigger picture.

I finished my morning looking out at the ocean, smoking a nice Churchill. One of the 'not sure what it is but it's Cuban and good' cigars I had saved from the original batch I packed at home. I had intended on smoking it after tomorrow. But an old RSM had taught me the folly of that years ago. 'Smoke 'em if you got em, and when you can.'

I needed to check in at the other hotel to see if my helicopter had been approved. I also needed to make an appearance at the football pitch. The day wasn't getting any younger so I finished my cigar and tossed the butt in my nearly empty coffee mug.

The parking lot was nearly full as people arrived for the big game. I looked for our watchers and hoped to slip in unnoticed, but the watchers were not there. I guess two days of coverage had convinced them we were on the up and up.

I went in the end fire door and made my way to the top floor. I walked into the hall and could hear the noise of the TV coming from my room. I only had a pistol and the thought of just bypassing the room and carrying on crossed my mind. The devil you knew about was far better than the one you didn't. I pulled out a knife and, keeping it low by my thigh, opened the door. Someone was in the room.

I moved in quickly. They moved off the bed, reaching for something. I prepared to throw the large knife ahead of my rush. The figure on the bed froze and I saw the hand holding the handle of the machine gun come free in a wave. I was mid-way through an underhand toss and couldn't stop. I could only adjust the point of aim. The knife slid free of my hand and flew at the target, imbedding itself deeply into the headboard with a loud, hollow thunk.

"Shit, Sir. Sorry this room was larger." It was one of the men, who, having opting for better accommodation, had chosen my room.

The man put down his MP5. I was glad we didn't just test the armour for blade penetration.

"Someone could have let me know," I growled.

My heart rate was still elevated and I went to look out the window and calm down. The young man said nothing, as he used two hands to pull my knife out of the headboard.

"Here ya go, Sir. Thanks for missing."

He handed me my knife with an unsteady hand.

"I didn't miss," I corrected him "Any packages arrive for me?"

I turned back away from the window and sheathed the knife.

"There was a knock on the door an hour ago but I didn't answer it."

He returned to the bed, unsteadily.

"Thanks. Good job security-wise. Carry on."

I left the room and walked down the hall to the lifts.

The lobby was busy, but Madrid saw me and immediately came around the counter with a package.

"This came for you from the President's office. I was supposed to give it to you personally, so I couldn't slide it under the door earlier."

"Thanks, Madrid." I took the package and thanked him with a 30-Franc tip..

I sat on one of the lobby couches to read the package. It said I had been cleared by the Department of the Military to put into service one Hind helicopter from the hours of 1100 until 1500. The cost was $130,000 thousand US. Payment could be made in advance to at the Bank of Equatorial Guinea to an account for which they provided the number. .

I could not fly off the territorial island, and I couldn't fly over any restricted military or Presidential air space. It went on to confirm the pilot would know where these were. It finished with: "This letter, with attached confirmation of deposit, serves as authorization to the pilot. It was signed by the President.

The morning had just become a whole lot better. I went back out to the truck.

The bank was empty when I arrived and I thought it might be closed. I walked in and went to the service counter.

"Good afternoon, sir, how can I be of assistance today?" the woman of obvious Fang descent asked in a very professional tone.

"I need to see the manager to facilitate a large transaction into the President's account. I have the number here."

I showed her the letter.

"May I take this to show the manager?" she asked, her face registering surprise as she read the contents.

She held the letter as if it were made of glass.

"Certainly," I replied.

She moved quickly toward the back of the bank.

It was only a few seconds before she returned with a balding short, fat man in tow. It looked as though he might break a sweat keeping up with her long stride.

"Sir, this is Samuel Itondo. He's the branch manager and can help you."

"Afternoon Samuel, I'm André. My football club is playing your National team tomorrow."

"Pleasure to meet you André," he stated.

"If you will follow me we can take care of that transfer right away."

He shook my hand, hard.

I followed him into the back and past his office to a sealed room. The door was very thick and the frame secure.

"This is our international money transfer room. Normally we don't allow clients back here, but as you are a guest of the President, I'm sure you're pretty safe." He moved to one of the three terminals.

"Completely." I offered.

While he started the computer I looked around. The walls were a completely different construction and material from the rest of the bank. The room looked like it was built to hold people out — no doubt to allow staff to get as much money transferred as they could before being overrun. The place looked like it could hold off a tank. I spotted the chink in the armour, a small thin window at the top of the wall. It was much too small to allow access and was made of block glass, judging from the light distortion. But it could be breeched.

I sat down in front of the screen Samuel had brought up. I wondered if money was still available in Tom's account. I was surprised to see there was. I arranged the transfer and gave the terminal back to Samuel. He completed the transaction and printed a receipt for me.

"Would you like a certified photocopy of those two documents?" he asked, ushering me out of the room.

"That would be great. Thanks," I responded with enthusiasm.

He took the two pieces of paper and made for his office. Inside he photocopied and stapled the documents. On the photocopy he stamped "Certified Copy" and signed it.

"Here you are, Andre. Good luck tomorrow."

"Thanks. You, too." I said as I left his office.

"Sir?" I heard him as I left.

I turned and noticed that he looked confused.

"Good luck tomorrow — against my team. You're going, right?"

"No, sir. I shall be here, working. But I do have money riding on its outcome."

I closed his office door thinking, "More than you know, buddy; more than you know."

I made my way back to the airport and parked in the now almost full lot. There were a group of journalists doing lead ins, using the airport as a backdrop. I even saw a CBC stringer outfit. This game was getting worldwide attention.

I walked over to the military checkpoint and produced the photocopy of the letter. The man took it and disappeared without a word. He came back in a few moments with another man of unknown, but higher rank.

"I will escort you. No pictures. Leave your cell phone in your pocket."

I had already turned on the video recorder in the iPod that was sitting on my hip. It was taking everything in.

"Of course, sir," I responded with a smile.

He nodded and walked toward the hangar.

We made our way back to the Hind hangar, taking a different route than yesterday, skirting the dusty and non-functional aircraft. The route allowed me to see the new Gator fighting vehicles that EG had stolen from the UN mission.

We reached the hangar and went in and directly to the office. The man handed the paperwork to the pilot whom I had met yesterday.

The pilot scanned the order confirmation.

"Hmm,," he commented. "You must have friends in high places, Mr. André, to get this moved so swiftly through our government."

The last bit was spit out with disdain.

"TIA sir, and everything is negotiable.

"At the right price," I answered sitting on the corner of the other desk.

"Everything is in order. I'll see you tomorrow at 1100 sharp."

He went to an old photocopier to make a copy.

"Would you be able to leave at 1100 and pick me up at the Bahia hotel shortly after that?" I asked.

"TIA Sir, everything is negotiable." He looked at me, brow up, the question obvious.

"Ten thousand." I offered.

"Done." He accepted.

"I shall see you tomorrow, sir. Please have the money with you or I shall develop engine problems very quickly. These old Russian birds are finicky."

He handed back the paperwork.

Everyone was in it for the money. Some things never changed, only the locations were different. I reached into my bag and took out the last envelope of US cash. $10,000 in various denominations. I handed it to him.

"I like to be up front, and I always come prepared," I explained.

"Thanks." He put the envelope into his flight suit.

Thankfully, the military man had stayed out of the office and as I passed him he locked into step beside me and I followed the same route out, iPhone on my hip, shooting video the whole way.

The drive back was less congested and I was in a far better mood. We had air support and I would be able to call the whole thing in while in the air. This had gone far better than I hoped or believed possible. But, ever the cynic, I waited to see what would go wrong. There were a million uncontrollable issues that I could only mitigate. Now I could be anyplace in a few moments, and that made it better.

I stopped by the football pitch and went in to meet the men and the coaches one last time before the game. I found them on the pitch running drills and looking very much like a pro team. I walked over and waited for the coaches to see me, not wanting to interrupt.

The head coach saw me and walked over.

"Hey André, you're not going to believe this, but they pulled a fast one and called a start time of 1100 instead of noon." He was tapping his clipboard.

"Really? That isn't good. So half time will start at 1145?"

"Yeah. And end at 1300. Apparently the President has a fucking parade planned for after the game and needs to be on a plane at 1400.

They just arbitrarily changed the times. It's going out on all the news broadcasts as we speak. Everything is going to shut down — a day of celebration they're calling it and one of my players is down again today with food poisoning. I think they are fucking with the food, the bloody sods."

He was obviously a very angry and suspicious man at heart.

"Well, TIA again. Why don't we take the men down to the fish place down by the main docks? It's a great restaurant. I ate there with Sunday at the start of the week. I'll stop by and make the reservations and foot the bill myself. Remember to bring something back for the men who are ill. I always need to eat more when I've been poisoned."

"Good idea. Great really, a pre-celebration dinner. Where is Sunday? We haven't seen him for a couple of days now."

He seemed genuinely concerned.

"Sorry, I thought one of the lads would have told you. He flew home with urgent health issues. Didn't say what they were, only that he needed to go home."

"Oh, that's bad luck. Is he ok?"

"Yeah, feeling much better now. I talked to him this morning and he wanted me to pass some stuff on to the men. May I?" He looked at the other training staff.

"By all means we're done here. It will give us a chance to hit the showers before all the hot water is gone from this lot." He gestured at the men running drills.

"Thanks." He walked away blowing his whistle and waving the staff over. I used a hand sign to get the men around me. They circled me and went down to one knee. I did the same.

I decided to speak in a common Bantu everyone would understand, but prevented casual listeners from eavesdropping.

"Life is good. Everything is in place for tomorrow. You have your targets: the bank and the radio and TV station. Try to keep civilian injuries to a minimum and anything wearing a uniform gets done. Tom has some private types near city hall, so be careful. The bank is easy to take and there's a small glass window at the rear you need to pay special attention to.

Most of you got some grenades off the sub when you picked up your gear. One has to be taped to that back glass window and another needs to go in. The wall will hold the explosion. I figure a team of six is enough for the bank.

The radio and TV stations are in the same complex. A 12-man team can take that. I will have a small squad arrive with a tape and video that need to go out on a constant loop. Get the professionals to do it, as we need to get the word out about the events here as fast as we can. I have two more teams for support. There's going to be mass panic, but we have Myron's Command and Control gear to help us. I will be airborne in a Hind D, watching and controlling from above. I'm in direct command contact with Myron. If it comes through him it started with me. The loose seven should take and hold the city hall. Use a tight perimeter. The bank team has to go right by there so work together and then let the bank team carry on.

It all goes into play at high noon. Questions in thirty seconds."

There were none.

I continued with the briefing.

"Ok, my friends. Let's focus on the outcome and not get sloppy. Enjoy your special dinner tonight. Remember, when you get inside the dressing room that after 45 minutes the playing is over. You need to get kitted and dressed and ready to go in less than fifteen minutes. But wait for the explosions before you leave the stadium. I need to make sure the fox is in the hen house. That also means you have to keep the game close, so you need to fucking play your asses off. Your teamwork is the key to all of this —even the professionals see it.

Think of your families and think of the sacrifices made to get here to this moment, right now. Nothing else in the world matters.

Dismissed!"

I stood and they all pounded the ground instead of saluting. They stayed there as I walked off the pitch and out of the stadium.

On the way back I stopped by the restaurant and gave them an imprint of my card and made a reservation for thirty. They said they would just close the restaurant for the night. I thought briefly about sneaking the other team down for a final dinner together. Not everyone was likely to make it tomorrow. But the gesture, while a good one, was foolhardy. Discipline was the key and we needed to maintain operational discipline.

CHAPTER SEVENTY-FOUR

I drove back to the Bahia and parked the truck for the last time. I figured the men would use it tomorrow to infiltrate downtown, but I was off diesels forever. How the black soot-belching things were more environmentally friendly than my Aston was beyond me.

I went back up to the suite where there was another poker game going on. Myron hadn't done so well. He was sitting at his computer shooting glares into the other room. The players who had busted out were preparing food. I needed to give them all the same briefing but the game looked to be at a very intense point so I waited, walking in to talk with Myron instead.

"Bust out early?" I asked pulling up a chair.

"Yeah. Dumb bloody luck. It was a community pot and everyone was playing loose. I had pocket aces and was the option so I raised it pre flop and got called by almost everyone. The flop was shit so I raised it again and Ronan came over the top. That got everyone off the pot but me. So I figured it's easier to go all in, than it's to call an all in, so I pushed."

"Pushed" I was a blackjack player and pushes sucked, so I imagined it meant something else in Texas Hold 'Em.

"You know, went all in. He called with kings and tripped up on the river. Dumb luck." He looked back at his screen.

"How you coming with things of an impeding nature?" I asked, trying to draw his attention away from the game.

"Great, I got the overlays done and found the drawings for the radio and TV complex on the internet. I added those too. I also found your Russian torpedo sound and it's a nuke fish as well. There was one of a new high-speed solid propellant rig but I thought that might be too recent."

"Can I hear them?"

"Sure, got them right here, hang on."

He typed away and pulled windows around and closed others.

"The nuke fish." He tapped the play icon and the speakers let out a poof, whish, whining sound.

"The solid one" He pushed play again and this time the sound was like a bubbling that got faster till it was a roar of sound.

"Myron, could you combine those two sounds?" I asked leaning forward.

"Easy."

He tapped away and then pushed play a third time and the two combined to sound like a really dangerous weapon.

"I like that combined. That is what we will play for the US ships," I said.

It sounded good and was just enough of a lie to be believable. They wouldn't know where the sub was. The fish could be a silent swim-out version. Those made no launch sound and would start their attack run a few hundred meters from the sub. No one was going to believe a propeller fish could go twenty miles. But perhaps a two-stage propeller, solid fuel one could. It was brilliant.

"Ok. You're the boss." He saved the file to one of the desktops.

"Next I need you to contact a man at this number. I need an audio and video file of him giving an acceptance style speech. Tell him you're working for me and to keep it short, to the point and reassuring. You can also tell him that my plane will be picking him up at 1200 his time from the Madrid airport. The plane can take ten people. He should have a security detail included in that number."

"What do you want to do with the files and who is he?" Myron asked as he took the number.

"He's the next President and I will need to play it over the LRAD devices and the radio and television stations."

"The radio and TV are easy. I can put it on thumb drive in enough formats one will work even in this backward country, but I don't know anything about the LRAD things. What format do they take?"

"I don't know. Let's go see." I got up and walked into the living room and picked up the duffle bag containing one of the LRAD units.

Myron and I took it out and he looked at the back.

"It takes a standard audio jack? Shit, that is easy. You can play it from my MP3 Shuffle." We went back into the bedroom.

"I will get on this, but I'll need some quiet to get the signal clean." He grabbed a laptop and went to the bed.

"Hopefully the guy has a web cam or something. Quality is going to be a problem, unless it's a good one, but I will work it out."

He pulled out his cell phone.

"Here use mine, he knows the number." I tossed him my phone and left the room, closing the door behind me.

The poker game had ended, with Ronan taking the title. Now the men were enjoying some food and gentle, good-natured banter. I went to the bar and poured myself a drink. No one else was drinking. I imagined Chiwa had ordered them not to. RHIP, Rank Has Its Privileges. I moved to the coffee table and tapped it to get everyone's attention. The noise died down and I spoke softly.

"Myron is on an important call, so I thought I would take this opportunity to brief you all. Move in so you can hear me."

I gave them a moment to get closer.

"Everything is good. Better than good, actually. The game has been pushed back to 1100, so our go time will be high noon. You guys go when the island fires its guns. I'm going to split you into four teams of six. The main objectives for you are the radio and television station complex. Twelve men from the other team will be going there as well. If that area gets secured then we will receive confirmation and orders over Myron's Command and Control system. I will be the direct command link with him and his system. If the orders come over the system, treat them as coming from me. The new President should be here within four hours of the start. I want this place secured and locked down tight by then. Surprise and devastating firepower is how we will achieve this. Limit civilian targets and drop anything in uniform. If in doubt, take them out! This is not a UN engagement! The truck is available for any team. The keys will be on the table.

I want one person to hang back here to protect Myron. He's our eyes and ears so we need to keep him alive. I will be in a Hind D attack helicopter for the duration of the battle, broadcasting the New President's message in an effort to keep the civilians off the streets.

The secondary target is city hall. I will have a team set up in a close perimeter and when the stations are secure we will move to that location, leaving a small security force in place at the stations. Expand and control that location and we will put a new President into power. Questions in thirty seconds."

Again there were none. "The food smells great," I remarked. "I need to eat. Let's share this last meal together. Tomorrow we will be leaders of men!"

The evening was spent in remarkably relaxed fashion. We spent the time sitting around talking about past adventures and the end of being unwanted citizens. A common theme amongst the lads was what the world should or would look like tomorrow. Their wants were really very simple; a safe country to raise children, who could be educated close to home and be treated when they were sick. A state that viewed its citizens as community and its children as something to be taken care of and nurtured to succeed. Rather, than a commodity to be used or sold. These were the same ideas the President in exile and I talked about. Simple notions really, in a country that could afford to do it. Tomorrow we opened the door on simple ideals. Unfortunately, the key we had to use was made of blood and violence. Then again, it was Marx who proposed that real change came only from violent revolution.

The lads were all going over their gear and I was getting ready. I packed all my gear into the two duffle bags; they were heavy and I would need a hand to load everything. Myron came into the room and approached me; obviously happy he could share with the group.

"We're all set, boss. The file is saved and ready to go. I just pulled the audio off the video file for your LRAD units. The total time is six minutes and it is pretty good quality. Not high definition or anything but it is good broadcast quality." He handed me three thumb drives and an Ipod shuffle.

"Great work, Myron. Thanks. Is there any difference between these drives?" The lads had gone quiet and were looking at Myron.

"Nope, just figured four units were better than one. There is no video on the shuffle." We all nodded at his thinking.

"Good work." A few of the lads tapped him on the shoulders and back as he returned to the computers.

"Myron, could you put out a situational report that I will be in a Hind tomorrow for the lads in the field? I don't want them to target me."

"Sure thing, Rhys." He disappeared into the bedroom and I looked around at the lads who were shaking their heads. They had really accepted Myron as a leader.

The gear was packed and ready and everyone sat pondering their own thoughts in solitude. I thought about firing them up a little with a speech but thought better of it. A good sleep was probably a better idea.

I got up and wished the lads a good sleep and went into my bedroom. Myron was at the desk working with the finished overlays doing a virtual run through.

"You're going to go nuts if you keep running scenarios, no plan survives past three seconds of contact with the enemy." I said, stripping down to my shorts and getting into bed.

"Yeah, so I've been told. I can't remember what boxer said something similar about getting punched in the face. I have found and highlighted the window you were talking about. That room was an add on after the bank was constructed. It took a bit but I found it on the Internet. So I tagged it. You really going to give me the helm here at the suite?" He spun round to look at me.

"Yes, does that make you nervous?

"No, not really. I am going to treat it like a game, like I don't know they're real people. Real people I played poker with. Seems like that will be easier." He looked down and away.

"Only till the day after. They all know why they're here and believe me; know the risk far more than you do. They made the decision and I think you can give them the best chances. I will be distracted at times and that hampers the team's situational awareness. This way you keep everyone on the plan and I will interject if I need to. I won't let you get too fast and loose, Myron. Don't worry" He looked back up at me.

"What happens Sunday, Rhys?'

"Sunday, the new president takes over and we start making some changes. We all get diplomatic passports and get on with making this country one of the best in Africa if not the world. I guess you'll have a decision to make that day too."

"Decision, me? What the hell do you mean?" Confusion etched his face.

"Well, I figure we are going to need a Minister of Technology. Know anyone better suited for the job?"

"No, not really. But I am not sure I want to work under a dictatorship either." The confusion replaced with stern resolve.

"It is only going to be a dictatorship for six, or perhaps eight, years then we will hold elections. Open and informed free elections. We need the time to set up the infrastructure and government policies so people get a real look of what they are voting for. Give them an idea of what a well-run country looks like. This place has a reported gross domestic product of over 26 billion dollars this year but the scary number; the one that shows how fucked up this place is the GDP per person ratio. This country's figures are higher than the United Kingdom, Germany, Japan, and even Finland. The fucking place is only five spots below Canada! Do you see free education, health care, social services, anything? No, because the President and his elite are raping this country dry! The world points at me and calls me a butcher, mercenary, a dog of war. Meanwhile, the yellow media paints pictures of nice football matches and the United Nations turns a blind eye and lets things go unchecked. The fucking US Navy comes in and gives them training to help secure their borders and revamp their Navy for Christ's sake. I spent more on this coup than he spent on his entire military last year. Why? Because big daddy, the USA, will come running full speed to his aid. Why would a country founded on the principles of Justice and Freedom for all support such a man? Money. So who are the real mercenaries here? Really, who is in it for the cash and to hell with the little black skinny monkeys? These little black bastards are people just like you and I. A great deal of whom will never get to grow up, get educated, buy a car. Why? Because the current President, and his children need to drive six each. The US needs cheap oil, and the rest of the world could give a flying fuck. There is a black man in the White House, but real African blacks are different. What a crock of shit. The media would rather do an article on this football game or which debutant socialite is sucking whose cock. The world has the Internet and the information and would rather ignore it and buy another fucking Escalade to drive their kid four blocks to school. Yet, we are the bad guys. The filthy profiteering dogs of war. Fuck that! Tomorrow I am going to open the eyes of the journalists that are here to cover this event. I am going to show them the hypocrisy of this. Five years from now this country will have a level of government responsibility that will be a model to the rest of the world. Sorry, got on a bit of a soapbox didn't I?" I got into bed with Myron still looking at me.

"Is that true?" He stammered out, feeling the effects of a barrage.

"What part? Yes fuck, it is all true every bit of it. All there on the Internet to find. The real scam is how much more money this place is really making." I blurted.

"I didn't know. I guess I never made the time to look. Do you want me to write the press release?" He looked serious.

"Press release? What are you talking about?"

"Rhys if you're going to show the journalists anything you have to play by their rules. You need to have a press release with facts and figures they can check and verify."

"Never thought much about it, Myron. Yeah sure, write a release." He turned away from me and he started doing research.

I let my body relax into sleep.

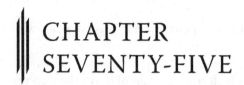

CHAPTER SEVENTY-FIVE

THE MORNING STARTED EARLY AS I woke to a loud racket in the other room. I climbed out of bed praying the housekeeping staff had not wandered in. I opened the door to find several of the lads laughing at Chiwa who seemed to be dancing around pulling off his pants.

"What the fuck is going on?" My voice a little harsh, no doubt from my snoring.

The room went quiet and Chiwa continued his odd strip tease.

"I tripped and spilled your coffee Sir."

"You spilled MY morning fucking coffee! Somebody shoot this man." There were odd looks amongst the men.

"Are you fucks losing your sense of humour?" I walked to the kitchen in my underwear and made myself a cup.

While it brewed I checked my watch and addressed the men.

"Ok, this is it. It is nine right now and I have to be at the field by ten and then back here by eleven. By three we want to be in control of this place. By this time tomorrow I want your families on planes. I know it's odd to have me address you in my underwear but there is an historical precedent for this. Are we ready to do this?"

The men all turned and snapped a salute my way and held it as I returned the honour.

"Chiwa, ya, skinny black monkey, put some clothes on. You look ridiculous" The room erupted in laughter with the lads pointing at me as much as Chiwa.

I took my coffee back into my bedroom and read what Myron had written, as he had seen fit to commandeer the bathroom during my absence. The press release looked like every other one I had seen. It was worded well and probably said what I had wanted to say better than if I had said it myself.

"Morning, Rhys. Sorry, I had to piss like a racehorse. Those look ok?" He walked back to his computers.

"No, it looks great; thanks again, Myron." I left him and headed for the can.

Ten minutes later I was dressed in an Armani suit and heading for the parking lot. The lot had more cars and there was a huge bus blocking the turn around. It was loading people for the game, I guessed. I jumped in the truck and headed down to the stadium. I arrived and the place was already in utter chaos. I bypassed the huge lines of people and made for the VIP entrance. My pass was checked like it was a passport and I was granted access. I made my way through four more checkpoints to the visiting team's locker room. The lads were getting dressed for the game, uniforms clean and bright.

"Morning lads, coaches, and trainers. I see everyone made it."

"Morning, Sir." Came the reply from all.

I signed with my hand at my thigh whether there were any issues. I wondered if they had to drop their gear for fear of being searched. The three identified leaders all flipped their thumbs indicating all was as planned.

"Great, well I am not the one for long speeches. You're here to change minds and make me a great deal of money. The bet Tom and I have with the President is huge. So win or you'll all be swimming to the mainland." This brought laughs from everyone and I made my way to the head coach.

"This is a third world country. If anything out of the ordinary happens your safest place is right here in this change room. Grab the players and your staff and get back here as fast as possible. Brace the door, move away from it, and sit tight. Tom has security people on the ground that will come help."

"Yeah ok, but what could go wrong?" He asked, tapping his ever-present clipboard.

"Anything, TIA. Remember?" I left him nodding his head. It had seemed like the decent and right thing to do. By giving him a heads up he and the others stood a much greater chance of survival.

I made my way out of the building and the crowds were increasing. It hadn't seemed possible the mass could get any bigger, but it had.

My truck was now swarmed with people waiting to pass through the lines. I checked my watch. The game was scheduled to start in thirty minutes.

The truck rattled to life and for once I was happy for the loud sound. The mass of humanity crushed together to let me pass. I drove slowly, as some people had to duck away from the truck's mirrors. It was that tight of a fit. I got clear of the area and increased speed up to the hotel.

The busses had all left the parking lot and it was once again quiet and deserted looking. I scoped out the most likely landing spot for the Hind and checked the ground for debris that could get pulled up into the wash. It was clear. I hurried upstairs.

The lads were primed and ready to go when I entered the great room. I checked with the individual team leaders and they quickly went over their plan. They were going to place a group of men in the back, covered with a comforter from one of the beds, and drive the two groups down to the Radio and TV complex, and hit it about the same time we hit the stadium. It was a slightly risky plan but the team leaders successfully argued that the police presence would be focused in the other direction near the stadium and city hall area for the big parade.

I changed into my combat clothing, and dumped on the armour. It was warm and I needed another loose fitting shirt to wear over it in order to hide the added bulk from casual observation. I immediately started to sweat. I went to the bar and pulled a few bottles of water to add to my kit.

I checked with Myron. I could see he was ready to go. He had five liters of water and a large assortment of pastries on the desk and one of the waste paper baskets.

"What is the basket for?" I walked up, adjusting the pistol for concealed carry while wearing the vest.

"Old online gamer trick. Washroom, I don't want to have to walk away from the action." He looked a little embarrassed.

"Ok. What is the unit's status?" He tapped a key and the unit report options flew up on the three screens.

"All green and operational. We got good connections all over the theatre through voice over IP. and normal radios. I just sent a test tone via radio, for security. I didn't transmit on the cellular or satellite channels for the same reason. But they came up online for each man.

We're golden there. The sub is on lockdown mode, all quiet, and my connection to the sub LRAD is five by five. The island has locked in the first shoot coordinates and is standing by for your order. The airport is locked into the Gator attack vehicles, or at least where they were yesterday from the videos you shot of the place. They are only going to go with a quarter capacity volley for the initial. So they have three shots in reserve if the fighting vehicles moved. They can do a pretty accurate firing solution on the fly. One of the lads has moved to a spotter position near the bottom of the tree line. They also have firing solutions for the tower, refinery, and runways." He sat back and grabbed a Danish.

"Sounds good, really good. Ok, can the island hit the Presidential buildings?" Myron punched up some ranges.

"Just, but it is a huge complex. If they only use a half load from one of the units on the stadium they could cover a great deal of it. But I don't know what kind of coverage numbers you need to get effective kill numbers." He took another bite of his Danish.

"It is on the peninsula, so start inland and work toward the sea. Same battle strategy that has been used for years." I pointed to the map.

"Oh, 300." He nodded.

"Far longer than three hundred years, my friend." I grabbed his shoulder.

"No, not years. The movie 300." Swivelling in his chair.

"Don't think I saw it. But it is a standard procedure. Anyway, I got a chopper to catch."

"Good luck, Rhys." He turned back to his computer game. He had really stepped up to the plate; his use of military jargon and the way he picked up things highlighted his intelligence. He was very vulnerable in this position and he had to know it.

"You too Myron. If your escort tells you it is time to move, you need to follow his lead and get the fuck out of dodge. The remote pick up is on the road we parked on to deliver lunch to the lads." I walked out the door, leaving Myron wearing his CC rig over his trendy computer programmer clothes.

Three lads were still in their normal clothes when I entered the room, standing next to my bags. I walked through the tight collection of warriors and rubbed heads or squeezed shoulders as I passed. Silently the four of us hefted the heavy bags and brought them down the fire escape and out to the area I had picked as a landing zone.

"Anyone got any green smoke?" I said tongue in cheek. The lads laughed and the tension fell away only for a second.

"Think they know we're coming Sir?"

"The thing with arrogance is it clouds your perception in everything you do. So I doubt it." The loud, thump, thump, thump, cut off his answer but I could see him shaking his head as the big catalogued Russian attack chopper cleared the tree line coming up from the south.

There was a good wind coming off the water and the pilot was good. He came in fast and steady and seemed to approve of our landing area as he nearly put the skids on our toes. He was good and testing us. A test I had just intentionally failed. I hadn't crouched down or moved back as he landed. I could see the gunner's position was vacant and I counted my blessings.

The gear was tossed into the large area behind the pilot and I jumped in and put on the old headset.

"Morning, Mr. Andre. Spent times in these birds, have you?" He cycled up and we took off banking into the wind and gaining altitude quickly.

"Yes, quite a bit of time. Been a while since I have flown one but I have probably eighty hours in your chair." I gabbed a handle without looking at it and watched him.

"An odd hobby for a rich football team owner." He turned towards the stadium.

"I have some very odd friends. Here, I have a picture of one on my phone." I brought up the picture of Mbando and I taken by the lawyer at the airport lounge. I felt him cut power and nose the machine up to a position knife-edge to a stall. So the game seemed to be mutually assured destruction.

"Easy, no need to get jumpy, it is just an iPhone." He took the phone from me and looked at the picture. He let out a snort and laughed.

"What?"

"I was thinking this was a fake until I read what Mbando wrote on the little sign." He handed the phone back and relaxed the position of the machine, continuing to the stadium.

"What did he write?" I settled down on one of the jump seats.

"It is an old saying, that even if you spoke the language well you wouldn't get. It means it's easy to trust in the devil when you're on the tip of his fork. Literally translated it sounds like and ad for hot sauce. Mbando used it a lot when we were kids. Ok so you're in tight with the ex boss, and a competent mercenary. Why should I cooperate and jam up my gig here?"

"Well, I am putting your current President up on a cross, and you can hand me the nails or join him. Tough enough mercenary line for you? Look, I could hand you this press release but you're flying. This country falls today. My real name is Rhys Munroe and this team is comprised of the last of the Greys." I watched him closely; I needed him in for the ride, but I needed him in control.

"You're a Grey? I've heard of them. I just thought they were stories men told each other to stay awake. Don't fall asleep or a Grey will get you." He was relaxed and began a slow circle of the new stadium. The game was being played and so was the one up here.

"Asleep or awake, never did make much of a difference. You don't have to do much more than what I paid you to do till the battle happens. Once it does you have a choice to make." I looked down on the field and could see we were holding our own.

"If you're thinking about using my guns or missiles to hit the President's bunker, forget about it. I am light and they were built it to withstand an attack by this very craft. Otherwise we would not have been cleared to fly over the game." He said, dipping lower and rotating left around the stadium.

"Nothing of the sort. Just do what you're doing and keep us in the air and make your decision to help or not based on the first card I play." Most of the spectator seats were full but there was still a throng of people outside the stadium.

"Ok Rhys, you have a pilot and a machine. My name is Linoo Mackuba. But if I don't like the looks of the first card, I am heading back to the airport, or you'll shoot me and we will crash as I doubt you can climb up here fast enough to arrest the fall." He looked back at me.

"Sounds good to me. I am going to outfit your machine with some sound gear, and get changed if you're cool with that, Linoo." I waited for his response.

"Yeah, go ahead, I am going to fly a little higher and south as the wind is a little annoying right here at low altitude. Stay in the back and we're fine." He turned the machine.

I zipped open the smaller bag and started pulling out gear. I shed the top that covered my vest and tossed on my load-bearing rig with Myron's CC system already attached. It was heavy with rounds but allowed the wind to reach my shoulders and underarms and I felt myself cooling down.

I clipped the MP5 to the rig's weapon holder and cinched up the sling so it was firmly held to my side and out of the way. Despite checking it when I loaded it I silently pulled the chamber back to check it was ready. It was.

I pulled out the two LRAD units and using the anchor hooks I secured them to the floor with the transmitting heads pointed down. I plugged them both into the auxiliary power and hoped the circuitry was the same as in all the other Hinds I'd flown in. They powered up and the ready lights came on. I plugged Myron's little shuffle to the two unit's auxiliary input ports and with the system set to the lowest setting, tested it. The LRAD's were so directional that I had to hang half my body out of the machine to be able to hear it. It worked. I pressed return on the shuffle and using a strip of duct tape off my vest taped the little shuffle to the back of one of the LRAD's.

I pulled my goggles on and switched on the CC unit. The headset had an auxiliary plug and I pulled the one out of my old Russian one and tried it in the newer one. It fit. The system took a while to come online and for a few seconds I thought the rotor and metal might be interfering with the reception. I pushed the auxiliary talk button.

"Hey Linoo, you hear me?" I looked toward the front, little green and red arrows floating in the distance beyond the cockpit bubble window.

"Five by Five, Captain Rhys." The sound crystal clear in my earpiece. He had used my rank, so he had heard of me. Well, the level of gear and that prior history should have cleared up the 'how full of shit' question he had been asking himself for the past little bit.

"Roger that, five by five." I looked toward the airport and could see little green dots. Two near a large Lego catapult and one near the bottom of the tree line. Words appeared at the bottom of my field of vision. I read them.

"Welcome to the party, Captain. Signal strength is poor but good enough for text. Everything is go but if you use talk function you will switch to a cellular connection. I would advise against words but a tone to confirm function would be ok."

I pushed the regular PPT (push to talk) button and made a tone the best I could and waited. The words started scrolling again.

"Signal good. Hope the game is going well."

I pushed the auxiliary PTT.

"Ok Linoo, I am good to go, let's roll back to the stadium to see how it is going?" I moved back to the jump seat.

"You can't hear the game? Oh sorry, got you on the wrong setting. There, how's that?" The announcer's voice screamed into my headset.

"GOAL! The game is now tied with 28 seconds remaining in the first half and I think the visiting team from London is surprising the National team. They are likely to bring in the next squad full of regulars to stop this surprisingly good professional team."

As we were heading toward the Stadium I figured a loose circle would be better. So I hit the PTT auxiliary button.

"Linoo, keep us loose up here. Any other traffic in the area?"

"Roger that Captain. No traffic, but then this is a restricted airspace. Want to listen in on the international frequencies for the play by play?"

"Sure." I looked out the doors getting used to the overlay system as the opinions and commentary about the first half provided background noise.

The minutes ticked by like hours. It hadn't moved this slow since I was in high school. I did a bunch of isometric exercises to force my blood to move and muscles to work. When the announcers commented on the home team taking the pitch I told Linoo to fly over and check the bunker and confirm the President was there.

The chopper arced and powered up, running in from the southeast. We came in low and I could see a great deal of people in the box. But I wasn't close enough to see faces and I strained and thought about an upgrade option for Myron.

"Yes, he is there. Front and center, standing up." The words made my heart jump.

"Positive?" I could see a well-dressed man standing up and looking toward the visitor's opening to the field.

"Yes, positive, President is in the box." The voice was now tight.

"I hit the regular PTT button. Commence operation, fire, fire, fire." The words rushed, tight and loud." I watched as one of the island catapults went from yellow to flashing yellow.

One of the referee's was running across the field toward the visitors opening. The sky to the northwest took on a shimmering appearance and it looked as if a little grey cloud was moving toward the field. But much faster.

The first volley of rounds hit the bunker square, with very few rounds going wide. I yelled into the mike.

"Direct hit, fire, fire, fire. Hit it again!"

While I was yelling I could see the thirty millimetres explosive rounds were flattening the structure. The thick windows had blown out and were being hurled toward the field, smashing bodies against it as it flew. The rounds that had gone wide had erased seats and people as completely as an artist dropping black paint on a canvas. The next volley hit four seconds after the first and tossed up a cloud of debris that was quickly obscuring that end of the stadium.

People were running to escape the cloud and the deadly spray of rubble whipped in every direction from the first strike. The section itself had seemed to collapse backwards in on itself. Fire could be seen licking up from the structure. The strewn burning plastic seats, and candling human bodies adding to the conflagration.

"Holy fucking shit! What the fuck kind of gun was that? Jesus." Linoo's expletives reached my ears as I moved to the LRAD.

I cranked the volume to ninety percent and pushed the button to start the sound. The exiled President's message, reflected back from the streets, was loud in the chopper. On the ground it was painful. I looked down and saw people covering their ears; some of them were on fire. I dialled it back to seventy five percent.

"Lino, circle the area. I'm guessing my first card was good enough?"

"Roger that Sir. Circling on radius and expanding." He understood what I was trying to do. The President's message was clear that a coup against the President, and not the people, was taking place. It advised citizens to return to their homes or places non-governmental in nature and to sit down and not get involved. They would not be fired upon unless they were combative. It went on to urge government police and soldiers to lay down their arms and take off their uniforms, providing them the same promise. I thought to myself the first lie, ringing hollow to the shattered bodies in the football field. The new government wasn't even formed yet.

My heads up display sort of overwhellmed me for a second as information cluttered the screen. The lads at the TV and radio station were seeing a little resistance.

"Media center under control." The sound burst through my earpiece. I looked up the street and saw the crowds had yet to make their way out of the gates yet the lads had moved out of the stadium as a group of twenty five. The progress was swift and they quickly broke into groups. They fired selectively at the police officers and various security people, leap frogging one another up toward the bank and the City Hall. Some Officers took the advice from above and tore off their shirts as if they were on fire.

"Take this thing once around the stadium at this speed and then roll up toward City Hall like you're going to do a strafing run." I grabbed a handle to steady myself in the door.

"Yes Sir, but I won't fire, too many friendlies." The machine pitched and went into the looping turn.

"You keep questioning my orders and we're going to have a problem. I said make like you're going to do a run. You're not clear to fire. I want to draw fire from the security contractors on the ground. They're used to American birds, not titanium bathtubs." My HUD displayed the men on the move on three different streets toward City Hall, while the tickertape message ran on the bottom. It read: "Message going out on radio and TV as per plan, no issues securing building."

The large machine dove across the top of the stadium and dipped on the far side even lower. I hung on as the large machine shuddered under the effort. We rolled on City Hall like a Valkrie and I heard a few impacts as we picked up some small arms fire from the ground.

"Figure eight turn, Linoo and bring us back round from behind. Then head toward the Presidential buildings." I could see on my heads up the lads had used the distraction well to move faster up the streets.

"Yes sir." Came the response from the front.

The machine did a perfect figure eight turn and came in even lower before flaring over the main building, and then running up to full power and shooting almost straight up. Rocking like a boat first back then forward we pulled a ton of dust into the air and shot off toward the coast.

"Sorry, Sir, I improvised a little on that one. Figured your fancy head gear would give you an advantage in the dust." He banked and kept our speed constant toward the coast"

Good thinking Linoo." I looked past him into the cockpit to see how many pounds of fuel we still had. This kind of flying would eat up fuel very quickly.

"You hitting the hired guns at the palace?" The question asked as he flipped switches bringing weapons live.

"Yeah, if I find any targets. I thought you said you were light, weapons wise?" I pulled the door shut to the second detent, as far as I could with the LRAD's positioned as they were.

"I lied. The off duty contractors should all be in that building with the red roof and satellite gear. They have some Suburban trucks located in that big garage. The trucks have mounted gattling guns that could give your men hell. See, that is one, coming out now. Am I clear to fire?" I could see the black four-door truck speeding down the double lane road.

"Clear to fire but maintain distance and steady. I am painting a target." I stepped out on the strut and using my eye-activated menu selected paint and looked at the red roof. Then I keyed the PTT.

"Target painted. Change in fire mission. Fire, fire, fire." The Hind's big front mounted cannon came to life at the same time and I watched shell casings fall as if poured from a bucket and the ground in front of the truck moved as if some beast were under it. The black truck ran into the dust cloud and came apart as if gravity was reversed. The hood was smashed flat and the tires each took different courses into the ocean. The cab windows blew out and the contents ejected, as if someone had stuffed a child's piñata with tomatoes instead of candy.

The second PR unit's one-third capacity shot hit the building and once again it just ceased to exist. Devastating firepower had meant many things. But this thing just erased targets. The remains were stark contrast to the other buildings around it. The fifty-calibre armour piercing rounds cutting like a torch while the thirty millimetre grenades pounded all in under half a second. I hit the PPT button again.

"Shifting fire, target painted. Fire, fire, fire." I looked at the garage.

The sky again turned dark as the volley came in and hit the garage. This time some of the rounds fell short. They ripped apart the gate and shredded the road back towards the point. The rounds that did come in must have hit something, as we got secondary explosions and large gouts of flame that shot across the road and didn't stop.

I pulled myself back inside and immediately the sound of rockets streaking past the half open door followed me inside. The fire was coming from us as Linoo tied a bow on the palace by effectively rendering the road useless to anything but tracked vehicles.

"Let's roll back to the city central, I want to try and keep as many civilians inside watching the television as I can." I pulled the side door back open and watched as we moved back over the docks and towards the centre of the city. The goggle information displayed two of the lads were down at City Hall, one permanently. I looked at the Media center, and while things were quiet now, that would change as soon as the authorities arrived. The police had remained at their posts despite being out gunned. Protecting their way of life, no doubt. I couldn't spare anyone from there.

There was a loud squeal over the headset and I almost took it off before it ended. The display came up. "We are being jammed. Radio and cellular is offline. You need to get close to the ground to use the VOIP network. Or relay orders through me. Your Satellite connection should still work. But only till they catch on. Broad-spectrum jam, coming from offshore or overhead."

This new information allowed me to adapt the plan to a small degree. Being airmobile allowed a great deal more flexibility then I imagined. There was shouting from the cockpit and I looked forward.

"We're being jammed. Probably from outside but it could be the tower. The brass at the refinery probably got the word out to the US boats. They will be on their way. Full power and burning oil." Lino circled back over the city hall, shouting. I saw the shooting was sporadic but it was still a hot landing zone.

"Get me close to the top of City Hall, time for me to join the party. Go get the lads from Media center and bring them back here." I yelled over the wash of the heavy prop.

"Too hot for me to put down in there! Radios are jammed so your boys are likely to fire on me if you can't get them word." He yelled back as he slipped closer to the rooftop.

"Follow your fucking orders, lads will be at the helipad and it will be cool enough to land, when you get back." I grabbed the strut and held on for a second as he dropped the bird quickly over the roof of City Hall. I dropped and landed on the soft gravel roof I had been on two days ago.

I rolled to the wireless router, although I knew it was working, as I could hear the various lads chiming in on their command branches. I could hear everything and it was a little distracting. I looked at the media group in my goggles and then my command radio function and squeezed the PTT module affixed to the MP5 while I scanned over the roof.

"Listen up lads, bird is on the way. We are being jammed and taking heavier than expected fire at City Hall. I need two squads to meet the hind at the helipad on the roof. You should be getting a map overlay from command. Move! The remainder of you make it look as though you have more people; use the dead, do what you can to look entrenched." I heard the replies as I spotted one of the contractors. He was under a car, firing across the field, the natural dip making him very hard to see. I aimed at the front tire and squeezed off a three round burst. The light weapon barely moved, and as it was suppressed, it whispered.

"Taking target under, car west of your position." When I slipped onto the frequency of the lads here I noticed that my target was already identified and highlighted on the overlay. The sniper locator system was alive and well.

When I fired the system heard and marked me, identifying me as a friendly at about the same time the explosively deflating tire pinned and then slowly, like a python, suffocated the man.

I could see two other targets on the overlay, but the positions were blocked from my angle.

"Joining your party lads. I see the two marked snipers. Anything else you're worried about?" I put two rounds through the doorknob and made my way inside.

"We're pinned down behind the bank, cops at either end of the alley, and the others are needed at the hall." The location of the lad showed he and four others were pretty much stuck directly in the middle of the alley behind the bank.

"I am coming to get you. Listen up, everyone else, the Hind is coming back with two teams and he doesn't like to get his bird dirty. Let's grab some local firepower and get those snipers heads down when he comes in." I let the PTT switch go and yelled loudly.

"Lay on the floor, and you won't be shot." I approached the first corner at the middle of the hall and holding the MP5 at my hip, level as I could, fired four rounds through the corner. The quiet chunks of soft lead slammed through the weak drywall and kept right on going. I rounded the corner and descended the stairs putting three more rounds through the walls on either side of the staircase. There was a low grunt and a figure rolled forward into the opening at the bottom of the stairs. He was holding his throat with one hand and in the other was trying to bring a weapon to bear. He wasn't being effective in either endeavour. Sliding down with his back against the wall, his weapon tip would raise slightly toward me as his heartbeat caused a spray of blood to course through his fingers and cover the area. Not wanting to waste rounds, I kicked him hard on the chin as I came off the staircase. He went out and his hand fell from his wound, which was only a pooling hole, erratic as the heart lost the ability to make pressure. I cleared the hallways, left and right, and continued quickly down the hall, putting three rounds into every corner starting three feet out from the junction. The rounds found no other hiding targets.

I reloaded from a box of rounds and made my way out of City Hall and ran crouched across the street and down to the next road. No rounds came my way. I turned north and sprinted toward the main road and the bank. I reached the corner and could see the bank was a mess. The glass front façade was lying in the street, as was the nice secretary from the other day. The fat man was nowhere to be seen but I imagined he had been turned into parts and generously infused into everything is the computer transfer room. I moved to the front and slowly looked around the corner keeping my head low. I could see three cops firing down the narrow alleyway. I looked to see the men's status. They were all yellow, hurt, injured, and no doubt running low on rounds.

CHAPTER
SEVENTY-SIX

THE CRUISER WAS HALF ON the sidewalk with its lights flashing. The one right rear tire rested on the curb, lifting the car like a dog peeing. Great idea, I thought, as I lay the machine gun sideways in front of me and watched the one officer squeeze off another round. Timing it. I fired when I saw his gun buck in his hand. My three round burst slammed into the gas tank at an angle. One split the bottom seam; the other made a hole at the midway point, the last barely hitting the corner. All three rounds hit and as the top round had hit high enough to let air in the gas gushed out of the tank. I keyed the PPT.

"Listen up, cavalry is here lads, tighten up and wait for my opening. Clearing left flank."

I pulled out my lighter and balled up some deposit slips and lit the ball. Tossing it into the flood of petrol in the gutter. It caught and chased itself up and down the street.

I leaned out around the corner just as the tank caught fire with a loud whoosh. It caught the three cops attention as well and I ended it for them. Rising to the kneeling position, I snap fired at the distracted three, hitting two in the head and one in the throat. They all fell where they were standing. I rushed the corner, scooped up a police cap and in the local dialect yelled.

"Grenade!"

I jumped on the hood of the burning car and into the alley and sprinted full speed. There were three targets at the end of the alley. To be crouched behind the police cruiser doors, with only their lower legs visible, waiting for the explosion. The third had just his head sticking around the corner, looking at what appeared to be a backlit silhouette of a cop running from a grenade.

I fired a three round burst and hit the wall in front of him with two rounds, causing brick and flattened lead to smash into his eyes and forehead. Reflexively he threw his head back and the last round ripped at his lower chin, smashed into his ruined eyes and split his skull open. Training told him to run for the safety of the police car and he did, howling with a ruined tongue and insane with pain.

The other officer tried to retreat from the creature that was running for him, and they tangled together in the front seat. The other hiding cop stood up to look and I intentionally dropped my shot from his ear to his neck. I had wanted to create as much of a visual distraction as I could and it was working.

The faceless cop was on the right, gurgling, quickly fading black to ashen. Hiding cop was spraying blood all over cop in the middle who never saw the window go white, ending his life. I continued up onto the roof of the car and checked the area. It was free of combatants.

"Clear!" I yelled down the alley and the men helped each other move to my position. I assessed the injuries as they moved toward me. None of them were life threatening if treated, as they were mainly lower leg wounds and injuries to the arms. I opened the police car parked on the streets rear door and ushered them in.

I went back to the dead cops and ran my hand along their belts at their bellies. On faceless cop I found the keys for the other cruiser. You had to love American TV programs. All the cops on reality TV shows tucked their keys there. I jumped in, started the car and rolled down the street, flipping the sirens on as I went.

"I am arriving shortly with a borrowed police car. Hold your fire." I voiced over the system and got a series of Rogers back. The Hind had brought the lads back and had left, saying he was low on fuel. The added numbers had made it easier to flank the two other snipers and take out the threat. The injured went into City Hall and one of the medics went with them.

"Sir, the Hind pilot said he was going to refuel and then continue the "hearts and minds" broadcast, and then go to your landing zone with two thirds fuel. That was what he said, word for word. I didn't understand so I memorized it." The lad, Javier Balboa, slipped down on the step holding his shattered arm, hand gone below the wrist.

"Thanks Javier, You know the two good things about that kind of an injury, solider? The men got quiet, and Javier Balboa looked at me, a puzzled look creasing his face.

"The great creator saw fit to give us two, and you weren't holding your cock, taking a slash, when it happened." Javier laughed first, and the rest joined in, till Myron interrupted us.

"Listen up guys, just had a contingent of vehicles pass our airport fire point and head down across the airfield. They parked against the far fence and are going for the fighting vehicles in a hurry. We also have the Coast Guard ship Dallas trying us on all bands, unjamming each as he does, wanting to talk to the man in charge of the coup. There are also cops searching the hotel. We have two bleeding out in the kitchen. I could really use some help here." He wasn't near panic but he was a little past terrified and it showed in his voice.

"Myron, thanks my man, You're at the helm, my friend. Relax, that thing you're feeling is fear and it's good for you. Makes everything taste better. Respond to the Dallas, and tell her to hold position and not to enter EG territorial waters or we will view it as an act of war by the United States of America and treat its citizens as hostile. Use whatever you got to get me a fix on that boat. Fire point airport, you are weapons free, your call using two thirds load, and stand by with secondary firing solution. All stations acknowledge."

I got a Roger for the airport and an OK from Myron. The mounting constant pressure was getting to him and I knew I had to go back.

"Chiwa, sort this mess out. We got 38 of the finest here and only seven are wounded. Round up our dead, who are only one by the way, gentlemen, and secure this fucking location. I will be at the Command Post. We will need to keep the wounded here but there is a ton of food and blankets, and no one is really messed up past the point of repair so treat, eat, and get out the marshmallows. Should be an easy day." Chiwa saluted me by way of an answer and I bit the end off one of my cigars and lit it before walking out into the street. I couldn't help myself and I whistled the theme from; "The Good, The Bad, and The Ugly. "

There was laughter behind me as I made my way to the cop car. I started it and began to drive back to the Bahia. Myron joined me in my ear.

"Rhys, ah, I got a position for you. On the boat, or ship. Anyway she is already inside our waters, currently inside outer exclusion zone by two kilometres." I saw thick black smoke off to my right, the direction of the airport, and needed to ask.

"Myron what happened at the airport?" I passed the main road to the airport and continued north.

"Oh Yeah shit, lots of info, trying to keep it all straight. They hit it, as some of the vehicles looked like they were going to leave early, not in stratification."

"Formation Myron. Take a deep breath close your eyes and tell me what happened." Tires spun on gravel as I made the final turn up to the Bahia.

"Right, sorry, same geological thing. Ok, they blew the hell out of the hangers. Huge flames, lots of planes on fire with no one responding to the problem. Total loss. The Hind was in the air when it went down, so you're golden."

"Ok I will be there in three minutes. Contact the Dallas and tell him to stop the ships mission and leave the area at once or we will view it as an act of war. Tell the airport fire point to hit building CH32 on the map and overlay." I swung into the drive and was greeted by waves from other cop cars."

"But Sir, shouldn't we give the Dallas a chance to stop?"

"Nope, I have faith they won't. This is someone who thinks they're the biggest bully on the block." Pulling into a spot near the back and side of the other cars I realized this was kind of a makeshift command center. I was still wearing the police hat but the disguise wouldn't last long.

"Island fire point, new target. Target is current position squared pattern no wider than twenty-five meters wide. Fire on one word, that being 'light'. Please confirm." I waited, feeling like the only white kid in Durban.

"Roger Sir, twenty five meters squared, centered on your current location. Shoot order is the word 'light.'"

I moved quickly. Already some of the police officers were noticing I was dressed significantly different than them and was, in fact, white. The doors were open into the hotel lobby and I moved past the doors and to a larger man, built like a lineman, wearing the most colourful uniform.

"Don't do it." I yelled, bringing my weapon to bear looking at the man directly. His sense of self preservation prevailed and I moved behind him driving, my pistol into his waistband and grabbing his belt at the small of his back.

"Come now Commander, dance with me. I pulled him against me and rotated slowly to the right. The circles of men displayed various stages of response. Some were standing stunned, while others were training weapons on us.

"Sorry I don't have the time for polite introductions. But shall we dispense with that in the sprit of brevity? My name is Rhys Munroe, I am one of the last Greys and I have just assassinated your president and likely most of his upper echelon. The contract security men are dead as are many of the elite President's rapid response men. Unfortunately, some of your men got caught up in the exchange as well, not listening to what the large hind was broadcasting." We had made several circles, like a deadly barn dance and now were standing by the large windows that framed an ancient couch in the south lobby. The commander's men had followed like a good procession and had us ringed in a semi circle.

"Are you familiar with my name, my good man?" I moved the pistol in his pants to give weight to the question.

"Yes I am familiar with you and your kind. This is a sovereign country and…"

Cutting him off I continued. "Great, so while I don't know your name, I am going to chance a guess that with your position you have learned to be a practical man. This war is over and the only reason for more to die is to create examples or beat dogs that don't have the good practical sense to know they're done. You don't strike me as a dog, sir, but I am guessing with the radios all jammed you're still trying to get a handle on what is happening. Allow me to help. We are reinstalling President Mbando to power. As we chat my men have taken the media center and the city hall as well as the government buildings and the airport. I can destroy at will any location I want on this cute little island. Our intelligence gathering included all the personal houses of anyone that held a position of authority, I'm afraid that included Police Commanders as well. However, there is really no need to crucify anyone else. I need the police to maintain order and frankly, sir, your police force is better disciplined than the military. We both know this. So my question is, can I expect your cooperation in this endeavour?"

"You have a gun to my balls and your asking for my help? There is no way for you to get out of here I have twenty-five men outside and another twenty in this hotel. We will find your comrades and we will maintain order." He pushed out his chest and looked at his men who, at his urging spread out a little farther. I was getting flanked.

"Commander that is what I would like you to do. Go and maintain order. I want to avoid anymore-unnecessary blood shed. This is the beginning of a new page here for you and the people you are sworn to protect. If you know what the Greys are, you know I didn't come in here without a plan. I am asking you to respect that and cooperate." I moved back with him in tow to the side of the window frame, my back to the wall.

"It is only a matter of time before the elite forces take your men, and then I or one of my men here, will arrest you. For treason! Here it still carries the death penalty." He nodded to a few of his men as they spread out in front of us.

"Commander, I am afraid you really have no concept of what a Grey is. I need you to understand your position. I wished I had the time to negotiate you into seeing the light, but I don't." With the word light I pushed the PTT switch in and out for the one word.

The sky outside went a little darker, as the close position of the PR units made it necessary for the rounds to go higher into the sky to reach the correct trajectory. This also meant the rounds were coming almost straight down. The dimming light caught the Commander's attention and he turned his head, ever so slightly, as the faster moving fifty-calibre armour piercing rounds impacted a fraction of a second first. The big hard rounds ripped through the non-armoured vehicles like hot embers dropped on tissue paper. Men exploded outwards as their bodies failed to contain the energy as the rounds tried to move vertically through them.

Then came the 30 millimetre grenades. They hit and flattened the vehicles as effectively as any car crusher designed. The hard steel panels flew like piles of leaves yielding to a moving car. The remaining men that had been missed by the bullets simply tore apart like paper lanterns caught in a gale. The large hotel windows blew in, and while the shear curtains caught some of the deadly shards, a few found a home. Several of the cops went down sporting cuts or holding their chest, trying to stem the spreading stain of death.

"Commander, now you have less than twenty men. The next volley of fire targets those personal houses we identified. Do you need any further motivation to do your job for the new President?" I pushed the gun harder into his crotch and pulled him from his silent revelation of the utter destruction he had just witnessed.

"No, Mr. Rhys Munroe, I do not." His shoulders slumped forward with the effort of his words.

"Great, so call off your men, rally up those you have left and get into the community and start calming people down." I removed the pistol but kept it trained on his back.

"Everyone, we must accept what we all do not like. However, our duty is to those citizens in which we are trusted to protect. Perhaps the US military will sort this out or perhaps they are behind it. But in either case, we need to insure the safety of the citizens of Malabo. We will move from here and gather at the hospital with as many cars as we can. I will send cars out broadcasting a general curfew for all private citizens. No one is to fire or try to arrest any foreign force. That we will leave for the military. Get the wounded and yourselves outside. Now!" The big man's voice boomed in the lobby and the men immediately began gathering their wounded and leaving the lobby. The commander walked away from me, not looking back. I picked up one of the radios from a dead man.

"I'll contact you on this radio if the USA stops jamming our frequencies. I never caught your name, Commander?" I watched as he stopped at the lobby doors.

"Fuck you butcher, you can just call me Commander." He continued out the door without another word.

I watched them all leave and then made for the stairs. I got to the suite and knocked.

"It's Munroe."

"Door's open." Came a voice from inside.

I pushed the door open and walked in, ignoring the muzzle pointed at my head.

"As you were, lad. Myron, send out a message that cops are now listed as potentially hostile and are not to be fired on without first receiving fire. Get ready to get me up to speed, I'll be in there in a moment." I walked past the lad, patting his shoulder, towards the bar and poured myself a stiff three fingers of vodka.

CHAPTER
SEVENTY-SEVEN

"OK, WHERE ARE WE AND what is going on?"

"Zombie checked in, he is en route and on time and wants to know status. The satellite connection is working, but I don't want to put too much traffic through it and let the yanks know we're using it. The lads at the airport have hit that building you asked for and the Captain of the Dallas is having fucking kittens about it. The lads were empty and so moved down to the airport and have taken the tower and the airport security people. They apparently have their compliance. The sub is standing by and all is fine on it and the lads on the island want to know if it is ok for them to swim into shore and help out. The media center is getting the word out and we have been getting a bunch of press worldwide. I guess a few of the sports journalists have computers and uplinks and are doing some reporting on the fly. Been pretty positive, considering. I scooped a few of their email addresses and sent them the press releases. We have lost five men total. Another five are fighting wounded and two can't fight but are stable."

"Myron, you're getting pretty good at this mercenary thing. Ok, let's get ready for our show down with the Dallas. Key up all the data you have on her and I'll call Zombie." I walked over and pulled out my Sat phone and made the call. I noticed I had two messages, both from Tom.

"Zombie, all is five by five. Airport is green and secure. Transfer will be by Hind to government house. I have a pilot so you can stay with the lads at the airport." I tried to be as quick as I could and his response was even quicker.

"Roger, thirty five minutes." The line went dead.

Next I called Tom. The phone rang once.

"Rhys, what the fuck are you doing? Are you mad? Did you fucking slip the fucking plot here? We have a fucking international fucking incident and I am getting looked at very closely, you fucking shit for brains retarded sod."

"Good afternoon, Tom. I regret to inform you, in my capacity as the head of security for the new government of Equatorial Guinea, that your Gulfstream 550 has been involved in a coup and as a result is being seized by the new government. Further, you are given official notice by the new state that you are officially 'persona non gratis' unless you wish to come and entertain these charges of treason."

"Fuck you, Rhys. I am gonna…what my plane? Listen you…" I cut him off.

"Good day, Sir." I hung up the phone.

"That went well. I have the Commander of the Dallas. Just push the t key to talk it is like a radio." Myron got up and went to the bathroom.

"Dallas, this is the Rhys Munroe, I am the current head of security for the Nation of Equatorial Guinea. Over."

"Hello, Rhys Munroe, this is the United States Coast Guard vessel Dallas. We do not recognise your status. You are to cease and desist current military actions against Equatorial Guinea and actions against US held assets and civilians. Over."

"I thought you would say that, Dallas. How about you get me on the line with someone who can pick up the horn and get the commander of the sixth fleet. Perhaps the Captains of the Ashland or the Higgins would be more appropriate than a puddle pirate. Over." Myron came back out of the bathroom and I signalled for him to pass me my cigar case and grab me another vodka.

"Munroe, I have your complete sheet in front of me. We are the closest boat and I have operational authority until one of the other vessels arrive. You're dealing with me. Over."

"Dallas, that sheet must be a short read. But I am kind of busy right now so let's speed up this dick size contest, shall we? Put me through to the big boys, Captain, you are dealing with a Bent Spear scenario. I repeat you're dealing with a Bent Spear. Over."

The line was dead for ten seconds as Myron came back into the room with my drink. I lit the cigar and took the drink from him.

"Rhys, this is Dallas. I understand Bent Spear. Where are you supposed to have got access to said weapon? Over"

"Come on, Dallas, perhaps we got the nukes from the ones you missed at Project Jennifer in 1970 or maybe we picked them up in the bay of Biscayne. You haven't been too good at keeping track of these, have you? Over."

"Stand by, Munroe. Over."

"Well that got their attention." Myron grabbed a Danish and proceeded to stuff most of it in his mouth.

"Munroe, this is Dallas. I am patching you in with Admiral Dickson of the Higgins. Go ahead Admiral." "Munroe, am I to understand you are currently threatening the United States of America with a nuclear torpedo? Over."

"Admiral. Pleasure to finally talk with someone in the loop to make decisions. We asked the Dallas to respect our sovereignty and stay out of our waters and she refused. She is currently jamming radio communications, making it difficult for our emergency personnel to help the injured. Despite my requests as the head of National Security and Protection, she continues to steam toward us in an act of war. Over."

"Listen here, you piss ant mercenary asshole. We do not recognize your authority to speak for the country. That is a nation protected by the United Nations and I am about to bring the entire hurt of the Sixth fleet down upon you like the holy hand of God, son." He didn't say over so I waited.

"You didn't say 'over' Admiral, were you done? Over."

"Yes I am done. Done with talking to you, and done with listening to you. OVER!"

"Very well Admiral, sorry we couldn't move this to a better resolution. Would you tell the powers that be that you have an official Broken Arrow? Over. The difference was lost on Myron, who held up his hands in the form of a question.

"A Bent Spear is where a radiological device, or weapon is lost and could be in hostile hands. A Broken Arrow is when that device is in hostile hands and they intend to use it" Myron nodded his head, understanding the difference and then his eyes went wide.

"Your threatening the US with a fucking nuke?"

"Yes I am, Myron."

"Where did you get a fucking nuke, Rhys?" He jumped off the bed and grabbed my glass, taking a long drink.

"Listen up, Rhys, I know a little bit about those two salvage operations and it is highly unlikely we lost nukes. So basically, son I'm not buying what you all are selling. Over."

"Admiral, I don't want a fight with the US, hell I hope we can normalize relations after your incursion today, but look at it this way. I fire one at the Dallas and one at you. Dallas doesn't have counter measures so she is dead. You have counter measures but not for nuke fish so if it hits the counter measures and misses your boat you're still going down. If it avoids the counter measures it will break your boats' back with the initial blast and melt your crew like Barbie left in the sun. Then the third boat has to mount a rescue mission. You're three days from landing on my shores and by that time Russia and Canada will recognize this new government and the US will have to or be froze out of the oil. Over."

"Son you must be slow. I don't buy the Broken Arrow. It just isn't possible. Like they say in the game of Texas; I am coming along to see your bluff. Over."

"You famous, Admiral? Cause if you're not you're going to be, for starting a nuclear war. Over." I looked at Myron.

"Hey Myron, can you tighten the beam or something to make the sub sound like it is out in the bay, closer to the tanker?"

"Ah Yeah, I can pull in the focus and it will start getting wider much farther away from the sub. I was thinking about doing it anyway, just in case they decided to hit the sub. If I manipulate the frequency and the focus I should be able to make the boat appear to be way out there. If they have a sub or a towed array deployed we're done. But the Dallas is coming much too fast for an array." He sat behind his laptop and checked some figures.

"Ready to do some acting? Pretend we are on a sub's bridge and play along." I got ready to push the T button again. Something said wait and I took another sip of my drink and checked the TV display to see what the lads were up to.

"Rhys, you got any other play than this nuke bluff?"

"No, Myron, I do not. They come in we lose the city as fast as we took it." He sat and looked out the window thinking.

"They likely to buy the show? I mean there is not going to be a radioactive cloud or anything." He looked up at the screen and did a check on the lads too.

"There wouldn't be much radioactive material in the air. The bomb goes off several feet below the water line and salt water is a pretty damn good shield. Besides, there is probably radioactive material on that boat. Lots of stuff has it, even that." I pointed to the smoke detector. "It is going to be one hell of a big explosion too."

"How big, Rhys?" He was watching me now, closely.

"Well if everything mixes right and goes off at close to the same time, about four times larger than the atomic bomb they dropped on Nagasaki." I relit my cigar and checked the tip.

"What! Are you for real? Four times larger! I had no idea that it was going to be that big." Myron was standing

"Well, that is actually a little conservative. It could be the full sixty-kiloton explosion. Little Boy was only thirteen." I tipped the rest of my vodka down. "Ready to play make believe sub?" I pushed the T button.

"Dallas, this is the department of Homeland Protection. I see you're not changing course. We have no choice but to view your actions as hostile. Please respond. Over"

"Munroe, this is Admiral Anderson. We have been ordered to take the city of Malabo by force. Son I told you, I didn't buy it and I told you we're looking for trouble and boy, you found it." Myron was typing away on his screen and gesturing helicopters and pointing to the sea. I checked the status of Zombie's flight and saw he was on the ground.

"They're launching helicopters off the Dallas, I caught some of the broadcast." He continued to listen on another earphone.

"Hey Admiral, the Dallas is making a great deal of noise up there. Recall your choppers or you're going to lose two machines. I am all in, Anderson, and I'll even show you one of my cards. Flood and open tubes one through four."

Myron parroted my orders, just like he had seen, either on the Russian boat or TV. He sounded convincing and I hoped they bought it.

"Swim out launch hybrid one, fire." Parroting as he ran over to the computer, he tapped a couple of keys and transmitted the sound to the Sub's LRAD embedded at the nose. Right where tube one would have been.

"Munroe, a hybrid, swim out? I don't…Sir, I detect a high-speed prop in the water. Confirm, Sir, mark 48 nuke fish, nuke fish, broken arrow." The Admiral had tipped his hand; now I knew he had been told it was a nuke fish.

I selected the Satellite number for Sunday and made the call. Only one person had the number but Sunday would still answer just as a failsafe. I found myself wishing he wouldn't answer. He did, with one word; "Now?" I looked at the time display on Myron's sound loop and answered.

"Twenty five seconds." I said through clenched teeth.

"Ah, less than thirty, how sweet, see ya Pinkie." The line went dead. I hit the all call command channel and said very clearly. "Arc light, Arc light, Arc light, grab the floor and don't look north east. I pushed Myron out of the way of the window and slipped down behind the table in front of the window. I wanted to watch and figured the goggles would protect me. I just pulled them on in time.

The whole sky froze gold and I could see the white clouds chased away from a point off in the distance. As if to highlight this point a geyser of fire streaked and seemed to mix with the very sky, and then it too rolled away from the center as if the heat could not contain itself. It got larger and would have been easier to believe that the entire atmosphere was catching fire. The shock wave rattled the window hard and then came the boom. A few minutes later the cloud had changed to the mushroom white cloud so familiar and I could see large waves breaking over the breakwater near the palace. I was glad it had been nearly thirty miles away. The Dallas had been about ten miles away.

"Equatorial Guinea Department of Homeland Protection, this is Admiral Anderson. Over" The radio came to life quicker than I thought it would.

"Admiral Anderson, go ahead. Over."

"Formally requesting permission to enter your territorial waters to perform a search and recovery mission for the pilots of our two downed aircraft and recover the Dallas. Over"

"Certainly Admiral what, is the status of the Dallas, can we be of assistance? Over."

"She was hit amidships by an 18 meter wave and she fell through a double crest. Heavy structural damage and casualties. No help is required at this time. Over"

"Roger that, no help required. Admiral, please stay at least one mile off shore. The next time will not be a lightly crewed freighter. Extend to your government my desire to enter into normalization talks that could include returning this quiet nation to a non-nuclear one. Over"

"Certainly Captain Munroe. Over." I looked at Myron and started laughing.

CHAPTER SEVENTY-EIGHT

IT TOOK TWO WEEKS TO return the city of Malabo to a new normal. But, only in the way of structure. The ideas of development and free healthcare and school were so foreign it was easier for the locals to believe we were aliens conducting experiments.

The various heads of state were told this was what the train looked like and it was leaving the station and they were in or out. Many decided to cut and run with the profits they had already stole while others liked the air of the new open and "for the people" government. The coffers had been left unplundered, the lads had effectively stopped the exchange of funds in four dummy accounts that combined had a figure that was truly hard to imagine. It also gave us a real number for the yearly-undiverted GDP.

The lad's families had all arrived as the US families had left. Many of which had moved into the homes left by the Americans. Many of the Americans had figured they were coming back and locked the doors and pushed the keys through the mail-slots of there palatial homes.

The act of setting up government and confirming to projects had been full sixteen-hour days and most of us were tired from burning the candle at both ends.

I contacted Minister Chiwa and told him I would be taking three weeks of personal time. The talks and full disclosure with the US had finished. They had sent in inspectors and paid a huge dollar to do so, only to conclude there were no weapons of mass destruction. The press had jumped on this "once again cry wolf" story and boosted our status and version of events.

The Canadians and the Russians were working together well and

Viktor had donated the Sub to the people of EG. It was currently booked solid for months, giving rides for the locals and school kids.

The long flight home was made significantly better in the Gulfstream, yet even here Z and I spent most of the flight talking about the needs of both the civil and military aviation. Planes and parts were ordered as we streaked toward Canada.

The GPS tracking software had been left in the plane and Tom had filed no less than twenty suits to try and retrieve his gorgeous toy and in doing so brought bad attention and press upon himself. In fact, he became the new whipping boy for corporate greed and those who rape the less fortunate countries and each court held that his plane had been used in a coup and as such was legal for the government to seize. The fact he could track its movement was merely salt in the wound.

I yearned to hold and kiss Andrea and was looking forward to seeing Ruben and the Aston. The downtime would allow her to graduate with her degree and into our lives as a couple. Ruben would be his pissed normal self for a few days till he forgave me for the long absence. The drives in the Aston would be all the more sweet with my new Diplomatic passport. Diplomatic immunity extended to speeding tickets.